READER'S DIGEST
SELECT EDITIONS

READER'S DIGEST
SELECT EDITIONS

www.readersdigest.co.uk

The Reader's Digest Association Limited
11 Westferry Circus Canary Wharf London E14 4HE

For information as to ownership of copyright in the material of this book, and acknowledgments, see last page.

Printed in Germany
ISBN 0 276 42990 7

SELECTED AND CONDENSED
BY READER'S DIGEST

THE READER'S DIGEST ASSOCIATION LIMITED, LONDON

from the editors

Fifty years ago, Reader's Digest launched a ground-breaking new product. The idea behind it was simple: to select the best of the hundreds of books published every year and republish them, four at a time, in one attractive hardback. As a result, Condensed Books—as they've been called for five decades—were born. There was soon a huge readership for them, not only in the UK but all round the world. Interesting, isn't it, that fifty years on, the best-selling formula remains the same? It just shows that you can't beat a good idea.

Back then, the selections included some of the great authors of the twentieth century: John Steinbeck, Winston Churchill, Harper Lee and Elspeth Huxley, among many others. They were also a showcase for books that later became lasting favourites: Jack Higgins's *The Eagle Has Landed*, Frederick Forsyth's *The Day of the Jackal* and Peter Benchley's *Jaws*, to name but three. And, time and time again, writers who were selected early on in their careers went on to become household names. For example, Wilbur Smith, Catherine Cookson, James Herriot, Dick Francis and Ken Follett, whose latest novel appears in this anniversary collection.

It's a fine heritage, and one that we're proud to continue. We are celebrating fifty years with a new look, bigger and better than ever, and a new name: Select Editions. The design may be different, but what hasn't changed is the promise made fifty years ago. Every collection, including this one, contains the very finest reading we can find for you—books and writers you'll want to return to again and again.

We hope you enjoy them.

CONTENTS

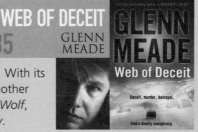

WHITEOUT
KEN FOLLETT

IT'S CHRISTMAS EVE AND THREE
GENERATIONS OF OXENFORDS ARE GATHERED
AT STEEPFALL, THE FAMILY HOME ON THE
EAST COAST OF SCOTLAND.

IT SHOULD BE A TIME OF PEACE AND
GOODWILL BUT TENSIONS ARE ALREADY
SIMMERING BETWEEN SIBLINGS, AND OLD
HURTS ARE ABOUT TO HAVE
TERRIBLE REPERCUSSIONS . . .

CHRISTMAS EVE

1 A.M.

Two tired men looked at Antonia Gallo with resentment and hostility in their eyes. They wanted to go home, but she would not let them.

All three were in the personnel department of Oxenford Medical. Antonia, always called Toni, was facilities director, and her main responsibility was security. Oxenford was a small pharmaceuticals company that did research on viruses that could kill. Security was deadly serious.

Toni had organised a spot check of supplies, and had found that two doses of an experimental drug were missing. The drug, an antiviral agent, was top secret, its formula priceless. It might have been stolen for sale to a rival company. But another, more frightening possibility, had brought the look of grim anxiety to Toni's freckled face. A thief might have stolen the drug for personal use. And there was only one reason for that: someone had become infected by one of the lethal viruses used in Oxenford's laboratories.

The labs were located in a vast nineteenth-century house built as a Scottish holiday home for a Victorian millionaire. It was nicknamed the Kremlin, because of the double row of fencing, the razor wire, the uniformed guards and the state-of-the-art electronic security. But it looked more like a church, with pointed arches and a tower and rows of gargoyles along the roof.

Toni and the two men were phoning everyone who had a pass to the top-security laboratory. There were four biosafety levels. At the highest, BSL4, the scientists worked in space suits, handling viruses for which there was no vaccine or antidote. Because it was the most secure location in the building, samples of the experimental drug were stored there.

Biohazard training was compulsory for everyone who went into BSL4. Toni herself had undergone the training, so that she could enter the lab to check security. Only twenty-seven of the company's eighty staff had access, but many had already departed for Christmas, and Monday had turned into Tuesday while the three people responsible doggedly tracked them down.

Toni got through to a resort in Barbados called Le Club Beach and persuaded the manager to look for a laboratory technician called Jenny Crawford.

As she waited, Toni glanced at her reflection in the window. She was holding up well, considering the late hour. Her brown chalk-stripe suit still looked businesslike and her face did not betray fatigue. Her father had been Spanish, but she had her Scottish mother's pale skin, green eyes and red-blonde hair. She was tall and looked fit. Not bad, she thought, for thirty-eight.

'It must be the middle of the night back there!' Jenny said when at last she came to the phone.

'We've discovered a discrepancy in the BSL4 log,' Toni explained crisply. 'When was the last time you entered BSL4?'

'Tuesday, I think. Won't the computer tell you that?'

It would, but Toni wanted to know whether Jenny's story would match the computer record. 'And when was the last time you accessed the vault?' The vault was a locked refrigerator within BSL4.

Jenny's tone became surly. 'I really don't remember, but it will be on video.' The touchpad combination lock on the vault activated a security camera, which rolled the entire time the door was open.

'Do you recall the last time you used Madoba-2?' This was the virus the scientists were working on right now in BSL4.

Jenny was shocked. 'Bloody hell, is that what's gone missing?'

'No, it's not. All the same—'

'I've never handled an actual virus. I mostly work in the tissue-culture lab.'

That agreed with the information Toni had. 'Just one more question. Is your temperature normal?'

'Are you saying I might have Madoba-2?'

'Have you got a cold or fever?'

'No!'

'Then you're all right. You left the country a week ago—by now you would have flu-like symptoms if anything were wrong. Thank you, Jenny. It's probably just an error in the log, but we have to make sure.'

'Well, you've spoilt my night.' Jenny hung up.

'Shame,' Toni said to the dead phone. She put the receiver down and said, 'Jenny Crawford checks out. A cow, but straight.'

The laboratory director, Howard McAlpine, leaned back in his chair. 'The overwhelming likelihood is that the material unaccounted for was used perfectly legitimately by someone who simply forgot to make entries in the log.' His tone of voice was testy. He was responsible for the log, and should have discovered the discrepancy himself. Toni's efficiency made him look bad.

'I hope you're right,' Toni said. She got up and went to the window.

The personnel office overlooked the extension that housed the BSL4 laboratory. The new building was on three levels and the labs were on the ground floor. As well as research space and storage there was an intensive-care medical isolation facility that had never been used. On the floor above was the air-handling equipment. Below, elaborate machinery sterilised all the building's waste. Nothing left the place alive, except human beings.

Toni turned to the other man, who was the director of human resources. 'How far down your list are we, James?'

James Elliot looked up from his computer screen. 'We've spoken to all but one of the twenty-seven staff who have access to BSL4,' he said.

'Who's the missing one?'

'Michael Ross, a lab technician. He's worked here for eight years.'

McAlpine ran his finger down a print-out and said, 'He last entered the lab three Sundays ago, for a routine check on the animals.'

'What's he been doing since?'

'Holiday,' Elliot said. 'He was due back today.' He looked at his watch. 'Yesterday, I should say. But he didn't show up, or call in sick.'

Toni raised her eyebrows. 'And we can't reach him?'

'No answer from his home phone or his mobile.'

'Doesn't that strike you as odd?'

McAlpine looked worried. 'He's very conscientious. It's surprising that he should take unauthorised leave.'

'Who was with Michael when he last entered the lab?' Toni asked. There was a two-person rule in BSL4; no one could work there alone.

McAlpine consulted his list. 'Dr Monica Ansari, a biochemist.'

Toni picked up the phone. 'What's her number?'

Monica Ansari spoke with an Edinburgh accent and sounded as if she had been fast asleep. 'Howard McAlpine called me earlier, you know.'

'I'm sorry to trouble you again. It's about Michael Ross. We can't track him down. I believe you were in BSL4 with him two weeks ago last Sunday.'

'Yes. Let me put the light on.' There was a pause. 'God, is that the time?'

Toni pressed on. 'Michael went on holiday the next day.'

'He told me he was going to see his mother in Devon.'

'That's helpful,' Toni said. 'Just hold on.' She turned to James Elliot. 'Do we have his mother's contact details on file?'

Elliot clicked his mouse. 'She's listed as next of kin.' He picked up the phone.

'Did Michael seem his normal self that afternoon?' Toni asked Monica.

'Totally.'

'Did you enter BSL4 together?'

'Yes. Then we went to separate changing rooms, of course, and he changed quicker than I did. When I entered the lab itself, he was already there.'

'Did you work alongside him?'

'No. I was in a side lab, dealing with tissue cultures. He was checking on the animals. And he left a few minutes before I did.'

'So he could have accessed the vault without your knowing about it?'

'Easily.'

Beside Toni, Elliot was asking to speak to Michael Ross or his mother.

'Do you know if Michael has a girlfriend?' Toni asked.

'I don't think so.'

'Anything odd about him, in your experience?'

'No.' Monica hesitated, then added, 'I mean, the fact that someone lives alone in an isolated cottage doesn't make them a nutcase, does it?'

Toni ended her call and hung up. 'Michael Ross had plenty of time to open the vault.' She looked at Elliot. 'Did you reach his mother's house?'

'It's an old folks' home,' Elliot said. He looked frightened. 'And Mrs Ross died last winter.'

TWO VANS drove out through the Kremlin gates at 3 a.m. and turned south, going dangerously fast. Both were marked with the international biohazard symbol: four broken black circles on a vivid yellow background.

Toni Gallo was at the wheel of the lead vehicle, and with her were three men trained in decontamination. The second vehicle was a mobile isolation unit with one paramedic at the wheel and one in the back, and a doctor, Ruth Solomons, in the passenger seat.

Toni was afraid she might have been wrong to have activated a red alert. Michael Ross might be safely asleep in bed with his phone turned off, and she winced to think what she would then say to her boss, Stanley Oxenford, in the morning. But it would be much worse if she turned out to be right. Toni could hardly bear to think of the consequences if the Madoba-2 virus had somehow escaped. It was highly infectious, spreading fast through coughs and sneezes. And it was fatal. A shudder of dread went through her, and she pushed down on the accelerator pedal.

The road was deserted and it took only twenty minutes to reach Michael Ross's stone cottage. Toni turned into a short drive and stopped the van next to a Volkswagen Golf, presumably Michael's. The place was dark.

She sounded her horn long and loud. Nothing happened. No lights came on, no one opened a door or window. Toni turned off the engine. Silence.

If Michael had gone away, why was his car here?

'Bunny suits, please, gentlemen,' she said.

They all climbed into orange space suits, including the medical team from the second van. It was an awkward business. The suit was made of a heavy plastic that did not easily yield. It closed with an airtight zip. They helped each other attach the gloves to the wrists with duct tape. Finally they worked the plastic feet of the suits into rubber overboots.

The suits were completely sealed. The wearer breathed through a High Efficiency Particulate Air (HEPA) filter, which would keep out any breathable particles that might carry germs or viruses, and took out all but the strongest smells. A headset in the helmet enabled them to speak to one another and to the switchboard at the Kremlin over a scrambled radio channel.

'I'll go first,' Toni said, and walked stiffly up to the front door.

She rang the bell and banged the knocker. After a few moments, she went round to the back. There was a neat garden with a wooden shed. She found the back door unlocked and stepped inside, then walked quickly through the house, turning on lights. The place was clean, tidy and empty.

Toni spoke to the others over the headset. 'No one home.'

She went back out into the garden. She tried the door of the garden shed. It, too, was unlocked. When she opened it, she caught the trace of a smell, unpleasant but vaguely familiar. Blood, she thought. The inside of the little wooden building was black; there were no windows. She fumbled in the dark and found a switch. When the light came on, she cried out in shock.

'Come quickly!' she said. 'To the garden shed. Ruth first.'

Michael Ross lay on the floor, face up. He was bleeding from his eyes, ears, nose and mouth. Blood pooled around him. Toni knew that multiple haemorrhage was a symptom of Madoba-2 and similar infections. Michael's body was an unexploded bomb full of the deadly virus. But he was alive. His chest was going up and down, and a weak bubbling sound came from his mouth.

She bent down and looked closely at him. 'Michael!' she said, shouting to be heard through the plastic of her helmet. 'It's Toni Gallo from the lab!'

There was a flicker of intelligence in his bloody eyes. He opened his mouth and mumbled something.

'What?' She leaned closer, kneeling in the sticky puddle of fresh blood.

'No cure,' he said. Then he vomited. A jet of black fluid exploded from his mouth, splashing Toni's faceplate. She jerked back and cried out in alarm.

She was pushed aside, and Ruth Solomons bent over Michael.

'The pulse is very weak,' she said. 'I need a laryngoscope—fast!'

Seconds later, a paramedic rushed in with the implement. Ruth pushed it into Michael's mouth, clearing his throat so that he could breathe more easily.

'Bring the isolation stretcher.' She opened her medical case and took out a syringe—loaded with morphine and a blood coagulant, Toni assumed. Ruth pushed the needle into Michael's neck and depressed the plunger.

'OK,' Ruth said. 'Let's get him out of here.'

Two paramedics carried Michael out to a trolley enclosed in a transparent plastic tent. They wheeled the trolley across Michael's garden. One of Toni's team had already got out a shallow plastic tub. Now Dr Solomons and the paramedics took it in turns to stand in the tub and be sprayed with a powerful disinfectant that destroyed any virus by oxidising its protein.

Toni watched, distraught that a deadly virus had escaped from her laboratory. Her job was to prevent this happening and she had failed.

Dr Solomons jumped into the back of the ambulance with the patient. One of the paramedics slammed the doors and they roared off into the night.

Toni shook herself to get rid of her gloomy torpor. 'Let's clean up,' she said.

One of the men took a roll of yellow tape that read BIOHAZARD—DO NOT CROSS LINE, and began to run it round the entire property. Luckily there were no houses nearby. The others got out rolls of refuse bags, garden sprayers filled with disinfectant, boxes of cleaning cloths, and large white plastic drums. Every surface had to be sprayed and wiped. Hard objects and precious possessions would be sealed in the drums and taken to the Kremlin to be sterilised by high-pressure steam in an autoclave. Everything else would be double-bagged and destroyed in the medical incinerator underneath the BSL4 lab.

Toni got one of the men to help her wipe Michael's black vomit off her suit and spray her. Then, while the men cleaned up, she looked around, searching for clues. What had Michael done to expose himself to the Madoba-2 virus?

In the shed was a glass case with an air extractor, rather like an improvised biosafety cabinet. There was a dead rabbit in the case. It looked as if it had died of the illness that had infected Michael. Beside it was a water bowl labelled JOE. Had it come from the laboratory?

Toni went into the house. Michael had turned the second bedroom into his study. Toni sat at his desk and read his emails. He had ordered a book called *Animal Ethics* from Amazon. She checked his Internet browser, and found he had recently visited animal-rights websites. Clearly, he had become troubled about the morality of his work. Toni sympathised with him. But, in her opinion, animal research was a sad necessity. Her father had suffered a brain tumour in his fifties and had died bewildered, humiliated, and in pain. His condition might one day be curable, thanks to research on monkey brains.

Toni found Michael's address book in a drawer. As she was opening it, a blue flash caught her eye through the window, and she looked out to see a grey Volvo saloon with a police light on its roof. Toni had been expecting them. In accordance with the Critical Incident Response Plan that Toni had devised, the security guards at the Kremlin had phoned regional police headquarters at Inverburn to notify them of a red alert. She hoped it would be Superintendent Jim Kincaid, who was responsible for what they called CBRN—chemical, biological, radiological and nuclear incidents. He had worked with Toni on her plan. The two of them would implement a careful, low-key response to this incident.

Toni had been a police officer herself until two years ago. She had been a golden girl—promoted rapidly, shown off to the media and tipped to be Scotland's first woman chief constable. Then she had clashed with her boss over racism in the force. He maintained that it was not institutionalised. She said that officers routinely concealed racist incidents, and that amounted to institutionalisation. The row had been leaked to a newspaper; she had refused to deny what she believed, and had been forced to resign.

At the time she had been living with Frank Hackett, another detective. They had been together eight years, although they had never married. When she fell out of favour, he left her. It still hurt.

She got one of the team to decontaminate her again. Then she took off her helmet to talk to the superintendent. However, the man in the Volvo was not Jim but Superintendent Frank Hackett—her ex. Her heart sank. Although he was the one who had left, he always acted as if he had been the injured party.

He got out of the car and came towards her. She said, 'Please don't cross the line—I'll come out,' then realised her error right away. He was the police officer and she was the civilian—he would feel that he should be giving orders to her. The frown on his face showed her that he had felt slighted.

'What's going on here?' he asked.

'A technician from the lab appears to have caught a virus. We've just taken him away in an isolation ambulance. Now we're decontaminating his house. Where's Jim Kincaid?'

'He's on holiday in Portugal.'

A pity, Toni thought. Kincaid knew about biohazards, but Frank did not.

Reading her mind, Frank said, 'Don't worry. I've got the protocol here.' It was the plan Toni had agreed with Kincaid. 'I don't like it—it puts civilians in charge of a crime scene.'

'What makes you think this is a crime scene?'

'Samples of a drug were stolen.'

'Not from here.'

Frank let that pass. 'How did your man catch the virus, anyway?'

'The local health board must figure that out,' Toni said, prevaricating.

'Were there any animals here when you arrived?'

Toni hesitated.

That was enough for Frank. 'So an animal got out of the lab and infected the technician when he wasn't wearing a suit?'

Before she could react, Toni heard a chime from her helmet. 'I'm getting a phone call,' she said to Frank. 'Sorry.' She took the headset out of the helmet and put it on. A voice said, 'Dr Solomons is calling Ms Gallo.'

Toni said, 'Hello?'

The doctor came on the line. 'Michael died, Toni.'

Toni closed her eyes. 'Oh, Ruth, I'm so sorry.'

'He would have died even if we'd got to him twenty-four hours earlier. I'm almost certain he had Madoba-2. Have you any idea how it happened?'

Toni didn't want to say much in front of Frank. 'He seems to have been troubled about cruelty to animals,' she said. 'Ruth, I've got the police here. I'll talk to you later.'

'OK.' The connection was broken. Toni took off the headset.

Frank said, 'So he died.'

'His name was Michael Ross and he appears to have contracted a virus called Madoba-2.'

'What kind of animal was it?'

On the spur of the moment, Toni decided to set a little trap for Frank. 'A hamster,' she said. 'Named Fluffy.'

'Could others have become infected?'

'Michael lived here alone. Anyone who visited him before he got sick would be safe, unless they did something intimate, like sharing a hypodermic needle. Anyone who came here when he was showing symptoms would surely have called a doctor. So there's a good chance he has not passed the virus on.' Toni was playing it down; she didn't trust him not to start a scare. 'But obviously our first priority must be to contact everyone who might have met Michael in the last sixteen days. I've found his address book.'

Frank tried a different tack. 'I heard you say he was troubled about cruelty to animals. How do you know?'

'I've been checking his personal stuff.'

'That's a job for the police.'

'I agree. But you can't go into the house. You have to undergo biohazard training before you're allowed to wear a suit.'

Frank was becoming angry again. 'Then bring the stuff out here to me.'

'Why don't I get one of my team to fax all his papers to you? We could also upload the entire hard disk of his computer.'

'I want the originals! What are you hiding in there?'

'Nothing, I promise you. But everything in the house has to be decontaminated, either with disinfectant or by high-pressure steam. Both processes destroy papers and might well damage a computer.'

'I'm going to get this protocol changed. I wonder whether the chief constable knows what Kincaid has let you get away with.'

'Oh, Frank, for God's sake—you might be right, but this is what we've got, so could we try to forget the past and work as a team?'

'Your idea of teamwork is everyone doing what you say.'

She laughed. 'Fair enough. What do you think should be our next move?'

'I'll inform the health board. They're the lead agency, according to the protocol. Meanwhile, we should start contacting everyone who might have seen Michael Ross. I'll get a detective to phone every number in that address book. I suggest you question all employees at the Kremlin.'

'All right.' Toni hesitated. Frank's best friend was Carl Osborne, a local television reporter. If Carl got hold of this story he would start a riot. 'There's a paragraph in the protocol I've got to mention,' she began. 'It says that no statements should be made to the press without first being discussed by the main interested parties, including the police, the health board and the company.'

Frank grinned. 'You're frightened of tabloid stories about killer hamsters roaming the highlands.'

'You owe me, Frank. I hope you remember.'

His face darkened. 'I *owe* you?'

She lowered her voice. 'You remember Farmer Johnny Kirk.' Kirk had been a big-time cocaine importer. He had never seen a farm in his life, but got the nickname from the oversize green rubber boots he wore to ease the pain of the corns on his feet. Frank had put together a case against Farmer Johnny. During the trial, Toni had come across evidence that would have helped the defence. She had told Frank, but Frank had not informed the court. Johnny was as guilty as sin, and Frank had got a conviction—but, if the truth ever came out, Frank's career would be over.

Now Frank said angrily, 'Are you threatening to bring that up again?'

'No, just reminding you of a time when you needed me to keep quiet about something, and I did.'

'We all bend the rules from time to time. That's life.'

'Yes. And I'm asking you not to leak this story to your friend Carl Osborne.'

Frank grinned again. 'Why, Toni,' he said in a tone of mock indignation, 'I never do things like that.'

7 A.M.

Kit Oxenford woke early, feeling eager and anxious at the same time.

Today he was going to rob Oxenford Medical.

The idea filled him with excitement. It would be the greatest prank ever. Even better, it would be revenge on his father. The company would be destroyed, Stanley Oxenford would be ruined financially and would never know who had done this to him. It would be Kit's secret gratification.

He lay in bed with his eyes closed, thinking of the obstacles he had to overcome. First, there was the physical security round the Kremlin: the double row of fencing, the razor wire, the tamper-proof intruder alarms connected to regional police headquarters at Inverburn.

None of that would protect the place against Kit and his collaborators.

Then there were the guards, watching important areas on closed-circuit television monitors, patrolling hourly. Finally there was the access control scheme: plastic credit-card passes, each bearing a photo of the authorised user plus details of the user's fingerprint embedded in a chip. Defeating this system would be complicated, but Kit knew how to do it.

His degree was in computer science, and he had been top of his class, but he had an even more important advantage. He had designed the software that controlled the entire security set-up at the Kremlin. It was his baby. He had done a terrific job for his ungrateful father.

At around midnight tonight, he would walk into the BSL4 laboratory, the most secure location in Scotland. With him would be his client, a quietly menacing Londoner called Nigel Buchanan, and two collaborators. Once there, Kit would open the refrigerated vault with a four-digit code. Then Nigel would steal samples of Stanley Oxenford's precious new antiviral drug.

They would not keep the samples long. Nigel had to hand them over by ten o'clock tomorrow morning, Christmas Day. Kit did not know who the customer was but he could guess. It had to be one of the pharmaceutical multinationals. Having a sample to analyse would save years of research. The company would be able to make its own version of the drug, instead of paying Oxenford millions in licensing fees. It was dishonest, of course, but men found excuses for dishonesty when the stakes were high.

The best part of Kit's plan, he felt, was that the intrusion would go unnoticed until long after he and Nigel had left the Kremlin. Today, Tuesday, was Christmas Eve. Tomorrow and the next day were holidays. There was a good chance the theft would not be spotted then or at the weekend, giving Kit and the gang until next Monday to cover their tracks. So why was he frightened? The face of Toni Gallo, his father's security chief, came into his mind. Once before he had underestimated her—with disastrous results.

He opened his eyes and sat on the edge of the bed. The digital clock on the hi-fi said 07:10. He wanted to be at his father's house in time for lunch. He was going there ostensibly for the Christmas holiday, actually to steal something he needed for tonight's robbery.

He walked to the kitchen and started to make coffee.

While he was working for his father, designing and installing protection for the BSL4 laboratory, he had pulled off one of his best scams. With the help of Ronnie Sutherland, then head of security, Kit had rigged the accounting software so that, in summing a series of suppliers' invoices, the computer added one per cent to the total, then transferred the one per cent to Ronnie's bank account in a transaction that did not appear on any report. The scam relied on no one checking the computer's arithmetic—and no one had, until one day

Toni Gallo saw Ronnie's wife parking a new Mercedes coupé outside Marks & Spencer's in Inverburn.

Kit had been astonished by the dogged persistence with which Toni had investigated. Worse, when she figured out what was going on, nothing would prevent her from telling the boss, Kit's father.

Kit had not found employment since being fired by his father. Unfortunately, he had continued to gamble. Ronnie had introduced him to an illegal casino where he was able to get credit, doubtless because his father was a famous millionaire scientist. He tried not to think of how much money he now owed; it made him sick with fear and self-disgust. But his reward for tonight's work would pay off the entire sum and give him a fresh start.

He took his coffee into the bathroom and looked at himself in the mirror. At one time he had been lean and fit. Now he saw a little softness in his outline. But he still had thick brown hair that flopped over his forehead. He tried his Hugh Grant expression, head down bashfully, looking up out of the corners of his blue eyes with a winning smile. Yes, he could still do it.

After shaving he went back into the bedroom and turned on the TV. He found a local news programme. The British Prime Minister had arrived in his Scottish constituency for Christmas. A fierce blizzard in the Norwegian Sea was drifting south. Then he heard the voice of Carl Osborne. Kit glanced at the screen. Osborne was broadcasting from outside the gates of the very building Kit was planning to rob tonight.

'What the hell is this?' Kit said worriedly.

Osborne was wearing a bulky anorak and a woolly hat. 'Scientists experiment with some of the world's most dangerous viruses,' he said, 'right here in the building behind me, dubbed "Frankenstein's Castle" by local people.'

Kit had never heard anyone call it 'Frankenstein's Castle'. Osborne was making that up. Its nickname was the Kremlin.

'But today, in what seems to some observers to be Nature's retribution for Mankind's meddling, a young technician died of one of these viruses.'

This would be woundingly bad publicity for Oxenford Medical. Normally, he would have gloated, but today he was more worried about the effect of such publicity on his own plans.

'Michael Ross, thirty-one, was struck down by a virus called Ebola. This agonising affliction causes painful, suppurating boils all over the victim's body.' Kit was pretty sure Osborne was getting the facts wrong, but his audience would not know. This was tabloid television.

'Oxenford Medical has always claimed its research poses no threat to local people or the surrounding countryside, but the death of Michael Ross throws that claim into serious doubt. Ross may have been bitten by a hamster named Fluffy that he stole from the laboratory here and took to his home.'

'Oh, no,' said Kit. This was getting worse and worse.

'Did Michael Ross work alone, or was he part of a group that may attempt to free more plague-carrying animals from Oxenford Medical's laboratories? Do we face the prospect of innocent-seeming dogs and rabbits roaming over the Scottish landscape, spreading the lethal virus? No one here is prepared to say,' said Osborne.

The studio anchor, an attractive blonde with carved hair, now said to camera: 'A very worrying story. Carl Osborne with that report. And now football.'

In a fury, Kit turned off the television. This was a catastrophe. Security at the Kremlin would be watertight. Tonight was the worst possible time to try to rob the place. Kit would have to call it off. There was no point in going ahead when failure was so likely.

The clock on the hi-fi said 07:28. It was early to telephone, but this was urgent. He picked up the handset and dialled.

The call was answered immediately. A man's voice said simply, 'Yes?'

'This is Kit. I need to speak to him. It's important.'

'He's not up yet.'

'Shit. Tell him I'm coming round,' Kit said. He hung up without waiting for a reply.

TONI GALLO thought she would be out of work by lunchtime.

She looked around her office. She had only just begun to make the place her own. Just last week she had put a photograph on the desk of her with her mother and her sister, Bella, taken a few years ago when Mother was still in good health. Toni could hardly believe she had already lost this job.

She now knew that Michael Ross had devised an elaborate way of getting round her security precautions. There was no one to blame but herself.

She had not known this two hours ago, when she had phoned Stanley Oxenford, chairman and majority shareholder in Oxenford Medical, to give him the terrible news. She had been dreading the call, and steeled herself for his disappointment, indignation, or perhaps rage.

He had said, 'Are you all right?'

She almost cried. She had not anticipated such kindness. 'I'm fine,' she had said. 'We all put on bunny suits before we went into the house.'

'But you must be exhausted.'

'I snatched an hour's sleep.'

'Good,' Stanley said, and briskly moved on. 'I knew Michael Ross. Quiet chap, experienced technician. How the hell did this happen?'

'I found a dead rabbit in his garden shed, in an improvised biosafety cabinet. I think he brought home a laboratory animal and it bit him.'

'I doubt it,' Stanley said crisply. 'Michael can't have been working alone, in BSL4. Even if his buddy wasn't looking, he couldn't have stolen a rabbit without being seen on the CCTV monitors. I presume we have video footage of the last time Michael was in BSL4?'

'Next thing on my checklist.'

'I'll be there at about eight. Have some answers for me then, please.'

'One more thing. As soon as the staff begin arriving, rumours will spread. May I tell people that you'll be making an announcement?'

'Good point. I'll speak to everyone in the Great Hall at, say, nine thirty.' The grand entrance hall of the old house was the biggest room in the building, always used for large meetings.

Toni had then summoned Susan Mackintosh, one of the security guards, a pretty girl in her twenties with a boyish haircut.

'I need you to set up a desk in the Great Hall,' Toni told her, 'and stop all employees as they arrive. Tell them there's been a virus security breach and that Professor Oxenford will give them a full briefing this morning. Ask them when they last saw Michael Ross. If anyone has seen him since Sunday two weeks ago, tell me immediately.'

That was almost two hours ago. Toni had spent most of the time since then viewing video footage of Michael Ross on his last visit to BSL4. She now had the answers Stanley wanted. She was going to tell him what had happened, and then he would probably ask for her resignation.

She recalled her first meeting with Stanley. She had been at the lowest point of her life. She was pretending to be a freelance security consultant, but she had no clients. Frank had left her. And her mother was becoming senile.

Stanley had offered her a short-term contract. He had invented a drug so valuable that he feared he might be the target of industrial espionage. He wanted her to check. She had not told him it was her first real assignment.

After combing the premises for listening devices, she had looked for signs that key employees were living above their means. No one was spying on

Oxenford Medical, as it turned out—but, to her dismay, she had discovered that Stanley's son, Kit, was stealing from the company.

She had been shocked. Kit had struck her as charming and untrustworthy; but what kind of man robs his own father? Kit had tried to persuade her to hush it up. But she had told Stanley everything.

She would never forget the look on his face. He had gone pale, grimaced, and said, 'Aah,' as if feeling a sudden internal pain. In that moment, as he struggled to master his profound emotion, she saw both his strength and his sensitivity, and she felt strongly drawn to him.

Stanley had fired Kit and rewarded Toni by giving her a full-time job. She was fiercely determined to repay his trust.

And life had improved. Stanley quickly promoted her from head of security to facilities director and gave her a rise. She bought a red Porsche.

When she mentioned one day that she had played squash for the national police team, Stanley challenged her to a game. She beat him, but only just, and they began to play every week. He took a game from her now and again, but she usually won. He was competitive, but good-humoured about losing. The more she got to know him, the better she liked him. Until, one day, she realised that she did not just like him. It was more than that. Now she felt that the worst part of losing this job would be not seeing him any longer.

She was about to head down to the Great Hall when her phone rang.

A woman's voice with a southern English accent said, 'This is Odette.'

'Hi!' Toni was pleased. Odette Cressy was a detective with the Metropolitan Police in London. They had met on a course at Hendon five years ago, and had they not lived so far apart they would have been best friends.

Odette said, 'It's about your virus victim.'

'Why would you be interested?' Odette was on the antiterrorist team, Toni knew. 'I suppose I shouldn't ask.'

'Correct. I'll just say that the name Madoba-2 rang an alarm bell here.'

Toni frowned. She guessed that Odette had intelligence indicating that some group was interested in Madoba-2. 'I don't think Ross was a terrorist,' Toni said. 'I think he just became attached to a particular laboratory animal.'

'What about his friends?'

'I found his address book, and the Inverburn police are checking the names. I kept a copy.' It was on her desk. 'I can fax it to you right away.'

'Thanks—it will save me time.' Odette recited a number and Toni wrote it down. 'How are you getting on with your handsome boss?'

Toni had not told her how she felt about Stanley, but Odette was telepathic. 'You know I don't believe in sex at work. Anyway, his wife died recently—'

'Eighteen months ago, as I recall.'

'Which is not long after nearly forty years of marriage.'

'Listen, if you decide you don't want him, I'll have him. Meanwhile, let me know personally if you find out anything new about Michael Ross.'

'Of course.' Toni hung up and glanced out of the window.

Stanley Oxenford's dark blue Ferrari F50 was pulling into his parking space. She put the photocopied pages of Michael's address book into the fax machine and dialled Odette's number. Then, feeling like a criminal about to be sentenced, she went to meet her boss.

THE GREAT HALL was like the nave of a church, with an open hammerbeam roof and tall arched windows. In the middle was a modern oval reception desk. A uniformed security guard sat on a stool inside the oval.

Stanley Oxenford came through the grand entrance. He was a tall man of sixty with thick grey hair and blue eyes. He dressed well without seeming stuffy. Today he wore a soft grey tweed suit with a waistcoat, a light blue shirt and—out of respect for the dead, perhaps—a black knitted tie.

Susan Mackintosh had placed a trestle table near the front door. She spoke to Stanley as he came in. He replied briefly then turned to Toni. 'Good idea— buttonholing everyone as they arrive and asking when they last saw Michael.'

'Thank you.' I've done one thing right, at least, Toni thought.

'Have you found out what happened?'

'Yes. Let me show you the video footage.'

They walked along a wide, oak-panelled corridor, then down a side passage to the Central Monitoring Station, normally called the control room. One wall was a bank of CCTV monitors showing key areas of the site, including every room within BSL4. On a long desk were touch screens controlling alarms. Thousands of control points monitored temperature, humidity and air-management systems in the laboratories. A uniformed guard sat at a work station that gave access to the central security computer. In the adjacent equipment room was the central processing unit for the phone system. It was brightly lit. Each of a thousand cables was clearly labelled with easy-to-read tags, to minimise downtime in case of technical failure.

They sat in front of a monitor in the control room, and Toni tapped the keyboard to bring up the pictures she wanted Stanley to see. On the monitor, she showed him Michael arriving at the main gate and presenting his pass. She tapped the keyboard, and the screen showed a green Volkswagen Golf pulling into a parking space. A slight man got out and took a duffle bag from the back of the car. 'Watch that bag,' Toni said. 'There's a rabbit in it.'

'How did he manage that?'

'I guess it's tranquillised, and probably wrapped up tightly.'

The next shot showed Michael presenting his pass at Reception. A pretty Pakistani woman of about forty came into the Great Hall.

'That's Monica Ansari,' said Stanley.

'She was his buddy. She needed to do some work on tissue cultures, and he was performing the routine weekend check on the animals.'

They walked along the corridor Toni and Stanley had taken, but went past the turning for the control room and continued to the door at the end. It looked like all the other doors in the building, with four recessed panels and a brass knob, but it was made of steel. On the wall beside the door was the yellow-and-black biohazard symbol.

Dr Ansari waved a plastic pass in front of a remote card reader, then pressed the forefinger of her left hand to a small screen. There was a pause, while the computer checked that her fingerprint matched the information on the microchip embedded in the smart card. Then the door opened and she stepped though. Michael followed.

Another camera showed them in a small lobby. A row of dials on the wall monitored the air pressure inside BSL4. The further you went, the lower the pressure. This ensured that any leakage of air was inward, not outward. From the lobby they went to separate men's and women's changing rooms.

'This is when he took the rabbit out of the bag,' Toni said. 'There are no cameras in the changing rooms.'

'But, damn it, you can't put security cameras in changing rooms,' Stanley said. 'No one would work here.'

'Absolutely,' said Toni. 'We'll have to think of something else. Watch this.'

The next shot came from a camera inside the lab. It showed conventional rabbit racks housed in a clear plastic isolation cover. Toni froze the picture. 'Could you explain to me what the scientists are doing in this lab, exactly?'

'Our new drug is effective against many viruses, but not all. Here it was being tested against Madoba-2, a variant of the Ebola virus that causes a lethal haemorrhagic fever in both rabbits and humans. Two groups of rabbits were infected with the virus. Then one group was injected with the drug.'

'What did you find?'

'The drug doesn't defeat Madoba-2 in rabbits. We're a bit disappointed. Almost certainly, it won't cure this type of virus in humans either.'

'But you didn't know that sixteen days ago.'

'Correct. '

'In that case, I think I understand what Michael was trying to do.'

She touched the keyboard. A figure stepped into shot wearing a light blue plastic space suit with a clear helmet. He pushed his feet into rubber over-boots. Then he connected a curly yellow air hose hanging from the ceiling to an inlet on his belt. As air was pumped in, the suit inflated.

'This is Michael,' Toni said. 'He changed faster than Monica, so at the moment he's in there alone.'

On screen Michael went up to the rabbit rack. His back was to the camera, and the pumped-up suit shielded what he was doing. Then he stepped away and dropped something on a stainless-steel laboratory bench.

'Notice anything?' Toni asked.

'No.'

'Nor did the security guards who were watching the monitors. But look again.' She went back a couple of minutes and froze the frame as Michael stepped into shot. 'One rabbit in that top right-hand cage.'

'I see.'

'Look harder at Michael. He's got something under his arm.'

'Yes—wrapped in blue plastic suit fabric.'

She ran the footage forward, stopping again as Michael moved away from the rabbit rack. 'How many rabbits in the top right-hand cage?'

'Two, damn it.' Stanley looked perplexed. 'I thought your theory was that Michael took a rabbit out of the lab. You've shown him bringing one in!'

'A substitute. Otherwise the scientists would have noticed one was missing.'

'Then what's his motivation? In order to save one rabbit, he has to con-demn another to death!'

'In so far as he was rational at all, I imagine he felt there was something special about the rabbit he saved.'

Toni ran the video footage forward. 'He did his chores as usual, ticking his tasks on a checklist. Monica came in, but she went to a side laboratory to work on her tissue cultures, so she could not see him. He went next door, to take care of the macaque monkeys. Then he came back. Now watch.'

Michael disconnected his air hose, as was normal when moving from one room to another within the lab—the suit contained three or four minutes' worth of fresh air, and when it began to run out the faceplate would fog, warning the wearer. He stepped into a small room containing the vault, a locked refrigerator used for storing live samples of viruses and the stocks of the priceless antiviral drug. He tapped a combination of digits on its keypad. A security camera inside the refrigerator showed him selecting two doses of the drug, already measured and loaded into disposable syringes.

'The small dose for the rabbit and the large one, presumably, for himself,' Toni said. 'Like you, he expected the drug to work against Madoba-2. He planned to cure the rabbit and immunise himself.'

'The guards could have seen him taking the drug from the vault.'

'He's authorised to handle these materials.'

'They might have noticed that he didn't write anything in the log.'

'They might have, but remember that one guard is watching thirty-seven screens, and he's not trained in laboratory practice.'

Stanley grunted.

'Michael must have figured that the discrepancy wouldn't be noticed until the annual audit, and even then it would be put down to clerical error.'

On the screen, Michael closed the vault and returned to the rabbit lab, reconnecting his air hose. 'Now he returns to the rabbit racks,' Toni said. Once again, Michael's back concealed what he was doing from the camera. 'Here's where he takes his favourite rabbit out of its cage. I think he slips it into its own miniature suit, probably made from parts of an old worn-out one.'

Michael turned his left side to the camera. As he walked to the exit, he seemed to have something under his right arm, but it was hard to tell.

Leaving BSL4, everyone had to pass through a chemical shower that decontaminated the suit, then take a regular shower before dressing. 'The suit would have protected the rabbit in the chemical shower,' Toni said. 'My guess is that he then dumped the rabbit suit in the incinerator. The water shower would not have harmed the animal. In the dressing room he put the rabbit in the duffle bag. As he exited the building, the guards saw him carrying the same bag he came in with, and suspected nothing.'

'Well, I'm damned,' Stanley said. 'I would have sworn it was impossible.'

'He took the rabbit home. I think it may have bitten him when he injected it with the drug. He injected himself and thought he was safe. But he was wrong.'

Stanley looked sad. 'Poor boy,' he said. 'Poor, foolish boy.'

'Now you know everything I know,' Toni said.

He gave her a level look. 'There's one obvious security precaution we could have taken that would have prevented this.'

'I know,' she said. 'A bag search. I've instituted it from this morning.'

'Thereby closing the stable door after the horse has bolted.'

'I'm sorry,' she said. 'You pay me to stop this kind of thing happening. I've failed. I expect you'd like me to tender my resignation.'

He looked irritated. 'If I want to fire you, you'll know soon enough.'

She stared at him. Had she been reprieved?

His expression softened. 'All right, you're a conscientious person and you feel guilty, even though neither you nor anyone else could have anticipated what happened. Since you came, our security has been tighter than ever before. You're damn good, and I aim to keep you. So, please, no more self-pity.'

She suddenly felt weak with relief. 'Thank you,' she said.

'Now, we've got a busy day ahead—let's get on with it.'

MIRANDA OXENFORD ordered a cappuccino Viennoise, with a pyramid of whipped cream on top. At the last moment she asked for a piece of carrot cake. She pocketed her change and carried her breakfast to the table where her older sister, Olga, was seated with a double espresso and a cigarette.

Miranda often ran into Olga first thing in the morning at this coffee bar in Sauchiehall Street, in the centre of Glasgow. They both worked nearby: Miranda was managing director of a recruitment agency specialising in IT personnel, and Olga was an advocate.

They did not look like sisters. Miranda was short and plump, with curly blonde hair. Olga was tall and slim like Daddy, but had the same black eyebrows as their late mother, who had been Italian by birth and was always called Mamma Marta. Olga was dressed in a dark grey suit and sharply pointed shoes. Miranda took off her coat and scarf. She wore a pleated skirt and a sweater embroidered with small flowers.

As she sat down, Olga said, 'You're working on Christmas Eve?'

'Just for an hour,' Miranda replied. 'Have you heard the news? A technician at the Kremlin died of a virus.'

'Oh God, that's going to blight our Christmas.'

Olga could seem heartless, but she was not really so, Miranda thought. 'It was on the radio. It seems the poor boy became fond of a lab hamster and took it home. It probably bit him. He lived alone, so nobody called for help. It's awful for Daddy. He's sure to feel responsible.'

'He should have gone in for a less hazardous branch of science—something like atomic-weapons research.'

Miranda smiled. 'I hope this doesn't spoil the holiday,' she said. The whole family was about to gather at Steepfall, their father's house, for Christmas. She was bringing her fiancé, Ned Hanley. 'I've been looking forward to it so much. You know Kit's coming?'

'I'm deeply sensible of the honour our little brother is doing us. Daddy will be pleased.' Olga spoke with a touch of sarcasm.

'He will, actually,' Miranda said reproachfully. 'You know it broke his heart to fire Kit. And now he wants to forgive and forget.'

'I know. Daddy's magnanimity is boundless. Has Kit stopped gambling?'

'He must have. He promised Daddy he would. And he's got no money,' said Miranda. 'Anyway, enough of Kit. You're going to get to know Ned much better this Christmas. I want you to treat him as one of the family.'

'Ned should *be* one of the family by now. When are you getting married? You're too old for a long engagement. And you've both been married before.'

This was not the response Miranda was hoping for. She wanted Olga to feel warm towards Ned. 'Oh, you know what Ned's like,' she said defensively. 'He's lost in his own world.' Ned was editor of the *Glasgow Review of Books*, a respected cultural-political journal, but he was not practical.

'I don't know how you stand it. I can't abide vacillation.'

'Believe me, it's a blessed relief after Jasper.' Miranda's first husband had been a bully and a tyrant. Ned was the opposite, and that was one of the reasons she loved him. 'And Ned's very good with Tom,' she added. Tom was her eleven-year-old son. 'Jasper hardly spoke to Tom. Ned takes an interest in him.'

'Speaking of stepchildren, how are you getting along with Sophie?' Ned's daughter by his first marriage was fourteen.

'She's coming to Steepfall too—I'm picking her up later.' Miranda took a sip of coffee. 'Sophie can be difficult, but it's not her fault. Her mother resents me, and the child is bound to pick up that attitude.'

'You shouldn't have let him move in without committing to a wedding date.'

The same thought had occurred to Miranda, but she was not going to admit it. Instead she said, 'He thinks Sophie needs more time to get used to the idea.'

'And she reflects her mother's attitudes, you've already admitted. So what you're saying is that Ned won't marry you until his ex gives permission.'

'Olga, please take off your advocate's wig when you're talking to me. I'm your sister, not a hostile witness.'

'I'm sorry I spoke.'

'I'm glad you spoke, because this is just the kind of thing I *don't* want you to say to Ned. He's the man I love and I'm asking you to be nice to him.'

Olga touched Miranda's hand. 'I get the message. I'll be good.'

9 A.M.

Oxenford Medical was under siege. Reporters, photographers and television crews massed outside the gates, harassing employees as they arrived for work. To make matters worse, a group of animal-rights protestors were holding a demonstration at the gates. The cameramen were filming them, having little else to shoot. Toni Gallo watched, feeling angry and helpless.

She was in Stanley Oxenford's office. His computer work station stood on a scratched wooden table he had had for thirty years, and on a side table was an optical microscope from the sixties that he still used from time to time. On the wall hung a photograph of a striking black-haired girl in a wedding dress—his late wife, Marta.

Stanley stood beside Toni at the window, their shoulders not quite touching. They watched with dismay as the crowd became noisier and more aggressive.

'I'm so sorry about this,' Toni said miserably. 'I know you said no more self-pity, but I let a rabbit get through my security cordon, then my bastard ex-partner leaked the story to Carl Osborne.'

'I gather you don't get on with your ex.'

'I honestly don't know why Frank hates me. I never rejected him. He left me—and he did it at a moment when I really needed help and support. You'd think he'd punished me enough for whatever I did wrong. But now this.'

'I can understand it. You're a standing reproach to him. Every time he sees you, he's reminded of how weak and cowardly he was when you needed him.'

'That's perceptive,' Toni said. She felt a warm surge of gratitude.

He shrugged. 'We never forgive those we've wronged.' He put a hand on her shoulder lightly. 'Frank may not have leaked the story merely to spite you. I suspect he would have done it anyway. I imagine Osborne will show his gratitude by reporting favourably on the Inverburn police in general and Superintendent Frank Hackett in particular.'

'It's generous of you to look at it that way,' she said. His hand warmed her skin through the silk of her blouse. Was this a casual gesture of reassurance, or was it something more?

There was a knock at the door. Stanley took his hand off Toni's shoulder as Cynthia Creighton, the company's public-relations officer, came in.

Cynthia was a thin woman of fifty. Normally hesitant, she was now on the edge of hysteria. 'Those people are *animals*!' she said. 'Where are the police?'

'A patrol car is on its way,' Toni said. 'They should be here in ten minutes.'

'They should arrest the lot of them.'

Toni realised with a sinking feeling that Cynthia was not capable of handling this crisis. She had never dealt with the jackal pack that was the British press in full cry, and she was too distressed to make good decisions.

Stanley was thinking the same thing. 'Cynthia, I want you to work with Toni on this,' he said. 'She has a lot of experience with the media.'

Cynthia looked relieved and grateful. 'Have you?'

'I did a year in the press office when I was with the police.'

'What do you think we should do? Should we apologise?' Cynthia asked.

'No,' Toni said quickly. 'It will be interpreted as confirmation that we've been careless. That's not true.' She thought for a moment. 'I think you should call a press conference in a couple of hours. Alert the people outside. It might calm them down a bit. Then phone the Press Association and Reuters and ask them to put it on the wire.'

'Right,' Cynthia said uncertainly.

As Cynthia left, Stanley's secretary buzzed him and said, 'Laurence Mahoney from the United States Embassy in London is on line one.'

'I remember him,' Toni said. 'He was here a few months ago. I showed him round.' The US Department of Defense was financing much of Oxenford Medical's research, being keenly interested in Stanley's new antiviral drug, which promised to be a powerful counter to biological warfare. Mahoney was the press officer who kept an eye on things for the Defense Department.

'Just a minute, Dorothy.' Stanley did not pick up the phone. He said to Toni, 'Mahoney is more important to us than all the British media put together. I don't want to talk to him cold. I need to think about how to handle him.'

'Do you want me to stall him?'

'Feel him out.'

Toni picked up the handset and touched a button. 'Hello, Larry, this is Toni Gallo. We met in September. How are you?'

'I'm worried,' Mahoney said. 'And I was hoping to speak to Professor Oxenford,' he added with an edge to his voice.

'He's with the laboratory director right now,' Toni said. 'He'll call you as soon as he has the complete picture—which will certainly be before midday.'

'How the hell did you let something like this happen?'

'The young man sneaked a rabbit out of the laboratory in his duffle bag. We've already instituted a compulsory bag search at the entrance to BSL4 to make sure it can't happen again.'

'My concern is bad publicity for the American government. We don't want to be blamed for unleashing deadly viruses on the population of Scotland.'

'There's no danger of that,' Toni said with her fingers crossed.

'Sooner or later the media will pick up on the fact that this research is American-financed. The most damaging angle is the one that says the research is done here because Americans think it's too dangerous to be done in the United States. I don't want to get into a situation where the only way to prove our goodwill is to transfer the research to Fort Detrick.'

Toni was shocked into silence. Fort Detrick, Maryland, housed the US Army Medical Research Institute of Infectious Diseases. If the research were transferred there, it would mean the end of the Kremlin. After a long pause, she said, 'We're not in that situation, not by a million miles.'

'I sure hope not. Have Stanley call me.'

'Thank you, Larry.' She hung up and said to Stanley, 'They can't transfer your research to Fort Detrick, can they?'

He went pale. 'There's certainly no provision in the contract to that effect,' he said. 'But they are the government of the most powerful country in the world, and they can do anything they want. What would I do—sue them?'

Toni was rocked by seeing Stanley appear vulnerable. 'Would they do it?'

'I'm sure the microbiologists at Fort Detrick would prefer to be doing this research themselves, if they had the choice.'

'Where would that leave you?'

'Bankrupt,' Stanley said grimly. 'I've invested everything in the new laboratory. I have a personal overdraft of a million pounds. If they pull the rug now, I've got no way of paying the debts.'

Toni could hardly take it in. 'But the new drug is worth millions.'

'It will be, eventually. I'm sure of the science—that's why I was happy to borrow so much money.' Stanley stood up. 'No point in whining. We've just got to manage our way out of this.'

'Yes. You're due to speak to the staff. Are you ready?'

'Yes.' They walked out of his office together. 'It will be good practice for the press later.'

KIT OXENFORD waited more than an hour for Harry McGarry.

McGarry, known as Harry Mac, had been born and raised in a tenement in Govan, a working-class district of Glasgow. With his profits from illegal gambling, drugs, theft and prostitution, he had moved—only a mile geographically, but a long way socially—across the Paisley Road to Dumbreck. Now he lived in a large, newly built house with a pool.

Kit waited nervously in the spacious hall, watched by a fat bodyguard.

Harry Mac's empire covered Scotland and the north of England. He owned the illegal casino where Kit played.

Most gamblers were stupid, Kit believed, but an intelligent player should always win. In blackjack there was a correct way to play every possible hand—a system called Basic—and he knew it backwards. Then, he improved his chances by keeping track of the cards that were dealt from the six-pack deck. Knowing the odds told him when to bet heavily.

But Kit had suffered a run of bad luck and, when the debt reached fifty thousand pounds, Harry had asked' for his money. Kit had gone to his father and begged to be rescued. It was humiliating, of course, after Stanley had fired him. But it was worth it. His father had paid. Kit had promised he would never gamble again, and meant it, but the temptation had been too strong.

Next time his debt reached fifty thousand he had gone back to his father, but Stanley put his foot down. 'I haven't got the money,' he had said. 'I could borrow it, perhaps, but you'd lose it and come back for more until we both were broke.' Kit had accused him of heartlessness and sworn never to speak to him again. The words had hurt, but Stanley had not changed his mind.

At that point, Kit should have left the country. But instead he had tried to win back what he owed. His debt went up to a quarter of a million.

For that much money, Harry Mac would pursue him to the North Pole. Kit thought about killing himself and eyed tall buildings in Glasgow, wondering if he could get up on the roofs in order to throw himself to his death.

Three weeks ago he had been summoned to this house. He had felt sick with fear. He was sure they were going to beat him up. When he was shown into the drawing room, with its yellow silk couches, he wondered how they would prevent the blood spoiling the upholstery.

'There's a gentleman here wants to ask you a question,' Harry had said.

The gentleman was Nigel Buchanan, a quiet type in his forties wearing expensive casual clothes. Speaking in a soft London accent, he had said, 'Can you get me inside the Level Four laboratory at Oxenford Medical?'

There had been two other people in the yellow drawing room at the time. One was Harry's daughter, Daisy, a muscular girl of about twenty-five with a shaved head, broken nose, bad skin and a ring through her lower lip. She was wearing leather gloves. The other was Elton, a handsome black man about the same age as Daisy, apparently a sidekick of Nigel's.

Kit was so relieved at not being beaten up that he would have agreed to anything. Nigel offered him a fee of £300,000 for the night's work. Kit could hardly believe his luck. It would be enough to pay his debts and more.

Later, Harry had talked about Nigel in reverent tones. A professional thief, Nigel stole only to order for a prearranged price. 'He's the greatest,' Harry said. 'You're after a painting by Michelangelo? No problem. A nuclear warhead? He'll get it for you—if you can afford it.'

Kit had spent the next three weeks planning the theft of the antiviral drug. He felt the occasional twinge of remorse, but mostly he felt a delirious glee at the thought of revenge on his father and Toni Gallo.

Nigel had gone over the details with him meticulously. Occasionally he would consult with Elton. Kit got the impression that he was a valued technical expert who had worked with Nigel before. Daisy was to join them on the raid, ostensibly to provide extra muscle—though Kit suspected her real purpose was to take £250,000 from him as soon as the fee was in his hands.

Kit had suggested that they rendezvous at a disused airfield near the Kremlin. Nigel looked at Elton.

'That's cool,' Elton said. He spoke with a broad south London accent. 'We could meet the buyer there after—he might want to fly in.'

Nigel had pronounced the plan brilliant, and Kit had glowed with pleasure.

Now, today, Kit had to tell Harry the whole deal was off. He felt wretched.

At last he was summoned to Harry's presence. Nervous, he followed the bodyguard through the laundry at the back of the house to the pool pavilion.

Harry was a stocky man of fifty with the grey skin of a lifelong smoker. He sat at a wrought-iron table, dressed in a purple towelling robe, drinking coffee and reading the *Sun*. Daisy was in the water, swimming laps tirelessly. Kit noticed she was wearing diver's gloves. She always wore gloves.

'I don't need to see you, laddie,' Harry said. 'I don't know anything about you or what you're doing tonight. Are you catching my drift?'

The air was hot and humid. Kit was wearing a blue mohair suit, with a white shirt open at the neck. His skin felt uncomfortably damp under his clothes. He realised that he had broken some rule of criminal etiquette by contacting Harry on the day of the robbery. 'I had to talk to you,' Kit said. 'Haven't you seen the news? A technician at Oxenford Medical died of a virus.'

'What do you want me to do, send flowers?'

Kit had not been asked to sit down, so he leaned on the back of a chair, feeling awkward. 'They'll be tightening security. This is the worst possible time to rob the place. We have to call it off.'

'Let me explain something to you.' Harry took a cigarette from a packet on the table and lit it with a gold lighter. 'For one thing, I've said it's going to happen. Now you may not realise this but when a man says something's going to happen, and then it doesn't, people think he's a wanker.'

'Yes, but—'

'Don't even dream of interrupting me.'

Kit shut up.

'For another thing, Nigel Buchanan is a legend, and more important, connected with some highly respected people in London. When you're dealing with folk like that, even more you don't want to look like a wanker.'

He paused, as if daring Kit to argue. Kit stood paralysed, saying nothing.

'And for a third thing, you owe me a quarter of a million pounds. No one has ever owed me that much money for so long and still been able to walk without crutches. I trust I'm making myself clear.'

Kit nodded silently. He was so scared he felt he might throw up.

'So don't tell me we have to call it off.'

Kit forced himself to speak. 'I meant postpone it, not call it off,' he managed. There's no point in doing it if we're going to get caught!' he said desperately. Harry did not respond. 'Everyone can wait a little longer, can't they?' It was like talking to the wall. 'Better late than never.'

Harry glanced towards the pool and made a beckoning gesture. Daisy climbed out of the pool.

'Kit wants us to wait for our money, Daisy,' Harry said. He stood up and tightened the belt of his robe. 'Explain to him how we feel about that—I'm too tired.' He put the newspaper under his arm and walked away.

Daisy grabbed Kit by the lapels of his best suit.

'Look,' he pleaded. 'I just want to make sure this doesn't end in disaster.'

Daisy jerked him sideways and threw him into the pool.

It was a shock, but if the worst thing she did was ruin his suit he would count himself lucky. Then, as he got his head above the surface, she jumped on him. He cried out and swallowed water as his head went under.

They were at the shallow end. When his feet touched the bottom he struggled to stand upright, but his head was clamped by Daisy's left arm, and he was pulled off balance again. She held him face down under the water.

Needing to breathe, he tried to break her hold, but she was too strong, and he lashed out feebly with his arms and legs. Daisy tightened her grip on his head. Panic overcame him. His body, starved of oxygen, forced him to gasp for air, and water rushed into his lungs. He found himself coughing and vomiting at the same time. After each spasm more water poured down his throat.

Terror gave him strength, and Daisy struggled to hold him, but he could not get his head up. He no longer tried to keep his mouth shut, but let the water flood into him. The sooner he drowned, the sooner the agony would be over. His struggles weakened. His eyes were open, showing him only a green blur; then his vision began to darken, as if night were falling.

NED DID NOT KNOW how to drive, so Miranda took the wheel of the Toyota Previa. Her son, Tom, sat behind with his Game Boy. The back row of seats had been folded away to make room for a stack of presents. As they pulled away from the Georgian terrace off the Great Western Road, where Miranda had her flat, a light snowfall began.

They were to pick up Ned's daughter, Sophie, before driving to Steepfall. Miranda drove to the suburb where Ned's ex-wife lived and turned into a street of old stone-built workers' cottages. She pulled up outside the largest one, where Ned had lived with Jennifer until they had split up two years ago.

She left the engine running and stayed in the car with Tom while Ned walked up the path to the house. Miranda never went inside. Although Ned had left the marital home before he met Miranda, Jennifer was hostile and avoided meeting her.

The door was opened by Sophie, a fourteen-year-old in jeans and a skimpy sweater. Ned kissed her and went inside.

Miranda turned on the radio. A choir was singing a Christmas carol. In the back, Tom's Game Boy beeped irregularly. Snow blew round the car in flurries. She turned up the heater. Ned came out of the house, looking annoyed.

He came to Miranda's window. 'Jennifer's out,' he said. 'Sophie hasn't even begun to get ready. Will you come in and help her pack?'

'Oh, Ned, I don't think I should,' Miranda said unhappily. She felt uncomfortable about going inside when Jennifer was not there.

Ned looked panicked. 'To tell you the truth, I'm not sure what a girl needs.'

Miranda sighed and killed the engine. 'Tom, you'll have to come too.'

Sophie was in the living room, lying on a couch in front of the television. She had a pierced navel with a cheap jewel in it. Miranda smelt cigarette smoke.

Ned said, 'Sophie, Miranda's going to help you get ready, OK, poppet?'

Sophie stood up reluctantly and walked slowly from the room. Miranda followed her upstairs to a messy bedroom decorated with posters.

Sophie opened the top drawer of a chest and began taking items out.

Miranda opened the door of a closet. 'You'll need a couple of frocks for the evenings.' She took out a red dress with spaghetti straps, much too sexy for a fourteen-year-old. 'This is nice,' she lied.

Sophie thawed a little. 'It's new.'

'We should wrap it so that it doesn't crease. Where do you keep tissue paper?'

'In the kitchen drawer, I think.'

'I'll fetch it. You find a couple of clean pairs of jeans.'

Miranda went downstairs. Ned and Tom were in the living room, watching TV. Miranda entered the kitchen and called out, 'Ned, do you know where tissue paper is kept?'

'I'm sorry, I don't.'

Miranda began opening drawers and eventually found some at the back of a cupboard. As she knelt on the floor to reach it she heard the back door of the house open, then a woman's footsteps. She looked up to see Jennifer.

'What the hell do you think you're doing?' Jennifer said. She was a formidable woman, smartly dressed in a tailored coat and high-heeled boots.

Miranda got to her feet, panting slightly. 'I was looking for tissue paper.'

'I can see that. I want to know why you're in my house at all.'

Ned appeared in the doorway. 'Hello, Jenny, I didn't hear you come in.'

'Obviously I didn't give you time to sound the alarm.'

'Sorry,' he said, 'but I asked Miranda to come in and—'

'Well, don't!' Jennifer interrupted. 'I don't want your women here.'

Miranda blushed hotly. 'I was just trying to help Sophie,' she said.

'I'll take care of Sophie. Please leave my house.'

Ned said, 'I'm sorry if we startled you, Jenny, but—'

'Don't bother to apologise, just get her out of here.'

'I'd better leave,' Miranda said, and turned angrily towards the hall.

'You can use the back door,' Jennifer said.

Miranda hesitated, then she looked at Jennifer and saw on her face the hint of a smirk. That gave Miranda an ounce of courage. 'I don't think so,' she said quietly. She went to the front door. 'Tom, come with me,' she called.

'Just a minute,' he shouted back.

She stepped into the living room. Tom was watching TV. She grabbed his wrist, hauled him to his feet and dragged him out of the house.

'That hurts!' he protested.

She slammed the front door. 'Next time, come when I call.'

She felt like crying as she got into the car. Ned had been hopeless. He had let Jennifer insult her without a word of protest. He just kept apologising. And then, worst of all, Miranda had taken out her anger on her son.

She looked round. 'Tommy, I'm sorry I hurt your wrist,' she said.

'It's OK,' he said. 'I'm sorry I didn't come when you called.'

'All forgiven, then,' she said. A tear rolled down her cheek, and she quickly wiped it away.

'VIRUSES KILL thousands of people every day,' Stanley Oxenford said. 'In 1918, flu caused more deaths than the whole of World War One. In 2002, three million people died of AIDS, caused by human immunodeficiency virus. And viruses are involved in ten per cent of cancers.'

Toni listened intently, sitting beside him in the Great Hall. She watched the faces of the reporters. Would they understand the importance of his work? If enough of these hacks chose to portray him as a mad scientist, the Americans might be sufficiently embarrassed to pull the finance.

'Viruses are a fact of life,' Stanley went on, 'but scientists can defeat them. Before AIDS, the great killer was smallpox—until a scientist called Edward Jenner invented vaccination in 1796. Now smallpox has disappeared from human society. In time, we will defeat influenza, and AIDS, and even cancer— and it will be done by scientists like us, working in laboratories such as this.'

A woman put up a hand. 'Edie McAllan, science correspondent, *Scotland on Sunday*,' she said. 'What are you working on here—exactly?'

Stanley said, 'We have developed an antiviral drug. That's rare. There are plenty of antibiotic drugs, which kill bacteria, but few that attack viruses. That's why a new antiviral drug is such good news.'

Edie McAllan asked, 'What viruses is your drug effective against?'

'That's the question we're trying to answer. We're testing the drug against a variety of viruses to determine its range.'

Clive Brown, from the tabloid newspaper the *Daily Record,* asked, 'Does that include dangerous viruses?'

'Yes,' Stanley replied. 'No one is interested in drugs for safe viruses.'

The audience laughed. It was a witty answer to a stupid question, but Brown looked annoyed and Toni's heart sank. A humiliated journalist would stop at nothing to get revenge.

'Thank you for that question, Clive,' Toni said, trying to mollify the tabloid reporter. 'At Oxenford Medical we impose the highest possible standards of security. In BSL4, which stands for Biosafety Level Four, the alarm system is connected with police headquarters at Inverburn. There are guards on duty twenty-four hours a day, and this morning I doubled the number of guards.'

Brown was not appeased. 'If you've got perfect security, how did the hamster get out?'

Toni was ready for this. 'Let me make three points. One, it was not a hamster. You've got that information from the police, and it's wrong.' Frank had betrayed himself as the source of the leaked story. 'Please rely on us for the facts about what goes on here. It was a rabbit, and it was not called Fluffy.'

They laughed at this, and even Brown smiled.

'Two, the rabbit was smuggled out of the laboratory in a bag, and we have today instituted a compulsory bag search at the entrance to BSL4, to make sure this cannot happen again. Three, I didn't say we had perfect security. I said we set the highest possible standards. That's all human beings can do.'

'So you're admitting your laboratory is a danger to the Scottish public?'

'No. You're safer here than you would be driving on the M8 or taking a flight from Prestwick. Viruses kill many people every day, but only one person has ever died of a virus from our lab, and he was an employee who deliberately broke the rules and knowingly put himself at risk.'

Frank's friend Carl Osborne spoke. He was a good-looking man of about Toni's age. 'Exactly what danger did this rabbit pose to the general public?'

Stanley answered. 'The virus is not very infectious across species. In order to infect Michael, we think the rabbit must have bitten him.'

'What if the rabbit had got loose?'

Stanley looked out of the window. A light snow was falling. 'It would have frozen to death.'

'Suppose another animal had eaten it. Could a fox have become infected?'

'No. Viruses are adapted to a small number of species, usually one, sometimes two or three. This one does not infect foxes, or any other forms of Scottish wildlife, as far as we know. Just humans, macaque monkeys and certain types of rabbit.'

'But Michael could have given the virus to other people.'

'By sneezing, yes. This was the possibility that alarmed us most. However, Michael seems not to have seen anyone during the critical period. We have already contacted his colleagues and friends. Nonetheless, we would be grateful if you would use your newspapers and television programmes to appeal for anyone who did see him to call us immediately.'

'I understand your work is financed by the American army,' Osborne said.

'The Department of Defense, yes,' Stanley said. 'They are naturally interested in ways of combatting biological warfare.'

'Isn't it true that the Americans have this work done in Scotland because they think it's too dangerous to be done in the United States?'

'On the contrary. A great deal of work of this type goes on in the States, at the Center for Disease Control in Atlanta, Georgia, and at the US Army Medical Research Institute of Infectious Diseases at Fort Detrick.'

'So why was Scotland chosen?'

'Because the drug was invented here at Oxenford Medical.'

Toni decided to quit while she was ahead and close the press conference. 'I don't want to cut the questioning short, but I know some of you have midday deadlines,' she said. 'You should all have an information pack and Cynthia here has extra copies.'

'One more question,' said Clive Brown. 'What's your reaction to the demonstration outside?'

Stanley said, 'They offer a simple answer to a complex ethical question. Like most simple answers, theirs is wrong.'

Toni added, 'And we hope they don't catch cold.'

While the audience was laughing at that, Toni stood up to indicate the conference was over. Then she was struck by inspiration. She beckoned to Cynthia Creighton. Turning her back on the audience, she said something to Cynthia in a low, urgent voice. Cynthia nodded and hurried away.

Toni turned to Stanley and said, 'Well done. You handled that perfectly.'

'I hope it's done the trick.'

'We'll know when we see the lunchtime TV news. Now you should slip away, otherwise they'll all try to corner you for an exclusive interview.'

'Good thinking. I need to get home, anyway.' He lived in a farmhouse on a cliff five miles from the lab. 'I'd like to be there to welcome the family.'

That disappointed her. She had been looking forward to reviewing the press conference with him. 'OK,' she said. 'I'll monitor the reaction.'

Stanley nodded over her shoulder. 'Here comes Osborne.'

'I'll head him off at the pass.' She moved to intercept the reporter, and Stanley left by a side door. 'Hello, Carl. I hope you got everything you needed?'

'I think so.' He changed tack. 'I've hardly seen you since you split up with Frank. We should get together and catch up.'

She had no desire to spend time with Carl, but she said, 'Sure, why not.'

He surprised her by following up quickly. 'Would you like to have dinner?'

It was the last thing she had expected. 'No!' she said. Then she remembered how dangerous this man could be and tried to soften her rejection. 'I'm sorry, Carl, you took me by surprise. I've known you so long that I just don't think of you that way.'

'I might change your thinking.' He looked boyishly vulnerable.

'I'm flattered,' she lied. 'But no.' Carl was handsome, charming, a local celebrity. But he had no integrity. Toni was not even mildly attracted to him.

He was not ready to give up. 'The truth is, I always fancied you, even when you were with Frank. You must have sensed that.'

'You used to flirt with me, but you did that with most women.'

'It wasn't the same. Have dinner with me tonight. I even have a table booked at La Chaumière.' It was a swanky restaurant. He must have made the reservation some time ago.

'I'm busy tonight.'

'You're not still carrying a torch for Frank, are you?'

Toni laughed. 'I did for a while, fool that I am, but I'm over him now.'

'Someone else, then?'

'I'm not seeing anyone.'

'But you're interested in someone. It's not the old professor, is it?'

'Don't be ridiculous,' Toni said.

'You're blushing. My God, you fancy Stanley Oxenford.' Carl was not good at taking rejection and his face became ugly. 'He's a widower, isn't he? Children grown up. All that money and just the two of you to spend it.'

'This is really offensive, Carl.'

'The truth so often is.'

She had to end this before she lost her temper. 'Thank you for coming to the press conference,' she said. She held out her hand and he shook it automatically. 'Goodbye.' She turned and walked away.

Toni was shaking with anger. But she had a crisis to deal with and could not let her emotions get in the way. She put on her coat and went outside. The snow was falling more heavily, but she could see the demonstration. She walked to the guard booth at the gate, where Toni had asked Cynthia to organise the distribution of hot drinks by three canteen staff. The protesters had stopped chanting and waving their banners, and were smiling and chatting.

And all the cameras were photographing them. Everything had gone perfectly, she thought. So why did she feel so depressed?

She returned to her office, closed the door and stood still, grateful to be alone for a minute. The phone rang. She looked at it for a moment, resenting its cheerful warble, not wanting to talk. Then she picked it up.

It was Stanley, calling from his car. 'Why don't you drop in at the house in an hour or so? We could watch the news, and learn our fate together.'

Her mood lifted instantly. 'Of course,' she said. 'I'd be delighted.'

12 NOON

The snow became heavier as Miranda drove north. It seemed to soundproof the Toyota Previa, and there was no more than a background swish of tyres to compete with the music from the radio.

The atmosphere inside was subdued. In the back, Sophie was listening to her own music on headphones, while Tom was lost in the beeping world of Game Boy. Ned was quiet, gazing into the snow. As Miranda watched his tranquil, bearded face, she realised that he had no idea how badly he had let her down.

He sensed her discontent. 'I'm sorry about Jennifer's outburst,' he said.

Miranda said, 'Jennifer was bloody rude. But it's not her behaviour that bothers me. It's yours. You didn't defend me!'

'I thought you were well able to defend yourself.'

'That's not the point! Of course I can look after myself. But you should be my champion.'

'I thought it was more important to get things calmed down.'

'Well, you thought wrong. When the world turns hostile, I don't want you to take a judicious view of the situation—I want you to be on my side.'

'I'm afraid I'm not the combative type.'

'I know,' she said, and they both fell silent. Miranda felt depressed. Even if her family embraced Ned, did she want to marry such a passive man? She had longed for someone gentle and cultured and bright, but she now realised that she also wanted him to be strong. Was it too much to expect?

Her mood lifted as they approached Steepfall. The house was reached by a long lane that wound through woods. Emerging from the trees, the drive swept round a headland with a sheer drop to the sea.

The garage came into view first. It was an old cowshed that had been renovated and given three up-and-over doors. Miranda drove past it to the house.

Her father's dark blue Ferrari was at the front of the house, where he always left it for Luke, the handyman, to put away.

Miranda parked the Toyota. Tom rushed in. Sophie followed more slowly; she had not been here before, though she had met Stanley once, at Olga's birthday party. Miranda decided to forget about Jennifer for now. She took Ned's hand and they went in together. They entered, as always, by the kitchen door at the side of the house. To Miranda this always felt like coming home.

A full-size black standard poodle called Nellie wagged her whole body with joy and licked everyone. Miranda greeted Luke and Lori, the Filipino couple who were preparing lunch.

Lori said, 'Your father just got home; he's washing.'

Miranda told Tom and Sophie to lay the table. She did not want them to put down roots in front of the TV. 'Tom, you can show Sophie where everything is.' And having a job to do would help Sophie feel part of the family.

There were several bottles of Miranda's favourite white wine in the fridge. She opened a bottle and poured a glass for Ned. Perhaps this, she thought, rather than the scene with Jennifer, would set the tone for the holiday. He had never brought Sophie before and he had never stayed overnight.

The phone rang. Miranda picked up the extension on the wall. 'Hello?'

'Miranda, it's Kit.'

She was pleased. 'Hello, little brother! How are you?'

'A bit shattered, actually.'

'How come?'

'I fell in a swimming pool. Long story. How are things at Steepfall?'

'We're just sitting around drinking wine, wishing you were with us.'

'Well, I'll be there in an hour or so. But, listen, can I have the cottage?'

'I'm sure you can. It's up to Daddy, but I'll talk to him.'

As Miranda replaced the handset, her father came in. He wore the waistcoat and trousers of his suit, but he had rolled the cuffs of his shirt. He shook hands with Ned and kissed Miranda and the children. He looked at his watch distractedly. 'I have to watch the lunchtime news on television.'

The door opened and Olga came in. As always, she entered speaking. 'This weather is a nightmare! People are skidding all over the place. Is that wine you're drinking? Let me have some before I explode. Daddy, how are you?'

'*Nella merde*,' he said.

Miranda recognised one of her mother's expressions. It meant 'in the shit'.

Olga said, 'I heard about the guy who died. Is it so bad for you?'

'We'll see when we watch the news.'

Olga was followed in by her husband, Hugo, a small man with impish charm. When he kissed Miranda, his lips lingered on her cheek a second too long.

Olga said, 'Where shall Hugo put the bags?'

'Upstairs,' said Miranda.

'I suppose you've staked your claim to the cottage.'

'No, Kit's having it.'

'Oh, please!' Olga protested. 'That big double bed and nice bathroom all for one person, while the four of us share the poky old bathroom upstairs?'

Miranda felt irritated with her sister. 'You know Kit hasn't been here since . . . that whole mess. I just want to make sure he has a good time.'

'So he's getting the best bedroom because he stole from Daddy—is that your logic?'

'You're talking like an advocate again. Save it for your learned friends.'

'All right, you two,' their father said, pulling up a chair and sounding just as he had when they were small. 'In this case, I think Olga's right. It's selfish of Kit to demand the cottage all to himself. Miranda and Ned can sleep there.'

Olga said, 'So no one gets what they want.'

'It will teach you not to quarrel.'

'No, it won't. You've been imposing these judgments of Solomon for thirty years, and we still haven't learned.'

Stanley smiled, and the argument was ended by the entrance of Caroline and Craig, the children of Hugo and Olga. Caroline, seventeen, was carrying a cage containing several white rats. Nellie sniffed it excitedly.

Craig, fifteen, carried two plastic rubbish bags crammed with wrapped gifts. He had Hugo's wicked grin, though he was tall like Olga. He put the bags down, greeted the family perfunctorily, and made a beeline for Sophie. They had met before, Miranda recalled, at Olga's birthday party. 'You got your bellybutton pierced!' Craig said to Sophie. 'Cool! Did it hurt?'

Miranda became aware that there was a stranger in the room. The newcomer, a woman, stood by the door to the hall, so must have come in by the front entrance. She was tall, with striking good looks: high cheekbones, lush red-blonde hair and marvellous green eyes. She was gazing with amusement at the scene in the kitchen. Miranda wondered how long she had been there.

The others began to notice her, and slowly the room fell silent. At last, Stanley turned round. 'Ah! Toni!' he said, jumping up from his seat, and Miranda was struck by how pleased he looked. 'Kind of you to drop in. Kids, this is my colleague, Antonia Gallo.'

The woman smiled. This was the ex-cop who had caught Kit stealing from the company, Miranda realised. Despite that, Stanley seemed to like her.

Stanley introduced everyone, and Miranda noticed the pride in his tone.

Toni said, 'I'm very glad to meet you all.' She sounded as if she meant it, but at the same time she seemed to be under strain.

'You must be having a difficult day,' Miranda said. 'I'm so sorry about the technician who died.'

Stanley said, 'It was Toni who found him.'

'Oh God!'

Toni nodded. 'We're pretty sure he didn't infect anyone else, thank Heaven. Now we're just hoping the media won't crucify us.'

Stanley looked at his watch. 'Excuse us,' he said to his family. 'We're going to watch the news in my study.' He held the door for Toni and they went out.

The children started to chatter again, and Miranda turned to Olga, their quarrel forgotten. 'Attractive woman,' she said musingly.

'Yes,' Olga said. 'About, what, my age?'

'Thirty-seven, thirty-eight, yes. A shared crisis brings people together.'

'Doesn't it just?'

'So what do you think?'

'I think what you think.'

Miranda drained her glass of wine. 'I thought so.'

TONI WAS OVERWHELMED by the scene in the kitchen. It had been like walking into a really good party where she knew nobody. She had stood there for several minutes, bemused but fascinated.

When at last they noticed her, she got a hard look from both daughters, Olga and Miranda. It was a careful scrutiny: detailed, unapologetic, hostile. Was Stanley sensing these undercurrents? As she followed him into his study, she felt again the frustration of not knowing what was in his mind.

It was a masculine room, with a Victorian pedestal desk, where she laid her bag, a bookcase full of weighty microbiology texts, and a worn leather couch in front of a log fire. The dog followed them in and stretched out by the fire.

On the mantelpiece was a framed photograph of a dark-haired teenage girl in tennis whites—the same girl as the bride in the picture on his office wall.

Sitting on the couch beside Stanley, she tried to concentrate on the crisis at hand. 'Did you call the US Embassy?' she asked him.

'Yes. I got Mahoney calmed down, but he'll be watching the news like us.'

The Scottish news came on before the UK bulletin. The death of Michael Ross was still the top story, but the report was introduced by a newsreader. There was no more of Carl Osborne's laughably inaccurate science.

'So far, so good,' Stanley murmured.

The picture switched to the gates of the Kremlin. 'Animal-rights campaigners took advantage of the tragedy to stage a protest outside Oxenford Medical,' the anchor said. The sentence was more favourable than Toni would have hoped. It implied the demonstrators were cynical media manipulators.

After a brief shot of the demo, the report cut to the Great Hall. Toni heard her own voice, outlining the security system at the laboratory. Then there was a shot of Carl Osborne asking, 'Exactly what danger did this rabbit pose to the general public?' Toni leaned forward on the couch. This was the crunch.

They played the interchange between Carl and Stanley, with Carl posing disaster scenarios and Stanley saying how unlikely they were. The final press conference shot was a close-up of Stanley, saying, 'In time, we will defeat influenza, and AIDS, and even cancer—and it will be done by scientists like us, working in laboratories such as this.'

'That's good,' Toni said. 'You look so reassuring.'

Then there was a shot of the canteen staff giving out steaming hot drinks to the demonstrators in the snow. 'Great—they used it!' said Toni.

'I didn't see this,' Stanley said. 'Whose idea was it?'

'Mine.'

Carl Osborne thrust a microphone into the face of a woman employee and said, 'These people are demonstrating against your company. Why are you giving them coffee?'

'Because it's cold out here,' the woman replied.

Toni and Stanley laughed, delighted with the woman's wit and the positive way it reflected on the company.

The anchor reappeared and said, 'The First Minister of Scotland issued a statement this morning, saying, "I have today spoken to representatives of Oxenford Medical, the Inverburn police and the Inverburn regional health authority, and I am satisfied that everything possible is being done to ensure that there is no further danger to the public." And now other news.'

Toni said, 'My God, I think we saved the day.'

'Giving out hot drinks was a great idea—when did you think of that?'

'At the last minute. Let's see what the UK news says.'

In the main bulletin, the story of Michael Ross came second, after an earth-quake in Russia. The report used some of the same footage. There was a low-key statement from the British Environment Minister in London. The report continued the same unhysterical tone of the Scottish news.

Stanley said, 'It's good to know that not all journalists are like Osborne.'

'He asked me to have dinner with him.' Toni wondered why she was telling him this.

Stanley looked surprised. 'What did you say to him?'

'I turned him down, of course.'

'I should think so, too.' Stanley looked embarrassed and added, 'Not that it's any of my business, but he's not worthy of you, not by a light-year.' He returned his attention to the television and switched to an all-news channel.

They watched footage of the Michael Ross story again, then Stanley turned off the set. 'Well, we escaped crucifixion by TV.'

'No newspapers tomorrow, as it's Christmas Day,' Toni observed. 'By Thursday the story will be old. I think we're in the clear—barring unexpected developments.'

'Yes. If we lost another rabbit, we'd be right back in trouble.'

'There will be no more security incidents in the lab,' Toni said firmly. 'I'll make sure of that.'

Stanley nodded. 'I have to say, you've handled this whole thing extraordi-narily well. I'm very grateful to you.'

Toni glowed. 'We told the truth, and they believed us,' she said.

They smiled at one another. It was a moment of happy intimacy.

Then the phone rang. Stanley reached across his desk and picked it up.

'Oxenford,' he said. 'Yes, patch him through here, please, I'm keen to speak to him.' He looked up at Toni and mouthed, 'Mahoney.'

Toni stood up nervously. She and Stanley were convinced they had con-trolled the publicity well—but would the US government agree?

He spoke into the phone. 'Hello again, Larry, did you watch the news? . . . I'm glad you think so . . . We've avoided the kind of hysterical reaction that you feared . . . Absolutely right, we must keep a very tight grip on security from now on . . . yes. Good of you to call. Bye.'

Stanley hung up and grinned at Toni. 'We're in the clear.' Exuberantly, he put his arms round her and hugged her.

She pressed her face into his shoulder and breathed in the warm, faint smell of him. She wrapped her arms round him and hugged him back.

She would have stayed like that for ever, but after a few seconds he gently disengaged, looking bashful. As if to restore propriety, he shook her hand. 'All credit to you,' he said, then added, 'Shall we get a breath of air?'

'Sure.'

Toni put on her parka and Stanley picked up an old blue anorak. They stepped outside to find the world painted white. The dog headed for the cliff and Stanley and Toni followed.

'What are your Christmas plans?' Stanley asked.

'I'm going to a health spa with some friends, all singles or childless couples, for a grown-up Christmas. No turkey, no crackers, no stockings, no Santa. Just gentle pampering and adult conversation.'

'It sounds wonderful. I thought you usually had your mother?'

'I have done for the past few years. But this Christmas my sister Bella is taking her—somewhat to my surprise.'

'Surprise?'

Toni made a wry face. 'Bella has three children, and she feels that excuses her from other responsibilities. I'm not sure that's fair, but I accept it.'

'Do you want to have children, one day?'

She caught her breath. It was a deeply intimate question. 'Maybe. It was the one thing my sister always wanted. The desire for babies dominated her life. I'm not like that. I envy you your family—they obviously love and respect you and like being with you. But I don't necessarily want to sacrifice everything else in life in order to become a parent.'

'I'm not sure you have to sacrifice everything,' Stanley said.

'And what about you? You could start another family.'

'Oh, no,' he said quickly. 'My children would be most put out.'

Toni felt a little disappointed that he was so decisive about that.

They reached the cliff. To the left, the headland sloped down to a beach. To the right, the ground dropped sheer into the sea. On that side, the edge was barred by a low wall four feet high. They both leaned on the wall and looked at the waves a hundred feet below.

'What a lovely spot,' Toni said.

'Four hours ago I thought I was going to lose it. I had to pledge the house as security for my overdraft. If I go bust, the bank takes my home.'

'But your family . . .'

'They would be heartbroken. And now, since Marta went, they're all I really care about.'

She looked at him. His expression was serious. Why was he telling her this? As a message, Toni assumed. An awful lot had happened in the last few hours, but all of it was ambiguous. He had touched her, hugged her, asked her if she wanted children. Did it mean anything? She had to know. She said, 'You're telling me you'd never do anything to jeopardise what I saw in your kitchen, the togetherness of your family.'

'Yes. They all draw their strength from it, whether they realise it or not.'

She faced him and looked directly into his eyes. 'And that's so important to you that you would never start another family?'

'Yes.'

The message was clear, Toni thought. He liked her, but he was not going to take it any further. The hug in the study had been a spontaneous expression of triumph, and now he was pulling back. Reason had prevailed. Feeling tears come to her eyes, she turned away, saying, 'This wind . . .'

She was saved by young Tom, who came running through the snow, calling, 'Grandpa! Grandpa! Uncle Kit's here!'

They went with the boy back to the house, not speaking, both embarrassed.

Kit was in the kitchen, being welcomed by his family—like the prodigal son, Toni thought. Toni stood at the kitchen door and watched Stanley greet his son. Kit looked wary, and held out a hand to shake, but his father embraced him.

'I'm very glad you came, my boy,' Stanley said. 'Very glad indeed.'

Kit said, 'I'd better get my bag from the car. I'm in the cottage, yeah?'

Miranda looked nervous and said, 'No, you're upstairs.'

'But—'

'Don't make a fuss,' Olga said. 'Daddy has decided, and it's his house.'

Toni saw a flash of pure rage in Kit's eyes, but he covered up quickly. 'Whatever,' he said. He was trying to give the impression that it was no big deal, but that flash said otherwise, and Toni wondered what secret project he had that made him so keen to sleep outside the main house tonight.

She slipped into Stanley's study. The memory of that hug came back to her. That was the closest she was going to get to making love to him, she thought.

Her bag lay on his desk where she had left it. She picked it up and slung it over her shoulder and returned to the hall. Looking into the kitchen, she saw

Stanley saying something to the cook. She waved to him. He came over.

'Toni, thanks for everything. Happy Christmas.'

'To you, too.' She went out quickly.

Kit was outside, opening the boot of his black Peugeot coupé. She hoped to pass him without speaking but, as she was opening her car door, he looked up.

'Happy Christmas, Kit,' she said politely.

He lifted a small suitcase from the boot and slammed the lid. 'Get lost, bitch,' he said, and he walked into the house.

CRAIG WAS THRILLED to see Sophie again. He had been captivated by her at his mother's birthday party. She was pretty in a dark-eyed, dark-haired way, but it was not her looks that had bewitched him; it was her attitude. Nothing impressed her: not Grandpa's Ferrari F50, nor Craig's football skills. Sophie wore what she liked, she ignored NO SMOKING signs, and if someone was boring her she would walk away in mid-sentence.

It made her difficult to get on with. Showing her around Steepfall, Craig found that nothing pleased her. Silence was as near as she got to praise.

He took her to the barn. The ground floor was a playroom with a billiard table, a bar football game and a TV. 'This is an OK place to hang out,' he said.

'Quite cool,' she said—the most enthusiasm she had yet shown.

Craig pointed to two camp beds. 'Tom and I are sleeping here,' he said. 'Come upstairs. I'll show you your bedroom.'

A ladder led to the hayloft. There was no wall, just a handrail for safety. Two single beds were neatly made up. The only furniture was a rail for hanging clothes and a cheval mirror. Caroline's suitcase was on the floor, open.

He sat on one of the beds. 'It's comfortable—better than our camp beds.'

She looked around the bare hayloft with an expression of distaste.

'The bathroom's underneath here, at the back. There's no bath, but the shower works all right.'

'How luxurious.' She went down the ladder.

He followed her down. There was one more thing that might get her excited. 'I've got something else to show you.' He led the way outside.

They stepped into a big square yard with one building on each of its four sides: the main house, the guest cottage, the barn they had just left, and the three-car garage. Craig led Sophie round the house to the front door. He led her up the stairs to Grandpa's suite in the new extension, and tapped on the door in case Grandpa was inside. There was no reply and he went in.

He walked through the bedroom into the dressing room beyond. He opened a closet door and pushed aside a row of suits, then got down on his knees, reached into the closet and shoved at the back wall. A panel two feet square swung open on a hinge. Craig crawled through it. Sophie followed.

Craig reached back through the gap and pulled the closet door shut, then closed the panel. Fumbling in the dark, he found a switch and turned on the light, a single unshaded bulb hanging from a roof beam.

They were in an attic. There was a big old sofa with stuffing bursting out of holes in the upholstery. A stack of mouldering photograph albums stood on the floorboards next to a collection of cardboard boxes and tea chests.

'This part of the house used to be the dairy, when the place was a farm,' Craig said. 'Grandpa turned the dairy into the kitchen, but the roof was too high, so he put a ceiling in and used this space for storage. You can see into the kitchen,' he persisted. 'Over here, where the flue from the Aga comes through the ceiling.' He lay flat and looked through a wide gap between the boards and a metal shaft. He could see the entire kitchen: the hall door at the far end, the long scrubbed-pine table, the side doors into the dining room and the laundry, and two doors at this end, one to the pantry and the other to the boot lobby and side entrance. Most of the family were round the table. Craig's sister, Caroline, was feeding her rats, Miranda was pouring wine, Ned was reading the *Guardian*. Lori was poaching a salmon in a fish kettle. 'I think Aunt Miranda's getting drunk,' Craig said.

That caught Sophie's interest. She lay down beside Craig to look. 'Can't they see us?' she said quietly.

He studied her as she stared through the gap. The skin of her cheek looked unbearably soft. 'Have a look, next time you're in the kitchen,' he said. 'You'll see that there's a ceiling light right behind the gap, which makes it difficult to make out, even when you know it's there.'

'So, like, nobody knows you're here?'

'Well, everyone knows there's an attic. And Nellie will look up and cock her head, listening, as soon as you move. She knows you're here—and anyone watching her may catch on.'

'Still, this is pretty cool. Look at my father. He's pretending to read the paper, but he keeps making eyes at Miranda. Yech.'

Craig looked through the gap again. Lori was sprinkling chopped parsley over a steaming bowl of potatoes. Suddenly he felt hungry. 'Lunch is ready,' he said. 'I'll show you the other way out.'

He went to the end of the attic and opened a large door. A narrow ledge overhung a drop of fifteen feet to the yard.

Sophie said, 'I can't jump from here.'

'No need.' Craig walked along the ledge to the end and stepped two feet down onto a lean-to roof over the boot lobby. 'Easy.'

Looking anxious, Sophie followed in his footsteps. When she reached the end of the ledge, he offered her his hand. She took it, gripping unnecessarily hard. He handed her down onto the lean-to roof, stepped back up on the ledge to close the big door, then returned to Sophie's side. They went cautiously down the slippery roof. Craig lay on his front and slid over the edge, then dropped the short distance to the ground. Sophie followed suit. When she was lying on the roof with her legs dangling over the edge, Craig reached up with both hands, held her by the waist, and lifted her down. She was light.

'Thanks,' she said, looking triumphant, as if she'd come successfully through a trying experience.

It wasn't that difficult, Craig thought as they went into the house for lunch. Perhaps she's not as confident as she pretends.

3 P.M.

The Kremlin looked pretty. Snow clung to its gargoyles and window ledges, outlining the Victorian ornamentation in white. Toni parked and went inside. The place was quiet. Most people had gone home.

She felt hurt and sensitive. But she had to put thoughts of love firmly out of her mind: she had work to do. Stanley's words repeated in her brain: *If we lost another rabbit, we'd be right back in trouble.* It was true. Another incident of the same kind would bring the story back to life but ten times worse. No amount of public-relations work could keep the lid on it.

She went to her office. The only threat that she could imagine was from the animal-rights activists. Michael Ross might have been working with other activists, and might have given them inside information.

She dialled Odette Cressy, her friend at Scotland Yard.

'I saw you on the news,' Odette said.

'How did I look?'

'Authoritative.' Odette giggled. 'Like you would *never* go to a nightclub in a see-through dress. But I know better.'

'Just don't tell anyone.'

'Anyway, your Madoba-2 incident appears to have no connections with . . . my kind of interest.' She meant terrorism.

'Good,' Toni said. 'What about Animals Are Free? Did you check them out?'

'Of course. They're harmless. The worst they're likely to do is block a road.'

'That's great news. I just want to make sure there's not another incident of the same kind.'

'It looks unlikely from my end.'

'Thanks, Odette. You're a friend.'

They hung up, and Toni summoned Steve Tremlett, the guard supervisor. He arrived within a minute, a small, neat man of thirty-five with receding fair hair. He carried a cardboard folder. Toni pointed to a chair and he sat down.

'The police don't think Michael Ross was working with others,' she said. 'All the same, we have to have this place buttoned up tight tonight.'

'No problem.'

'Let's make doubly sure of that. You have the duty roster there?'

Steve handed over a sheet of paper. Normally there were three security guards on duty overnight and on weekends and holidays: one in the gatehouse, one in Reception, and one in the control room, watching the monitors. Every hour, the guard from Reception made a tour of the main building, and the guard from the gatehouse walked round the outside. Toni had doubled the guard for this Christmas holiday, so that there would be two people at each of the three stations and they would patrol every half-hour.

'I see you're working tonight.'

'I need the overtime.'

'All right. Let me check your emergency call list.'

Steve passed her a laminated sheet from the folder. It listed the agencies he was to phone in case of fire, flood, power cut, computer crash, phone-system faults and other problems.

Toni said, 'I want you to ring each of these in the next hour. Ask them if the number will be operational over Christmas.' She handed back the sheet. 'Don't hesitate to call the police at Inverburn if you're worried about anything.'

He nodded. 'My brother-in-law Jack is on duty tonight, as it happens.'

'You don't happen to know who the duty superintendent is?'

'Yes. It's your Frank. He's on call.'

Toni did not comment. 'I'll have my mobile phone with me day and night. I want you to call me if anything unusual happens, regardless of the time, OK?'

'Of course.'

'That's all. I'll be leaving in a few minutes.' She checked her watch: it was almost four. 'Happy Christmas, Steve.'

'To you, too.'

Steve left. Toni closed down her computer and locked her filing cabinet. She needed to get going. She had to return home and change, then drive to the spa, fifty miles away. The sooner she hit the road, the better: the forecast said the weather would not get worse, but forecasts could be wrong.

KIT WAS FURIOUS about the sleeping arrangements. He had *specifically* told Miranda he needed to be in the cottage. She had practically gone down on her knees to plead with him to come, but had failed to fulfil the one condition he had made. The old man had obviously overruled her.

Kit sat in the living room, with his father, his nephew Tom, his brother-in-law Hugo, and Miranda's fiancé, Ned. The women of the family were preparing tomorrow's Christmas dinner, and the older children were in the barn. The men were watching a movie on TV. Kit was too tense to follow the plot.

He had to leave Steepfall tonight and come back tomorrow morning without anyone knowing he had been away. If he had been sleeping in the cottage, he could have sneaked away quietly. He had already moved his car to the garage forecourt, away from the house, so that no one would hear the engine.

Now it would be much more difficult. His room was in the creaky old part of the main house, next to Olga and Hugo. He would have to wait until everyone had retired and then creep out of his room and tiptoe down the stairs. If someone should open a door, what would he say? 'I'm just going to get some fresh air.' In the middle of the night, in the snow? And in the morning someone would almost certainly see him coming in.

He tried to put that worry out of his mind. He had a more immediate problem. He had to steal the smart card his father used to enter BSL4.

The chip inside Stanley's card would contain the site code for the Kremlin, but it would have Stanley's fingerprint data, not Kit's. However, he had thought of a way round that.

Kit got up, grunted something about the bathroom and went out. From the hall, he glanced into the kitchen, where Olga was stuffing a huge turkey while Miranda cleaned Brussels sprouts. He stepped into his father's study and closed the door. The old man's briefcase was on the floor beside the desk. Kit went through it quickly. It contained a file of graphs, today's *Times* and a small leather notebook.

The top of the pedestal desk was tidy, and Kit could not see a card or anything that might contain one. He started opening the drawers and he felt his heartbeat speed up. But if he were caught, what would they do—call the police? He carried on, his hands unsteady. The smart card wasn't there.

Kit left the room and went quietly up the stairs. The only remaining possibility was the bedroom. He went inside and closed the door. On either side of the double bed were a pair of Victorian mahogany commode chests, used as bedside tables. His father had always slept on the right of the bed. Kit opened the drawers on that side. In one of them he found a flashlight, presumably for power cuts, and a volume of Proust, presumably for insomnia. He checked the drawers on his mother's side of the bed, but they were empty.

Kit went into the dressing room, a square space lined with closets. Outside it was twilight, but he could see well enough, so he did not switch on the lights. He opened the door of his father's suit cupboard. There on a hanger was the jacket of the suit Stanley was wearing today. Kit reached into the inside pocket and drew out a black leather wallet. It contained a small wad of banknotes and a row of plastic cards. One was a smart card for the Kremlin.

'Bingo,' Kit said softly.

The bedroom door opened. Kit had not closed the door to the dressing room, and he was able to look through the doorway and see his sister Miranda step into the bedroom, carrying an orange plastic laundry basket.

He quickly moved behind the dressing-room door. If he peeked round the side of the door, he could see her reflected in the mirror on the bedroom wall. She switched the lights on and began to strip the bed. She and Olga were obviously doing some of Lori's chores. Kit decided he would just have to wait.

Miranda began to make up the bed with fresh sheets, and at that moment Hugo came in. He had changed into a red pullover and green corduroy trousers, and he looked like a Christmas elf. He closed the door behind him.

Miranda said, 'Hugo, what do you want?' She sounded wary.

Hugo gave her a conspiratorial grin. 'I just thought I'd give you a hand.' He went to the opposite side of the bed and started tucking in the sheet.

Miranda tossed a clean pillowcase across the bed. 'Here,' she said.

Hugo stuffed a pillow into it. Together they arranged the bed cover. 'It seems ages since we've seen you,' Hugo said. 'I miss you.'

'Don't talk rubbish,' Miranda said coolly.

Kit was puzzled but fascinated. What was going on here?

Miranda smoothed the cover. Hugo came round the end of the bed. She picked up her laundry basket and held it in front of her like a shield. Hugo gave his impish grin and said, 'How about a kiss, for old times' sake?'

Kit was mystified. What old times was Hugo talking about?

'Stop that, right now,' Miranda said firmly.

Hugo grasped the laundry basket and pushed. The backs of Miranda's legs came up against the edge of the bed. Involuntarily, she sat down, released the basket and used her hands to balance herself. Hugo tossed the basket aside and shoved her back, kneeling on the bed with his legs either side of her.

'Get off me now,' she said.

Kit did not know what to do. Could he sneak past them while they were wrestling? No, the room was too small. He just stood paralysed, looking on.

'Just a quickie,' Hugo said, pushing up her skirt. 'No one will know.'

Miranda drew back her right arm and swung at Hugo's face, hitting him on the cheek with a mighty slap. Then she lifted her knee sharply, making contact with his groin. She twisted, threw him off, and jumped to her feet.

Hugo remained lying on the bed. 'That hurt!' he protested.

'Good,' she said. 'Now listen to me. Never do anything like that again.'

He stood up. 'Why not? What will you do—tell Ned?'

'I ought to tell him, but I haven't got the courage. I slept with you once, when I was lonely and depressed, and I've regretted it bitterly ever since.'

Kit was shocked. Miranda had slept with Olga's husband. He was not surprised by Hugo's behaviour but Miranda was prissily moral about such things.

Miranda went on, 'It was the most shameful thing I've done in my life, and I don't want Ned to find out about it, ever.'

'So what are you threatening to do? Tell Olga?'

'She would divorce you and never speak to me again. It would explode this family.' Miranda was always anxious about keeping the family together.

'That leaves you a bit helpless, doesn't it?' Hugo said, looking pleased. 'Since we can't be enemies, why not just kiss me nicely and be friends?'

Miranda's voice went cold. 'Because you disgust me.'

'Ah, well.' Hugo sounded resigned but unashamed. 'I still adore you.' He gave her his most charming smile and left the room, limping slightly.

As the door slammed, Miranda said, 'You fucking bastard.'

Kit had never heard her swear like that.

She picked up her laundry basket then, instead of going out as he expected, she turned towards him. There was no time to move. In three steps she reached the entrance to the dressing room and turned on the lights.

Kit was just able to slip the smart card into his trouser pocket. An instant later she saw him. She gave a squeal of shock.

'Kit! What are you doing there? You gave me a fright!' She went white, and added, 'You must have heard everything.'

'Sorry.' He shrugged. 'I didn't want to.'

Her complexion changed from pale to flushed. 'You won't tell, will you?'

'Of course not.'

She saw the wallet in his hand. 'What are you up to?'

'I needed money.' He showed her the banknotes in the wallet.

'Oh, Kit!' She was distressed, not judgmental.

He tried to look ashamed. 'I'm a bit desperate.'

'I'll give you money!' she said. 'But you must never steal from Daddy.'

'OK.'

'And, for pity's sake, don't ever tell anyone about me and Hugo.'

'I promise,' he said.

TONI HAD BEEN sleeping heavily for an hour when her alarm clock woke her.

It was 5 p.m. She was lying on the bed fully dressed. She had been too tired even to take off her jacket and shoes. But the nap had refreshed her.

She lived on one floor of a subdivided Victorian house in Inverburn, which was a ferry port, although she could not see the sea from the house. She was not fond of her home. It was the place to which she had fled when she broke up with Frank. Even after two years, she still regarded it as temporary.

She got up, stripped off the business suit she had been wearing for two days and a night, and dumped it in the dry-cleaning basket. With a robe on over her underwear she moved rapidly round the flat, packing a case for five nights at a health spa. She had planned to leave at midday today.

Her mother should be at Bella's place by now. Mother was an intelligent woman who was losing her mind. She had been a maths teacher and had always been able to help Toni with her studies, even when Toni was in the final year of her engineering degree. Now she could not check her change in a shop. Toni loved her intensely and was deeply saddened by her decline.

Bella was a bit slapdash. She cleaned the house when the mood took her and cooked when she felt hungry. Her husband, Bernie, was a hairdresser, but worked infrequently because of some vague chest ailment. Mother never seemed to mind Bella's ways and had always been happy to visit the windy Glasgow council estate and eat undercooked chips with her grandchildren.

After Toni had packed, she took a bath and washed her hair. As she was putting on jeans and a dark green sweater, the phone rang. It was her sister.

'Hi, Bella,' said Toni. 'How's Mother?'

'She's not here.'

'What? You were supposed to pick her up at one o'clock!'

'I know, but Bernie had the car and I couldn't get away.'

'And you still haven't left?' Toni looked at her watch. It was half past five.

'The thing is, the weather's turned bad.'

'It's snowing all over Scotland, but not heavily.'

'Well, Bernie doesn't want me to drive sixty miles in the dark.'

'You wouldn't have had to if you'd picked her up when you promised!'

'Oh dear, you're getting angry. I knew this would happen.'

'Never mind how I feel,' Toni said. 'What about Mother? What are you going to do?'

'There isn't anything I can do.'

'So you're going to leave her in the home over Christmas?'

'Unless you have her. You're only ten miles away.'

'Bella, I'm booked into a spa! My friends are expecting me to join them. I've paid four hundred pounds deposit and I'm looking forward to a rest.'

'That sounds a bit selfish.'

'Just a minute. I've had Mother the last three Christmases, but I'm selfish?'

'You don't know how hard it is with three children and a husband too ill to work. You've got plenty of money and only yourself to worry about.'

'So you're asking me to cancel my holiday, drive to the home, pick up Mother and look after her over Christmas?'

'It's up to you,' Bella said in a tone of elevated piety. 'You must do what your conscience tells you.'

Toni's conscience said she should not let Mother spend Christmas in an institution, and Bella knew that. 'All right, I'll go and fetch her now,' she said.

'I'm just sorry you couldn't do it more graciously,' said her sister.

'Oh, fuck off, Bella,' said Toni, and she hung up the phone.

Now she would have to call the spa to cancel her reservation and explain to her friends. 'What a miserable life,' she said aloud. 'What a miserable bloody life.'

CRAIG'S RELATIONSHIP with Sophie was advancing very slowly. He had spent all afternoon with her. They had agreed about music. They both read horror fiction. But she talked of a world of nightclubs and friends who took drugs and boys who had motorcycles. All this talk implied that he was just a kid, even though he was older than Sophie by a year and seven months. He had to find some way to prove he was as mature and sophisticated as she.

At six o'clock, slumped on the couch in the barn, he decided he had watched as much MTV as he needed for one day. 'Want to go over to the house?' he asked her.

'What for?'

'They'll all be sitting round the kitchen table.'

'So?'

Well, Craig thought, it's nice. The kitchen is warm, and you can smell dinner cooking, and my dad tells funny stories, and it just feels good. But he knew that would not impress Sophie, so he said, 'There might be drinks.'

She stood up. 'Good. I want a cocktail.'

Dream on, Craig thought. Grandpa was not going to serve hard liquor to a fourteen-year-old. They put on coats and went out.

It was now full dark, but the yard was lit by lamps on the walls of the surrounding buildings. Snow swirled in the air, and the ground was slippery. They crossed to the main house and approached the back door. Just before they went in, Craig glanced towards the front of the house and saw Grandpa's Ferrari under two inches of snow. Luke must have been too busy to put it away.

'Last time I was here, Grandpa let me drive his car into the garage.'

'You can't drive,' Sophie said sceptically.

'I haven't got a licence, but that doesn't mean I can't handle a car.' He was exaggerating. He had driven his father's Mercedes estate a couple of times, once on a beach and once on a disused airstrip, but never on a road.

'All right, then, park it now,' Sophie said.

Craig knew he should ask permission. But he said, 'All right, then,' and walked towards the car. It was unlocked, and the key was in the ignition.

Sophie followed, then stood, arms folded, her stance saying, OK, show me.

'Why don't you come with me?' Craig said. 'Or are you scared?'

They both got into the car. Craig turned the ignition key and the Ferrari started with a roar. Craig half hoped that the noise would bring Luke running out of the house, arms raised in protest. However, the Ferrari was at the front door, and the family were in the kitchen at the back of the house, overlooking the yard. The thunder of the car did not penetrate the thick stone walls.

The whole car seemed to tremble as the big engine turned over.

'This is cool!' Sophie said excitedly.

The garage stood at a right angle to the house, and now its doors were ahead and to the left of the Ferrari. Kit's car was parked in front of the garage block at its far end. Craig found a remote control under the Ferrari's dashboard and clicked. The furthermost of three garage doors swung up and over.

Craig moved the gear stick into first gear and drove the car forward. He depressed the accelerator another millimetre, and the car picked up speed, just enough to feel exciting. He swung right, aiming for the open door, but he was going too fast. He touched the brake.

That was his mistake. As soon as the brakes bit, the rear wheels lost traction and the car slid sideways across the snow. Sophie let out a scream of fear. Craig spun the steering wheel further to the right, but that made the skid worse. He stamped on the brake and the clutch at the same time, but the car drifted inexorably over the slippery surface, missing Kit's Peugeot by inches.

Losing momentum, it slowed down. But just before the car came to a complete stop, its front nearside wing touched a tree on the far side of the apron.

'That was great!' Sophie said.

'No, it bloody was not.' Craig sprang out of the car. To his dismay, he saw a large dimple in the gleaming blue wing. 'Shit,' he said miserably.

Sophie got out and looked. 'It's not a very big dent,' she said. 'They might not notice it.'

'Of course they'll bloody notice it,' he said angrily. 'Grandpa will see it as soon as he looks at the car.'

'That might not be for a while. He's not likely to go out in this weather.'

'What difference does that make?' Craig said impatiently.

'Better if you're not here when the shit hits the fan.'

'I don't see . . .' He paused. He did see. If he confessed now, Christmas would be blighted. If he confessed later, perhaps there would be less fuss.

'I'll have to put it in the garage,' he said, thinking aloud.

'Park it with the dented side right up against the wall,' Sophie suggested. 'That way, it won't be noticed by anyone just walking past.'

Sophie's idea was beginning to make sense, Craig thought. There were two other cars in the garage: a massive Toyota Land Cruiser Amazon off-road car, and Luke's old Ford Mondeo. Luke would certainly enter the garage this evening to get his car and drive home, but if the Ferrari were hard up against the wall the dent would not be visible.

The engine was still running. Craig sat in the driver's seat and drove slowly forward. On his first attempt he was no closer than eighteen inches from the wall. That was not good enough. He had to try again. On his third attempt he managed to position the car four or five inches away from the wall. He got out and looked. It was impossible to see the dent from any angle.

He closed the door, then he and Sophie headed for the kitchen. Craig felt jangled and guilty, but Sophie was in high spirits.

'That was awesome,' she said.

Craig realised he had impressed her at last.

KIT SET UP his computer in the box-room, a small space that could be reached only by going through his bedroom. He plugged in his laptop, a fingerprint scanner, and a smart-card reader-writer he had bought for £270 on eBay.

He took the pass he had stolen from his father and slid it into the reader-writer. Its top stuck out of the slot, showing the printed words: OXENFORD MEDICAL. He hoped no one would come into the room. They were all in the kitchen, where Lori was making osso bucco according to Mamma Marta's famous recipe—Kit could smell the oregano.

The chip in the card contained details of his father's fingerprint. Kit had built a device that measured twenty-five points of the fingerprint, using minute electrical differences between ridges and valleys. He had also written a program that stored these details in code. At his apartment he had several prototypes of the fingerprint scanner, and he had kept a copy of the software.

Now he set his laptop to read the smart card. After a few seconds, the screen shimmered and displayed a page of code: Stanley's fingerprint details. Kit saved the file, then switched the software into Read mode, and pressed the forefinger of his left hand to the glass of the scanner. The program scrutinised his fingerprint and encoded the details. Kit saved that file.

Finally, he uploaded his own fingerprint details to the smart card, overwriting his father's. The card now carried Kit's fingerprint details, not Stanley's. 'Yes!' he said aloud, mutedly triumphant. He removed the card from the machine and put it in his pocket. It would now give him access to BSL4.

After he returned from the lab he would reverse the process before he replaced the card in his father's wallet. The computer at the Kremlin would record that Stanley Oxenford had entered BSL4 in the early hours of December 25. It pleased him to think how baffled they would all be.

He took his phone from his pocket and rang Hamish McKinnon, who was one of the security guards on duty at the Kremlin. Hamish was the company dope dealer, supplying marijuana and Ecstasy to the younger scientists. Kit had asked him to be his inside man tonight, confident that Hamish would not dare to spill the beans, having his own secrets to conceal.

'It's me,' Kit said when Hamish answered. 'Can you talk?'

'And a happy Christmas to you too, Ian,' Hamish said cheerily. 'Just a tick, I'm going to step outside . . . that's better.'

'Everything all right?'

Hamish's voice became serious. 'Aye, but she's doubled the guard, so I've got Willie Crawford with me in the gatehouse. And there are two at Reception and two in the control room.'

'OK. We can cope with that. Let me know if anything unusual happens.'

Kit ended the call and dialled a number that gave him access to the telephone system computer at the Kremlin. The number was used by Hibernian Telecom, the company that had installed the phones, for remote diagnosis of faults. Kit had worked closely with Hibernian, and he knew the number and the access code. He had a moment of tension, worrying that the number or the code might have been changed since he left. But they had not.

His mobile phone was linked to his laptop by a wireless connection. Now he used the laptop to access the central processing unit of the Kremlin's phone system. First he closed down every phone on the site except the one on the desk in Reception. Next, he diverted all calls into and out of the Kremlin to his mobile. He had programmed his laptop to recognise the numbers likeliest to come up, such as Toni Gallo's. He would be able to answer the calls himself, or play recorded messages to the callers, or even redirect calls and eavesdrop on the conversations. Finally, he caused every phone in the building to ring for five seconds, to get the attention of the security guards.

Then he disconnected and sat on the edge of his chair, waiting.

The guards had a list of people to call in the event of different emergencies. Their first action now should be to call the phone company.

He did not have to wait long. His mobile rang. After a moment, a message appeared on the screen of his laptop: KREMLIN CALLS TONI.

He quickly activated a recorded message. The security guard trying to reach Toni Gallo heard a voice saying that the mobile he was calling might be switched off or out of range, and advising him to try later. The guard hung up.

Kit's phone rang again almost immediately. The screen said: KREMLIN CALLS RPHQ. They were ringing regional police headquarters at Inverburn. Kit redirected the call to the correct number and listened in.

'This is Steven Tremlett, security guard supervisor at Oxenford Medical.

We have a problem with our phone lines. I'm not sure the alarms will work.'

'I'll log it, Mr Tremlett. Can you get your phones fixed?'

'I'll call out a repair crew, but God knows when they'll get here.'

'Do you want a patrol to call?'

'It wouldn't do any harm, if they've not much on.'

'They'll be busy later, when the pubs chuck out, but it's quiet the noo.'

'Right. Tell them I'll give them a cup of tea.'

They hung up. Kit's mobile rang a third time and the screen said: KREMLIN CALLS HIBERNIAN. At last, he thought with relief. He touched a button and said into his phone, 'Hibernian Telecom, can I help you?'

Steve's voice said, 'This is Oxenford Medical, we have a problem with our phone system.'

Kit exaggerated his Scots accent to disguise his voice. 'What's the problem?'

'All the phones are out except this one. The place is empty, of course, but the alarm system uses the phone lines, and we need to be sure that's working.'

At that point, Kit's father walked into the room.

Kit froze. Stanley looked at the computer and raised his eyebrows. Kit pulled himself together. He said into the phone, 'Let me call you back in two minutes.' He touched the keyboard of his laptop and the screen went dark.

'Working at Christmas?' his father said, crossing the room.

'I said I'd deliver this piece of software by December the 24th.'

'By now your customer will have gone home, like all sensible folk.'

'But his computer will show that I emailed the program to him before midnight on Christmas Eve, so he won't be able to say I was late.'

Stanley smiled. 'Well, I'm glad you're being conscientious.' He stood silent for several seconds then said, 'Is our quarrel really behind us now?'

Trying to hide his frantic impatience, Kit said, 'I think so, yes.'

'I know you think you've been unjustly treated,' his father said. 'And I, too, feel unfairly done by. But we have to try to forget that, and be friends again. I'm just not sure you have put it behind you. I sense you holding something back.'

Kit tried to keep his face wooden. 'I'm doing my best,' he said. 'It's not easy.'

Stanley seemed satisfied. 'Well, I can't ask for any more than that,' he said. He put his hand on Kit's shoulder. 'I came to tell you supper's almost ready.'

'I'm nearly done. I'll come down in five minutes.'

'Good.' Stanley went out.

Kit slumped in his chair, shaking with a mixture of shame and relief. When his hands were steady enough, he dialled the Kremlin again.

Steve Tremlett's voice said, 'Oxenford Medical.'

'Hibernian Telecom here.' Kit remembered to change his voice. 'I can't access your central processing unit.'

'That line must be down also. You'll have to send someone.'

This was what Kit wanted, but he was careful not to sound eager. 'It's going to be difficult to get a repair crew out to you at Christmas.'

'Don't give me that,' Steve said angrily. 'You guarantee to attend to any fault within four hours, every day of the year. That's what we pay you for.'

'All right, keep your shirt on. I'll try to get a crew to you by midnight.'

Kit put down his mobile. He was perspiring. So far, it had all gone perfectly.

8.30 P.M.

Miranda felt mellow. The osso bucco was hearty and satisfying, and her father had opened two bottles of Brunello di Montepulciano to go with it. Kit was restless, dashing upstairs every time his mobile rang, but everyone else was relaxed. The four kids ate quickly then retired to the barn to watch a DVD movie called *Scream 2*, leaving the adults in the dining room. Lori served coffee while Luke loaded the dishwasher in the kitchen.

Then Stanley said, 'How would you all feel if I started dating again?'

Everyone went quiet. Lori stopped pouring coffee and stared at him.

Miranda said, 'I suppose we're talking about Toni Gallo.'

He looked startled and said, 'No. I'm not talking about anyone in particular, I'm discussing a general principle. Marta has been dead for a year and a half. For almost four decades she was the only woman in my life. But I'm sixty, and probably have another twenty or thirty years to live. I may not want to spend them alone.'

Olga said bad-temperedly, 'So why consult us? You don't need our permission to sleep with your secretary or anyone else.'

'I'm not asking permission. I want to know how you would feel *if* it happened. And it won't be my secretary, by the way. Dorothy is happily married.'

Miranda spoke, mainly to prevent Olga saying something harsh. 'I think we'd find it hard, Daddy, to see you with another woman in this house. But we want you to be happy, and we'd do our best to welcome someone you loved.'

He gave her a wry look. 'Not exactly a ringing endorsement, but thank you for trying to be positive.'

Olga said, 'For God's sake, what are we supposed to say to you? Are you thinking of marrying this woman? Would you have more children?'

'I'm not thinking of marrying anyone,' he said tetchily, then added, 'But I'm not ruling anything out.'

'It's outrageous,' Olga stormed. 'When I was a child I hardly saw you. You were always at the lab. Well, I want a reward for my sacrifice. I want my children to inherit your money, and I don't want them to share it with a litter of brats bred by some tart who knows how to take advantage of a widower.'

Stanley's expression darkened. 'I wasn't planning to date *some tart*,' he said.

Olga saw that she had gone too far. She said, 'I didn't mean that last part.' For her, that amounted to an apology.

Stanley said, 'I thought you might feel badly about your mother being replaced by someone new. It never occurred to me that your main concern would be my will.'

'The important thing is to keep the family together,' Miranda said to Olga. 'Whatever Daddy decides, we mustn't let it break us up.'

'Don't lecture me about the family,' Olga said angrily. 'Talk to your brother. He's the one who has come closest to destroying the family.'

Kit said, 'Get off my case!'

'I don't want to rake all that up again,' Stanley said firmly.

'Come on, Daddy,' Olga said. 'What could be more threatening to the family than one of us who steals from another?'

Kit was red with shame and fury. 'I'll tell you,' he said.

Miranda's heart missed a beat. 'Kit, calm down, please,' she said frantically.

'I'll tell you what could be more threatening to the family. Someone—'

Miranda stood up. 'Shut up!' she shouted.

'—someone who sleeps—'

Miranda snatched up a glass of water and threw it in Kit's face.

Kit wiped his face with his napkin. With everyone watching him in shocked silence, he said, '. . . sleeps with her sister's husband.'

Olga was bewildered. 'This makes no sense. I never slept with Jasper.'

Miranda held her head in her hands.

'I didn't mean you,' Kit said.

Olga looked at Miranda. Miranda looked away.

Lori, still standing there with the coffeepot, gave a gasp of comprehension.

Olga turned to Hugo. 'You and my sister?'

He tried his bad-boy grin. Olga swung her arm and slapped his face. 'Ow!' he cried, and rocked back in his chair.

Olga said, 'You lousy, lying . . .' She searched for words. 'You worm. You pig. You bloody bastard, you rotten sod.' She turned to Miranda. 'And you!'

Miranda could not meet her eye.

'How could you?' Olga said to her. 'How could you?'

Miranda would try to explain, one day, but now she just shook her head.

Olga stood up and walked out of the room.

Hugo looked sheepish. 'I'd better . . .' He followed her.

Stanley suddenly realised that Lori was standing there listening to every word. Belatedly, he said, 'Lori, you'd better help Luke in the kitchen.'

She started as if awakened. 'Yes, Professor Oxenford.'

Stanley looked at Kit. 'That was brutal.' Anger made his voice shake.

'Oh, that's right, blame me,' Kit said petulantly. 'I didn't sleep with Hugo, did I?' He threw down his napkin and left.

Ned was mortified. 'Um, excuse me,' he said, and he went out.

Only Miranda and her father were left in the room. Stanley got up and came to her side. He put his hand on her shoulder. 'They'll all calm down about it, eventually,' he said. 'This is bad, but it will pass.'

She turned to him and pressed her face into the soft tweed of his waistcoat. 'Oh, Daddy, I'm sorry,' she said, and she began to cry.

THE WEATHER was getting worse. Toni's drive to the old folks' home had been protracted, but the return journey was even slower. There was a thin layer of snow on the road, beaten hard by car tyres and frozen solid. Drivers went at a crawl. Toni's red Porsche Boxster was not at its best in slippery conditions.

Mother sat contentedly beside her, wearing a green woollen coat and a felt hat. She was not in the least angry with Bella. She seemed to think it was Toni's fault she had been kept waiting so long.

Toni kept thinking of her friends at the spa. They would all be having so much fun, while Toni drove through the snow with her mother. She told herself to stop being pathetic. I'm a grown-up, she thought, and grown-ups have responsibilities. Besides, Mother might not be alive for many more years, so I should enjoy having her with me while I can.

She found it harder to look on the bright side when she thought about Stanley. She had felt so close to him this morning, and now the gulf between them was bigger than the Grand Canyon.

Up ahead she saw the lights of a petrol station. 'Do you need the toilet, Mother?' she said.

'Yes, please.'

Toni slowed down and pulled onto the forecourt. She topped up her tank, then took her mother inside. Mother went to the ladies' room while Toni paid. As Toni returned to the car, her mobile phone rang. 'Toni Gallo.'

'This is Stanley Oxenford.'

'Oh.' She was taken aback. She had not been expecting this.

'Perhaps I'm phoning at an inconvenient time,' he said politely.

'No, no, no,' she said quickly, sliding behind the wheel. 'I imagined the call was from the Kremlin, and I was worried that something might have gone wrong there.' She closed the car door.

'Everything's fine, as far as I know. How's your spa?'

'I'm not there.' She told him what had happened.

'How terribly disappointing,' he said.

Her heart was beating faster. 'What about you—is everything all right?'

'Family dinner ended in an upset.'

'What was it about?'

'In brief, Kit revealed that Miranda had slept with Olga's husband.'

'Good God!' It was a ripe tale, but what was more surprising was that Stanley should repeat it to her as if they were intimate friends.

'But I don't want to burden you with all that,' he said. 'I called to say something else. After Christmas, will you have dinner with me one evening?'

What does this mean? she thought. She said, 'Of course. I'd be delighted.'

'I've been thinking about our conversation this morning, on the cliff. I said something to you then that I've been regretting ever since.'

'What . . .' She could hardly breathe. 'What was that?'

'That I could never start another family.'

'You didn't mean it?'

'I said it because I had become . . . frightened. Strange, isn't it? At my time of life, to be scared.'

'Scared of what?'

There was a long pause, then he said, 'Of my feelings.'

Toni felt a flush spread from her throat to her face. 'Feelings,' she repeated.

'If this conversation is embarrassing you dreadfully, you just have to say so, and I'll never refer to it again.'

'Go on.'

'When you told me Osborne had asked you out, I realised you wouldn't be single for ever, probably not much longer. If I'm making a complete fool of myself, please tell me right away, and put me out of my misery.'

'No—' Toni swallowed. He was finding this extraordinarily difficult, she realised. 'No, you're not making a fool of yourself, not at all.'

'I thought this morning that you might feel warmly towards me, and that's what scared me. Am I right to tell you this? I wish I could see your face.'

'I'm very glad,' she said in a low voice. 'I'm very happy.'

'Really? When can I see you? I want to talk some more.'

'I'm with my mother. We're at a petrol station. She's just coming out of the toilet.' Toni got out of the car. 'Let's talk tomorrow morning.'

'Don't hang up yet. There's so much to say.'

Toni waved at her mother and called, 'Over here!' Mother saw her and turned. Toni opened the passenger door and helped her in, saying, 'I'm just finishing off this phone call.' She closed the door.

'I want us to meet tomorrow. We've both got family obligations, but we're entitled to some time to ourselves.'

'We'll work something out. I must go—Mother's getting cold.'

'Goodbye,' he said. 'Call me any time you feel like it. Any time.'

'Goodbye.' She flipped the phone shut and got into the car.

'That's a big smile,' Mother said. 'Who was on the phone—someone nice?'

'Yes,' Toni said. 'Someone very nice indeed.'

KIT SAT WAITING at the old desk in the box-room, impatient for everyone to settle down for the night. It was half past ten and he needed to get away.

He had dealt with three calls to and from the Kremlin. Two had been personal calls to guards, and he had let them through. The third had been a call from the Kremlin to Steepfall. He had played a recorded message saying there was a fault on the line.

While he waited, he could hear Olga and Hugo having a row in the next bedroom. Downstairs, Luke and Lori clattered pots in the kitchen for half an hour, then the front door slammed as they left to go to their house a mile away. The children were in the barn, and Miranda and Ned had presumably gone to the guest cottage. Then Kit heard Stanley climb the stairs and close his bedroom door. Olga and Hugo both went to the bathroom, and afterwards they were quiet—either reconciled or exhausted. The dog, Nellie, would be in the kitchen, lying next to the Aga.

He wondered if he dared leave yet. He was ready to go. He was dressed in jeans and a warm black sweater; he would carry his boots and put them on downstairs. Kit waited a little longer, giving them all a chance to go to sleep. He stood up—then heard the back door slam. He cursed with frustration as footsteps mounted the stairs. A moment later he heard his bedroom door open. Miranda came in, carrying a sheet and a duvet. Without speaking, she crossed to the sleepchair in the box-room and unfolded it.

Kit was irate. 'For God's sake, what are you doing?'

'I'm sleeping here,' she replied calmly.

'You can't!' he said, panicking. 'You're supposed to be in the cottage.'

'I've had a row with Ned, thanks to your dinnertime revelation.'

'I don't want you here!'

'I don't give a damn what you want.'

Kit watched with dismay as Miranda made up a bed on the sleepchair. How was he going to sneak out of his bedroom with her in here? And then, in the morning, she was sure to get up before he returned, and notice his absence.

He had to go now. He would pretend to be even angrier than he really was. 'Fuck you,' he said. He unplugged his laptop and closed the lid. 'I'm not staying here with you.' He stepped into the bedroom.

'Where are you going?'

Out of her sight, he picked up his boots. 'I'm going down to watch TV.'

'Keep the volume low.' She slammed the door between the two rooms.

Kit went out. He tiptoed across the dark landing and down the stairs. Nellie came out of the kitchen and stood by the door, wagging her tail, hoping with irrepressible canine optimism to be taken for a walk.

Kit sat on the stairs and put his boots on, listening for the sound of a door opening above him. He tied his bootlaces and put on his black Puffa jacket, then shoved Nellie away from the door, opened it and stepped outside. It was bitterly cold, and the snow was falling heavily. He pushed Nellie's nose back inside and closed the door behind him.

His car was on the far side of the garage, a duvet of snow on its roof. He got in, putting his laptop on the passenger seat beside him and turned the key in the ignition. The car coughed and spluttered, but after a few seconds the engine turned over. Kit hoped no one had heard it.

The snow was blinding. He switched on his headlights, praying that no one was looking out of a window, and pulled away. The car slid alarmingly. He coaxed it onto the drive, then followed the lane all the way to the main road.

He headed north, and after ten minutes turned onto a side road that wound over hills. At last he saw a sign that read INVERBURN SCHOOL OF FLYING.

Double wire gates stood open. He drove through, his headlights picking out a hangar and a control tower.

The place appeared deserted, but the hangar door stood partly open. Kit drove slowly in. There were no planes inside—the airfield operated only in the summer months—but he saw a light-coloured Bentley Continental that he recognised as Nigel Buchanan's. Beside it stood a van marked HIBERNIAN TELECOM. The others were not in sight, but a faint light came from the stair-well. Carrying his laptop, Kit followed the stairs up to the control tower.

Nigel sat at the desk, wearing a pink rollneck sweater and a sports jacket, holding a mobile phone to his ear. Elton leaned against the wall, dressed in a trench coat, a big canvas bag at his feet. Daisy slumped on a chair, heavy boots on the windowsill. She wore tight-fitting gloves of light tan suede.

Nigel spoke into the phone in his soft London voice. 'The forecast says the worst of the storm will pass us by . . . Yeah, you'll be able to fly tomorrow morning, no problem . . . We'll be here well before ten . . . I'll be in the con-trol tower, I'll talk to you as you come in . . . There won't be any trouble, so long as you've got the money, in mixed notes, as agreed.'

The talk of money gave Kit a shiver of excitement. In twelve hours and a few minutes, he would have £300,000 in his hands, True, he would have to give most of it to Daisy immediately, but he would keep £50,000.

'Thank *you*,' Nigel was saying. 'Goodbye.' He turned round. 'What-ho, Kit. You're bang on time.'

Kit said, 'Who was on the phone—our buyer?'

'His pilot. He'll be arriving by helicopter.'

Kit frowned. 'What will his flight plan say?'

'That he's taking off from Aberdeen and landing in London. No one will know that he made an unscheduled stop at the Inverburn Flying School.'

'Good.'

'I'm glad you approve,' Nigel said with a touch of sarcasm.

Elton said, 'Let's get dragged up, shall we?'

He took from his bag four sets of overalls with HIBERNIAN TELECOM printed on the back. They all climbed into them.

Kit said to Daisy, 'The gloves look odd with the overalls.'

'Too bad,' she said.

Kit stared at her for a few moments, then dropped his gaze. He wished she were not coming tonight. He was scared of her after what had happened in the swimming pool that morning.

Next, Elton handed out faked identity cards that said HIBERNIAN TELECOM FIELD MAINTENANCE TEAM. Kit's card bore a photograph of an older man, with black hair that grew over his ears, plus a heavy moustache and glasses.

Elton reached into his bag again and handed Kit a black wig, a black moustache, and a pair of heavy-framed glasses. He also gave him a hand mirror and a tube of glue. Kit glued the moustache to his upper lip and put on the wig. Looking in the mirror, he was satisfied that the disguise altered his appearance radically. Tonight Kit planned to avoid any guards who had been employed at the Kremlin when he had been there. However, if he had to speak to them, he felt confident they would not recognise him.

Elton also had disguises for Nigel, Daisy and himself, to ensure that the descriptions that the security guards would later give to the police bore no relation to their actual faces. Nigel also had glasses and a wig. His own hair was sandy-coloured and short, but his wig was mid-grey and chin-length. Daisy had a long blonde wig over her shaved head. Tinted contact lenses turned her eyes from brown to blue. She was even more hideous than usual. As Kit looked, she removed the ring from her lower lip.

Elton's own disguise was the subtlest. All he had was a set of false teeth that gave him an overbite—but he looked completely different. The handsome dude had gone, and in his place was a nerd.

Finally, he gave them all baseball caps with HIBERNIAN TELECOM printed on them. 'Most of those security cameras are placed high,' he explained. 'A cap with a long peak will make sure they don't get a good shot of your face.'

They were ready. There was a moment of silence while they looked at one another. Then Nigel said, 'Showtime.'

They left the control tower and went down the stairs to the van.

TONI'S MOTHER had fallen asleep the moment they pulled out of the petrol station, and she was still asleep when they reached the outskirts of Inverburn. Using her mobile, which became a hands-free carphone when slotted into a cradle on the dashboard, she called the Kremlin, just to check in.

The call was answered by Steve Tremlett. 'Oxenford Medical.'

'This is Toni. How are things?'

'Hi, Toni. We have a slight problem, but we're dealing with it. Most of the phones are out. Only this one works, at Reception.'

Toni felt a chill. 'How did that happen?'

'No idea. The snow, probably.'

Toni shook her head, perplexed. 'That phone system cost hundreds of thousands of pounds. It shouldn't break down because of bad weather.'

'I've called out a crew from Hibernian Telecom. They should be here soon.'

'What about the alarms?'

'I don't know whether they're functional or not.'

'Damn. Have you told the police?'

'Yes. A patrol car dropped in earlier. The officers had a look round, didn't see anything untoward. They've left now. Where are you?'

'Inverburn.'

'I thought you were going to a health farm?'

'I was, but a family problem cropped up. Let me know what the repairmen find, OK? Call me on the mobile number.'

Toni hung up. 'Hell,' she said to herself. First Mother, now this.

She wound her way through the web of streets that climbed the hill overlooking the harbour. When she reached her building she parked, but did not get out.

She had to go to the Kremlin. She could not go home while something strange was going on at Oxenford Medical. The only problem was Mother. She could not be left alone, and Toni could not ask neighbours to look after her at this hour. Mother would just have to come along to the Kremlin.

As she put the gearshift into first, a man got out of a light-coloured Jaguar saloon parked a few cars further along the kerb. There was something familiar about him, she thought as he walked towards her. He came to her window and she recognised Carl Osborne. He was carrying a small bundle.

She put the gearshift back into neutral and wound down the window. 'Hello,' she said. 'What are you doing here?'

'Waiting for you. I was ready to give up.'

'Why were you waiting for me?'

'I brought you a present,' he said, and he showed her what was in his hand. It was a puppy. 'Merry Christmas,' he said, and tipped it into her lap.

'Carl, for God's sake, don't be ridiculous!' She looked at the pup. It was an English sheepdog, white with grey patches, about eight weeks old. She hardened her heart, picked up the furry bundle and handed it back to him.

'Well, think about it,' he said, looking disappointed. 'I'll keep him tonight, and call you tomorrow.'

She put the gear stick into first again. 'Don't call me, please.'

'You're a hard woman,' he said as she pulled away.

For some reason, that gibe got to her and unexpected tears came to her eyes. She rubbed them with the back of her hand and peered ahead into the swirling snowflakes, heading for the main road out of town. Manoeuvring carefully through a series of roundabouts, she looked in her rearview mirror and noticed the Jaguar close on her tail. Carl Osborne was following her.

She pulled over and he stopped right behind her. She got out and went to his window. 'What now?'

'I'm a reporter, Toni,' he said. 'It's almost midnight on Christmas Eve, and you're looking after your elderly mother, yet you're in your car and you seem to be heading for the Kremlin. This has to be a story.'

'Oh shit,' said Toni.

CHRISTMAS EVE

MIDNIGHT

Kit felt relieved as the van with HIBERNIAN TELECOM on its side approached the main gate of the Kremlin. The storm was turning into a full-scale blizzard and the journey from the airfield had taken longer than expected.

The phone call from Toni Gallo worried him. He had put her through to Steve Tremlett, fearing that if he played her a fault message she might drive to the Kremlin to find out what was going on. But having listened in to the conversation, Kit thought she might do that anyway.

The first of the two barriers lifted and Elton moved the van forward and drew level with the gatehouse. He wound down the window.

A guard leaned out and said, 'We're glad to see you laddies.'

Recalling his conversation with Hamish, Kit realised it must be Willie Crawford. Looking past him, Kit saw Hamish himself.

Willie said, 'It's good of you to come out at Christmas.'

'All part of the job,' Elton said.

Willie said, 'I need to see identification for everyone, please.'

They all took out their fake cards. Willie scrutinised the cards, wrote down the names from them and handed them back without comment.

'Drive to the main entrance,' Willie said. 'You'll be all right if you stay between the lampposts.' The road ahead was invisible, covered with snow. 'At

Reception you'll find a Mr Tremlett who can tell you where to go.'

The second barrier lifted and Elton pulled forward. They were inside.

Kit felt sick with fear. He swallowed hard and thought of the enormous sum he owed Harry Mac. He had to go through with this.

Elton parked at the main entrance and they got out. Kit carried his laptop. Nigel and Daisy took toolboxes from the back of the van. Elton had an expensive-looking burgundy leather briefcase, very slim with a brass catch— typical of his taste, but a bit odd for a telephone repairman, Kit thought.

They passed between the stone lions on the porch and entered the Great Hall. At the reception desk were two more guards. One was an attractive young woman Kit did not recognise, and the other was Steve Tremlett. Kit hung back, not wanting Steve to look at him too closely.

'You'll want to access the central processing unit,' Steve said.

Nigel answered. 'That's the place to start.'

'Susan will show you the way—I need to stay by the phone.'

Susan gave them a friendly smile and led them along a corridor.

A fatalistic calm seemed to descend on Kit. The cards had been dealt, he had placed his bet, there was nothing to do now but play out his hand, win or lose.

They entered the control room. Here also there were two guards instead of one. They sat at the long desk, watching the monitors. Susan introduced them as Don and Stu. Don was a dark-skinned south Indian with a thick Glasgow accent, and Stu was a freckled redhead. Kit did not recognise either one.

Susan opened the door to the equipment room. 'The CPU is in there.'

A moment later Kit was inside the inner sanctum. Here were the computers and other devices that ran not just the phone system but also the lighting, the security cameras and the alarms. Even to get this far was a triumph.

He said to Susan, 'Thanks very much—we'll take it from here.'

'If there's anything you need, come to Reception,' she said, and she left.

Kit put his laptop on a shelf and connected it to the security computer. He felt Daisy's eyes on him, suspicious and malevolent. 'Go into the next room,' he said. 'Keep an eye on the guards.'

She glared resentfully at him for a moment, then did as he said.

Kit took a deep breath and accessed the program that controlled the video feed from thirty-seven closed-circuit cameras. He looked at the entrance to BSL4, which appeared normal. He checked the reception desk and saw Steve there, but not Susan. Scanning the input from other cameras, he located Susan patrolling elsewhere in the building. He noted the time. Nigel and Elton watched him in tense silence. The computer stored the camera images for four weeks before overwriting them. Kit located the video from the cameras in BSL4 this time last night, and checked the footage to make sure no crazy scientist had been working in the lab in the middle of the night. He then fed last night's images into the monitors the guards were currently watching. Now someone could walk round BSL4 doing anything he liked without their knowing.

Kit stepped into the main control room. Daisy was slumped in a chair. Kit studied the bank of screens. All appeared normal.

The dark-skinned guard, Don, looked at him with an enquiring expression. As a cover, Kit said, 'Are any of the phones in here working?'

'None,' said Don.

Along the bottom of each screen was a line of text giving the time and date. The time was the same on the screens showing yesterday's footage. But they showed yesterday's date. He was betting that no one ever looked at that date.

Kit's mobile phone rang. He stepped back into the equipment room. The message on the screen of his laptop said: KREMLIN CALLING TONI. He put the call through, then listened in on his mobile.

'This is Toni Gallo.' She was in her car: Kit could hear the engine.

'Steve here. The maintenance team from Hibernian Telecom have arrived.'

'Have they fixed the problem?'

'They've just started work. I hope I didn't wake you.'

'No, I'm not in bed; I'm on my way to you.'

Kit cursed under his breath. It was what he had been afraid of.

'Where are you now?' Steve asked.

'I'm only a few miles away, but the roads are terrible. It's going to take me at least half an hour, maybe an hour.'

They hung up and Kit cursed again. Now the risk of something going wrong would increase tenfold. But there was nothing he could do except hurry.

His next task was to get Nigel into the lab without any of the guards seeing. The main problem here was the patrols. Once an hour, a guard from Reception made a tour of the building, which took twenty minutes. Having passed the entrance to BSL4, the guard would not come back for an hour.

Kit had seen Susan patrolling a few minutes ago, when he had connected his laptop to the surveillance program. Now he checked the feed from Reception and saw her sitting with Steve at the desk, her circuit done. Kit checked his watch. He had a comfortable thirty minutes before she went on patrol again.

Kit had dealt with the cameras inside BSL4, but there was still one outside the door. He called up yesterday's feed, ran the footage at double fast-forward, and stopped when the patrolling guard appeared. Beginning after the guard left the picture, he fed yesterday's images into the monitor in the next room. Don and Stu should see an empty corridor for the next hour, or until Kit returned the system to normal.

Kit looked at Nigel. 'Let's go.'

Elton stayed in the equipment room to make sure no one interfered with the laptop. Nigel picked up Elton's smart burgundy leather briefcase.

Passing through the control room, Kit said to Daisy, 'We're going to get the nanometer from the van. You stay here.' There was no such thing as a nanometer, but Don and Stu would not know that.

Daisy grunted and looked away. She was not much good at acting the part. Kit hoped the guards would simply assume she was bad-tempered.

Kit and Nigel walked quickly to BSL4. Kit waved his father's smart card in front of the scanner then pressed the forefinger of his left hand to the screen. He waited while the computer compared the information from the screen with that on the card.

Then a woman's voice behind them said, 'I'm afraid you can't go in there.'

Kit and Nigel turned. Susan was standing behind them. She appeared friendly but anxious. She should have been at Reception, Kit thought in a panic. She was not due to patrol for another thirty minutes . . .

Unless Toni Gallo had doubled the patrols as well as doubling the guard.

There was a chime like a doorbell. All three of them looked at the light over the door. It turned green, and the heavy door swung slowly open.

Susan said, 'How did you open the door?' Her voice betrayed fear now.

Involuntarily, Kit looked down at the stolen card in his hand.

Susan followed his gaze. 'You're not supposed to have a pass!' she exclaimed.

Nigel moved towards her. She turned on her heel and ran. Nigel went after her, but he was twice her age. He'll never catch her, Kit thought. How could everything go so wrong, so quickly?

Then Daisy emerged from the passage leading to the control room. Kit realised that she must have been watching the monitors in the control room. She would have seen Susan leave the reception desk and walk towards BSL4.

Susan saw Daisy and hesitated, then ran on, apparently determined to push past. The hint of a smile touched Daisy's lips. She drew back her arm and smashed her gloved fist into Susan's face. The blow made a sound like a melon dropped on a tiled floor. Susan collapsed as if she had run into a wall.

Daisy rubbed her knuckles, looking pleased. Susan got to her knees. Sobs bubbled through the blood covering her nose and mouth. Daisy pulled a flexible cosh from her pocket and raised her arm.

Kit shouted, 'No!'

Daisy hit Susan over the head with the cosh. The guard collapsed again.

Kit yelled, 'Leave her!'

Daisy raised her arm to hit Susan once more, but Nigel stepped forward and grabbed her wrist. 'No need to kill her,' he said.

Daisy stepped back reluctantly.

'You mad cow!' Kit cried. 'We'll all be guilty of murder!' He stared at the crumpled body on the floor. 'Now what are we going to do with her?'

Daisy straightened her blonde wig. 'Tie her up and hide her somewhere.'

'Right,' Kit said. 'Put her inside BSL4. The guards aren't allowed in there.'

Nigel said to Daisy, 'Drag her inside. I'll find something to tie her up with.' He stepped into a side office.

Kit's mobile phone rang. He ignored it. He used his card to reopen the door, which had closed automatically. Daisy got her arms round Susan's chest and pulled her along the carpet. Nigel emerged from the office with a long power lead. They all passed into BSL4. The door closed behind them.

They were in a small lobby leading to the changing rooms. Daisy propped Susan against a wall and Nigel tied her hands and feet with the lead.

Kit's phone stopped ringing.

The three of them went outside. No pass was needed to exit: the door opened at the push of a green button set into the wall.

Kit was trying desperately to think ahead. There was no possibility now that the theft would remain undiscovered. 'Susan will be missed quite soon,' he said, making himself keep calm. 'Even if Don and Stu don't notice that she's disappeared off the monitors, Steve will be alerted when she fails to return from her patrol. We don't have time to get into the laboratory and out again before they raise the alarm. Shit, it's all gone wrong!'

'Calm down,' Nigel said. 'We can handle this, so long as you don't panic. We just have to deal with the other guards, like we dealt with her.'

TONI WAS DRIVING at ten miles an hour, leaning forward over the steering wheel to peer into the blinding snowfall, trying to see the road. She had been staring so long that her eyelids hurt. She had dialled the Kremlin on her hands-free mobile, and now she listened as it rang out unanswered. The repair people must have downed the entire system, Toni thought. Were the alarms working? Feeling troubled and frustrated, she touched a button to end the call.

'Where are we?' Mother asked.

'Good question.' Toni was familiar with this road but she could hardly see it. She glanced to the side from time to time, looking for landmarks. She thought she recognised a stone cottage with a distinctive wrought-iron gate. It was only a couple of miles from the Kremlin, she recalled. That cheered her up. 'We'll be there in fifteen minutes, Mother,' she said.

She looked in the rearview mirror and saw the headlights that had been with her since Inverburn: Carl Osborne in his Jaguar, following her at the same sluggard pace. She came to a right-hand bend and headlights appeared coming towards her. She could make out a hundred yards of road between the two cars. The oncoming car was travelling quite fast, she noted nervously as she rounded the long, wide bend. She held her line through the curve. But the other car did not. It drifted across the carriageway to the crown of the road, then Toni realised with horror that it was heading straight for her.

The car crossed the middle of the road and came at her broadside. It was a hot hatch with four men in it. They were laughing and, in the split second for which she could see them, she divined that they were young merrymakers too drunk to realise the danger they were in.

'Look out!' she screamed uselessly.

The front of the Porsche was about to smash into the side of the skidding hatchback. Toni jerked her steering wheel to the left, then pushed down the accelerator pedal. The car leapt forward and skidded. For an instant the hatchback was alongside her, inches away. The Porsche was angled left and sliding forward. Then there was a loud clang and she realised her bumper had been hit.

It was not much of a blow, but it destabilised the Porsche, and the rear swung left, out of control again. Toni desperately tugged the steering wheel to the left, turning into the skid, but, before her corrective action could take effect, the car hit the dry-stone wall at the side of the road. There was a terrific bang and the sound of breaking glass, then the car came to a stop.

Toni looked worriedly at her mother. She was staring ahead, mouth open, bewildered—but unharmed. Toni felt a moment of relief.

Then she thought of Osborne. She looked fearfully in the rearview mirror, thinking the hatchback must smash into Osborne's Jaguar. She could see the red rear lights of the hatchback and the white headlights of the Jag. The hatchback fishtailed, the Jag swung hard over to the side of the road and came to a stop, then the hatchback full of drunk young men went on into the night.

Mother said in a shaky voice, 'I heard a bang—did that car hit us?'

'Yes,' Toni said. 'We had a lucky escape.'

'I think you should drive more carefully,' said Mother.

KIT WAS FIGHTING down panic. There was now no way the robbery would go undetected until after the holiday. At most, it might remain a secret until six o'clock this morning, when the next shift of security guards arrived. But if Toni Gallo was still on her way here, the time left was even shorter.

If his plan had worked, there would have been no violence. The guard Susan could have been captured and tied up without Daisy's brutality. Kit hoped desperately that the other guards could be rounded up without injury.

Now, as they ran to the control room, both Nigel and Daisy drew guns.

Kit was horrified. 'We agreed no weapons!' he protested.

'Good thing we ignored you,' Nigel replied.

They came to the door. Nigel turned the handle and kicked it open.

Daisy burst into the room, yelling, 'On the floor! Now! Both of you!'

There was only a moment's hesitation, while the two security guards went through shock and bewilderment to fear; then they threw themselves down.

Kit felt powerless. He had lost control. There was nothing he could do, now, but string along and try to make sure nothing else went wrong. Elton appeared in the doorway of the equipment room.

Daisy screamed at the guards, 'Face down, hands behind your backs, eyes closed! Quick, quick, or I'll shoot you in the balls!'

They did as she said but, even so, she kicked Don in the face with a heavy boot. He cried out and flinched away, but remained prone.

Kit placed himself in front of Daisy. 'Enough!' he shouted.

Elton shook his head in amazement. 'She's loony tunes.'

The gleeful malevolence on Daisy's face frightened Kit, but he had too much at stake to let her ruin everything. 'Listen to me!' he shouted. 'You're not in the lab yet, and you won't ever get there at this rate. If you want to be empty-handed when we meet the client at ten, just carry on the way you are.'

Nigel backed him. 'Ease up, Daisy,' he said. 'Do as he says. See if you can tie these two up without kicking their heads in.'

Kit said, 'We'll put them in the same place as the girl.'

Daisy tied their hands with electrical cable, then she and Nigel forced them to their feet and herded them out at gunpoint. Elton stayed behind, watching the monitors. Kit followed the prisoners to BSL4 and opened the door. They put Don and Stu on the floor next to Susan and tied their feet. Don was bleeding from a cut on his forehead. Susan seemed conscious but groggy.

'One left,' said Kit as they stepped outside. 'Steve, in the Great Hall. And no unnecessary violence!'

Daisy gave a grunt of disgust.

Nigel said, 'Kit, try not to say any more in front of the guards about the client and our ten o'clock rendezvous. If you tell them too much, we may have to kill them.'

Kit realised aghast what he had done. He felt a fool.

His phone rang. 'That might be Toni,' he said. 'Let me check.' He ran back to the equipment room. His laptop screen said: TONI CALLING KREMLIN. He transferred the call to the phone on the desk at Reception, and listened in.

'Hi, Steve, this is Toni. Any news?'

'The repair crew are still here.'

'Everything all right otherwise?'

With the phone to his ear, Kit stepped into the control room and watched Steve on the monitor.

'Yeah, I think so. Susan Mackintosh should have finished her patrol by now, but maybe she went to the ladies' room.'

Toni asked anxiously, 'How late is she?'

On the monitor, Steve checked his wristwatch. 'Five minutes.'

'Give her another five minutes, then go and look for her.'

'OK. Where are you?'

'Not far, but I've had an accident. A car full of drunks clipped the Porsche.'

Steve said, 'Are you OK?'

'Fine, but my car's damaged. Fortunately, another car was following me, and he's giving me a lift.'

'When will you be here?'

'Twenty minutes, maybe thirty.' Toni said goodbye and hung up.

Kit ran out into the corridor. 'She'll be here in twenty or thirty minutes,' he said. 'And there's someone with her, I don't know who. We have to move fast.'

They ran along the corridor. Daisy, going first, burst into the Great Hall and yelled, 'On the floor—now!'

Kit and Nigel ran in after her and stopped abruptly. The room was empty.

Steve had been at the desk twenty seconds ago. He could not have gone far. While Nigel and Daisy ran along radiating corridors, opening doors, Kit ran across the hall to the toilets. A short corridor led to separate men's and ladies' rooms. Kit went into the men's room. It appeared empty.

'Mr Tremlett?' He pushed open all the cubicle doors. No one was there.

As he stepped out, he saw Steve returning to the reception desk. The guard must have been in the ladies' room—searching for Susan.

Steve turned round, hearing Kit. 'Looking for me?'

'Yes.' Kit realised he could not apprehend Steve without help. He turned away and shouted, 'Hey! Back in here!'

Steve looked troubled. 'What's going on? You lot aren't supposed to be wandering around the building. I don't like this.' He picked up the phone on the desk and dialled. The mobile in Kit's pocket rang. Steve heard it. He frowned, thinking, then a look of shocked understanding came over his face. 'You messed with the phones!'

Kit said, 'Stay calm and you won't get hurt.'

Steve acted quickly. He leapt nimbly over the desk and ran for the door.

Kit yelled, 'Stop!'

Daisy came running into the hall, saw Steve, and turned towards the main door, heading him off. Steve turned instead into the corridor leading to BSL4. Daisy and Kit ran after him.

Daisy was well ahead of Kit, arms pumping, but Steve was running like a hare and pulling away from them. There was an exit towards the rear of the building, Kit recalled. If Steve made it outside, they might never catch him.

Then, as Steve drew level with the door leading to the control room, Elton stepped into the corridor in front of him. Steve was going too fast to take evasive action. Elton stuck out a foot and tripped Steve, who went flying.

As Steve hit the ground, face down, Elton fell on him, with both knees in the small of his back, and pushed the barrel of a pistol into his cheek. 'Don't move, and you won't get shot,' Elton said. His voice was calm but convincing. He stood up, keeping the gun pointed at Steve, who lay still. 'That's the way to do it,' he said to Daisy. 'No blood.'

Nigel came running up. 'What happened?'

'Never mind!' Kit shouted. 'We're out of time!'

'What about the two guards in the gatehouse?' Nigel said.

'Forget them! They stay in the gatehouse all night.' Kit pointed at Elton. 'Get my laptop from the equipment room and wait for us in the van.' He turned to Daisy. 'Bring Steve, tie him up in BSL4, then get into the van. We have to go into the laboratory—now!'

IN THE BARN, the youngsters were sitting in front of the television set, watching an old horror movie. Caroline was stroking a white rat, Tom was pigging out on chocolates and trying to stay awake, and Craig was worrying about the dented Ferrari. Then Sophie went up the ladder to the hayloft, where her bag was, and came back down with a half-bottle of Smirnoff.

'Who wants some?' she said.

They all did. They had plastic tumblers and a fridge with soft drinks and ice. Tom and Caroline mixed their vodka with Coca-Cola. Craig copied Sophie and drank it straight with ice. The taste was bitter, but he liked the warm glow as it went down his throat.

The movie was going through a dull patch. Craig said to Sophie, 'Do you know what you're getting for Christmas?'

'Two decks and a mixer, so I can deejay. You?'

'Snowboarding holiday at Easter with some guys I know. So you want to be a deejay? Is that, like, your career plan?'

'Dunno.' Sophie looked scornful. 'What's your *career plan*?'

'I'd like to be a scientist like Grandpa.'

'A bit boring.'

'No! He discovers fantastic new drugs, he's his own boss, he makes piles of money, and he drives a Ferrari F50—what's boring?'

She shrugged. 'I wouldn't mind the car.' She giggled. 'Except for the dent.'

The thought of the damage he had done to his grandfather's car no longer depressed Craig. He was feeling pleasantly relaxed and carefree.

Sophie drained her glass. 'Another?'

They all had another.

Craig began to realise that the movie was, in fact, hilarious. 'That castle is so obviously made of plywood,' he said with a chuckle.

Caroline suddenly said, 'I'm so sleepy.' She got to her feet, climbed the ladder with some difficulty, and disappeared.

The old witch in the story had to bathe in the blood of a virgin to make herself young again. Craig and Sophie giggled helplessly.

'I'm going to be sick,' said Tom.

'Oh, no!' Craig sprang to his feet. He felt dizzy for a second, then recovered. 'Bathroom, quick,' he said. He took Tom's arm and led him there.

Tom started to throw up a fatal second before he reached the toilet.

Craig ignored the mess on the floor and guided him to the bowl. Tom puked some more. Craig held the boy's shoulders and tried not to breathe.

Sophie came to the door. 'Is he all right?'

'Yeah.' Craig put on the air of a snooty schoolteacher. 'An injudicious combination of chocolates, vodka and virgin's blood.'

Sophie laughed. Then, to Craig's surprise, she grabbed a length of toilet
roll, got down on her knees and began to clean the tiled floor.

Tom straightened up.

'All done?' Craig asked him.

Tom nodded. Craig flushed the toilet. 'Now clean your teeth.'

Tom brushed his teeth, then Craig led him out of the bathroom to his camp
bed. 'Get undressed,' he said. He opened Tom's suitcase and found a pair of
Spiderman pyjamas.

Tom put them on and climbed into bed. 'I'm sorry I heaved,' he said.

'It happens to the best of us,' Craig said. 'Forget it.' He pulled the blanket
up to Tom's chin. 'Sweet dreams.'

He returned to the bathroom. Sophie had cleaned up with surprising efficiency. Craig washed his hands, and she stood beside him at the basin and did
the same. She looked the most beautiful she had all day, Craig thought, as she
smiled at him. He took a towel and handed her one end. They both dried their
hands. Craig pulled the towel, drawing her to him, and kissed her lips.

She kissed him back, but she seemed tentative, unsure how to respond.
Could it be that, for all her talk, she had not done much kissing?

'Let's go back to the couch,' he murmured. 'I never like snogging in the bog.'

She giggled and led the way out.

Craig sat close to Sophie on the couch and put his arm round her. They
watched the film for a minute, then he kissed her again.

AN AIRTIGHT submarine door led from the changing room into the biohazard
zone. Kit turned the four-spoked wheel, opened the door and stepped into the
shower room. Nigel followed him, carrying Elton's burgundy briefcase.

Kit closed the door behind them. The doors were electronically linked so that
the next would not open until the last was shut. They passed through another
doorway into a room where blue plastic space suits hung from hooks.

Kit took off his shoes. 'Find one your size and get into it,' he said to Nigel.
'We've got to short-cut the safety precautions.'

'I don't like the sound of that.'

Kit did not either, but they had no choice. 'The normal procedure is too
long,' he said. 'You have to take off all your clothes and put on surgical scrubs

before you suit up.' He took a suit off a hook and began to climb into it. 'Coming out takes even longer. You shower in your suit, first with a decontamination solution, then with water, on a five-minute cycle. Then you take off the suit and scrubs and shower naked for five minutes. You clean your nails, blow your nose, clear your throat and spit. Then you get dressed. If we do all that, half the Inverburn police could be here by the time we get out. We'll skip the showers, take off our suits and run.'

Nigel was appalled. 'How dangerous is it?'

'It probably won't kill you, so long as you don't make a habit of it. Hurry up, get a suit on.' Kit closed his helmet then helped Nigel.

He used a roll of duct tape to attach the suit gauntlets to the rigid circular wrists of Nigel's suit, then got Nigel to do the same for him.

From the suit room they stepped into the decontamination shower, and then into the lab proper. Kit suffered a moment of pure fear. There was something in here that could kill him. He breathed slowly and made himself calm. You're not exposed to the atmosphere here in the lab, you'll be breathing pure air from outside, he told himself. No virus can penetrate this suit. Get a grip.

Curly yellow air hoses dangled from the ceiling. Kit grabbed one and connected it to the inlet on Nigel's belt, and saw Nigel's suit begin to inflate. He did the same for himself, and heard the inward rush of air. His terror abated.

Kit pointed to a door. 'The vault is through there.' He crossed the room, his air hose extending as he moved. He opened the door to a small room containing an upright refrigerator with a keypad combination lock. But Kit had installed the lock, so he knew the combination. He keyed the numbers and pulled the handle. The door opened. Nigel looked over his shoulder.

Measured doses of the antiviral drug were kept in disposable syringes, packed in small cardboard boxes. Kit pointed to the shelf. He raised his voice so that Nigel could hear him through the suit. 'This is the drug.'

Nigel said, 'I don't want the drug.'

Kit was astounded. 'What are you talking about? Why are we here?'

Nigel did not respond. On the second shelf were samples of various viruses ready to be used to infect laboratory animals. Nigel looked carefully at the labels, then selected a sample of Madoba-2.

Kit said, 'What the hell do you want that for?'

Without answering, Nigel took all the remaining samples of the same virus from the shelf, twelve boxes altogether.

One was enough to kill someone. Twelve could start an epidemic.

Kit said, 'I thought you were working for one of the pharmaceutical giants.'

'I know.'

Nigel could afford to pay Kit £300,000 for tonight's work. Even if Elton and Daisy were getting a smaller fee, Nigel had to be spending something like half a million. To make that worth his while, he must be getting a million from the customer. The drug was worth that, easily. But who would pay a million pounds for a sample of a deadly virus?

As soon as Kit asked himself the question, he knew the answer.

Nigel carried the sample boxes across the laboratory and placed them in a biosafety cabinet. This was a glass case with a slot at the front through which the scientist could put his arms in order to perform experiments.

Next, Nigel opened the burgundy leather briefcase. The top was lined with blue plastic cooler packs. The bottom half was filled with white polystyrene chips. Lying on the chips was an ordinary perfume spray bottle, empty. Kit recognised the bottle. It was a brand called *Diablerie*. His sister Olga used it.

Nigel put the bottle in the cabinet. It misted over with condensation. 'They told me to turn on the air extractor,' he said. 'Where's the switch?'

'Wait!' Kit said. 'What are you doing? You have to tell me!'

Nigel found the switch and turned it on. 'The customer wants the product in deliverable form,' he said. 'I'm transferring the samples to the bottle here, in the cabinet, because it's dangerous to do it anywhere else.' He took the top off the perfume bottle, then opened a sample box. Inside was a clear Pyrex vial with gradation marks printed on its side. Working awkwardly with his gauntleted hands, Nigel unscrewed the cap of the vial and poured the liquid into the *Diablerie* bottle. He recapped the vial and picked up another one.

Kit said, 'Do you know what your customer wants it for?'

'I can guess.'

'It will kill people—hundreds, maybe thousands!'

'I know.'

The perfume spray was the perfect delivery mechanism. Filled with the colourless liquid that contained the virus, it would pass unnoticed through all security checks. A woman could take it out of her handbag in a public place and look quite innocent as she filled the air with a fatal vapour. She would kill herself too, and slaughter more people than any suicide bomber. Horrified, Kit said: 'You're talking about mass murder!'

'Yes.' Nigel turned to look at Kit. 'And you're in it now, and as guilty as anyone, so shut your mouth and let me concentrate.'

Kit groaned. Nigel was right. There was nothing Kit could do. If he tried to stop the heist now, Nigel would probably kill him or Harry McGarry would have him killed for not paying his debt. He had to follow it through to the end and pick up his payment. Otherwise he was dead.

If Nigel did not handle the virus properly, Kit was dead anyway.

With his arms inside the biosafety cabinet, Nigel emptied the contents of all the sample vials into the perfume bottle, and replaced the spray-top. He then put the bottle into the pass-out tank, which was full of decontamination fluid, and removed it from the other side. He wiped the bottle dry then took two Ziploc food bags from the briefcase. He put the perfume bottle into one, sealed the bag, then put the bagged bottle into the second. Finally he put the double-bagged bottle back into the briefcase and closed the lid.

'We're done,' he said.

They left the lab, Nigel carrying the briefcase. They passed through the decontamination shower without using it—there was no time. In the suit room they climbed out of the cumbersome plastic space suits and put their shoes back on. Kit kept well away from Nigel's suit—the gloves were sure to be contaminated with minute traces of the virus. They moved through the normal shower, again without using it, through the changing room and into the lobby. The four security guards were tied up and propped against the wall.

Kit checked his watch. It was thirty minutes since he had listened to Toni Gallo's conversation with Steve. He pressed the green button that opened the door. He and Nigel ran down the corridor and into the Great Hall. To Kit's relief, it was empty: Toni Gallo had not yet arrived. We made it, he thought.

The van was outside the main door, its engine running. Elton was at the wheel, Daisy in the back. Nigel jumped in, and Kit followed him, shouting, 'Go! Go! Go!' Elton roared off before Kit got the door shut.

They stopped at the gate. Elton wound down the window.

Willie Crawford leaned out. 'All fixed?' he said.

'Not quite,' Elton said. 'We need some parts. We'll be back.'

'It's going to take you a while, in this weather,' the guard said.

'We'll be as quick as we can,' Elton said calmly. Then he closed the window.

After a moment the barrier lifted, and they pulled out. As they did so, headlights flashed. A car was approaching from the south. Kit made it out to be a light-coloured Jaguar saloon. Elton turned north and drove away.

Kit looked in the mirror and watched the headlights of the car. It turned into the gates of the Kremlin. Toni Gallo, Kit thought. A minute too late.

1.15 A.M.

TONI WAS in the passenger seat beside Carl Osborne when he braked to a halt alongside the gatehouse of the Kremlin. Her mother was in the back.

She handed Carl her pass and her mother's pension book. 'Give these to the guard with your press card,' she said.

Carl slid the window down and handed over the documents.

Looking across him, Toni saw Hamish McKinnon. 'Hi, Hamish, it's me,' she called. 'I've got two visitors with me.'

'Hello, Ms Gallo,' said the guard. 'Is that lady in the back holding a dog?'

'Don't ask,' she said.

Hamish copied down the names and handed back the press card and the pension book. 'You'll find Steve in Reception.'

'Are the phones working?'

'Not yet. The repair crew just left to fetch a spare part.' He lifted the barrier and Carl drove in.

Toni suppressed a wave of irritation at Hibernian Telecom. On a night such as this, they really should carry all the parts they might need. The roads might soon be impassable. She doubted they would be back before morning.

Carl pulled up at the main entrance. 'Wait here,' Toni said, and sprang out before he could argue. She did not want him in the building if she could avoid it. She ran up the steps, passed between the stone lions and pushed through the door. She was surprised to see no one at the reception desk. One of the guards might be on patrol, but they should not both have gone.

She headed for the control room. The monitors would show where the guards were. She was astonished to find the control room empty. Her heart seemed to go cold. Four guards missing? Something was wrong.

She looked again at the monitors. They all showed empty rooms. If four guards were in the building, one of them should appear on a monitor within seconds. But there was no movement anywhere.

Then something caught her eye. She looked closely at the feed from BSL4.

The dateline said December 24. She checked her watch. It was after one o'clock in the morning. Today was Christmas Day, December 25. She was looking at old pictures. Someone had tampered with the feed.

She sat at the work station and accessed the program. In three minutes she established that all the monitors covering BSL4 were showing yesterday's footage. She corrected them and looked at the screens.

In the lobby outside the changing rooms, four people were sitting on the floor. Toni stared at the monitor, horrified. Please, God, she thought, don't let them be dead. One moved. She looked more closely. They were the guards and their hands were behind their backs, as if they were tied up.

'No, no!' she said aloud. But there was no escaping the dismal conclusion that the Kremlin had been raided.

She felt doomed. First Michael Ross, now this. Where had she gone wrong? She had failed to make this place secure. She had let Stanley down.

Her first instinct was to rush to BSL4 and untie the captives. Then her police training reasserted itself. Stop, assess the situation, plan the response. Whoever had done this could still be in the building, though her guess was that the villains were the Hibernian Telecom repairmen who had just left. She picked up the phone on the desk.

It was dead, of course. The fault in the phone system was part of whatever was going on. She took her mobile from her pocket and called the police. 'This is Toni Gallo, in charge of security at Oxenford Medical. There's been an incident here. Four of my security guards have been attacked.'

'Are the perpetrators still on the premises?'

'I don't think so, but I can't be sure.'

'Anyone injured?'

'I don't know. I'll check—but I wanted to tell you first.'

'We'll try to get a patrol car to you—though the roads are terrible.' He sounded like an unsure young constable.

Toni tried to impress him with a sense of urgency. 'This could be a biohazard incident. A young man died yesterday of a virus that escaped from here.'

'We'll do our best.'

'I believe Frank Hackett is on duty tonight. Is he in the building?'

'He's on call.'

'I strongly recommend you phone him at home and tell him about this.'

'I've made a note of your suggestion.'

'We have a fault on the phones, probably caused by the intruders. Please take my mobile number.' She read it out. 'Ask Frank to call right away.'

'I've got the message.'

'May I ask your name?'

'PC David Reid.'

'Thank you, Constable Reid. We'll be waiting for your patrol car.' Toni hung up. She hurried out of the control room and ran along the corridor to

BSL4. She swiped her pass through the card reader, held her fingertip to the scanner and went in. There were Steve, Susan, Don and Stu, in a row against the wall, bound hand and foot. Susan's nose was swollen and there was blood on her chin and chest. Don had a nasty abrasion on his forehead.

Toni knelt down and began to untie them. 'What the hell happened here?'

THE HIBERNIAN TELECOM van was ploughing through snow a foot deep. Elton drove at ten miles an hour in high gear to keep from skidding. Snowflakes bombarded the vehicle, forming two steadily growing wedges at the bottom of the windscreen. The wipers described an ever-smaller arc, until Elton could no longer see out and had to stop the van to clear the snow away.

Kit thought about opening the van door and jumping out. He might disappear into the blizzard before they could catch him. But then they would still have the virus and he would still owe Harry a quarter of a million pounds.

Peering ahead through the snowstorm, he saw an illuminated sign that read DEW DROP INN. Elton turned off the road. There was a light over the door, and eight or nine cars in the car park. The place was open.

Elton pulled up next to a Vauxhall Astra estate. 'The idea was to ditch the van here,' he said. 'It's too easily identifiable. We're supposed to go back to the airstrip in that Astra, but I don't know if we're going to make it.'

From the back, Daisy said, 'You prick, why didn't you bring a Land Rover?'

'Because the Astra is one of the most popular and least noticeable cars in Britain, and the forecast said no snow, you ugly cow.'

'Knock it off, you two,' Nigel said calmly. He pulled off his wig and glasses. 'Take off your disguises. We don't know how soon those guards will be giving descriptions to the police.' The others followed suit.

Elton said, 'We could stay here, take rooms, wait it out.'

'Dangerous,' Nigel replied. 'We're only a few miles from the lab. Besides, we have an appointment to meet our customer.'

'He's not going to fly his helicopter in this muck.'

Kit's mobile rang. He checked his laptop. It was a regular call, not one diverted from the Kremlin system. He picked it up. 'Yeah?'

'It's me.' Kit recognised the voice of Hamish McKinnon. 'I'm on my mobile, I've got to be quick, while Willie's in the toilet.'

'What's happening?'

'She arrived just after you left. She found the other guards tied up and called the police. She just came up to the gatehouse and told us to expect a patrol. When they'll get here— Sorry, gotta go.' He hung up.

Kit pocketed his phone. 'Toni Gallo has found the guards,' he announced. 'She's called the police, and they're on their way.'

'That settles it,' Nigel said. 'Let's get in the Astra.'

AS CRAIG slipped his hand under the hem of Sophie's sweater, he heard steps. He broke the clinch and looked round.

His sister was coming down from the hayloft in her nightdress. 'I feel a bit strange,' she said, and crossed the room to the bathroom.

Thwarted, Craig turned his attention to the film on TV. The old witch, transformed into a beautiful girl, was seducing a handsome knight.

Caroline emerged, saying, 'That bathroom smells of puke.' She climbed the ladder and went back to bed.

'I'm sorry about this,' Craig murmured.

'There's no privacy here,' Sophie said. 'Why don't we go somewhere else?'

'Like where?'

'How about that attic you showed me earlier?'

TONI SAT in the control room, watching the monitors. Steve and the guards had related everything that had happened. Don had told her how one of the men had tried to stop the violence. The words he had shouted were now burnt into Toni's brain: *If you want to be empty-handed when we meet the client at ten, just carry on the way you are.*

Clearly, they had stolen something from the laboratory, and they had taken it away in a briefcase. Toni had a dreadful feeling she knew what it was.

She was running the BSL4 footage from 0.55 to 1.15. Although the monitors had not shown these images at the time, the computer had stored them. Now she was watching two men inside the lab, wearing biohazard suits.

She gasped when she saw one of them open the door to the little room that contained the vault. He tapped numbers into the keypad—he knew the code! He opened the fridge door, then the other man began to remove samples.

Toni froze the playback. The camera was above the door, and looked over the man's shoulder into the vault. His hands were full of small white boxes. Toni enlarged the picture on the monitor. She could see the biohazard symbol on the boxes. He was stealing virus samples. She ran the image-enhancement program. Slowly, the words on one of the boxes became clear: MADOBA-2.

It was what she had feared, but the confirmation hit her like the cold wind of death. She restarted the footage, and watched with horror while one of the intruders emptied the contents of the vials into a perfume spray marked *Diablerie*. The ordinary perfume bottle was now a weapon of mass destruction. She watched him carefully double-bag it and place it in the briefcase.

Toni sat staring at the screen in despair. Madoba-2 was now in the hands of a gang of thieves who were carrying it around in a damn briefcase. The risks were horrendous. And even if they did not release it by accident, their 'client' would do so deliberately. Someone was planning to use the virus to murder people in hundreds and thousands.

And they had obtained the murder weapon from her.

She had seen enough. She knew what needed to be done. The police had to gear up for a massive operation—and fast. If they moved quickly, they could still catch the thieves before the virus was handed over to the buyer. She returned the monitors to their default position and left the control room.

The security guards were in the Great Hall, sitting on the couches normally reserved for visitors, drinking tea.

'We have important work to do,' Toni said briskly. 'Stu, go to the control room and resume your duties, please. Steve, get behind the desk. Don, stay where you are.' Don had a makeshift dressing over the cut on his forehead.

Susan Mackintosh, who had been coshed, was lying on a couch. The blood had been washed from her face but she was severely bruised.

'I'm so sorry this happened,' Toni said. 'How do you feel?'

Susan smiled weakly. 'Pretty groggy.'

Toni's mother was sitting next to Don. The puppy sat on a newspaper at her feet. She fed it a piece of biscuit. 'That nice boy Steven made me a cup of tea,' she said. 'He'd make a nice boyfriend for you.'

'He's married,' Toni replied. She turned to Steve. 'Where's Carl Osborne?'

'Men's room.'

Toni nodded and took out her phone. It was time to call the police.

She got David Reid again. When she identified herself, he said, 'We sent you a car, but they turned back. The weather—'

She was horrified. 'Are you serious?' she said, raising her voice. 'Christ! What kind of wimps are the police recruiting nowadays?'

'There's no need for that kind of talk, madam.'

Toni got herself under control. 'You're right, I'm sorry. Here's the situation. The thieves stole a significant quantity of a virus called Madoba-2 which is lethal to humans, so this is a biohazard emergency.'

'Biohazard,' he said, obviously writing it down.

'The perpetrators are three men—two white and one black—and a white woman. They're driving a van marked HIBERNIAN TELECOM.'

'Can you give me fuller descriptions?'

'I'll get the guard supervisor to call you with that information—he saw them, I didn't. We have two injured people here. They need to see a doctor.'

'Right.'

'The intruders were armed.'

'What sort of weapons?'

Toni turned to Steve. 'Did you get a look at their firearms?'

Steve nodded. He was a gun buff. 'Nine-millimetre Browning automatic pistols, all three of them—the kind that take a thirteen-round magazine. They looked like ex-army stock to me.' Toni repeated the description to Reid.

'Armed robbery, then,' he said.

'Yes—but the important thing is that they can't be far away, and that van is easy to identify. If we move quickly, we can catch them.'

'Nobody can move quickly tonight.'

Toni was ready to scream with frustration, but she bit her tongue. 'Is Frank Hackett there?'

'Superintendent Hackett is not available.'

'If you won't wake him up, I will,' she said. She dialled his home number. He picked it up. 'Hackett.'

'Toni. Oxenford Medical has been robbed of a quantity of Madoba-2, the virus that killed Michael Ross.'

'How did you let that happen?'

It was the question she was asking herself, but it stung when it came from him. She retorted, 'If you're so smart, figure out how to catch the thieves.'

'Didn't we send a car out to you an hour ago?'

'It never got here. Your tough coppers saw the snow and got scared.'

'Well, if we're stuck, so are our suspects.'

'You're not stuck, Frank. You can get here with a snowplough.'

There was a long pause. 'I don't think so,' he said at last.

Toni could have killed him. But she bit back the retort that was on the tip of her tongue and said, 'What's your thinking, Frank?'

'I can't send unarmed men chasing after a gang with guns. We'll need to assemble our firearms-trained officers and get them kitted out with Kevlar vests, guns and ammunition. That's going to take a couple of hours.'

'While the thieves get away with a virus that could kill thousands!'

'I'll put out an alert for the van.'

'They might switch cars. They could have an off-road vehicle somewhere.'

'They still won't get far.'

'What if they have a helicopter?'

'Curb your imagination. There are no thieves with helicopters in Scotland.'

'Frank, use *your* imagination. These people want to start a plague!'

'Don't tell me how to do the job. You're not a cop any more.'

'Frank—' She stopped. He had broken the connection. 'Frank, you're a dumb bastard,' she said into the dead phone, then she hung up.

She frowned at her phone, racking her brains. How was she going to put a bomb under Frank? She scrolled through the memory of her mobile and found the home number of Odette Cressy, her friend at Scotland Yard.

The phone was answered after a long wait.

'This is Toni,' she said. 'I'm sorry to wake you.'

'It's OK. What's new?'

Toni told her.

Odette said, 'Jesus Christ, this is what we were afraid of.'

'I can't believe I let it happen.'

'Is there anything to give us a hint about when and how they plan to use it?'

'Two things,' Toni said. 'One: they didn't just steal the stuff, they poured it into a perfume spray. *Diablerie.* It's ready to use—in any crowded place.'

'At least we know what we're looking for. What else?'

'A guard heard them talk about meeting the client at ten.'

'At ten o'clock. They're working fast.'

'Exactly. It could be in London tonight. They could release it in the Albert Hall tomorrow.'

'Good work, Toni. Anything else?'

'I saw their van turn north when they left. But there's a blizzard and the roads are becoming impassable, so they probably aren't far from here.'

'Then we have a chance of catching them before they deliver the goods?'

'Yes—but I haven't been able to persuade the local police of the urgency.'

'Leave that to me. Terrorism comes under the Cabinet Office. Your hometown boys are about to get a phone call from Number Ten Downing Street. What do you need—helicopters?'

'I don't think helicopters can fly in this blizzard. What I need is a snowplough. They should clear the road from Inverburn to here, and the police should make this their base. Then they can start looking for the fugitives.'

'I'll make sure it happens. Keep calling me, OK?'

'Thanks, Odette.' Toni hung up.

She turned round. Carl Osborne was standing behind her, making notes.

ELTON DROVE the Vauxhall Astra estate car at bicycle pace, ploughing through more than a foot of fresh snow. Nigel sat beside him, clutching the burgundy leather briefcase with its deadly contents. Kit was in the back with Daisy. He was maddened with impatience. He wanted to get to the airfield fast.

The snow became so heavy that little was visible through the windscreen but whiteness. Their speed dropped to the pace of a brisk walk. Kit longed for a more suitable car. In his father's Toyota Land Cruiser Amazon, parked only a couple of miles away, they would have had a better chance.

'Is this car going to get us there?' Nigel asked.

'We might be all right on this road,' Elton said. 'But there are three or four miles of country lane before you get to the airfield.'

Kit made up his mind. He said, 'There's a Toyota Land Cruiser in my father's garage.'

'How far?'

'A mile back along this road, then another mile down a side turning. We could park in the woods near the house, borrow the Land Cruiser and drive to the airfield. Afterwards, Elton could bring it back and take the Astra.'

Nigel said, 'Has anyone got a better idea?'

No one did. Elton turned the car round and went back down the hill.

After a few minutes, Kit said, 'Take that side road.'

Elton pulled up. 'No way,' he said. 'The snow's eighteen inches thick down that lane and there's been no traffic on it for hours. We won't get fifty yards.'

Kit had the panicky feeling he got when losing at blackjack, that a higher power was dealing him all the wrong cards.

Nigel said, 'How far are we from your father's house?'

'A bit—' Kit swallowed. 'A bit less than a mile. You three could wait here while I go and get the Land Cruiser.'

Nigel shook his head. 'Something might happen to you. You could get stuck in the snow and we wouldn't be able to find you. Better to stay together.'

There was another reason, Kit guessed: Nigel did not trust Kit alone. He probably feared that Kit might have second thoughts and call the police.

They sat in silence, reluctant to leave the warmth blasting from the car's heater. Then Elton turned off the engine and they all got out of the car.

Nigel held on tightly to the briefcase. Kit was carrying his laptop. Elton found a flashlight in the glove box and gave it to Kit. 'You're leading the way,' he said.

Kit headed off, ploughing through snow up to his knees. It was painfully cold. None of them was dressed for this. Nigel had a sports jacket, Elton a raincoat and Daisy a leather jacket. Kit was the most warmly dressed, in his Puffa jacket. Kit wore Timberlands and Daisy had motorcycle boots, but Nigel and Elton wore ordinary shoes.

Soon Kit was shivering. His hands hurt and the snow soaked his jeans up to the knees and melted into his boots. The familiar lane was buried out of sight, and no hedge or wall marked the edge of the road. Kit stopped, and with his bare hands dug down into the snow.

'What now?' Nigel said bad-temperedly.

'Just a minute.' Kit found frozen turf. That meant he had strayed from the paved road. But which way? He blew on his icy hands, trying to warm them. The land to his right seemed to slope up. He guessed the road was that way. He trudged a few yards in that direction, then dug down again. This time he found tarmac. 'This way,' he said with more confidence than he felt.

The others followed him in silence. Even Daisy had stopped bitching. At last they reached the woods near the house. Kit had lost all feeling in his fingers and toes, but the snow was not so thick on the ground here, in the shelter of the trees, and he was able to walk faster. A faint glow ahead told him he was approaching the house. He headed for the light and came to the garage.

The big doors were closed, but there was a side door that was never locked. Kit found it and went inside. The other three followed.

'Thank God,' Elton said. 'I thought I was going to die in sodding Scotland.'

Kit shone his torch. Here was his father's Ferrari, parked very close to the wall. Next to it was Luke's Ford Mondeo. That was surprising: Luke normally drove himself and Lori home in it. Had they stayed the night, or . . . ?

He shone his torch at the far end of the garage, where the Toyota Land Cruiser was usually parked. The bay was empty.

'Oh shit,' said Kit. 'Now we're in trouble.'

CARL OSBORNE was speaking into his mobile phone. 'Is anyone on the newsdesk yet? . . . Good—put me through.'

Toni felt desperate. She had to stop him. Steve was behind the desk. She called him over and they crossed the Great Hall to where Carl sat.

'I'm sorry, you can't use that here,' she said. 'Please hang up.'

'Get ready to do a voice-record,' Carl said into his mobile. 'You can run it with a still photo of me holding a phone. Ready?'

She put her hand between his phone and his mouth.

Carl turned away and said into the phone, 'They're trying to stop me filing a report. Are you recording this?'

Toni spoke loud enough for the phone to pick up her words. 'Mobile phones may interfere with delicate electronic equipment operating in the laboratories.' It was untrue, but it would serve as a pretext. 'Please turn it off.'

He held it away from her and said loudly, 'Get off me!'

Toni nodded at Steve, who snatched the phone from Carl and turned it off.

'You can't do this!' Carl said.

'Of course I can. You're a visitor here and I'm in charge of security.'

'Then I'll go outside.'

'You'll freeze to death.'

'You can't stop me leaving.'

Toni shrugged. 'True. But I'm confiscating your phone. We'll mail it to you.'

'I'll find a phone box.'

'Good luck.' There was no public phone within five miles.

Carl pulled on his coat and went out. Toni and Steve watched him through the windows. He got into his car and started the engine. He got out again and scraped several inches of snow off the windscreen. The wipers began to operate. Carl got in and pulled away.

A mound of snow grew in front of the Jaguar as it climbed the rise. A hundred yards from the gate, it stopped.

Steve smiled. 'I didn't think he'd get far.'

The car's interior light came on. Toni frowned, worried.

'What's he doing?' Steve said. 'Looks like he's talking to himself.'

Toni's heart sank. 'Shit,' she said. 'That means he has another phone in the car.' She thought for a moment, then said, 'When he comes back in, sneak outside and see whether he's left the keys in the ignition. If he has, take them—then at least he won't be able to phone again.'

'OK.'

Her mobile rang and she picked up. 'Toni Gallo.'

'This is Odette.' She sounded shaken. 'We have fresh intelligence. A terrorist group called Scimitar has been actively shopping for Madoba-2.'

'Scimitar? An Arab group?'

'Sounds like it, though we're not sure—the name might be intentionally misleading. But we think your thieves are working for them.'

'My God. Do you know anything else?'

'They aim to release it tomorrow, Boxing Day, at a public location in Britain.'

Toni gasped. On Boxing Day, all over Britain, families would go to soccer matches, race meetings, cinemas and theatres and bowling alleys. The opportunities were endless. 'But where?' Toni said. 'What event?'

'We don't know. So we have to stop these thieves. The local police are on their way to you with a snowplough.'

'That's great!' Toni's spirits lifted.

'The guy in charge there is called Frank Hackett. The name rang a bell—he's not your ex, is he?'

'Yes. That was part of the problem. He likes to say no to me.'

'Well, you'll find him a chastened man. He's had a phone call from the Chancellor of the Duchy of Lancaster, who's in charge of the Cabinet Office Briefing Room. He's the antiterrorism supremo. Your ex must have jumped out of his bed as if it was on fire.'

'Don't waste your sympathy, he doesn't deserve it.'

'Since then, he's heard from my boss, another life-enhancing experience. The poor sod is on his way to you with a snowplough.'

DAISY WAS SHIVERING so much she could hardly hold the ladder. Elton climbed the rungs, grasping a pair of garden shears in one frozen hand. The exterior lamps shone through the filter of falling snow. Kit watched from the garage door, his teeth chattering. He felt as if he were in a nightmare. Nigel was in the garage, arms wrapped round the burgundy leather briefcase.

They had to go to Luke and Lori's cottage, which was more than a mile away, and take the Land Cruiser, which Stanley must have let Luke drive home. But Kit knew they could not go immediately. They were nearly falling down with exhaustion. Worse, Kit was not sure he could find Luke's place. He had almost lost his way looking for Steepfall. They had to wait until the blizzard eased, or until daylight gave them a better chance. And to make sure no one could find out that they were here, they were cutting off the phones.

When Elton had succeeded in snipping the telephone wires, he carried the ladder and shears back into the garage, where Kit had found them.

Nigel looked around the bare stone walls of the converted stable. 'We can't stay here,' he said. 'We're cold and wet and there's no heat. We could die.'

Daisy said, 'I want a cup of tea and a dram. I'm going in the house.'

'No!' The thought of these three in his family home filled Kit with horror. And how could he let them carry the briefcase into the kitchen?

Elton said, 'I'm with her. Let's go into the house.'

'But how would I explain you?' Kit demanded.

'They'll all be asleep.'

'And if it's still snowing when they get up?'

Nigel said, 'Tell them you don't know us. You met us on the road. Our car is stuck in a snowdrift. You took pity on us and brought us back here.'

'They aren't supposed to know I've left the house!'

'You'll think of a plausible story, Kit,' said Nigel. 'Let's get inside.'

'You left your disguises in the van. My family will see your real faces.'

'It doesn't matter. We're just unfortunate stranded motorists. There'll be hundreds like us, it will be on the news. We'll just be polite and not say much.'

'Say nothing at all would be the best plan. Any rough stuff and the game will be up.' He turned to Daisy. 'You keep your hands to yourself.'

Nigel backed Kit. 'Yeah, Daisy, try not to give the bloody game away, OK?'

She said, 'Yeah, yeah,' and turned away.

Kit realised that at some point in the argument he had given in. 'Shit,' he said. 'Just remember that you need me to show you where the Land Cruiser is. If any harm comes to my family, you can forget it.'

With a fatalistic feeling, he led them round the house to the back door. It was unlocked, as always. As he opened it, he said, 'All right, Nellie, it's me.'

When he entered the boot lobby, warm air washed over him. He led them into the kitchen. 'Be nice, Nellie,' he said quietly. 'These are friends.'

Nigel patted Nellie and she wagged her tail. They took off their wet coats. Nigel stood the briefcase on the table and said, 'Put the kettle on, Kit.'

Kit put down his laptop and turned on the small TV set on the kitchen counter. He found a news channel, then filled the kettle.

A pretty newsreader said, 'An unexpected change in the prevailing wind has brought a surprise blizzard to most of Scotland.'

Kit put out mugs, a sugar bowl and a jug of milk. Nigel, Daisy and Elton sat round the scrubbed pine table, just like family. The kettle boiled. Kit made a pot of tea and a cafetière of coffee.

A weather forecaster appeared in front of a chart. 'Tomorrow morning the blizzard will die away as quickly as it came,' he said.

'Yes!' Nigel said triumphantly.

'The thaw will follow before midday.'

Elton poured tea and added milk and sugar. 'We can still make it,' he said. 'If we leave at first light,' Kit added. Seeing the way ahead cheered him up. Daisy got to her feet. She opened the door to the dining room and peered in. Kit said, 'Where do you think you're going?'

'I need a shot of booze in this tea.' She turned on the light and went in. A moment later Kit heard her opening the cocktail cabinet.

Kit's father walked into the kitchen from the hall, wearing grey pyjamas and a black cashmere dressing gown. 'Good morning,' he said. 'What's all this?'

'Hello, Daddy,' Kit said. 'Let me explain.'

Daisy came in from the dining room holding a full bottle of Glenmorangie. Stanley raised his eyebrows at her. 'Do you want a glass of whisky?'

'No, thanks,' she replied. 'I've got a whole bottle here.'

TONI CALLED Stanley at home as soon as she had a spare moment. It was a conversation she dreaded. She had to tell him that she was responsible for a catastrophe that could ruin his life. How would he feel about her after that?

She dialled his number and got the 'disconnected' tone. It must be out of order. Perhaps the snow had brought down the lines. He did not carry a mobile, but there was a phone in his Ferrari. She dialled that and left a message.

She stared impatiently out of the windows of the Great Hall. Where were the police with their snowplough? It should be here by now.

Once it had arrived, she hoped it would leave again almost immediately, and get on the track of the Hibernian Telecom van. But the thieves had probably switched vehicles soon after leaving the Kremlin. That was how she would have done it. She would have picked a nondescript car and left it in a location where a vehicle might be parked for hours without attracting attention. What were the possibilities? she wondered. She went to the reception desk and got a notepad and pen. She made a list:

Inverburn Golf Club
Dew Drop Inn
Greenfingers Garden Centre
Scottish Smoked Fish Products
Williams Press (Printing & Publishing)

She did not want Carl Osborne to know what she was doing. He had returned from his car to the warmth of the hall, and was listening to everything.

Unknown to him, he could no longer phone from the car—Steve had sneaked out and taken the keys from the ignition—but Toni was taking no chances.

She spoke quietly to Steve. 'We're going to do some detective work.' She tore her sheet of paper in two and gave half to Steve. 'Ring these places. You should find a caretaker or security guard. Tell them we've had a robbery, but don't say what's missing. Say the getaway vehicle may have been abandoned on their premises. Ask if they can see a Hibernian Telecom van outside.'

Steve nodded. 'Smart thinking—maybe we can get on their trail and give the police a head start.'

'Exactly. But don't use the desk phone. Go to the far end of the hall, where Carl can't eavesdrop. Use the mobile you took from him.'

Toni moved well away from Carl and took out her mobile. She called enquiries and got the number for the golf club. She dialled and waited. After more than a minute, a sleepy voice answered, 'Yes? Golf club. Hello?'

Toni introduced herself and told the story. 'I'm trying to locate a van with HIBERNIAN TELECOM on its side. Is it in your car park?'

'Well, it wasn't when I came on duty at seven yesterday evening.'

'Could a van have parked there since then?'

'Well, maybe . . . I've no way of telling.'

'Could you have a look?'

'Aye, I could look!' He spoke as if it were an idea of startling originality. 'Hold on, I'll just be a minute.' There was a knock as he put the phone down.

Toni waited. Footsteps receded and returned.

'No, there's no van there.'

'OK. You've been very helpful. I appreciate it.'

Toni hung up. Steve was talking and clearly had not yet struck gold. She dialled the Dew Drop Inn.

A cheerful voice answered. 'Vincent speaking, how may I help you?'

Toni went through her routine again.

'There are lots of vehicles in our car park—we're open over Christmas,' Vincent told her. 'I'm looking at the closed-circuit television monitor, but I don't see a van. Unfortunately, the camera doesn't cover the entire car park.'

'Would you mind going to the window and having a good look?'

'Just hold on,' he said. He went away and came back. 'Yes, it's here. Ford Transit van, blue, with HIBERNIAN TELECOM in large white letters on the side. It can't have been there long, because it's not under as much snow as the rest of the cars—that's how come I can see the lettering.'

'That's tremendously helpful, thank you.' It seemed a long time since Toni had enjoyed a piece of luck. 'I don't suppose you noticed whether another car is missing—possibly the car they left in?'

'No, sorry.'

'OK—thanks again!' She hung up and looked across at Steve. 'I've found the getaway vehicle!'

He nodded towards the window. 'And the snowplough's here.'

DAISY DRAINED her cup of tea and filled it up again with whisky.

Kit felt unbearably tense. Nigel and Elton might be able to keep up the pretence of being innocent travellers accidentally stranded, but Daisy was hopeless. She looked like a gangster and acted like a hooligan.

When she put the bottle down on the kitchen table, Stanley picked it up. 'Don't get drunk, there's a good girl,' he said mildly. He stoppered the bottle.

Daisy was not used to people telling her what to do. She looked at Stanley as if she was ready to kill him. The tension was broken by Kit's sister Miranda, who came in wearing a pink floral nightgown.

Stanley said, 'Hello, my dear, you're up early.' It was 4.30 a.m.

'I couldn't sleep. I've been on the sleepchair in Kit's box-room. Don't ask why.' She looked at the strangers. 'It's early for Christmas visitors.'

'This is my daughter Miranda,' Stanley said. 'Mandy, meet Nigel, Elton and Daisy.'

A few minutes ago, Kit had introduced them to his father and, before he realised his mistake, he had given their real names.

Miranda nodded to them. 'Did Santa bring you?' she said brightly.

Kit explained. 'Their car died on the main road near our turn-off. I picked them up, then my car gave out too, and we walked the rest of the way here.'

'I didn't know you'd left the house—where on earth did you go, in the middle of the night, in this weather?'

'Oh, you know.' Kit put on a sheepish grin. 'Couldn't sleep, felt lonely, went to look up an old girlfriend in Inverburn.'

'Which one?'

'I don't think you know her.' He thought of a name quickly. 'Lisa Fremont.' He almost bit his tongue. She was a character in a Hitchcock movie.

Miranda did not react to the name. 'Was she pleased to see you?'

'She wasn't in.'

Miranda picked up the coffeepot. Kit wondered whether she believed him.

'Where are you from?' Stanley asked Nigel. 'You don't sound Scots.' It seemed like small talk, but Kit knew his father was probing.

Nigel answered in the same relaxed tone. 'I live in Surrey, work in London. My office is in Canary Wharf.'

'You're in the financial world?'

'I source high-tech systems for Third World countries, mainly the Middle East,' he said. It sounded pat.

Miranda brought her coffee to the table and sat opposite Daisy. 'What nice gloves.' Daisy's suede gloves were soaking wet. 'Why don't you dry them?'

Kit tensed. Any conversation with Daisy was hazardous.

Daisy gave a hostile look, but Miranda did not see it, and persisted. 'You need to stuff them, so they'll keep their shape,' she said. She took a roll of kitchen paper from the counter. 'Here, use this.'

'I'm fine,' Daisy muttered angrily.

Miranda raised her eyebrows. 'Have I said something to offend you?'

Kit thought, Oh God, here it comes.

Nigel stepped in. 'Don't be daft, Daisy, you don't want to spoil your gloves.' There was an edge of insistence in his voice. He was as worried as Kit. 'Do what the lady says; she's being nice to you.'

Kit waited for the explosion. But, to his surprise, Daisy took off her gloves. Kit was astonished to see that she had small, neat hands. The rest of her was brutish, but her hands were beautiful, and she obviously knew it, for they were well manicured, with clean nails and a pale pink nail varnish. Kit was bemused. Somewhere inside that monster there was an ordinary girl, he realised.

Miranda helped her stuff the wet gloves with kitchen paper. 'How are you three connected?' she asked Daisy, her tone conventionally polite.

Daisy looked panicked. After a moment, Nigel spoke. 'Daisy's father is an old friend of mine. And Elton works for me.'

Miranda smiled at Elton. 'Right-hand man?'

'Driver,' he replied brusquely. Kit reflected that it was a good thing Nigel was personable—he had to supply enough charm for the three of them.

Kit could not sit still any longer; the strain was unbearable. He jumped up. 'I'm hungry,' he said. 'Dad, is it OK if I scramble some eggs for everyone?'

'Of course.'

'I'll give you a hand,' Miranda said. She put sliced bread in the toaster.

Stanley said, 'Anyway, I hope the weather improves soon. When were you planning to return to London?'

'Heading back on Boxing Day,' Nigel said.

'A short Christmas visit,' Stanley commented, gently challenging the story. Nigel shrugged. 'Work to do, you know.'

'You may have to stay longer than you anticipated. I can't see them clearing the roads by tomorrow.'

The thought seemed to make Nigel anxious. He pushed up the sleeve of his pink sweater and looked at his watch.

Kit realised he needed to do something to show he was not in league with Nigel and the other two. As he began to make breakfast he resolved not to defend or excuse the strangers. On the contrary, he should question Nigel sceptically, as if he mistrusted the story.

But, before he could put his resolution into practice, Elton suddenly became talkative. 'How about your Christmas, Professor?' he said. Kit had introduced his father as Professor Oxenford. 'Got your family all around you, it seems. This must be a big house, to sleep, what, ten of you?'

'Yes. We have some outbuildings.'

'Oh, handy.' He looked out of the window, although the snow made it difficult to see anything. 'Guest cottages, like?'

'There's a cottage and a barn.'

'Very useful. And staff quarters, I presume?'

'Our staff have a cottage a mile or so away. I doubt if we'll see them today.'

'Oh. Shame.' Elton lapsed into silence again—having carefully established exactly how many people were on the property.

Kit wondered if anyone else had noticed that.

5 A.M.

THE SNOWPLOUGH was a Mercedes lorry with a blade hooked to its front attachment plate. It quickly cleared the drive from the gatehouse, and by the time it stopped at the entrance to the Kremlin, Toni had her coat on, ready to go.

The snowplough was followed by three police cars and an ambulance. The ambulance crew came in first. They took Susan out on a stretcher, though she said she could walk. Don refused to go. 'If a Scotsman went to hospital every time he got a kick in the head, the doctors could never cope,' he said.

Frank came in wearing a dark suit and a grim expression on his face.

Toni's mother said, 'Hello, Frank! This is a surprise. Are you and Toni getting back together?'

'Not today,' he muttered.

'Shame.'

Frank was followed by two detectives carrying large briefcases—a crime-scene team, Toni presumed. Frank nodded to Toni and shook hands with Carl Osborne, but spoke to Steve. 'You're the guard supervisor?'

'Aye. Steve Tremlett. You're Frank Hackett, I've met you before.'

'I gather four guards were assaulted.'

'Me and three others, aye.'

'Did all the assaults take place in the same location?'

'Susan was attacked in the corridor. I was tripped up in about the same place. Don and Stu were held at gunpoint and tied up in the control room.'

'Show me both places, please.'

Toni was astonished. 'We need to go after these people, Frank. Why don't you leave this to your team?'

'Don't tell me how to do the job,' he replied, then turned back to Steve and said, 'Lead the way.'

Toni suppressed a curse and followed along. So did Carl Osborne.

The detectives put crime-scene tape across the corridor where Steve had been tripped up and Susan had been coshed. Then they went to the control room, where Stu was watching the monitors. Frank taped the doorway.

Steve said, 'All four of us were tied up and taken inside the BSL4 facility. Not the laboratory itself, just the lobby.'

'Which is where I found them,' Toni added. 'But that was four hours ago—and the perpetrators are getting further away every minute.'

'We'll take a look at that location.'

'No, you won't,' Toni said. 'It's a restricted area. No one is allowed past the door without biohazard training. You can see it on a monitor.'

Frank turned on his heel.

Toni followed him. Back in the Great Hall were two police officers in yellow jackets and rubber boots. 'Check every vehicle you pass,' Frank said. 'Radio in the registration number and tell us if there's anyone in the cars. We're looking for three men and a woman. Don't approach the occupants. These laddies have guns and you don't. There's an armed-response unit on its way. If we can locate the perpetrators, we'll send them in. Is that clear?'

The two men nodded.

'Go north and take the first turnoff. I think they headed east.'

Toni knew that was wrong. 'The thieves didn't head east,' she said.

'I suppose you reached that conclusion by feminine intuition?'

One of the constables laughed.

Toni said calmly, 'The getaway vehicle is in the car park of the Dew Drop Inn, on this road five miles north.'

Frank reddened. 'And how did you acquire this information?'

'Detective work. I phoned around. Better than intuition.'

The constable laughed again, then smothered it when Frank glared at him.

Toni added, 'The thieves probably switched cars at the motel and drove on.'

Frank suppressed his fury. 'Go to the motel,' he said to the two constables. 'I'll give you further orders when you're on the road.' Then he summoned a plain-clothes detective and told him to follow the snowplough to the motel.

Relieved, Toni turned her mind to the next step. She wanted to stay in close touch with the police operation, but she had no car. And Mother was here.

She saw Carl Osborne talking quietly to Frank. Carl pointed at his Jaguar, still stuck halfway up the drive. Frank nodded and said something to a uniformed officer, who went outside and spoke to the snowplough driver.

Toni addressed Carl. 'You're going with the snowplough.'

He looked smug. 'It's a free country.'

'Don't forget to take the puppy.'

'I was planning to leave him with you.'

'I'm coming with you. I need to get to Stanley's house. It's five miles beyond the Dew Drop Inn. You can leave me and Mother there.'

'Forget it,' Carl said, putting on his coat.

Toni nodded. 'Let me know if you change your mind.'

He frowned, suspicious of her ready acceptance of his refusal, but said no more. Steve Tremlett opened his mouth to speak, but Toni discreetly flapped her hand at him in a 'Keep quiet' gesture. Carl went to the door.

Toni said: 'Don't forget the puppy.'

He picked up the dog and went out to his car.

Toni watched through the windows as the convoy moved off. The snowplough cleared the pile in front of Carl's Jaguar, then climbed the slope to the gatehouse. One police car followed. Carl sat in his car for a moment, then got out again and returned to the Great Hall.

'Where are my keys?' he said angrily.

Toni smiled sweetly. 'Have you changed your mind about taking me?'

Steve jingled the bunch of keys in his pocket.

Carl made a sour face. 'Get in the damn car,' he said.

MIRANDA FELT UNEASY about the weird threesome of Nigel, Elton and Daisy. Were they what they claimed to be? Did Nigel and Elton have no family who wanted to see them at Christmas? Nigel was not a friend of Daisy's family, Miranda decided. There was no warmth between them. They were more like people who had to work together. But if they were colleagues, why lie about it?

Her father looked strained, too. She wondered if he was also suspicious.

The kitchen filled with delicious smells: frying bacon, coffee and toast. Cooking was one of the things Kit did well, Miranda mused. Now he handed each of them a plate with crisp bacon, slices of tomato, scrambled eggs sprinkled with chopped herbs, and hot buttered toast. The tension in the room eased a little. Perhaps, Miranda thought, that was what Kit had been aiming at.

Kit made conversation. 'So, Daisy, what do you do for a living?'

She took a long time to reply. 'I work with my father,' she said.

'And what's his line of business?'

She seemed baffled by the question.

Nigel laughed and said, 'My old friend Harry has so many things going, it's hard to say what he does.'

'Well, give us an example of one of the things he does, then.'

It was not like Kit to question people aggressively, Miranda thought. Perhaps he, too, found the guests' account of themselves hard to believe.

Daisy brightened and, as if struck by inspiration, said, 'He's into property development.' She seemed to be repeating something she had heard.

The tension spoiled Miranda's breakfast. She had to talk to her father about this. She swallowed, coughed, and pretended to have something stuck in her throat. Coughing, she got up from the table. 'Sorry,' she spluttered.

Her father snatched up a glass and filled it at the tap.

Still coughing, Miranda left the room. As she intended, her father followed her into the hall. She closed the kitchen door and motioned him into his study. She coughed again, for effect, as they went in.

He offered her the glass, but she waved it away. 'I was pretending,' she said. 'I wanted to talk to you. What do you think about our guests?'

He put the glass down on his desk. 'A strange bunch. I wondered if they were shady friends of Kit's, until he started questioning the girl.'

'Me, too. They're lying about something, though.'

'But what? If they're planning to rob us, they're getting off to a slow start.'

Miranda felt a stab of fear. 'I don't know, but I feel threatened.'

'I'll call the police.' Stanley picked up the phone on his desk and put it to his ear. He frowned. 'No dialling tone,' he said. He tapped the keyboard of his computer. 'No email, either. It's probably the weather. Where's your mobile?'

'In the cottage. Don't you have one?'

'Only the phone in the Ferrari.'

'Olga has one.'

'No need to wake her.' Stanley glanced out of the window. 'I'll just throw on a coat over my pyjamas and go to the garage.'

'Where are the keys?'

'Key cupboard.'

The key cupboard was in the boot lobby. 'I'll fetch them for you.'

They stepped into the hall. Stanley went to the front door and bent down to put on his boots. Miranda put her hand on the knob of the kitchen door, then hesitated. She could hear Olga's voice coming from the kitchen. Miranda had not spoken to her sister since last night.

She opened the door. Nigel, Elton and Daisy were sitting at the table and Kit was hovering behind them. Olga was leaning against the kitchen counter, wearing a black silk wrap. Miranda noticed a rectangular bulge in the pocket: Olga never went anywhere without her phone.

She was in full courtroom mode, interrogating the strangers across the table. She said to Nigel, 'What on earth were you doing out so late?' He might have been a delinquent teenager.

Nigel frowned. 'We were on our way to Glasgow.'

'What was the occasion?'

'A party.'

Olga raised her dark eyebrows. 'You come to Scotland to spend Christmas with your old friend, then you and his daughter go off to a party and leave the poor man alone?'

'He wasn't feeling too well.'

Olga turned the spotlight on Daisy. 'What sort of a daughter are you, to leave your sick father at home on Christmas Eve?'

Daisy stared back in mute anger. Miranda suddenly feared that Daisy could be violent.

Kit seemed to have the same thought, for he said, 'Take it easy, Olga.'

Olga ignored him. 'Well?' she said to Daisy. 'Haven't you got anything to say for yourself?'

Daisy picked up her gloves. For some reason, Miranda found that ominous. Daisy put the gloves on then said, 'I don't have to answer your questions.'

'I think you do.' Olga looked back at Nigel. 'Three complete strangers, sitting in my father's kitchen filling yourselves with his food, and the story you tell is highly implausible. I think you need to explain yourselves.'

Nigel's anger showed as he said, 'I don't like being interrogated.'

'If you don't like it, you can leave,' Olga said. 'But if you want to stay in my father's house, you need to tell a better story.' She reached for the coffeepot, then pointed to the burgundy briefcase on the table. 'What's this?'

'It's mine,' Nigel said.

'Well, we don't keep luggage on the table.' She reached out and picked it up. 'Not much in it—ow!' Nigel had grabbed her arm. 'That hurts!' she cried.

Nigel spoke quietly but distinctly. 'Put the case down. Now.'

Stanley appeared beside Miranda. 'Take your hands off my daughter!' he said to Nigel.

Nellie barked loudly. Elton reached down and grabbed the dog's collar.

Daisy grabbed the briefcase. Olga tried to keep hold of it, and somehow the case flew open. Polystyrene packing chips scattered all over the kitchen table. Kit gave a shout of fear and Miranda wondered momentarily what he was so frightened of. Out of the case fell a perfume bottle in a polythene bag.

With her free hand, Olga slapped Nigel's face.

Nigel slapped her back. Everyone shouted at once. Stanley pushed past Miranda and strode towards Nigel. Miranda shouted, 'No—'

Daisy stood in Stanley's way. He tried to push her aside. There was a blur of movement and Stanley cried out and fell back, bleeding from his mouth.

Then, suddenly, both Nigel and Daisy were holding guns.

Everyone went quiet except Nellie, who was barking frantically. Elton twisted her collar, throttling her, until she shut up. The room was silent.

Olga said, 'Who the hell are you people?'

Stanley looked at the perfume spray on the table and said fearfully, 'Why is that bottle double-bagged?'

Miranda slipped out through the door.

Kit stared in fear at the *Diablerie* bottle on the kitchen table. But the glass did not smash; the top did not fall off; the double plastic bags stayed intact. The lethal fluid remained safely inside its fragile container.

But now that Nigel and Daisy had pulled guns, they could no longer pretend to be innocent victims of the storm. As soon as the news from the laboratory got out, they would be connected with the theft of the virus.

Kit thought furiously, trying to devise a way out. Then, as everyone stood frozen, staring at the vicious little dark grey pistols, Nigel moved his gun a fraction of an inch, mistrustfully pointing it at Kit.

Slowly, Kit raised his hands. 'Dad, I'm so sorry I brought these people into the house,' he said. 'I had no idea . . .'

His father gave him a long look, then nodded. 'There was no way you could have known,' he said. 'You can't turn strangers away in a blizzard.'

Nigel jumped in to back up Kit's pretence. 'I'm sorry to return your hospitality this way . . . Kit, is it? Yes . . . You saved our lives in the snow, now we're pointing guns at you. This old world never was fair.'

Elton frowned. Daisy turned away with a scornful expression. But to Kit's relief, the gang did not betray him. Fortunately, they still needed him. He knew the way to Luke's cottage and the Toyota Land Cruiser.

Kit's mobile phone rang.

He stood paralysed, not knowing what to do. The caller was probably Hamish. How could he speak to him without betraying himself to his family?

Nigel solved the problem. 'Give me that,' he said.

Kit handed over his phone and Nigel answered it. 'Yes, this is Kit,' he said, in a fair imitation of a Scots accent. The person at the other end seemed to believe him, for there was a silence while Nigel listened. 'Got it,' he said. 'Thanks.' He hung up and pocketed the phone. 'Someone wanting to warn you about three dangerous desperadoes in the neighbourhood,' he said. 'Apparently the police are coming after them with a snowplough.'

CRAIG AND SOPHIE were in a universe of their own, lying under their coats on the old sofa in the attic, when they heard the noise from the kitchen.

'Oh my God, what's that?' Sophie asked.

Craig had been aware of people in the kitchen below. He had vaguely heard the murmur of voices but he had taken no notice, confident that no one would interrupt them here in the attic. Now the sounds could not be ignored. First he heard Grandpa shout—an unusual event in itself. Nellie started barking like a fiend; there was a scream, and several voices yelling at once.

Sophie said in a frightened voice, 'What's going on?'

Below them, the kitchen went quiet as suddenly as it had burst into sound.

Craig stood up and stepped across the attic to the hole in the floor. He lay down and looked through the gap in the floorboards. He saw his mother looking shocked and frightened. Grandpa was wiping blood off his chin. Uncle Kit had his hands in the air. Three strangers were in the room. At first he thought they were all men, then he realised one was an ugly girl with a shaved head. The older man and the girl held guns.

Craig murmured, 'Bloody hell, what's happening down there?'

Sophie lay down beside him. 'Are those things guns?' she gasped.

'Yes.' Craig thought. 'We have to call the police. Where's your phone?'

'I left it in the barn. Oh God, what can we do?'

'Think. Think. A phone. We need a phone.' Craig hesitated. Where was the nearest phone? 'There's an extension beside Grandpa's bed.'

Sophie said, 'I can't do anything, I'm too scared.'

'You'd better stay here.' Craig stood up, and went to the low door. He was frightened. He took a breath, then opened the door. He crawled into Grandpa's suit cupboard, pushed at the door and emerged into the dressing room. The lights were on. Craig stepped into the bedroom. On the bedside table was a copy of *Scientific American* magazine, open—and the phone.

Craig picked up the handset. There was no dialling tone. Why were the phones out? He replaced the handset and pulled open the bedside drawers. In one of them he found a flashlight and a book, but no mobile phone. Then he remembered: Grandpa had a phone in his car, but did not carry a mobile.

He heard a sound from the dressing room. Sophie poked her head out of the suit cupboard, looking frightened. 'Someone's coming!' she hissed. A moment later, Craig heard a heavy footstep on the landing.

He darted into the dressing room. Sophie ducked back into the attic. Craig fell on his knees and crawled through the suit cupboard just as he heard the bedroom door open. He had no time to close the cupboard door. He wriggled through the low door, then quickly turned and closed it softly behind him.

Sophie whispered, 'The older man told the girl to search the house. He called her Daisy.'

'I heard her boots on the landing.'

'Did you get through to the police?'

He shook his head. 'The phone's dead.'

'No!'

Craig heard Daisy's heavy tread in the dressing room. She would see the open cupboard door. Would she spot the low door behind the suits? The silence dragged out. He thought he heard her step into the bathroom. After a shorter pause, her boots crossed the dressing room and the bedroom door slammed.

'Oh God, I'm so scared,' Sophie said.

'Me, too,' said Craig.

MIRANDA WAS in Olga's bedroom with Hugo.

When she left the kitchen she had not known what to do. She could not go outside—she was in her nightdress and bare feet. She had raced up the stairs and then just come to a standstill on the landing. She was so frightened she wanted to vomit. She had to call the police—that was the priority. Olga had her mobile in the pocket of her silk robe, but Hugo probably had his own.

She opened Hugo's door, slid inside the room and closed the door quietly.

Hugo was standing at the window, looking out. He was naked and had his back to the door. 'Would you look at this bloody weather?' he said, obviously thinking his wife had come back.

Miranda was momentarily arrested by his casual tone. Clearly Olga and Hugo had made up their quarrel.

'It's me,' she said.

Hugo spun round, startled, then smiled. 'And in *déshabillé*—what a lovely surprise! Let's get into bed, quick.'

He looked like a little round gnome and Miranda wondered how she could have found him attractive. Then she heard heavy footsteps on the stairs. 'We have to phone the police right now,' she said. 'Where's your mobile?'

'Just here,' he said, pointing to the bedside table. 'What on earth is wrong?'

'People with guns in the kitchen—dial nine-nine-nine, quickly!'

The footsteps had reached the landing. She froze, terrified that the door would burst open, but the steps went by.

'Who are they?'

'Never bloody mind!' Her voice became a kind of low scream. 'They're probably looking for me. Get on with it!'

Hugo snatched up his phone and jabbed at the ON button. 'Damn thing takes for ever!' he said in frustration. 'How did these people get in?'

'Said they were stranded . . . What is the matter with that phone?'

'Searching,' he said. 'Come on, come on!'

Miranda heard the footsteps outside again. She flung herself on the floor and slid sideways under the double bed just as the door flew open.

She could see Hugo's bare feet and a pair of black motorcycle boots with steel-tipped toes. She heard Hugo say, 'Hello, gorgeous, who are you?'

His charm did not work on Daisy. She said, 'Give me that phone.'

'I was just—'

'Now, you fat fool! . . . Now come with me.'

'Let me put something on.'

Miranda saw Hugo's feet step away from Daisy. She moved quickly towards him, then there was the sound of a blow and he let out a cry. Both pairs of feet moved towards the door together. They passed out of Miranda's sight and a moment later she heard them going down the stairs.

Miranda said to herself, 'Oh God, what do I do now?'

CRAIG AND SOPHIE lay side by side on the floorboards of the attic, looking down through the hole into the kitchen, as Craig's father was dragged naked into the room by Daisy. Craig was shocked. It was like a scene from a nightmare. He could hardly grasp that this humiliated figure was his *father*, the master of the house, the only person with the nerve to stand up to his domineering mother, the man who had ruled Craig for all fifteen years of his life.

Sophie began to cry softly. 'We're all going to be murdered,' she whispered.

Craig put his arm round her narrow shoulders. She was trembling. 'We're not dead yet,' he said. 'We can get help. Where is your phone, exactly?'

'I left it in the barn. I think I dropped it into my suitcase when I changed.'

'We have to go there and use it to call the police.'

'What if those terrible people see us?'

'We'll stay away from the kitchen windows.'

'We can't—the barn door is right opposite!'

She was right, Craig knew, but they had to take the risk. 'They probably won't look out. Anyway, you can hardly see across the back yard in this snow.' He squeezed her shoulders and kissed her cheek. 'Come on. Be brave.'

She wiped her nose on her sleeve. 'I'll try.'

They stood up and put on their boots and coats. Moving softly, for fear of being heard below, they walked to the big loft door. When Craig opened it, a freezing wind blew a dense flurry of snow into the attic.

'Come on,' Craig said.

Sophie stood beside him and looked down. 'You go first.'

Craig swept the snow off the ledge with his hand, then walked along it to the lean-to roof of the boot lobby. He swept a section of the roof clear, then stood upright and reached out to her. He held her hand as she pushed the loft door closed and then inched along the edge. 'You're doing fine,' he said softly. At last she stepped down to the lean-to roof. 'Well done,' Craig said.

Then Sophie's feet skidded from under her. Craig still had hold of her hand, but he could not keep her upright, and she landed awkwardly and tipped over backwards, sliding down the icy slates on her bottom.

Craig grabbed a handful of her anorak and tugged, but his feet were on the same slippery surface and she drew him down the roof after her. He let go of her coat, waving his arms to stay upright.

Sophie screamed and fell off the roof. She dropped ten feet and landed in soft new snow behind the dustbin.

Craig leaned over the edge. Little light fell in that dark corner and he could hardly see her. 'Are you all right?' he said. There was no reply. 'Sophie!'

'I'm OK,' she said miserably.

The back door opened. Quickly, Craig lowered himself to a sitting position. A man stepped out. Craig could just see a head of short dark hair. He glanced over the side. The extra light spilling from the open door made Sophie just visible. Her pink anorak disappeared into the snow, but her dark jeans showed. She lay still. He could not see her face.

A voice from inside called, 'Elton! Who's out there?'

Elton waved a torch from side to side, but the beam showed nothing but snowflakes. He turned to the right, away from Sophie, and walked a few steps into the storm, shining his torch in front of him.

Craig pressed himself to the roof, hoping Elton would not glance up.

The voice came from inside again. 'Elton?'

'I can't see nothing,' Elton shouted back irritably. He stopped at the dustbin. If he peeked round the angle of the lobby and shone his torch into the corner, he would see Sophie.

After a long moment, Elton turned away. 'Nothing out here but fucking snow,' he called out. He stepped back inside the house and slammed the door.

Craig groaned with relief. He found he was shaking. He tried to make himself calm. Thinking about Sophie helped. He jumped off the roof and landed beside her. Bending down, he said, 'Did you hurt yourself?'

She sat up. 'No, but I'm so scared. Are you sure he's gone?'

'I saw him go in and close the door. They must have heard your scream, or maybe the bump as you slipped on the roof—but in this storm they probably aren't sure it was anything.'

She struggled to her feet. 'Oh God, I hope so.'

MIRANDA LAY STILL for a long time, terrified that Daisy would return. In the end it was the thought of Tom that made her move. Somehow she had to protect her eleven-year-old son. She had to find a phone and get help.

That meant she had to go to the guest cottage and get the phone she had left in her handbag on the floor by the door. Shaking, she slid out from under the bed. The bedroom door was open. She peeped out, then stepped onto the landing. She could hear voices from the kitchen and looked down.

There was a hat stand at the foot of the stairs. Most of the family's coats and boots were kept in a closet in the boot lobby, but Daddy always left his in the hall. She could see his old blue anorak hanging from the stand and below it his rubber boots. They should keep her from freezing to death.

She started to tiptoe down the stairs. The voices from the kitchen became louder. There was an argument going on. She heard Nigel say, 'Well, bloody well look again, then!' She turned and ran back, going up the stairs two at a time. As she reached the landing, she heard heavy boots in the hall—Daisy.

It was no good hiding under the bed again. If Daisy was being sent back for a second search, she was bound to look harder this time. Miranda stepped into her father's bedroom. There was one place she could hide: the attic.

The door of the suit cupboard stood open. As she heard Daisy's steps on the landing, she fell to her knees, crawled inside and opened the low door that led to the attic. Then she turned and closed the cupboard door behind her. She backed into the attic and closed the low door.

She realised her error immediately. Daisy had searched the house a quarter of an hour or so ago. She must have seen the cupboard door standing open.

Miranda heard footsteps in the dressing room. She held her breath as Daisy walked to the bathroom and back. She heard the sound of cupboard doors being flung open. She bit her thumb to keep from screaming with fear. There was a brushing sound as Daisy rummaged among suits and shirts.

There was a long moment of quiet. Then Daisy's footsteps receded through the bedroom. Miranda felt so relieved that she wanted to cry. She stopped herself: she had to be brave. What was happening in the kitchen? She remembered the hole in the floor. She crawled slowly across to take a look.

HUGO LOOKED so pathetic that Kit almost felt sorry for him. He was a short man, and podgy. Dressed in natty suits that flattered his figure, he was poised and self-assured. Now he looked foolish and mortified.

The family were crowded together at one end of the kitchen, by the pantry door: Kit himself, his sister Olga in her black silk wrap, their father with swollen lips where Daisy had punched him, and the naked Hugo. Stanley was sitting down, holding Nellie, stroking her to keep her calm. Nigel and Elton stood on the other side of the table and Daisy was searching the upstairs.

Hugo stepped forward. 'There are towels and things in the laundry,' he said. The laundry was off the kitchen, on the same side as the dining room. 'Let me get something to wrap round me.'

Daisy heard this as she returned from her search. She picked up a tea towel. 'Try this,' she said, and flicked it at his crotch. Hugo let out an involuntary yelp and skipped away, into the corner. Daisy laughed.

Hugo's humiliation was unpleasant to see and Kit felt slightly sick.

'Stop playing around,' Nigel said angrily. 'I want to know where the other sister is—Miranda. She must have slipped out. Where did she go?'

Daisy said, 'I've looked all over the house twice. She's not in the building.'

Kit knew where she was. A minute ago he had seen Nellie cock her head and lift one black ear. Someone had entered the attic and it had to be Miranda. She was no great threat, up there with no phone, wearing only a nightdress. Still, Kit wondered if there was a way he could warn Nigel about her.

Elton said, 'Maybe she went outside. The noise we heard was probably her.'

Nigel replied, 'So how come you didn't see her when you went to look?'

'Because it's bloody dark!' Elton was irritated by Nigel's hectoring tone.

Kit guessed the noise outside had been some of the kids, fooling around. What if they had looked through the window and seen the guns? Nigel needed to capture the rest of the family before anyone made a phone call. But there was nothing Kit could do without blowing his cover.

'She was only wearing a nightdress,' Nigel said. 'She can't have gone far.'

Elton said, 'Well, I'll go and check the outbuildings, shall I?'

Nigel frowned, thinking. 'Yes,' he said. 'Round up the rest of the family and bring them here. Make sure you get all their phones. And check the garage—there could be phones in the cars.'

Daisy said, 'I'll check the garage if Elton goes to the other buildings.' She pocketed her gun and zipped up her leather jacket.

Nigel said, 'Before you go, let's shut this lot up somewhere.'

That was when Hugo jumped Nigel.

Everyone was taken by surprise. Kit had written Hugo off, as had the gang. But he leapt forward with furious energy, punching Nigel in the face again and again with both fists. He had chosen his moment well, for Daisy had put her weapon away, and Elton had never drawn his, so Nigel was the only one with a gun in his hand, and he was too busy dodging blows to use it.

Nigel staggered back, bumping against the kitchen counter, but he did not drop the gun. Elton grabbed Hugo and tried to pull him off Nigel. Being naked, Hugo was hard to grasp and, for a moment, Elton could not get a grip.

Stanley released Nellie, who was barking furiously, and the dog flung herself on Elton, biting his legs.

As Daisy reached for her gun, Olga picked up a plate and threw it across the room at her. Daisy dodged, and the plate hit her glancingly on the shoulder.

Kit stepped forward to grab Hugo, then stopped himself.

He would intervene on Nigel's side, against his own family, if he had to, but he wanted to maintain the fiction that he had never seen Nigel before tonight. So he stood helplessly looking on as contrary impulses clashed within him.

Daisy kicked Nellie in the ribs with a heavy boot, and the dog whimpered and fled to the corner of the room.

Elton put both arms round Hugo in a powerful bear hug. Hugo struggled gamely, but he could not shake Elton off. Elton lifted Hugo's feet off the ground and stepped back, pulling him away from Nigel.

Nigel was bleeding from his nose and mouth, and there were angry red marks round his eyes. He glared malevolently at Hugo and raised his right hand, which still grasped the gun.

Olga took a step forward, shouting, 'No!'

Instantly, Nigel swung his arm and pointed the gun at her.

Stanley grabbed her and held her back, saying, 'Please don't shoot.'

Nigel kept the gun pointed at Olga. 'Daisy, have you still got that sap?'

Looking pleased, Daisy took out her cosh.

Nigel nodded towards Hugo. 'Hurt this bastard.'

Hugo began to struggle, but Elton tightened his hold. Daisy drew back her right arm and smashed the cosh into Hugo's face. It hit his cheekbone with a sickening crunch. He screamed. With a spiteful grin, Daisy kicked him in the groin, then hit him with the cosh on the top of his head. He fell unconscious, but that made no difference to Daisy. She hit him full on the nose.

Olga let out a wail of grief and rage, broke free of her father's grasp, and threw herself at Daisy. Daisy swung the cosh at her, but Olga was too close, and the blow whistled behind her head.

Elton dropped Hugo, who slumped on the tiled floor. As he made a grab for Olga, she got her hands on Daisy's face and scratched.

Nigel had his gun pointed at Olga but he hesitated to shoot, no doubt fearing that he would hit Elton or Daisy.

Stanley turned to the stovetop and picked up the heavy frying pan in which Kit had scrambled the eggs. He raised it high then brought it down on Nigel, aiming at the man's head. Nigel saw it coming, and dodged. The pan hit his right shoulder. He cried out in pain, and the gun flew from his hand.

Stanley tried to catch the gun, but missed. It landed on the kitchen table an inch from the perfume bottle. It bounced onto the seat of a pine chair, rolled over, and dropped to the floor at Kit's feet. Kit bent down and picked it up.

Nigel and Stanley looked at him. Sensing the dramatic change, Olga, Daisy and Elton stopped fighting and turned to look at Kit holding the gun.

Kit hesitated, torn in half by the agony of the decision.

They all stared at him for a long moment of stillness. Then at last he turned the gun round, holding it by the barrel, and gave it back to Nigel.

6.30 A.M.

CRAIG AND SOPHIE had circled round the guest cottage and approached the barn from behind. They were now following the front wall of the barn, in full view from the kitchen. In the dark and the snow he could not see the building itself, just the lighted windows, and vague figures moving in the kitchen.

He pulled the big door open. They stepped inside and he closed it gratefully. Warm air washed over him. He was shivering and Sophie's teeth were chattering like castanets. She threw off her snow-covered anorak and sat on one of the big hospital-style radiators.

The place was dimly lit by a nightlight next to the camp bed where Tom lay. The boy was sleeping peacefully. There was no point in waking him, Craig decided. There was nothing the boy could do and he would only be terrified.

Craig went quickly up the ladder that led to the hayloft. On one of the beds, he could make out the heap of blankets that covered his sister Caroline. She seemed fast asleep. Like Tom, she was better off that way.

On the floor next to the second bed he could see the shape of an open suitcase. Craig crossed the room, moving cautiously in the near dark. As he bent down to search Sophie's case, he heard the soft rustle and squeak of Caroline's rats moving in their cage.

Working by touch, he rummaged in the suitcase until his hand closed over the oblong shape of a mobile phone. He flipped its lid, but no lights came on. He could not see well enough to find the ON–OFF switch.

He hurried back down the ladder with the phone in his hand. There was a standard lamp by the bookshelf. He turned it on and held Sophie's phone under the light. He found the power button and pressed it, but nothing happened. 'I can't get the bloody thing to come on!' he whispered.

Sophie took the phone. She pressed the same button, frowned, then jabbed at it repeatedly. At last she said, 'The battery has run down.'

'Where's the charger?'

'I don't know. I . . . ' Sophie's voice went small. 'I think I left it at home.'

'Shit!' Craig controlled his temper with an effort. He was silent for a moment. The memory of kissing her came back to him and he could not be angry. He put his arms round her. 'All right,' he said. 'Never mind.'

She rested her head on his chest. 'I'm sorry.'

'Let's think of something else.'

'There must be more phones, or a charger we can use.'

'Caroline and I don't carry mobiles—my mother won't let us have them.'

'Tom hasn't got one. Wasn't there one in your grandfather's car?'

Craig snapped his fingers. 'The Ferrari—right! And I left the keys in. All we have to do is get to the garage and we can phone the police.'

'You mean we have to go outside again?'

'You can stay here. You wouldn't be alone—Tom and Caroline are here.'

'No. I want to come with you.'

Craig tried not to show how pleased he was. 'You'd better get your coat on again, then.' He picked her anorak up from the floor and helped her into it. She looked up at him, and he tried an encouraging smile. 'Ready?'

A trace of her old spirit came back. 'Yeah. Like, what can happen? We could be murdered, that's all. Let's go.'

They went outside. It was still pitch-dark, and the snow fell in bursts of stinging pellets. Once again, Craig looked nervously across the yard to the house, but he could see no more than before. He took Sophie's hand and led her to the end of the barn, then crossed the yard to the garage.

The side door was unlocked, as always. It was as cold inside as out. There were no windows, so Craig risked switching on the lights.

Grandpa's Ferrari was where Craig had left it, parked close to the wall to hide the dent. He went to the Ferrari and pulled the door handle. It would not open. 'The car's locked,' he said. He looked inside. 'And the keys have gone.'

'Oh, no! How did that happen?'

'Luke must have locked it and taken the keys back to the house.'

'Where are they kept?'

'In the key box, on the wall of the boot lobby,' he said grimly. 'About two yards from those people with guns.'

THE SNOWPLOUGH moved slowly along the two-lane road in the dark. Carl Osborne's Jaguar followed it. Toni was at the wheel of the Jag, peering ahead as the wipers struggled to clear away the thickly falling snow.

Mother was asleep in the back with the puppy on her lap. Beside Toni, Carl was quiet, dozing or sulking. He had told Toni that he hated other people driving his car, but she had insisted and she had the keys.

They had found the getaway vehicle at the Dew Drop Inn. It had contained wigs, false moustaches and plain-lensed spectacles, but no clues as to where the gang might be headed. The police car had stayed there while the officers questioned the staff. The snowplough continued north, on Frank's instructions. For once, Toni agreed with him. It made sense for the gang to switch cars at a location en route, rather than delay their getaway with a diversion.

The snowplough did not stop when it passed stationary vehicles. The two police officers in the cab with the driver were under strict instructions to observe only. Some of the cars were abandoned, others had one or two people inside, but so far none contained three men and a woman. Most of the occupied cars started up and fell in behind the snowplough, following the track it cleared. There was now a small convoy behind the Jaguar and, as it moved north, Toni worried that her guess was wrong and the thieves had driven south.

She spotted a sign saying BEACH, and realised they must be near Steepfall. Now she had to go to the house and brief Stanley. She was dreading it.

Using Osborne's carphone, Toni dialled Frank's mobile. His voice came out of the Jaguar's speakers. 'Detective Superintendent Hackett.'

'Toni here. The snowplough is approaching the turnoff for Stanley Oxenford's house. I'd like to brief him on what's happened. I can't get him on the phone, but the house is only a mile down a side road—'

'Forget it. I've got an armed-response team here now, bristling with fire-power and itching to go. I'm not going to delay finding the gang.'

'It will take the snowplough five or six minutes to clear the lane—and you'll get me out of your hair. And my mother.'

'Tempting though that is, I'm not holding up the search for five minutes.'

'Stanley may be able to assist the investigation. After all, he is the victim.'

'The answer's no,' Frank said.

Toni played her ace. 'Remember Farmer Johnny.'

'Go to hell.'

'I'm using a hands-free phone, and Carl is beside me, listening to us both.'

'Pick up the phone.'

Toni detached the handset from its cradle and put it to her ear, so that Carl could not hear Frank. 'Call the snowplough driver, Frank, please.'

'You bitch. You know Farmer Johnny was guilty.'

'Everyone knows that. But only you and I know what you did to get a conviction. And Carl is listening to everything I say.'

'I suppose there's no point in talking to you about loyalty.'

'Not since the moment you told Carl about Fluffy the hamster.'

That shot went home. Frank began to sound defensive. 'Carl wouldn't do the Farmer Johnny story. He's a mate.'

'Your trust is deeply touching—him being a journalist and all.'

There was a long silence.

Toni said, 'Make up your mind, Frank—the turning is just ahead. Either the snowplough diverts, or I spend the next hour briefing Carl on Farmer Johnny.'

There was a click and a hum as Frank hung up.

Carl said, 'What was that all about?'

'If we drive past the next left turn, I'll tell you.'

A few moments later, the snowplough turned left onto the road to Steepfall.

HUGO LAY BLEEDING on the tiled floor, unconscious but breathing. Olga was weeping, close to hysterics. Stanley Oxenford was grey with shock. He stared at Kit, his face showing despair and bewilderment and suppressed rage. His expression said: *How could you do this to us?*

Kit could hardly contain his own fury. Everything was going wrong. His family now knew he was in league with the thieves, and there was no way they would lie about it, which meant the police would eventually know the whole story. He was doomed to a life on the run from the law.

He was also afraid. The virus sample in its perfume bottle lay on the kitchen table, protected only by two transparent plastic bags.

Nigel ordered Stanley and Olga to lie face down beside Hugo, threatening them with his gun. Elton searched out improvised ropes—appliance leads, a length of clothes line and a ball of stout cord. Daisy tied up Olga, the unconscious Hugo, and Stanley, binding their feet together and their hands behind their backs. She pulled the cords tight, so that they cut into the flesh.

Kit said to Nigel: 'I need my phone. in case there's a call to the Kremlin that I need to intercept.'

Nigel hesitated.

Kit said: 'For Christ's sake, I gave you your gun!'

Nigel shrugged and handed over the phone.

'How can you do this, Kit?' Olga said, as Daisy knelt on their father's back. 'How can you watch your family being treated this way?'

'It's not my fault!' he rejoined angrily. 'If you'd behaved decently to me, none of this would have happened.'

'Not your fault?' his father said in bewilderment.

'I owed money to gangsters. I was forced into this!'

'No one is forced into something like this.' He spoke in a voice of authoritative contempt that was familiar to Kit from childhood. 'What is it all about, anyway?'

'Shut your gob,' Daisy said.

He ignored her. 'What in God's name are you up to with these people, Kit? And what's in the perfume bottle? Why is it double-bagged?'

'I said shut up!' Daisy kicked Stanley in the face.

He grunted with pain, and blood came out of his mouth.

That will teach you, Kit thought with savage satisfaction.

Nigel said, 'Turn on the TV, Kit. Let's see when this snow is going to stop.'

They watched advertisements: January sales, summer holidays, cheap loans. Elton shut Nellie in the dining room. Hugo stirred and appeared to be coming round, and Olga spoke to him in a low voice.

A newscaster appeared on screen wearing a Santa hat. 'A freak blizzard hit Scotland last night, bringing a surprise white Christmas to most of the country this morning,' he said. 'The storm is expected to ease around daybreak, and the thaw should set in by midmorning.'

Kit was cheered. They could still make it to the rendezvous.

Nigel had the same thought. 'How far away is that four-wheel-drive, Kit?'

'About a mile.'

'We'll leave here at first light.' He looked worried. 'But then we have to walk a mile in the snow, and drive another ten. We're going to be cutting it fine.' He took a phone out of his pocket. He began to dial, then stopped. 'Dead battery,' he said. 'Elton, give me your phone.' He took Elton's phone and dialled. 'Yeah, it's me. What about this weather, then?'

Kit guessed he was speaking to the customer's pilot.

'Yeah, should ease up in an hour or so . . . I can get there, but can you?' Nigel was pretending to be more confident than he really felt. 'Good. So I'll see you at the appointed time.' He pocketed the phone.

The newscaster said, 'At the height of the blizzard, thieves raided the laboratories of Oxenford Medical, near Inverburn.'

The kitchen went silent. That's it, Kit thought; the truth is out.

'They got away with samples of a dangerous virus.'

Stanley spoke through smashed lips. 'So that's what's in the perfume bottle . . . Are you people mad?'

'Carl Osborne reports from the scene.'

The screen showed a photo of Osborne with a phone to his ear, and his voice was heard over a phone line. 'The deadly virus that killed laboratory technician Michael Ross only yesterday is now in the hands of gangsters. In a meticulously planned Christmas caper, three men and a woman defeated the laboratory's state-of-the-art security and penetrated to Biosafety Level 4, where stocks of incurable viruses are kept in a locked refrigerator.'

Stanley said, 'Kit, you didn't help them do this, did you?'

Olga spoke up. 'Of course he did,' she said disgustedly.

'The armed gang overcame security guards, injuring two, one seriously. But many more will die if the Madoba-2 virus is released into the population.'

Stanley rolled over with an effort and sat up. 'You're going to kill your-selves,' he said, raising his voice over the commentary. 'If you really have Madoba-2 in that bottle on the table, there's no antidote. If you drop it and the bottle smashes and the fluid leaks out, you're dead. Even if you sell it to someone else and they release it after you've left, it spreads so fast that you could easily catch it and die. Surely no amount of money is worth that risk?'

Nigel said, 'I won't be in Britain when it's released.'

Kit was shocked. Nigel had not previously mentioned this. Had Elton also made plans to go abroad? What about Daisy and Harry Mac?

Stanley turned to Kit. 'You can't possibly think this makes sense.'

He was right, Kit thought. The whole thing bordered on insane. But then, the world was crazy. 'I'm going to be dead anyway if I don't pay my debts.'

'Come on, they're not going to kill you for a debt.'

Daisy said, 'Oh, yes, we are.'

'How much do you owe?'

'A quarter of a million pounds.'

'Good God!'

'I told you I was desperate three months ago, but you wouldn't listen.'

'How did you manage to run up a debt—? No, never mind, forget I asked.'

'Gambling on credit. My system is good. I just had a long run of bad luck.'

Olga spoke up. 'Luck? Kit, wake up—you've been had! These people lent you the money then made sure you lost, because they needed you to help them rob the laboratory!'

Kit did not believe that. He said scornfully, 'How would you know that?'

'I'm a lawyer, I meet these people. I know more about them than I care to.'

Stanley spoke again. 'Look, Kit, surely we can find a way out of this.'

'Too late, now. I made my decision and I've got to see this through.'

'But think about all the innocent people you are going to kill.'

'I see you're willing for me to be killed. You'd protect a crowd of strangers, but you wouldn't rescue me.'

Stanley groaned. 'God knows I love you, and I don't want you to die, but are you sure you want to save your own life at that price?'

As Kit opened his mouth to reply, his phone rang.

No one moved. Kit took the phone out of his pocket. It was Hamish. 'Toni's following the snowplough and she's persuaded them to divert to your place. She'll be there any minute. And there are two police officers in the lorry.'

Kit ended the call and looked at Nigel. 'The police are coming here, now.'

CRAIG OPENED the side door of the garage, then glanced back to where Sophie sat. He had turned out the lights in the garage, but he knew she was in the front passenger seat of Luke's Ford, her pink anorak pulled close around her against the cold. He waved in her direction, then stepped outside.

Lifting his feet high as he stepped in the deep snow, he went along the blind wall of the garage and on towards the front of the house. He was going to get the Ferrari keys from the key box in the boot lobby.

As he hesitated at the corner of the house, his hands were shaking and his legs felt strangely weak. He looked along the front of the house. He was going to have to pass the living-room and dining-room windows, where the curtains were not drawn. He forced himself to move forward.

He passed the snow-covered cars, Miranda's Toyota Previa and Hugo's Mercedes-Benz estate, and rounded the corner of the house. There was a light in the boot-lobby window. Cautiously, he peeped round the edge of the window frame. He could see the cupboard where anoraks and boots were kept, a yard brush leaning in a corner—and the steel key box, screwed to the wall.

The door from the lobby to the kitchen was closed. That was lucky.

He listened, but he could not hear anything from inside the house. Forcing himself to move, he grasped the handle of the back door, turned it gently and pushed. The door swung open and he stepped inside. The lobby was a small room, six feet long, narrowed by the massive old chimney and the deep cupboard beside it. The key box hung on the chimney wall. Craig opened it. There were twenty numbered hooks, some with single keys and some with bunches, but he instantly recognised the Ferrari keys. He grasped them and lifted, but the fob snagged on the hook. He jiggled it, fighting down panic. Then someone rattled the handle of the kitchen door.

Craig's heart leapt in his chest. The person had turned the handle, but was pushing instead of pulling. In the moment of delay, Craig stepped into the coat cupboard and closed the door behind him. He held his breath and listened.

NIGEL RATTLED the handle until he realised that the door opened inwards, not out. He pulled it wide and looked into the boot lobby. 'No good,' he said. 'Door and two windows.' He crossed the kitchen and flung open the door to the pantry. 'This will do. Only one window. Elton, put them in here.'

'It's cold in there,' Olga protested.

'Oh, stop it, you'll make me cry,' Nigel said sarcastically.

'My husband needs a doctor.'

'He's lucky he doesn't need an undertaker.' Nigel turned back to Elton. 'Stuff something in their mouths so they can't make a noise.'

Elton found a drawer full of clean tea towels. He gagged Stanley, Olga and Hugo, who was now conscious, though dazed. Then he got the bound prisoners to their feet and pushed them into the pantry.

'Listen to me,' Nigel said to Kit. He was superficially calm, but beneath the surface, Kit saw, he was wound as tight as a guitar string. 'When the police get here, go to the door. Speak to them nicely, look relaxed. Say that nothing's wrong here and everyone in the house is still asleep except you.'

Kit felt as if he were facing a firing squad. 'What if they want to come in?'

'If they insist, bring them into the kitchen. We'll be in that little back room.' He pointed to the boot lobby. 'Just get rid of them as fast as you can.'

'Toni Gallo is coming along with the police,' Kit said. 'She's head of security at the lab. She'll want to see my father.'

'Say she can't.'

'She may not take no for an answer—'

Nigel raised his voice. 'For crying out loud, what is she going to do? Knock you down and walk in over your unconscious body? Just tell her to fuck off.'

'All right,' Kit said. 'But we need to keep my sister Miranda quiet. She's hiding in the attic.'

'Attic? Where?'

'Directly above this room. Look inside the first cupboard in the dressing room. Behind the suits is a low door leading into the roof space.'

Nigel looked at Daisy. 'Take care of it.'

MIRANDA SAW her brother speaking to Nigel and heard his words as he betrayed her. She crossed the attic in a moment and crawled through the door into Daddy's suit cupboard. Her heart was racing but she was not in a panic, not yet. She jumped out of the cupboard into the dressing room.

She had heard Kit say the police were coming and, for a joyful moment, she had thought they were saved. All she had to do was sit tight until men in blue uniforms walked in through the front door and arrested the thieves. Then she had listened with horror as Nigel rapidly devised a way of getting rid of the police. She had decided she would open a bedroom window and start screaming if they started to leave without arresting anyone.

She was terrified of meeting Daisy again, but she held on to her reason, just. She could hide in Kit's bedroom while Daisy searched the attic. That might give Miranda just long enough to open a window and yell for help.

She ran through the bedroom. As she put her hand on the doorknob, she heard heavy boots on the stairs. She was too late.

The door flew open. Miranda hid behind it. Daisy stormed through the bedroom and into the dressing room without looking back.

Miranda slipped out of the door. She crossed the landing and stepped into Kit's room. She ran to the window and pulled back the curtains, hoping to see police cars with flashing lights. There was no one outside.

She almost despaired. Daisy would take only a few seconds to make sure no one was in the attic. Miranda needed more time. How far away could the police be? Was there any way she could shut Daisy in the attic?

She did not give herself a second to worry about risks. She ran back to her father's room. She could see the door of the suit cupboard standing open. Daisy must be in the attic. Without forethought, Miranda closed the door.

There was no lock, but it was made of solid wood. If she could jam it shut, Daisy would have trouble busting it open, especially as she would have little room to manoeuvre inside the cupboard. There was a narrow gap at the bottom of the door. What could she wedge into it to make the door stick? She pulled open her father's bedside drawers and found a volume of Proust in one of them. She started ripping pages out.

KIT HEARD the dog bark in the next room. Someone was coming. He pushed through the swing door that led to the dining room. Nellie was standing with her forepaws on the windowsill. Kit went to the window.

The snow had eased to a light scatter of flakes. He looked towards the wood and saw, emerging from the trees, a big truck with a flashing orange light on top and a snowplough blade in front. 'They're here!' he called out.

Nigel came in. The dog growled, and Kit said, 'Shut up.' Nellie retreated to a corner. Nigel stood against the wall beside the window and peered out.

The snowplough cleared a path ten feet wide. It passed the front door and swept away the snow in front of Hugo's Mercedes and Miranda's Previa. Then it reversed to the garage block, turned off the drive and cleared a swath of the concrete apron in front of the garage doors. As it did so, a light-coloured Jaguar S-type came past it and pulled up at the front door.

A woman in a leather flying jacket got out of the car. In the reflected light from the headlamps, Kit recognised Toni Gallo.

'Get rid of her,' said Nigel. He retreated into the boot lobby with Elton.

Kit went to the front door and opened it.

Toni was helping someone out of the back of the car. Kit frowned. It was an old lady in a green woollen coat and a felt hat.

'Hello, Kit,' Toni said. She walked the old woman towards the house.

'What do you want?' Kit asked.

'I've come to see your father. There's an emergency at the laboratory.'

'Daddy's asleep.'

'He'll want to wake up for this, trust me.'

'Who's the old woman?'

'This lady is my mother, Mrs Kathleen Gallo.'

'And I'm not an old woman,' said the old woman. 'I'm seventy-one, and as fit as a butcher's dog, so mind your manners.'

'All right, Mother, he didn't mean to be rude.'

Kit ignored that. 'What's she doing here?'

'I'll explain to your father.'

The snowplough had turned round in front of the garage, and now it returned along the track it had cleared, heading back through the woods towards the main road. The Jaguar followed.

Kit felt panicked. What should he do? 'You can't come in,' he said to Toni.

'This is not your house, it's your father's,' she replied, 'and he'll want to see me.' She continued walking slowly towards him with her mother on her arm.

He was stymied, he realised. If he persisted in trying to obey Nigel's orders, he might bring the police back. Toni on her own was more manageable. 'You'd better come in,' he said.

'Thanks.' Toni and her mother stepped into the hall. 'Do you need the bathroom, Mother?' Toni asked. 'It's just here.'

Kit watched the lights of the snowplough and the Jaguar disappear into the woods. He relaxed slightly. He was saddled with Toni, but he had got rid of the police. He closed the front door.

There was a loud bang from upstairs, like a hammer hitting a wall.

'What the heck was that?' said Toni.

MIRANDA HAD TAKEN a thick sheaf of pages from the book and folded them into a wedge, which she had shoved into the gap under the cupboard door. Then she dragged one of the heavy mahogany bedside chests across the carpet, tilted it at a forty-five-degree angle and jammed it against the door. Almost immediately, she heard Daisy pushing at the other side of the door. When pushing failed, she banged. Miranda guessed that Daisy was lying with her feet in the cupboard, kicking the door.

The door shuddered but did not fly open. Miranda had won a few precious seconds. She flew to the window. To her dismay, she saw two vehicles—a lorry and a car—driving *away* from the house. 'Oh, no!' she said aloud. The vehicles were already too far for the people inside them to hear her scream.

She ran out of the bedroom and stopped at the top of the stairs. Down in the hall, an old woman she had never seen before was going into the cloakroom. What was happening? Next she recognised Toni Gallo, closing the cloakroom door, then taking off a flying jacket and hanging it on the hat stand.

Kit came into view. There was another bang from the dressing room and he said to Toni, 'The children must be awake.'

He was hoping to make Toni think that all was well, Miranda realised. Then he would either persuade her to leave, or overpower her and tie her up with the others. Meanwhile, the police were driving away.

Kit said to Toni, 'You'd better come into the kitchen.'

There was a crash from the bedroom: Daisy had broken out of the cupboard.

Miranda acted without thinking. 'Toni!' she screamed.

Toni looked up the stairs and saw her.

Kit said, 'Shit, no—'

Miranda yelled: 'The thieves, they're here, they've got guns—'

Daisy burst out of the bedroom and crashed into Miranda, sending her tumbling down the stairs.

For an instant, Toni froze.

Kit stood beside her, an expression of rage on his face, looking up the stairs. With a twisted mouth he said, 'Get her, Daisy!'

MIRANDA WAS falling down the stairs. Running after her was an ugly young woman with a shaved head and Gothic eye make-up, dressed in leather.

And Mother was in the cloakroom.

In a flash of comprehension, Toni realised that these must be the people who had robbed the Kremlin. The bald woman at the top of the stairs would be the blonde Toni had seen on the security video—her wig had been found in the getaway van. And Kit was in league with them—

As that thought struck her, Kit hooked his arm round her neck and pulled, trying to yank her off her feet. At the same time, he yelled, 'Nigel!'

She elbowed him forcefully in the ribs, and heard him grunt with pain. His grip on her neck eased and she turned and punched him in the midriff with her left fist. He lashed out at her, but she dodged the blow and drew back her right arm for a knockout punch. But before she could strike, Miranda reached the foot of the stairs and crashed into the back of Toni's legs. Toni fell backwards. A moment later, the woman in leather tripped over Miranda and Toni and collided with Kit, and all four of them ended up in a heap on the flagstone floor.

Toni realised she could not win this fight. She was up against Kit and the woman he had called Daisy, and soon she might have others to contend with. She had to get away, catch her breath and figure out what to do.

She wriggled out of the scrum and rolled over. Kit was flat on his back. Miranda was curled up in a ball, appearing bruised and winded but not seriously injured. As Toni looked, Daisy got to her knees and, apparently in a fury, punched Miranda on the arm with a fist encased in a tan suede glove.

Toni leapt to her feet. She jumped over Kit, reached the front door and threw it open. Kit grabbed her ankle. She twisted, and kicked out with the other foot. She connected with his elbow. He cried out and released his grip. Toni jumped through the doorway and slammed the door behind her.

She turned right and dashed along the track made by the snowplough. She heard a gunshot and then a crash as a pane of glass shattered in a window near her. Someone was shooting at her from inside the house.

She ran to the garage and turned onto the concrete apron in front of the doors. Now the garage block was between her and the person with the gun.

The snowplough would be too far away for her to catch it on foot. What was she going to do? Where could she hide? She had taken off her flying jacket just before Miranda yelled her warning—so she would not last long in the open. The garage itself would be almost as cold.

She ran to the other end of the building and looked round the corner. A few yards away, she could see the door to the barn. Did she dare to risk crossing the courtyard, in view of the house? She had no other choice.

As she was about to set off, the barn door opened and a small boy emerged. He was wearing a coat over his pyjamas and a pair of rubber boots. Toni recognised Tom, Miranda's son. He did not look round, but turned left and trudged through the snow towards the guest cottage. Tom disappeared inside.

Still Toni hesitated. Was there someone behind one of the house windows, covering the courtyard with an automatic pistol? She was about to find out.

She set off through the deep snow, each big step taking painfully long. She looked fearfully at the house, but could see no one at any of the windows. At last she reached the barn, stepped inside and swung the door closed behind her, shaking with relief that she was still alive.

A small lamp revealed a billiard table, an assortment of elderly couches, a television set and two empty camp beds. A ladder led to a loft. Toni made herself stop shaking and climbed up it. She peeped over the top and was startled by several pairs of small red eyes staring at her: Caroline's rats. She climbed the rest of the way. There were two more beds here. The somnolent lump in one was Caroline. The other had not been slept in.

It would not be long before the gang in the house came looking for Toni. She had to get help fast. She reached for her mobile phone. Then she realised she did not have it. It was in the pocket of the flying jacket, which she had hung up in the hall. What was she going to do now?

'WE'VE GOT to get after her,' Nigel said. 'She could be phoning the police.'

'Wait,' Kit said. He stepped across the hall to the hat stand. He was rubbing his left elbow where Toni had kicked him, but he stopped to search her jacket. Triumphantly, he produced a phone from one of her pockets. 'She can't!'

'Thank God for that.' Nigel looked around the hall. Daisy had Miranda face down on the floor with her arm bent behind her back. Elton stood in the kitchen doorway. Nigel said, 'Elton, get some more rope so Daisy can tie up this cow.' He turned back to Kit. 'Your sisters are a right bloody pair.'

'Never mind that,' Kit said. 'We can get away now, can't we? We can use any car and take the path cleared by the snowplough.'

'Your man said there were coppers in that snowplough.'

'The one place they won't look for us is right behind them.'

Nigel nodded. 'Clever. But the snowplough's not going all the way to . . . where we need to be. What do we do when it turns off our route?'

'Look out of the window,' Kit said. 'The snow has stopped. It will start to thaw soon, the forecast said. And we're in worse danger here, now that the road has been cleared. Toni Gallo might not be the only visitor to show up.'

Elton returned with a length of electric cable. 'Kit's right,' he said. 'We can easily get there by ten o'clock, barring accidents.' He handed the cable to Daisy, who tied Miranda's hands behind her back.

'OK,' Nigel said. 'But first we have to round everyone up and make sure they can't call for help for the next few hours.'

Daisy dragged Miranda through the kitchen and shoved her into the pantry.

Kit said, 'Miranda's phone must be in the cottage, otherwise she would have used it by now. Her boyfriend, Ned, is there.'

Nigel said, 'Elton, go to the cottage.'

Kit went on, 'There's a phone in the Ferrari. I suggest Daisy goes to the garage to make sure no one is trying to use it. Leave the barn till last. That's where the kids are. Caroline, Craig and Tom don't have phones. I'm not sure about Sophie, but she's only fourteen.'

'All right,' Nigel said. 'Let's get it done as fast as possible.'

The cloakroom door opened and Toni Gallo's mother came out.

Kit and Nigel stared at her. Kit had forgotten she was in there.

Then Nigel said, 'Stick her in the pantry with the others.'

'Oh, no,' the old woman said. 'I think I'd rather sit by the Christmas tree.' She crossed the hall and went into the living room.

Kit looked at Nigel, who shrugged.

CRAIG OPENED the door of the boot cupboard a crack. Peeping out, he saw that the lobby was empty. Then one of the gangsters, Elton, came in from the kitchen. Craig pulled the door an inch towards himself and held his breath.

It had been like this for a quarter of an hour. One of the gang was always in view. The cupboard smelt of damp anoraks and old boots. He worried about Sophie, sitting in Luke's Ford in the garage, getting cold.

A few minutes ago Nellie had barked, which had to mean someone at the door. Craig's heart had lifted in hope, and he wanted to burst out of the cupboard and run to the door yelling for help, but Nigel and Elton had stood inches away from him, talking in whispers that he could not quite make out.

There was a banging from upstairs, as if someone was trying to bash a door down. Then there was a different bang, more like a firework—or a gun going off. Craig was dismayed. If they had started shooting, where would it end?

At the gunshot Nigel and Elton went, but left the door open. Elton remained in sight at the far end of the kitchen, talking urgently to someone in the hall. Then he returned, but went out the back way, leaving the door wide open.

This was Craig's chance. He stepped out of the cupboard, flipped open the key box and snatched the Ferrari keys. This time they came off the hook without snagging. In two strides he was out of the door.

The snow had stopped and somewhere beyond the clouds dawn was breaking. To his left he could see Elton trudging through the snow to the guest cottage. Craig went the other way and turned the corner, so that the house hid him from Elton.

He was shocked to see Daisy only yards away.

She had obviously come out of the front door and was walking away from him. There was a cleared path and he realised that a snowplough had been here while he was hiding in the boot cupboard. Daisy was heading for the garage. He ducked behind his father's Mercedes. Peeping round the wing, he saw Daisy turn the corner of the house.

He went after her, moving as fast as he could along the front of the house. Daisy was heading for the side door of the garage. If she went in there, she would find Sophie sitting in Luke's Ford.

She reached into the pocket of her leather jacket and took out her gun.

Craig watched, helpless, as she opened the door.

7.45 A.M.

The pantry was cold. The Christmas turkey, too large to fit into the kitchen refrigerator, stood in a baking tray on a marble shelf, stuffed and seasoned by Olga, ready for roasting. Miranda wondered dismally if she would live to eat it.

She stood with her father, her sister and Hugo, the four of them trussed like the turkey and crammed into a space three feet square, surrounded by food.

Hugo was in the worst state, drifting in and out of consciousness. He was leaning against the wall and Olga was pressing herself to his naked body, trying to keep him warm. Stanley's face looked as if he had been hit by a truck, but he was standing erect and his expression was alert.

The others had tea towels stuffed into their mouths, but Daisy had not gagged Miranda. She realised that she could remove the gags.

'Daddy, lean down,' she said.

He bent his tall figure over her obediently, the end of the gag trailing from his mouth. She tilted her head, caught a corner of the tea towel between her teeth and tugged. She pulled it out and it fell to the floor.

'Thank you,' he said. 'By God, that was ghastly.'

Miranda did the same for Olga, who then removed Hugo's gag by the same method. 'Try to stay awake, Hugo,' Olga said urgently. 'Keep your eyes open.'

Stanley asked Miranda, 'What's going on out there?'

'Toni Gallo came here with a snowplough and some policemen,' she explained. 'Kit went to the door as if everything was all right, and the police left, but Toni insisted on staying.'

'That woman is incredible.'

'I was hiding in the attic. I managed to warn Toni.'

'Well done!'

'That frightful Daisy pushed me down the stairs, but Toni got away. I don't know where she is now.'

'She can phone the police.'

Miranda shook her head. 'Kit's got her phone. She left it in her coat pocket.'

'She'll think of something—she's remarkably resourceful. Anyway, she's our only hope. No one else is free, except the children, and Ned, of course.'

'I'm afraid Ned won't be much use,' Miranda said gloomily. She looked out of the pantry window. Dawn had broken and the snow had stopped, so she could see the cottage and the barn.

A moment later, she was horrified to see Ned emerge from the cottage with Elton close behind, holding a gun to the back of his head. With his left hand, Elton held Tom by the arm.

Miranda gasped with shock. She had thought Tom was in the barn. He must have woken up and gone looking for her. She fought back tears.

The three of them were heading for the house, but then there was a shout, and they stopped. A moment later Daisy came into view, dragging Sophie by the hair. Sophie was bent double, stumbling in the snow, crying with pain.

Daisy said something to Elton that Miranda could not hear. Then Tom screamed at Daisy, 'Leave her alone! You're hurting her!'

'Be quiet, Tommy,' Miranda murmured fearfully, although he could not hear her. 'It doesn't matter if she gets her hair pulled.'

Elton laughed. Daisy grinned and yanked more viciously at Sophie's hair.

Tom suddenly went berserk. He jerked his arm out of Elton's grasp and threw himself at Daisy.

Miranda shouted, 'No!'

Daisy was so surprised that when Tom crashed into her she fell backwards, letting go of Sophie's hair, and sat down in the snow. Tom dived on top of her, pummelling her with his small fists.

Miranda found herself shouting uselessly, 'Stop! Stop!'

Daisy pushed Tom away and got to her feet. Tom jumped up, but Daisy hit him with her gloved fist on the side of the head and he fell down again. She heaved him up off the ground and, in a fury, held him upright with her left hand while she punched him with her right, hitting his face and body.

Miranda screamed.

Suddenly Ned moved. Ignoring the gun that Elton was pointing at him, he stepped between Daisy and Tom. He said something that Miranda could not hear and put a restraining hand on Daisy's arm.

Miranda was astonished: weak Ned standing up to thugs!

Without letting go of Tom, Daisy punched Ned in the stomach. He doubled over in agony. But when Daisy drew back her arm to punch Tom again, Ned straightened up and stood in her way. She punched Ned in the mouth. He cried out, and his hands flew to his face, but he did not move.

Miranda was profoundly grateful that Ned had distracted Daisy from Tom—but how long could he stand this beating?

When Ned took his hands away from his face, blood poured out of his mouth. Daisy punched him a third time.

Miranda was awestruck. Ned was like a wall. He simply stood there and took the blows. And he was doing it, not for his own child, but for Tom. Miranda felt ashamed of thinking he was weak.

At that moment Ned's own child, Sophie, acted. She had been standing still, watching in a stunned way, since Daisy had let go of her hair. Now she turned round and moved away.

Elton made a grab for her, but she slipped through his grasp. He lost balance and Sophie broke into a run, crossing the deep snow with balletic leaps.

Hastily, Elton righted himself, but Sophie had disappeared.

Elton grabbed Tom and shouted at Daisy, 'Don't let that girl get away!' Daisy looked disposed to argue. Elton yelled, 'I've got these two. Go! Go!'

With a malevolent look at Ned and Tom, Daisy turned and went after Sophie.

CRAIG TURNED the key in the ignition of the Ferrari. Behind him, the huge rear-mounted V12 engine started, then died.

Craig closed his eyes. 'Not now,' he said aloud. 'Don't let me down now.'

He turned the key again. The engine fired, faltered, then roared like an angry bull. Craig pumped the throttle and the roar turned into a howl.

He looked at the phone's display. It said: SEARCHING . . . 'Come on,' he urged. 'I don't have much time—'

The side door of the garage flew open and Sophie stumbled in.

Craig was taken by surprise. He thought Sophie was in the hands of the dreadful Daisy. He had struggled to remain calm as he watched Daisy dragging Sophie out of the garage by the hair. He kept telling himself that the best thing he could do for Sophie was to stay free and phone the police.

Now she seemed to have escaped unaided. She was sobbing and panicky, and he guessed that Daisy must be on her tail.

The car was so close to the wall that the passenger door could not be opened. Craig threw open the driver's door and said, 'Get in quick—climb over me!'

She staggered over to the car and fell in.

Craig slammed the door. He did not know how to lock it and he was too rushed to find out. Daisy could not be more than a few seconds away. There was no time to phone—they had to get out of there. As Sophie collapsed into the passenger seat, he fumbled under the dashboard and found the remote-control device for the garage door. He pressed it, and in the rearview mirror saw the up-and-over door begin to move slowly.

Then Daisy came in, her face red with exertion, her eyes wide with rage. She hesitated in the doorway, peering into the gloom of the garage. Then her staring eyes locked onto Craig in the driving seat of the car.

He depressed the clutch and shoved the gearshift into reverse.

Daisy ran across the front of the car and came to the driver's side. Her tan glove closed on the door handle. The garage door was not yet fully open, but Craig could wait no longer. Just as Daisy opened the car door, he released the clutch and trod on the accelerator pedal.

The Ferrari leapt backwards as if fired from a catapult. Sophie gave a yell of fear as it flew out of the garage like a champagne cork. Craig stamped on the brake. The snowplough had cleared the snow from in front of the garage, but more had fallen since and the concrete apron was slippery. The car went into a backwards skid and stopped with a bump against a bank of snow.

Daisy came out of the garage into the grey dawn light.

The phone suddenly spoke in a female voice. 'You have one new message.'

Craig pushed the gearshift into what he hoped was first. He eased the clutch out and, to his relief, the tyres found purchase and the car moved forward. He turned the wheel, heading for the drive.

Daisy fumbled in the pocket of her jacket and brought out a gun.

'Get down!' Craig yelled at Sophie. 'She's going to shoot!'

As Daisy levelled the gun, he stamped on the accelerator and swung the steering wheel, desperate to get away. The car went into a skid, slipping across the icy concrete. Sophie was flung from side to side in her seat.

The car stopped, with great good luck, in the middle of the drive, facing away from the house and towards the lane. He had a clear road to freedom.

He pressed the accelerator pedal. Nothing happened. The engine had stalled.

Out of the corner of his eye, he saw Daisy raise the gun and take aim.

He turned the key and the car jerked forward: he had forgotten to take it out of gear. In the same instant, he heard the unmistakable firecracker bang of a gun. The side window of the car shattered. Sophie screamed.

Craig knocked the stick into neutral and turned the key again. The throaty roar filled his ears. He could see Daisy taking aim again as he pressed the clutch and found first gear. He ducked involuntarily as he pulled away, and it was lucky that he did, for this time his side window smashed.

The bullet also went through the windscreen, making a small round hole and causing the entire screen to craze over. Now he could see nothing ahead but blurred shapes. Nevertheless he kept the accelerator depressed, doing his best to stay on the driveway. Beside him, Sophie was curled up in a ball.

On the periphery of his vision, he saw Daisy running after the car. Another shot banged. The carphone said, 'Stanley, this is Toni. Bad news—a break-in at the lab. Please call my mobile as soon as you can.'

Craig guessed that the people with guns must be connected to the break-in, but he could not think about that now. He tried to steer by what he could see out of the smashed side window, but after a few seconds the car went off the cleared path and the shape of a tree appeared in the crazed glass of the windscreen. Craig slammed on the brakes, but he was too late.

As the car hit the tree, Craig was thrown forward. His head hit the broken windscreen, knocking out shards of glass, cutting his forehead. The steering wheel bruised his chest. Sophie was flung against the dashboard. She swore and tried to right herself, so he knew she was all right.

The engine had stalled again. Craig looked in the rearview mirror. Daisy was ten yards behind him, walking across the snow towards the car, holding the gun in her suede-gloved hand. He knew she was going to kill him and Sophie. He had only one chance left. He had to kill her.

He started the engine again. Daisy, five yards away and directly behind the car, raised her gun arm. Craig put the gearshift into reverse and closed his eyes.

He heard a bang just as he stamped on the throttle. The rear window shattered. The car leapt backwards, straight at Daisy. There was a heavy thump, as though someone had dropped a sack of potatoes on the boot.

Craig took his foot off the throttle and the car rolled to a stop. Where was Daisy? He pushed broken glass out of the windscreen and saw her. She had been thrown sideways by the impact and was lying on the ground with one leg at an odd angle. Her gun lay on the snow nearby.

Then she moved.

As she reached out and picked up the gun, Craig put the car into first gear.

Daisy looked into his eyes and pointed the gun at him.

Craig let out the clutch and stamped on the throttle. He heard the bang of the gun over the bellow of the engine, but the shot went wild. He kept his foot down. Daisy tried to drag herself out of the way, and Craig deliberately turned the wheel in her direction. An instant before the impact he saw her face, staring in terror, her mouth open to scream. Then the car hit her with a thud. She disappeared beneath its curved front. The low-slung chassis scraped over something lumpy. Craig saw that he was headed straight for the tree he had hit before. He braked, but too late. Once again, the car crashed into the tree.

The carphone, which had been telling him how to save messages, stopped in mid-sentence. He tried to start the engine, but nothing happened, not even the click of a broken starter motor.

And where was Daisy?

He got out of the car. In the driveway behind him was a pile of ripped black leather, white flesh and gleaming red blood. Daisy was not moving.

Sophie got out and stood beside him. 'Oh God, is that her?'

Craig felt sick. He could not speak, so he nodded.

Sophie whispered, 'Do you think she's dead?' Then he turned aside and vomited into the snow.

KIT WATCHED as Elton brought Ned and Tom into the kitchen at gunpoint. Ned was bleeding from several places on his face and Tom was bruised and crying, but they were walking steadily, Ned holding Tom's hand.

Kit reckoned up who was still at large. Sophie had run away, and Craig would not be far from her. Caroline was probably still asleep in the barn. Then there was Toni Gallo. Four people, three of them children—surely it could not take long for three tough criminals to capture them? But time was running out. Kit and the gang had less than two hours to get to the airfield.

Elton threw Miranda's phone onto the kitchen table. 'Found it in a handbag in the cottage,' he said. 'The guy doesn't seem to have one.' The phone landed beside the perfume spray. Kit longed for the moment when the bottle would be handed over and he would get his money.

Elton made Ned lie on the floor, then tied him up. Nigel tied Tom, who was still snivelling. When Elton opened the pantry door to put them inside, Kit saw to his surprise that the prisoners had managed to remove their gags.

Olga spoke first. 'Please, let Hugo out of here,' she said. 'He's so cold, I'm afraid he'll die. Just let him lie on the floor in the kitchen, where it's warm.'

Kit shook his head in amazement. Olga's loyalty to her unfaithful husband was incomprehensible.

Nigel said, 'He shouldn't have punched me in the face.'

Elton pushed Ned and Tom into the pantry with the others.

Olga said, 'Please, I'm begging you!'

Elton closed the door and Kit put Hugo out of his mind. 'We've got to find Toni Gallo,' he said. 'She's the dangerous one.'

Nigel said, 'Where do you think she is?'

'Well, she's not in the cottage because Elton's just searched it, and not in the garage because Daisy's just been there. So either she's out of doors, where she won't last long without a coat, or she's in the barn.'

'All right,' Elton said. 'I'll go to the barn.'

TONI WAS LOOKING out of the barn window. She had now identified three of the four people who had raided the Kremlin. One was Kit, of course. He would have told them how to defeat the security system. There was the woman Kit had called Daisy. A few minutes ago Daisy had addressed the young black man as Elton. Toni had not yet seen the fourth, but she knew that his name was Nigel, for Kit had shouted to him in the hall.

They had the virus, and were clearly tough professional criminals who would kill her if necessary. But Toni was tough, too, and she had a chance to redeem herself by catching them.

The best plan would be to get help, but she had no phone, and the house phones had been cut off, presumably by the gang. Toni had seen two cars parked in front of the house but she had no idea where the keys were.

That meant she had to capture the thieves on her own. The odds against her were fearsome. Three of them were armed with automatic pistols. Her only chance would be to pick them off one by one.

As she was racking her brains, she lost the initiative. Elton emerged from the house and came across the courtyard towards the barn.

He was younger than Toni, probably twenty-five. He was tall and looked fit. In his right hand he carried a pistol, pointed down at the ground. She had a few seconds to find some weapons. She looked at the things around her. She considered a billiard cue, but it was too light. Billiard balls were much more dangerous. She stuffed two into her jeans pockets.

She scrambled up the ladder to the hayloft. Caroline was fast asleep. On the floor between the two beds was an open suitcase. On top of the clothes was a plastic shopping bag. Next to the case was a cage of white rats.

The barn door opened and Toni dropped to the floor and lay flat. The main lights came on. Toni could not see the ground floor from her prone position. She listened hard, trying to hear Elton's footsteps over the thunder of her heart. Elton was overturning the camp beds. Then he opened the bathroom door. There was nowhere left to look but the hayloft. He would be coming up the ladder any second now. What could she do?

Toni heard the squeak of rats, and was struck by inspiration. Still lying flat, she took the plastic bag from the open suitcase and removed the gift-wrapped package from inside. Then she opened the rats' cage. Gently, she picked the rats up one by one and put them in the bag. There were five.

An ominous vibration in the floor told her that Elton had started to climb the ladder. It was now or never. She reached forward with both arms and emptied the bag of rats over the top of the ladder.

She heard Elton give a roar of shock and disgust as five live rats dropped on his head. His shout woke Caroline, who let out a squeal and sat upright. There was a crash as Elton lost his footing on the ladder and fell to the floor.

Toni sprang to her feet and looked down. Elton had fallen on his back. He was yelling in panic and frantically trying to brush rats off his clothing.

Toni could not see his gun.

She hesitated a fraction of a second, then jumped off the loft. She came down with both feet on Elton's chest. He gave an agonised grunt as the air was knocked out of him. Toni landed like a gymnast, rolling forward.

From above, she heard a scream: 'My babies!' Looking up, she saw Caroline at the top of the ladder. The rats scattered, apparently unhurt.

Toni struggled to her feet. Where was the gun? He must have dropped it.

Elton was hurt, but perhaps not immobilised. She fumbled in her jeans for a billiard ball, but it slipped through her fingers as she tried to pull it out of her pocket. She suffered a moment of terror, a feeling that her body would not obey her brain. Then she used both hands, one to push from outside her pocket and the other to grasp the ball as it emerged.

The delay had allowed Elton to recover from the shock of the rats. As Toni raised her right hand above her head, he rolled away from her. Instead of bringing the heavy ball down on his head, she was forced to throw it at him.

The throw was too weak. She hit the target, and there was an audible thud as the billiard ball connected with Elton's skull, causing him to roar in pain, but he did not slump unconscious. Instead he struggled to his feet.

Toni took out the second ball.

Elton looked at the floor all around him, searching for his gun.

Caroline had climbed halfway down the ladder and now she leapt to the floor. As Caroline stooped to grab one of the rats, which was hiding behind a leg of the billiard table, something caught Toni's eye. She looked again and saw the gun, dull grey against the dark wood of the floor.

Elton saw it at the same time and dropped to his knees. As he reached under the table, Toni raised her arm high and brought the ball down with all her might, squarely on the back of his head. He slumped unconscious.

Toni picked up the gun, turned the safety catch to the locked position, then stuffed the gun in the waist of her jeans. She unplugged the television and ripped the cable out of the back of the set, then used it to tie Elton's hands behind his back. Then she searched him, looking for a phone, but to her intense disappointment he did not have one.

IT TOOK CRAIG a long time to work up the courage to look again at Daisy's mangled body. Sophie came to him and put her arms round his waist, and he hugged her, keeping his back to Daisy. They had stood like that until at last his nausea passed and he felt able to turn and see what he had done.

Sophie said, 'What are we going to do now?'

Craig swallowed. It was not over yet. Daisy was only one of three thugs—and then there was Uncle Kit. 'We'd better take her gun,' he said.

She looked unhappy. 'Do you know how to use it?'

'How hard can it be?'

He took her hand and they walked towards the body, stopping six feet away.

Daisy was lying face down, her arms beneath her. Her leather trousers had been ripped to shreds. One leg was twisted unnaturally and the other was gashed and bloody. The leather jacket seemed to have protected her arms and body, but her shaved head was covered with blood.

'I can't see the gun,' Craig said. 'It must be underneath her.'

They stepped closer. Sophie bent down to look. Quick as a snake Daisy lifted her head, grabbed Sophie's wrist and brought her right hand out from under her with the gun in it. Sophie screamed.

Craig shouted, 'Christ!' and jumped back.

Daisy jammed the snout of the little grey pistol into the soft skin of Sophie's throat. 'Stand still, laddie!' she yelled.

Craig froze.

Daisy wore a cap of blood. One ear hung from her head by a narrow strip of skin. But her face was unmarked, and now showed an expression of pure hatred. 'If you want to save your little girlfriend's life,' she said, 'just do everything I tell you, instantly. Hesitate, and she dies.'

Craig felt she really meant it.

'Get over here,' she said, 'and kneel down.'

He had no choice. He stepped closer and knelt beside her.

She turned her hateful eyes on Sophie. 'Now, you little whore, I'm going to let go of your arm, but don't move or I'll shoot you.' She took her left hand off Sophie's arm, but kept the gun pushed into the flesh of her neck. Then she put her left arm round Craig's shoulders. 'Hold my wrist, lad,' she said.

Craig grasped Daisy's wrist as it dangled over his shoulder.

'You, lassie, get under my right arm.'

Sophie changed her position slowly, and Daisy put her right arm over the girl's shoulders, managing all the time to keep the gun pointed at her head.

'Now, you're going to lift me up and carry me to the house. But do it gently. I think I've got a broken leg. If you jog me it might hurt, and if I flinch I might accidentally pull the trigger. So, easy does it . . . and lift.'

Craig tightened his grip on Daisy's wrist and raised himself from the kneeling position. To ease the burden on Sophie, he put his right arm round Daisy's waist and took some of her weight. The three of them slowly stood upright.

Daisy was gasping with pain and as pale as the snow all around them, but when Craig looked sideways he saw that she was watching him intently.

TONI CIRCLED the guest cottage and approached the main house from the side. The back door stood open, but she did not go in. She needed to reconnoitre.

She had left Caroline in the barn searching tearfully for her pet rats. Elton was trussed up under the billiard table, blindfolded and gagged.

Toni crept along the back of the house and peeped in at the first window.

Six people were crammed into the pantry, bound hand and foot but standing: Olga, Hugo, who seemed to be naked, Miranda, her son Tom, Ned and Stanley. A wave of happiness washed over Toni when she saw Stanley, till she noticed his bruised and bloody face. He spotted her, and his eyes widened with surprise and pleasure. He opened his mouth to speak. Quickly, Toni raised a finger to her lips. Stanley closed his mouth and nodded understanding.

Toni moved to the next window and looked into the kitchen. Two men sat with their backs to the window. One was Kit. The other man wore a pink sweater. He must be the one Kit had called Nigel. They were looking at a small television set, watching the news.

Toni chewed her lip, thinking. She had a gun now but, even so, it could be difficult to control the two of them. But she had no choice.

As she hesitated, Kit stood up, and she quickly ducked back out of sight.

NIGEL SAID, 'That's it. They're clearing the roads. We have to go *now*.'

'I'm worried about Toni Gallo,' Kit said.

'Too bad. If we wait any longer, we'll miss the rendezvous.'

Kit looked at his watch. Nigel was right. 'Shit,' he said 'We'll take that Mercedes outside. Go and find the keys.'

Kit left the kitchen and ran upstairs. In Olga's bedroom, he spotted Hugo's blazer draped over the back of a chair. He found the Mercedes keys in the pocket, and ran down to the kitchen. Nigel was looking out of the window.

'Why is Elton taking so long?' Kit said. 'And what the hell's happened to Daisy?' He could hear a note of hysteria in his own voice.

'I don't know,' said Nigel. 'Try to stay calm. Go and start the engine.'

'Right.' As Kit turned away, his eye was caught by the perfume spray, in its double bag, lying on the kitchen table. On impulse, he picked it up and stuffed it into his jacket pocket. Then he went out.

TONI PEEPED round the corner of the house and saw Kit emerge from the back door. He went in the opposite direction, to the front of the building. She followed him and saw him unlock the Mercedes estate car.

This was her chance. She took Elton's pistol from the waist of her jeans and unlocked the safety catch. There was a full magazine in the grip—she had checked. She held the gun pointing skywards, and breathed slowly. She ran through the back door into a small lobby, then threw open a second door and ran into the kitchen. Nigel was at the window, looking out.

'Freeze!' she screamed.

He spun round.

She levelled the gun at him. 'Hands in the air!'

He hesitated. His pistol was in the pocket of his trousers—she could see the lumpy bulge it made, the right size and shape for an automatic.

'Don't even think about reaching for your gun,' she said.

Slowly, he raised his hands.

'On the floor! Face down! Now!'

He went down on his knees, hands still held high. Then he lay down, his arms spread. Toni stood over him. She had to get his gun.

She transferred her pistol to her left hand and thrust its nose into the back of his neck. 'The safety catch is off and I'm feeling jumpy,' she said. She went down on one knee and reached into his trouser pocket.

He moved very fast. Rolling over, he swung his right arm at her. For a split second she hesitated to pull the trigger, then it was too late. He knocked her off balance and she fell sideways—dropping her gun.

He kicked out at her wildly, his shoe connecting with her hip. She regained her balance and scrambled to her feet, coming upright before he did. As he got to his knees, she kicked him in the face. He fell back, his hand flying to his cheek, but he recovered fast and looked at her with an expression of fury.

She snatched up the gun and pointed it at him. 'Let's try again,' she said. 'This time, *you* take the gun out. Slowly. And, please—give me an excuse to blow your head off.'

He took the gun out of his pocket.

'Drop it on the floor.'

He smiled. 'Have you ever actually shot a man?'

'Drop it—now.'

'I don't think you have.'

He had guessed right. She had been trained to use firearms and she had

WHITEOUT | 143

carried a gun on operations, but she had never shot at anything other than a target. The idea of making a hole in another human being revolted her.

'You're not going to shoot me,' he said.

'You're a second away from finding out.'

Her mother walked in. She said, 'We haven't had any breakfast, dear.'

Nigel raised his gun.

Toni shot him in the right shoulder.

She was only six feet away, so it was not difficult to wound him in exactly the right place. She pulled the trigger twice, as she had been taught. The double bang was deafening in the kitchen. Two round holes appeared in the pink sweater, side by side where the arm met the shoulder. The gun fell from Nigel's hand. He cried out in pain and staggered back against the refrigerator.

Toni felt sick. She had not really believed she could do it.

Nigel screamed, 'You fucking bitch!'

Like magic, his words restored her nerve. 'Be glad I didn't shoot you in the belly,' she said. 'Now lie down.'

He slumped to the floor and rolled over on his face, clutching his wound.

Mother said, 'I'll put the kettle on.'

Toni picked up his dropped gun and locked the safety catch. She stuffed both guns into her jeans and opened the pantry door.

Stanley said, 'What happened? Was someone shot?'

'Nigel,' she said calmly. She took a pair of kitchen scissors from the knife block and cut the washing line that bound Stanley's hands and feet.

When he was free, he put his arms round her and squeezed her hard. 'Thank you,' he murmured in her ear.

She closed her eyes and hugged him hard for a precious second, then broke the clinch. Handing him the scissors, she said, 'You free the rest.' She drew one of the pistols from her waistband. 'Kit's not far away. He must have heard the shots. Does he have a gun?'

'I don't think so,' Stanley replied.

Toni was relieved. That would make it easier.

Olga said, 'Get us out of this cold room, please!'

Stanley turned to cut her bonds.

Kit's voice rang out: 'Nobody move!'

Toni spun round, levelling the gun. Kit stood in the doorway. He was holding a glass perfume spray in his hand as if it were a weapon. Toni recognised the bottle she had seen, on the security video, being filled with Madoba-2.

Kit said, 'This contains the virus. One squirt will kill you.'

Everyone stood still.

Kit stared at Toni. She was pointing the gun at him, and he was pointing the spray at her. He said, 'If you shoot me, I'll drop the bottle and the glass will break on these tiles.'

She said, 'If you spray us with that stuff, you'll kill yourself as well.'

'I don't care,' he said. 'I made the plan, I betrayed my family, and I became a party to a conspiracy to murder thousands of people. After all that, how can I fail? I'd rather die.' As he said it, he realised it was true. Even the money had diminished in importance now. All he really wanted was to win.

He looked at Nigel, sitting on the floor, holding his bleeding right shoulder with his left hand. That explained the two gunshots that had caused Kit to arm himself with the spray before coming back into the kitchen.

Nigel struggled to his feet. 'Ah, bollocks, it hurts,' he said.

Stanley said, 'How did we come to this, Kit?'

Kit met his father's gaze. He saw anger there, as he expected, but also grief. Stanley looked the way he had when Mamma Marta died. Too bad, Kit thought angrily; he brought this on himself.

'Put the guns on the table, Toni,' Kit said. 'Quick, or I'll press this nozzle.'

Toni hesitated.

Stanley said, 'I think Kit means what he says.'

She put the guns on the kitchen table, beside the empty briefcase.

Kit said, 'Nigel, pick them up.'

With his left hand, Nigel picked up a gun and stuffed it into his pocket. He took the second, and smashed it across Toni's face. She cried out and fell back.

Kit was furious with him. 'What do you think you're doing?' he cried. 'There's no time for that! We have to get going.'

'Don't you give me orders,' Nigel said harshly. 'This cow shot me.'

Kit could tell from Toni's face that she thought she was about to die. But there was no time to enjoy revenge. 'That cow ruined my life, but I'm not hanging around to punish her,' Kit said. 'Let's go!'

Nigel hesitated, then turned away from Toni. 'What about Elton and Daisy?'

'To hell with them.'

'We should tie up your old man and his tart.'

'You stupid fool, don't you realise we're out of time?'

The stare Nigel gave him was sulphuric. 'What did you call me?' Nigel wanted to kill someone, Kit realised, and right now he was thinking of shooting Kit. It was a terrifying moment. Kit raised the perfume spray high in the air and stared back, waiting for his life to end.

Then Nigel looked away and said, 'All right, let's get out of here.'

9 A.M.

Kit ran outside. The engine of the Mercedes was throbbing low, and the snow on its bonnet was already melting from the heat. He jumped in, stuffing the perfume spray into his jacket pocket. Nigel clambered into the passenger seat, grunting with the pain of his gunshot wound.

Kit put the automatic gearshift into drive and touched the accelerator pedal. He felt a soaring elation as he accelerated along the cleared driveway. He passed the garage—and saw Daisy. He braked reflexively.

Nigel said, 'What the hell?'

Daisy was walking towards them, supported by Craig on one side and Sophie on the other. Daisy's legs dragged uselessly behind her, and her head was a mass of blood. Beyond them was Stanley's Ferrari, its sensuous curves battered and deformed. What the hell had happened there?

'Stop and pick her up!' Nigel said.

Kit remembered how Daisy had humiliated him and almost drowned him in her father's pool only yesterday. He was at the wheel, and he was not going to delay his escape for her. He put his foot down.

As the Mercedes leapt forward, Craig grabbed the hood of Sophie's anorak with his right hand and pulled her to the side of the drive. Because they were tangled up with Daisy, she moved with them, and all three fell into the soft snow beside the track, Daisy screaming in pain and rage.

The car shot past, missing them by inches, and Craig glimpsed his Uncle Kit at the wheel. He was flabbergasted.

Kit accelerated past the crashed Ferrari and along the curving driveway that ran beside the cliff top. Craig watched, frozen, as Daisy levelled her pistol and took aim. Her hand was steady, despite the pain she was in. She squeezed off a shot and Craig saw a rear side window shatter.

Daisy tracked the speeding car with her arm and fired repeatedly, cartridge cases spewing from the ejection slot of the gun. A line of bullet holes appeared in the car's side, then there was a different kind of bang. A front tyre blew out and a strip of rubber flew through the air.

The car continued in a straight line for a second, then the back swung out and skidded into the low wall that ran along the cliff edge. Daisy kept firing and the windscreen shattered. The car rolled onto its side, then toppled over onto its roof. It slid a few feet upside-down before it came to a stop.

Daisy stopped shooting and fell backwards, her eyes closed. Craig stared at her. The gun fell from her hand. Sophie started to cry.

Craig reached across Daisy. He watched her eyes, terrified that they would open at any moment. His hand closed over the warm gun. He picked it up.

He held it in his right hand and put his finger into the trigger guard. He pointed it at a spot exactly between Daisy's eyes. All he cared about was that this monster should never threaten him and Sophie and their family ever again. Slowly, he squeezed the trigger. The gun clicked on an empty magazine.

KIT WAS LYING flat on the inside roof of the overturned car. He felt bruised all over and his neck hurt, but he could move all his limbs. He managed to right himself. Nigel lay beside him, unconscious, possibly dead.

Kit tried to get out. He pulled the handle and pushed at the door, but it would not move. He suffered a moment of panic, then saw that the windscreen was crazed. He shoved at it with his hand and pushed out a section of broken glass. He crawled through the windscreen, careless of the broken glass, and a shard cut the palm of his hand. He cried out and sucked the wound. He slithered out from under the bonnet of the car and scrambled to his feet. The wind off the sea blew madly in his face. He looked around.

His father and Toni Gallo were running along the drive towards him.

TONI STOPPED to look at Daisy. She seemed to be out cold. Craig and Sophie appeared scared but unhurt. 'What happened?' Toni said.

'She was shooting at us,' Craig replied. 'I ran over her.'

Toni followed Craig's gaze and saw Stanley's Ferrari, dented at both ends and with all its windows smashed.

Stanley said, 'Good God!'

Toni felt for a pulse in Daisy's neck. It was there, but weak. 'She's still alive—just.'

Craig said, 'I've got her gun. It's empty, anyway.'

They were all right, Toni decided. She looked ahead to the crashed Mercedes. Kit had climbed out. She ran towards him. Stanley followed close behind.

Kit started to run away, along the drive, heading for the woods, but he was battered and shaken by the crash, and after a few paces he staggered and fell.

He seemed to realise that he could not escape that way. Scrambling to his feet, he changed direction and turned towards the cliff.

Toni glanced into the Mercedes as she passed it. Nigel lay in a crumpled heap, eyes open with the blank stare of the dead. That accounted for the three thugs, Toni thought: one tied up, one unconscious and one dead. Only Kit was left.

Kit slipped on the icy drive, staggered, regained his balance and turned round. He took the perfume spray from his pocket and held it out like a gun. 'Stop, or I'll kill us all,' he said.

Toni and Stanley stopped.

Kit's face was all pain and rage. Toni saw a man who had lost his soul. He might do anything: kill his family, kill himself, destroy the world.

Stanley said, 'It won't work out here, Kit.'

Toni wondered if that were true.

Kit had the same thought, and said, 'Why not?'

'Feel this wind. The droplets will disperse before they can do any harm.'

'To hell with it all,' Kit said, and he threw the bottle high in the air. Then he turned round, jumped over the low wall and ran full tilt at the cliff edge.

Stanley jumped after him.

Toni caught the perfume bottle before it hit the ground.

Stanley leapt through the air, hands stretched out in front of him. He almost got Kit by the shoulders, but his hands slipped. He hit the ground, but managed to grab one leg and grip it tight. Kit fell to the ground with his head and shoulders jutting out over the edge of the cliff. Stanley jumped on top of him, holding him down with his weight. Kit struggled, but his father held him down and eventually he became still.

Stanley got slowly to his feet and pulled Kit up. Kit's eyes were shut. He was shaking with emotion, like someone in a fit. 'It's over,' Stanley said. He put his arms round his son and held him. 'It's all over now.' They stood like that on the edge, with the wind blowing their hair, until Kit stopped shaking. Then, gently, Stanley turned him around and led him back towards the house.

THE FAMILY were in the living room, stunned and silent. Stanley was talking to the Inverburn ambulance service on Kit's mobile phone, while Nellie tried to lick his hands. Hugo lay on the couch, covered in blankets, while Olga bathed his wounds. Miranda was doing the same for Tom and Ned. Kit lay on his back on the floor, eyes closed. Craig and Sophie talked in low voices in a corner. Caroline had found all her rats and sat with their cage on her knees.

Toni's mother sat next to Caroline with the puppy on her lap.

Toni called Odette. 'How far away did you say those helicopters were?'

'They're at Inverburn, waiting for instructions,' Odette replied. 'Why?'

'I've caught the gang and I've got the virus back, but—'

'What, on your own?' Odette was amazed.

'Never mind that. The important man is the customer, the one who's trying to buy this stuff and use it to kill people. I think we can find him, if we act fast. Could you send a helicopter to me at Steepfall? It's right on the cliff, fifteen miles north of Inverburn. There are four buildings in a square, and the pilot will see two crashed cars in the garden.'

'My God, you have been busy.'

'I need the chopper to bring me a miniature radio-tracking beacon. It has to operate for forty-eight hours and be small enough to fit into a bottle cap.'

'No problem. They should have that at police headquarters in Inverburn.'

'One more thing. I need a bottle of perfume—*Diablerie.*'

'They won't have *that* at police headquarters. They'll have to break into Boots in the High Street.'

'We don't have much time— Wait.' Olga was saying something.

'I can give you a bottle of *Diablerie*, just like the one that was on the table. It's the perfume I use.'

'Thanks.' Toni spoke into the phone. 'Forget the perfume, I've got a bottle. How soon can you get the chopper here?'

'Ten minutes. Where's it going after it picks you up?'

'I'll get back to you on that,' Toni said, and she ended the call.

She knelt on the floor beside Kit. He was pale. His eyes were closed, but he was not asleep: his breathing was shallow and he trembled intermittently. 'Kit,' she said. 'I need to ask you a question. It's very important.'

He opened his eyes.

'You were going to meet the customer at ten o'clock, weren't you?'

A tense hush fell on the room as the others turned and listened.

Kit looked at Toni but said nothing.

She said, 'I need to know where you were going to meet them.'

He looked away.

'Kit, please.'

His lips parted. Toni leaned closer. He whispered, 'No.'

'Think about it,' she urged. 'You might earn forgiveness, in time.'

His eyes moved as he looked from one family member to the next.

Reading his mind, Toni said, 'You've done a great wrong to them, but they don't yet seem ready to abandon you. They're all around you. You could begin to redeem yourself right now.'

Stanley opened his mouth to speak, but Miranda stopped him with a raised hand. 'Kit, please,' she said. 'Do one good thing, after all this rottenness. Do it for yourself, so you'll know you're not all bad. Tell her what she needs to know.'

Kit closed his eyelids tight, and tears appeared. At last he said, 'Inverburn Flying School.'

'Thank you,' Toni whispered.

AT 10 A.M. Toni sat in the control tower at the flying school. With her in the little room were Frank Hackett, Kit Oxenford and a local police detective. In the hangar, parked out of sight, was the military helicopter that had brought them here. It had been close, but they had made it with a minute to spare.

Kit clutched the burgundy briefcase. He was pale, his face expressionless. He obeyed instructions like an automaton.

They all watched through the big windows. The clouds were breaking up, and the sun shone over the snow-covered airstrip. There was no sign of a helicopter.

Toni held Nigel Buchanan's mobile phone, waiting for it to ring.

'The pilot should have called by now,' she said anxiously.

Frank said, 'He may be a few minutes late.'

As he spoke, a helicopter came down through the clouds.

Toni took out her own mobile and called Odette, who was now in the operations room at Scotland Yard. 'Customer in sight.'

'Give me the tail number,' Odette said, with excitement in her voice.

'Just a minute . . .' Toni peered at the helicopter until she could make out the registration mark, then read the letters and numbers to Odette.

The helicopter descended. It landed a hundred yards from the control tower. Frank looked at Kit and nodded. 'Off you go.'

Toni said, 'Just do everything as planned. Say: "We had some problems with the weather, but everything worked out OK in the end." You'll be fine.'

Kit went down the stairs, carrying the briefcase.

Toni had no idea whether he would perform as instructed. He had been up for more than twenty-four hours, he had been in a car crash, and he was emotionally wrecked. He might do anything.

There were two men in the front of the helicopter. One of them, presumably the copilot, opened a door and got out, carrying a large suitcase.

A moment later, Kit appeared outside and walked towards the helicopter.

The two men met halfway. There was some conversation. Kit pointed to the control tower. What was he saying?

Toni's mobile rang. It was Odette. 'The helicopter is registered to Adam Hallan, a London banker,' she said. 'The pilot and copilot are employees of his. They filed a flight plan to Battersea Heliport—just across the river from Mr Hallan's house in Cheyne Walk.'

'He's Mister Big, then?'

'Trust me. We've been after him for a long time.'

The copilot pointed at the burgundy briefcase. Kit opened it and showed him a *Diablerie* bottle in a nest of polystyrene chips. The copilot put his suitcase on the ground and opened it to reveal closely packed stacks of banded fifty-pound notes—at least a million pounds, Toni thought, perhaps two million. As he had been instructed, Kit took out one of the stacks and riffled it.

Toni told Odette, 'They've made the exchange. Kit's checking the money.'

The two men on the airfield looked at one another, nodded, and shook hands. Kit handed over the burgundy briefcase, then picked up the suitcase. The copilot walked back to the helicopter and Kit returned to the control tower.

As soon as the copilot got back into the aircraft, it took off.

Toni was still on the line to Odette. 'Are you picking up the signal from the transmitter in the bottle?'

'Loud and clear,' Odette said. 'We've got the bastards.'

BOXING DAY

7 P.M.

London was cold. No snow had fallen here, but a freezing wind whipped the ancient buildings, and people hunched their shoulders as they hurried to the warmth of pubs and restaurants and cinemas.

Toni Gallo sat in the back of a grey Audi beside Odette Cressy, who was a blonde woman of Toni's age. Two detectives sat in the front, one driving, one studying a direction-finding radio receiver and telling the driver where to go.

The police had been tracking the perfume bottle for thirty-three hours. The helicopter had landed, as expected, in southwest London. The pilot had got into a waiting car and driven across Battersea Bridge to the riverside home of Adam Hallan. All last night the radio transmitter had beeped steadily from somewhere in the elegant eighteenth-century house. Odette did not want to arrest Hallan yet. She wanted to catch the maximum number of terrorists in her net.

When Toni had lain down in her flat just before noon on Christmas Day, she felt too tense to sleep. Her thoughts were with the helicopter as it flew the length of Britain, and she worried that the tiny radio beacon would fail.

In the evening, she had driven to Steepfall to see Stanley. They had held hands and talked for an hour in his study, then she flew to London. She slept heavily all night at Odette's flat in Camden Town.

As well as following the radio signal, the Metropolitan Police had Adam Hallan and his pilot and copilot under surveillance. In the morning Toni and Odette joined the team watching Hallan's house.

Toni had achieved her main objective. The deadly virus samples were back in the BSL4 laboratory at the Kremlin. But she also hoped to catch the people responsible for the nightmare she had lived through. She wanted justice.

Today Hallan had given a lunch party, and fifty people of assorted nationalities and ages had visited the house. One of the guests had left with the perfume bottle. Toni and Odette and the team tracked the radio beacon to Bayswater and kept watch over a student rooming-house all afternoon.

At seven o'clock in the evening, the signal moved again.

A young woman came out of the house. In the light of the street lamps, Toni could see that she had lustrous dark hair. She carried a shoulder bag. She turned up the collar of her coat and walked along the pavement. A detective in jeans and an anorak got out of a tan Rover and followed her.

'I think this is it,' Toni said. 'She's going to release the spray.'

'I want to see it,' Odette said. 'For the prosecution, I need witnesses.'

Toni and Odette lost sight of the young woman as she turned into a tube station. The radio signal weakened as she went underground. It remained steady for a while, then the beacon moved, presumably because the woman was on a train. They followed the feeble signal till she emerged at Piccadilly Circus, the detective still tailing her. Then the detective called Odette on his mobile phone and reported that the woman had entered a theatre.

Toni said, 'That's where she'll release the spray.'

The unmarked police cars drew up outside the theatre. Odette and Toni went in, followed by two men from the second car. The girl with beautiful hair was standing in the queue for collection of prepaid tickets. While she waited, she took from her shoulder bag a perfume bottle. With a gesture that looked entirely natural, she sprayed her head and shoulders. The theatregoers around her paid no attention.

'That's good,' said Odette. 'But we'll let her do it again.'

The bottle contained plain water, but all the same Toni shivered with dread as she breathed in. Had she not made the switch, the spray would have contained live Madoba-2, and that breath would have killed her. Toni shuddered as she thought how close it had been.

The woman collected her ticket and went inside. Odette spoke to the usher and showed him her police card, then the detectives followed the woman. She went to the bar, where she sprayed herself again. She did the same in the ladies' room. At last she took her seat in the stalls and sprayed herself yet again.

A nervous man in a tuxedo approached them. 'I'm the theatre manager,' he said. 'What's happening?'

'We're about to make an arrest,' Odette told him. 'You may want to delay the curtain for a minute.'

'I hope there won't be a fracas.'

'Believe me, so do I.' The audience was seated. 'All right,' Odette said to the other detectives. 'We've seen enough. Pick her up, and gently does it.'

The two men from the second car walked down the aisles and stood at either end of the row. The woman with beautiful hair looked at one, then the other. 'Come with me, please, miss,' said the nearer of the two detectives. The theatre went quiet as the waiting audience watched.

The woman remained seated, but took out her perfume bottle and sprayed herself again. The detective, a young man in a short Crombie coat, pushed his way along the row to where she sat. 'Please come immediately,' he said. She stood up, raised the bottle, and sprayed it into the air. 'Don't bother,' he said. 'It's only water.' Then he took her by the arm and led her along the row and up the aisle to the back of the theatre.

Toni stared at the prisoner. She was young and attractive. She had been ready to commit suicide. Toni wondered why.

Odette took the perfume bottle from her and dropped it into an evidence bag. '*Diablerie*,' she said. 'French word. Do you know what it means?'

The woman shook her head.

'The work of the devil.' Odette turned to the detective. 'Put her in handcuffs and take her away.'

CHRISTMAS DAY

a year later

5.50 P.M.

Toni came out of the bathroom naked and walked across the hotel room to answer the phone.

From the bed, Stanley said, 'My God, you look good.'

She grinned at her husband. He was wearing a short towelling bathrobe that showed his long, muscular legs. 'You're not so bad yourself,' she said, and she picked up the phone. It was her mother. 'Happy Christmas,' she said.

'Your old boyfriend is on the television,' Mother said.

'What's he doing, singing carols in the police choir?'

'He's being interviewed by that Carl Osborne. He's telling how he caught those terrorists last Christmas.'

'*He* caught them?' Toni was momentarily indignant, then thought, What the hell. 'Well, he needs the publicity—he's after a promotion. How's Bella?'

'She's just getting the supper.'

Toni looked at her watch. On this Caribbean island it was a few minutes before six in the evening. For Mother, in England, it was coming up to ten at night. Meals were always late at Bella's. 'What did she give you for Christmas?'

'We're going to get something in the January sales, it's cheaper.'

'Did you like my present?' Toni had given Mother a pink cashmere cardigan.

'Lovely, thank you, dear. I must go now; the grandchildren are running around breaking their presents.'

'Bye, Mother. Thank you for calling.'

There was a knock at the door. Stanley called out, 'Who is it?'

'Olga. Toni was going to lend me a necklace.'

Toni could see that Stanley was about to tell his daughter to go away, but she put a hand on his mouth. 'Just a minute, Olga,' she called.

Stanley got off the bed and went into the bathroom. Toni pulled on a green silk robe and opened the door.

Olga strode in, dressed for dinner in a black cotton dress with a low neckline. 'You said you'd lend me that jet necklace.'

'Of course. Let me dig it out.'

In the bathroom, the shower ran.

Olga lowered her voice. 'I wanted to ask you—has he seen Kit?'

'Yes. He visited the prison the day before we flew out here.'

'How is my brother?'

'Uncomfortable, frustrated and bored, as you would expect, but he hasn't been beaten up or raped, and he isn't using heroin.' Toni found the necklace and put it round Olga's neck. 'It looks better on you than me—black really isn't my colour. Why don't you ask your father directly about Kit?'

'He's so happy, I don't want to spoil his mood. You don't mind, do you?'

'Not in the least.' On the contrary, Toni was flattered. She said, 'Did you realise that Elton and Hamish are in the same jail?'

'No—how awful!'

'Not really. Kit's helping Elton learn to read.'

'My god, how things work out. Did you hear about Daisy?'

'No.'

'She killed another inmate of the women's prison, and she was tried for murder, and convicted. She got a life sentence added to her existing term. She'll be in jail until she's seventy. I wish we still had the death penalty.'

Toni understood Olga's hatred. Hugo had never completely recovered from the beating Daisy had given him with the cosh. He had lost the sight in one eye. Worse, he had never regained his old ebullience.

'A pity her father is still at large,' Toni said. Harry Mac had been prosecuted as an accomplice, but Kit's testimony had not been enough to convict him. He had been found not guilty and gone straight back to his life of crime.

Olga said, 'There's news of him, too. He's got cancer. Started in his lungs, but now it's everywhere. He's been given three months to live.'

'Well, well,' said Toni. 'There is justice, after all.'

MIRANDA PUT out Ned's clothes for the evening: black linen trousers and a check shirt. He did not expect her to do it but, if she did not, he might absent-mindedly go down to dinner in shorts and a T-shirt. He was not helpless, just careless. She had accepted that.

She had accepted a lot about him. She understood that he would never be quick to enter a conflict, even to protect her; but, to compensate for that, she knew that in a real crisis he was a rock. The way he had taken punch after punch from Daisy to protect Tom proved that.

She was dressed already, in a pink cotton frock with a pleated skirt. It made her look a bit wide across the hips, but then she was a bit wide across the hips. Ned said he liked her that way.

She went into the bathroom. He was sitting in the tub, reading a biography of Molière in French. She took the book from him. 'The butler did it.'

'Now you've spoilt the suspense.' He stood up.

She handed him a towel. 'I'm going to check on the kids.'

GRANDPA HAD RESERVED a private room in the hotel restaurant for the ten members of the Oxenford family. A waiter poured champagne. Grandpa stood up, and they all went quiet. 'There's steak for dinner,' he said. 'I ordered a turkey, but apparently it escaped.' They all laughed.

He continued in a more sombre tone. 'The last twelve months have been the worst year of my life, and the best. None of us will ever completely get over what happened at Steepfall one year ago today.'

Craig looked at his father. He certainly would never recover. One eye was permanently half-closed and he often seemed just to tune out, nowadays.

Grandpa went on, 'Had it not been for Toni, God alone knows how it would have ended.'

Craig glanced at Toni. She looked terrific, wearing a chestnut-brown silk dress that showed off her red hair. Grandpa was nuts about her. He must feel almost the same way I do about Sophie, Craig thought.

Grandpa said, 'The whole nightmare reminded me that life is short, and I realised that I should tell you all how I felt about Toni and waste no more time. I need hardly say how happy we are. Then my new drug was passed for testing on humans, the future of the company was secured, and I was able to buy another Ferrari—and driving lessons for Craig.'

They laughed and Craig flushed. He had never told anyone about the *first* time he had dented the car. Only Sophie knew. He thought he might confess when he was really old, like thirty or something.

'Enough of the past,' said Grandpa. 'Merry Christmas, everybody.'

KEN FOLLETT

Born: Cardiff, June 5, 1949
Favourite hobby: Playing the Blues
Website: www.ken-follett.com

It was a cash crisis over car repairs, back in the seventies, that first prompted Ken Follett to start writing. A friend had earned £200 from producing a mystery novel, and Follett, then a young reporter on the *London Evening News*, decided to do the same in order to supplement his income. Written under a pseudonym, his first books brought him modest success and some useful extra cash, but it wasn't until 1978 that he finally hit the jackpot with *Eye of the Needle* (published under his own name). It was greeted by rave reviews, then made into a successful film, and the sales figures were dazzling.

The twenty-nine-year-old Follet was, however, loath to rest on his laurels. 'Although I had made all this money, I was very worried that I might not be able to do it again. So I worked very hard on the next, *Triple* (1979), to try to make it just as exciting.' The string of thrillers that subsequently emerged from Follett's fertile imagination quickly became best sellers, and many, like *The Key to Rebecca* (1980), *The Man*

'It is a little initimidating to climb into one of those protective suits and breathe through a pipe.'

from St Petersburg (1982) and *Lie Down with Lions* (1986), went on to become popular classics. Remarkably, for someone so prolific, Ken Follett doesn't fall into the trap of repeating his ideas. He's been bold enough to tackle subjects as diverse as the building of a medieval cathedral in *The Pillars of the Earth* (1989), Victorian banking in *A Dangerous Fortune* (1993), the Cold War in *Code to Zero* (2000), and the Danish Resistance during the Second World War in *Hornet Flight* (2002).

'I get a lot of my ideas from research,' he explains, ' but I am always working my imagination to elaborate the story.' For *Whiteout,* he not only visited two Biosafety Level 4 laboratories, one in London and one in Winnipeg in Canada, but actually tried out the equipment. 'The experience is in some ways reassuring, because you see how carefully controlled everything is. But it is a little intimidating to climb into one of those protective suits and breathe through a pipe.' When he visited the Winnipeg laboratory, he spent fifteen minutes inside a suit in the training lab and says he was very glad to get out of it. 'It's claustrophobic in there. You can breathe, but your mind tells you that you can't.' He is the first to admit that it would be 'very difficult indeed' to actually steal a virus sample from a research laboratory, like the one in *Whiteout*, as their security really is topnotch. 'But anything is possible,' he adds. 'And, after all, thrillers are about extraordinary events.'

One of the things that makes *Whiteout* such a good read is the clever way in which the author combines terrorism with a family drama. What inspired him to come up with this combination? 'I had the idea of a house on a cliff, and a family celebrating Christmas and then, of course, something terrifying happening to them. I've always believed that a thriller is only gripping if the reader cares about the people who are in danger in the story.'

Ken Follett's wife is the Labour MP for Stevenage and he is a long-time supporter of the Party. He says that politics is an important factor in their marriage and he is very happy to get involved in campaigning—just so long as it doesn't interfere too much with his writing. Have his wife's experiences in Parliament inspired any plot ideas? 'Not yet,' he says, 'but watch this space.'

ON THE SUBJECT OF . . .

Routine: 'I am a morning person. As soon as I'm up, I want to get to my desk. In the evening I want to relax and eat and drink and do all that sort of low-tension stuff.'

Imagination: 'My mother told me stories all the time. I don't know whether I inherited it from her, or just acquired it under her influence, but by the time I was seven years old I was an imaginative child.'

Reading: 'I have got tremendous pleasure out of good storytelling: good yarns that have taken me to places I have never been and shown me life styles and periods that I have never known. When

I started writing fiction, my impulse was to give the same pleasure to others that I had enjoyed myself.'

Music: 'I've always played the guitar quite badly. I think it's important to have something that you do badly, especially if you are the over-achiever type of personality.'

Champagne socialism: 'I deserve both halves of that label. I've always been enthusiastic about champagne.'

JOSEPH FINDER

PARA

NOIA

Lose the job, or agree to become a company spy—that's the stark choice facing Adam Cassidy.

No choice at all, really.

Best learn to play the game, put all scruples aside . . . gather the information without leaving any traces. Then get out quickly.

Try to ignore that unsettling feeling of being watched.

PART ONE
The Fix

Fix: A CIA term, of Cold War origin, that refers to a person who is to be compromised or blackmailed so that he will do the Agency's bidding.

—*The Dictionary of Espionage*

Until the whole thing happened, I never believed the old line about how you should be careful what you wish for because you might get it.

I believe it now. I believe all those cautionary proverbs. I believe that pride goeth before a fall, the apple doesn't fall far from the tree, misfortune seldom comes alone, all that glitters isn't gold. Man, you name it, I believe it.

I could try to tell you that what started it all was an act of generosity, but that wouldn't be quite accurate. It was more like an act of stupidity.

All I did was make a couple of phone calls. Impersonated the VP for Corporate Events and called the outside caterer that did all of Wyatt Telecom's parties. I told them to make it exactly like the bash they'd done the week before for the Top Salesman of the Year award. I gave them all the right disbursement numbers, authorised the transfer of funds in advance. The whole thing was surprisingly easy.

I think what really pissed off Wyatt Telecom was that Jonesie was an assistant foreman. Paying for his retirement party—a *loading-dock guy, for Christ's sake!*—was a violation of the natural order. If, instead, I'd used the money as a down payment on a Ferrari 360 Modena convertible, Nicholas Wyatt might have almost understood.

Still, I have to say, it was pretty cool. I loved seeing the loading-dock guys finally getting a taste of how the execs lived. Most of the guys and their wives didn't know what to make of the weird food, the caviar and saddle of veal

Provençal, but they devoured it. The ice sculptures were a big hit and the Dom Pérignon flowed, though not as fast as the Budweiser. I'd hired an excellent Jamaican reggae group, and everyone got right into it.

This was after the big tech meltdown, of course, and companies everywhere were laying people off and instituting 'frugality' policies. Jonesie was slated to just stop work one Friday, spend a few hours at HR signing forms, and go home for the rest of his life, no party, no nothing. Meanwhile, the Wyatt Telecom E-staff were planning to head down to the island of St Barthélemy in their Learjets and discuss companywide frugality policies over buffet breakfasts of papayas and hummingbird tongues. Jonesie and his friends didn't question who was paying for the retirement party, but it did give me some kind of twisted secret pleasure—until around one thirty in the morning, when the sound of electric guitars and drunken screams attracted the curiosity of a security guard who wasn't inclined to cut anyone any slack. He gripped his walkie-talkie as if it were a Glock and said, 'What the hell?'

And my life as I knew it was over.

THE VOICEMAIL was waiting for me when I got into work.

I felt queasy, my head thudded and my heart was going too fast from the cup of cheap coffee I'd gulped down on the subway. I'd considered calling in sick, but that little voice of sanity in my head told me that the wiser thing to do was to show up and face the music. Thing is, I fully expected to get fired—almost looked forward to it—and as I walked the half-mile through the cubicle farm to my work station, I could see heads popping up, prairie-dog style, to catch a glimpse of me.

The little LCD screen display on my phone said, 'You have eleven voice-mails.' I put it on speaker and zipped through them. Just listening to the messages increased the pressure behind my eyeballs. I got out the Advil bottle from the bottom desk drawer and dry-swallowed two as I heard the clipped voice of a man named Arnold Meacham, who identified himself as Director of Corporate Security and asked me to 'come by' his office the moment I got in.

I had no idea who Arnold Meacham was, beyond his title. I didn't even know where Corporate Security was located.

I stared at my cubicle walls. I kept the panels free of any evidence of human habitation—no photos of the wife and kids (easy, since I didn't have any), no Dilbert cartoons, nothing ironic that said I was here under protest, because I was way beyond that. I would not miss this cubicle. I picked up the phone and called Meacham's office, told his assistant that I was on my way, and asked how to get there.

My throat was dry, so I stopped at the break room to get one of the formerly-free-but-now-fifty-cent sodas. I surveyed the glass case, decided against my usual Diet Pepsi—I really didn't need more caffeine right now—and pulled out a Sprite. I popped the drink open and headed for the elevator.

I was a junior product line manager for routers in our Enterprise Division. You don't want the English translation, it's too mind-numbingly boring. I spent my days hearing phrases like 'dynamic bandwidth circuit emulation service' and 'integrated access device' and 'ATM backbones', and I didn't know what half of it meant. I truly despised my job, so the thought of losing it wasn't exactly bumming me out. On the other hand, it wasn't as if I had a trust fund, and I sure did need the money.

I had moved back here, essentially, to help with my dad's medical care—my dad, who considered me a fuckup. In Manhattan, bartending, I had made half the money but lived better. Now I was living in a ratty street-level studio apartment that reeked of traffic exhaust. Granted, I was able to go out a couple of nights a week with friends, but I usually ended up dipping into credit a week or so before my pay cheque appeared each month.

Not that I was exactly busting my ass. I coasted. I put in the minimum required hours, got in late and left early, but I got my work done. My performance review numbers weren't so good, just one band up from 'lowest contributor', when you should start packing your stuff.

I got into the elevator, looked down at what I was wearing—black jeans and a grey polo shirt, sneakers—and wished I'd put on a tie.

WHEN YOU WORK at a big corporation, there's always a lot of tough, macho talk. They're always telling you about 'killing the competition', or putting a 'stake in their heart', and after a while you start to think that somehow you got mixed up with one of those aboriginal tribes in Papua New Guinea that wear boar's tusks through their noses, when the reality is that if you email a politically incorrect joke to your buddy in IT you can end up in a sweaty HR conference room for a gruelling week of Diversity Training.

Thing is, of course, I'd done something a little more serious than emailing an off-colour joke.

They kept me waiting in an outer office for forty-five minutes. The receptionist tapped away at a keyboard, glanced over at me furtively from time to time, the way you might try to catch a glimpse of a grisly car accident while you're trying to keep your eyes on the road. My confidence began to waver. The monthly pay-cheque thing was beginning to look like a good idea. Maybe defiance *wasn't* the best approach.

Arnold Meacham didn't get up from his giant black desk when the receptionist brought me in. He was around forty, thin, with a long nose, no lips. He wore a double-breasted blue blazer and a blue striped tie, and glared at me through oversized steel aviator glasses. His office was big and spare, and at one end a half-opened door let onto a darkened conference room.

'So you're Adam Cassidy,' he said. He had a prissy, precise way of speaking. 'Party down, dude?' He pressed his lips into a smirk.

Oh God. This was not going to go well. 'What can I do for you?' I said. I tried to look perplexed, concerned.

'What can you *do* for me? How about start with telling the truth?'

Generally I'm pretty good at winning people over—the pissed-off maths teacher, the customer whose order is six weeks overdue, you name it. But I could see that this wasn't a Dale Carnegie moment. The odds of salvaging my odious job were dwindling by the second.

'The truth about what?'

He snorted with amusement. 'How about last night's catered event?'

I paused, considered. I didn't know how much they knew. 'You're talking about the little retirement party?' I said. 'It was a much-needed morale boost. Believe me, sir, it'll do wonders for departmental productivity.'

His lipless mouth curled. '"Morale boost". Your fingerprints are all over the funding for that "morale boost".'

'I'm not sure I'm understanding you, sir.'

Meacham's pasty face flushed. 'You think it's funny, hacking into proprietary company data bases to obtain confidential disbursement numbers? You think it's recreation, it's *clever*? It doesn't *count*?'

I tried to look chastened. 'No, sir—'

'You stole *seventy-eight thousand dollars* from the Corporate Events account for a goddamned party for your buddies on the *loading dock*!'

I swallowed hard. Shit. Seventy-eight thousand dollars? I knew it was pretty high-end, but I had no idea how high-end.

'This guy in on it with you? The old guy, "Jonesie"?'

'Jonesie had nothing to do with it,' I shot back. 'If you want to fire me, go ahead, but Jonesie was totally innocent.'

'Fire you?' Meacham looked as if I'd said something in Serbo-Croat. 'You think I'm talking about *firing* you? You're a smart guy, good at maths, right? So add up these numbers. Embezzling funds gets you five years of imprisonment and a two-hundred-fifty-thousand-dollar fine. Wire fraud, that's another five years in prison, but wait—if the fraud affects a financial institution—and lucky you, you fucked with our bank *and* the recipient bank—that brings it up to thirty years and a one-million-dollar fine. What's that, thirty-five years? And we haven't even got into computer crimes. That'll get you anywhere up to twenty years in prison. So what have we got so far, *fifty-five* years? You're twenty-six now. You'll be, let's see, *eighty-one* when you get out.'

Now I was sweating through my polo shirt. I felt cold and clammy and my legs were trembling. 'But,' I began, my voice hoarse. 'Seventy-eight thousand dollars is a rounding error in a thirty-billion-dollar corporation.'

'I suggest you shut your mouth,' Meacham said quietly. 'Our lawyers are confident that they can get a charge of embezzlement in a court of law. The US Attorney was a college room-mate of our house counsel, Mr Cassidy, and we have every assurance he intends to throw the book at you.'

I stared at him. I felt a trickle of sweat run down the inside of my shirt.

'We've *got* you, pure and simple. It's just a matter of how hard we're going to hit you. Let's hear what you have to say, pal, and you'd better make it good.'

I swallowed, but my saliva had stopped flowing.

In my college years I got stopped fairly often for speeding, and I developed a reputation as a virtuoso at getting out of tickets. The trick is to make the cop feel your pain. Even cops are human beings. I used to keep a couple of law-enforcement textbooks on the front seat and tell them I was studying to be a police officer and I sure hoped this ticket wouldn't hurt my chances. Or I'd show them a prescription bottle and tell them I was in a rush because I needed to get Mom her epilepsy medication. Basically, I learned that if you're going to start, you have to go all the way, you have to put your heart into it.

I took a deep breath. 'Look,' I said, 'I'm going to level with you.'

'About time.'

'Here's the thing. Jonesie—well, Jonesie has cancer.' I sighed, like I was spilling something I really didn't want to. 'Pancreatic cancer. Inoperable. I mean, there's nothing they can do—the guy's dying. And so Jonesie, you know—well, he's always putting on a brave front. He says to the oncologist, "You mean I can stop flossing?"' I gave a sad smile. 'That's Jonesie.'

Meacham stared at me, stone-faced.

Was I getting to him? I couldn't tell. I had to amp it up, really go for it.

'There's no reason you should know any of this,' I went on. 'Jonesie's not exactly an important guy around here. But he's important to me, because . . .' I closed my eyes, inhaled deeply. 'The thing is—I never wanted to tell anyone this, but Jonesie's my father.'

Meacham's chair came forward. Now he was paying attention.

'Different last name and all—my mom changed my name to hers when she left him twenty years ago, took me with her. I was a kid, I didn't know any better. But Dad, he . . .' I bit my lower lip. I had tears in my eyes now. 'He kept on supporting us, worked two, sometimes three jobs. Never asked for anything. Mom didn't want him to see me at all, but every Christmas . . .' A sharp intake of breath. 'Every Christmas, Dad came by the house with a present for me, some big expensive thing he couldn't afford. Later on, when Mom said she couldn't afford to send me to college, not on a nurse's salary, Dad started sending money. He—he said he wanted me to have the life he never had. Mom had sort of poisoned me against him, you know? So I never even thanked the guy. I didn't even invite him to graduation, but he showed up anyway in an ugly old suit—he must have got it at the Salvation Army—because he really wanted to see me graduate and he didn't want to embarrass me.'

Meacham's eyes actually seemed to be getting moist.

I was on a roll. 'When I started working here at Wyatt, I never expected to find Dad working on the loading dock. Mom died a couple of years ago, and here I am, connecting up with my father, this sweet guy who supported an ungrateful son he never got to see. It's like fate, you know? And then when he gets this news about the cancer, I mean . . . I just had to show him what he meant to me. I told him I'd hit the jackpot at the track, I didn't want him to worry or anything. Believe me, what I did was wrong, totally wrong, in a hundred different ways. But maybe in just one small way it was right.'

Meacham was looking down, unable to meet my gaze. I was giving *myself* chills.

Then I heard a door open at the far end of the office and what sounded like clapping. Slow, loud clapping. I looked up, startled.

It was Nicholas Wyatt, founder and CEO of Wyatt Telecommunications. He approached, smiling broadly. 'Brilliant performance. Absolutely brilliant.'

Wyatt was a tall man, around six foot six, with a wrestler's build. He was wearing some kind of Armani-looking grey suit with a subtle pinstripe. He wasn't just powerful, he *looked* powerful.

'Mr Cassidy, let me ask you a question.'

I didn't know what to do, so I stood up, extended my hand.

Wyatt didn't shake it. 'What's Jonesie's first name?'

I hesitated, a beat too long. 'Al,' I finally said.

'Al? As in—what?'

'Al—Alan,' I said. 'Albert. Shit.'

'Details, Cassidy,' Wyatt said. 'They'll get you every time. But I have to say, you moved me. You got me right here.' He tapped his chest with a fist and smiled. 'You're a supremely gifted young man. A goddamned Scheherazade. And I think we should have a talk.'

NICHOLAS WYATT was one scary dude. I had never met him before, but I'd seen him on TV and on the corporate website, the video messages he'd recorded. I'd even caught a few glimpses of him, during my three years working for the company he founded. Up close he was even more intimidating. He had a deep tan, perfect teeth and black hair that was gelled and combed straight back.

I had no idea why he was here. What could the CEO of the company threaten me with that Meacham hadn't already pulled out? Death by a thousand paper cuts? Being eaten alive by wild boar? I had this fleeting fantasy that he was going to high-five me, congratulate me for pulling off a good one, say he liked my spirit. But that little daydream shrivelled as quickly as it popped into my desperate mind. I'd heard Nicholas Wyatt was a vindictive son of a bitch, famous for his rages and shouting matches. At his staff meetings he always picked one person to humiliate, and he was known to fire people on the spot. He was viciously competitive, a weightlifter and triathlete, and guys who worked out in the company gym said he was always challenging the serious jocks to chin-up competitions. He never lost.

His top guys all dressed like he did, in $7,000 suits, and they put up with his shit because they were disgustingly well compensated for it. There was a joke about him: What's the difference between God and Nicholas Wyatt? God doesn't think he's Nicholas Wyatt.

He slept three hours a night, seemed to eat nothing but Power Bars, was a nuclear reactor of nervous energy. He managed by fear and never forgot a slight. The quote he's famous for, the one thing he repeated so often it should have been carved in granite above the main entrance, was: 'Of course I'm paranoid. I want everyone who works for me to be paranoid. Success *demands* paranoia.'

AS MEACHAM and I followed Wyatt down the hall from Corporate Security to his executive suite, the walls went from white plasterboard to mahogany; the carpeting became soft and deep-pile. We were at Wyatt's office, his lair. And it was vast. An entire Bosnian village could live there. Two of the walls were glass, floor to ceiling, and the views of the city were unbelievable. The other walls were dark wood, covered with framed magazine covers with his mug on them: *Fortune*, *Forbes*, *Business Week*.

He led us to a group of black leather chairs and an enormous sofa, and sank down at one end of the sofa.

I couldn't imagine why I was here, in Nicholas Wyatt's office. Maybe he'd been one of those boys who liked to pull the legs off insects one by one with tweezers, then burn them to death with a magnifying glass.

'So this is some pretty elaborate scam you pulled off,' he said. 'Impressive.'

I smiled, ducked my head modestly. *Thank God*, I thought. It looked like we were going the high-five route.

'But no one kicks me in the balls and walks away, you should know that by now. I mean *nobody*.'

Maybe not. He'd got out the tweezers and the magnifying glass.

'So what's your deal? You've been a product line manager here for three years, your performance reviews suck, you haven't gotten a raise the whole time you've been here. Not exactly an ambitious guy, are you?'

I smiled again. 'I guess not. I sort of have other priorities.'

'Like?'

I hesitated. I'm almost never speechless, but this time I couldn't think of anything clever to say. Meacham was watching me too, a nasty, sadistic little smile on his knife-blade face.

'You an actor or something in your spare time?'

I shook my head.

'Well, you're good, anyway. You may suck at marketing routers, but you are one *Olympic*-level bullshit artist.'

'If that's a compliment, sir, thank you.'

'Anyway, bottom line, you ripped me off and you seem to think you're going to get away with it.'

I looked appalled. 'No, sir, I *don't* think that.'

'Spare me another demonstration.' He flicked his hand like a Roman emperor, and Meacham handed him a folder. He glanced at it. 'Your aptitude scores are in the top percentile. You were an engineering major in college. What kind?'

'Electrical. My dad wanted me to major in something I could get a real job with. I wanted to play lead guitar with Pearl Jam.'

'Any good?'

'No,' I admitted.

He half smiled. 'Why did you do college on the five-year plan?'

'I got kicked out for a year. I pulled a stupid prank. I had a bad semester, so I hacked into the college computer system and changed my transcript.'

'So it's an old trick.' He glanced at Meacham, then back at me. 'I've got an idea for you, Adam.' I didn't like the way he said my name; it was creepy. 'A very good idea. An extremely generous offer, in fact.'

'Thank you, sir.' I had no idea what he was talking about, but I knew it couldn't be good or generous.

'What I'm about to say to you I'm going to deny I ever said. In fact, I won't just deny it, I'll sue you for defamation if you ever repeat it, are we clear? I will crush you.' Whatever he was talking about, he had the resources. He was a billionaire, like the third- or fourth-richest man in America, and he had been number two before our share price collapsed.

My heart thudded. 'Sure.'

'Are you clear on your situation? Behind door number one you've got the certainty of at least twenty years in prison. So it's that, or else whatever's behind the curtain. You want to play *Let's Make a Deal*?'

I swallowed. 'Sure.'

'Let me tell you what's behind the curtain, Adam. It's a very nice future for a smart engineering major like you, only you have to play by my rules.'

My face was prickly-hot.

'I want you to take a job at Trion.'

'At Trion Systems?' I didn't understand. Trion was our biggest competitor. 'They'd never hire me.'

'No, they'd never hire a lazy fuckup like you. But a Wyatt superstar on the verge of going supernova, they'd hire you in a nanosecond.'

'I don't follow.'

'Come on, dipshit. The Lucid—that was your baby, right?'

He was talking about Wyatt Telecom's flagship product, an all-in-one personal digital assistant, or PDA, sort of a Palm Pilot on steroids. An incredible toy. I had nothing to do with it. I didn't even own one.

'They'd never believe it,' I said.

'Listen, Adam. I make my biggest decisions on gut instinct, and my gut tells me you've got the brass balls to do it.' His eyes bore down on me, steely. 'I want you to get information. Only a Trion insider can get the information I want, and not just any insider. A major player.'

'And what if I'm caught?'

'If you screw up—well, we'll be here to protect you,' Meacham said.

Somehow I doubted that. 'They'll see right through me.'

'Not if you do your job right,' said Wyatt. 'And with a coach like me, you won't have any excuses. But, you're going to have to learn product marketing, you're going to have to work harder than you've ever worked in your whole sorry life.'

'What if I don't get hired?'

'Door number one.' He gave an ugly smile.

'What kind of money are we talking about?'

'A hell of a lot more than you get here. Six figures anyway.'

I tried not to gulp visibly. 'Plus my salary here,' I said.

He gave me a dead stare. He didn't have any expression in his eyes.

'I'm taking an enormous risk,' I went on.

He turned to Meacham. 'I don't believe this.'

Meacham looked like he'd swallowed a turd. 'You little prick,' he said. 'I ought to pick up the phone right now—'

Wyatt held up an imperial hand. 'That's OK. He's ballsy. I like that. You do your job right, you get to double-dip. But if you fuck up—'

'I know. Door number one. Let me think it over, get back to you tomorrow.'

Wyatt's jaw dropped. He paused, then said, all icy, 'I'll give you till nine a.m. When the US Attorney gets into his office.'

'I advise you not to say a word about this to anyone,' Meacham put in. 'Or you won't know what hit you.'

'I understand,' I replied. 'No need to threaten me.'

'Oh, that's not a threat,' said Nicholas Wyatt. 'That's a promise.'

THERE DIDN'T seem to be any reason to go back to work, so I went home. It felt strange to be on the subway at one in the afternoon, with the old people and the students, the moms and kids. I still felt queasy.

My keys jingled as I unlocked the three locks on my apartment door. The old lady in the unit across the hall opened her door a crack, the length of her security chain, then slammed it; she was too short to reach the peephole.

The room was dark even though the blinds were wide open, and the air smelt of stale cigarettes. Since the apartment was at street level, I couldn't leave the windows open during the day to air it out.

The one room was dominated by a beer-encrusted sleeper sofa, which faced a Sanyo nineteen-inch TV that was missing its remote. A tall, narrow pine bookcase stood lonely in one corner. I sat down on the sofa, and a cloud of dust rose in the air. I wondered if Nicholas Wyatt had ever lived in such a dump. The story was that he came up from nothing, but I didn't believe it. I found my Bic lighter, lit a cigarette, looked over at the pile of bills on the table. I didn't even open the envelopes any more. My two MasterCards and three Visas all had whopping balances, and I could barely make the minimum payments.

I had already made up my mind, of course.

'You get busted?'

Seth Marcus, my best buddy since high school, bartended three nights a week at a yuppie dive called Alley Cat. During the day he was a paralegal at a law firm. He said he needed the money, but I was convinced that secretly he was bartending in order to keep from turning into the sort of corporate dweeb we both liked to make fun of.

'Busted for what?' I replied. How much had I told him? Did I tell him about the call from Meacham, the security director? I hoped not. Now I couldn't tell him a goddamned thing about the vice they'd got me in.

'Your big party.'

I shook my head.

'You got away with it, huh? You actually pulled it off. Amazing. What can I get you to celebrate? How about a draught? They don't keep track of those.'

I shrugged. 'Sure.'

He pulled me a beer. He was a tall, dark-haired, good-looking guy with a ridiculous goatee and an earring. He was half-Jewish but wanted to be black. He played and sang in a band called Slither, which I'd heard a couple of times; they weren't very good, but he talked a lot about 'signing a deal'.

Seth was the only guy I knew who was more cynical than me. That was probably why we were friends. That plus the fact that he didn't give me grief about my father, who had coached (and tyrannised) the high-school football team. Later, when my dad was hired as the coach at Bartholomew Browning & Knightley, a fancy prep school, I was offered free tuition there. So for two years I rarely saw Seth, until Dad got fired for breaking a kid's right forearm and the free tuition tap got shut off, and I went back to the public school.

For a couple of summers, Seth and I worked cleaning windows for a company that did a lot of downtown skyscrapers, until we decided that dangling from ropes on the twenty-seventh floor sounded cooler than it actually was. Not only was it boring, but it was scary as hell, a lousy combination.

Someone down at the other end of the bar was whistling, two fingers in his mouth, loud and shrill. It was a chubby balding guy in a suit.

'That guy whistling at *me*? Like I'm a *dog*?' Seth said. He headed for the other end of the bar. I took out a cigarette and lit it as I watched him lean over the bar, glowering at the whistler, looking like he was going to grab the guy's lapel but stopping short. He said something. There was laughter from the whistler's general vicinity. Looking cool and relaxed, Seth headed back.

'I don't believe you're still smoking,' he said. 'That's so stupid, with your dad.' He took a cigarette from my pack, lit it, and took a drag.

'Thank you for not thanking me for not smoking. So what's *your* excuse?'

He exhaled through his nostrils and put the cigarette in the ashtray. 'Dude, I like to multitask. Also, cancer doesn't run in my family. Just insanity.'

'He doesn't have cancer.'

'Emphysema. Whatever the hell. How is the old man?'

'Fine.' I shrugged. I didn't want to go there, and neither did Seth.

He went off for a couple of minutes, banging things around, the blender screaming. Served a pair of beautiful women with one of his killer smiles. Stayed to chat a while. They both turned to look at me and smiled.

When he came back, he said, 'What are you doing later?'

'Later?' It was already close to ten, and I had to meet with a Wyatt engineer at seven thirty in the morning. A couple of days training with him, some big shot on the Lucid project, then a couple more days with a new-products marketing manager. But I couldn't tell Seth; I couldn't tell anyone.

'I'm done at one,' he said. 'Those two chicks asked if I wanted to go to Nightcrawler with them after. I told them I had a friend. They just checked you out, they're into it.'

'Can't,' I said.

'What? What's going on?'

'Early day tomorrow. Big project.'

Seth looked alarmed, disbelieving. 'You becoming one of Them? One of the pod people?'

I grinned. 'Time to grow up. No more kid stuff.'

'Dude, it's *never* too late to have a happy childhood.'

AFTER TEN gruelling days of tutoring by engineers and product marketing types who'd been involved with the Lucid handheld, my head was stuffed with information. I'd been given a tiny 'office' in the executive suite that used to be a supply room, though I was almost never there. I didn't know how long I'd be able to keep this up without flipping out, but the image of a prison bunk bed kept me motivated.

You wouldn't have recognised me any more. I was a changed man. I drove a silver Audi A6, leased by the company. I had a new wardrobe, too. One of Wyatt's administrative assistants had taken me clothes shopping at a very expensive place I had only seen from the outside. She picked out suits, shirts, ties and shoes, and put it all on a company Amex card. And this wasn't the crap I usually wore; you could tell it had all been hand-stitched by Italian widows listening to Verdi.

Also, no more of the scraggly bed-head look. She took me to a fancy salon, and I came out looking like a Ralph Lauren model. I dreaded next time Seth and I got together; I knew I'd never hear the end of it.

A cover story was devised. My co-workers and managers were informed that I had been 'reassigned'. Rumours circulated that I was being sent to Siberia because the manager of my division was tired of my attitude, but no one knew the truth.

Then one morning I was summoned to an office two doors down from Nicholas Wyatt's. The brass plate on the door said JUDITH BOLTON. The office was all white—white rug, white upholstered furniture, white marble slab for a desk, even white flowers.

On a white leather sofa, Nicholas Wyatt sat next to an attractive, fortyish woman who was chatting away familiarly with him, touching his arm, laughing. Coppery red hair, blue eyes, glossy lips, a slender body in a navy suit. She'd obviously once been a knockout, but she'd gotten a little hard.

I realised I'd seen her before, over the last week or so, at Wyatt's side, when he paid his quick visits to my training sessions, but we were never introduced. Later, I learned that she was a senior VP who'd been brought into Wyatt Telecom a few years earlier to advise Nicholas Wyatt on sensitive personnel issues, 'conflict resolution' in the uppermost echelons of the company. She had a PhD in behavioural psychology, and she advised Wyatt on who was executive material and who wasn't, who should be fired, who was plotting behind his back. She had an X-ray eye for disloyalty.

Without getting up, she extended a hand as I approached—long fingers, red nail polish—and gave me a firm, no-nonsense shake. 'Judith Bolton.'

'Adam Cassidy.'

'You're late,' she said. 'You have a problem with punctuality. I don't ever want you to be late again, are we clear?'

I smiled back, the same smile I give cops when they ask if I know how fast I was going. 'Absolutely.' I sat down in a chair facing her.

'Judith is one of my most valuable players,' Wyatt said. 'My "executive coach". I suggest you listen to every word she says. I do.' He stood up, excused himself. She gave him a little wave as he left.

Judith turned back to me and continued. '*If* you're hired by Trion, you're to arrive at your cube forty-five minutes early. Under no circumstances will you have a drink at lunch or after work. No "hanging out" with friends from work. If you have to attend a work-related party, drink club soda.'

'You make it sound like I'm in AA.'

'Getting drunk is a sign of weakness. Now, about your handshake.' She shook her head. 'You blew it. Hiring decisions are made in the first five seconds—at the handshake. You get the job with the handshake, and then the rest of the job interview you fight to keep it. Since I'm a woman, you went easy on me. Don't. Be firm. Hold the shake a second or two longer. Look me in the eye, and smile. Aim your heart at me. Let's do it again.'

I stood up, shook Judith Bolton's hand again.

'Better,' she said. 'You're a natural. People meet you and think, there's something about this guy I like.' She leaned towards me, her chin resting in a cupped hand, checking me out. 'I can tell you're an athlete, Adam, by the way you carry your body. I like it. But you're not synchronising.'

'Excuse me?'

'You've got to synchronise. *Mirror.* I'm leaning forward, so you do the same. I lean back, you lean back. I cross my legs, you cross your legs. Even synchronise your *breathing* with mine. Just don't be blatant about it. This is how you connect with people on a subconscious level, make them feel comfortable with you. *People like people who are like themselves.* Are we clear?'

I grinned disarmingly, or what I thought was disarmingly, anyway.

'And another thing.' She leaned in even closer and whispered, 'You're wearing too much aftershave.'

My face burned with embarrassment.

'Let me guess: Drakkar Noir.' She didn't wait for my answer; she knew she was right. 'Very high-school stud. Bet it made the cheerleaders weak at the knees. Now, our first assignment is to learn how to do a job interview.'

'I got hired here,' I said, feebly.

'We're playing in a whole new league, Adam,' she said. 'You have to interview like a hotshot, someone Trion's going to fall all over themselves to steal away from us. How do you like working at Wyatt?'

I looked at her, feeling stupid. 'Well, I'm trying to leave there, aren't I?'

She rolled her eyes, inhaled sharply. 'No. Keep it positive.' She turned her head to one side, then did an imitation of my voice: 'I *love* it! It's *inspiring*! My co-workers are *great*!' The mimicry was so good, it weirded me out.

'So why am I interviewing at Trion?'

'*Opportunities*. You're just taking the logical next step in your career, and there are more opportunities at Trion to do *even bigger, better things*. What's your greatest weakness, Adam?'

I thought for a second. 'Nothing, really,' I said. 'Never admit to a weakness. It's a trick question.'

'Of *course* it's a trick question. Job interviews are *minefields*. You *have* to "admit" to weaknesses, but you must *never* tell them anything derogatory.' She did the Adam-voice again: 'Sometimes when little things bother me, I don't always speak up, because I figure most things tend to blow over. *You don't complain enough!* Or how about this: I tend to get *really absorbed in a project*, so I sometimes put in long hours, too long. Maybe I work on things more than is necessary. Get it? They'll be salivating, Adam.'

I smiled, nodded. Man, oh man, what had I gotten myself into?

'You're a natural,' she said. 'You're going to do just fine.'

THE NIGHT before my first interview at Trion I went over to see my dad. I did this at least once a week, more if he called and asked me to come over. He called a lot, partly because he was lonely—Mom had died six years earlier—and partly because he was paranoid from the steroids he took and convinced his caregivers were trying to kill him. So his calls were never friendly; they were complaints, rants, accusations.

To say that it was hard to retain people to take care of him was an understatement. Francis X. Cassidy had always been a bad-tempered man, and had only grown angrier as he grew older and sicker. He'd always smoked a couple of packs a day and was always getting bronchitis. So it came as no surprise when he was diagnosed with emphysema, which was now what they called 'end stage', meaning that he could die at any time.

Unfortunately, it fell to me, his only offspring, to arrange his care. He hadn't saved any money, and his pension was pitiful; he barely had enough to cover his medical expenses. That meant part of my pay cheque went to pay his rent (he still lived in the same apartment I'd grown up in), the home health-care aide's salary, whatever. I never expected any thanks, and never got any.

When I arrived, he was sitting in his favourite Barcalounger in front of the huge TV, his main occupation.

'Hey, Dad,' I said.

He didn't look up for a minute or so—he was hypnotised by some infomercial, like it was the shower scene in *Psycho*. He'd gotten thin, though he still had a barrel chest, and his crew cut was white. When he did look up at me, he said, 'The bitch is quitting, you know that?'

The 'bitch' in question was his latest home healthcare aide, a moody Irish woman in her fifties named Maureen. She limped through the living room as if on cue—she had a bad hip—with a plastic laundry basket heaped with neatly folded white T-shirts and boxer shorts, my dad's wardrobe. The only surprise about her quitting was that it had taken her so long.

'Why don't you tell him what you called me?' she said, setting the laundry down on the couch.

'Oh, for Christ's sake,' he said. He spoke in short, clipped sentences, since he was always short of breath. 'You've been putting antifreeze in my coffee. I can taste it. They call this eldercide, you know. Grey murders.'

'If I wanted to kill you I'd use something better than antifreeze,' she snapped back.

'She deserved whatever I called her. She assaulted me. I sit here hooked up to air tubes, and this bitch is slapping me around.'

'I grabbed a cigarette out of his hands,' Maureen said. 'He was trying to sneak a smoke when I was in the basement doing the laundry. As if I can't smell it throughout the house.' She looked at me. 'I don't even know where he hides the cigarettes—he's hiding them somewhere, I *know* it!'

My father smiled triumphantly but said nothing.

'Anyway, what do I care?' she said bitterly. 'This is my last day.'

'Like I'm going to notice,' Dad said. 'I should have fired her the minute I met her,' he grumbled. 'I could tell she was one of those grey-murderers.'

Maureen picked up the laundry basket. 'I should never have taken this job.' She left the room.

I didn't know what I was going to do now. The guy couldn't be alone and he refused to go into a nursing home; he said he'd kill himself first.

I put my hand on his, and said, 'We'll get someone, Dad, don't worry.'

He lifted his hand, flung mine away. 'What kind of nurse is she anyway?' he said. 'She doesn't give a shit about anyone else.' He went into a long coughing fit, and spat into a balled-up handkerchief. 'I don't know why you don't move back in. The hell you got to do anyway in that go-nowhere job?'

I shook my head, said gently, 'I can't, Dad. I got student loans to pay off.' I didn't want to mention that someone had to make money to pay for the help that was always quitting.

'Fat lot of good college did you,' he said. 'Huge waste of money, all it was. Spent your time carousing with all your fancy friends.'

I smiled to let him know I wasn't offended.

'Your mother, rest in peace, spoiled you rotten.' He sucked in some air. 'You're wasting your life. When you gonna get a real job, anyway?'

Dad was skilled at pushing the right buttons. I let a wave of annoyance pass over me. When I was a kid, small enough not to fight back, he'd whip off his leather belt at the slightest provocation and whomp me. As soon as he finished the beating, he'd invariably mutter, 'See what you made me do?'

'I'm working on that,' I said.

'These companies can smell a loser a mile off, you know. Nobody wants a loser. Go get me a Coke, would you?'

This was his mantra, and it came from his coaching days—that I was a 'loser', that the only thing that counted was winning. There was a time when that sort of talk used to piss me off. But now I barely even heard it.

I went to the kitchen, thinking about what we were going to do. He needed round-the-clock help, but none of the agencies would send anyone any more. We were reduced to whoever we could find through ads in the paper.

I filled two glasses with ice, poured the contents of a can into each. I'd have to sit Maureen down, apologise on Dad's behalf, beg her to stay until I found a replacement. The truth was, I was desperate. If I blew the interviews tomorrow, I'd be behind bars. That wouldn't help.

I came back out holding the glasses, the ice tinkling as I walked, and I set them down on a little end table.

'Dad, don't worry about anything,' I said, but he'd passed out.

I stood before him for a few seconds, watching to see if he was still breathing. He was. I kissed the old man's blotchy red forehead. 'We'll get someone,' I said quietly.

THE HEADQUARTERS of Trion Systems looked like a brushed-chrome Pentagon. Each of the five sides was a seven-storey 'wing'. Underneath was a parking garage filled with BMWs, Range Rovers, you name it. When I gave the B Wing 'lobby ambassador' my name, she printed out an ID sticker that said VISITOR. I pasted it onto the breast pocket of my grey Armani suit and waited. I tried to relax. I reminded myself that I couldn't ask for a better set-up. Trion was looking to fill a product marketing manager slot—a guy had left suddenly—and I'd been custom-tooled for the job. In the last few weeks, the word had been spread, casually, on the grapevine. A few selected head-hunters had been told about this amazing young guy at Wyatt who was just ripe for the picking. And I began to get all sorts of calls from recruiters.

I'd done my homework on Trion Systems. I'd learned it was a consumer-electronics giant founded in the early 1970s by the legendary Augustine Goddard, whose nickname was not Gus but Jock. He was almost a cult figure. He graduated from Cal Tech, served in the navy, went to work for Fairchild Semiconductor then Lockheed, and invented some kind of breakthrough technology for manufacturing colour TV picture tubes. He was generally considered to be a genius, but unlike some of the other geniuses who founded huge corporations, he apparently wasn't an asshole. He was kind of a distant, paternal presence. People liked him, were fiercely loyal to him.

Later Trion had moved into electronic communications—and these days they made cellphones and pagers, computer components, colour laser print-ers, personal digital assistants, all that kind of stuff.

A woman with frizzy brown hair came into the lobby. 'You must be Adam.'

I gave her a nice firm handshake. 'Good to meet you.'

'I'm Stephanie,' she said. 'I'm Tom Lundgren's assistant.' She took me to the elevator and up to the sixth floor. We made small talk. I tried to sound enthusiastic but not geeky.

On the sixth floor cubicles were spread out as far as the eye could see, high as an elephant's eye. The route she led me down was a maze; I couldn't have retraced my steps to the elevator bank if I'd dropped breadcrumbs.

Eventually we came to a conference room with a plaque on the door that said STUDEBAKER.

'Studebaker, huh?' I said.

'Yeah, all the conference rooms are named after classic American cars. Mustang, Thunderbird, Camaro, Corvette. Jock loves them.' She said Jock with a little twist, almost with quotation marks round it, as if indicating that she wasn't really on a first-name basis with the CEO but that's what everyone called him. 'Can I get you something to drink?'

'Coke, Pepsi, whatever,' I said. I didn't want to sound too fussy. 'Thanks.'

I sat down at one side of the table and a couple of minutes later a compact guy wearing khakis and a navy-blue golf shirt with the Trion logo on it came bounding into the room. Tom Lundgren. I recognised him from the dossier that Dr Bolton had prepared for me. The VP of the Personal Communications Sector business unit. Forty-three, five kids, an avid golfer. Right behind him followed Stephanie, holding a can of Coke and a bottle of water.

He gave me a crusher handshake. 'Adam, I'm Tom Lundgren.'

'Nice to meet you.'

'Nice to meet *you*. I hear great things about you.'

I smiled, shrugged modestly.

Stephanie shut the door behind her quietly as she left, and Lundgren sat down next to me.

'So working at Wyatt's pretty intense, I bet.' He had thin lips and a quick smile that clicked on and off and his right leg pistoned up and down. He was a bundle of nervous energy. I'd hate to see him after a pot of coffee.

'Intense is how I like it,' I said.

'Good to hear it. So do we.' His smile clicked on, then off. 'I think there's more type A people here than anywhere else. Everyone's got a faster clock speed.' He unscrewed the top of his water bottle and took a sip. 'I always say Trion's a great place to work, but, man, you pay a price for taking time off. You come back, your voicemail box is full, you get crushed like a grape.'

I nodded, smiled conspiratorially. 'Sounds familiar,' I said. I was mirroring his body language, almost aping him, but he didn't seem to notice.

'Absolutely. Now, we're not really in hiring mode these days—no one is. But one of our new-product managers got transferred suddenly.'

I nodded again.

'The Lucid is genius—really saved Wyatt's bacon in an otherwise dismal quarter. That's your baby, huh?'

'I was just part of the team. Wasn't running the show.'

He seemed to like that. 'You're too modest. You were a pretty key player, from what I've heard. How'd you do it? What's the secret?'

I blew out a puff of air through pursed lips, as if recalling running a marathon. 'No secret. Teamwork. Driving consensus, motivating people.'

'Be specific.'

'The idea started as a Palm-killer, to be honest.' I was talking about Wyatt's wireless PDA, the one that buried the Palm Pilot. 'At the early concept-planning sessions, we got together a cross-functional group—engineering, marketing, our internal ID folks.' ID was jargon for industrial design. I was jamming; I knew this answer by heart. 'And we looked at the market research, what the flaws were in the Trion product, in Palm, BlackBerry and other handhelds.'

'And what was the flaw in our product?'

'Speed. The wireless sucks, but you know that.' Judith had downloaded for me some candid remarks Lundgren had made at industry conferences, in which he confessed as much. My bluntness was a calculated risk on Judith's part. In her assessment, he despised toadyism, grooved on straight talk.

'Correct,' he said. He flashed a millisecond of a smile. 'The only serious weakness with the Lucid, far as I can see, is the the lack of a flash slot.'

'I absolutely agree.' I had been well prepped with stories of 'my' success. And pseudofailures I managed so well that they might as well have been victories. 'A big screwup. That was the biggest feature that got jettisoned. It was in the original product definition, but it grew the form factor outside of the bounds we wanted, so it got scrapped midway through the cycle.'

'Doing anything about it in the next generation?'

'Sorry, I can't say. That's proprietary to Wyatt Telecom. This isn't just a legal nicety, it's a moral thing with me—when you give your word, it's got to mean something. If that's a problem . . .'

He gave what looked like a genuine, appreciative smile. 'Not a problem at all. I respect that. Anyone who leaks proprietary information from their last employer would do the same to me.'

I noted the words 'last employer'—Lundgren had already signed me on.

He pulled out his pager and quickly checked it. 'I don't need to take any more of your time, Adam. I want you to meet Nora.'

NORA SOMMERS WAS BLONDE, around fifty, with wide-set, staring eyes. She had the carnivore look of a wild pack animal. Or maybe I was biased by her dossier, which described her as ruthless, tyrannical. She was a director, the team leader of the Maestro project, a sort of scaled-down BlackBerry rip-off that was running into some heavy weather. No one wanted to be on her team, which was why they were having a hard time filling the job internally.

'So Nick Wyatt must be no fun to work for, huh?' she began.

I didn't need Judith Bolton to tell me you're never supposed to complain about your previous employer. 'Actually,' I said, 'he's demanding, but he brought out the best in me. I have nothing but admiration for him.'

She nodded wisely, smiled as if I'd selected the right multiple-choice answer. 'Well, the word has certainly spread about you. What was the hardest battle you had to wage on the Lucid project?'

I rehashed the story I'd just told Tom Lundgren.

She sounded underwhelmed. 'Doesn't sound like much of a battle to me,' she countered. 'I'd call that a tradeoff.'

'Maybe you had to be there,' I said. Lame. I scrolled through my mental list of anecdotes about the Lucid. 'Also, there was a pretty big tussle over the five-way directional joy pad with built-in speaker. Our design people wanted that as a focal point of the product—it really drew your eye to it. But I was getting pushback from the engineers, who said it was way too tricky to make. I had to put my foot down. I said this was cornerstone. The design not only made a visual statement, but it also made a major technology statement— told the market we could do something our competitors couldn't.'

She was lasering in on me with her wide-set eyes. 'Engineers,' she said with a shudder. 'They can really be impossible. No business sense at all.'

'Actually, I never have problems with engineers,' I said. 'I think they're the heart of the enterprise. I never confront them; I *inspire* them, or try, anyway. That's one of the things that appeals to me about Trion—engineers reign supreme here, which is as it should be. It's a real culture of innovation.'

All right, so I was pretty much parroting an interview Jock Goddard once gave to *Fast Company*, but I thought it worked. Trion's engineers were famous for loving Goddard because he was one of them. They considered it a cool place to work, since so much of Trion's funding went into R&D.

'So tell me, Adam—what's your greatest weakness?'

I smiled and mentally uttered a prayer of gratitude to Dr Bolton.

Man, it all seemed almost too easy.

MORE THAN A WEEK went by before I got the news from Nick Wyatt. When I was shown into his office by his admininstrative assistant, I found him on his elliptical trainer. He was wearing a sweat-soaked tank top and gym shorts and was barking orders into a wireless headset.

I knew the Trion interviews had gone well and I figured, wrongly, that once they were done I'd be given time off from KGB school, but no such luck. The training went on, including what they called 'tradecraft'—how to steal stuff without getting caught, copy computer files, search data bases, and so on. Meacham and another of Wyatt's corporate security staff, who'd spent two decades in the FBI, taught me how to contact them by email, using an 'anonymiser', a remailer based in Finland that buries your real name and address, how to encrypt my email, and how to make copies of the ID badges most corporations use these days, the ones that unlock a door when you wave them at a sensor. I was beginning to feel like a real spy.

But after a few days of waiting and waiting for some word from Trion, I was scared shitless. Meacham and Wyatt had been pretty clear about what would happen if I didn't land the job.

Now, Nick Wyatt didn't even look at me.

'Congratulations,' he said eventually. 'I got the word from the head-hunter. You just got an offer. A hundred seventy-five thousand to start, stock options, the whole deal. You're being hired in at the manager level, grade ten.'

I was relieved, and amazed by the amount. That was about three times what I was making now. Adding in my Wyatt salary, it took me to two hundred and thirty-five thousand. Jesus.

'Sweet,' I said. 'Now what do we do?'

'Now you show 'em how amazing you are,' Wyatt said. 'If you can't blow 'em away after graduating our little charm school here, then you're an even bigger loser than I thought.' He stepped off the machine, grabbed a white towel off the handlebars, and blotted his face. He stood so close to me I could smell his perspiration. 'Now, listen carefully,' he said. 'About sixteen months ago, Trion's board of directors approved an extraordinary expenditure of five hundred million dollars to fund some kind of skunkworks.'

'A what?'

He snorted. 'A top-secret in-house project. Now, it's highly unusual for a board to approve an expenditure that large without a lot of information. In this case they approved it blind, based solely on assurances from Goddard that the technology, whatever the hell it is, will be a monumental breakthrough. I mean huge. Disruptive beyond disruptive. He assured them that anyone who's not a part of this gets left behind.'

'What is it?'

'If I knew, you wouldn't be here, idiot. I've invested far too much in this firm to let it go the way of the mastodon and the dodo. So your assignment is to find out everything you can about this skunkworks. Clear?'

'How?'

'That's your job.' He turned, walked across the vast expanse of office and opened a door, revealing a gleaming marble bathroom. I stood there awkwardly, not sure whether I was supposed to wait, or leave, or what.

'You'll get the call later on this morning,' Wyatt said without turning round. 'Act surprised.'

PART TWO
Backstopping

Backstopping: An array of bogus cover identifications issued to an operative that will stand up to fairly rigorous investigation.
  —*The Dictionary of Espionage*

I placed an ad in three local papers looking for a home healthcare aide for my dad and six responses came in. Three were from people who had misunderstood the ad and were themselves looking to hire someone. Two phone messages were in foreign accents so thick I couldn't even be sure they were speaking English. One was from a pleasant-voiced man who said his name was Antwoine Leonard.

I arranged to meet Antwoine for coffee. I wasn't going to have him meet my father until I'd hired him, so he couldn't back out so easily.

Antwoine turned out to be a huge, scary-looking black dude with prison tattoos and dreadlocks. Just as soon as he could, he told me he'd just got out of prison for auto theft, and it wasn't his first stint in the slammer. He gave me the name of his parole officer as a reference. I liked the fact that he was so open about it. In fact, I just liked the guy. He had a gentle voice, a surprisingly sweet smile, a low-key manner. I figured that if anyone could handle my dad, he could, and I hired him on the spot.

THE MORNING I started at Trion, the alarm clock went off at five thirty, and it was like something was wrong with the clock—it was still night-time. When I remembered, I felt a jolt of adrenaline. This was it; practice time was over.

I got into the silver Audi A6, which still had that new smell. In my perfect Zegna suit and tie and Cole Haan shoes, I was pumped, and to celebrate my new station in life I stopped at a Starbucks and got a triple grande latte.

Almost four dollars for a cup of coffee, but hey, I was making big bucks now.

Amazingly, there were a fair number of cars in the underground garage at Trion, even at seven thirty. I parked two levels down.

For the next two hours I sat in the Human Resources reception area on the third floor of E Wing filling out form after form. They took my picture and gave me an ID badge, then one of them took me on a tour of Trion, which was pretty impressive. A great fitness centre, ATM cash machines, a place to drop off your laundry and dry cleaning, break rooms with free sodas, cappuccino machines. You could get your car washed; you could get discount tickets to movies, concerts and baseball games.

I noticed that the elevator in D Wing didn't stop on the fifth floor—'Special Projects,' the HR girl explained. 'No access.' I tried not to register any particular interest. But I wondered if this was where the 'skunkworks' was housed.

Finally, Stephanie came by to take me up to the sixth floor of B Wing.

Tom Lundgren was on the phone but waved me in. His legs were pistoning away like crazy, and his face looked like it had been scrubbed raw with a Brillo pad. 'Steph,' he said, 'can you ask Nora to come by?'

A few minutes later he slammed down the phone, sprang to his feet and shook my hand. 'Hey, Adam, welcome to the team!' he said. 'Man, am I glad we bagged you! Sit down, sit down.' I did. 'We need you, buddy. Bad. We're covering twenty-three products, we've lost some key staff, and we're stretched way thin. The gal you're replacing got transferred. You're going to be joining Nora's team, working on the refresh of the Maestro line. There are some serious fires to put out, and—here she is!'

Nora Sommers was standing in the doorway, one hand on the doorjamb, posing like a diva. She extended the other hand coyly. 'Hi, Adam, welcome! *So* glad you're with us.'

'Nice to be here.'

'It was not an easy hire, frankly. We had a lot of strong candidates. But, as they say, cream rises to the top. Well, shall we get right to it?'

Her voice, which had almost had a girlish lilt to it, seemed to deepen instantly as soon as we walked away from Tom Lundgren's office. 'All right, Adam,' she said. 'I should warn you, we don't hold hands around here. It's a pretty steep learning curve, but I have no doubt you're up to it. We throw you right in the pool, sink or swim.' She looked at me challengingly.

'I'd rather swim,' I said with a sly smile.

'Good to hear it,' she said. 'I like your attitude.'

I HAD a bad feeling about Nora. She was the type who'd put cement boots on me, bundle me into the trunk of a Cadillac and throw me in the East River. Sink or swim, tell me about it.

She left me at my new cubicle to finish reading orientation stuff, learn the code names for all the projects. Every high-tech company gives their products code names; Trion's were types of storms—Tornado, Typhoon, Tsunami, and so on. Maestro was code-named Vortex. It was confusing, all the different names, and on top of it, I was trying to get the lie of the land for Wyatt.

Around noon, when I was starting to get really hungry, a stocky guy in his forties, greying black hair in a ponytail, wearing a vintage Hawaiian shirt and black, heavy-framed glasses, appeared at my cubicle. 'You must be the latest victim,' he said. 'The fresh meat hurled into the lion cage.'

'And you all seem so friendly,' I said. 'I'm Adam Cassidy.'

'I know. I'm Noah Mordden. Trion Distinguished Engineer. It's your first day, you don't know who to trust, who wants to play with you, and who wants you to fall flat on your face. Well, I'm here to answer all your questions. How would you like to grab some lunch in the cafeteria?'

Strange guy, but I was intrigued. As we walked to the elevator, he said, 'So, they gave you the job no one else wanted, huh?'

'That right?' Oh, great.

'Nora wanted to fill the slot internally, but no one wanted to work for her. Alana, the woman whose job you're filling, actually begged to get out from under her thumb, so they moved her somewhere else in-house. Word on the street is, Maestro's on the slide,' he muttered as he strode towards the elevator bank. 'They're always quick to pull the plug when something's failing. Catch a cold and they're measuring you for a coffin.'

I nodded. 'The product's redundant.'

'A piece of crap. Doomed. Trion's also coming out with an all-in-one cellphone that has the exact same text-messaging packet, so what's the point? Plus, Nora's a bitch on wheels. If you didn't figure that out within ten seconds of meeting her, you're not as bright as your advance billing. But do not underestimate her: she's got a black belt in corporate politics.'

'Thank you.'

'Goddard's into classic American cars, so she's into them too. Owns a couple to show Jock Goddard that she's cut from the same cloth.'

The cafeteria was buzzing with the electricity of hundreds, maybe thousands, of Trion employees. It was like a food court in a fancy shopping mall—a sushi bar, a gourmet pizza counter, Chinese food, steaks and burgers, an amazing salad bar, even a vegetarian/vegan counter.

'"Give the people bread and circuses",' Noah said. 'Juvenal. Keep the peasants well fed and they won't notice their enslavement.'

'I guess,' I said, looking around. 'So much for frugality, huh?'

'Last year the CFO, a man named Paul Camilletti, tried to eliminate the weekly beer bashes, but someone circulated an email that set out a business case for keeping them. Beer costs X per year, whereas it costs Y to hire and train new employees, so given the morale-boosting and employee-retaining benefits, costs, the return on investment, ya de ya de ya, you get it. Camilletti gave in. Still, his frugality campaign rules the day.'

'Same way at Wyatt,' I said.

'Trion doesn't have a corporate jet—but, let's be clear, Goddard's wife bought one for him for his birthday, so we don't have to feel sorry for him.'

I got a burger and Diet Pepsi and he got some kind of Asian stir-fry and a Dr Pepper. It was ridiculously cheap. We looked around the room, but Mordden didn't find anyone he wanted to sit with, so we sat at a table by ourselves.

'Goddard's not too in-your-face about his money,' Noah went on. 'He drives his own car—though granted he has a dozen or so, all antiques he's restored himself. Also, he gives his top fifty execs the luxury car of their choice, and they all make obscene amounts of money.'

'What about you Distinguished Engineers?'

'Oh, I've made an obscene amount of money here myself.' He sighed. 'When I struck gold, a few years after I started here, I quit and sailed around the world, packing only my clothes and several heavy suitcases containing the greatest hits of Western literature. However, once I'd read everything, I realised that I'm constitutionally unable to not work, and I returned to Trion. Have you read Étienne de la Boétie's *Discourse on Voluntary Servitude*?'

'Man, I slept through that class in college.'

He smiled. 'The only power tyrants have is that relinquished by their victims.'

'That and the power to hand out free Pepsis,' I said, tipping my can towards him. 'So you're an engineer.'

He gave a grimace. 'Not just any engineer, take note, but, as I said, a Distinguished Engineer. That means I have a low employee number and I can pretty much do whatever I want. If that means being a thorn in toxic Nora's side, so be it. Now, as for the cast of characters on the marketing side of your business unit . . . Let's see, Tom Lundgren, your exalted VP, lives for the church, his family and golf. Then there's Phil Bohjalian, old as Methuselah and just about as technologically up-to-date, who started when computers were as big as houses and ran on IBM punch cards. His days are surely numbered. And—lo and behold, it's Elvis himself, venturing into our midst!'

I turned. Standing by the salad bar was a white-haired guy with a heavily lined face, heavy white eyebrows and a sort of pixieish expression. He was wearing a black mock turtleneck. You could sense the energy in the room change, rippling around him in waves, as people turned to look, whispered.

Augustine Goddard, Trion's founder and CEO, in the flesh.

He looked older than in the pictures I'd seen. Next to him was a much younger and taller guy, lean and really fit, Italian-looking, movie-star handsome but with deeply pitted cheeks. Except for the bad skin, he reminded me of Al Pacino in the first couple of *Godfather* movies.

'That Camilletti?' I asked.

'Cutthroat Camilletti,' Mordden said, digging into his stir-fry with chopsticks. 'Our chief financial officer. The tsar of frugality. They're together a lot, those two.' He spoke through a mouthful of food. 'You see his face, those *acne vulgaris* scars? Rumour has it they say "eat shit and die" in Braille. Anyway, Goddard considers Camilletti to be the man who's going to launch Trion stock back into the stratosphere. Some say Camilletti is Jock Goddard's id, the bad Jock. His Iago. I say he's the bad cop who lets Jock be the good cop.'

I finished my burger.

'It's very Camilletti to get lunch in the employee dining room,' Mordden continued, 'to demonstrate to the masses his commitment to slashing costs. No executive dining room at Trion. No personal executive chef. Oh no. Break bread with the peasants.' He took a swallow of Dr Pepper. 'Where were we in my little Who's Who? Ah, yes. There's Chad Pierson, Nora's golden-haired protégé and professional suck-up. No doubt he'll consider you a threat to be eliminated. And there's Audrey Bethune, the only black woman in . . .'

Noah fell silent suddenly and I saw a handsome blond guy, around my age, gliding up to our table, a shark through water. Button-down blue shirt, preppy-looking, a jock. One of those white-blond guys you see in magazines, consorting with other specimens of the master race at a cocktail party on the lawn of their baronial estate.

Noah Mordden stood up. 'Pardon me,' he said uncomfortably. 'I have a one-on-one.' He left his dishes spread out on the table and bolted just as the white-blond guy got there, hand outstretched.

'Hey, man, how you doing?' the guy said. 'Chad Pierson.'

I went to shake his hand, but he did one of those too-cool-to-shake-hands-the-normal-way hand-slide things. 'I've heard so much about you!'

'All bullshit,' I said. 'Marketing, you know.'

He laughed conspiratorially. 'Nah, you're supposed to be the *man*. I'm hangin' with you, learn a trick or two.'

'I'm going to need all the help I can get. They tell me it's sink or swim around here, and it definitely looks like the deep end.'

'Mordden give you his cynical egghead bit? I wouldn't pay much attention.'

I realised that I'd just sat with the unpopular kid on the first day of school, but it made me want to defend Mordden. 'I like him,' I said.

'He's an engineer. They're all weird. So, bud, you're going to be at the two o'clock meeting, right?'

'Wouldn't miss it.'

'Cool. Nice having you on the team. We're gonna do some damage, you and me.' He gave me a big smile.

CHAD PIERSON was standing at a whiteboard, writing up a meeting agenda with red and blue markers, when I walked into Corvette later. It was a conference room like every other I'd ever seen—big table, Polycom speakerphone console, a basket of fruit and an ice bucket of soft drinks.

Chad gave me a quick wink as I sat down on one of the long sides of the table. There were already a couple of other people there. Nora Sommers was at the head of the table, reading through a file.

Next to me sat a grey-haired guy in a blue Trion polo shirt tapping away on a Maestro. He was thin with skinny arms and knobbly elbows poking out of his short-sleeved shirt. This had to be Phil Bohjalian, the old-timer. He kept sneaking nervous, furtive glances at me through his bifocals.

Noah Mordden slipped quietly into the room and opened his notebook computer at the far end of the conference table. More people filed in, laughing and talking. There were maybe a dozen people now.

Nora Sommers stood up, walked over to the whiteboard. 'Let's get started. I'd like to introduce our newest team member. Adam Cassidy. Welcome.'

All heads turned. I smiled modestly, ducked my head.

'We were very fortunate in being able to steal Adam away from Wyatt, where he was one of the key players on Lucid. We're hoping he'll apply some of his magic to Maestro.' She smiled beatifically.

Chad looked from side to side as if he were sharing a secret. 'This boy's a genius. Everything you've heard is true.' He turned to me and shook my hand.

Nora went on, 'As we all know far too well, we're getting some serious pushback on Maestro. The knives are out throughout Trion, and I don't have to name names.' There was some low chortling. 'We have a deadline looming—a presentation before Mr Goddard himself, where we will make the case for maintaining the Maestro. Our enemies want to put us in the electric chair; we're pleading for a stay of execution. Are we clear about that?' She looked around menacingly, saw obedient nods. Then she turned to the whiteboard and slashed through the first item in the agenda with a purple marker. Whipping back round, she handed a sheaf of stapled papers to Chad, who began passing them round. They looked like some kind of product definition or protocol, but the name of the product had been removed.

'Now,' she said, 'I'd like us to do an exercise—a demonstration, if you will. If any of you recognise this product protocol, keep it to yourselves. As we work to refresh the Maestro, I want us all to think outside the box for a moment, and I'd like to ask our newest star to look this over and give us his thoughts.'

I touched my chest and said stupidly, 'Me?'

She smiled. 'You. Tell us what you think, Adam. Do we go for it, or not?'

My stomach dropped. My heart started thudding. I tried to control my breathing, but I could feel my face flushing as I thumbed through it. I didn't know what the hell it was for. In the silence I could hear little nervous noises—Nora clicking the top of the marker off and on, someone playing with the little plastic flex-straw on his apple juice box. I nodded slowly, as I scanned it, trying not to look like a deer caught in headlights.

'Well, Adam? Go or no-go?'

I nodded again. 'I like it,' I said. 'It's clever.'

'Hmm,' she said. There was some low chuckling. Something was up. Wrong answer, I guessed, but I could hardly change it now.

'I've always believed in being bold,' I said. 'I'm intrigued. I like the form factor, the handwriting recognition specs . . . Given the usage model, the market opportunity, I'd certainly pursue this further.'

'Aha,' she said. One side of her mouth turned up in an evil smile. 'And to think the guys at Cupertino didn't even need Adam's wisdom to greenlight this stink bomb. Adam, these are the specs for the Apple Newton. Cost Cupertino over five hundred million dollars to develop, and *then*, when it came out, they lost sixty million bucks a *year* on it.'

More chuckles. People were looking away from me. Chad was biting the inside of his cheek, looking grave. Mordden seemed to be in another world. I wanted to rip Nora Sommers's face off, but I did the good-loser thing.

Nora looked round the table. 'There's a lesson here. You've always got to look beyond the hype, get under the hood. And, believe me, when we present to Jock Goddard in two weeks, he's going to be getting under the hood.'

Polite smiles all round: everyone knew Goddard was a car nut.

'All right,' she said. 'I think I've made my point. Let's move on.'

Yeah, I thought. Let's move on. Welcome to Trion. You've made your point. I felt a hollowness in the pit of my stomach.

What the hell had I gotten myself into?

I ARRIVED at Dad's apartment right after I finished my first day at Trion. I parked the Audi down the block, because I didn't want to get grief from Dad about it. Even if I told him I'd gotten a big raise or something, he'd find a way to put some nasty spin on it.

I got there just in time to see Maureen putting her suitcase in the trunk of a cab. I handed her a final cheque, thanked her profusely for her loyal service, and even tried to give her a ceremonial peck on the cheek but she turned away and got in the cab, slamming the door. The cab took off.

'When's this new guy getting here?' Dad said when I walked in. 'He's already late, isn't he?'

'Not yet.' Maureen had refused to spend a minute showing him the ropes, so unfortunately there'd be no overlap.

'What're you all dressed up for? You look like an undertaker.'

'I told you, I started a new job today.'

He shook his head in disgust. 'You got fired, didn't you?'

'From Wyatt? No, I left.'

'You tried to coast like you always do, and they fired you. I know how these things work. They can smell a loser a mile off.' He took a couple of heavy breaths. 'Your mother always spoiled you. Like hockey—you coulda gone pro if you applied yourself.'

'I wasn't that good, Dad.'

'Easy to say that, isn't it? Makes it easier if you just say that. I put you through that high-priced college just so you could spend all your time partying.' He was only partly right, of course: I did work-study to put myself through college. But he remembered what he wanted to remember.

Fortunately the doorbell rang, and I almost ran to answer it.

'Who's that?' Dad shouted hoarsely.

'It's Antwoine,' I said.

'*Antwoine?* You hired some French faggot?' But Dad had already turned to see Antwoine standing at the front door, and his mouth fell open in horror.

'How's it going?' Antwoine said, giving me a bone-crushing handshake. 'So this must be the famous Francis Cassidy,' he said, approaching the Barcalounger. 'I'm Antwoine Leonard. Pleasure to meet you, sir.' He spoke in a deep, pleasant baritone and was dressed in pale blue hospital scrubs.

Dad kept staring. Finally he said, 'Adam, I wanna talk to you.'

'Sure, Dad.'

'No—you tell *An-twoine*, or whatever the hell his name is, to get outta here, let you and me talk.'

Antwoine looked at me, puzzled, wondering what he should do.

'Why don't you bring your stuff to your room?' I said to him. 'It's the second door on the right. You can start unpacking.'

He carried two nylon duffle bags down the hall. Dad didn't even wait for him to get out of the room before he said, 'Number one, I don't want a *man* taking care of me, you understand? Number two, I don't want a *black* man here. They're unreliable. What were you thinking? You were gonna leave me alone with Leroy? I mean, look at your *homeboy* here, the tattoos, the braids. I don't want that in my house.' He was puffing harder than ever.

I kept my voice down. 'Dad, we don't really have a choice here, because the agencies won't even *deal* with us any more. I can't stay with you, because I've got a day job, remember? And you haven't even given the guy a chance.'

Antwoine came back down the hall towards us. He approached my father, and he spoke in a soft, gentle voice. 'Mr Cassidy, you want me to leave, I'll leave. I don't got no problem with that. As long as my parole officer knows I made a serious attempt to get a job, I'm cool.'

Dad stared at Antwoine. 'You're a *convict*?'

'*Ex*-con.'

He turned his glare on me. 'The *hell* you trying to do to me?' he said. 'You trying to kill me before the disease does? I can't hardly move, and you put me alone with a fucking *convict*?'

Antwoine didn't even seem to be annoyed. 'You ain't got nothing worth stealing, even if I wanted to,' he said calmly. 'If I wanted to pull off some kinda scam, I wouldn't take a job *here*.'

'You hear *that*?' Dad puffed, enraged. 'You hear *that*?'

'Plus, if I'm going to stay, we gotta come to agreement on a couple of things, you and me.' Antwoine sniffed the air. 'I can smell the smokes, and you're going to have to cut that out right now.' He reached out one huge hand and tapped the arm of the Barcalounger. A compartment popped open, which I'd never seen before, and a red-and-white pack of Marlboros popped up like a jack-in-the-box. 'Thought so. That's where my dad hid his.'

'Hey!' Dad yelled. 'I don't believe this!'

'And you're gonna start a workout routine. Your muscles are wasting away. Your problem isn't your lungs, it's your muscles.'

'Are you out of your mind?' Dad said.

'You gotta exercise. Can't do anything about the lungs, those are gone, but the muscles we can do something about. We're gonna start with some leg lifts in your chair. My old man had the emphysema, and me and my brother—'

'You tell this big . . . tattooed nigger,' Dad said between puffs, 'to get his stuff . . . out of that room . . . and get the hell out of my house!'

I almost lost it. For months and months I'd been busting my ass trying to find someone who'd put up with the old guy, and here he was, summarily dismissing the latest who, granted, may not have been an ideal candidate, but was the only one we had. I wanted to let fly, but I couldn't. I couldn't scream at my father, this pathetic dying old man. So I held it in.

Before I could say anything, Antwoine turned to me. 'I believe your son hired me, so he's the only one who can fire me.'

I shook my head. 'No such luck, Antwoine. You're not getting out of here—not so easy. Why don't you get started?'

I NEEDED to blow off steam. So I showed up at Alley Cat, knowing that Seth would be working there that night.

'Hey!' he said, delighted to see me. 'Your first day at the new place, huh?'

'Yeah. I don't want to talk about it.'

'That bad, huh? Wow.' He poured me a Scotch. 'Love the haircut, dude. Don't tell me you got drunk and woke up with that haircut.'

I ignored him. The Scotch went straight to my head. It felt great.

'How bad could it be, bud? They showed you where the bathroom is, right?'

I told him about Nora Sommers and her cute little Apple Newton trick.

'What a bitch, huh? What'd she come down on you so hard for? What'd she expect—you're new, you don't know anything, right?'

I shook my head. 'No, she—' Suddenly I realised that I'd left out a key part of the story, the part about my allegedly being a superstar at Wyatt Telecom. The anecdote only made sense if you knew the dragon lady was trying to take me down a peg. Fortunately someone caught Seth's eye, signalled to him.

'Sorry, man, it's half-price hamburger night,' he announced to me as he went to fetch the guy a couple of beers.

By the time he came back, he'd forgotten what we were talking about. Seth, like most guys, tends to focus more on his own stuff than on anyone else's.

'God, women love bartenders,' he said. 'Why is that?'

'I don't know, Seth. Maybe it's you.' I tipped my empty glass towards him.

'No doubt. No doubt.' He glugged another few ounces of Scotch in there, refreshed the ice. In a low, confiding voice, barely audible over the din of whooping voices and the blaring ball game on the TV, he said, 'So, you think you've got it bad at work. Shapiro, my boss at the law firm, gives me hell if I'm ten minutes late. He doesn't know how to use the copier, or how to send a fax. He'd be sunk without me. Did I tell you about my latest scam?'

'Tell me.'

'Get this—*jingles*!' He pointed up at the TV, some cheesy ad for a mattress company with a stupid song they were always playing. 'I met this guy who works for an ad agency, he told me all about it. Told me he could get me an audition with one of those jingle companies.'

'You can't even read music, Seth.'

'Neither can Stevie Wonder. I mean, how long does it take to learn a thirty-second piece of music? I just got to put a reel together, a CD, and pretty soon I'll be on the A list. No work, mucho bucks!'

'Sounds great,' I said.

I took a long swig of the Scotch as he went to serve someone, enjoyed the burn at the back of my throat. Now it was starting to kick in and I felt a little unsteady on the bar stool. Nora Sommers and Chad Pierson and all the others had begun to recede, to take on a harmless, cartoon-character aura. Everyone felt a little out of their element on the first day in a new job. I was *good*, I had to keep that in mind. If I weren't, Wyatt would never have chosen me for his mission. He'd have just tossed me into the legal system to fend for myself.

I began to feel a pleasant, alcohol-fuelled surge of confidence bordering on megalomania. As if I'd been parachuted into Nazi Germany with little more than K rations and a short-wave radio, and the success of the Allies, nothing less than the fate of Western civilisation, was riding entirely on me.

Seth returned and was soon reminding me of some awful trick we'd played on a preppy kid we'd both hated at school. The story struck me as hilarious, and I was laughing so hard I lost my balance and sprawled onto the floor.

Someone grabbed me by the shoulder, someone else by the elbow. Seth and a guy were helping me out of the bar. Everyone seemed to be watching me.

'Sorry, man,' I said, feeling a wave of embarrassment wash over me. 'Thanks. My car's right here.'

'You're not driving, bud.'

'It's right *here*,' I insisted feebly.

'That's not your car. That's an Audi or something.'

'It's mine,' I said with a vigorous nod. 'Audi—A6, I think. New car.'

'Man, this new job, they paying you a lot more?'

'Yeah, I said, then added, my words slurred, 'Not that much more.'

He whistled for a cab, and he and the other guy hustled me into it. 'You want a coffee for the ride home, sober you up a little?'

'Nah,' I said. 'I got to get to sleep. Work tomorrow.'

Seth laughed. 'I don't envy you, man,' he said.

IN THE MIDDLE of the night my cellphone rang, earsplittingly loud. Only it wasn't the middle of the night. I could see a shaft of light behind the shades. I grabbed the phone. 'Yeah?'

'You left the Audi in a tow zone.' Arnold Meacham, I realised at once. Wyatt's security Nazi. 'It's not *your* car, it's leased by Wyatt Telecom, and the least you can do is take decent care of it—not leave it lying around.'

It came back to me: last night, getting wasted at Alley Cat, somehow getting home, forgetting to set the alarm . . . Trion!

I jolted upright. My head throbbed, felt enormous.

'We set out the rules quite clearly,' Meacham said. 'No more carousing. No partying. This is not an auspicious start.'

'It was real—real busy yesterday. My first day, and my father—'

'I don't give a shit. What have you turned up on the skunkworks?'

'Skunkworks?' I flung my legs round to the floor, sat on the edge of the bed, massaged my temples with my free hand. 'It's too early,' I said. 'Too soon, I mean.' Slowly my brain was starting to function. 'I was escorted everywhere yesterday. You don't want me blowing this assignment on the first day.'

Meacham was silent for a few seconds. 'Fair enough,' he said. 'But I want a report by close of business *today*, are we clear?'

BY LUNCHTIME I began to feel less like the walking wounded, and I decided to go up to the gym—the 'fitness centre', excuse me—to get in a quick workout. The fitness centre was on the roof of E Wing, with all sorts of cardio equipment, treadmills and elliptical trainers fitted with individual TV/video screens. I had finished with the machines and the weights and was changing when Chad Pierson sauntered into the locker room.

'There he is,' Chad said. 'How's it going, big guy?' He opened a locker near mine. 'Anything I can do to help?'

I thought for a moment. There's nothing people love to part with more than advice. 'Maybe a Nora tip or two?'

His eyes lit up. 'Aw, she does that to all the newbies. It's nothing personal, believe me—I got the same treatment when I started here. Just stay on your toes, and she'll move on. She likes you. She wouldn't have fought to get you on her team if she didn't.'

'OK.' I couldn't tell if he was holding out on me or not.

'I mean, if you wanna . . . like, this afternoon's meeting—Tom Lundgren's going to be there, reviewing the product specs, right? And we've been stuck in some dumbass debate for weeks over whether to add GoldDust functionality.' He rolled his eyes. 'Like, give me a break. Don't even get Nora started on that crap. Anyway, you don't have to agree with her that GoldDust is total bullshit and a huge waste of money. The important thing is to just have an opinion on it. She likes informed debate.'

Wyatt's engineers had ridiculed GoldDust, a low-power, short-range wireless transmission technology that was supposed to let you connect your Palm or BlackBerry or Lucid to any phone, laptop or printer within twenty feet. It was going to free us all from wires and cables. What the industry geeks who invented it didn't figure on was the explosion in Wi-Fi—802.11 wireless.

'Yeah, there was always someone at Wyatt trying to push that on us.'

He shook his head. 'Engineers want to pack everything into everything, no matter what it costs. Anyway, that'll come up at the meeting—I'll bet you can really whale on it. Earn a couple of brownie points with the boss.'

Chad was a snake and I knew I could never trust him, but he was obviously trying to establish an alliance with me, probably on the theory that it was better for him to be aligned with the hot new talent, be my buddy, than to appear to be threatened by me, which of course he was.

'All right, man, thanks,' I said.

'Least I can do.'

By the time I got back to my cube there was half an hour before the meeting, so I got on the Internet and did some research on GoldDust so I could sound like I knew what I was talking about. I was whipping through dozens of websites when I noticed someone standing over my shoulder.

It was Phil Bohjalian. 'Eager beaver, huh?' he said. He introduced himself. 'Only your second day, and look at you.' He shook his head in wonderment. 'Don't work too hard; you'll make us all look bad.' He made a sort of chortle, and exited stage left.

THE MAESTRO marketing group met after lunch again in Corvette, everyone sitting pretty much in the same place. But this time, just before Nora called the meeting to order, in walked Paul Camilletti, Trion's CFO, looking like a matinée idol, wearing a dark grey hound's-tooth jacket over a black mock turtleneck. He took a seat, and you could feel the entire room go still.

Even Nora looked a little rattled. 'Well,' she said, 'why don't we get started? I'm pleased to welcome Paul Camilletti, our chief financial officer . . .'

He ducked his head in acknowledgment.

'Who else is with us today? Who's teleconning in?'

A voice came over the intercom speaker: 'Ken Hsiao, Singapore.'

Then: 'Mike Matera, Brussels.'

'All right,' she said, 'so the gang's all here.' She looked excited, but it was hard to tell how much of that was a show she was putting on for Tom Lundgren and Paul Camilletti. 'This seems as good a time as any to take a look at forecasts, get a sense of where we stand. None of us wants to hear that old cliché, "dying brand", am I right? I hope we're all on board on that.'

'Nora, this is Ken in Singapore. Uh, we're feeling some pressure here, I have to say, from Palm and Sony and BlackBerry. Advance orders are looking a little soft.'

'Thank you, Ken,' she said hastily, cutting him off. 'Kimberly?'

Kimberly Ziegler, wan and nervous-looking with a head of wild curls, looked up. 'My take is quite different from Ken's. I'm seeing product differentiation that's benefiting us. We've got a better price point than either BlackBerry or Sony. It's true there's a little wear and tear on the brand, but the upgrade in the processor and the flash memory are really going to add value. So I think we're hanging in there.'

'Excellent,' Nora beamed. 'Good to hear. I'd also be quite interested to hear whatever feedback has come in on GoldDust—'

'GoldDust?' I said with a knowing smirk. 'It's the Betamax of wireless. It's up there with New Coke, XFL football and the Yugo.'

There were appreciative titters.

I went on, 'The compatibility problems are massive—no standardised code. And the transfer rate is, what, less than one megabit per second? Pathetic. Less than a tenth of Wi-Fi. This is horse-and-buggy stuff. And let's not even talk about how easy it is to intercept—no security whatsoever.'

'Right on,' someone said in a low voice, though I didn't catch who it was. Mordden was beaming. Phil Bohjalian was watching me through narrowed eyes, his expression unreadable. Then I looked over and saw Nora. Her face was flushing, a wave of red rising from her neck to her wide-set eyes.

'Are you finished?' she snapped.

I felt queasy. This was not the reaction I'd expected. 'Sure,' I said warily.

An Indian-looking guy sitting across from me said, 'Why are we revisiting this? I thought you made a final decision on this last week, Nora. You seemed to feel very strongly that the added functionality was worth the cost.'

Chad, who'd been studying the table, said, 'Hey, come on, guys, give the newbie a break. He doesn't even know where the cappuccino machine is yet.'

'I think we don't need to waste any more time here,' said Nora. 'The matter's decided. We're adding GoldDust.' She gave me a look of darkest fury.

When the meeting ended twenty minutes later, and people began filing out of the room, glancing at me curiously, Mordden gave my shoulder a quick, furtive pat, which should have told me everything. I'd fucked up, big time.

As I walked out, Chad came up to me and spoke in a low voice. 'Sounds like she didn't take it well,' he said, 'but that was really valuable input, big guy.'

Yeah, right.

MAYBE FIFTEEN minutes after the meeting broke up, Mordden stopped by my cubicle. 'Well, I'm impressed,' he said. 'Taking on your manager, the dread Nora, on her pet project . . .' He shook his head. 'Talk about creative tension. But you should be aware that Nora does not forget slights. You should be on the alert for subtle signs of her displeasure: empty boxes stacked next to your cubicle; being unable to log on to your computer; HR demanding your badge back. Fear not, however, Trion outplacement services are provided *gratis*.'

'I see. Thanks.'

I noticed that I had a voicemail. When Mordden left, I picked up the phone. It was a message from Nora, ordering me to come to her office at once.

She was tapping away at her keyboard when I got there. She gave a quick, sidelong, lizardlike glance and went back to her computer, ignoring me for a good two minutes. Her face had started flushing again.

Finally she wheeled round in her chair, her eyes glistening, but not with sadness. Something almost feral.

'Listen, Nora,' I said gently. 'I want to apologise for my—'

'I suggest *you* listen, Adam. You've done quite enough talking today.'

'I was an idiot. I should have kept my mouth—'

'And to make such a remark in the presence of Camilletti, Mister Profit Margin . . . I've got some serious damage control to do, thanks to you.'

'If I'd known—'

'Don't even go there. Phil Bohjalian told me he passed by your cube and saw you feverishly doing research on GoldDust before the meeting, before your "casual" dismissal of this vital technology. You may think you're hot stuff because of your track record at Wyatt, Mr Cassidy, but I wouldn't get too comfortable here at Trion. If you don't get on the bus, you're going to get run over. And mark my words, I'm going to be behind the wheel.'

I stood there for a few seconds while she bore down on me with those predator eyes. I looked down at the floor. 'I really owe you a huge apology. Obviously if anyone had told me the decision had been made, I certainly would have kept my big mouth shut. I guess I was going on the assumption that folks here at Trion had heard about Sony, that's all.'

'Sony?' she said. 'What do you mean, "heard about Sony"?'

Wyatt's competitive-intelligence people had sold him this titbit, which he'd given me to use at a strategic moment. I figured that this counted as a strategic moment. 'Just that they're scrapping their plans to incorporate GoldDust in all their new handhelds.'

'Why?' she asked suspiciously.

'The latest release of Microsoft Office isn't going to support it. Sony figures if they incorporate GoldDust, they lose out on millions of dollars of enterprise sales, so they're going with BlackHawk, the local-wireless protocol that Office *will* support.'

'You're sure about this? Your sources are completely reliable?'

'I'd stake my life on it.'

'You'd stake your career on it as well?' Her eyes drilled into me.

'I think I just did.'

'Very interesting,' she said. 'Thank you, Adam.'

I STAYED late that evening. By eight the place was empty, so I sat at my cubicle and started poking around the Trion internal website.

If Wyatt wanted to know about a 'skunkworks' that had been started in the last two years, I figured I should try to find out who Trion had *hired* in the last two years. Luckily for my purposes, Trion had been in a slow period, so there weren't that many new hires, and I could identify them by employee number—a lower number meant you were hired earlier. I downloaded all the names that came up, and their bios, to a CD. So that was a start, at least.

Trion had its own instant-messaging service called InstaMail, which told you when colleagues were online. I noticed that Nora Sommers was logged in but she wasn't here, which meant she was working from home. That meant that I could break into her office without the risk of her showing up.

The thought of doing it made my guts clench, but I knew I had no choice. Arnold Meacham wanted tangible results, like yesterday. Nora Sommers was on several Trion new-product marketing committees. Maybe she'd have information on any new technology that Trion was secretly developing.

The plaque on the door said N. SOMMERS. I summoned up the nerve to try the doorknob. It was locked. That didn't surprise me. I could see through the plate glass into her darkened ten-by-ten office. It was fanatically neat.

I knew there had to be a key somewhere in her administrative assistant's cluttered desk. I looked around, saw no one, and began to pull open the desk drawers. After a few minutes I found the key ring hidden inside a paperclip holder. I took a deep breath, took the key ring—it must have had twenty keys on it—and began trying the keys, one by one. The sixth opened Nora's door.

I flipped on the lights, sat down at Nora's desk, and powered up her computer. In case anyone happened to come by unexpectedly, I was prepared. Arnold Meacham had pumped me full of strategies—go on the offensive, ask *them* questions—but for now I focused on the task at hand.

Unfortunately it wasn't so easy. USER NAME/PASSWORD blinked on the screen. I typed in NSommers; that was standard. Then I typed NSommers in the password space. Seventy per cent of people, I'd been taught, make their password the same as their user name.

But not Nora.

I tried just Sommers; I tried her birth date, the first and last seven digits of her Social Security number, a range of combinations. DENIED. After the tenth try, I stopped. Each attempt was logged, I had to assume. This was not good.

But there were other ways to crack the password. Meacham had supplied me with a device called a 'keystroke logger', a tiny cable connector that got plugged in between a computer keyboard and the PC. You'd never notice it. It had a chip embedded in it that recorded and stored up to 2 million keystrokes. You just came back for it later and you had a record of everything the person had typed in. In about ten seconds, I had unplugged Nora's keyboard, attached it to the little KeyGhost thing, and then plugged that into her computer. She'd never see it, and in a couple of days I'd come back and get it.

But I wasn't going to leave her office empty-handed. There were the filing cabinets to go through. Even in a high-tech place like Trion, important files almost always exist on paper. I quickly located the filing-cabinet key on the admin's key ring and unlocked the drawers. I found a lot of HR files on Nora's subordinates, which might have made for interesting reading if I'd had the time. I found my file, which was thin and contained nothing of interest.

Then I came across a few print-outs of emails Nora had received from someone high up at Trion. From what I could tell, when Alana Jennings, who'd had my job before me, had abruptly been transferred somewhere else inside the company, Nora had escalated a complaint all the way up to the senior vice-president level:

SUBJ: Re: Reassignment of Alana Jennings
FROM: GAllred
TO: NSommers

Nora,

I am in receipt of your emails protesting the transfer of ALANA JENNINGS to another division of the company. I understand your upset, since Alana is a valued player on your team, but I regret that your objections have been overruled on the highest authority. Alana's skill set is urgently needed in Project AURORA and, since AURORA is a classified R&D project of the utmost sensitivity, I would respectfully ask you not to pursue the matter further.

Let me assure you that you will not lose your head count. I am happy to tell you that you are, in this instance, permitted to disregard the general companywide ban on hiring from outside. This slot is therefore designated a 'silver bullet' position, enabling you to hire from outside Trion. I trust and hope this will allay your concerns about filling Alana's position with someone appropriately qualified.

Please let me know if I can do anything further to help.

Best,

Greg Allred, Senior VP, Advanced Research Business Unit

Whoa. Suddenly things were starting to make a little sense. I'd been hired to replace this Alana woman, who'd been moved into a top-secret undertaking called Project AURORA. I'd found the skunkworks.

It didn't seem a good idea to take the email out to the copy machine, so I got a yellow legal pad from a stack in Nora's supply closet and began taking notes.

I don't know how long I'd been sitting there on the carpeted floor of her office, writing, but suddenly I became aware of something in my peripheral vision. I glanced up, saw a security guard, a tall, beefy black man wearing a navy blazer, standing in the doorway watching me.

'I see what you got there,' the guard said. He wasn't looking at me; he was staring right at Nora's computer.

Despite all the time I'd spent mentally rehearsing what I'd say if I was caught, I went blank. I'm hosed, I thought.

Had he seen me install the KeyGhost? No, God, please, *no*. And then I was suddenly seized by another, equally sickening thought: Wouldn't he wonder why a man was in a woman's office, thumbing through her files?

I glanced over at the name plaque on the open door. It said N. SOMMERS— could be male *or* female. Then again, for all I knew he'd been patrolling the halls for ever, and he and Nora went way back. I ran through a series of explanations in my head: I was Nora Sommers's new assistant. I was her direct report—well, I *was*—working late at her behest.

The security guy took a few steps into the office, shook his head. 'Man, I thought I'd seen everything.'

'Look, we've got a project due tomorrow morning—' I started to say.

'You got a Bullitt there. That's a genuine Bullitt.'

Then I saw what he was staring at. It was a framed photograph, hanging on the wall, of a beautifully restored vintage car. 'Shit, that's a genuine 1968 Mustang GT three-ninety,' he breathed, like he'd just seen the face of God.

The relief seeped out of my pores. 'Yep,' I said proudly. 'Very good.'

'Man, look at that 'Stang. That pony a factory GT?'

What the hell did I know? I couldn't tell a Mustang from a Dodge Dart. 'Sure,' I said.

'Lotta fakes out there, you know. You ever check under the rear seat, see if it got those reinforcements for the dual exhaust?'

'Oh yeah,' I said airily. I stood up, extending my hand. 'Nick Sommers.'

His handshake was dry, his hand large, engulfing mine. 'Luther Stafford,' he said. 'I haven't seen you 'round here before.'

'Yeah, I'm never here at night. But this damned project—it's always "We need it at nine a.m., big rush".' I tried to sound casual. 'Glad to see I'm not the only one working late.'

But he wouldn't drop the car. He moved in closer. 'Got the rear spoiler and everything.' He shook his head. 'You restore it yourself?'

'Nah, I wish I had the time.'

He laughed, a low, rumbling laugh. 'I know what you mean.'

'Got it from a guy who'd been keeping it in his barn.'

'Three-twenty horsepower on that pony?'

Jesus, could we move off this topic? 'Truth is, Luther, I know nothing about Mustangs. I don't deserve to own one. My wife got it for me for my birthday. Course, it'll be *me* paying off the loan for the next seventy-five years.'

He chuckled a little more. 'I hear you. I've been there.' I noticed him looking down at the desk, and realised what he was looking at.

It was a big manila envelope with Nora's name on it in bold red capital letters. NORA SOMMERS. Trying to act casual, I slid the legal pad over the envelope with my left hand. Real cool, Adam. The yellow paper had a few notes on it in my handwriting, but nothing that would make any sense to anyone.

'Who's *Nora* Sommers?' he said.

'Ah, that's my wife.'

'Nick and Nora, huh?' he chortled.

'Yeah, we get that all the time.' I smiled broadly. 'It's why I married her. Well, better get back to the files or I'll be here all night. Nice to meet you, Luther.'

'Same here, Nick.'

By the time the security guy left I was so nervous I couldn't do more than finish copying the email, then turn off the light and relock Nora's office door. As I turned to return the key ring to the admin's cubicle, I noticed someone walking not too far away. Luther again?

But it wasn't Luther; it was a paunchy guy with black-rimmed glasses and a ponytail. Noah Mordden. Had he seen me locking up Nora's office, or maybe even *in* it? What was he *doing* here?

He didn't say anything to me. I wasn't even sure he noticed me at all. But I was the only other person around, and he wasn't blind. He turned into the next aisle down and left a folder in someone's cubicle. Quickly, I deposited the key ring where I'd found it, then kept moving.

I was halfway to the elevators when I heard, 'Cassidy.'

I turned back.

'And I thought only engineers were nocturnal creatures.'

'Just trying to get caught up,' I said lamely.

'*I* see,' Mordden said. The way he said it sent a chill up my spine. Then he asked, 'What are you caught up *in*?'

'I'm not sure I understand,' I said, my heart pounding.

'Try to remember that.'

'Come again?'

But Mordden was already on his way out, and he didn't answer.

Part Three
Plumbing

Plumbing: Tradecraft jargon for various support assets such as safe houses, dead drops, et al. of a clandestine intelligence agency.
—*The International Dictionary of Espionage*

By the time I got home I was a wreck. I wasn't cut out for this line of work. I wanted to go out and get smashed again, but I had to get some sleep. My apartment seemed even smaller and more squalid than ever. I was making a six-figure salary, so I should have been able to afford one of those apartments in the tall buildings on the wharf, but I didn't have the time to look for a new place.

I hit the light switch by the door and the room stayed dark. Damn. That meant the bulb in the big ugly lamp by the sofa, the main light source in the room, had burned out. I always kept the lamp switched on so I could turn it on and off at the door. Now I had to stumble through the dark apartment to the closet where I kept the spare bulbs. I felt around in the cardboard box for a new bulb, then navigated across the room to the sofa table, and replaced the old one. Still no light came on. I found the little switch on the lamp's base and turned it, and the room lit up.

I was halfway to the bathroom when the thought hit me: How did the lamp get switched off? I never turned it off there—never. Had someone been in the apartment? It was a creepy feeling, a flicker of paranoia. Someone *had* been here. How else could the lamp have been switched off at its base? I had no room-mates, no girlfriend, and no one else had the key.

Looking over at the phone directly beneath the lamp, I saw something else was off. The black phone cord lay on top of the phone's keypad, instead of coiled to one side of the phone the way it always was.

Someone had *definitely* been in here.

And then I realised the cassette that recorded incoming messages was gone. Someone had removed it. Someone, presumably, who wanted a copy of my phone messages. Or—the idea suddenly hit me—who wanted to make sure I hadn't used the answering machine to *record* any phone calls I'd received.

The question was, who? If it was Wyatt and Meacham's people, that was infuriating, totally outrageous. But what if it wasn't them? What if it was *Trion*? That was so scary I didn't even want to think about it. I remembered Mordden's blank-faced question: *What are you caught up in?*

NICK WYATT'S house was easily the biggest, fanciest, most outrageously high-end place in a town known for big, fancy, outrageously high-end estates. No doubt it was important to Wyatt to live in the house that everyone talked about, that *Architectural Digest* put on its cover. From time to time his PR guy put out stories about the estate, which was how I knew it had cost $50 million, that it was a replica of a fourteenth-century Japanese palace built in Osaka and shipped in pieces to the US. That it was surrounded by forty acres of Japanese gardens full of rare flowers, rock gardens, a waterfall and antique wooden bridges. The fake Zen serenity and simplicity clashed grotesquely with Wyatt's own totally un-Zen stridency, I thought as I drove up the endless stone driveway. I'd gotten the order to report for this meeting from Meacham by secure email—a message to my Hushmail account from 'Arthur', sent through the Finnish anonymiser. I was instructed to drive to a Denny's parking lot and wait for a dark blue Lincoln, which I then followed to Wyatt's house. I guess the point was to make sure *I* wasn't being followed there. They were being a little paranoid about it, I thought, but who was I to argue? After all, I was the guy in the hot seat.

As soon as I got out of the car, the Lincoln pulled away. A Filipino man answered the door, told me to take off my shoes. He led me down a long hallway towards an almost-empty room where I could see Wyatt seated at the head of a long, low, black lacquered dining table.

I suddenly heard a high-pitched alarm go off. I looked around in bewilderment, but before I could figure out what was going on I was grabbed by the Filipino while another guy, who appeared out of nowhere, patted me down.

What were they looking for, weapons? The Filipino guy found my iPod MP3 music player, yanked it out of my workbag. He looked at it, said something in whatever they speak in the Philippines, handed it to the other guy.

'This how you welcome all Mr Wyatt's guests?' I said. The houseman took the iPod and, entering the dining room, handed it to Wyatt, who was watching the action. Wyatt handed it right back to the Filipino without looking at it.

'Afraid I might be packing?' I asked.

Wyatt was wearing a black linen shirt that probably cost more than I made in a month. 'I'm not "afraid" of anything, Cassidy,' he said. 'I like everyone to play by the rules. If you're smart, everything will go fine. Don't even think about trying to take out an "insurance policy", because we're way ahead of you.'

'I don't follow.'

'If you plan to do something foolish like try to tape-record our meetings or phone calls, things will not go well for you,' he went on. 'You don't need insurance, Adam. *I'm* your insurance.'

A Japanese woman in a kimono appeared with a tray, and used silver tongs to hand him a rolled hot towel. He wiped his hands and handed it back to her.

'You're to initiate contact with us only in an emergency, except in response to a request from us. All other times you'll be contacted by secure, encrypted email. Now, may I see what you have?'

I gave him the CD of all recent Trion hires I'd downloaded from the website, and a couple of sheets of paper, covered with typed notes. After reading my notes for a few minutes, he picked up a small black phone on the table, which I hadn't noticed before, and said something in a low voice.

Finally he looked at me. 'Very interesting. You've done a good job,' he said. 'Are you comfortable at Trion in your new role?'

'I'm learning the ins and outs. My boss is a serious bitch—'

'Not your cover, your *real* job—the penetration.'

'Comfortable? No, not yet.'

'I assume I don't need to remind you of the consequences of failure.'

'I don't need to be reminded. Actually, I sort of like being at Trion. My team is making a presentation to Augustine Goddard in a couple of weeks.'

'Good old Jock Goddard, huh. Well, you'll see quickly that he's a sententious old gasbag. I think he actually believes all the "conscience of high tech" bullshit that you read in *Fortune*.'

I nodded; what was I supposed to say? I didn't know Goddard, so I couldn't agree or disagree, but Wyatt's envy was pretty transparent.

The phone rang, and he picked it up. 'Yes?' He listened for a minute. 'All right,' he said, then hung up. 'You hit something. Soon you'll be receiving a complete background on this Alana Jennings. She's your way in. I want the names of everyone connected in any way with AURORA.'

'All right,' I said, with just a little defiance creeping into my voice. 'But then you'll have what you need, right? And we'll be done.'

'Oh, no,' he said. He smiled, flashing his big white chompers. 'This is only the beginning. We've barely scratched the surface.'

I WAS constantly zonked. In addition to my normal workdays at Trion, I was spending long hours, late into the night, every night, doing Internet research or going over more competitive-intelligence files that Wyatt sent over, the ones that made me sound so smart. I was so busy trying to stay on top of things that I barely had time to skulk around and gather information on AURORA. I'd get an email from 'Arthur' every couple of nights asking me how things were going, what the hell was taking me so long.

Every once in a while I'd see Mordden, and he'd stop to chat. But he never mentioned that night when he did or didn't see me coming out of Nora's office.

I was hardly ever at home. Seth left a bunch of phone messages for me and after a week or so gave up. Most of my other friends had given up on me, too.

I'd try to squeeze in half an hour here or there to drop by Dad's apartment and check in on him, but whenever I showed up he was so pissed off he barely looked at me. A sort of truce seemed to have settled in between him and Antwoine. At least Antwoine wasn't threatening to quit. Yet.

One night I got back into Nora's office and removed the little keystroke logger thing, quickly and uneventfully. That tiny cable now stored thousands of Nora's keystrokes, including all her passwords, and it was just a matter of plugging the device into my computer and downloading text. But I didn't dare do it there at my cubicle. Instead, I logged on to the corporate website and in the search box typed in Alana Jennings's name. Her page came up immediately. There was no photo, but there was some basic information like her telephone extension, her job title (Marketing Director, Disruptive Technologies Research Unit) and her department number.

This little number, I knew, was extremely useful. All I had to do was punch it into the corporate data base and I had a list of everyone who worked directly with Alana Jennings—on AURORA. Forty-seven names.

I printed out the forty-seven web pages that showed basic information on those people and slipped the sheets into a folder in my workbag. That, I figured, should keep Wyatt's people happy for a while.

When I got home that night, around ten, intending to sit down at my computer and download all the keystrokes from Nora's computer, something else grabbed my attention. Sitting in the middle of my Formica-topped kitchen table was a thick, sealed manila envelope.

Once again, someone from Wyatt had slipped into my apartment. OK, maybe it was the safest way to get something to me without being observed. But it seemed almost like a threat.

The envelope contained a fat dossier on Alana Jennings, just as Wyatt had promised. I opened it and saw a whole bunch of photos of the woman. Suddenly I lost interest in Nora Sommers's keystrokes. This Alana Jennings was, not to put too fine a point on it, a real hottie.

After an hour, I knew more about her than I ever knew about any girlfriend. She had glossy black hair and blue eyes, and a slim body. Sometimes she wore heavy-framed black glasses, the kind that beautiful women wear to signal that they're smart and yet so beautiful that they can wear ugly glasses. And she wasn't just beautiful, she was rich—a double threat. She'd grown up in Connecticut, went to Yale, where she'd majored in English, specialising in American literature. She also took some classes in computer science and electrical engineering, and according to her college transcript got mostly As. OK, so she was smart, too; make that a triple threat. She had a trust fund of several million dollars, but her father, the CEO of a small manufacturing company, had a portfolio worth a whole lot more than that.

She was single, didn't seem to be seeing anyone regularly, and owned her own condo not far from Trion headquarters. She seemed to be a vegetarian, and she ate like a bird—lots of fruits, berries, nuts. She did get the occasional delivery from a liquor store in her neighbourhood, so she had at least one vice. Her house vodka seemed to be Grey Goose; her house gin was Tanqueray Malacca. She ate at Thai restaurants, and high-end places with names like Chakra, Buzz and Om. She went out to movies at least once a week, occasionally bought books online, mostly trendy serious fiction and books on Buddhism and Eastern wisdom. She'd also bought movies on DVD, including some forties noir classics like *Double Indemnity*. She seemed to have bought every record ever made by Ani DiFranco and Alanis Morissette.

I stored these facts away. I was beginning to get a picture of Alana Jennings. And I was beginning to come up with a plan.

SATURDAY AFTERNOON, dressed in tennis whites (which I'd bought that morning) and wearing a ridiculously expensive Italian diver's watch I'd recently splurged on, I arrived at the hoity-toity, exclusive tennis club where, according to the dossier, Alana Jennings played most Saturdays. I confirmed her court time by calling the day before, saying I was supposed to play her tomorrow and had forgotten the time, couldn't reach her, when was that again? Easy. She had a four thirty doubles game.

Half an hour before then, I had a meeting with the club's membership director to get a quick tour of the place. That had taken a little doing. I had got Arnold Meacham to ask Wyatt to arrange to have some rich club member—a friend of a friend of a friend—contact the club about sponsoring me. The guy's name obviously pulled some weight, because the membership director, Josh, seemed thrilled to take me around. He even gave me a guest pass for the day so I could check out the courts, maybe pick up a game.

I shook off Josh at the café by pretending to wave at someone I knew. He offered to arrange a game for me, but I told him I knew people here; I'd be fine.

A couple of minutes later I saw her. You couldn't miss this babe. Her blue eyes were dazzling. She came into the café with another woman around her age, and both of them ordered San Pellegrinos. I found a table close to hers, but not too close, so I could observe without being noticed.

And then her cellphone rang. 'This is Alana.' She had a velvety-smooth voice, cultured without being too affected.

'You did?' she said. 'Well, it sounds like you've solved it.'

My ears pricked up.

'Keith, you've just slashed the time in half; that's *incredible.*'

She was definitely talking business. I moved a little closer so I could hear more clearly over the clinking of dishes and the *thop thop* of tennis balls. I heard her say in a hushed voice: 'Well, thanks for letting me know—great stuff.' A little beep tone, and she ended the call. 'Work,' she said apologetically to the other woman. 'Sorry, I'm on call round the clock. There's Drew!'

A tall guy came up to her—early thirties, bronzed, the broad and flat body of a rower—and gave her a kiss on the cheek. 'Hey, babe,' he said.

Great, I thought. So Wyatt's goons didn't pick up on the fact that she was seeing someone after all.

'Hey, Drew,' she said. 'Where's George?'

'He didn't call you? He forgot he's got his daughter for the weekend.'

'So we don't have a fourth?' the other woman said.

'We can pick someone up,' said Drew.

A light bulb went on over my head. Jettisoning my carefully worked-out plan of anonymous observation, I made a bold, split-second decision, stood up and said, 'Excuse me. You guys need a fourth?'

I INTRODUCED myself, told them I was checking the place out, didn't mention Trion. They seemed relieved I was there. I think they assumed from my titanium pro racket that I was good, though I told them I was just OK, that I hadn't played in a long time. Basically true.

We had one of the outdoor courts. The teams were Alana and Drew versus me and the other woman, whose name was Jody. Jody and Alana were about evenly matched, but Alana was by far the more graceful player.

Unfortunately, I'd underestimated Pretty Boy, who was playing like he was at Wimbledon. I started out pretty rusty, and double-faulted my first serve, to Jody's visible annoyance. Soon, though, my game came back, and the more it returned the more aggressive he got, until it was ridiculous. He started poaching at the net, crossing over the court to get shots that were meant for Alana, really hogging the ball. Then he started serving right at me, hitting them really hard. Though his serves were viciously fast, he didn't have much control, and so he and Alana started losing.

He came up to the net and shook my hand at the end. 'You're a good player,' he said in this fake-chummy way.

'You too,' I said.

He shrugged. 'I had to cover a lot of court.'

Alana heard that, and her blue eyes flashed with annoyance. She turned to me. 'Do you have time for a drink?'

It was just Alana and me, on the 'porch', as they called the wooden deck overlooking the courts. Jody had excused herself, saying that she had to get going. Then Drew saw what was happening and he excused himself too.

The waitress came round, and Alana told me to go first; she hadn't decided what she wanted. I asked for a Tanqueray Malacca G & T.

Alana gave me a startled glance, just a split second, before she regained her composure. 'I'll second that,' she said.

We talked for a while, about the club, the members ('snotty', she said), the courts ('best around by *far*'), but she didn't mention Trion, so neither did I. I wasn't sure how I'd smooth over the bizarre coincidence that we both worked there, and hey, you used to have my very exact job! But the gin went to my head pretty quickly, it was a beautiful sunny day, and the conversation really flowed. I still couldn't believe I'd vaulted myself right into her orbit.

'I'm sorry about Drew being so out of control,' she said. 'You were a threat. Must be a male thing. Combat with rackets.'

I smiled. 'It's like that Ani DiFranco line, you know? "'Cause every tool is a weapon if you hold it right."'

Her eyes lit up. 'Exactly! Are you into Ani? Not many men are.'

'I'm a sensitive guy, I guess,' I said, deadpan.

'I *guess*. We should go out sometime,' she said.

Was I hearing right? Had she just asked *me* out?

'Good idea,' I said. 'So, do you like Thai food?'

I GOT to my dad's apartment so exhilarated from my mini-date with Alana Jennings that I felt like I was wearing a suit of armour. Nothing he did or said could get to me now.

I found him in the first-floor bathroom, which was filled with steam billowing out of a vaporiser. He was lying face down on a bench, a bunch of pillows under his head and chest. Antwoine, his pale blue scrubs soaking wet, was thumping on Dad's naked back with his huge hands.

He looked up when I opened the door. 'Yo, Adam.'

'This son of a bitch is trying to kill me,' Dad screeched.

'This is how you loosen the phlegm in the lungs,' Antwoine said.

'The bastard lied to me,' Dad said, his voice muffled by the pillows. 'He told me I was just going to breathe in steam. He didn't say he was going to crack my goddamned *ribs*. My bones are fragile, you goddamned nigger!'

'Hey, Dad,' I yelled, 'enough! This man is a whole lot bigger and stronger than you. I don't think it's a good idea to alienate him.'

Antwoine looked up at me with sleepy, amused eyes. 'Hey, man, I had to deal with Aryan Nation every day I was in prison. Believe me, a mouthy old cripple's no big deal.'

I winced.

LATER, DAD was parked in front of the TV, hooked up to the bubbler by a tube in his nose.

'This arrangement is not working out,' he said, scowling. 'Have you seen the kind of rabbit food he tries to give me?'

'It's called fruit and vegetables,' Antwoine said. He was sitting in the chair a few feet away. 'I know what he likes—I can see what's in the pantry. Beef stew, Vienna sausages and liverwurst. Well, not as long as I'm here. You need the healthy stuff, Frank, build up your immunity. You catch a cold, you end up with pneumonia, in the hospital, and then what am I going to do? You're not going to need me when you're in the hospital.'

'Like you really give a shit,' Dad said.

'You think I'm here to help you die?'

'Looks that way to me.'

'If I wanted to kill you, why would I do it the slow way?'

'This is a blast, isn't it?' I said.

'Hey, wouldja check out the watch on that man?' Antwoine suddenly said. 'Let me see that. Man, that's gotta be a five-thousand-dollar watch.' He came up to me, inspected it, marvelling. I was embarrassed—it had cost more than he made in two months. 'That one of those Italian diving watches?'

'Yep,' I said hastily.

'Oh, you gotta be kiddin' me,' Dad said, his voice like a rusty hinge. 'I don't *believe* this. You threw away five thousand dollars on a goddamned *watch*? What kinda money they paying you?'

'They're paying me a lot, Dad. And if I want to throw my money away, I'll throw it away. I've earned it.'

'You've earned it,' he repeated with thick sarcasm. 'Any time you want to pay me back for'—he took a breath—'I don't know *how* many tens of thousands of dollars I dumped on you, be my guest.'

I came this close to telling him then how much money I threw *his* way, but I pulled back just in time. The momentary victory wouldn't be worth it.

Dad took a loud breath. 'You think just 'cause you buy the two-thousand-dollar suits and the five-thousand-dollar watches you're going to become one of *them*, don't you?' He took another breath. 'Well, let me tell you something, 'cause you're my son and no one else is going to give it to you straight. You're nothing more than an ape in a tuxedo.'

'What's that supposed to mean?' I mumbled. I noticed Antwoine tactfully walking out of the room. My face went all red.

He's a sick man, I told myself. He doesn't know what he's saying.

'They know who you are, son, and where you come from. Maybe they'll let you play in their sandbox for a while, but as soon as you start to forget who you really are, someone's going to remind you.'

I couldn't restrain myself any longer. 'It doesn't work that way in the business world, Dad,' I said patiently. 'If you help them make money, you fulfil a need. I'm where I am because they need me.'

'Oh, they *need* you,' Dad repeated, drawing out the word, nodding. 'That's a good one. They need you like a guy taking a shit needs a piece of toilet paper, you unnerstand me? Then when they're done, they flush.'

I rolled my eyes, shook my head, didn't say anything.

A breath. 'And you're too stupid and full of yourself to know it. You're living in a goddamned fantasy world just like your mother. You went to a fancy prep school for a couple of years, and you got a high-priced do-nothing college degree, but you still ain't shit.' His voice seemed to soften a little. 'I tell you this because I don't want you to be fucked over the way they fucked me over, son. Like that candy-ass prep school, the way all the rich parents looked down on me, like I wasn't one of them. Well, guess what. Took me a while to figure it out, but they were right. I wasn't one of them. Neither are you, and the sooner you figure it out, the better off you'll be.'

'Better off, like you,' I said. It just slipped out.

He stared at me, his eyes beady. 'At least I know who I am,' he said.

THE NEXT MORNING was Sunday, my only chance to sleep late, so of course Arnold Meacham insisted on meeting me early. I'd replied to his daily email using the name 'Donnie', which told him I had something to deliver. He emailed right back, telling me to be at the parking lot of a particular Home Depot at 9 a.m. sharp.

When his black BMW 745i pulled into the space next to mine, I saw he was wearing a baby-blue cardigan and looked like he was on his way to play golf. He signalled for me to get into his car, which I did, and I handed him a CD and a file folder. 'And what do we have here?' he asked.

'List of AURORA Project employees,' I said.

'All of them?'

'I don't know. There might be others in separate departments on the same floor. But it's forty-seven names. It's a decent start.'

'I think it's time to penetrate AURORA,' Meacham said.

I shook my head. 'Too risky right now. The badge access is separate.'

'For Christ's sake, follow someone in, steal a badge, whatever.'

'They log all entries, every entrance has a turnstile and there's closed-circuit TV cameras trained on every entry point. It's not so easy. You don't want me to get caught, not now.'

He seemed to back down. 'What about HR files?'

'HR's pretty well protected too,' I said.

'Not like AURORA. Get us the personnel files on everyone you can who's associated in any way with AURORA.'

'I can try for it next week.'

'Do it tonight. Sunday night's a good time to do it.'

'I've got a big day tomorrow. We're making a presentation to Goddard. I've got to be up to speed.'

He looked disgusted. 'I hope you haven't forgotten who you really work for. Anyway, all the more reason why you'd be in the office working tonight,' he said, and turned the key in the ignition.

EARLY THAT EVENING I drove to Trion headquarters. The parking garage was almost entirely empty, the only people there probably security, the people who manned the twenty-four-hour ops centres, and the odd work-crazed employee, like I was pretending to be. I didn't recognise the lobby ambassador, a Hispanic woman, and she barely looked at me as I let myself in.

I went up to my cubicle and did a little real work, massaging the sales figures for Maestro. Most of the floor was dark. I even had to switch on the lights in my area. It was unnerving.

Meacham and Wyatt wanted the personnel files of everyone on AURORA in order to suss out what AURORA was all about. But it wasn't as if I could just saunter into Human Resources, pull open some filing cabinets, and pluck out files. For one thing, their computers were on a whole separate network. And HR was located on the third floor of E Wing, a long hike from New Product Marketing. My badge would probably open each one of the locked doors along the way, but it wouldn't look good that on a Sunday night, for some reason, I had walked from New Products to Personnel.

So I left the building by one of the back entrances, because the security system only kept track of entrances, not exits. And as I walked round to E Wing, I saw someone coming out of a shadowy service entrance.

'Hey, can you hold the door?' I shouted at the guy, who looked like he was on the cleaning crew. 'Damned badge isn't working right.'

The man held the door open for me and I walked right in. Nothing recorded. As far as the system was concerned, I was still at my cubicle.

I took the stairs to the third floor and found the door unlocked, thanks to a fire department law of some kind: in buildings above a certain height you had to be able to go from floor to floor by the stairs, in case of emergency. I walked right into the HR reception area.

It had just the right kind of HR look—a lot of dignified mahogany, to say we're serious about your career, and colourful, welcoming chairs. As far as I could see there were no closed-circuit TV cameras. Not that I was expecting any—this wasn't the skunkworks—but I wanted to make sure.

I stood there for a few seconds, thinking. There weren't any cleaning people around to let me into the offices, so I'd have to try the old my-badge-won't-work trick again. I went back downstairs and headed into the lobby through the back way, where a female lobby ambassador sat in front of the security monitors.

'And I thought I was the only one who had to work on Sunday,' I said to her.

She laughed politely. I looked like I belonged: I had a badge clipped to my belt and I was coming from the inside, so I was supposed to be there, right?

'Hey, listen,' I said, 'sorry to bother you, but do you have that machine to fix badges? It's not like I *want* to get into my office but I have to or I'm out of a job, and the damned badge reader won't let me in. It's like it *knows* I should be home watching football.'

She smiled. 'I'm sorry, the lady who does that won't be in until tomorrow.'

'Oh, man. How am I supposed to get in? I'm totally screwed.'

She picked up her phone. 'Stan, can you help us out here?'

Stan, the security guard, showed up a couple of minutes later. I gave him some blather about how HR was on a hierarchically separate badging system, but he wasn't too interested. As we took the elevator up to the third floor he just wanted to talk sports with me, and that I could do. When we got to HR, he waved his badge at the card reader. 'Don't work too hard,' he said.

'Thanks, brother,' I said.

And I was in.

ONCE YOU GOT past the reception area, HR looked like every other office at Trion, the same generic cube-farm layout. From what I could see, all the cubicles were empty, as were all the offices.

It didn't take long to figure out where the records were kept: in the centre of the floor were long aisles of beige filing cabinets. The question was: How were they organised? The more I looked over the drawer labels, the more discouraged I got. There were titles like BENEFITS ADMINISTRATION; CLAIMS, LITIGATED; IMMIGRATION AND NATURALISATION. Mind-numbing.

I tried one of the drawers, and of course it was locked; they all were. Each filing cabinet had a lock at the top, and they had to be all keyed alike. I looked for an admin's desk, and sure enough, a key to the files was there, on a ring in an unlocked top drawer.

I went for one of the alphabetised employee files.

Choosing one name from the AURORA list—Yonah Oren—I looked under O. Nothing there. I looked for another name—Sanjay Kumar—and found nothing there either. Strange. Just to be thorough, I checked under those names in the pension files. Nothing.

What was particularly strange was that, in the places where the records *should* have been, there seemed to be gaps, as if the files had been removed. Just when I was about to give up, I noticed an alcove—a separate, open room. Above the entrance was a sign that read: CLASSIFIED PERSONNEL RECORDS— ACCESS ONLY BY DIRECT AUTHORISATION OF JAMES SPERLING OR LUCY CELANO.

I entered the alcove, and was relieved to see that things were simple here: the drawers were organised by department number. James Sperling was the director of HR, and Lucy Celano, I knew, was his assistant. It took me a couple of minutes to find Lucy's desk, and maybe thirty seconds to find her key ring (bottom right drawer). I returned to the restricted filing cabinets and found the drawer that held the department numbers, including the AURORA Project. I unlocked the cabinet, and pulled it open. It made a kind of metallic *thunk* sound, as if some castor at the back of the drawer had dropped.

And then I saw something truly bizarre: *all* the files for the AURORA department were gone. There was a gap of two feet between the number before and the number after. For a second it felt as if my heart had stopped.

Out of the corner of my eye I saw a bright light start to flash. It was high on the wall, just outside the file alcove. A few seconds later came the loud *hoo-ah, hoo-ah* of a siren. Somehow I'd triggered an intrusion-detection system.

I raced to the door to the reception area, slammed my side against the crash bar, and the door didn't move. The impact hurt like hell. I tried another door, and that too was locked from inside.

Now I realised what that funny metallic thunking sound had been a minute or two earlier—by opening the file drawer I must have set off some kind of mechanism that autolocked all the exit doors. I ran to the other side of the floor but found even the emergency fire-escape door locked.

I was trapped like a rat in a maze. My mind raced. I had to hide. Security would be here any second now, and if I was caught, it was over. I wouldn't just lose my job at Trion. Far worse. It was a disaster.

I grabbed the nearest metal trash can. It was empty, so I snatched a piece of paper from a nearby desk, crumpled it up, took my lighter and lit it, then dropped it in the trash can. Running back towards the classified-records alcove, I set the can against the wall. Then I took out a cigarette from my pack and tossed it in. Maybe they'd blame that. Maybe.

I heard footsteps, voices coming from the back stairwell. No, please, God.

I found a supply closet, not very wide but maybe twelve feet deep, crowded with shelves stacked with reams of paper and the like. I could just squeeze myself in. As I pulled the door shut behind me I heard another door open, and then muffled shouts. I froze. The alarm kept whooping. People were running back and forth, shouting louder, closer.

'Over here!' someone bellowed.

My heart was thundering. I held my breath, forced myself to remain still.

'*Cigarette!*' I heard, to my relief.

For a long, long time—it could have been ten minutes, it could have been half an hour—I stood there squirming uncomfortably. I could hear a fire extinguisher going off. The shouts had diminished, and finally everything went quiet.

Slowly I extricated myself from the closet. I stood for a few moments, listening intently. I couldn't hear a sound. It seemed a safe bet that they'd gone, satisfied that there hadn't been a break-in after all. They'd blame it on some alarm-system glitch and, if I were really lucky, no one would wonder why the *intrusion*-detection alarm had gone off before the *smoke* alarm.

The place smelt of smoke, and also some kind of chemical, probably from the fire extinguisher. Quietly, I made my way to one of the rear exit doors.

Locked. They hadn't deactivated the autolock. Adrenaline surging again, I went to the reception-area doors and pushed against the crash bars. Those too were locked. Now what?

I'd just have to stay here until morning, when the cleaning crew came in. Or worse, when the first HR staff arrived.

I found a cubicle far from any door or window, and sat down. I was totally fried. I needed sleep badly. So I folded my arms and, like a frazzled student at the college library, passed out.

AROUND FIVE in the morning I was woken by a clattering noise. I sat bolt upright. The cleaning crew had arrived, wheeling big yellow plastic buckets and mops, and the kind of vacuum cleaners you strap to your shoulder. There were two men and a woman, speaking rapidly to each other in Portuguese.

I knew a little: a lot of our neighbours when we were growing up had been Brazilians. I sauntered over to the exit doors, which they'd propped open.

'*Bom dia, como vai?*' I said. I glanced at my watch, looking embarrassed.

'*Bem, obrigado e o senhor?*' the woman replied. She grinned, exposing a couple of gold teeth. She seemed to get it—poor office guy, working all night.

'*Cançado,*' I said to the lady: I'm tired, that's how I am. '*Bom, até logo.*' See you later.

'*Até logo, senhor,*' the woman said as I walked out of the door.

I left E Wing and re-entered B Wing and went up to my cubicle. OK, so if anyone checked the entrance records, they'd see that I'd come in to the building Sunday night around seven, then returned around five thirty in the morning on Monday. Eager beaver. I made a pot of coffee, then went to the men's room to wash. My shirt was a little wrinkled, but overall I looked presentable, even if I felt like shit. Today was a big day, and I had to be at my best.

An hour before the big meeting with Augustine Goddard, we gathered in Packard, one of the bigger conference rooms, for a dress rehearsal. Nora was wearing a beautiful blue suit and she looked like she'd had her hair done specially for the occasion. She crackled with nervous energy.

She and Chad were rehearsing in the room while the rest of us gathered. Chad was playing Jock. They were doing this back-and-forth like an old married couple going through the paces of a long-familiar argument, when suddenly Chad's cellphone rang.

'This is Chad,' he said. His tone abruptly warmed. 'Hey, Tony.' He went off into a corner of the room.

'Chad,' Nora called after him with annoyance. He turned back, held up his index finger as if telling her to wait. A minute or so later I heard him snap his phone closed, and then he came up to Nora, speaking in a low voice.

'That's a buddy of mine in the controller's office,' he said quietly, grim-faced. 'The decision on Maestro has already been made. The controller just put through the order to do a write-off of fifty million bucks for Maestro. This meeting is just a formality.'

Nora flushed deep crimson and walked over to the window.

THE EXECUTIVE Briefing Centre was on the seventh floor of A Wing, just down the hall from Goddard's office. We trooped over there in a group, the mood pretty low. Nora said she'd join us in a few minutes.

The room itself was a truly impressive sight. There was a huge wooden conference table that took up most of the space. One entire end of the room was a screen for presentations. Built into the table were speakerphones, and little screens that slid up in front of each chair when a button was pushed.

There was a lot of whispering and nervous laughter as the marketing team sat waiting. I didn't have to make any part of the presentation, but I was nervous anyway. And looking forward to seeing the famous Jock Goddard up close and personal.

At two minutes before ten, Nora came in, looking calm and radiant. Maybe she'd been meditating, because she seemed transformed.

Then, at exactly ten o'clock, Jock Goddard and Paul Camilletti entered, and everyone went quiet. 'Cutthroat' Camilletti, in a black blazer and an olive silk T-shirt, had slicked his hair back and looked like Gordon Gekko in *Wall Street*. He took a seat at a corner of the immense table. Goddard, in his customary black mock turtleneck under a tweedy brown sports jacket, walked up to Nora and whispered something that made her laugh. She was acting girlish, sort of flirtatious; it was a side of Nora I'd never seen before.

Goddard then sat down at the head of the table, facing the screen. His white hair, parted on one side, was unruly, his eyebrows bushy, white. His forehead was deeply creased, and he had an impish look in his eyes.

There were a few seconds of awkward silence, and he looked around. 'You all look so nervous,' he said. 'Relax! I don't bite.' He glanced at Nora, winked. 'Not often, anyway.'

She laughed. 'Only when you're threatened,' she said and he smiled. 'Jock, do you mind if I start off here?'

'Please.'

'Jock, we've all been working so incredibly hard on the refresh of Maestro that I think sometimes it's just hard to get any real perspective. I've spent the last thirty-six hours thinking about nothing else. And it's clear to me that there are several important ways in which we can update Maestro.'

Goddard nodded, made a steeple with his fingers.

She tapped her notebook. 'We've come up with a strategy, adding twelve new functionalities. But I have to tell you quite honestly that, if I were sitting where you're sitting, I'd pull the plug.'

Goddard turned suddenly to look at her, his great white eyebrows aloft. We all stared at her, shocked. She was burning her entire team.

'Jock,' she went on, 'if there's one thing you've taught me, it's that sometimes a true leader has to sacrifice the thing he loves most. It kills me to say it. But I simply can't ignore the facts. Maestro was great for its time. But its time has come—and gone.'

Goddard looked surprised, impressed. After a few seconds he nodded with a shrewd I-like-what-I-see smile. 'Is everyone in agreement on this?'

Gradually people started nodding, jumping on the moving train as it pulled out of the station. Mordden was nodding vigorously, like he was finally able to express his true opinion.

'I must say, I'm surprised to hear this,' Goddard said. 'I was expecting the Battle of Gettysburg this morning. I'm impressed.'

'What's good for any of us as individuals in the short term,' Nora added, 'isn't necessarily what's best for Trion.'

I couldn't believe the way Nora was leading this immolation, but I had to admire her cunning, her Machiavellian skill.

'Well,' Goddard said, 'before we pull the trigger, hang on for a minute. You—I didn't see you nodding.' He seemed to be looking directly at me. 'You got some kind of problem with the decision we're making here?'

I glanced around, then back at him. He *was* looking at me. 'Huh? No.'

'So you're in agreement on pulling the plug.'

I shrugged. 'I certainly see where Nora's coming from.'

'And if you were sitting where I'm sitting?' Goddard prompted.

I took a deep breath. 'If I were sitting where you're sitting, I wouldn't pull the plug. And I wouldn't add those twelve new features, either.'

'You wouldn't?'

'No. Just one.'

'And what might that be?'

I caught a quick glimpse of Nora's face, and it was beet red. She was staring at me as if an alien were bursting out of my chest. I turned back towards Goddard. 'A secure-data protocol.'

Goddard's brows sunk all the way down. 'Secure data? Why the hell would that attract consumers?'

Chad cleared his throat and said, 'Come on, Adam. Secure data's like what? Number seventy-five on the list of features consumers are looking for.' He smirked. 'Unless you're Austin Powers, International Man of Mystery.'

There was some snickering from the far reaches of the table.

I smiled. 'No, Chad, you're right—the average consumer has no interest in secure data. But I'm talking about the military.'

'Adam—' Nora interrupted in a flat, warning sort of voice.

Goddard fluttered a hand towards Nora. 'No, I want to hear this. The military, you say?'

I tried not to look as panicked as I felt. 'Look, the whole defense establishment in the US, Canada and the UK recently overhauled their global communications system, right?' I pulled out some newspaper clippings and held them up. Wyatt had prepared me for this, and I hoped I had the details right. 'It's called the Defense Message System, the DMS—the secure messaging system for millions of defense personnel around the world. It's all done via desktop PCs, and the Pentagon is desperate to go wireless. Imagine what a difference that could make—secure wireless remote access to classified data and communications, end-to-end secure encryption. Nobody owns that market. And Maestro's the perfect product for it. It's small, sturdy and totally reliable, and its dated technology is totally compatible with the military's five-year-old wireless transfer protocols. All we need to add is secure data. The cost is minimal, and the potential market is *huge*.'

Goddard was staring at me, though I couldn't tell if he was impressed or thought I'd lost my mind.

I went on: 'So instead of trying to tart up this old product, we remarket it. Throw on a hardened plastic shell, pop in secure encryption, and we're golden. Forget about writing off fifty mil—now we're talking about hundreds of millions in added revenue per year.'

At his end of the table, Camilletti was scrawling notes.

Goddard started nodding. 'Most intriguing,' he said. He turned to Nora. 'What's this young man's name?'

'Adam Cassidy,' Nora said crisply.

'Thank you, Adam,' he said. 'That's not bad at all.'

Don't thank me, I thought; thank Nick Wyatt.

And then I caught Nora's expression of pure, undisguised hatred.

THE OFFICIAL WORD came down by email before lunch: Goddard had ordered a stay of execution for Maestro. The Maestro team was instructed to rush through a proposal for retooling and repackaging to meet the military's requirements. Meanwhile, Trion would start negotiating a contract with the Pentagon's Defense Information Systems Agency. Not only had the old product been taken off life support, but it had also got a massive blood transfusion.

And the shit had hit the fan. A voicemail from Nora was waiting for me when I returned from lunch, asking me to go to her office immediately.

'Adam,' she said softly as I entered. 'Sit down, please.' She was smiling, a sad, gentle smile. This was ominous.

'Nora, can I say—?'

'Adam, one of the things we pride ourselves on at Trion is always striving to fit the employee to the job—to make sure our most high-potential people are given responsibilities that best suit them.' She smiled again, and her eyes glittered. 'That's why I've just put through an employee transfer request form. We're all awfully impressed with your talents, your resourcefulness. And we feel that someone of your calibre could do a world of good at our supply-chain management unit down in Raleigh-Durham, North Carolina.'

'You're transferring me to North *Carolina*?' Was I hearing her right?'

'Adam, you make it sound like it's Siberia. Have you ever been to Raleigh-Durham? It's really such a lovely area.'

'I—but I can't move, I've got responsibilities here, I've got—'

'Employee Relocation will coordinate the whole thing for you. They cover all your moving expenses—everything within reason, of course.' Her smile broadened. 'You're going to love it there, and they're going to love *you*!'

'Nora,' I said, 'Goddard asked me for my honest thoughts, and I'm a big fan of the Maestro line. The last thing I intended to do was piss you off.'

'On the contrary, Adam,' she said, 'I was grateful for your input. I only wish you'd shared your thoughts with me *before* the meeting. But that's water under the bridge. We're on to bigger and better things. And so are *you*!'

THE TRANSFER was to take place within the next three weeks. I was completely freaked out. I'd be useless to Wyatt at the North Carolina site, which was strictly for back-office stuff. And he'd blame me for screwing up. But it wasn't until I walked out of Nora's office that I thought about my dad, and then it really hit me. I *couldn't* move. I couldn't leave the old man here. Yet if I refused to go where Nora was sending me, I'd have to resign from Trion, and then all hell would break loose. I had to sit down, had to think.

As I passed by Noah Mordden's office, he waggled his finger at me to summon me in. In his signature Aloha shirt and his big black glasses he was looking more and more like a caricature.

'Ah, Cassidy,' he said. 'You might want to read Sun Tzu.' When I looked puzzled he went on, 'My point is, and this is wisdom from the Roman emperor Domitian, if you strike at a king, you must kill him. Instead, you waged an attack on Nora without arranging air support in advance.'

'I didn't intend to wage an attack.'

'Whatever you intended, my friend, she will surely destroy you.'

'She's transferring me to Raleigh-Durham, North Carolina.'

He cocked an eyebrow. 'Could have been much worse, you know. Have you ever been to Jackson, Mississippi?'

I had, and I liked the place, but I didn't feel like engaging in a long conversation with this strange dude. I pointed to a large, ugly doll with curly blonde hair that was sitting on a shelf and said, 'That yours?'

'Love Me Lucille,' he said. 'A huge flop and one that, I'm proud to say, was my initiative.'

'You engineered . . . *dolls*?'

He reached over and squeezed the doll's hand, and it came to life. Its scarily realistic eyes opened and its Cupid's-bow mouth turned down into a scowl.

'Lucille is fully robotic, and has a wide range of human facial expressions. She whines, gurgles, coos, even tinkles in her diaper. And she exhibits alarming signs of colic. She has speech-localisation, which means she looks at whoever's talking to her. You teach her to speak.'

'I didn't know you did dolls.'

'Hey, I can do anything I want. I'm a Trion Distinguished Engineer. I invented it for my little niece, but she thought it was creepy.' He turned to the doll and spoke slowly. 'Lucille? Say hello to our CEO.'

Lucille turned her head slowly to Mordden. She blinked, and began speaking in a deep voice, her lips forming the words: 'Eat my shorts, Goddard.'

'*Jesus*,' I blurted out.

Lucille turned slowly to me, blinked again, and smiled sweetly.

'The technological guts inside this butt-ugly troll were way ahead of its time,' Mordden said. 'I developed a full multithreaded operating system that runs on an eight-bit processor, and there are three separate ASICs in her fat tummy, which I designed.'

An ASIC, I knew, was geek-speak for a fancy custom-designed computer chip that does a bunch of different things.

He pulled up her frilly pink pyjama top, exposing a small rectangular LCD screen. 'Mommy and Daddy can program her and see the settings on this little proprietary Trion LCD here. One of the ASICs drives this LCD, another drives the motors, another drives the speech.'

'Incredible,' I said. 'All this for a doll.'

'Correct. And let this be a lesson to you. The toy company we partnered with didn't ship the dolls until the last week in November, which is about eight weeks too late—Mommy and Daddy have already made up their Christmas lists by then. Moreover, the price point sucked—in this economy, Mommy and Daddy don't like spending over a hundred bucks for a toy. Of course, the marketing geniuses at Trion thought I'd invented the next Beanie Baby, so we stockpiled several hundred thousand of these custom chips, manufactured for us in China at enormous expense and good for nothing else. Which means we got stuck with almost half a million ugly dolls that no one wanted.'

'Ouch.'

'It's OK. Nobody can touch me. I've got kryptonite.'

He didn't explain what he meant, but Mordden was borderline crazy so I didn't pursue it. I returned to my cubicle, where I found that I had several voice messages. When I played the second one, I recognised the voice with a jolt even before he identified himself.

'Mr Cassidy. This is Jock Goddard. I was very much taken by your remarks at the meeting today, and I wonder if you might be able to stop by my office. Do you think you could call my assistant, Flo, and set something up?'

PART FOUR
Compromise

Compromise: The detection of an agent, a safe house, or an intelligence technique by someone from the other side.

—*The Dictionary of Espionage*

Jock Goddard's office was no bigger than Tom Lundgren's or Nora Sommers's. It was maybe a few feet bigger than my own pathetic cubicle. I walked right by it once, sure I was in the wrong place. But the name was there—AUGUSTINE GODDARD—on a brass plaque on the door, and he was in fact standing right outside his office, talking to a large, formidable-looking black woman who I assumed was Flo. He had on one of his black mock turtlenecks, no jacket, and wore a pair of black-rimmed reading glasses.

They both looked up as I approached. It took Goddard a minute, then he recognised me—it was the day after the big meeting—and said, 'Oh, Mr Cassidy, great, thanks for coming.'

Flo handed him a manila file—I could see it was my HR file—and he showed me into his office. He sat down on the leather chair behind his desk and leaned back. I took one of two chairs on the other side of the desk, looked around and saw a photograph of an unglamorous, white-haired woman I assumed was his wife. One entire shelf was taken up with old-fashioned tin models of cars, convertibles with big tail fins and swooping lines.

He saw me looking at them and said, 'What do you drive?'

'Drive? Oh, an Audi A6.'

'Audi,' he repeated. 'I would have thought you'd drive a Porsche 911, or at least a Boxster. Fella like you.'

'I'm not really a gearhead,' I said. It was a calculated response. Although Wyatt's *consigliere*, Judith Bolton, had devoted part of a session to talking about cars so I could fit in with the Trion corporate culture, my gut now told me that, one-on-one, I wasn't going to pull it off. Better to avoid the subject.

'I thought everyone at Trion was into cars,' Goddard said, and I could see he was making a jab at the slavishness of his cult following. I liked that.

'The ambitious ones, anyway,' I said, grinning.

'Well, you know, cars are my only extravagance, and there's a reason for that. Back in the early seventies, when I started making more money than I knew what to do with, I went out one day and bought a boat, a sixty-one-footer. I was so pleased with this boat until I saw a seventy-footer in the marina. Nine damned feet longer, and my competitive instincts were aroused. Suddenly I'm feeling—I need a bigger boat. So you know what I did?'

'Bought a bigger boat.'

'Nope. Could have done, but there'd always be some other jackass with a bigger boat. Can't win that way. So I sold the damned thing.' He chuckled. 'That's why this office is small. I figured if the boss's office is the same as every other manager's, at least we're not going to have much office-envy in the company. Let people focus on something else. So, Elijah, you're a new hire.'

'It's Adam, actually.'

'Damn, I'm sorry. Adam.' He leaned forward in his chair and scanned my HR file. 'We hired you away from Wyatt, where you saved the Lucid.'

'I didn't "save" the Lucid, sir.'

'No need for false modesty here.'

'I'm not being modest. I'm being accurate.'

He smiled as if I amused him. 'How does Trion compare to Wyatt? Oh, forget I asked that. I wouldn't want you to answer it anyway.'

'That's OK, I'm happy to answer it,' I said, all forthrightness. 'I like it here. It's exciting. I like the people.' I thought for a split second, realising how kiss-ass this sounded. 'Well, most of them.'

His pixie eyes crinkled. 'You took the first salary package we offered you,' he said. 'You could have negotiated a good bit more.'

I shrugged. 'The opportunity interested me.'

'Maybe, but it tells me you were eager to get the hell out of there.'

This was making me nervous, and anyway, I knew Goddard would want me to be discreet. 'Trion's more my kind of place, I think.'

'Paul, my CFO, mentioned to me your intervention on GoldDust. You've obviously got sources.'

'I stay in touch with friends.'

'Adam, I like your idea for retooling the Maestro, but I worry about the ramp-up time of adding the secure encryption protocol. The Pentagon's going to want working prototypes yesterday.'

'Not a problem,' I said. The details were still fresh in my head. 'Kasten Chase has already developed the RASP secure access data security protocol. It might add two months to incorporate it into the Maestro. Long before we're awarded the contract, we'd be good to go.'

Goddard shook his head, looked befuddled. 'The whole goddamned market has changed. It's the age of all-in-one. Consumers don't want a TV and a VCR and a fax and computer and stereo and phone and you-name-it. Convergence is the future. Don't you think?'

I took a deep breath and said, 'The long answer is . . . No.'

He smiled. I'd done my homework. I'd read a transcript of remarks Goddard had made at a conference recently. He'd gone on a rant against 'creeping featurism', as he called it.

'How come?'

'That's just featuritis. Loading on the chrome at the expense of ease of use, simplicity, elegance. I think we're all getting fed up with having to press thirty-six buttons, in sequence, just to watch the evening news. Plus, this whole convergence thing is a myth anyway. Bad for business. Canon's fax-phone was a flop—a mediocre fax and an even lousier phone. Fifty years after the computer was invented, it's converged with—what? Nothing. The way I see it, this convergence stuff is just bullshit.'

'You don't mince words, do you?'

'Not when I'm convinced I'm right, sir.'

'What about Trion as a whole? Any other strong opinions?'

'Some, sure.'

'Let's hear 'em.'

Wyatt was always commissioning competitive analyses of Trion, and I'd committed them to memory. 'Well, Trion Medical Systems is a pretty robust portfolio, real best-in-class technologies in magnetic resonance and ultrasound, but a little weak in service stuff like patient information management.'

He smiled, nodded. 'Agreed. Go on.'

'Trion's Business Solutions unit obviously sucks—I don't have to tell *you* that—but you've got most of the pieces in place there for some serious market penetration, especially in circuit-switched voice and ethernet data services.'

'But what about Consumer Electronics?'

'Obviously it's our core competency, which is why I moved here. I mean, our high-end DVD players beat Sony's hands down. Cordless phones are strong, always have been. Our mobile phones rule the market. But it's crazy that we don't have a real BlackBerry-killer. Wireless devices should be our playground. Instead, it's like we're just ceding the ground to RIM and Palm.'

I noticed he was looking at me with a cryptic smile on his crinkly face. 'How would you feel about priming the retooling of the Maestro?'

'Nora owns that. I wouldn't feel comfortable about it, frankly.'

His grin got crooked. 'She'd get over it. Nora knows what side her bread's buttered.'

'I won't fight you on it, sir, but I think it might be bad for morale.'

'Well, then, how would you like to come work for me?'

'Don't I already?'

'I mean here, on the seventh floor. Special assistant to the chairman for new-product strategy. Dotted line responsibility to the Advanced Technology unit. Interested?'

I couldn't believe what I was hearing. I felt like bursting from excitement and nerves. 'Well, sure. Reporting directly to you?'

'That's right. So, do we have a deal?'

I gave a slow smile. In for a penny, I thought, and all that. 'I think more responsibility calls for more money, sir, don't you?'

He laughed. 'Oh, does it?'

'I'd like the additional fifty thousand I should have asked for when I started here. And I'd like forty thousand more in stock options.'

He laughed again, a robust, almost Santa Clausy ho-ho. 'You've got balls, young man. I'll tell you what. I'm not going to give you fifty thousand more. I'm going to *double* your salary. *Plus* your forty thousand options. That way you'll feel pressure to bust your ass for me.'

To keep from gasping, I bit the inside of my lip.

'Where do you live?' he asked.

I told him.

He shook his head. 'Not quite appropriate for someone at your level. Also, you're going to be working late nights, so I want you living close by. Why don't you get yourself one of those condos in the Harbor Suites? You can afford it now. We've got a lady in Trion E-staff who specialises in corporate housing. She'll set you up with something nice.'

I swallowed. 'Sounds OK,' I said, suppressing a little nervous chuckle.

'Now, I know you've said you're not a gearhead, but this Audi . . . I'm sure it's perfectly nice, but why don't you get yourself something fun? I think a man should love his car. Give it a chance, why don't you? Flo can make the arrangements.' He stood up. 'So, are you on board?' He stuck out his hand.

I shook. 'I'm not an idiot,' I said good-naturedly.

'No, that's obvious. Well, welcome to the team, Adam.'

I stumbled out of his office and towards the bank of elevators, my head in a cloud. And then I caught myself, remembered why I was here and what my real job was. I'd just been promoted way, way above my ability.

I DIDN'T have to break the news to anyone: the miracle of email and instant messaging had already taken care of that for me. By the time I got back to my cubicle, the word was all over the department. Obviously Goddard was a man of immediate action.

No sooner had I reached the men's room for a much-needed pee than Chad burst in and unzipped at the urinal next to me.

'So, are the rumours true, dude?' he said.

I looked at the wall tile. 'Which rumours?'

'I take it congratulations are in order. I underestimated you,' he said.

'I'm lucky,' I replied. 'Or maybe I just have a big mouth, and for some reason Goddard likes that.'

'No, I don't think so. You've got some kind of Vulcan mind-meld going with the old guy. I'll bet you two don't even need to talk. I'm impressed, big guy, seriously impressed.' He zipped up, clapped me on the shoulder. 'Let me in on the secret, will ya?' But he didn't wait for a reply.

When I got back to my cubicle, Noah Mordden was standing there holding a gift-wrapped package.

'Cassidy,' he said. 'Our too-cool-for-school Widmerpool.'

'Excuse me?' Man, was the guy into cryptic references.

'I want you to have this,' he said.

I thanked him and unwrapped the package. It was a book, an old one that smelt of mildew. *Sun Tzu on the Art of War.*

'Not a first edition,' he said, 'but an early printing at least.'

I was touched. 'When did you have time to buy this?'

'Last week, online, actually. I didn't intend it to be a departure gift, but there you are. At least now you'll have no excuse.'

'Thank you,' I said. 'I'll read it.'

'Please do. I suspect you'll need it all the more. Recall the Japanese *kotowaza*, "The nail that sticks up gets hammered down." You're fortunate that you're being moved out of Nora's orbit, but there are great perils in rising too quickly in any organisation. Ambition is a useful quality, but you must always cover your tracks.'

I nodded. 'I'll keep that in mind.' He was definitely hinting at something— he *had* to have seen me coming out of Nora's office—and it scared me.

'THIS BETTER not be a joke,' Nicholas Wyatt said. For a split second his polished, deep-tanned shell of arrogance had cracked open. He gave me a look that seemed to border on respect. 'It's unbelievable.'

We were sitting on his private plane, waiting for his latest bimbo girlfriend to show up so the two of them could take off for Hawaii. I wasn't flying with them; Arnold Meacham and I would get off before the plane went anywhere. I'd never been in a private jet before, and this one was sweet, a Gulfstream G-IV, interior cabin twelve feet wide, over sixty feet long. I'd never seen all this empty space in an airplane. You could practically play football in it.

Wyatt picked up his cellphone, hit two keys. 'Judith,' he said. 'Our boy is now working directly for Mister Big himself. The Big Kahuna. Special executive assistant to the CEO.' He paused, smiled at Meacham. 'I kid you not.' Another pause. 'Judith, sweetheart, I want you to do a crash course with our young man here.' Pause. 'I want Adam to be the best special assistant the guy's ever hired. Right.' And he ended the call with a beep. Looking back at me, he said, 'You just saved your own ass, my friend. Arnie?'

Meacham was waiting for this cue. 'We ran all the AURORA names you gave us,' he said darkly. 'Not one popped up with anything. No Social Security numbers, no nothing.'

'What? I downloaded them straight from the Trion directory on the website.'

'Yeah, well, the admin names are real, but the research-division names are obviously cover names. That's how deep they're buried.'

'That doesn't sound right,' I said, shaking my head.

'Are you being straight with us?' Meacham said. 'Because if you aren't, so help me, we will crush you.' He looked at Wyatt. 'He totally screwed up the personnel records—got diddly-squat.'

'The records were *gone*, Arnold,' I shot back. 'Removed.'

'What do you have on the broad?' Wyatt broke in.

I smiled. 'I'm seeing "the broad" next week.'

To my surprise, Wyatt just nodded. 'Nice.'

'I don't think we need to be paying him his old salary,' Meacham said to Wyatt. 'Not with what he's making at Trion now. Hell, this kite's making more than *me*. Plus there's a security risk in transferring corporate funds into the kid's account, no matter how many shells it goes through.'

Wyatt seemed amused. 'Nah, we made a deal.'

'What'd you call me?' I asked Meacham.

Meacham wasn't even listening, but Wyatt looked at me and muttered, 'It's corporate-spy talk. A kite's a "special consultant" who gathers the intel by whatever means necessary, does the work. You fly a kite, and if it gets caught in a tree, you just cut the string. Plausible deniability, you ever hear of that?'

'Cut the string,' I repeated dully. On one level I wouldn't mind that at all, because that string was really a leash. But I knew that when they talked about cutting the string, they meant leaving me high and dry.

I WENT OUT and got myself a $90,000 Porsche. Thedealership only had only two 911 Carrera coupés on the lot, one in Guards Red and one in metallic Basalt Black. It came down to the stitching on the leather. The red car had black leather with red stitching on it, which looked cowboy-western and gross. Whereas the Basalt Black model had a terrific Natural Brown supple leather interior, with a leather gearshift and steering wheel. I came right back from the test drive and said let's do it.

It was like flying a jet. When you floored it, it even *sounded* like a 767. Three hundred twenty horsepower, zero to sixty in five seconds, unbelievably powerful. It made me feel like everything was happening right.

GODDARD'S PEOPLE found me a new apartment on the twenty-ninth floor of the south tower of the Harbor Suites. It looked like something out of an *In Style* photo shoot. It was around 2,000 square feet, with hardwood parquet and stone floors. There was a 'master suite' and a 'library' that could also be used as a spare bedroom, a formal dining room and a giant living room. There were floor-to-ceiling windows with staggering views. The living room looked over the city in one direction, and over the water in another.

If you didn't want to cook, all you had to do was pick up the phone and press a button, and you could get a room service meal from the swanky hotel below the towers. There was an immense, state-of-the-art health club, valet parking, and the elevators were about the same size as my old apartment. The security here was a whole hell of a lot better, too. Wyatt's goons wouldn't be able to break in so easily and search my stuff. I liked that.

The apartment cost over $2 million, but it was all free—furnishings included—courtesy of Trion Systems, as a perk.

I kept almost nothing from my old apartment—just my computer, my clothes, and my mother's black cast-iron frying pan (for sentimental reasons). The Salvation Army came and took away what I left behind.

I ordered big, puffy, overstuffed couches, matching chairs, a dining table and chairs that looked like they came out of Versailles, a huge iron bed, Persian rugs. Everything. Hey—I wasn't paying for any of it.

The furniture was being delivered when the doorman called up to me to tell me that I had a visitor, a Mr Seth Marcus. I told him to send Seth right up.

The front door was already open for the delivery people, but Seth rang the doorbell and stood there in the hall. He was wearing a Sonic Youth T-shirt and ripped jeans. His normally lively brown eyes looked dead. He was subdued— I couldn't tell if he was intimidated, jealous, pissed off that I'd disappeared from his radar screen, or a combination of all three.

'Hey, man,' I said, and gave him a hug. 'Welcome to my humble abode.' I didn't know what else to say. For some reason I was embarrassed.

He stayed where he was. 'You weren't going to tell me you were moving?'

'It kind of happened suddenly,' I said. 'I was going to call you.'

He pulled a bottle of cheap champagne from his canvas bicycle-courier bag, handed it to me. 'I'm here to celebrate.'

'Excellent!' I said, taking the bottle. 'Come on in.'

'You dog. This is great,' he said in a flat, unenthusiastic voice. 'Huge, huh?'

'Two thousand square feet. Check it out.' I gave him the tour.

He said funny, cutting stuff like 'If that's a library, don't you need books?' and 'Now all you need to furnish the bedroom is a babe.' Then he helped me take the plastic wrap off one of the couches and we sank into it, facing the ocean.

'Nice,' he said. 'But what's with the hair?'

'What about it?'

'You putting mousse in it or something?'

'A little gel,' I said defensively, and changed the subject. 'I thought you worked tonight.'

'You mean bartending? Nah, I quit that. I got a better gig, on the "mobile energy team" for Red Bull. They give you this cool car to drive around in, and you hand out samples. Hours are flexible. I can do it after the paralegal gig.'

'So, you're still working at the law firm too?'

'Believe me, man, I do as little as possible. I do just enough to keep Shapiro off my back—faxes, copies, searches, whatever. I get twenty bucks an hour for playing web games, burning music CDs and pretending to work.'

'You're really getting one over on them,' I said. It was pathetic, actually.

'You got it.'

And then I don't know why, but I said, 'So, who do you think you're cheating the most, them or yourself? I mean, you scam by, doing as little as possible. You ever ask yourself what you're doing it for, what's the point?'

Seth's eyes narrowed in hostility. 'What's up with you?'

'At some stage you got to commit to something, you know?'

He paused. 'Whatever. Hey, you want to get out of here, go somewhere? This is sort of too grown-up for me, it's giving me hives.'

'Sure.' I called down to the valet and asked them to bring my car round.

It was waiting for me by the time we got down there.

'That's *yours*?' he gasped. His cynical, aloof composure had finally cracked. 'This baby must cost like a hundred grand!'

'Less than that,' I said. 'Way less. Anyway, the company leases it for me.'

He approached the Porsche slowly, awe-stricken. 'All right, buddy,' he demanded, 'what's your scam? I want a piece of this.'

'Not a scam,' I said uncomfortably as we got in. 'I sort of fell into this.'

'Oh, come on, man. This is *me* you're talking to—Seth. Remember me? You selling drugs or something? Because if you are, you better cut me in.' He leaned back in the leather seat, took a deep breath of the new-car smell. 'This is great. I think I want your life. Wanna trade?'

I laughed hollowly as we roared away.

IT WAS out of the question, of course, for me to meet again with Dr Judith Bolton at Wyatt headquarters, but now that I was hunting with the big cats I needed an in-depth session. Wyatt insisted, and I didn't disagree.

So I met her at a Marriott the next Saturday, in a suite set up for business meetings. They'd emailed me the room number to go to and she was already there when I arrived, her laptop hooked up to a video monitor. I'd forgotten how intense she was—the ice-blue eyes, the coppery red hair, the glossy red lips and red nail polish—and how hard-looking. I gave her a firm handshake.

'You're right on time,' she said, smiling.

I half smiled back to say I got it but I wasn't really amused.

We sat at a fancy conference table and she asked me how it was going. I filled her in, the good stuff and the bad, including about Chad and Nora.

'You're going to have enemies,' she said. 'That's to be expected, and we'll talk about how to handle that later. But right now I want to focus on Jock Goddard. And if you take away nothing else today, I want you to remember this: he's *pathologically honest*. He's singled you out not because he likes your mind, your ideas, but because he finds your honesty refreshing. The blunter you are, the less calculating you seem, the better you'll play.'

I wondered if Judith saw the irony in what she was doing—counselling me in how to pull the wool over Jock Goddard's eyes by feigning honesty. One hundred per cent synthetic honesty, no natural fibres.

'If he starts to detect anything shifty or calculating in your manner, he'll cool on you fast. And once you lose that trust, you may never regain it.'

'Got it,' I said impatiently. 'So from now on, no gaming the guy.'

'Sweetheart, what planet are you living on?' she shot back. 'Of *course* we game the old geezer. That's lesson two in the art of "managing up". You'll mess with his head, but you have to be supremely artful about it. You've got to come across as the ultimate straight shooter. You tell him the bad news other people try to sugar-coat. Show him a plan he likes—then be the one to point out the flaws. Integrity's a pretty scarce commodity in our world—once you figure out how to fake it, you'll be on the good ship *Lollipop*.'

'Where I want to be,' I said drily.

She had no time for my sarcasm. 'People always *say* that nobody likes a suck-up, but the truth is, the vast majority of senior managers *adore* being sucked up to. It makes them feel powerful, bolsters their fragile egos. Jock Goddard, on the other hand, has no need for it. Believe me, he thinks quite highly of himself already. He's not blinded by need, by vanity.'

Like anyone we know? I wanted to say.

'Look who he surrounds himself with—bright, quick-witted people who can be abrasive and outspoken.'

I nodded. 'You're saying he doesn't like flattery.'

'No, I'm not saying that. Everyone likes flattery. But it's got to feel real to him. Do it subtly and indirectly, and make sure that Goddard thinks he can always get the unvarnished truth from you. He realises what a lot of other CEOs don't—that candour from his aides is vital if he's going to know what's going on inside his company. And let me tell you something else: in every male mentor–protégé relationship there's a father–son element—but I suspect it's even more germane in this case. You likely remind him of his son, Elijah.'

Goddard had called me that by mistake, I recalled. 'He was my age?'

'Would have been. He died a couple of years ago at the age of twenty-one. The point is, just as you may come to idealise Goddard as the father you wish you had'—she smiled, she *knew* about my dad somehow—'you may remind him of the son he wishes *he* still had. You should be aware of this, because you may be able to use it.'

She turned to her laptop and tapped at a few keys. 'Now, we're going to watch some television interviews Goddard has given over the years. Your intelligence-gathering assignment has just become *hugely* more difficult, so you're going to need all the ammunition you can collect. Before we finish today, I want you to know this fellow *inside and out*, are you with me?'

'I'm with you.'

'Good,' she said, whirling round in her chair to face me. 'I *know* you are.' She lowered her voice. 'Adam, I have to tell you—for your own sake—that Nick is getting very impatient for results. You've been at Trion for how many weeks?—and he has yet to know what's going on in the skunkworks.'

'There's a limit,' I began, 'to how aggressive—'

'Adam,' she said quietly. 'He's is *not* someone you want to fuck with.'

I PULLED UP in front of Alana Jennings's duplex apartment in my Porsche that evening, climbed the steps and rang the doorbell. Her voice chirped over the speaker, said she'd be right down.

She was wearing a white embroidered peasant blouse and black leggings and her hair was up, and she wasn't wearing the scary black glasses. She looked spectacularly beautiful.

'Hey,' I said.

'Hi, Adam.' She had on glossy red lipstick and was carrying a tiny square black handbag over one shoulder.

'My car's right here,' I said, trying to be subtle about the brand-new Porsche ticking away right in front of us. She gave it an appraising glance but didn't say anything. She was probably putting it together in her mind with my Zegna jacket and trousers, maybe the $5,000 Italian watch too. And thinking I was either a show-off or trying too hard.

I opened the passenger's door for her. There was a Trion parking sticker on the left rear side of the car, which she hadn't yet noticed but would soon enough. That was just as well. She had to find out one way or another that I worked at Trion, and that I'd been hired to fill the job she used to have.

There were a few moments of awkward silence as I drove towards her favourite Thai restaurant. She glanced at the speedometer. 'You should probably watch it around here. This is a speed trap.'

I smiled, nodded, then remembered a riff from one of her favourite movies, *Double Indemnity*, which I'd rented the night before. 'How fast was I going, Officer?' I said in a sort of flat, film-noir, Fred MacMurray voice.

She got it immediately. Smart girl. She grinned. 'I'd say around ninety.' She had the vampish Barbara Stanwyck voice down perfectly.

'Suppose you get down off your motorcycle and give me a ticket.'

'Suppose I let you off with a warning this time,' she came back, playing the game, her eyes alive with mischief.

The line came to me. 'Suppose it doesn't take.'

'Suppose I have to whack you over the knuckles.'

I smiled. 'Suppose I burst out crying and put my head on your shoulder.'

'Suppose you try putting it on my husband's shoulder.'

She laughed delightedly. 'How do you *know* that?'

'Too much wasted time watching old black-and-white movies.'

'Me too! And *Double Indemnity* is probably my favourite.'

I wanted to quit while I was ahead, because I'd pretty much exhausted my supply of memorised film trivia. So I moved the conversation into tennis, which was safe. When I pulled up in front of the restaurant, her eyes lit up again. 'You know about this place? It's the best!'

'For Thai food, it's the only place, as far as I'm concerned.'

A valet parked the car. So she never saw the Trion sticker.

It was actually a great date for a while. That *Double Indemnity* stuff seemed to have set her at ease, made her feel that she was with a kindred spirit. We ordered green papaya salad and vegetarian spring rolls. I considered telling her I was a vegetarian, like she was, but I decided that was too much; besides, I didn't know if I could stand to keep up the ruse for more than one meal. So I ordered Masaman curry chicken and she ordered a vegetarian curry.

The talk moved on to summer vacations. She used 'summer' as a verb, and figured out pretty quickly that we came from different sides of the tracks. She must have felt a little uncomfortable about her privileged upbringing, because she said she'd spent part of her summers doing scutwork 'at the company where my dad worked', neglecting to mention that her father was the CEO. Also, I knew that her summers were spent on a ranch in Wyoming, on safari in Tanzania, or interning at the Peggy Guggenheim museum in Venice.

When she mentioned the company where her father 'worked', I braced myself for the inevitable subject of what-do-you-do. But it didn't happen until much later. And I was surprised when she brought it up.

She sighed. 'Well, I suppose now we have to talk about our jobs, right? Well, I'm in high-tech, OK? And you—wait, don't tell me.'

My stomach tightened.

'You're a chicken farmer.'

I laughed. 'How'd you guess?'

'Yep. A chicken farmer who drives a Porsche and wears Fendi.'

'Zegna, actually.' My cellphone started vibrating in my jacket pocket. 'Excuse me,' I said, taking it out and glancing at the caller ID.

'One quick second,' I apologised, and answered the phone.

'Adam,' came Antwoine's deep voice. 'Better get over here. It's your dad.'

OUR DINNERS were barely half eaten. I drove her home, apologising profusely all the while. She could not have been more sympathetic.

Once I'd dropped her off, I took the Porsche up to eighty miles an hour and made it to the hospital in fifteen minutes. I raced into the emergency room, hyper-alert, scared. I pretty much shouted out Dad's name at the triage nurse, and when she told me where he was I took off running.

I saw Antwoine first, standing outside the green curtains. His face was for some reason scratched and bloodied, and he looked scared.

'What's up?' I called out. 'Where is he?'

Antwoine pointed to the curtains, behind which I could hear voices. 'All of a sudden his breathing got all laboured. Then he started turning kind of bluish. That's when I called the ambulance.'

'Is he—?'

'Yeah, he's alive. Man, for an old cripple he's got a lot of fight left in him.'

'He did that to you?' I asked, indicating his face.

Antwoine nodded, smiling sheepishly. 'He refused to get into the ambulance. I spent like half an hour fighting with him, when I should have just thrown him in the car. I hope I didn't wait too long to call the ambulance.'

A small guy in scrubs came up to me. 'I'm Dr Patel. Are you his son?'

'Yeah. Hi.' I paused. 'Um, is he going to make it?'

'Looks like it. Your father has a cold, that's all. But he doesn't have any respiratory reserve. So a minor cold, for him, is life-threatening.'

'Can I see him?'

'Of course,' he said, stepping to the curtain and pulling it back.

A nurse was hooking up an IV bag to Dad's arm. He had a clear plastic mask on over his mouth and nose, and was connected to a bunch of monitors. He saw me and pulled the mask off. 'Look at all this fuss,' he said weakly.

'How're you doing, Mr Cassidy?' Dr Patel said.

'Oh, great,' Dad said, heavy on the sarcasm. 'Can't you tell?'

'I think you're doing better than your caregiver.'

Antwoine was sidling up to take a look. Dad looked suddenly guilty. 'Oh, that. Sorry about your face, there, Antwoine.'

Antwoine must have realised this was as elaborate an apology as he was ever going to get from my father. 'Next time I'll fight back harder.'

Dad smiled like a heavyweight champ.

'This gentleman saved your life,' Dr Patel said.

'Did he?' Dad said.

'He sure did.'

Dad shifted his head slightly to stare at Antwoine. 'What'd you have to go and do that for?' he said.

'Didn't want to have to look for another job,' Antwoine said back.

Dr Patel spoke softly to me. 'His chest X-ray was normal, for him, and his white count is eight point five, which is also normal. His blood gases indicated impending respiratory failure, but he appears to be stable now. We've got him on a course of IV antibiotics, some oxygen, and IV steroids.'

'What's the mask?' I said. 'Oxygen?'

'It's a nebuliser. Albuterol and Atrovent, which are bronchodilators.' He leaned over my father and put the mask back. 'You're a fighter, Mr Cassidy.'

'*That's* an understatement,' Antwoine said, laughing huskily.

I STARTED my first official day of working for Jock Goddard having been up all night. I'd gone from the hospital to my new apartment around four in the morning, considered trying to grab an hour of sleep, then rejected the idea because I knew I'd oversleep. So I took a shower, shaved, and spent some time on the Internet reading the latest tech news.

I dressed, in a lightweight black pullover, a pair of dress khakis and a brown hounds-tooth jacket. Now I looked like a fully fledged member of Goddard's inner posse. I called down to the valet and asked them to have my Porsche brought round.

I drove a couple of blocks to Starbucks and bought a latte, and while I was waiting for the kid to steam a quart of milk I picked up a *Wall Street Journal*. Right on the front page was an article about Trion. Or, as they put it, 'Trion's woes'. Under the headline ARE AUGUSTINE GODDARD'S DAYS NUMBERED? was an article by a *Journal* regular named William Bulkeley, who obviously had good contacts at Trion. The gist of it was that Trion's stock price was slipping, its products were long in the tooth, the company was in trouble, and Jock Goddard, Trion's founder, seemed to be out of touch and headed for a fall.

Great, I thought. If Goddard falls, guess who falls with him.

Then I remembered: Goddard was not my real employer. He was the *target*. My real employer was Nick Wyatt. It was easy to forget where my true loyalties lay, in the excitement of the first day and all.

Finally my latte was ready, and I took a big gulp, which scalded the back of my throat, and sat down at a table to finish the article. The journalist seemed to have the goods on Jock Goddard. The knives were out for the old guy, even at Trion. I wondered whether he really was in trouble.

Then I thought: The guy *must* be in bad shape—he hired me, didn't he?

As I PASSED the newsstand in the lobby of A Wing, it was barely seven in the morning. I noticed that the normally towering pile of *Wall Street Journal*s was already half gone. Obviously everyone at Trion was reading it. I said hi to the lobby ambassador and took the elevator to the seventh floor.

My new office was just down the hall from Goddard's. Sitting at her desk outside it was my new administrative assistant, Jocelyn Chang, a fortyish Chinese-American woman with perfectly arched eyebrows, short black hair, and a tiny bow-shaped mouth.

As I approached, she stuck out her hand. 'You must be Mr Cassidy.'

'Adam,' I said.

'I'm Jocelyn,' she said. 'Nice to meet you.'

'You too. I gather you've been here for ever, which I'm glad to hear.' Oops. Was that my first mistake?

'Fifteen years,' she said warily. 'The last three for your predecessor. He was reassigned a couple of weeks ago, so I've been floating.'

'Fifteen years. Excellent. I'll need all the help I can get.'

She glanced at her watch. 'You've got a seven thirty with Mr Goddard. Oh, hold on.' She handed me a leatherette-bound document, easily a hundred pages long, that said BAIN & COMPANY on the front. 'Flo said Mr Goddard wanted you to read this before the meeting.'

'In two and a half minutes . . .'

She shrugged and left me to it.

Was this my first test? There was no way I could read even a page of this incomprehensible gibberish before the meeting. Bain & Company is a high-priced global management-consulting firm that takes guys around my age and works them until they're drooling idiots, making them visit companies and write reports and bill hundreds of thousands of dollars for their bogus wisdom. This one was stamped TRION SECRET. I skimmed it quickly and all the clichés and buzz words jumped right out at me—'cost inefficiencies', 'diseconomies of scale', 'minimising non-value-adding work', blah blah blah—and I knew I didn't even have to read the thing to know what was up. Layoffs. Head-harvesting on the cubicle farm.

Groovy, I thought. Welcome to life at the top.

WHEN FLO escorted me in, Goddard was already sitting at a round table in his office with Paul Camilletti and a guy I recognised as Jim Colvin, Trion's chief operations officer. I said hi, smiled nervously, sat in a chair near Goddard and took out a yellow pad and pen, ready to take notes. Goddard had on a pair of black half-glasses on a string round his neck and looked even older and more tired than last time I'd seen him. Spread out on the table were several copies of the *Wall Street Journal* article.

Camilletti scowled at me as I sat down. 'Who's this?' he said.

'You remember Mr Cassidy, don't you? From the Maestro meeting?'

'Your new assistant,' he said without enthusiasm. 'Right. Welcome to damage control central, Cassidy.'

'Jim, this is Adam Cassidy,' Goddard said. 'Adam, Jim Colvin, our COO.'

Colvin nodded. 'Adam.'

'We were just talking about how to handle this darned *Journal* piece,' Goddard said.

'Well,' I said sagely, 'it'll blow over in a couple of days, no doubt.'

'Bullshit,' Camilletti snapped, glaring at me with an expression so scary I thought I was going to turn to stone. 'It's the *Journal*. It's front-page. Everyone reads it. This is a train wreck.'

I told myself to keep my mouth shut from now on.

'The worst thing to do is to over-rotate,' Colvin said. 'We don't want to send out panic signals.' I liked 'over-rotate'. He was obviously a golfer.

'I want to get Investor Relations in here now, and draft a letter to the editor,' Camilletti said.

'Forget the *Journal*,' Goddard said. 'I think I'd like to offer a face-to-face exclusive to the *New York Times*. An opportunity to address issues of broad concern to the whole industry, I'll say. They'll get it.'

'Whatever,' said Camilletti. 'But let's not protest too loudly. We don't want to force the *Journal* to do a follow-up, stir up the mud even more.'

'Sounds to me like the *Journal* reporter must have talked to insiders here,' I said, forgetting the part about keeping my mouth shut. 'Do we have any idea who might have leaked?'

'The guy may have called me—I don't know, I can check my voicemail— but I surely didn't return his call,' said Camilletti.

'I can't imagine that anyone at Trion would knowingly have any part in this,' Goddard said.

'One of our competitors,' Camilletti said. 'Wyatt, maybe.'

No one looked at me. I wondered if the other two knew I came from Wyatt.

'Anyway,' Goddard said, 'it's all water under the bridge. And however skewed and unfair it might be—well, how terrible is this asinine piece, really? Apart from the grim-reaper headline, what's in here that's new? OK, revenue growth is flat, but good Lord, all this tripe about how we may be facing our first quarterly loss in fifteen years, that's pure invention—'

Camilletti shook his head. 'No,' he said quietly. 'It's even worse than that.'

'What are you talking about?' Goddard said. 'I just came from our sales conference in Japan, where everything was hunky-dory!'

'Last night when I got the alert about this article,' Camilletti said, 'I fired off emails to the VP/Finance for Europe and for Asia/Pacific telling them I wanted to see all the revenue numbers as of this week. Brussels got back to me an hour ago, Singapore in the middle of the night. And the numbers look like crap. The sell-through has been terrible. The fact is, Jock, we're going to miss this quarter, and miss big. It's a flat-out disaster.'

Goddard glanced at me. 'You're obviously hearing some privileged information, Adam, let's be clear about that, not a word—'

'Of course.'

'We've got . . .' Goddard began, faltered, then said, 'for God's sake, we've got AURORA—'

'The revenue from AURORA is several months off,' said Camilletti. 'We've got to manage for *now*. And let me tell you, when these numbers come out, the stock's going to take a *huge* hit. Our revenues for the fourth quarter are going to be off by *twenty-five per cent*.' He gave Goddard a significant look. 'I'm estimating a pretax loss of close to half a *billion* dollars.'

Goddard winced. 'It's absurd, given what we *know* we have in the pipeline.'

'That's why we need to take another look at this,' Camilletti said, jabbing his copy of the Bain document with his index finger.

'Quite the handsomely bound report it is, too,' Goddard said. 'You never told me what it cost us.'

'You don't want to know.'

Goddard grimaced. 'Paul, I swore I would never do this. I gave my word.'

'Well, you should never have made such a promise. We're one of the few high-tech companies that *hasn't* gone through layoffs yet.'

'Adam,' Goddard said, turning to me and looking over his glasses, 'have you had a chance to plough through all this gobbledegook?'

I shook my head. 'Just got it a few minutes ago. I've skimmed it.'

'I want you to look closely at the projections for consumer electronics. Page eighty-something. You have some familiarity with that.'

'Right now?' I asked.

'Right now. And tell me if they look realistic to you.'

'Jock,' said Colvin, 'it's impossible to get honest projections from division heads. They're all protecting their head count, guarding their turf.'

'That's why Adam's here,' Goddard replied. 'He doesn't have turf to protect.'

I was frantically thumbing through the Bain report, trying to look like I knew what I was doing.

'Paul,' Goddard said, 'we've gone through all this before. You're going to tell me we have to slash eight thousand jobs if we want to be lean and mean.'

'No, Jock, if we want to remain *solvent*.'

'Right. So tell me something. Nowhere in this darned treatise does it say that a company that downsizes or rightsizes or whatever the hell you want to call it is ever better off in the long run. Hell, Paul, you know as well as I do that as soon as the skies clear up again we just end up hiring most of 'em back. Is it really worth all the goddamned *turmoil*? Do layoffs ever really lead to a *sustained* increase in share price, or market share?'

'Jock,' Jim Colvin said, 'you know the Eighty-Twenty Rule—twenty per cent of the people do eighty per cent of the work. We're just cutting the fat.'

'That "fat" is dedicated Trion employees,' Goddard shot back. 'We expect loyalty from them, but they don't get it back from us? Far as I'm concerned, you go down this road, you lose more than head count. In fact *I'll* give you an eighty-twenty rule. If we do this, eighty per cent of my remaining employees are going to be able to focus no more than about twenty per cent of their mental abilities on their work. Adam, how do the forecasts look to you?'

'Mr Goddard—'

'I fired the last guy who called me that.'

I smiled. 'Jock. Look, I'm not going to dance around here. I don't *know* most of the numbers, and I'm not going to shoot from the hip. Not on something this important. But I do know the Maestro numbers, and I can tell you these look overly optimistic, frankly. Until we start shipping to the Pentagon—assuming we land that deal—these numbers are way high.'

'Meaning the situation could be even worse than our hundred-thousand-dollar consultants tell us.'

'Yes, sir.'

He nodded. 'But you see my point, don't you?'

For a moment I felt like a deer frozen in the headlights. It was obvious what Goddard wanted to hear from me. But after a few seconds I shook my head. 'To me,' I said slowly, 'it looks like if you don't do it now, you'll probably have to cut even more jobs a year from now.'

Camilletti patted me on the shoulder. I recoiled a little. I didn't want it to look like I was choosing sides—against my boss. Not a good way to start.

'You want the layoffs effective June the 1st, is that right?' Goddard said with a sigh.

Camilletti nodded warily.

'All right,' Goddard said mournfully. 'Sometimes you just gotta get in the car. But we're doing this only once. I'm not slicing twice. And first I want to run this by the entire management team. I also want to get on the horn to our investment bankers. If it flies, as I fear it will, I'll tape a webcast announcement to the company, and we'll release it tomorrow, after close of trading. I don't want a word of this leaking out before then—it's demoralising.'

'If you'd prefer, I'll make the announcement,' Camilletti said. 'That way you keep your hands clean.'

Goddard glared at Camilletti. 'This is my decision—I get the credit, and I get the blame too. It's only right.' He looked miserable. 'Now I suppose they're all going to be calling me Chainsaw Goddard or something.'

'I think "Neutron Jock" has a better ring to it,' I said, and for the first time Goddard actually smiled.

I LEFT Goddard's office feeling both relieved and weighed down. I'd survived my first meeting with the guy, didn't make too big a fool of myself. But I was also in possession of a serious company secret, inside information that was going to change a lot of lives.

Here's the thing: I'd made up my mind that I wasn't going to pass this on to Wyatt and company. It had nothing to do with the skunkworks. Let them find out about the layoffs when everyone else did.

Preoccupied, I stepped off the elevator on the third floor of A Wing to grab a late lunch in the dining room when I saw a familiar face coming at me.

'Hey, Adam!' said the tall, skinny young guy as he got into the elevator. He had one hand on the doors to keep them from closing.

Even in that fraction of a second before I could put a name to the face, my stomach clenched. I kept on walking. My face was burning.

His name was Kevin Griffin, I used to shoot hoops with him at Wyatt. He was in the Enterprise Division and I remembered him as very sharp, very ambitious behind his laid-back demeanour. He used to joke with me, in a good-natured way, about my casual attitude towards work.

In other words, he knew who I really was.

'Adam!' he persisted. 'Adam Cassidy! Hey, what are *you* doing here?'

I couldn't exactly ignore him any more, so I turned back. 'Oh, hey, Kevin,' I said. 'You work here now?'

'Yeah, in Sales. Didn't they kick you out of Wyatt because of that party?' He sniggered, not nasty or anything, just kind of conspiratorial.

'Nah,' I said, trying to sound light-hearted. 'It was a big misunderstanding.'

'Yeah,' he said dubiously. 'Where're you working here?'

'Same old, same old,' I said. 'Hey, nice to see you. Sorry, I've got to run.'

He looked at me curiously as the elevator doors closed.

I WAS SCREWED. Kevin Griffin knew I wasn't on the Lucid project back at Wyatt, knew I wasn't any superstar. He knew the real story. He was probably already back at his cubicle looking me up on the Trion intranet, amazed to see me listed as executive assistant to the president and CEO. How long would it be before he started asking around? Five minutes?

How the hell could this have happened, after all the careful planning, the laying of the groundwork by Wyatt's people?

I looked around, dazed, at the cafeteria's deli counter. Suddenly I didn't have an appetite, but I took a ham-and-cheese sandwich anyway.

I went back to my new office and saw Jock Goddard standing in the hall talking to some other executive type. He caught my eye, held up an index finger to let me know he wanted to talk to me, so I stood there awkwardly while he finished his conversation.

After a couple of minutes Jock put a hand on the other man's shoulder, looking solemn, then led the way into my office.

'I'd say you passed with flying colours,' Goddard said as he sat down in the visitor's chair. 'Congratulations.'

'Really? I thought I blew it,' I said. 'I didn't exactly feel comfortable taking someone else's side.'

'That's why I hired you. To speak truth to power, as it were.'

'It wasn't truth,' I said. 'It was just one guy's opinion.'

Goddard rubbed his eyes with a stubby hand. 'The easiest thing in the world for a CEO—and the most dangerous—is to be out of touch. No one ever really wants to give me the unvarnished truth. They've all got their own agenda. But I need candour. Now more than ever. That *Journal* piece was a shot across the bow. It wouldn't surprise me if it came from disgruntled board members, some of whom think it's time for me to step down, retire to my country house, and tinker with my cars full-time.'

'You don't want to do that, do you?'

He scowled. 'I'll do whatever's best for Trion. This company is my whole life.' He handed me a thick manila folder. 'This is our strategic plan for the next eighteen months—new products, upgrades, the whole kit and caboodle. I want you to give me your blunt, unvarnished take on it. Soon as you can. You'll see there are all kinds of interesting things in the pipeline. Some of which are quite closely held. My God, there's one thing in the works, code-named Project AURORA, that may reverse our fortunes entirely.'

'AURORA?' I said, swallowing hard. 'You mentioned that in the meeting.'

'I've given it to Paul to manage. Truly mindblowing stuff. A few kinks still need to be ironed out, but it's just about ready to be unveiled.'

'Sounds intriguing,' I said, trying to sound casual. 'I'd love to help out on that, if I may.'

'Oh, you will. But all in good time. I don't want to send you in too many directions at once, spread you too thin.' He stood up, clasped his hands together. 'Now I've got to head over to the studio to tape the webcast, which is *not* something I'm looking forward to, let me tell you.'

I smiled sympathetically.

'Anyway,' Goddard said, 'sorry to plunge you in that way, but I have a feeling you're going to do just fine.'

I ARRIVED at Wyatt's house at the same time as Meacham, who made some crack about my Porsche. We were shown in to a gym in the basement, where Wyatt was lifting weights—150 pounds. He wore only a skimpy pair of gym shorts, and looked more bulked up than ever. This guy was Quadzilla.

He finished his set, then got up and towelled himself off. 'So you get fired yet?' he said.

'Not yet.'

'No, Goddard's got things on his mind. Like the fact that his company's falling apart.' He looked at Meacham, and the two men chortled, then Wyatt turned back to me. 'How much of the article's true?'

'You mean, you didn't plant it?' I said.

Wyatt gave me a look. 'Are they going to miss the quarter or not?'

'I have no idea,' I lied. 'It's not like I was in Goddard's office all day.' I don't know why I was so stubborn about not revealing the disastrous quarter numbers, or the news about the impending layoffs. When they were announced tomorrow, Wyatt would go medieval on me for holding back. He wouldn't believe I hadn't heard. So I fudged a little. 'But there's something going on,' I said. 'Something big. Some kind of announcement coming.' I handed Wyatt a folder containing a copy of the strategic plan Goddard had given me to review. 'That's Trion's strategic plan for the next eighteen months. Including detailed descriptions of all the new products in the pipeline.'

Wyatt leafed through the document. 'Including AURORA?'

I shook my head. 'Goddard did mention it, though. He said it would turn the company around. Said he'd given it to Camilletti to run.'

'Huh. Camilletti's in charge of all acquisitions, and my sources say Project

AURORA was put together from a collection of companies Trion's secretly bought over the last few years. Did Goddard say what it was?'

'No. But I told him I'd be interested in taking part in something so significant.'

Wyatt was silent. His eyes were scanning the pages rapidly.

Meanwhile, I handed Meacham a scrap of paper. 'Goddard's personal cell number. It should help you trace a lot of his most important calls.'

Meacham took it without thanks.

'One more thing,' I said to Meacham as Wyatt continued reading. 'There's a problem. There's a new hire at Trion, a kid named Kevin Griffin, in Sales. They hired him away from you—from Wyatt.'

'He knew you at the company?'

'Yep. We were sort of friends. We played hoops together.'

'Shit,' Meacham said. 'That *is* a problem.'

Wyatt looked up from the document. 'Nuke him,' he said.

Meacham nodded.

'What does that mean?' I said.

'It means we'll take care of him,' Meacham said.

'This is valuable information,' Wyatt said at last. 'Very, *very* useful. What does he want you to do with it?'

'He wants my overall take on the product portfolio.'

'Adam Cassidy, marketing genius,' Wyatt said, amused. 'Well, get out a notepad and pen and start taking notes. I'm going to make you a star.'

I WAS UP most of the night in my Harbor Suites apartment, putting together my presentation to Goddard.

The odious Nick Wyatt had spent more than an hour giving me his whole take on the Trion product line, including all sorts of inside information that he was willing to give up for the sole purpose of making Goddard impressed with me. His short-term strategic loss would be his long-term strategic gain.

When I finally crashed for the night, my mind was racing, running through the presentation. What if Goddard asked my opinion on something and I revealed my true, ignorant self. What then? After a couple of hours of tossing and turning I decided to just get up, take a shower and get dressed, and head into work. My Goddard work was done; it was my *Wyatt* work, my espionage, that was way behind. If I got in early enough, maybe I could try to find out something about AURORA. Goddard had mentioned that it was Paul Camilletti's turf. So maybe his office would yield some information.

I glanced in the lobby mirror as I walked out. I looked—like shit.

'You up already?' Carlos, the concierge, said. 'Man, you can't keep hours like this, Mr Cassidy. You get sick.'

'Nah,' I said. 'Keeps me honest.'

AT A LITTLE after five in the morning the Trion garage was deserted. The fluorescent lights buzzed and washed everything in a kind of greenish haze, and the place smelt of gasoline and motor oil.

I took the back elevator to the seventh floor, which was also deserted, and walked down the dark executive corridor until I came to Paul Camilletti's office. I was about to cross a line, do something risky at a whole new level.

What if Camilletti's admin came in really early, to get a jump on the day? Or, more likely, what if Camilletti *himself* wanted to get an early start? Given the big announcement, he might well have to start placing calls, writing emails to Trion's European offices, which were six or seven hours ahead.

So to break into his office today, I realised, was insanely risky.

But for some reason I decided to do it anyway.

I checked all the usual places for the key—every drawer in his admin's desk, inside the paperclip holder, even under her computer, but nothing.

Then, I suddenly remembered an odd detail about my own new office. Like all the offices on the executive floor, it was equipped with a motion detector, which is not as high-security as it sounds. It's actually a common safety feature—a way to make sure that no one ever gets locked inside their own office. As long as there's motion inside, the doors won't lock . . .

The door to Camilletti's office was solid mahogany, and there was no gap between it and the deep-pile carpet; I couldn't even slide a piece of paper under it. That made things more complicated—but not impossible.

I walked down to the sitting area and found a ladderback chair, which I brought back and placed beside the glass wall of Camilletti's office. Then I went back to the sitting area and grabbed a copy of *Barron's* from the fan of newspapers on the coffee table. After looking around once again to make sure I wasn't caught doing something I couldn't even *begin* to explain, I climbed up on the chair and pushed up one of the square acoustic ceiling panels.

I reached up into the empty space above the suspended ceiling, into that dark, dusty place choked with wires and cables and stuff, felt for the next ceiling panel, the one directly over Camilletti's office, and lifted that one too, propping it up on the metal grid thing.

Taking the *Barron's*, I reached over, lowered it slowly, waving it around. Nothing happened. Maybe the motion detectors didn't reach high enough. I stood up on tiptoe, crooked my elbow as sharply as I could, and managed to lower the newspaper another foot or so, waving it around wildly until I really began to strain some muscles.

There was a faint but unmistakable click.

I pulled the *Barron's* back through, put the ceiling panels back in place, then got down from the chair and moved it back where it belonged.

I tried Camilletti's doorknob. The door came open.

In my workbag I'd brought a couple of tools, including a Maglite flashlight. I immediately drew the venetian blinds, closed the door, then switched on the powerful beam.

Camilletti's office was as devoid of personality as everyone else's—the generic collection of framed family photos, the plaques and awards, the same old line-up of business books they all pretended to read.

The computer had been left on, but when I clicked the space bar on the black keyboard and the monitor lit up, I could see the ENTER PASSWORD screen, the cursor blinking. Just for kicks I entered his user name, PCamilletti, and then the same password, PCamilletti. Nope. He was more cautious than that. After looking in drawers, under the keyboard, on the back of the big monitor, for a note of his password, I gave up.

I'd have to get it by stealth. I figured he probably wouldn't notice if I swapped the cable between his keyboard and CPU with a KeyGhost. So I did.

I admit I was even more nervous being inside Camilletti's office than I'd been in Nora's. The guy himself was terrifying, and the consequences of being caught didn't bear thinking about. Plus I had to assume that the security precautions in the executive-level offices were more elaborate than in the rest of Trion. That scared me most of all.

I looked around, groping for inspiration. For some reason the office seemed neater, more spacious than others I'd been in at Trion. Then I realised why: there were no filing cabinets in here. Where *were* all his files?

Of course! Like Goddard, every top-level Trion executive had a double office, a back conference room the same size as the front. That was the way Trion got round the equality-of-office-space problem. Hey, everyone's office is the same size; the top guys just get *two* of them.

The door to Camilletti's conference room was unlocked. I shone the Maglite around and saw that each wall was lined with mahogany filing cabinets.

According to the labels, most of the drawers contained financial and account-ing records, but then I saw some labelled TRION CORPORATE DEVELOPMENT, and I lost all interest in anything else. Corporate development is just a busi-ness buzz word for mergers and acquisitions. And if Wyatt was right that Project AURORA was made up of a bunch of companies Trion had secretly acquired, then the solution to the mystery of AURORA had to be here.

Inside the drawers there were files on companies Trion had acquired out-right, bought a chunk of, or looked at closely and decided not to get involved in. How the hell was I supposed to know if some small start-up I'd never heard of was part of AURORA? It seemed impossible.

But then my problems were solved.

One of the drawers was labelled PROJECT AURORA.

And there it was. Simple as that.

Breathing shallowly, I pulled the drawer open. I half expected it to be empty, like the AURORA files in HR. But it wasn't. It was jam-packed with folders, each one stamped TRION SECRET AND CONFIDENTIAL. This was clearly the good stuff.

From what I could tell, these files were on several small start-ups—two in Silicon Valley, California, another couple in Cambridge, Massachusetts—that had recently been acquired by Trion. I didn't really get it. One company seemed to have developed a way to combine electronic and optical components in one integrated circuit. Another had figured out a way to mass-produce photonic circuits. OK, but what did that *mean*? A company called Delphos Inc. had come up with a process for manufacturing some chemical compound called indium phosphide, made of 'binary crystals from metallic and nonmetallic elements'. Apparently it was used for building a certain kind of laser.

Here was the interesting part: the Delphos file was stamped ACQUISITION PENDING. So Trion was in negotiations to buy the company. The file was thick with financials, just a blur before my eyes, but the bottom line seemed to be that Trion was offering *$500 million*. It looked like the company's officers, a bunch of research scientists from Palo Alto, as well as a venture-capital firm based in London that owned most of the company, had agreed to the terms, and an announcement was tentatively scheduled for a week from now.

How was I supposed to copy these files? By now it was nearly six o'clock in the morning, and if Jock Goddard got in at seven thirty, you'd better believe Paul Camilletti got in before that. So I really had to get the hell out of there. I didn't have *time* to make copies of everything. Instead, I took a key page or two from each of the eight company files, switched on the copying machine and photocopied them. In less than five minutes I had replaced the pages into the file folders and put the copies into my bag.

By a quarter past six, I was back in my own office.

MY BIG PRESENTATION to Goddard kept getting postponed. It was supposed to be at eight thirty but, ten minutes before, I got an InstaMail message from Flo telling me Jock's E-staff meeting was running over, let's make it nine. Then another message from Flo: the meeting shows no sign of breaking up, let's push it back to nine thirty.

I figured that all the top managers were duking it out over who'd get the brunt of the cuts. They were probably all in favour of layoffs in general, but not in their own division. In any corporation, the more people under you on the org chart the more power you have. Nobody wants to lose bodies.

I was exhausted, too wired to do anything but work some more on my PowerPoint presentation, make it even slicker. I kept paring down the text, making it shorter, punchier. But the special effects grew cooler and cooler. I put in an animated fade between slides. I figured out how to make the bar graphs shrink and grow before your eyes. Goddard would be impressed.

Finally, at eleven thirty I got a message from Flo saying I could head over to the Executive Briefing Centre now, since the meeting was wrapping up.

People were leaving as I got there. Some I recognised—Jim Colvin, the COO; Tom Lundgren; Jim Sperling, the head of HR. None of them looked very happy. Goddard himself looked terrible—red-rimmed, bloodshot eyes, the pouches under them even bigger than normal.

I busied myself hooking up my laptop to the projector built into the conference table. I pushed the button that lowered the blinds electrically.

Now it was just Goddard and me in the darkened room. 'What do we have here—a matinée?'

'Sorry, just a slide show,' I said.

'I'm not so sure it's a good idea to turn off the lights. I'm liable to fall fast asleep,' said Goddard. 'I was up most of the night, agonising over all this bushwa. I consider these layoffs a personal failure.'

'They're not,' I said, then cringed inwardly. Who the hell was I to try to reassure the CEO? 'Anyway,' I added quickly, 'I'll keep it brief.'

I started with a cool animated graphic of the Trion Maestro, all the pieces flying in from offscreen and fitting perfectly together. I said, 'The only thing more dangerous than being in today's consumer-electronics market is not to be in the market at all.' Then a slide came up that said TRION CONSUMER ELEC-TRONICS—THE GOOD, THE BAD AND THE UGLY.

'Adam.'

I turned round. 'Sir?'

'What the hell is this?'

Sweat broke out at the back of my neck. 'That was just intro,' I said. Obviously too much of it. 'Now we get down to business.'

He stood up, walked over to the light switch, and put the lights on. 'Adam, you're a smart, creative, original-thinking young man. You think I want you wasting your time trying to decide whether to go with Arial eighteen point or Times Roman twenty-four point, for God's sake? I hate that PowerPoint crap. How about you just tell me what you think?'

'I'm sorry—' I began again.

'No, I'm sorry. I shouldn't have snapped at you. Low blood sugar, maybe. It's lunchtime, and I'm starved.'

'I can go down and get us some sandwiches.'

'I have a better idea,' Goddard said.

GODDARD'S car was a perfectly restored 1949 Buick Roadmaster convertible, sort of a custardy ivory, beautifully streamlined, with a chrome grille that looked like a crocodile's mouth. It had whitewall tyres and a magnificent red leather interior and it gleamed like something you'd see in a movie. He powered down the cloth top before we emerged from the garage into the sunshine.

'This thing really moves,' I said, as we accelerated onto the highway.

'I call it my Ship of Theseus.'

I chuckled like I knew what he was talking about.

'You should have seen it when I bought it—it was a real junk heap. I must have spent five years of weekends and evenings rebuilding this thing from the ground up—I mean, I must have replaced every single part.'

I smiled, leaned back with the sun on my face. Here I was, sitting in this beautiful old convertible with the chief executive officer of the company I was spying on—I couldn't decide if it felt great, like I'd reached the mountaintop, or creepy and sleazy and dishonest. Maybe both.

Goddard wasn't some deep-pockets collector like Wyatt, with his planes, boats and Bentleys. He was a genuine gearhead who got grease on his fingers.

He said, 'You ever read *Plutarch's Lives*?'

'I don't think I even finished *To Kill a Mockingbird*,' I admitted.

'You don't know what the devil I'm talking about when I call this my Ship of Theseus, do you?'

'No, sir, I don't.'

'Well, there's a famous riddle the ancient Greeks loved to argue over. It first comes up in Plutarch. The Athenians decided to preserve the ship that once belonged to Theseus, the great hero who slew the Minotaur in the Labyrinth, as a monument. Over the years, of course, it began to decay, and they found themselves replacing each rotting timber with a new one, and then another, and another. Until every single plank on the ship had been replaced. And the question the Greeks asked was: Is this really the Ship of Theseus any more?'

'Or just an upgrade,' I said.

But Goddard wasn't joking around. 'I'll bet you know people who are just like that ship, don't you, Adam?' He glanced at me, then back at the road. 'People who move up in life and change everything about themselves until you can't recognise the original?'

My insides clutched. Jesus. We weren't talking Buicks any more.

'You know, you go from wearing jeans and sneakers to wearing suits and fancy shoes. You're living in a big fancy house, you go to fancy parties, you acquire new friends. You used to drink Budweiser; now you're sipping some first-growth Pauillac. You used to buy Big Macs at the drive-through; now you're ordering salt-crusted sea bass. The way you see things has changed, even the way you *think*.' He was speaking with a terrifying intensity, and when he turned to look at me his eyes flashed. 'At a certain point, Adam, you've got to ask yourself: Are you the same person or not? And if you have *integrity*, you know deep down that you're the same ship you always were.'

My stomach felt tied up in knots. He could see right through me. Or could he? How much *did* he see? How much did he *know*?

'A man has to respect the person he's been. Your past—you can't be a captive to it, but you can't discard it, either. It's part of you.'

I was trying to figure out how to respond when he announced breezily, 'Well, here we are.'

It was an old-fashioned, stainless-steel dining car from a passenger train, with a blue neon sign that said THE BLUE SPOON. Another neon sign said OPEN FOR BREAKFAST ALL DAY. He parked the car and we got out.

'You'll love this place,' he said. 'It's the real thing. Not one of those phoncy retro-repro things. It hasn't changed since 1952.'

WE SAT in a booth upholstered in red vinyl. The table was grey fake-marble Formica with a stainless-steel edge. There was a long counter with swivelling stools bolted to the floor, cakes and pies in glass domes. The breakfast was two eggs, home fries, sausage or bacon or ham, and hotcakes, for $4.85, but Goddard ordered a sloppy joe on a bun from a waitress who knew him, called him Jock. I ordered a cheeseburger and fries and a Diet Coke.

'So let's hear your thoughts,' Goddard said through a mouthful of food. 'Don't tell me you can't think without a computer and an overhead projector.'

I took a gulp of Coke. 'Well, to begin with, I think we're shipping way too few of the large flat-screen TVs,' I said.

'Too *few*? In *this* economy?'

'A buddy of mine works for Sony, and he tells me that NEC, which makes their plasma display panels, is having some kind of production glitch. We've got a sizable lead on them. Six to eight months easy.'

'I won't make a major production decision based on rumour.'

'Can't blame you,' I said. 'Though the news'll be public in a week or so. But we might want to secure a deal with another equipment manufacturer before the price on those plasma display panels jumps. And it sure will.'

His eyebrows shot up.

'Also,' I continued, 'Guru looks huge to me.'

He shook his head, turned his attention back to his sloppy joe. 'Guru's run into a production problem so serious the thing might not even ship.'

'What kind of problem?'

He sighed. 'Too complicated to go into right now. Though you might want to start going to some of the Guru team meetings, see if you can help.'

'Sure.' I thought about volunteering again for AURORA, but decided against it—too suspicious.

'Oh, and listen. Saturday's my annual barbecue at the lake house. In the old days we'd have everyone there, but we can't any more—so we have some of the old-timers, the top officers and their spouses. Think you can spare the time?'

'Love to.' I tried to act blasé, but this was a big deal. Goddard's barbecue was really the inner circle, the subject of major one-upmanship in the company.

'Now, on to more important matters,' he said. 'They have the best apple pie here you've ever tasted.' He caught the eye of the waitress. 'Debbie, bring this young man a slice of the apple. I'll have the usual.' He turned to me. 'If you don't mind, don't tell your friends about this place. It'll be our little secret.' He arched a brow. 'You can keep a secret, can't you?'

I GOT BACK to Trion on a high, wired from my lunch with Goddard. Not because my ideas has flown so well, but because I'd had the big guy's undivided attention. He took me seriously. Nick Wyatt's contempt for me seemed bottomless. He made me feel like a squirrel. With Goddard I felt as if his decision to single me out as his executive assistant might actually have been justified, and it made me want to work my ass off for the guy. It was weird.

Camilletti was in his office, door closed, meeting with someone important-looking, and I wondered briefly whether he'd type up notes on his meeting after his visitor left. Whatever he entered into his computer I'd soon have, passwords and all. Including anything on Project AURORA.

And then I felt my first real twinge of—of what? Of guilt, maybe. The legendary Jock Goddard, a truly decent human being, had just taken me out to his favourite diner and actually listened to my ideas, and here I was skulking around his executive suites and planting surveillance devices for the benefit of that sleazeball Nick Wyatt.

Jocelyn looked up from whatever she was doing. 'Good lunch?' she asked.

I nodded. 'Yes, thanks. You?'

'Just a sandwich at my desk. I had lots to do.' As I headed into my office, she added, 'Oh, some guy stopped by to see you.'

'He leave a name?'

'No. He said he was a "buddy" of yours. Blond hair, cute?'

'I think I know who you're talking about.' What could Chad possibly want?

'He said you left something for him on your desk, but I wouldn't let him into your office—you never said anything about that. Hope that's OK.'

'That's great, Jocelyn. Thank you.'

I logged on to my computer, wondering why Chad was trying to snoop around my office, and an instant message box popped onto my screen.

To: Adam Cassidy
FROM: ChadP
Yo Adam—I had a very interesting lunch with an old friend of yours from WyattTel. You might want to give me a call—C

I felt like the walls were closing in. Chad's message had a distinctly threatening tone. He wanted me to squirm, to sweat, to call him in a panic. And yet how could I not call him? Wouldn't I naturally call him out of simple curiosity about an "old friend"?

Right now I really needed to work out. I couldn't exactly spare the time, but

I needed a clear head to deal with the latest developments. On my way out of the office, I remembered my workbag and its radioactive contents. Jocelyn had a key to my desk so I couldn't lock the bag in one of my desk drawers. In fact, there was nowhere she couldn't get into if she wanted. So I retrieved the documents from my briefcase, put them in a manila folder, and took them with me to the gym. Goddard's webcast was going out at 5 p.m. so I'd watch it there. I'd have to carry the damned files around with me until I got home, when I could secure-fax them, and then destroy them.

AT A FEW minutes before five, the company gym still wasn't crowded. I grabbed an elliptical trainer, plugged in the headphones and switched to the Trion channel. Right at five the Trion logo came up, then a freeze-frame of Goddard in the Trion studio. I found myself getting kind of nervous, but why? I knew exactly what he was going to say. But I wanted him to do it well. I wanted him to make a case for the layoffs that was persuasive and powerful, because I knew that a lot of people in the company would be pissed off.

I didn't have to worry. He was amazing. In the whole five-minute speech there wasn't a phoney note. He opened simply, talked about the industry, about Trion's recent problems. He said, 'In our business, no one likes to admit when things aren't going well, when the leadership of a company has misjudged, goofed, made mistakes. Well, I'm here to tell you, as the CEO of the company, that *I've* goofed. *I've* made mistakes. I consider the loss of valuable employees to be a sign of grievous failure. Layoffs are like a terrible flesh wound—they hurt the entire body.' He said he'd been opposed to them for years but, well, sometimes you have to make the hard decision, just get in the car. He pledged that his management team was going to take good care of every person affected; he said that he believed the severance packages they were offering were the best in the industry. By the time he was done I had tears in my eyes and I'd forgotten all about moving my feet on the elliptical trainer. I was watching the tiny screen like a zombie. I heard loud voices nearby, looked around and saw knots of people gathered, looking stunned. Then I pulled off the headphones and went back to my workout as the place started filling up.

A few minutes later someone got on the machine next to mine, a woman in Lycra exercise togs. She plugged her headphones into the monitor, fooled with it for a while, and then tapped me on the shoulder. 'Do you have any volume on your set?' she asked. I recognised the voice even before I saw Alana's face. Her eyes widened. 'What are *you* doing here?' she said.

'Oh my God,' I said, truly startled. I didn't need to fake it. 'I work here.'

'You do? So do I. What an *amazing* coincidence. Which department?'

I didn't think my stomach could sink any lower, but it did. 'Uh, I was hired by Consumer Products Division—new products marketing?'

'You're *kidding*.' She stared in amazement as she got down off the machine. 'Don't tell me you're in the same division as me or something. That I'd *know*—I'd have seen you.'

'I used to be.'

'Where are you now?'

'I do marketing for something called Disruptive Technologies,' she said, somewhat reluctantly, I thought.

'Really? Cool. What's that?'

'It's boring,' she said, unconvincingly. 'Complicated, speculative stuff.'

'Oh.' I didn't want to seem too interested. 'You catch Goddard's speech?'

She nodded. 'Pretty heavy. I had no idea we were in such bad shape. I mean, you sort of figure layoffs are for everyone else, not for Trion. But it made sense, the way he presented it. Of course, that's easy for me to say, since I probably have some job security. You, on the other hand, as a recent hire—'

'I should be OK, but who knows.' I really wanted to get off the subject of what exactly I did. 'Hey, I'm sorry about the way our date ended.'

'Sorry? Nothing to be sorry about.' Her voice softened. 'How is your dad?'

I'd left her a voice message in the morning saying that Dad had made it.

'Hanging in there. In the hospital he has a fresh cast of characters to bully and intimidate, so he has a whole new reason for living.'

She smiled politely, not wanting to laugh at the expense of a dying man.

'But if you're up for it, I'd love to have another chance.'

'I'd like that too.' She got back on the machine and started moving her feet. 'You still have my number?' Then she smiled, genuinely, and her face was transformed. She was beautiful. Really amazing. 'What am I saying? You can look me up on the Trion website.'

CAMILLETTI WAS STILL in his office at seven o'clock. I just wanted the guy to go home so I could get into his office and collect the KeyGhost. I also wanted to get home and get some sleep, because I was crashing and burning.

I was trying to figure out how I could get Camilletti on my 'buddy list'—so I'd know when he was online and when he'd signed off—when an instant message from Chad popped up on my computer screen.

You never call, you never write. Don't tell me you're too important now for your old friends?—C

I wrote: Sorry, Chad, it's been crazy.

There was a pause, about half a minute, then he came back:

You probably knew about these layoffs in advance, huh? Lucky for you you're immune.

I wasn't sure how to answer, so for a minute or two I didn't, and then the phone rang. Jocelyn had gone home, so the calls were routed right to me.

I picked up. 'Cassidy.'

'I know *that*,' came Chad's voice, heavy with sarcasm. 'I just didn't know if you were at home or in your office. I should have figured an ambitious guy like you stays late, just like all the self-help books tell you to do.'

'How're you doing, Chad?'

'I'm filled with admiration for you, Adam. Especially after my lunch with your old friend Kevin Griffin.'

'Actually, I barely knew the guy.'

'Not what he said. You know, it's interesting—he was less than impressed with your track record at Wyatt. He said you were a big party-hearty dude. Also had no recollection of your being on the Lucid.'

'He's in—what, in *sales*, isn't he?' I said, figuring that if I was going to imply that Kevin was out of the loop it was at least better to be subtle.

'He *was*. Today was his last day. In case you didn't hear.'

'Didn't work out?' There was a little tremor in my voice, which I disguised by clearing my throat.

'Security got a call from someone at Wyatt saying that poor Kevin had a nasty habit of cheating on his expense sheets. They faxed the evidence right over. Of course, Trion dropped him like a hot potato. He denied it, but you know how these things work—it's not exactly a court of law, right?'

'Unbelievable,' I said. 'I had no idea. I mean, he seemed nice enough. Man. I guess you can't do that kind of stuff too often and hope to get away with it.'

'Oh, that's good. You're really good, big guy.' He laughed so loud I had to pull my ear away from the receiver. 'You are so right. You can't do that kind of stuff too often and hope to get away with it.' Then he hung up.

Five minutes earlier I'd wanted to lean back in my chair and doze off, but now I was way too freaked out. My mouth was dry, so I went to the break room and got an Aquafina. I took the long way, past Camilletti's office. He had gone, his office was dark, but his admin was still there. When I came by half an hour later, she had gone too. It was a little after eight.

I got inside quickly and easily this time, now that I had the technique down. I pulled the blinds closed, retrieved the KeyGhost cable, then lifted one slat to look around. I didn't see anyone, so I raised the blinds and opened the door.

Standing against the wall of Camilletti's reception area was Noah Mordden. He had a peculiar smile on his face. 'Cassidy,' he said.

'Oh, hi, Noah.' Panic flooded my body, but I kept my expression blasé. 'What are you up to?'

'I could ask you the same thing.'

'They've got me working for everyone here,' I said. It was the best I could think of, and it sucked.

'You have many masters,' he said. 'You must lose track of whom you really work for.'

My smile was tight. Inside I was dying. He knew. He'd seen me in Nora's office, now in Camilletti's, and he *knew*.

It was over. Mordden had found me out. So now what? Who would he tell? Once Camilletti learned I'd been in his office, he'd fire me in an instant, and Goddard wouldn't stand in his way.

'Noah,' I said. I took a deep breath, but my mind stayed blank.

'I've been meaning to compliment you on your attire,' he said. 'Very Goddard.' He smiled. 'And I notice you have a new Porsche.'

'Yeah.'

'It's hard to escape the car culture in this place, isn't it? But as you speed along the highway of life, Adam, you might pause and consider. When everything's coming your way, maybe you're driving in the wrong lane.'

'I'll keep that in mind.'

'Interesting news about the layoffs,' he went on.

'Well, you're safe, though.'

'Is that a question or a proposition?' Something about me seemed to amuse him. 'Never mind. I have kryptonite.'

'What does that mean?'

'Let's just say I wasn't named Distinguished Engineer simply because of my distinguished career.'

'What kind of kryptonite are we talking about? Gold? Green? Red?'

'At last a subject you know something about. But if I showed it to you, it would lose its potency, wouldn't it? Just cover your trail and watch your back, Cassidy,' he said, and he disappeared down the hall.

PART FIVE
Dead Drop

Dead Drop: Drop; hiding place. Tradecraft jargon for a concealed physical location used as a communications cut-out between an agent and a courier, case officer or another agent in an agent operation or network.

—*The International Dictionary of Intelligence*

I got home by nine thirty, an early night for me, feeling a nervous wreck, needing three days of uninterrupted sleep. Driving away from Trion, I kept replaying that scene with Mordden in my head, trying to figure it out. Was he planning to tell someone, turn me in? And if not, why not? Would he hold it over my head somehow? I didn't know how to handle it.

Before I could go to bed I had to get those Camilletti files to Wyatt. So I used the scanner Meacham had provided me with, turned them into pdf documents, encrypted them, and secure-emailed them through the anonymiser service. Once I'd done that, I got out the KeyGhost, hooked it up to my computer, and started downloading pages and pages of text. Everything the guy had tapped out on his computer that day, and there was a lot.

First things first: I'd captured his password. Six numbers, ending in 82—maybe it was the birth date of one of his kids, or the date of his marriage.

But far more interesting were all the emails, full of confidential information about the company, about the acquisition of Delphos, the company I'd seen in his files. The one that they were preparing to pay a load of money for.

There was an exchange of emails, marked TRION CONFIDENTIAL, about a secret new method of inventory control they'd put in place a few months ago to combat forgery and piracy. There was a lot of information about chip-fabrication manufacturers in Singapore that Trion had acquired.

Maybe it was because I was so wiped out, but I felt lousy about what I was doing. I could almost see Goddard's gnome-like head floating in the air, watching me. It sounds strange, I know—it was OK to steal stuff about the AURORA Project and pass it to Wyatt, but giving them stuff I hadn't been assigned to get felt like an outright betrayal of my new employers.

The letters WSJ jumped out at me. They had to stand for the *Wall Street Journal*. I wanted to see what Camilletti's reaction to the *Journal* piece was, so I zoomed in on the string of words, and I almost fell out of my seat.

He seemed to be using a number of different email accounts outside of Trion—for personal business, like dealing with his stockbroker, notes to his sister and father, stuff like that. One of the Hotmail emails was addressed to BulkeleyW@WSJ.com. It said:

> Bill—Shit has hit the fan around here. Will be lot of pressure on you to give up your source—hang tough. Call me at home tonite 9.30—Paul

So there it was. Paul Camilletti was—he *had* to be—the leaker, the guy who had fed the damaging information on Trion to the *Wall Street Journal*. He was helping them wreak serious damage on Jock Goddard, portraying the old man as over-the-hill. And when Trion's board of directors, as well as every analyst and investment banker, saw the *Journal*'s article, who would they appoint to take Goddard's place?

It was obvious, wasn't it?

Camilletti's disloyalty really got to me. I knew I had to tell Goddard about him, but how could I when I'd got my evidence by breaking into Camilletti's office? I was struck with a terrible knife-jab of anguish that I wasn't any better than Camilletti. I mean, there I was at Trion, pretending I could walk on water, when all the time I was breaking into offices and stealing documents.

Still, I'd been cornered into it. I didn't have a choice. Camilletti's treachery was of a different order. Goddard needed to know.

WHEN I GOT IN to my office the next day, I called Trion's Information Technology department and told them that the CEO's office wanted copies of all archived emails to and from the office of the chief financial officer in the last thirty days. I got instant cooperation. Without pointing a finger at Camilletti, I made it appear that Goddard was concerned about leaks from the CFO's *office*.

I'd learned that Camilletti used outside email for some of his more sensitive correspondence, including the *Wall Street Journal*, and that he deleted all copies from his computer, but I wondered whether he knew that Trion's computers captured a copy of *all* email that went through the company's fibre-optic cables, whether Yahoo or Hotmail or anything else.

My new friend in IT, who seemed to think he was doing a personal favour for Goddard himself, also agreed to get me the phone records of all calls in and out of the CFO's office. The results came back within the hour.

It was all there. Camilletti had received a number of calls from the *Journal* guy in the last ten days. But far more incriminatingly, he'd placed a bunch of calls *to* the guy. One or two he might be able to explain away as an attempt to return the reporter's calls—but twelve calls? That didn't look good.

And then came copies of the emails. 'From now on,' Camilletti wrote, 'call me only at home. Emails should go only to this Hotmail address.'

Explain *that* away, Cutthroat.

I could barely wait to show my little dossier to Goddard, but he was in meeting after meeting from midmorning to late afternoon.

It wasn't until I saw Camilletti coming out of Goddard's office that I had my chance.

The CFO didn't seem to notice me as he walked away; I could have been a piece of office furniture. Goddard caught my eye, however, and his brows shot up questioningly. Flo began talking to him, and I did the index-finger-in-the-air thing that Goddard always did, indicating I just needed a minute of his time. He did a quick signal to Flo, then beckoned me in.

'You got something on your mind?' he asked.

'It's about that *Wall Street Journal* article,' I said. 'Remember, we thought it had to be someone inside the company who was leaking information—'

'Yes, yes,' he said impatiently.

'It's—well, it's Paul. Camilletti.' I slid into a chair.

'What are you talking about?'

'I know it's hard to believe. But it's all here, and it's pretty unambiguous.' I slid the print-outs across his desk. 'Check out the email on top.'

He took his reading glasses from the chain round his neck and put them on. Scowling, he inspected the papers. 'Where's this from?'

I smiled. 'IT.' I fudged just a bit and said, 'I asked IT for phone records of all calls from anyone at Trion to the *Wall Street Journal*. Then when I saw all those calls from Paul's phone, I thought it might be an admin or something, so I requested copies of his emails.'

Goddard didn't look at all happy, which was understandable, so I added, 'I'm sorry. I know this must come as a shock.' The cliché just came barrelling out of my mouth. 'I don't really understand it, myself.'

'Well, I hope you're pleased with yourself,' Goddard said.

I shook my head. 'Pleased? No, I just wanted to get to the bottom of—'

'Because I'm disgusted,' he said, standing up and removing his glasses. 'What do you think this is, the goddamned *Nixon White House*? Invading people's privacy, digging up dirt! I find that kind of underhandedness reprehensible, and I don't ever want you doing that again. Now get the hell out of here.'

I got up unsteadily, light-headed, shocked. At the doorway I stopped, turned back. 'I want to apologise,' I said hoarsely. 'I thought I was helping out. I'll—I'll go clear out my office.'

'Oh, for Christ's sake, sit back down.' The storm seemed to have passed. His voice was gentler. 'I understand you were trying to protect me, Adam, and I appreciate it. And I won't deny I'm flabbergasted about Paul. But there's a right way and a wrong way to do things, and I prefer the right way. Now, I'll figure out some way of handling it. Meantime we've got something far more important going on. I'm going to need your input on a matter of the utmost secrecy.' He settled himself behind his desk, put on his reading glasses again, and took out his worn little black leather address book. He looked at me sternly. 'Don't ever tell anyone that the founder and chief executive officer of Trion Systems can't remember his own computer passwords. And *certainly* don't tell them about the specific type of handheld device I use to store them.' Looking closely at the little black book, he tapped at his keyboard.

In a minute his printer hummed to life and spat out a few pages. He removed them and handed them to me. 'We're in the final stages of a major acquisition,' he said, 'probably the most costly in Trion history. But it's probably also going to be the best investment we've ever made. I can't give you the details just yet, but we should have a deal by the end of next week. Those are the basic specs on the new company—number of employees, space requirements and so on, and since it's going to be integrated into Trion immediately, and located here in this building, something here has to go. I need you to figure out which division, or divisions, can be moved with the least disruption, to make room for the new acquisition. OK? Look over these pages, and when you're done, shred them. And let me know your thoughts as soon as possible.'

'OK.'

'Adam, I know I'm dumping a whole lot on you, but it can't be helped. I need you to call it as you see it. I'm counting on your strategic savvy.' He reached over and gave me a reassuring shoulder squeeze. 'And your honesty.'

THE NEXT TIME Jocelyn left her desk for a coffee break, I took the papers on Delphos that Goddard had given me—I knew it had to be Delphos, even though the company's name wasn't on the sheets—and made photocopies at the machine behind her desk. Then I slipped the copies into a manila envelope.

262 | JOSEPH FINDER

I fired off an email to 'Arthur', telling him, in coded language, that I had new stuff to pass on—that I wanted to 'return the clothing' I'd bought online. Sending an email from work was, I knew, a risk. Even using Hushmail, which encrypted it. But I didn't want to have to wait until I got home.

Meacham's reply came back almost instantly. He told me not to send the items to the post-office box but to the street address instead. Translation: he didn't want me to scan and email the documents; he wanted to see the hard copies, and I was to use one of the dead drops we'd worked out weeks before. He didn't say why.

At a little after six, I left work, drove over to a McDonald's about two miles from Trion headquarters. In the small, one-guy-at-a-time men's room, I locked the door, popped open the paper towel dispenser, put the rolled-up manila envelope inside and closed it again. Until the paper towel roll needed changing, no one would look inside—except Meacham.

On the way out I bought a Quarter Pounder—for cover, like I'd been taught. About a mile down the road was a 7-Eleven with a low concrete wall round its parking lot. I parked, went in and bought a Diet Pepsi, which I placed on the top of the concrete wall outside.

The Pepsi can was a signal to Meacham, who drove by this 7-Eleven regularly, that I'd loaded dead drop number three, the McDonald's. This simple bit of spy tradecraft would enable Meacham to pick up the documents without being seen with me. OK, so what I was doing made me feel sleazy, but at the same time I couldn't help feeling a little proud. I was getting good at this stuff.

BY THE TIME I got home there was an email on my Hushmail account from 'Arthur'. Wyatt wanted me to drive to a restaurant in the middle of nowhere, more than half an hour away, immediately.

The place turned out to be a famous foodie mecca called the Auberge.

I could see why Wyatt wanted to meet me here, and it wasn't just the food. The restaurant was set up for maximum discretion—for private meetings, extramarital affairs, whatever. In addition to the main dining room, there were small, separate alcoves for private dining which you could enter and leave directly from the parking lot. It reminded me of a high-class motel.

Wyatt was sitting at a table in a private alcove with Judith Bolton. Judith was cordial, and even Wyatt seemed a little less hostile than usual. Maybe because I'd been so successful in getting him what he wanted.

'Adam,' he said, 'those files you got from the CFO's office were very helpful.'

'Good,' I said. Now I was Adam? And an actual compliment? It gave me the heebie-jeebies.

'Especially that term sheet on this company Delphos,' he went on. 'Obviously it's a linchpin, a crucial acquisition for Trion. No wonder they're willing to pay five hundred million bucks for it. Anyway, that finally solved the mystery. We've figured out AURORA.'

I gave him a blank look, like I didn't really care, and nodded.

'This whole business—the training, the security measures, the *huge* risks—it was worth it, worth every penny,' he said, tipping his wineglass towards Judith, who smiled proudly. 'I owe you big-time,' he said to her.

I thought: And what am I, chopped liver?

'Now, I want you to listen to me very closely,' Wyatt said, 'because the stakes are immense. Trion Systems appears to have developed the most important technological breakthrough since the integrated circuit. They've managed somehow to develop an optical chip.'

'So?'

He stared at me with contempt. Judith spoke earnestly, quickly, as if to cover my gaffe. 'Intel's spent billions trying to crack this without success. The Pentagon's been working on it for over a decade. It'll revolutionise their missile navigation systems, so they'll pay almost anything to get their hands on it.'

'The opto-chip,' Wyatt said, 'handles optical signals—light—instead of electronic ones, using a substance called indium phosphide.'

I remembered reading something about indium phosphide in Camilletti's files. 'The stuff that's used for building lasers. Delphos make it, don't they?'

'That was the tip-off. Trion need indium phosphide for the semiconductor in the chip.'

'You've lost me,' I said. 'What's so special about these chips?'

'Let me put it to you in simple terms. A *single particle* of opto-chip one-*hundredth* the diameter of a human hair will now be able to handle all of a corporation's telephone, computer, satellite and television traffic at once. Or maybe you can get your mind round this: with the optical chip, you'll be able to download a two-hour movie in digital format in *one-twentieth of a second*. This is a quantum leap in the industry. It's amazing. It's the Holy Grail.'

'Excellent,' I said quietly. The import of what I'd done was beginning to sink in, and now I felt like a damned traitor to Trion, to Jock Goddard. I had just given the hideous Nick Wyatt the most valuable, paradigm-shifting technology since colour TV or whatever. 'I'm glad I could be of service.'

'I want every last spec,' Wyatt said. 'I want their prototype. I want the patent applications, the lab notes, everything. You're working directly for Goddard; you've got access to just about anything you want to get.'

'It's not that simple. You know that.'

'I don't want you holding back a single thing.'

'I'm not holding back—'

'I have to watch CNBC to find out about the layoffs at Trion when I've got a mole in the CEO's office?'

'I told you there was some kind of big announcement coming. I didn't know anything more than that at the time.'

Wyatt stared at me. 'Don't ever hold anything back from us, do you understand? *Ever*. Now, listen up. We've got excellent sources telling us that Goddard's people are putting on a major press conference at Trion headquarters in two weeks. The email traffic you handed me suggests they're on the verge of going public with this optical chip.'

'They're not going to announce it if they haven't locked down all the patents, right?' I said. I'd done a little late-night Internet research myself. 'I'm sure you've had your minions checking all Trion filings at the Patent Office.'

'Attending law school in your spare time?' Wyatt said with a thin smile. 'You file with the Patent Office at the last possible second, to avoid premature disclosure or infringement. Which means, until it's filed it's open season on the design specs. The clock's ticking. I don't want you to rest for a goddamned minute until you have every last detail on the optical chip. Are we clear?'

I nodded sullenly.

'Now, if you'll excuse us, we'd like to order dinner.'

I got up from the table and went out to use the men's room before I drove off. As I came out of the private dining room, a guy walking past glanced at me. I panicked. I spun round and went back through the private room to the parking lot. I wasn't one hundred per cent sure at the time, but the guy looked a whole lot like Paul Camilletti.

I HAD a meeting at seven thirty the next morning, so when I got in I headed straight over to Plymouth, one of the smaller conference rooms.

Goddard and Camilletti were seated at a small round table along with the COO, Jim Colvin, and the director of Human Resources, Jim Sperling, plus a couple of women I didn't recognise.

When I entered, Goddard looked up and said, 'Adam, do me a favour. I gave Flo the morning off—would you mind getting my, uh, handheld from my office? Seem to have forgotten it.' His eyes seemed to twinkle and I guess the joke was for my enjoyment. He meant his little black address book.

'Sure,' I said, and I swallowed hard. 'Be right back.'

Goddard's office door was closed but unlocked. The little black book was on his bare, neat desk, next to his computer.

I sat down at his desk and looked around at his stuff: the framed photographs of his white-haired wife, Margaret, and his lake house. No pictures of his son, Elijah, I noticed: probably too painful a reminder.

I was alone in Jock Goddard's office, and Flo had the morning off. Was there time to try to get into his computer?

No. Insanely risky.

But I'd probably never have this opportunity again.

Quickly I flipped the worn little book open and saw phone numbers, pencil scrawlings on calendar entries . . . and on the page inside the back cover was printed in a neat hand: GODDARD. And below that, '628582'.

It had to be his password.

I grabbed a pen and a scrap of paper and copied down the ID and password.

But why not copy the whole book? There might well be other important information here.

Closing Goddard's office door behind me, I went to the photocopier behind Flo's desk.

'You trying to do my job, Adam?' came Flo's voice.

I whipped round, saw Flo carrying a Saks Fifth Avenue bag. She was staring at me with a fierce expression.

'Morning, Flo,' I said offhandedly. 'No, fear not. I was just getting something for Jock.'

'That's good. Because I've been here longer, and I'd hate to have to pull rank on you.' A sweet smile broke out on her face.

AS THE MEETING broke up, Goddard sidled up to me, put his arm round my shoulder and led me to his office. He stopped for a moment before Flo's desk. 'Morning, sweetheart,' he said. 'I want to see the confirmation dress.'

Flo beamed, opened the Saks bag, pulled out a small, white silk girl's dress, and held it up proudly.

'Marvellous,' he said, 'just marvellous.'

Then we went into his office and he closed the door.

'I haven't said a word to Paul yet,' Goddard said, settling behind his desk, 'and I haven't decided whether I will. You haven't told anyone else, right? About the *Journal* business?'

'Right.'

'Keep it that way. Look, Paul and I have some differences of opinion, and maybe this was his way of lighting a fire under me. I just don't know.' A long sigh. 'If I do raise it with him—well, I don't want word of it getting round. We have far, far more important things going on.'

'OK.'

He gave me a sidelong glance. 'I've never been out to the Auberge, but I hear it's terrific. What'd you think?'

I felt a lurch in my gut. My face grew hot. That *had* been Camilletti there last night, of all the lousy luck.

'I just—I only had a glass of wine, actually.'

'You'll never guess who happened to be having dinner there the same night,' Goddard said. His expression was unreadable. 'Nicholas Wyatt.'

Camilletti had obviously done some asking around. To even try to deny that I was with Wyatt would be suicide. 'Oh, that,' I said, trying to sound weary. 'Ever since I took the job at Trion, Wyatt's been after me for—'

'Oh, I know how it goes,' Goddard interrupted. 'The other guy guilts you into taking a meeting with him, just for old times' sake, and you don't want to be rude to him, and then he lays it on nice and thick . . .'

'You know I had no intention of—'

'Of course not, of course not,' Goddard muttered. 'You're not that kind of person. Please. I *know* people. Like to think that's one of my strengths.'

WHEN I GOT back to my office, I sat down at my desk, shaken.

The fact that Camilletti had reported to Goddard that he'd seen me at the Auberge at the same time as Wyatt meant that Camilletti, at least, was suspicious of my motives.

I wondered, too, whether Goddard really did think the whole thing was innocent. 'I *know* people,' he'd said. Was he that naive? I didn't know what to think. This was a disaster. I took a deep breath, pressed my fingertips hard against my closed eyes. No matter what, I still had to keep plugging away.

After a few minutes, I did a quick search on the Trion website and found the name of the guy in charge of the Trion Legal Department's Intellectual Property Division: Bob Frankenheimer.

I called him from my desk, because I wanted him to see my caller ID, see I was calling from the office of the CEO. He answered his own phone, with a surprisingly mellow voice, like a late-night radio DJ.

'Mr Frankenheimer, this is Adam Cassidy in the CEO's office.'

'What can I do for you?' he said, sounding genuinely cooperative.

'We'd like to review patent applications for department three twenty-two.'

It was bold, and definitely risky. What if he happened to mention it to Goddard? That would be just about impossible to explain.

A long pause. 'The AURORA Project.'

'Right,' I said casually. 'I know we're supposed to have all the copies on file here, but I've just spent the last two hours looking all over the place, and I just can't find them, and Jock's really in a stew about this.'

Another pause. Frankenheimer's voice suddenly seemed cooler, less cooperative, like I'd pressed the wrong button. 'Why are you calling me?'

'Because I just started here, and I figure you're the one guy who can save my job,' I said with a mordant chuckle.

'Mr Cassidy, I've got a team of six top-notch intellectual-property attorneys here in house who can handle just about anything that's thrown at them. But the AURORA filings? Oh, no. Those have to be handled by outside counsel, allegedly for reasons of "corporate security".' He sounded really pissed off.

'So who *is* handling the filings?' I said.

Frankenheimer exhaled. 'I wish I could tell you. But obviously we can't be trusted with that information either.'

When I hung up, I passed by Camilletti's office on the way to the men's room, and then I did a double take.

Sitting with Camilletti in his office, a grave look on his face, was my old buddy. Chad Pierson.

I quickened my stride, not wanting to be seen by either of them through the glass walls. Though *why* I didn't want to be seen, I had no idea. I was running on instinct by now.

I couldn't think of any legitimate—or at least innocent—reason why the two of them might be talking. And it sure as hell wasn't social—Camilletti wouldn't waste his time on a worm like Chad. No, the only plausible explanation was the one I most dreaded, that Chad had taken his suspicions about me right to the top, or as close to the top as he could get.

My stomach was starting to ache. I wondered if I was getting an ulcer.

Even if I was, that would be the least of my problems.

THE NEXT DAY, Saturday, was Goddard's barbecue. It took me an hour and a half to get to the lake house, which stood at the end of a long dirt path through dense woods that broadened into a big circular drive. A kid in a green shirt was serving temporary valet duty, and I handed him the keys to the Porsche.

The house was a sprawling, grey-shingled place set on a bluff overlooking the lake, with four fat stone chimneys and ivy climbing on the shingles. In front was a huge, rolling lawn dotted with oaks and pines. Twenty or thirty people were standing around on the lawn in shorts and T-shirts, holding drinks.

A pretty blonde girl sitting at a table in front of the verandah smiled and handed me my name tag.

I wandered around, looking for a familiar face, and didn't see anyone. A stout woman of about sixty in a burgundy caftan came up to me.

'You look lost,' she said kindly. Her voice was deep and hoarse, and her face was as weathered and picturesque as the house.

I knew right away she had to be Goddard's wife.

'I'm Margaret Goddard. And you must be Adam,' she said.

I extended my hand, flattered that she'd somehow recognised me until I remembered that my name was on the front of my shirt. 'Nice to meet you, Mrs Goddard,' I said.

'Jock's told me quite a bit about you.' She held on to my hand for a long time and nodded, her small brown eyes widening. 'My husband's a cynical old codger, and he's not easily impressed. So you *must* be good.'

As I approached the verandah, I passed a couple of large black Cajun grills. A couple of girls in white uniforms were tending sizzling burgers, steaks and chicken. A bar had been set up nearby, where two college-age guys were pouring drinks into clear plastic cups. I began to recognise people. Nancy Schwartz, senior vice-president of the Business Solutions Unit, was playing a game of croquet with Rick Durant, the chief marketing officer. Goddard's admin, Flo, in a floral silk Hawaiian muumuu, was swanning around as if she were the real hostess.

Then I caught sight of Alana, long legs tan against white shorts. She saw me at the same instant and her eyes seemed to light up. She gave me a quick furtive wave and a smile, and turned away. I had no idea what that was supposed to mean, if anything. Maybe she wanted to be discreet about our relationship, the old don't-fish-off-the-company-pier thing.

I passed my old boss, Tom Lundgren, who was dressed in one of those hideous golf shirts with grey and bright pink stripes. He was clutching a bottle of water and listening with a fixed grin to an attractive black woman who was probably Audrey Bethune, the head of the Guru team.

Fifty feet away or so, Goddard was laughing with a small knot of guys. He was drinking from a bottle of beer and wearing a blue button-down shirt rolled up at the sleeves, a pair of cuffed khakis, and battered brown moccasins. The ultimate prepster country baron.

To one side of him was Paul Camilletti, in neatly pressed, faded jeans and a white button-down shirt, also with the sleeves rolled up. *He'd* gotten the appropriate-dress memo, even if I hadn't—I had on a pair of khaki shorts and a polo shirt. And facing Goddard was Jim Colvin, the COO, his legs pasty-white under plain grey Bermuda shorts. A real fashion show this was. Goddard looked up, caught my eye, and beckoned me over.

I reached Goddard's group and stood politely off to one side until he saw me. He reached out to put his arm round my shoulder, an awkward gesture since I was so much taller than him, and said quietly, 'Come with me.'

He guided me towards a screened porch that wrapped round the back of the house. 'In a while I'm going to be doing my traditional little ceremony,' he said as we climbed the wooden steps and I held the screen door open. 'I give out little gifts, silly little things.' I smiled, wondering why he was telling me this.

We passed through the porch, with its old wicker furniture, into the main part of the house. The floors were old wide-board pine, the walls were creamy white, and everything seemed bright and homey. This was the house of a rich man with no pretensions, I thought. We went down a wide hallway past a sitting room with a big stone fireplace, then turned a corner into a narrow hall, with trophies and stuff on shelves on either side. Finally we entered a small book-lined room with a long table in the centre, a computer and printer and several huge cardboard boxes on it. This was obviously Goddard's study.

'The old bursitis is acting up,' he apologised, indicating the big cartons, which were heaped with wrapped gifts. 'If you wouldn't mind carrying these out to the podium, near the bar . . .'

'Not at all,' I said, disappointed but not showing it.

'I'll guide you out of here,' Goddard said. I lifted one of the enormous boxes, which was not only heavy but bulky and unwieldy, and followed him into the narrow corridor. The box scraped against the shelves on both sides, and I had to turn it sideways and up to maneuvre it through. I could feel the box nudge something. There was a loud crash, the sound of glass shattering.

'Oh God, I'm sorry,' I said, setting down the box so I could see what had happened. I must have knocked one of the trophies off a shelf—it lay in a dozen golden shards all over the tiled floor. I crouched down to pick up the pieces.

Goddard turned white. 'Forget it,' he said in a strained voice.

I collected as many of the pieces as I could. It was—it had been—a statuette of a running football player made of some kind of gilt-painted ceramic. The base was wood with a brass plaque that said 1995 CHAMPIONS—LAKEWOOD SCHOOL—ELIJAH GODDARD—QUARTERBACK.

Elijah Goddard, according to Judith Bolton, was Goddard's dead son.

'Jock,' I said, 'I'm so sorry.' One of the shards sliced painfully into my palm.

'I said, forget about it,' Goddard said. 'It's nothing. Now let's get going.'

I didn't know what to do. I wanted to clean the mess up, but I didn't want to piss him off further. So much for all the goodwill I'd built up with the old guy.

The cut in my palm was now oozing blood.

'Mrs Walsh will clean this up,' he said, a hard edge to his voice. 'Come on, please take these gifts outside.' He went down the hall and disappeared somewhere. Meanwhile, I cautiously carried the box out of the house.

When I returned for the second box, I saw Goddard in a chair in a corner of his study. He was sitting hunched over, holding the wooden trophy base in both hands. I hesitated, not sure whether I should get out of here and leave him alone, or pretend I didn't see him and keep moving the boxes.

'He was a sweet kid,' Goddard suddenly said. I stopped moving. 'An athlete, tall and broad in the chest, like you. And he had a . . . gift for happiness. He made people feel good. He was beautiful, and he was kind, and there was this—this *spark* in his eyes.' He slowly raised his head and stared into the middle distance. 'You would have liked him,' he said.

'I'm sorry I never met him.'

'Everybody loved him. He had the best sm—' His voice cracked. 'The best smile . . .' Goddard lowered his head, and his shoulders shook. After a minute he said, 'One day I got a call at the office from Margaret. She was screaming . . . She'd found him in his bedroom . . . Elijah had moved back in after he dropped out of Haverford his junior year—really, they kicked him out. He'd stopped going to classes. I had a good idea he was on drugs, but I couldn't get him to talk about it. Later I heard from one of his friends that he'd gotten into heroin. This wasn't some juvenile delinquent, this was a gifted, sweetnatured fellow. But at some point he started . . . what's the expression, shooting up? And it changed him. The light in his eyes was gone. He started to lie all the time, as if he was trying to erase everything he was. Do you know what I mean?' Goddard looked up again. Tears were running down his face.

I nodded.

'The medical examiner ruled it an overdose. He said there was no question it was deliberate, that Elijah knew what he was doing.' He covered his eyes with a pudgy hand. 'You ask yourself, what should I have done differently? Was I too hard on him, too stern? Or not hard enough? Was I too involved in my own work, too busy building Trion, to be a real father to him?'

Now he looked directly at me, and the anguish in his eyes felt like a dagger in my gut. My own eyes got moist.

'I drove home, I couldn't think straight. He was lying on his bed, and I cradled him in my arms just like he was a baby. Do you know what it's like seeing your child in a coffin?' he whispered. 'I thought I'd never get over it. Margaret says I never have. I couldn't figure out the reason I was alive any more. Something like this happens and you—you question the value of everything.'

He pulled out a handkerchief from his pocket, and mopped his face. 'To this day I ask myself, did I ever know Elijah? Maybe not. I thought I did. I do know I loved him. But did I really *know* my boy?' He shook his head slowly, and I could see him begin to take hold of himself. 'Your dad's goddamned lucky, whoever he is, so goddamned lucky. He's got a son like you, a son who's still with him. I know he's got to be proud of you.'

'I'm not so sure of that,' I said softly.

'Oh, I am,' Goddard said. 'Because I know *I'd* be.'

PART SIX
Control

Control: Power exerted over an agent or double agent to prevent his defection or redoubling (so-called 'tripling').

—*The International Dictionary of Intelligence*

The next morning I showed up, unannounced, at my dad's apartment with a box of Krispy Kreme doughnuts. I parked in a space right out front. I'd just come from the car wash, and the Porsche was a gleaming hunk of obsidian, a thing of beauty. Dad hadn't seen it yet. His 'loser' son, a loser no more, was arriving in style—in a chariot of 450 horsepower.

My father was stationed in his usual spot in front of the TV, watching some investigative show about corporate scandals. Antwoine was sitting next to him, reading a colour supermarket tabloid.

Dad saw the doughnut carton I was waving at him, and shook his head.

'I'm pretty sure there's a chocolate frosted in here. Your favourite.'

'Nah,' he said. 'I can't eat that shit any more. Mandingo here's got a gun to my head. Why don't you offer him one?'

Antwoine shook his head too. 'No, thanks, I'm trying to lose a few pounds.'

'Soon as you leave this guy's going to start crackin' the whip, making me do laps around the room,' Dad said. His face was more amused than angry. 'Whatever floats his boat,' he added. 'Though nothing seems to get him off like keeping me off my smokes.' The tension between the two of them seemed to have ebbed into some kind of a resigned stalemate.

'Hey, you look a lot better, Dad,' I lied.

'Bullshit,' he said, his eyes on the TV. 'You still working at that new place?'

'Yeah,' I said. I figured it was time to tell him the big news. 'In fact—'

'Let me tell you something,' he said, finally giving me a rheumy stare. He pointed at the TV. 'These bastards will cheat you out of every last nickel if you let them. The CEOs, with their stock options and their big fat pensions, they're all out for themselves, every last one of them.'

I looked down at the carpet. 'Well,' I said quietly, 'not all of them.'

'Oh, don't kid yourself.'

'Listen to your father,' Antwoine said, not looking up from the tabloid. There almost seemed to be affection in his voice. 'The man's a fount of wisdom.'

'Actually, Dad, I happen to know a little something about CEOs. I just got a huge promotion—I was just made executive assistant to the CEO of Trion.'

There was just silence. I thought that might have sounded a little arrogant, so I softened it a bit: 'It's really a big deal, Dad.'

More silence. He was staring at the TV.

I was about to repeat it when he said, 'What's that, like a secretary?'

'No, no. It's, like, high-level stuff. Brainstorming and everything.'

'So what exactly do you do all day?'

The guy had emphysema, but he knew just how to take the wind out of me. 'Never mind, Dad,' I said. 'I'm sorry I brought it up.' I was, too.

'No, really. I'm curious what you did to get that slick new set of wheels.'

I smiled. 'Pretty nice, huh?'

'How much that vehicle cost you?' He took a long suck of oxygen.

'Nothing. Trion covers the lease. It's a perk of my new job.'

He breathed in again. 'A perk.'

'Same with my new apartment.'

'You moved?'

'I thought I told you. Two thousand square feet in that new Harbor Suites building. And Trion pays for it.'

Another intake of breath. 'You proud?' he said.

I was stunned. I'd never heard him say that word before, I didn't think. 'Yeah,' I said, blushing.

'Proud of the fact that they own you now?'

I should have seen the razor blade in the apple. 'Nobody owns me, Dad,' I said curtly. 'I believe it's called "making it". Look it up. You'll find it in the thesaurus next to "life at the top".' I couldn't believe what I was saying.

Antwoine put down his newspaper and excused himself, tactfully.

Dad laughed harshly, turned to look at me. 'So lemme get this straight.' He sucked in some more oxygen. 'You don't own the car *or* the apartment, that right? You call that a perk?' A breath. 'I'll tell you what that means. Every-thing they give you they can take away, and they will, too. None of it's yours. Your whole life ain't yours.'

I bit my lip. The old guy was dying, I told myself for the millionth time. He's an unhappy, caustic guy. But it just came out: 'Dad, some fathers would actually be proud of their son's success, you know?'

His tiny eyes glittered. 'Success, that what you call it, huh? See, Adam, you remind me of your mother more and more. Got the same social-type person-ality—everyone liked her, she fitted in anywhere.'

'Oh, that's real good, Dad. Too bad I'm not more like *you*, you know? Bitter, nasty. Pissed off at the world. You want me to grow up to be like you, that it?'

He puffed, his face growing redder.

I kept going. My heart was going a hundred beats a minute, and I was almost shouting. 'When I was broke and partying all the time you considered me a fuckup. OK, so now I'm a success by just about anyone's definition, and you've got nothing but contempt. Maybe there's a reason you can't be proud of me no matter what I do, Dad.'

He glared and puffed, said, 'Oh yeah?'

'Look at you.' There was like this runaway freight train inside me, unstop-pable. 'You're always saying the world's divided up into winners and losers. So let me ask you something, Dad. What are you, Dad? What are *you*?'

I headed for the door in a slip-stream of my own pent-up anger, feeling more miserable than ever. The last thing I saw, my parting image of the guy, was his big red face, puffing and muttering, his eyes staring in disbelief or fury or pain, I didn't know which.

I KNEW from the moment Alana said she wanted to eat at the restaurant at the Harbor Suites that we'd sleep together that night. It was there all along, that invisible line that we both knew we were going to cross; the question was when, and how, we were going to cross it. We came back up to my apartment after dinner, both a little unsteady from too much wine. I had my arm round her narrow waist, we sort of careened around, enjoying the views of the water, and I made us both martinis, which we definitely didn't need. She said, 'I can't believe I have to go to Palo Alto tomorrow morning.'

'What's up in Palo Alto?'

She shook her head. 'Nothing interesting.' She had her arm round my waist, too, but she accidentally-on-purpose let her hand slip down to my butt, and made a joke about whether I'd finished unpacking the bed.

The next minute I had my lips on hers, and she snaked a warm hand down to my groin. Both of us were quickly aroused, and we stumbled over to the couch. We kissed. She was wearing a white silk teddy under her shirt. Her breasts were ample, round, perfect. And she came loudly, with surprising abandon.

We made our way down the long corridor to my bedroom and did it again, this time more slowly.

'Alana,' I said when we were snuggling. 'That means "beautiful" in Gaelic or something, right?'

'Celtic, I think.' She was scratching my chest.

'Alana, I have to confess something.'

She groaned. 'You're married.'

'No—I hate Ani DiFranco.'

'But didn't you . . .? You quoted her.' She looked puzzled.

'I had an old girlfriend who used to listen to her a lot. Bad associations.'

'So why do you have one of her CDs out?'

She'd seen the damned thing next to the CD player. 'I was trying to make myself like her. For you.'

She furrowed her dark brow. 'You don't have to like everything I like. I don't like Porsches.'

'You don't?' I turned to her, surprised.

'They're dicks on wheels. Maybe some guys need that, but you don't.'

'No one "needs" a Porsche. I just thought it was cool.'

'Did your dad have a Porsche? My dad had one.' She rolled her eyes. 'Ridiculous. Like, his male-menopause, midlife-crisis car.'

'Actually, for most of my childhood we didn't even *have* a car. We took public transportation.'

'Oh.' Now she looked uncomfortable. After a minute she said, 'So all this must be pretty heady stuff.' She indicated the apartment with a wave.

'Yeah.'

'Hmm.'

Another minute went by. 'Can I visit you at work sometime?' I said.

'You can't. Access to the fifth floor is pretty restricted. Anyway, I think it's better if people at work don't know, don't you agree?'

'Yeah, you're right.'

Then she curled up next to me and drifted right off to sleep.

THE BEDSIDE CLOCK said three thirty-five when I got up. I walked across the carpet and noiselessly closed the bedroom door behind me. Alana remained asleep.

I signed on to my email and saw the usual assortment of work stuff that didn't look urgent, and one on Hushmail from 'Arthur' whose subject line said, 'Re: Consumer Devices.'

Boss extremely disappointed by your failure to make contact. Wants additional presentation materials by 6 p.m. tomorrow or deal is endangered.

I hit REPLY and typed, 'Unable to locate additional materials, sorry', and signed it 'Donnie.' Then I read through it and deleted my message. Nope. I wasn't going to reply at all. That was simpler. I'd done enough for them.

I noticed that Alana's little square black handbag was still on the granite bar where she'd left it. Inside were her badge, a lipstick, some breath mints, a key ring, and her Trion Maestro. The Maestro probably held phone numbers, addresses and diary appointments, and it would have been really easy for me to slip it into the recharging cradle attached to my desktop computer and hot-link it. It probably held information that could be very useful to Wyatt and Meacham. But there was a risk of her waking up and, no matter how cleverly I handled it, she'd know what I was up to. And I'd be caught, and the relationship would be over, and all of a sudden that mattered to me. After only a couple of dates and one night together I was smitten with Alana. I was just beginning to discover her earthy, expansive, wild side. I loved her loopy, unrestrained laugh, her boldness, her dry sense of humour. I didn't want to lose her because of something the loathsome Nick Wyatt was forcing me to do.

And then I realised I'd already quit working for Wyatt. I'd made the decision that afternoon in the study at Goddard's lake house. I wasn't going to keep betraying the guy. Not after the trust he'd put in me. Until that moment of revelation there'd been a part of me that was baffled as to why Goddard had singled me out. Now I got it, and it rocked my world. I didn't just want to impress the old man any more; I wanted his approval, maybe something deeper.

Already I'd handed over to Wyatt all kinds of valuable information on the AURORA Project. I'd done my job. I was finished with those assholes. Odds were they'd calculate that it wasn't worth hassling me further, and anyway what could they do to me?

So I put Alana's Maestro back into her handbag, I poured myself a glass of cold water from the dispenser on the refrigerator door, gulped it down, and climbed back into my warm bed. Alana muttered something in her sleep, and I snuggled right up next to her and, for the first time in weeks, actually felt good about myself.

GODDARD WAS SCURRYING down the hall to the Executive Briefing Centre, and I struggled to keep up with him. Man, the old guy moved fast. 'This darned meeting is going to be a circus,' he muttered. 'I called the Guru team here for a status update as soon as I heard they're going to slip their Christmas ship date. You're going to see a side of me now that's not so attractive.'

I didn't say anything—what could I say? I'd seen his flashes of anger, and they didn't even compare to what I'd seen in the only other CEO I'd ever met.

'Guru's prime is a very smart young woman named Audrey Bethune,' Goddard muttered. 'But this disaster may derail her career. I really have no patience for screwups on this scale.' As we approached the room, he slowed. 'Now, if you have any thoughts, don't hesitate to speak. But be warned—this is a high-powered group, and they're not going to show you any deference just because I brung you to the dance.'

The Guru team was assembled round the big conference table, waiting nervously. They looked like scared rabbits. Goddard sat at the head of the table, next to a black woman in her late thirties, the same woman I'd seen talking to Tom Lundgren at the barbecue.

Goddard patted the table next to him to tell me to sit by his side. My cell-phone had been vibrating in my pocket for the last ten minutes, so I furtively switched it off.

'Afternoon,' Goddard said. 'This is my assistant, Adam Cassidy.' A number of polite smiles, then I saw that one of the faces belonged to my old friend Nora Sommers. Shit, she was on Guru, too? She caught my eye, beamed like I was some long-lost playmate. I smiled back, savouring the moment.

Audrey Bethune, the programme manager, was beautifully dressed in a navy suit with a white blouse and small gold stud earrings. She had dark skin and her hair was perfectly coifed. She reached behind Jock's back to shake my hand. Her palm was dry and cool. I was impressed. Her career was on the line.

Guru—code-named TSUNAMI—was a supercharged handheld digital assistant, Trion's only convergence device. It was a PDA, a communicator, a mobile phone. It had the power of a laptop in an eight-ounce package. It had a full HTML Internet browser and a great TFT active-matrix colour screen.

Goddard cleared his throat. 'I understand we have a little challenge,' he said.

'That's one way of putting it, Jock,' Audrey said smoothly. 'Yesterday we got the results of the in-house audit, which indicated that we've got a faulty component. Apparently the LCD driver is defective.'

'In every single one?' asked Goddard.

'That's right.'

'A quarter of a million units have a bad LCD driver,' Goddard said. 'I see. The ship date is in—what is it, now?—three weeks. Hmm. Now, as I recall your plan was to ship these before the end of the quarter, thus bolstering earnings for the third quarter and giving us all thirteen weeks of the Christmas quarter to rake in some badly needed revenue. As we all know, Trion is experiencing some difficulties in the market, which means that it's all the more crucial that Guru ship on schedule.'

The chief marketing officer, Rick Durant, put in mournfully, 'This is a huge embarrassment. We've already launched a huge teaser campaign: "The digital assistant for the next generation".' He rolled his eyes.

'Yeah,' muttered Goddard. 'And it sounds like it won't *ship* until the next generation.' He turned to the lead engineer, Eddie Cabral, a round-faced, swarthy guy. 'Is it a problem with the mask?'

'I wish,' Cabral replied. 'No, the whole damned chip is going to have to be respun, sir. This is a complicated ASIC. It's got to drive our own, proprietary Trion LCD screen, and the cookies just aren't coming out of the oven right—'

'What about replacing the LCD?' Goddard interrupted.

'No, sir,' said Cabral. 'Not without retooling the whole casing.'

Goddard tightened his mouth. 'How long will it take to respin the ASIC?'

Cabral hesitated. 'Three months. If we're lucky.'

I suddenly sat up. The words jumped out at me. *ASIC . . . proprietary Trion LCD . . .*

'If we're *lucky*,' Goddard repeated. His voice was getting louder. 'Three months puts the ship date into December. That won't work at all, will it?'

'No, sir,' said Cabral.

I tapped Goddard on the arm, but he ignored me. 'Mexico can't manufacture this for us quicker?'

The head of manufacturing, a woman named Kathy Gornick, said, 'Maybe a week or two faster, but then the quality will be substandard at best.'

'This is a goddamned mess,' Goddard said.

I picked up a product spec sheet, then tapped Goddard's arm again. 'Will you please excuse me for a moment?' I said.

I rushed out of the room, flipped open my phone.

Noah Mordden wasn't at his desk, so I tried his cellphone, and he answered on the first ring: 'What?'

'It's me, Adam. You know that ugly doll you've got in your office?'

'Love Me Lucille. You can't have her. Buy your own.'

'Doesn't it have an LCD screen on its stomach?'

'What are you up to, Cassidy?'

'Listen, I need to ask you about the LCD driver. The ASIC.'

WHEN I RETURNED to the conference room a few minutes later, the head of engineering and the head of manufacturing were engaged in a heated debate. I sat down quietly and waited for a break in the argument. Finally I got my chance. I cleared my throat.

'Excuse me for a second. I know this is going to sound crazy, but remember that robotic doll Love Me Lucille?'

'Don't remind me,' grumbled Rick Durant. 'We shipped half a million of those hideous dolls and got 'em all back.'

'Right,' I said. 'That's why we have three hundred thousand ASICs, custom-fabricated for the Trion LCD, sitting in a warehouse in Van Nuys.'

A few chuckles, some guffaws. One of the engineers said to another, loud enough for everyone to hear, 'Does he know about connectors?'

Nora looked at me, wincing with fake sympathy, and shrugged.

Eddie Cabral said, 'I wish it were that easy, uh, Adam. But ASICs aren't interchangeable. They've got to be pin-compatible.'

I nodded. 'Lucille's ASIC is an SOLC-68 pin array. Isn't that the same pin layout that's in the Guru?'

Goddard stared at me.

There was another beat of silence, and the rustling of papers.

'SOLC-68 pin,' said one of the engineers. 'Yeah, that should work.'

Goddard looked around the room, then slapped the table. 'All right, then,' he said. 'What are we waiting for?'

Nora beamed moistly at me and gave me the thumbs-up.

On the way back to my office I pulled out my cellphone again. Five messages from a number I didn't recognise and another marked PRIVATE. I dialled my voicemail and heard Meacham's voice. 'This is Arthur. I haven't heard from you in over three days. Email me by noon or face the consequences.'

I felt a jolt. The fact that he'd actually *called* me, which was a security risk no matter how the call was routed, showed how serious he was. Sorry, buddy, I thought. But I had no plans to make contact.

The next message was from Antwoine, his voice high and strained. 'Adam, you need to get over to the hospital,' he said. The other four messages were all from Antwoine, his tone increasingly desperate. 'Adam, where the hell are you? Come *on*, man. Get over here *now*.'

I stopped by Flo's desk and said to her, 'Can you tell Jock I've got an emergency? It's my dad.'

I DROVE like a lunatic. Every red light, every left-turning vehicle—everything was conspiring to delay me from getting to the hospital before Dad died.

I parked illegally, ran into the emergency room entrance and rushed up to the triage desk.

'Frank Cassidy?' I said to the attendant. 'Where is he?'

She glanced at her computer screen and said, 'Room three.'

I raced through the waiting area into the ward, and saw Antwoine sitting on a chair next to a green curtain.

When he saw me he just looked blank, and I could see that his eyes were bloodshot. Then he shook his head slowly and said, 'I'm sorry, Adam.'

I yanked the curtain open and there was my dad sitting up in the bed, his eyes open, and I thought, *You see, you're wrong, Antwoine, he's still with us, the bastard*, until it sank in that the skin of his face was the wrong colour, and his mouth was open, frozen in an agonised last gasp.

'Oh, no,' I moaned.

I touched Dad's waxy cheek, and it was cool. A few degrees cooler than it should be. I couldn't breathe; I felt like I was in a vacuum. The lights seemed to flicker. Suddenly I cried out, 'Dad. No.'

Antwoine stood and moved behind me. 'I wanted you to have a chance to say goodbye to him,' he said. I could hear his voice, but I couldn't turn round and look. 'He went into that respiratory distress again and this time I didn't even waste time arguing with him, I just called the ambulance. They said he had pneumonia, probably had it for a while. I kept calling and calling. I wanted you to say goodbye to him.'

'I know. It's OK.' I swallowed. I didn't want to look at Antwoine, didn't want to see his face because it sounded like he was crying, and I couldn't deal with that. And I didn't want him to see me crying, which I knew was stupid. 'Did he . . . say anything?'

'No,' Antwoine said, really slowly. 'He didn't ask after you. But you know, he wasn't really saying anything, was mostly cursing the doctors . . .'

'Yeah,' I said, staring at Dad's face. His forehead was all wrinkled, angrily furrowed. I reached up and tried to smooth out the wrinkles but I couldn't. 'Dad,' I said. 'I'm sorry.'

The curtain on the other side of the bed pulled back. A dark-skinned guy in scrubs with a stethoscope. I recognised him as Dr Patel, from the last time.

'Adam,' he said. 'I'm so sorry.' He looked genuinely sad. 'He developed full-blown pneumonia and it was too much for him, in his condition.'

I nodded. 'I know. Thanks. I know you did everything you could.'

ANTWOINE CAME INTO THE waiting area, looking out of place, lost. 'You want me to clear my stuff out?' he asked gently.

'No, come on. You take your time. Stay in the apartment as long as you want.'

'You know, he did talk about you,' he said.

'Oh, sure,' I said. He was obviously feeling guilty about telling me that Dad hadn't asked for me at the end. 'I know that.'

A low, mellow chuckle. 'Not always the most positive guy, but I think that's how he showed his love, you know?'

'I know.'

'He was a tough old bastard, your father.'

'He was pretty nasty to you.'

'That was just his way. I didn't let it get to me. Towards the end we kind of had a relationship.'

'He liked you.'

'I don't know about that, but we had a relationship.'

'No, I think he liked you. I know he did.'

He paused. 'He was a good man, you know.'

I didn't know what to say in response to that.

IT'S FUNNY: after that first time I broke out crying at my dad's hospital bed, something in me shut down. I didn't cry again, not for a long while.

On the drive out to the funeral home I called Alana at work and got a voice-mail message saying she was 'out of the office' but would be checking her messages frequently. I remembered she was in Palo Alto. I called her cell-phone, and she answered on the first ring.

'This is Alana.' I loved her voice: velvety smooth with a hint of huskiness.

'It's Adam.'

'Hey, jerk.'

'What'd I do?'

'Aren't you supposed to call a girl up the morning after you sleep with her, to make her feel less guilty about putting out?'

'God, Alana, I—'

'Some guys even send flowers,' she went on. 'I've read about it in *Cosmo*.'

She was right, of course: I hadn't called her, which was truly rude. But what was I supposed to tell her—that I hadn't called her because I was frozen like some insect in amber and I didn't know what to do? That I couldn't believe how lucky I was to find a woman like her—and yet I felt like a complete and total fraud?

'How's Palo Alto?'

'Pretty, but you're not changing the subject so easily.'

'Alana,' I said, 'listen. I got some bad news. My dad just died.'

'Oh, Adam. Oh, I'm so sorry. Oh God. What can I do?'

'Don't worry about it. Nothing.'

'The funeral's in a couple of days.'

'I'll be out here till Thursday. Adam, I'm so sorry.'

I called Seth next, who said pretty much the same thing: 'Oh, man, buddy, I'm so sorry. What can I do?'

'Nothing, really. But thanks, man. I'll let you know about the funeral.'

'Take care, buddy, huh?'

Then the cellphone rang in my hand. Meacham didn't say hello or any-thing. His first words were, 'Where the *fuck* have you been?'

'My father just died. About an hour ago.'

A long silence. Then he said stiffly, 'Sorry to hear it. Timing really sucks.'

'Yep,' I said, my anger flaring up. 'I told him to wait.' Then I pressed END.

AT THE FUNERAL, Seth sat on one side of me in the pew, Antwoine on the other. There were maybe twenty people in the church, some of them regular parish-ioners who didn't know Dad. The others were friends of mine from high school and college, a few neighbours, a couple of elderly cousins I vaguely recognised. The priest, a silver-haired fellow named Father Joseph Iannucci, took me aside before the Mass and asked me a few questions about Dad—his 'faith', what he was like, that sort of thing. I was pretty much stumped.

Seth and I were pallbearers along with some other guys from the church and the funeral home. The Mass was long, and I didn't follow what Father Iannucci said. I felt depleted, shell-shocked. When it was over, Seth gave me a hug, and then Antwoine gave me a crushing handshake and hug, and I was surprised to see a single tear rolling down the giant's face. I hadn't cried during the whole service; I felt anaesthetised. Maybe I was past it.

I was leaving the church, about to get in the limousine to follow the hearse to the graveyard, when I saw a man sitting in the back row. I couldn't make out his face in the dark light of the church's interior—until he turned round and caught my eye.

It was Goddard.

I couldn't believe it. Astonished, and moved, I walked up to him slowly. I smiled, thanked him for coming. He shook his head, waved away my thanks.

'One of the very few things I've learned in life is the importance of getting your priorities straight.'

For a moment I was speechless. 'I'll be back in tomorrow,' I said. 'It might be on the later side, because I have some business to take care of—'

'Take your time,' he said. 'Somehow we'll manage without you for a little while, Adam.'

'It's not like—not at all like your son, Jock. I mean, my dad was pretty sick for a long time, and . . . it's really better this way. He wanted to go. And, I mean, we weren't all that close, really.' I smiled sadly. 'I probably shouldn't say it, but he was kind of a difficult guy, which makes it easier, his passing. It's not like I'm totally devastated or anything.'

'Oh, no, that makes it even harder, Adam. You'll see. It hits you later. The wasted opportunities. The things that could have been. But I want you to keep something in mind: your dad was fortunate to have you. Really.'

'I don't know about that,' I said, and all of a sudden, the shut-off valve in me gave way, the dam broke, and the tears welled up. I flushed with shame as the tears streamed down my face, and I blurted out, 'I'm sorry, Jock.'

He reached both of his hands up and placed them on my shoulders. 'If you can't cry, you're not alive,' Goddard said. His eyes were moist.

Now I was weeping like a baby, and I was mortified and somehow relieved at the same time. Goddard put his arms round me.

'I want you to know something, son,' he said, very quietly. 'You're not alone.'

THE DAY AFTER the funeral I returned to work. What was I going to do, mope around the apartment? I felt raw, like a layer of skin had been peeled off. I needed to be around people. And maybe, now that Dad was dead, there'd be some comfort in being around Goddard, who was beginning to look like the closest thing I ever had to a father.

At least by my reckoning, I'd done my service, paid my debt to Wyatt, and I deserved a clean slate. I'd stopped returning Meacham's phone calls and emails. Once I even got a message, on my cellphone voicemail, from Judith Bolton. 'Adam,' she said, 'I know you're going through such a difficult time. We all feel terrible about the death of your father, and please know you have our deepest condolences. But it's extremely important, even in this time of turmoil, for you to remain in contact. I need you to make contact today.'

I deleted her message as well as Meacham's. They would get the point eventually. I wasn't Nick Wyatt's kite any more.

AS SOON as I arrived in the office, Flo told me that Jock wanted to see me. He was in his back room with Camilletti, Colvin and Stuart Lurie, the senior VP for Corporate Development. Camilletti was talking as I entered. 'No, from what I hear the SOB just flew into Palo Alto yesterday with a term sheet already drawn up. He had lunch with Hillman, the CEO, and by dinner they'd inked the deal. He matched our offer dollar for dollar—but in cash!'

'How the *hell* could this happen?' Goddard exploded. I'd never seen him so angry. 'Delphos signed a no-shop provision, for Christ's sake!'

'The no-shop's dated tomorrow—it hasn't been signed yet. That's why he flew out there so fast, so he could do the deal before we locked it in.'

'Who are we talking about?' I asked softly, as I sat down.

'Nicholas Wyatt,' Stuart Lurie said. 'He just bought Delphos right out from under us for five hundred million in cash.'

My stomach sank. *Wyatt bought Delphos?*

I turned to Goddard with a questioning look.

'That's the company we were in the process of acquiring—I told you about them,' he said impatiently. 'Our lawyers were just about finished drawing up the definitive purchase agreement . . .' His voice trailed off, then grew louder. 'I didn't even think Wyatt had that kind of cash.'

'They had just under a billion in cash,' said Jim Colvin. 'Eight hundred million, actually.'

Goddard smacked his hand down on the table. 'God*damn* it to hell!' he thundered. 'What the hell *use* does Wyatt have for a company like Delphos? He doesn't have AURORA . . . and without it, Delphos is worthless!'

'Maybe he knows about AURORA,' said Colvin.

'Impossible!' said Goddard. 'And even if he knows, he doesn't *have* it!'

There was a long silence.

Camilletti spoke slowly, intensely. 'We're protecting AURORA with every goddamned safeguard known to man. There's just no way. Unless . . .' he paused. 'Unless he had someone inside.' An idea seemed to occur to him, and he looked at me. 'You used to work for Wyatt, didn't you? Are you still in touch with him?' His eyes drilled into me.

I could feel the blood rushing to my head, and to mask it I faked outrage. 'What are you trying to suggest?' I stood up.

'You had dinner with Wyatt at the Auberge not so long ago, correct?'

'Paul, that's enough,' said Goddard. 'Adam had no access whatsoever to AURORA. Or to the details of the Delphos negotiation. Today's the first time he's even heard the company's name.'

I nodded.

'Let's move on,' Goddard said. He seemed to have cooled off a little. 'Paul, I want you to talk to our lawyers, see if we can stop Wyatt. AURORA's scheduled launch is in four days. As soon as the world knows, there'll be a mad scramble to buy up materials and manufacturers up and down the whole damned supply chain. I do *not* want to be part of that scramble, so either we delay the launch, or look around for some other comparable acquisition—'

'*No one* has that technology but Delphos!' Camilletti said.

Goddard got to his feet. 'There are always other opportunities. You know, there's a story Ronald Reagan used to tell about the kid who found a huge pile of manure and said, "There must be a pony around here somewhere."' He laughed, and the others laughed as well, politely, appreciating his attempt to defuse the tension. 'Let's all get to work. Find the pony.'

I THOUGHT things through as I drove home that night, and the more I did the angrier I got, and the angrier I got the faster I drove.

If it weren't for the acquisition information I'd got from Camilletti's files, Wyatt wouldn't have known about Delphos, the company Trion was about to buy. The more I reminded myself of this, the worse I felt.

Damn it, it was time to let Wyatt know I wasn't working for them any more.

I unlocked my apartment door and headed for the computer.

But no.

Arnold Meacham was sitting at it, while a couple of tough-looking crewcut guys were tearing the place apart.

'What the fuck—?' I said.

Meacham looked up calmly. 'You think you can *hide* shit from me?' he said. 'I don't think so. You don't have a safe-deposit box that's safe from us. I see you've been saving all my emails. I didn't know you cared.'

'Of course I have. I keep back-ups of everything,' I said, trying to sound unfazed. 'Now, why don't you and your boys get the hell out of here before I call the police.'

Meacham snorted and made a hand signal that looked as if he was summoning me over.

'No.' I shook my head. 'I said, you and your buddies—'

There was a sudden movement that I could see out of the corner of my eye, lightning-fast, and something slammed into the back of my head. I sagged to my knees, tasting blood. Everything was tinged dark red. I flung my hand out to grab my attacker, but while my hand was flailing behind, a foot slammed into my right kidney. A jagged bolt of pain shot up and down my torso, knocking me flat on the Persian rug.

'No,' I gasped.

Another kick, this one to the back of my head, incredibly painful. Pinpoints of light sparkled before my eyes.

'We're going for a drive,' Meacham said.

MEACHAM and his goons hustled me out of my apartment, down the elevator to the garage, then out through a service entrance to the street. One of the guys was carrying my laptop; another had my desktop computer.

'We're going for a drive' usually means, at least in Mafia movies, cement boots and a dunk in the East River. It didn't look good.

I was manhandled into a waiting black Suburban, and forty-five minutes later we pulled into Nick Wyatt's driveway. I was searched for weapons or whatever, as if somehow between my apartment and here I could have picked up a Glock. They took my cellphone, watch, belt and keys and shoved me into the house.

Wyatt was sitting in front of a huge flat-panel TV in a spacious, sparely furnished room, watching CNBC with the sound muted. I glanced at myself in a mirror as I entered with my crewcut escorts. I looked pretty bad.

'Look at you,' Wyatt said. 'Walk into a door? Fall down a flight of stairs?'

'Something like that.'

'Sorry to hear about your dad. But, Christ, breathing through a tube, all that shit—I mean. Just as well he's dead, huh? Put him out of his misery?'

I wanted to lunge at him, throttle him. 'Thanks for your concern,' I said.

'I want to thank *you*,' he said, 'for the information on Delphos.'

'Sounds like you had to empty your piggy bank to buy it.'

'Yeah, but when we announce *we've* got the optical chip, our stock's gonna go into orbit.'

'I'm glad you've got it all figured out. You don't need me any more.'

'Oh, you're far from done, friend. Not until you get me the specs on the chip itself. And the prototype.'

'No,' I said, very quietly. 'I'm done now.'

'You think you're *done*? Man, you truly don't get it, do you? You think I'm going to let you walk away before you're finished?'

'You got all sorts of valuable intelligence from me,' I said. 'Your plan worked. It's over. From now on, you don't contact me any more. End of transaction. As far as anyone's concerned, this never happened.'

Sheer terror had given way to a kind of delirious confidence: I'd finally crossed the line. I'd jumped off the cliff and I was soaring in the air. I was going to enjoy the ride until I hit ground. 'Think about it,' I went on. 'You've got a whole lot more to lose than I do. Your company. And your fortune.'

His smile was broad. 'What are you going to do, go to "Jock" Goddard and tell him you're nothing but a little snoop whose brilliant ideas were spoonfed him by his chief competitor? And then what do you think he's going to do? Thank you, take you to lunch at his little *diner* and toast you with a glass of Ovaltine? I don't think so. Or maybe you think you can go to the FBI, is that it? Tell them you were a spy-for-hire for Wyatt? Oh, they'll love that. You know how *understanding* the FBI can be, right? I will deny *everything* and they'll have no choice but to believe me, and do you know why? Because you are a fucking little con man. It's on *record*, my friend, that I fired you from my company when you embezzled from me, and *everything*'s documented.'

'Then you're going to have a hard time explaining why everyone at Wyatt recommended me so enthusiastically.'

'But no one did, get it? You counterfeited our letterhead to forge your own recommendations when you applied to Trion. Those letters didn't come from us. Paper analysis and forensic document examination will establish that without a doubt. You used a different computer printer, different ink cartridges. You forged signatures.' A pause. 'You really think we weren't going to cover our asses?'

I tried to smile back, but I couldn't get the trembling muscles of my mouth to cooperate. 'Sorry, that doesn't explain the phone calls from Wyatt executives to Trion,' I said. 'Anyway, Goddard'll see through it. He knows me.'

Wyatt's laugh was more like a bark. 'He *knows* you! That's a scream. Man, you think anyone's going to believe that our HR department called Trion with glowing recommendations, after we bounced you out on your ass? Do a little investigative work, and you'll see that every single phone call from our HR department was rerouted. Phone records show they all came from your own apartment. You made all the HR calls yourself, impersonating your supervisors at Wyatt. You're sick, man. You're pathological. You made up a story about being some big honcho on the Lucid project, which is provably false.'

My head was spinning slowly, and I felt nauseated.

'And maybe you should check out that secret bank account where you think we've been depositing funds from some offshore account? Why don't you track down the real source of those funds?'

I stared at him.

'That money,' Wyatt explained, 'was routed directly from several discretionary accounts at Trion. With your digital fingerprints on it. You stole money from them, same way you stole from us.' His eyes bulged. 'Your head is in a goddamned jaw trap. Next time I see you, you'd better have all the technical specs for that optical chip, or your life is *over*. Now get *out* of my house.'

PART SEVEN
Black Bag

Black Bag Job: Slang for surreptitious entry into an office or home to obtain files or materials illegally.

—*Spy Book: The Encyclopedia of Espionage*

'This better be important, buddy,' Seth said. 'It's like after midnight.'

'This is. I promise.'

'Yeah, you only call when you want something these days. Or death of a parent, that kinda thing.'

He was joking, and he wasn't. Truth is, he had a right to be pissed off. I hadn't exactly kept in touch with him since I'd started at Trion. Yet he'd been there when Dad died. He'd been a much better friend than I'd been.

We met an hour later at an all-night Dunkin' Donuts near Seth's apartment. He stared at me. 'What the hell happened to you?'

I didn't keep any of the grisly details from him—what was the point?

At first he thought I was making it up, but when I'd wound up my story he said, 'Oh, man, you are so lost.'

I smiled sadly, nodded. 'I'm screwed,' I said.

'That's not what I mean.' He sounded testy. 'You went along with this. They got your balls in a vice, and you caved.'

'What other option did I have?'

'You could have told me, I could have gotten one of the lawyers I work for to help out. You could have threatened to go public.'

I was silent for a moment. 'Yeah, well, it's too late for that now. Anyway, even if one of your firm's lawyers agreed to represent me, Wyatt would have set the whole goddamned American Bar Association after me.'

'Maybe. Or maybe he would have wanted the whole thing to stay quiet. You might have been able to make it go away.'

'I don't think so.'

'So instead, you went along with their illegal scheme, agreed to become a spy, pretty much guaranteeing yourself a prison sentence, and fucking over the one guy in corporate America who ever gave you a chance.'

I sat there, feeling miserable. Finally I said, 'I need your help.'

I'D NEVER been to the law firm where Seth worked, or pretended to work. It took up four floors in one of those downtown skyscrapers, and it had all the trappings people want in a high-end law firm—mahogany panelling, expensive Aubusson carpets, modern art, lots of glass.

He got us an appointment first thing in the morning with his boss, a senior partner named Howard Shapiro who specialised in criminal defence work. Shapiro was a short, chubby guy, balding, round black glasses, a high voice and rapid-fire delivery. He kept interrupting me, prodding me, and looking at his watch. He took notes on a yellow pad. Seth mostly sat there watching.

'Who beat you up?' Shapiro said.

'His security guys.'

He made a note. 'When you told him you were pulling out?'

'Before. I stopped returning their calls and emails.'

'If this whole thing blows up in your face and you're caught, you're going to go to jail, simple as that. Guarantee it.'

I felt like I'd been punched in the stomach. Seth winced.

'So what do you suggest?'

'I've got a buddy in the US Attorney's office, guy I trust. Wyatt's a big fish. You can serve him up on a silver platter. They'll be very interested.'

'How do I know they won't arrest me, throw me in jail too?'

'I'll make a proffer. Call him up, tell him I've got something I think he might be interested in. I'll say, I'm not going to give you any names. If you want to deal, you give my guy a queen for a day.'

'What's a "queen for a day"?'

'We go in, sit down with the prosecutor and an agent. Anything that's said in that meeting cannot be directly used against you.'

I looked at Seth, raised my eyebrows, and turned back to Shapiro. 'Are you saying I could get off?'

Shapiro shook his head. 'With that prank you pulled at Wyatt, the loading-dock guy's retirement party, we'll have to fashion a guilty plea to something. You won't get a total pass. Could be probation, or possibly six months.'

'Prison,' I said.

Shapiro nodded.

'If they're willing to deal,' I said.

'Correct. Look, you're in a shitstorm of trouble, frankly. The theft of trade secrets is a federal criminal offence. You could get ten years in prison.'

'What about Wyatt?'

'If they catch him? Under the Federal Sentencing Guidelines, a judge has to take into account the defendant's role in the offence. If you're a ringleader, the offence level is increased by two levels.'

'So they'll hit him harder?'

'Right,' he said. 'So, you want me to make the call or no?'

I looked at Seth, who nodded. There didn't seem to be any other choice.

WE SAT in the waiting area, silent, while Shapiro made the call. My nerves were stretched to breaking point. I called my office and asked Jocelyn to reschedule a couple of appointments.

A few minutes later, the door opened. I could tell from Shapiro's face that things hadn't gone well.

'What'd your buddy say?' I asked.

'My buddy got transferred to Main Justice. His replacement is a real prick. He said that if you give him a great case, he's willing to write you a great Five-K. A Five-K is a letter the prosecutor writes to the judge asking him to depart from the sentencing guidelines. However, there's no guarantee this prick would really write you a decent Five-K. To be honest, I don't trust him.'

'What's his definition of a "great case"?' asked Seth.

'He wants Adam to introduce an undercover.'

'An undercover *agent*?' I said. 'That's *insane*! Wyatt'll won't meet with anyone but me. He's not an idiot. And anyway, what guarantee is there that I won't get jail time even if I do agree to introduce an undercover?'

'None,' Shapiro admitted. 'The judge may not go for it. But whatever you decide, they're giving you seventy-two hours to make up your mind. Or the chips fall where they may. Look, they don't trust you. They don't think you can do this on your own. And face it, it's their ball.'

'I don't need seventy-two hours. I've already decided. I'm not playing.'

Shapiro looked at me strangely. 'You're going to keep working for Wyatt?'

'No,' I said. 'I'm going to handle this my own way. Set my own terms.'

'How so?' Shapiro said.

'Let's say I get some really concrete evidence against Wyatt,' I said. 'Could we take that directly to the FBI and make a better deal?'

'Theoretically, sure.'

'Good,' I said. 'I guess the only one who's going to get me out of this is me.'

Seth half smiled, reached out and put a hand on my shoulder. '"Me" meaning "me" or "me", meaning "us"?'

I GOT an email from Alana saying that she was back from Palo Alto and she'd love to see me. I called her at home, and we talked a while about the funeral, and how I was doing and all that. And then she said, 'Are you aware you're in serious trouble with HR?'

My breath stopped. 'Am I?'

'Oh, boy. Trion's Personnel Policy Manual expressly forbids workplace romances. Inappropriate sexual behaviour in the workplace harms organisational effectiveness through its negative impact on co-workers.'

I let my breath out slowly. 'You're not in my management chain. Anyway, I felt that we were organisationally quite effective. And I thought our sexual behaviour was quite appropriate. We were practising horizontal integration.' She laughed, and I said, 'Don't you think we'll be better Trion employees if we take off a night? I mean really get out of town. Be spontaneous.'

'Sounds intriguing,' she said. 'Yes, that could definitely boost productivity.'

'Good. I booked a room for us tomorrow night.'

'Where?'

'It'll be a surprise. As our fearless leader likes to say, sometimes you just gotta get in the car.'

SHE PICKED me up in her blue Mazda convertible and drove us out to the country while I gave directions. In the silences I obsessed about what I was about to do. I was really into her, yet here I was, using her to try to save my own skin. I was *so* going to hell.

The drive took forty-five minutes, past identical shopping malls and gas stations, and then a narrow, winding road through woods. Finally we came to a big, rambling country inn, white clapboard with dark green shutters. The air was cool and fragrant, and you could hear birds chirping, and no traffic.

'Hey,' she said. 'Nice. This place is supposed to be excellent. You take all your girlfriends here?'

'Never been here before,' I said. 'I read about it, and it seemed like the perfect getaway.' I put my arm round her and gave her a kiss. 'Let me get your bags.'

'Just one,' she said. 'I travel light.'

I took our bags up to the front door. Inside, it smelt of wood fires and maple syrup. The couple who owned the place greeted us like old friends.

Our room was sweet, very country-inn. There was an enormous four-poster bed, antique furniture, braided rugs, chintz curtains and a huge old brick fireplace. The bathroom was enormous, with an old iron clawfoot tub in the middle of the room. The bed squeaked and groaned, as we found out when we both plopped down on it.

'A lot of chintz,' Alana said. 'Reminds me of my grandmother's house.'

'Is your grandmother's house as big as this place?'

She nodded once. 'This is cosy. Great idea, Adam.' She slipped a cool hand under my shirt, stroked my stomach, and then moved south. 'What were you saying about horizontal integration?'

A ROARING FIRE was going in the dining room when we came down for dinner.

I ordered an expensive red Bordeaux, and I could hear Jock Goddard's words echoing in my head: *You used to drink Budweiser; now you're sipping some first-growth Pauillac.*

The service was slow, but it didn't bother me. We were both sort of blissed out, floating on a postcoital high.

'I noticed your computer in the trunk of your car. Are you sort of tethered to the office?' I said. 'Computer, cellphone, email, all that?'

'Aren't you?'

'Having only one boss seems to cut down on some of that.'

'Well, you're lucky. I've got six direct reports and a bunch of really arrogant engineers I have to deal with. Plus a huge deadline.'

'What kind of deadline?'

She paused, but for just a moment. 'The roll-out's next week.'

'You're shipping a product?'

She shook her head. 'It's a demo—a big public announcement, demonstration of a working prototype of the thing we're developing. I mean, it's a really big deal. Goddard hasn't told you about it?'

'He might have, I don't know. He tells me about all kinds of stuff.'

'Not the kind of thing you'd forget. Anyway, it's taking up all my time. Night and day.'

'Not totally,' I said. 'You're taking tonight off.'

'And I'll pay for it tomorrow and Sunday.'

The waiter finally showed up with a bottle of white wine. I pointed out his error, and he apologised profusely and went off to get the right one.

'Why *didn't* you want to talk to me at Goddard's barbecue?' I asked.

She looked at me incredulously, her sapphire-blue eyes wide. 'We've got to be discreet. People talk. And then if something happens . . .'

'Like a breakup or something.'

'Whatever. Then it becomes awkward for everyone.'

'So I guess I can't just pop in on you one day at work. Show up on the fifth floor unannounced with a bouquet of lilies.'

'I told you, they'd never let you in.'

'I thought my badge lets me in anywhere in the building.'

'Maybe most places, but not the fifth floor.'

'You have your badge with you?'

'They've trained me not to go to the bathroom without it.' She pulled it out of her little black bag and flashed it at me. It was attached to her key ring.

I grabbed it playfully. 'Not as bad as a passport picture, but I wouldn't submit this head shot to a modelling agency,' I said. Her badge had the same stuff on it as mine, the 3-D holographic Trion seal, the pale blue background with TRION SYSTEMS printed over and over on it in tiny white letters. The chief difference seemed to be that hers had a red-and-white stripe across the front. Plus, the chip inside was encoded with information that got her into the fifth floor in addition to all the main entrances, the garage, and so on. The red-and-white stripe had to be for quick visual identification. Meaning that there must be at least one additional checkpoint beyond the electronic badge reader. Someone had to check you out as you entered.

'When you go down to lunch or up to the gym—must be a huge hassle.'

She shrugged, uninterested. 'It's not too bad. They get to know you.'

Right, I thought. That's the problem. You have to pass by a guard for facial confirmation. 'At least they don't make you go through that biometric crap,' I said. 'We had to do that at Wyatt. You know—the fingerprint scan.'

'Well, there's this one inner area with biometrics, but only the engineers go in there. It's where they do work on the prototype. Hey,' she said, 'you haven't touched your wine. Don't you like it?'

I dipped a couple of fingertips into my glass of wine. 'Delicious,' I said.

This little act of stupid juvenile male goofiness made her laugh, her eyes crinkling into slits. Some women—OK, most women—might have asked for the bill at that point. Not Alana.

I was into her.

BOTH OF US were stuffed from dinner and a little unsteady from too much wine. Alana fell back on the creaky bed, her arms outstretched as if to embrace the whole room, the inn, the night, whatever. That was the moment for me to follow her onto the bed. But I couldn't, not yet.

'Hey, you want me to get your laptop from the car?'

She groaned, rolled her eyes. 'Oh, I wish you hadn't mentioned it. You've been talking about work way too much.'

'The first step is always to admit you're powerless over your workaholism. Anyway, I left something in your car, so I'm going down there anyway.' I held out my hand. 'Keys?'

She was leaning back on the bed, looking too comfortable to move. 'Mmph. OK, thanks.' She rolled over to the edge of the bed, fished her car keys out of her bag, handed them to me. 'Come back soon, huh?'

The parking area was deserted by now. I looked back at the inn, made sure our room didn't look over the parking lot. She couldn't see me.

I popped open the trunk of her car and found her computer bag, a grey nylon satchel. I wasn't kidding; I had left something in here: a small knapsack. I swung the satchel and knapsack onto my shoulder and got into the dark interior of her car. I felt like a creep, but I didn't have a choice. Alana was my best way into AURORA, and I *had* to get inside if I was to save myself.

Quickly I unzipped the satchel, pulled out her laptop and powered it on. While I waited for it to boot up, I opened my knapsack and pulled out a first-aid kit. Inside, instead of Band-Aids and such, were a few small plastic cases. Each contained a soft wax. By the blue light of the computer screen I pressed each of the keys on her key ring onto a rectangle of wax. Maybe one of them would open filing cabinets on the AURORA Project floor.

Now the password prompt on her screen was blinking at me. Shit. Not everyone password-protected their laptops. Oh, well: at least this wasn't going to be a wasted errand. From the knapsack I pulled out the miniature pcProx reader that Meacham had given me and connected it to my handheld. I pressed the start button, then waved Alana's badge at it. The little device captured the data on Alana's card and stored it on my handheld.

Maybe it was just as well that her laptop was password-protected. There was a limit to how much time I could spend out in the parking lot without her wondering where the hell I'd gone. Just before I shut down her computer, just for kicks I decided to try some of the usual-suspect passwords—I typed in ALANA, and the password prompt disappeared.

Oh, man, that was easy. I was in. How could I pass the opportunity up? It might never come again.

Alana was an extremely well-organised person. Her computer was set up in a clear, logical hierarchy. One directory was labelled AURORA.

It was all there—a gold mine of technical specs on the optical chip, marketing memos, copies of emails she'd sent and received, meeting schedules, staff rosters with access codes, even floor plans . . .

I had some blank CDs in the knapsack. I popped one into her CD drive. It took a good five minutes to copy all the AURORA files to a disk.

'WHAT TOOK you so long?' she said poutily when I returned.

She was under the covers, and she looked sleepy.

'I couldn't figure out which was your trunk key.'

'A car guy like you? I thought you drove off and left me here.'

'Do I *look* stupid?'

'Appearances can be deceiving,' she said. 'Come to bed.'

I put her laptop on the oak desk next to the bathroom. 'There,' I said, taking off my clothes. 'In case you're seized with some brilliant inspiration, some brainstorm in the middle of the night.'

Naked, I approached the bed. 'Get up here,' she said in a dramatic whisper, staring at me. 'I just had a *brainstorm*.'

WE BOTH woke up after eight—unusually late for us hyper-driven type A workaholics—and fooled around in bed for a while before showering and going down to a country breakfast. I doubt people in the country actually eat this way, or they'd all weigh 400 pounds: rashers of bacon, mounds of grits, freshly baked hot blueberry muffins, eggs, French toast . . .

Around eleven we reluctantly left, and the date was over. I think we both wanted it to keep going, but we also needed to get back, get some work done, make up for this delicious night away from work.

As we drove, I found myself luxuriating in the country road, the trees dappled with sunlight, the fact that I'd just spent the night with the coolest and most gorgeous and funniest and sexiest woman I'd ever met.

What the hell was I doing?

BY NOON I was back in my apartment, and I immediately called Seth.

'I'm going to need some more cash, man,' he said.

I'd already given him several thousand dollars, from my Wyatt-funded account. I was surprised he'd run through it already.

'I didn't want to get cheap stuff,' he said. 'I got all professional equipment.'

'I guess you had to,' I said. 'Even though it's one-time use.'

'What about the badges?'

'I'm working on that,' I said.

'Aren't you nervous?'

I hesitated a moment, thought about lying just to bolster his courage, but I couldn't. 'Totally,' I said.

I didn't want to think about what might happen if things went wrong. My brain was now obsessively working through the plan I'd come up with after meeting with Seth's boss. And yet there was part of me that wanted just to escape into a daydream, and think about Alana.

I'd alternate between feeling guilty about my treachery, and being overwhelmed by my attachment to her, something I really hadn't felt before. Little details kept popping into my mind: the way she scooped up water from the tap with a cupped hand instead of using a glass; the graceful hollow of her lower back, the incredibly sexy way she applied her lipstick . . . I thought about her velvet-smooth voice, her crazy laugh, her sweetness. And I thought—this was by far the strangest thing—about our future together.

I didn't want to lose this woman.

MEACHAM'S goons had brought back my computers and such, which was fortunate, because I needed them.

I popped the CD into my computer with all the stuff I'd copied from Alana's laptop. A lot of it was emails concerning the vast marketing potential of AURORA, the huge increases in computing power it promised, and how it really would change the world, but there was also a note about the security measures all AURORA team members followed.

One of the more interesting documents was a schedule of the public demonstration of AURORA. It was to happen four days from now, at the Visitors' Centre at Trion headquarters. Email alerts, faxes and phone calls were to go out only the day before to all the media. It was going to be an immense public event. I printed the schedule out.

Then I opened one of the garbage drawers in the kitchen island. Wrapped in a trash bag were a couple of objects I'd stored in Ziploc bags. One was the glass Alana had used in the apartment. The other was the Ani DiFranco CD she had picked up on an earlier occasion.

Meacham had given me a fingerprint kit, containing little vials of latent print powder, transparent fingerprint lifting tape and a fibreglass brush. Putting on a pair of latex gloves, I dusted both the glass and the CD with a little of the black graphite powder. By far the best thumbprint was on the CD. I lifted it carefully on a strip of tape, and put it in a sterile plastic case.

Then I composed an email to Nick Wyatt, addressed, of course, to 'Arthur':

Monday evening/Tuesday morning will complete assignment & obtain samples. Tuesday early morning will hand over at time and place you specify. Upon completion of assignment I will terminate all contact.

But would Wyatt himself show up at the rendezvous? I guess that was the big question. It wasn't crucial that Wyatt was there, and insisting on it would probably just warn him *not* to show. But by now I knew enough of Wyatt's psychology to be fairly confident that he wouldn't trust anyone else.

You see, I was going to give Nick Wyatt what he wanted. I was going to give him the actual prototype of the AURORA chip, which I was going to steal, with Seth's help, from the secure fifth floor of D Wing.

And the moment Wyatt—or Meacham, if it had to be—took delivery of the pilfered chip, I had him. Without naming names, Howard Shapiro, Seth's boss, had struck a deal with the FBI, who would be waiting with a SWAT team. If everything came off successfully, and I delivered Nick Wyatt to them, I'd get probation and nothing more.

Well, I was going to deliver Wyatt. But it was going to be my way.

I GOT INTO WORK early on Monday morning, wondering whether this was going to be my last day at Trion.

On Sunday, I'd cloned a couple of copies of Alana's proximity badge, using a little machine Meacham had given me called a ProxProgrammer and the data I'd captured from Alana's ID badge.

Also, I'd found among Alana's files a floor plan for the fifth floor of D Wing. Almost half the floor was labelled 'Secure Facility C', which was where the prototype was being tested. Unfortunately, I had no idea *where* in that area the prototype was kept. Once I got in, I'd have to wing it.

The rest of Sunday, I'd done research on the Trion website. It was amazing, really, how much information was available to Trion employees—from floor plans to security badging procedures to the inventory of security equipment installed on the fifth floor of D Wing. From Meacham I'd got the radio frequency the Trion security guards used for their two-way radios.

Getting to the AURORA prototype was going to be grotesquely difficult. I wasn't even going to be able to get through the first, manned checkpoint. I couldn't use Alana's card, obviously, because after you'd waved your badge at an automated card reader, you then had to show your face to a guard, as Alana had told me—and nobody would mistake me for her. But her card might be useful in other ways once I got onto the fifth floor.

The biometric sensor was even tougher. Trion was on the cutting edge of most technologies, and biometric recognition—fingerprint scanners, hand readers, voice ID, iris scans, retina scans—was the next big thing in the security business. They all have their strengths and weaknesses, but finger scans are generally considered the best and most reliable. And mounted on the wall outside Secure Facility C was a fingerprint scanner.

In the late afternoon, I placed a call from my cellphone to the assistant director of the security command centre for D Wing.

'Hey, George,' I said. 'This is Ken Romero in Network Design.' Ken Romero was a real name, just in case George decided to look me up.

'What can I do for you?' the guy said.

'Just a courtesy call. Bob wanted me to give you guys a heads-up that we're going to be doing a fibre upgrade on D-Five early tomorrow morning.'

'Uh-huh.' Like: why are you telling me?

'I don't know why they think they need laser-optimised fifty-micron fibre, but hey, it's not coming out of my pocket, you know? I guess they've got some serious bandwidth-hog applications running up there, and—'

'What can I do for you—'

'Romero. Anyway, I guess the guys on the fifth floor didn't want any disruptions during the workday, so they put in a request to have it done early in the a.m. We wanted to keep you guys in the loop 'cause the work's going to set off proximity detectors between four and six in the morning.'

The assistant security chief actually sounded sort of relieved that he didn't have to *do* anything. 'You're talkin' the whole darned fifth floor?' he said. 'I can't shut off the whole darned fifth floor without—'

'No, no, no,' I said. 'We're aiming for areas . . . lemme see, areas twenty-two A and B, I think? Just the internal sections. Anyway, your boards are probably going to light up like Christmas trees, probably going to drive you guys bonkers, so I wanted to give you a heads-up—'

George gave a heavy sigh. 'If it's just twenty-two A and B, I suppose I can disable those . . . Yeah, I can give you three hours if you need it.'

'We shouldn't need three hours, but I guess better safe than sorry, you know? Anyways, appreciate your help.'

AROUND SEVEN that evening I checked out of the Trion building, as usual, and drove home. I got a fitful night's sleep.

Just before four in the morning, I drove back and parked on the street so there wouldn't be a record of my re-entering the Trion building. Ten minutes later, a truck labelled J.J. RANKENBERG & CO—PROFESSIONAL WINDOW CLEANERS pulled up. Seth was behind the wheel in a blue J.J. Rankenberg uniform.

'Howdy, cowboy,' he said.

'J.J. himself let you have this?'

'The old man's dead,' Seth said. He was smoking, which was how I could tell he was nervous. 'I had to deal with Junior.' He handed me a folded pair of blue overalls, and I slipped them over my chinos and polo shirt. 'Told him I needed it for a quickie job I got for my girlfriend's dad's company.'

'You don't have a girlfriend.'

'All he cared was, I was offering cash and he doesn't have to report the income. Ready to rock'n'roll, dude?'

'Press send, baby,' I said. I pointed out the D Wing service entrance to the parking garage, and Seth drove down into it. The night attendant in the booth glanced at a sheet of paper, found the company name on the admit list.

Seth pulled the truck over to the lower-level loading dock and we took out the big nylon tote bags stuffed with gear: the professional squeegees, the big green buckets, the ropes and hooks, the Ski Genie and bosun chair and the Jumar ascenders. I'd forgotten how much *junk* the job required.

I hit the big round steel button next to the steel garage door, and a few seconds later the door began rolling open.

A paunchy, pasty-faced security guard with a bristly moustache came out with a clipboard. 'You guys need any help?'

'We're all set,' I said. 'If you can show us to the freight elevator to the roof . . .'

'No problem,' he said. He stood there with his clipboard and watched us struggle with the equipment. 'You guys can really clean windows when it's dark out?' he said as he walked us over to the elevator.

'At time and a half, we clean 'em *better* when it's dark out,' said Seth.

The guard laughed. 'Just hit R,' he said. 'If the roof access door's locked, there should be a guy up there, I think it's Oscar.'

WHEN WE GOT to the roof, I remembered why I hated high-rise window cleaning. The Trion building was only seven storeys high but up there, in the middle of the night, it might as well have been the Empire State Building.

The wind was whipping around, it was cold and clammy, and there was distant traffic noise, even at that time of night.

Oscar, the security guard, was a short guy in a navy-blue uniform with a two-way radio clipped to his belt squawking static. He met us at the freight elevator, shifting his weight awkwardly from foot to foot as we unloaded our stuff, and showed us to the roof-access stairs.

We followed him up the short flight. While he was unlocking the roof door, he said, 'Yeah, I got the word you guys would be coming, but I was surprised, I didn't know you guys worked so early.'

Seth repeated his line about time and a half, and Oscar laughed. We looked like legit window cleaners, and who the hell else would be crazy enough to climb out on the roof of a tall building lugging all that equipment?

'I've only been on nights a couple weeks anyway,' he said. 'You guys been up here before? You know your way around?'

We said we hadn't done Trion yet, and he showed us the basics—power outlets, water spigots, safety anchors. Unfortunately he hung around, watching as we attached the locking steel carabiners to half-inch orange-and-white kernmantle climbing rope, then connected them to the safety anchors.

'Neat,' he said. 'You guys climb mountains in your spare time, huh?'

Seth looked at me, then said, 'You a security guard in your spare time?'

'Nah,' he said, and laughed.

Each of us had two separate lines, one to climb down on, the other a back-up safety line with a rope grab, in case the first one broke. I wanted to do it right, and not just for appearances' sake. I knew that what we were doing was dangerous. During those unpleasant couple of summers when Seth and I worked as window cleaners, we kept hearing about how there was an industry average of ten fatalities a year.

After another five minutes or so, Oscar finally got bored, and went back to his station.

The kernmantle rope attaches to a thing called a Sky Genie—gotta love the name—which is a descent-control device that works by friction and pays out the rope. It gets hooked up to a nylon safety harness attached to a waist belt and padded seat board. These Sky Genies were scratched and looked like they'd been used. I held it up and said, 'You couldn't buy us new ones?'

'Hey, they came with the truck, whaddaya want? What are you worried about? These babies'll support five thousand pounds. Then again, you look like you've put on a couple pounds the last few months.'

Seth mounted the electric winch to one of the roof anchors with a D-ring. This was a 115-volt model with a pulley capable of lifting 1,000 pounds. He connected it to each of our lines, making sure that there was enough play that it wouldn't stop us from climbing down. We got into the nylon safety harnesses and hooked up to the Sky Genies.

The only thing we'd set up that was slightly out of the ordinary was a pair of Jumar ascenders, which would enable us to climb back up the ropes. Most of the time when you're cleaning windows you have no reason to go back up—you just work your way down until you're on the ground.

But this would be our means of escape.

I tugged on the rope, hard, to check that everything was locked in place, and we both walked over to the edge of the building and looked down.

Seth smiled a what-the-hell-are-we-doing smile. 'You ready, buddy?'

'Yeah,' I said.

We climbed onto the guardrail slowly and then went over the side.

WE ONLY HAD to rappel down two storeys, but it wasn't easy. We were both out of practice, we were lugging some heavy tools, and we had to be careful not to swing too far to either side, into the range of the closed-circuit TV cameras, because if anyone looked closely they'd realise we weren't actually cleaning windows. They'd see that we weren't even positioning ourselves in front of a window; we were dangling in front of a steel ventilation grate.

Bracing our feet against a ledge, we got out our power tools and set to work on the hex bolts. They were fastened through the steel and into concrete, and there were a lot of them. Seth and I laboured in silence, sweat pouring down our faces. Each bolt took a good fifteen minutes to remove.

Then, on a signal from me, Seth loosened the last bolt, and we both carefully lifted the heavy grate away from the steel skin of the building and rested it on the window ledge. Then Seth, grasping the grille for leverage, managed to swing his legs into the air shaft. He dropped to the floor of the mechanical equipment room with a grunt.

'Your turn,' he said. 'Careful.'

I grabbed an edge of the grate, swung my legs into the shaft and dropped to the floor, looking around quickly.

The room was crowded with immense, roaring equipment, all kinds of air-conditioning stuff, lit only by the spill of light from the floodlights mounted on the roof. We unsnapped our harness belts and let go, so that they hung in midair from the double ropes. Obviously we couldn't just leave them out there, but we'd rigged them up to the electric winch up on the roof. Seth pulled out a little black remote-control garage-door opener and pressed the button. You could hear this whirring, grinding noise far off, and the harnesses and ropes began to rise slowly in the air, pulled by the electric winch.

'Hope we can get 'em back when we need 'em,' Seth said, and I couldn't help thinking that this whole thing was little more than a game to him. If he was caught, he'd be OK. I was the one who was in deep doodoo.

Now we pulled the grate in tight so that, from the outside, it looked like it was in place.

Seth took out a pair of Motorola walkie-talkies, handed me one, and then pulled out from his holster a compact black short-wave radio, a 300-channel police scanner. 'You remember the security frequency? In the four hundreds UHF, wasn't it?'

I took a little notebook from my shirt pocket and read off the frequency number. As he began to key it in, I unfolded the floor map and studied my route. I was even more nervous now. We had a pretty solid plan, but too many things could go wrong. For one, there might be people around, even this early. AURORA was Trion's top-priority programme, and engineers worked weird hours. And there was the remote possibility that I might run into someone who recognised me. So I'd brought along a yellow hard hat, jammed it down on my head, then put on a pair of safety glasses.

'Got it,' Seth said, staring at the police scanner's digital read-out. 'I just heard "Trion Security" and something else Trion.'

'OK,' I said. 'Alert me if there's anything I should know.'

'Be careful, Cas.'

I nodded.

'Wait, here you go.' He'd spotted a big yellow-wheeled cleaning bucket in the corner, rolled it over to me. 'Take this.'

'Good idea.' I looked at my old buddy for a moment, wanting to say something like 'Wish me luck', but decided it sounded too mushy. Instead, I gave him the thumbs-up, like I was cool about all this. 'See you back here,' I said.

'Hey, don't forget to turn your thingy on, will you' he said, pointing to my walkie-talkie.

I shook my head at my own forgetfulness and smiled.

I opened the door slowly, looked out, saw no one coming, stepped into the hall, and closed the door behind me.

FIFTY FEET up ahead, a security camera was mounted high on the wall, its tiny red light winking.

Wyatt said I was a good actor, and now I'd really need to be. I had to look casual, busy, and most of all not nervous.

My work boots squeaked softly as I walked down the carpeted hall, wheeling the cleaning bucket. I turned the corner into a large, open cubicle-farm area and made my way down the middle of the room. Except for a few emergency lights, it was dark.

On the other side of this open area, I knew from the map, was a short corridor leading directly to the sealed-off half of the floor. A sign on the wall, saying SECURE FACILITY C—ADMITTANCE ONLY TO CLEARED PERSONNEL and showing an arrow, confirmed it for me. I was almost there.

This was all going a lot more smoothly than I'd expected. Of course, there were motion detectors and cameras all round the entrance to the secure facility. But if the call I'd made to Security the day before had worked, they'd have shut off the motion detectors.

Suddenly a loud noise jolted me, a high-pitched trill from my walkie-talkie.

'Jesus,' I muttered, heart racing.

'Adam,' came Seth's voice, flat and breathy.

I pressed the button on its side. 'Yeah.'

'We got a problem.'

'What do you mean?'

'Just get the fuck *back* here.'

Oh, shit.

I spun round, left the cleaning bucket, started to run until I remembered I was being watched. I forced myself to slow down to a stroll. What the hell could have happened?

The walk back took for ever. An office door swung open just ahead, and a middle-aged guy came out. He was wearing brown double-knit polyester slacks and a short-sleeved yellow shirt, and he looked like an old-line mechanical engineer. Getting an extra-early start on the day. The guy glanced at me, then looked down at the carpet without saying anything.

I was a cleaning guy. I was invisible.

Finally I reached the mechanical room. I stopped in front of the door, listening for voices, but all I could hear was the faint squawk of the police scanner.

I pulled the door open. Seth was standing just on the other side of the door, the radio near his ear. He looked panicked.

'We gotta get out of here,' he whispered. 'The security guy who took us to the roof must have gone back out there. Curious, whatever. Looked down, saw the ropes and the harnesses, but no window cleaners, and he freaked.'

'What?'

'*Listen!*'

There was squawking over the police scanner, a babble of voices. I heard a snatch: 'Floor by floor, over!'

Then: 'Bravo unit, come in.'

'Bravo, over.'

'Bravo, suspected illegal entry, D David wing. Looks like window cleaners—abandoned equipment on the roof, no sign of the workers. I want a floor-by-floor search of the whole building. This is a Code Two. Bravo, your men cover the first floor, over.'

'They're searching the building,' Seth whispered, his voice barely audible over the roar of the machinery. 'We have to get *out* of here.'

'How?' I hissed back. 'We can't drop the ropes, even if they're still in place! And we sure as hell can't get out through the man trap on *this* floor!'

'What the hell are we going to *do*?'

I inhaled deeply, tried to think clearly. 'All right. Find a computer, any computer. Log on to the Trion website. Look for the company security procedures page, see where the emergency points of egress are. I'm talking freight elevators, fire stairs, whatever. Any way you can get out.'

'Me? So what are *you* going to do?'

'I'm going back out there.'

'What? This building is crawling with security guards, you moron!'

'They don't know where we are, only that we're *somewhere* in this wing—and there are seven floors.'

'Jesus, Adam!'

'I'll never get this chance again,' I said, running towards the door. 'Tell me when you find a way out. I'm going back to get what we came for.'

DON'T RUN. I had to keep reminding myself. Stay calm. I walked down the hall, trying to look blasé when my head was about to explode.

I was halfway to the big open cubicle area when my walkie-talkie bleeped at me, two quick tones.

'Yeah?'

'Listen, man. It's asking me for an ID. The sign-on screen.'

'Oh, shit, right, of course. I whipped out a little spiral notebook. 'Use CPierson.' I spelled it out for him as I kept walking.

'Password? Got a password?'

'MJ twenty-three,' I read off.

'All right, I'm in,' he said. 'The Security page, you said?'

'Company security procedures. See if we can get back down to the loading dock using the freight elevator. That might be our best escape route. I gotta go.'

Straight ahead of me was a door with a diamond-shaped window reinforced with wire mesh. A sign said AUTHORISED PERSONNEL ONLY.

I approached the door slowly, at an angle, and looked through the window. On the other side was a small waiting room. I counted two CCTV cameras mounted high on the wall near the ceiling, their red lights blinking. They were on. I could also see the little white pods in each corner of the room: the motion detectors. No LED lights on the motion detectors. Maybe Security really had shut them down for a few hours.

In one hand I was holding a clipboard, trying to look official. With my other hand I tried the doorknob. It was locked. Mounted on the wall to the left of the door was a little proximity sensor. Would Alana's badge open it? I took out my copy of her badge, waved it at the sensor, willing the red light to turn green.

And I heard a voice. 'Hey! You!'

I turned slowly. Two Trion security guards were running towards me.

'Freeze!' the first man shouted.

Oh, shit. My heart leapt in my chest.

I stared at the guards, my expression changing from startled to arrogant. I took a breath. In a quiet voice, I said, 'You find him yet?'

'Huh?' said the first guard, slowing to a stop.

'Your goddamned intruder!' I said. 'The alarm went off five minutes ago, and you guys are still running around like idiots!'

'Sir?' the second guard said, looking at me, bewildered.

'You morons have any idea where the point of entry was?' I was shouting at them like a drill sergeant. 'Could we have made it any easier for you guys? For Christ's sake, are we going to have to spray-paint the trail in DayGlo colours? Should we have given you guys engraved invitations to a surprise security audit? We've run this drill in three area buildings in the past week, and you guys are the worst bunch of amateurs I've seen.' I took the clipboard and the attached pen and began writing. 'OK, I want names and badge numbers.'

'McNamara,' the second guard said reluctantly.

'Valenti,' said the first.

I jotted down their names. 'Badge numbers? Aw, look—one of you get this goddamned door open, and then both of you get the hell out of here.'

The first one approached the card reader, waved his badge at it. There was a click and the light turned green.

I shook my head in disgust as I pulled the door open. The two guards turned and began loping back down the hall.

I knew that all I'd done was to buy a couple of minutes. The guards would radio in to their dispatch and find out the truth immediately—there was no 'surprise security audit' going on. Then they'd be back with a vengeance.

I watched the motion detector, waiting to see whether a light would flash on, but it didn't. If the motion detectors were off, that meant the cameras were fixed—they couldn't turn in the direction of a moving object. I could enter the little lobby area without being seen. I took a few tentative steps into the room, flattening my back against the wall, and sidled slowly over to one of the cameras from behind. I was in the camera's blind spot.

A blast of sound jolted me—a throaty mechanical *hoo-ah* blaring from an alarm horn somewhere very close.

Now what? I *couldn't* stop here, just feet from the entrance to the AURORA Project! Not this close!

I had to keep going. I pulled a spray can out of my overalls—a can of aerosol cooking oil—then leapt up at the camera and sprayed the lens. I could see an oil slick on the glass eyeball. Done.

The siren blared, *hoo-ah*, *hoo-ah*, deafeningly loud.

Now the camera was blind, its optics defeated, but not in a way that would attract attention. Anyone watching the monitor would see the image go blurry.

There were footsteps, shouts, but they sounded far away, just background chatter against the earsplitting siren.

Maybe I could still make it. If I hurried. Once I was inside the AURORA laboratory, they probably couldn't come after me. Not unless they had some kind of override.

I circled the room, keeping out of camera range until I reached the other camera. Standing in its blind spot, I leapt up, sprayed the oil, hit the lens dead on. Now Security couldn't see me.

I was almost in. Another few seconds and I'd be inside AURORA.

Mounted on the wall to the left of a shiny steel door was a small beige box: an Identix fingerprint scanner. From the front pocket of my overalls I pulled the clear plastic case. With trembling fingers, I removed the strip of tape with Alana's thumbprint on it, and pressed it gently on the scanner, right where you'd normally put your thumb. I waited for the LED to change from red to green.

And nothing happened.

No, please, God, I thought desperately. *Make it work. Please, God.*

The light stayed red, stubbornly red.

Meacham had given me a long session on how to defeat biometric scanners, and I'd practised countless times until I thought I'd gotten it down. This was one of the commonest types of fingerprint reader, with an optical sensor inside it. And what I'd just done was supposed to work.

Shit, it *wasn't* working!

What were the other tricks they'd taught me?

Something about old fingerprints remaining on the surface of the sensor like handprints on a mirror, the oily residue of people who'd been admitted. The old fingerprints could be reactivated with . . . moisture . . .

I leaned over, cupped my hands over the little sensor, *breathed* on it. My breath hit the glass, condensed at once. It disappeared in a second, but it was long enough—

A beep, almost a chirp. A happy sound. A green light on the box went on.

I'd passed. The moisture from my breath had activated an old fingerprint. I'd fooled the sensor.

The shiny steel door to Secure Facility C slid slowly open on tracks just as the other door behind me opened and I heard, 'Stop right there!'

I stared at the huge open space that was Secure Facility C, and I couldn't believe what I was seeing. My eyes couldn't make sense of it.

I was expecting laboratory equipment and banks of electron microscopes, clean rooms, supercomputers and coils of fibre-optic cable . . .

Instead, what I saw were naked steel girders, bare unpainted concrete floors, plaster dust and construction debris.

An immense gutted space.

There was *nothing* here.

Where was the AURORA Project? I was in the right place, but there was nothing here.

And then a thought came to me that made the floor beneath my feet buckle and sway: *Was there in fact no AURORA Project after all?*

'Don't move a *muscle*!' someone shouted from behind me.

I froze. I couldn't have moved if I'd wanted to.

PART EIGHT
Active Measures

Active Measures: Russian term for intelligence operations that will affect another nation's policies or actions. These can be either covert or open and can include a wide variety of activities, including assassination.

—*Spy Book: The Encyclopedia of Espionage*

It was close to six in the morning when the security guards put me in a locked conference room on the fifth floor—no windows, only one door. There was an overhead projector, a whiteboard and, fortunately, a computer.

I wasn't a prisoner, exactly. I was being 'detained'. They told me Goddard wanted to speak to me when he got in. It was made clear to me that if I didn't cooperate I'd be turned right over to the police there and then, and that didn't seem to be a very good idea. So I waited.

Later I learned that Seth had just made it out of the building, though without the truck.

I suddenly remembered that I still had my cellphone with me—I'd tucked it into one of my pockets, and they hadn't found it. I switched it on. There were five messages, but before I could check my voicemail the phone rang.

'Yeah,' I said.

'Adam. Oh, shit, man.' It was Antwoine. He sounded desperate, almost hysterical. 'These guys tried to break in your dad's apartment. Two of 'em got away, but I grabbed the slower guy—oh, man, I don't want to get in trouble now! I don't want to go back inside. You gotta help me.'

'Calm down,' I said. 'Take a deep breath and sit down.'

'I'm sittin' on him right now. What's freaking me out is he says he knows you.'

'*Knows* me?' Suddenly I got a funny feeling. 'Describe the guy, Antwoine.'

'I don't know, he's a white guy—' He sounded sheepish. 'Right now he looks kinda red and mushy. I think I broke his nose.'

I sighed. 'Antwoine, ask him what his name is.'

Antwoine put down the phone. I heard the low rumble of Antwoine's voice, followed by a yelp. Antwoine came back on. 'Says his name is Meacham.'

I flashed on an image of Arnold Meacham, lying on my dad's kitchen floor under 300 pounds of Antwoine, and I felt a brief, blessed spasm of pleasure.

'Oh, I wouldn't worry about it,' I said. 'I promise you he's not going to cause you any more trouble.'

Antwoine now sounded relieved. 'Look, I'm really sorry about this, man.'

'Sorry? Hey, don't apologise. Believe me, that's the first piece of good news I've heard in a long time.'

And it would probably be the last.

I hung up. I figured I had a few hours to kill before Goddard showed up, so to pass the time I went on the Internet.

That was how I began to put some things together.

THE DOOR to the conference room opened. It was one of the security guards.

'Mr Goddard's downstairs at the press conference,' the guard said. 'He said you should go down to the Visitors' Centre.'

I nodded.

The main lobby of Building A was hectic with people, loud voices, photographers and reporters swarming all over the place. I stepped out of the elevator and elbowed my way through the crowd. I thought I heard someone call my name, but I kept going, moving slowly, gnome-like.

The auditorium's floor sloped down to a glittering pod of a stage, where Goddard was standing in a spotlight, wearing his black mock turtleneck and brown tweed jacket. Behind him was a huge screen on which his talking head was projected five or six feet high.

The place was packed with journalists, glaringly bright with TV lights.

'This acquisition,' he was saying, 'will double the size of our sales force, and it will double and in some sectors even triple our market penetration. By bringing together two great companies, we're creating one world-class technology leader. Trion Systems is now without question one of the world's leading consumer electronics companies.

'And I'd like to make one more announcement,' Goddard went on. He gave a pixie smile. 'I've always believed in the importance of giving back. So this morning Trion is pleased to announce the establishment of a new charitable foundation. Over the next few years, this foundation hopes to put computers into thousands of public schools in America, in districts that don't have the resources to provide computers for their students. We call it the AURORA Project—for Aurora, the Greek goddess of the dawn. We believe this project will welcome the dawn of a bright new future for all of us in this great country.'

There was a smattering of polite applause.

'Finally, let me extend a warm welcome to all the talented and hard-working employees of Wyatt Telecommunications. Welcome to the Trion family. Thank you very much.' Goddard bowed his head slightly and stepped off the stage. More applause, which gradually swelled into an enthusiastic ovation.

The giant projection of Jock Goddard's face dissolved into a TV news broadcast—CNBC's morning financial programme, *Squawk Box*.

On the screen, Maria Bartiromo was broadcasting from the floor of the New York Stock Exchange. 'As trading in Trion Systems hit record volume,' she was saying, 'Trion shares have already almost doubled and show no sign of slowing down, after the announcement by Trion founder and CEO Augustine Goddard that it's acquiring the troubled Wyatt Telecommunications.'

I felt a tap on my shoulder. It was Flo, a grave expression on her face. 'Adam, can you please come with me? Jock wants to see you.'

I nodded but kept watching. I wasn't really able to think clearly.

Now the picture on the big screen showed Nick Wyatt being hustled out of Wyatt headquarters by a couple of guards. You could tell that he was both furious and humiliated. I knew the feeling.

'Wyatt Telecommunications was a debt-plagued company, nearly three billion dollars in debt, when the news leaked out late yesterday that the company's flamboyant founder, Nicholas Wyatt, had signed a secret agreement, without the vote or even knowledge of his board of directors, to acquire a small California-based start-up called Delphos, a tiny company without any revenue, for five hundred million dollars in cash,' Maria Bartiromo was saying.

The camera zoomed in closer on Nick Wyatt. Tall and burly, hair gleaming like black enamel, coppery tan.

'That left Wyatt without enough to cover its debt payments. The company's board met yesterday afternoon and announced the firing of Mr Wyatt for gross violations of corporate governance, just moments before bondholders forced the sale of the company to Trion Systems at a fire-sale price of ten cents on the dollar. Today Mr Wyatt was unavailable for comment.'

Another tap on my shoulder. 'I'm sorry, Adam, but he wants to see you right now,' Flo said.

ON THE WAY up to the penthouse the elevator stopped at the cafeteria, and a man in an Aloha shirt with a ponytail got in.

'Cassidy,' Mordden said. He was clutching a cup of coffee, and he didn't seem surprised to see me. 'Word has it that Icarus's wings have melted.'

I nodded.

He bowed his head and was silent while the doors closed and the cabin ascended. It was just me and him. 'I see you're going up to the Executive Reception Suite. I take it you're not receiving dignitaries.'

I just looked at him.

'Now perhaps you understand the truth about our fearless leader,' he said.

'No, I don't think I do. As a matter of fact, I don't even understand *you*. For some reason, you're the one person here who has utter contempt for Goddard, everyone knows it. You're rich. You don't need to work. Yet you're still here.'

He shrugged. 'By my choice. I told you, I'm fireproof.'

'What the hell does that mean, already? Look, you're never going to see me again. You can tell me now. I'm outta here. I'm dead.'

Mordden smirked, did a fairly passable imitation of Ernst Stavro Blofeld. 'Since you're about to die, Mr Bond—' He broke off. 'Oh, I wish I could lay it all out for you. But I'd never violate the nondisclosure agreement I signed eighteen years ago.'

'Mind putting it in terms my puny earthling mind can comprehend?'

The elevator stopped, the doors opened, and Mordden got out. He put his hand on one of the doors to hold it open. 'That nondisclosure agreement is now worth about ten million dollars to me in Trion stock. Perhaps twice that, at today's share price. It certainly wouldn't be in my interest to jeopardise that arrangement by breaking my contractually obligated silence.'

'What sort of NDA?'

'As I said, I surely don't wish to jeopardise my lucrative arrangement with Augustine Goddard by telling you that the famous Goddard modem was invented not by Jock Goddard, a rather mediocre engineer if brilliant corporate gamesman, but by yours truly. Goddard could have had it for free, as my corporate contract stipulated, but he wanted sole credit. That was worth a good deal of money to him. Why would I want to reveal such a thing? Why would I want to disillusion you—and risk my financial bounty?'

'You're telling me the truth?' was all I could think to say.

'I'm not telling you anything,' Mordden said. 'It wouldn't be in my interest. Adieu, Cassidy.'

I'D NEVER seen anything like Trion's Executive Reception Suite. It didn't look at all like the rest of Trion—no choked offices or cluttered cubicles, no industrial-grey wall-to-wall carpeting or fluorescent lights. Instead, it was a huge open space with floor-to-ceiling windows through which the sunlight sparkled. The floors were black granite, the walls some kind of tropical wood. The space was broken up by banks of ivy, clusters of designer chairs and sofas, and in the centre of the room, a giant freestanding waterfall rushed over rugged pinkish stones.

A small round dining table was being set in the area between the indoor waterfall and a fireplace with roaring gas flames on ceramic logs. A man and a woman in maroon uniforms were putting out silver coffee- and teapots, baskets of pastries, pitchers of orange juice.

Baffled, I looked around, but there was no one else. No one waiting for me.

All of a sudden there was a *bing*, and a small pair of brushed-steel elevator doors on the other side of the room slid open.

Jock Goddard and Paul Camilletti.

They were laughing loudly, both of them high as kites. Goddard saw me, stopped midlaugh, and said, 'Excuse us, Paul—*you* understand.'

Camilletti smiled, patted Goddard's shoulder and remained in the elevator as the old man emerged, the doors closing behind him.

Goddard strode across the big open space. 'Walk with me to the john, will you?' he said to me. 'Gotta wash off this damned make-up.'

Silently, I followed him over to a glossy black door that was marked with little silver male and female silhouettes. The lights went on as we entered.

Goddard looked at himself in the mirror. 'Christ, I look like Liberace,' he said as he worked up soapsuds in his hands and began splashing his face. 'You've never been up here, have you?'

I shook my head, watching him in the mirror as he ducked his head down towards the basin and then up again. I felt a strange tangle of emotions—fear, anger, shock—that was so complex that I didn't know what to feel.

'Congratulations,' I said softly. 'It's been a big morning.'

He towelled off his face. 'It's all theatrics,' he said dismissively.

'You knew Wyatt would buy Delphos, no matter what it cost,' I said. 'Even if it meant going broke.'

'He couldn't resist,' Goddard said. He tossed the towel, now stained orange-brown, onto the marble counter.

'No,' I said. 'Not when he believed you were about to announce this breakthrough on the optical chip. But there was no optical chip, was there?'

Goddard grinned. He turned, and I followed him out of the rest room.

I kept going: 'That's why there were no patents filed, no HR files . . .'

'The optical chip exists only in the fevered minds of a handful of third-raters at a tiny, doomed company in Palo Alto.' He sat at the table, gestured to the place next to his.

I sat, and the two uniformed attendants came forward, poured us each coffee. I was more than frightened and angry and confused; I was exhausted.

'They may be third-raters,' I said, 'but you bought their company more than three years ago.'

It was, I admit, an educated guess—the lead investor in Delphos was, according to the filings I'd come across on the Internet, a venture-capital fund based in London whose money was channelled through the Cayman Islands. Which indicated that Delphos was actually owned by a major player.

'You're a smart fellow,' Goddard said, grabbing a sweet roll and tucking into it greedily. 'The true ownership chain is pretty hard to unwind.'

Now I understood why Paul Camilletti had conveniently 'forgotten' to sign the no-shop clause on the term sheet. Once Wyatt saw that, he knew he had less than twenty-four hours to 'steal' the company from Trion—no time to get his board to approve it. Which they probably wouldn't have anyway.

'But the only way to make Wyatt swallow the hook,' I said, 'was to have it come from a spy he thought he'd planted.'

'Nick Wyatt's a very suspicious man,' Goddard said. 'He never believes a single damned scrap of intel unless he's gotten it by subterfuge.'

I took a sip of ice water, which was so cold it made my throat ache. The only sound in this vast space was the splashing and burbling of the waterfall. The bright light hurt my eyes. It felt cheery in here, weirdly so.

'I don't understand how you managed to convince Wyatt the mole idea could work,' I said.

Goddard glanced up as the elevator opened, the one he'd come up on.

Judith Bolton. My breath stopped.

She came up to Goddard, gave him a quick kiss on the lips. Then she reached over to me, and clasped my hand in both of hers.

She sat down on Goddard's other side, unfolded a linen napkin on her lap.

'Adam's curious how you convinced Wyatt,' Goddard said.

'Oh, I didn't have to twist Nick's arm,' she said with a throaty laugh.

'You're far more subtle than that,' Goddard said.

I stared at Judith. 'Why me?' I said finally.

'I'm surprised you ask,' she said. 'You're a natural.'

'That, and the fact that you had me by the balls because of the money.'

'Plenty of people in corporations colour outside the lines, Adam,' she said. 'We had lots of choices. But you were far and away the most qualified. A pitch-perfect gift of blarney, plus father issues.'

Anger welled up inside me until I couldn't sit there any more listening. I rose, stood over Goddard, and said, 'Let me ask you something. What do you think Elijah would think of you now?'

Goddard looked at me blankly.

'Elijah,' I repeated. 'Your son.'

'Oh, gosh, right, Elijah,' Goddard said, his puzzlement slowly turning to wry amusement. 'That. Elijah was Judith's inspiration.' He chuckled.

The room seemed to be spinning slowly and getting brighter, more washed out. Goddard peered at me with twinkling eyes.

'Sit down, Adam,' Judith said, all concern and empathy. 'We were worried you might start to get suspicious if it all seemed to come too easily. Everything had to make sense, or it would start to unravel. We couldn't risk that.'

I flashed on Goddard's lake-house study, the trophies that I now knew were fakes. The way the trophy somehow got knocked to the floor . . .

'Oh, *you* know,' Goddard said, 'the old man's got a soft spot for me, I remind him of his dead son, all that bullshit? Makes sense, right?'

'Can't leave these things to chance,' I said hollowly.

'Precisely,' said Goddard.

'Very, very few people could have done what you did,' Judith said. She smiled. 'Most wouldn't have been able to endure the doubleness, straddle the line the way you did. You're a remarkable person, Adam.'

'I don't believe this,' I whispered. My legs felt wobbly, my feet unsteady. My head was throbbing like an open wound. 'I'll go clear out my office.'

'You'll do no such thing,' Goddard cried out. 'You're not resigning. Clever young fellows like you are all too rare. I *need* you.'

A shaft of sunlight blinded me; I couldn't see their faces.

'And you'd trust me?' I said bitterly, shifting to avoid the sun.

Goddard exhaled. 'Corporate espionage, my boy, is as American as apple pie and Chevrolet.'

'I'm done being jerked around,' I said.

'Adam,' Goddard said. 'You're sounding like an embittered loser. Like your father was. And I know you're not—you're a *winner*, Adam. You're brilliant. You have what it takes.'

I smiled, then laughed quietly. 'Meaning I'm a lying scumbag, basically.'

'Believe me, you didn't do anything that isn't done every day in corpora-tions the world over.' His voice softened. 'The game is the same everywhere. You just play it better than anyone else. No, you're not a liar, Adam. You're a goddamned master strategist.'

I turned away, stepped across the granite floor towards the elevator.

Very quietly, Goddard said, 'Do you know how much money Paul Camilletti made last year?'

Without looking back I said, 'Twenty-eight million.'

'You could be making that in a few years. You're worth it to me, Adam.'

I snorted softly, but I don't think he heard it.

'Did I ever tell you how grateful I am that you saved our bacon on Guru? That and a dozen other things. Let me be specific about my gratitude. I'm giving you a raise—to a million a year. With stock options thrown in, you could pull in a neat five or six million next year. Double that the year after.'

I froze in my tracks. I didn't know how to react. If I turned round, they'd think I was accepting. If I kept on walking, they'd think I was saying no.

'Adam, turn round,' Goddard said angrily. 'Turn round, *now*.'

I obeyed, my expression sullen.

'Are you clear on what happens if you walk away?'

I smiled. 'Sure. You'll turn me in. To the cops, the FBI, or whatever.'

'I'll do no such thing,' Goddard said. 'I don't want a word of this ever made public. But without your car, without your apartment, your salary—you'll have nothing. What kind of life is that for a talented fellow like you?'

They own you now . . . Your whole life ain't yours . . . My dad was right.

Judith got up from the table, came over very close to me. 'Adam, I under-stand what you're feeling,' she said. 'You're hurt, you're angry. You want to retreat into the comforting anger of a small child. It's totally understandable. But now it's time to put away childish things. You see, you haven't fallen into something. You've *found* yourself. It's all good, Adam. It's all good.'

Goddard smiled benevolently. 'Don't throw it all away, son. I know you'll do the right thing.'

MY PORSCHE, fittingly, had been towed away. I'd parked it illegally last night; what did I expect?

I walked out of the Trion building and looked around for a cab, but none was anywhere to be found, so, carrying a white cardboard box filled with the few things from my office, I walked along the side of the highway.

A few minutes later a bright red car pulled over to the kerb, slowed down next to me. It was an Austin Mini Cooper, the passenger's side window rolled down, and I could smell Alana's lush floral scent wafting through the city air.

She called out to me. 'Hey, do you like it? I just got it. Isn't it *fabulous*?'

I nodded and attempted a smile. 'Red's cop bait. Cops see red cars and switch on their radar.'

She said, 'Suppose you get down off your motorcycle and give me a ticket?'

I nodded, kept walking, unwilling to play.

She inched her car alongside me. 'Hey, what happened to your Porsche?'

'Got towed.'

'Come on, get in then, I'll give you a ride.'

'No, thanks.'

She drove slowly alongside. 'Oh, come on, Adam, don't be *mad*.'

I stopped, went over to the car, set down my box, put my hands on the car's low roof. Don't be mad? All along I'd been torturing myself because I thought I was manipulating *her*, and she was just doing a goddamned job. 'You—they told you to sleep with me, didn't they?'

'Adam,' she said sensibly. 'Get real. That wasn't part of the job description. That's just what HR calls a fringe benefit, right?' She laughed her swooping laugh, and it chilled me. 'They just wanted me to guide you along, pass along leads, that sort of thing. But then you came after *me* . . .'

'They just wanted you to guide me along,' I echoed. 'Oh, man. Oh, man. Makes me ill.' I picked up the box and resumed walking.

'Adam, I was just doing what they *told* me to do. You of all people should understand that.'

'Like we'll ever be able to trust each other? Even now—you're just doing what they want you to, aren't you?'

'Oh, please,' said Alana. 'Don't be so goddamned paranoid.'

'And I actually thought we had a nice relationship going,' I said.

'It was fun. I had a *great* time.'

'Did you.'

'God, don't take it so seriously, Adam! It's just sex. *And* business. What's wrong with that? Now come on and get in the car.'

I kept walking.

'Oh, come on,' she said, her voice like velvet, suggesting everything, promising nothing. 'Will you just get in the *car*?'

JOSEPH FINDER

Born: Albany, New York, 1958
Area of expertise: Russian Studies
Website: www.josephfinder.com

Joseph Finder is the kind of writer who has you looking over your shoulder, just to check no one's watching . . . In *Paranoia* he brilliantly creates an almost tangible sense of unease as his hero grows more and more certain that someone's observing his every move at the high-tech company where he works. How does Finder make it all seem so very real? Well, for a start, he visited several big corporations in America and took notes. 'It required going to places like Apple Computer, Cisco Systems and Hewlett-Packard and seeing how people there live their lives. What I found is, the more you talk to people the more you find their lives are invested in the place they work . . . the colleagues, the politics and the gossip . . . in a lot of ways it's like high school except you get the pay cheque.'

Even the dialogue in *Paranoia* has a ring of authenticity. Again, that's apparently down to research. 'I listened with the ear of an outsider. I sort of felt like an anthropologist going to Fiji or Africa—it was a completely alien situation. I remember the first time I visited Cisco, someone talked about "escalating", and I learned that it means going above someone's head, or your immediate boss's head, to get something done. There's a whole vocabulary, a whole way that people talk.'

Finder first made a splash with a controversial nonfiction book that drew on his detailed knowledge of Soviet affairs (he has a degree in Russian Studies and a master's degree from the Harvard Russian Research Centre). Since then he's produced five best-selling thrillers, three of which turned out to be prophetic: *The Moscow Club* presaged the coup against Mikhail Gorbachev; *Extraordinary Powers* described the unmasking of a CIA mole just days before Aldrich Ames was named, while *The Zero Hour* described a terrorist attack on Manhattan that foreshadowed 9/11. It's no wonder Finder is regularly hired by America's top newspapers to report on international affairs.

His last word on developing gripping plotlines is this: 'Any good thriller-writer has to be able to summon up some kind of paranoia. I always remember Kissinger's line: "Just because you're paranoid, doesn't mean they're not out to get you."'

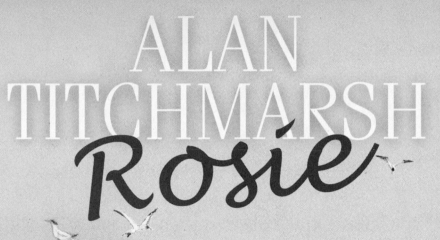

ALAN TITCHMARSH
Rosie

A picturesque seaside cottage,
wonderful views, an easel and
a set of paints . . . Nick Robertson
has settled for a quiet but
comfortable life, one that doesn't
hold too many surprises.
But all that changes when his
grandmother Rosie comes to visit.
At eighty-seven, she's about to
show her grandson how to really
live life to the full . . .

Chapter 1

'It's your grandmother.'

'Yes?'

'She's been arrested.'

This is not a conversation that many people expect to have. We know that grannies are not what they were, but even allowing for the fact that many are proficient on the Internet, lunatic behind the wheel and capable of doing full justice to the drinks cabinet, the discovery that our own had been detained at Her Majesty's pleasure would, if we are honest, come as a bit of a shock. A shock likely to provoke either disbelief or outrage.

As the policeman at the other end of the line delivered the grave news, in the particularly self-righteous manner that only someone wearing a uniform can, Nick Robertson found himself in the former camp. 'She's been what?'

'Arrested, sir. Well, detained, actually.'

'But what for?'

'Disturbing the peace.'

'Where?'

'In London, sir. She's at Bow Street police station. If you could come and collect her? We don't want to release her on her own and . . . well, I'd rather not say any more over the phone. We'll fill you in when you get here.'

'But why me?'

'Yours was the name and number she gave us, sir.'

There were many things Nick wanted to say, the first being: 'But I live on the Isle of Wight.' Instead he settled for: 'Right. It will take me a couple of hours to get there.'

'No problem, sir. We'll keep her comfortable.'

'She's all right, isn't she? I mean, she's not hurt?'

'Oh, no, sir. She's absolutely fine. Keeping my officers well entertained.'

'She would. I'll be there as soon as I can.'

And that was it. No more information. What had she done? And why hadn't she called his mother? She was nearer. But the answer to that was obvious: his mother would have given her mother-in-law what for. Or his father—her son? No again. Nick's dad would have been at the races—or at some meeting for his next money-making wheeze. Not much chance of finding him at the end of a telephone: his mobile number changed almost weekly.

Which was why, on a bright May morning, when he should have been staring out of the window and moping about the end of a three-year relationship with a girl, who was now sitting on a British Airways flight to New York, Nick found himself rattling into Waterloo Station on the eleven fifteen from Southampton. Briefly, he pictured his grandmother sitting in a cell, cowed and tearful, but, if he was honest with himself, he knew that was unlikely.

He wasn't wrong: he found her at the front desk of the police station, regaling a wide-eyed trio of uniformed officers with the reasons behind her forecast for a Chelsea victory over Manchester United. She looked round as he came in and smiled at him. 'Hello, love! Come to take me home?'

He nodded.

The desk sergeant broke away from the group, looking sheepish, negotiated the narrow opening to one side of the counter with some difficulty and beckoned Nick towards the room opposite. 'Would you mind, sir?' As the door closed behind them he heaved a sigh. 'Quite a character, your granny.'

'Yes.'

'I should think she takes a bit of looking after.'

'Well, most of the time she's fine.'

'Lives on her own, I gather.'

'Yes. She's not helpless,' Nick said defensively.

'Oh, I can see that. But it might be worth keeping an eye on her.'

Nick interrupted. 'What's she done? Nothing serious, surely?'

'Well, not serious. Just silly. We're letting her off with a caution. I think the Russian embassy was surprised more than anything. It's normally students who chain themselves to their railings. And dissidents. Not that we get many of them nowadays.' Then: 'We don't get many grannies either.'

'No. I suppose not,' Nick said, thoughtfully. Disbelief had been augmented by irritation. There were so many things he could have asked, but in the event he only managed, 'I mean . . . why did she do it?'

'Some sort of protest. Mind you, her equipment wasn't up to much. One of those bicycle safety chains. We just snipped it off.'

'I see.' He thought about it. It would once have been his grandfather's.

'The worry is that I think she rather enjoyed the attention and we've enough on without coping with protesting pensioners.'

'I'm sorry. I'll try to make sure she stays out of trouble.'

'If you would.'

'Can I take her home then?'

'Yes, of course.' He hesitated. 'Can I just ask you, sir . . . What your granny was saying. I suppose it's just her funny way, isn't it? I mean . . .' He looked at Nick sideways. 'She's not really related to the Russian royal family, is she?'

'What?' It was one of those defining moments: the moment when your granny, who you've always perceived as adorable and ever-so-slightly . . . *individual*, might have turned a corner.

Nick shook his head. 'No. I think you misunderstood. Her family *was* Russian. Gran left when there was all that bother with the Russian royal family when she was a baby. She's lived in Britain ever since.'

The policeman stared at Nick for a moment. 'Well, the embassy were very good about it. They had a particularly reasonable attaché on duty today. I suggested to him that your granny was just a bit—well, doolally.'

Nick's eyes widened.

'So, if you could just make sure she gets home safely. And maybe keep her away from bicycle chains for a while.'

'Yes. Yes, of course. It won't happen again,' he said, and added, under his breath, 'I hope.'

SHE WAS STANDING by the door of the police station, smiling, her silver-grey hair in its familiar soft curls, sensible shoes polished and tweed skirt pressed. Thanks to the morning's excitement, her pale blue eyes were sparkling as she pushed her hands deep into the pockets of her red, woolly jacket.

Nick's greeting came as a bit of a let-down.

'Come on, Granny.' Nick's tone was impatient.

She frowned. 'There's no need for that.'

'All right, then—Rosie.'

'Better.'

He sighed. 'Tea?'

'Ooh! Yes, please. Best thing anybody's said all day.'

'I thought police stations were famous for their tea.'

'Yes. But they don't do Earl Grey. Terrible stuff, theirs.'

'There's a café across the road. Come on, they'll probably do a range of designer teas.'

She stood quite still and shook her head.

'What's the matter?'

'I'm not having tea there, designer range or no.'

'Where, then?'

'The Ritz. As a celebration.'

'A celebration of what?'

'Mission accomplished.'

'What sort of mission? You've just been arrested.'

'I achieved what I set out to do.'

'Which was?'

She pulled up the collar of her jacket and held it with a leather-gloved hand. 'To draw attention to my life in exile.'

'Oh, Rosie!'

She fixed him with flashing eyes. 'I mean it.' The stern expression subsided and she grinned. 'Oh, go on, take me for tea at the Ritz. You look as though you could do with a bit of fun.'

He shook his head. 'What are you like?'

She put her head on one side. 'A duchess?'

'I DO WISH you wouldn't look so smug.'

Rosie sipped the Earl Grey in the china cup. 'Why shouldn't I?'

'Because you should be ashamed of yourself. Wasting police time.'

'Well, it was all in a good cause.' She picked up a tiny cucumber sandwich and popped it into her mouth, whole, chewing it purposefully and scrutinising her surroundings. 'Look at him. Over there.' She gestured towards a small, bespectacled man in a light grey suit. He was looking around the room as though he was waiting for someone. 'He looks suspicious. Do you think he's here to meet a lover?'

The reply was impatient. 'I really don't know.'

'Well, he might be. They come in the most unlikely disguises, you know.'

'Who do?'

'Lovers.'

'Like duchesses?'

She avoided his eye, then muttered, 'What, love?'

'What were you telling that policeman?'

'Have you finished with the sandwiches? Shall we go on to the cakes?'

'Is this how it's going to be now?'

'How what's going to be?' She was examining the cakestand.

'Are you going to carry on being childish?'

She looked hurt. 'That's a very mean thing to say.' He saw that her eyes were glistening with tears.

'Oh, don't do that!' He searched his pockets for a handkerchief, found it and handed it to her. 'You know what I mean.'

Rosie blew her nose. 'Oh, yes, I know what you mean. You're eighty-seven. Why can't you just be a normal granny? The usual stuff.'

'Well, what's wrong with that? Has Mum been at it again?'

She wiped the tears off her cheeks. 'A bit. But it's not just her.'

'But why chain yourself to the railings of the Russian embassy?'

'To scare myself.' She blew her nose again. 'To make myself feel as though I'm doing more than just sitting around waiting.' She sniffed. 'It's to prove to myself that I can still feel things.'

'Since Granddad?'

She nodded.

Nick reached forward and squeezed her hand. 'I know.'

'I'm glad he's not in pain any more. It wasn't much of a life at the end. But at least he minded. Once. Well . . . I think he did. About me.'

'Of course he did. We all do.'

'Huh! Some more than others.'

'Is that why you didn't ask the police to call Mum or Dad?'

She dabbed her cheek with the handkerchief. 'Not much point was there? Your mum would have given me what for, and your dad wouldn't have been there. No, I wanted you.'

'But you've got to find another way . . . You can't keep getting yourself arrested.'

'It was the first time!'

'You know what I mean.'

'If you mean will I promise I won't be any more trouble, the answer's no.'

'But why should you want to be trouble?'

'Because I want to do something with myself. It's time I had a life.'

'But you've had a life.' As soon as he'd said it he could have bitten out his tongue.

'So, that's it, then. Because I'm eighty-seven I shouldn't have expectations?'

'No, I didn't mean that—'

'Well, what did you mean? I've got a new hip and a new knee. It'd be a crime not to use them.'

'It *is* a crime when you chain them to railings.'

'It's just that I don't want to go quietly. To give in. I want to take risks.'

'Like imprisonment?'

She bit her lip, and her eyes brimmed with tears again. She mopped at them, then sniffed. 'Stupid old woman. I suppose it's hard for you to understand.'

'Not really. In one way, yes, but not in another.' He sat back in his chair. 'I just worry that—'

'That I'm getting dementia? Well, I'm not. At least, I don't think I am. But, then, I don't suppose you realise it when it's happening to you, do you?'

Nick watched her as she sipped her tea. She had looked confident in the police station, Nick thought. Now she looked crestfallen, fearful. He felt guilty: he was responsible for the change in her. He offered an olive branch. 'Tell me about it, then.'

She avoided his eyes. 'About what?'

'This Russian thing.'

'You know perfectly well what it's about.' She picked up another tiny sandwich, nibbled the corner, then finished it.

He spoke gently. 'The policeman said something about the royal family.'

She looked vague. 'Did he?'

'Can you remember what you said to him?'

'I have perfect recall.'

'Well?'

'Not telling you now. Wrong time. Wrong place. One day. When I'm ready.' She eyed the cakestand and settled on an elaborate cream horn. 'That'll put me right.' She began to dissect it. 'I know what you're thinking,' she murmured, through a mouthful of pastry, 'but I can't be bothered what people think any more.'

'Why?'

'Because people think what the newspapers and the television tell them to think. And, anyway, it's all geared to people under forty. Thirty, even. Get to my age and they think all you want to watch is repeats of *Miss Marple*. I can remember all the endings, you know.'

'So you do watch them?'

'Only once.' She snapped the end off the cream horn. 'Most of the time people just patronise you. Last week I was standing on the pavement looking at some may blossom. It was so pretty, but before I knew it I was halfway across the road with this man gripping me by the arm and booming in my ear. They treat you as though you're educationally subnormal. And deaf—they always shout at you. And I'm not deaf. Or daft.'

'No,' he said, with feeling.

She was warming to her theme now, and the cream horn was yielding to the pressure of a pastry fork. 'The trouble is, you get used to it. You do! You begin to believe that you *are* past it. You start acting like a child because you're expected to, and before you know it you've given up. It's a slippery slope.

'Take that over-sixties club I went to. What a waste of time. Arguing over the teapot, painting Christmas cards. Being fawned over. Heavens! There's more to life than that. I was twenty years older than most of them and I ended up running round after them—picking up their paints, passing them their coats, taking them to the toilet. It was like being back at school. No, thank you. I've still got a brain—what's left of it—and I still have opinions, but they don't seem to count any more. Who cares what I think?'

'I do.'

She looked at him suspiciously. 'Do you? Do you really?'

'Yes.'

'Even if it means being embarrassed?'

Nick leaned forward. 'I'd prefer to avoid that bit but, on the whole, yes, even if it means being embarrassed.'

Her face brightened. 'So will you help me?'

'Help you with what?'

'To live a bit.'

Her request took him by surprise. It seemed so innocent and plaintive. 'Well, I don't know . . .'

'I won't be a burden. I don't want to take over your life or anything. I just need a bit of support. Encouragement, I suppose.'

'I'll try.'

She smiled weakly. 'I know it must look like attention-seeking, but it's not that. It's just . . .' She sighed. 'Do you know that Peggy Lee song, "Is That All There Is"?'

He nodded.

'Well, I suppose I just want to keep dancing a bit longer. That's all.'

Nick put his arm round her and squeezed her gently. She smelt faintly of Chanel No. 5. Not like a granny at all.

He eased away and looked into her shimmering eyes. 'Well, no more chaining yourself to railings. Promise?'

She hesitated, then saw him raise his eyebrows in warning. 'I promise.'

He sat back in his chair. 'And this Russian thing. You'll talk to me about it when you're ready?'

'Yes. When I'm ready. I never told your dad when he was little. I was waiting until he was older but by then I knew there was no point. He was always a bit . . . well . . .'

'Cynical?'

'Yes. No imagination—except when he's dreaming he can make a fortune on some hare-brained scheme or a horse. I told him his grandmother was Russian and that she stayed behind during the revolution when I was brought over here. I never told him any more. I've never told anyone. No one would have believed me.'

'Why not?'

'Not now. I'll tell you when there's more time. And, anyway, there are other things I want to do as well.'

'What sort of things?' Nick asked uneasily.

'Things that nobody else has thought of. Like Marks and Spencer.'

'What?'

She hunched forward conspiratorially. 'I've had this brilliant idea. If Marks and Spencer change the labels on all their clothes, marking them as a size smaller than they really are, more people would shop there.'

'I'm sorry?'

She sighed impatiently. 'You're so slow. Think about it. Women don't like to think they're fat. They want to be a size eight, and most of them are a size ten—or more. All M and S have to do is change the labels on their clothes and then the size-ten women will be able to fit into a size eight.' She glanced about her to make sure they were not overheard, then carried on: 'Stands to reason that Mrs Smith will keep going back there, rather than to Next or Laura Ashley, because she feels better about herself in clothes from M and S.

Come to think of it,' she went on reflectively, 'maybe they should mark them down two sizes. Imagine a size-sixteen woman suddenly being able to fit into a twelve. Ha! Mind you, if I write and tell them, I don't expect I shall hear anything. Next thing you know they'll be doing it and won't pay me a penny.'

Nick gaped at her.

'Shut your mouth, dear, or you'll catch a fly.' She winked. 'Cakes have all gone. Shall we make a move?'

AS THEY WALKED down the street in Richmond towards his grandmother's flat, Rosie clung tightly to Nick's arm. 'Come in for a while?'

Nick looked at his watch. 'Just for a few minutes. I have to catch the ferry back to the island.'

'Aah! Doesn't that sound lovely? Almost like an adventure.'

Nick smiled. 'I suppose it does. I still like crossing the water to go home. Makes it a bit special.'

'Yes. And I've always liked the Isle of Wight. Ever since that holiday when you were little.'

'It's a bit quiet now.'

'Oh? I'd have thought it would have been busier than it was.'

'No. I mean quieter for me.'

Rosie looked at him enquiringly.

'Debs has gone.'

She stopped walking. 'What? But you'd been together such a long time.'

'Three years.'

'Oh, love! I'm so sorry.'

'Thanks.' He tried to sound noncommittal.

'What was it? You or her?'

'An estate agent, actually.'

'Huh. Never liked estate agents. Too smug by half. Wearing cufflinks during the day.' She took his arm and started walking again. 'Was it a shock?'

'Well, it was a bit of a surprise. I thought we were . . . comfortable.'

'I always think that's dangerous.'

'What do you mean?'

'Being comfortable can mean being taken for granted.' Rosie stopped at the kerb, looked right and left, then steered him across the road. Only when they had mounted the opposite pavement did she continue. 'Your trouble is that you always undersell yourself.'

'I'm a realist.'

'No, you're not. You're an apologist.'

'That's a big word.'

'Well, you're a big boy. Look at you—six foot what?'

'And a bit.'

'Good-looking, in a crooked sort of way.'

'Careful!'

'Well, no, you are—you're not George Clooney, but you've got a lovely smile and all your own hair.'

Nick winced. 'What is this? Are you starting up a dating agency?'

'Now, there's a thought . . .'

'Don't go there!'

'All right. Too much paperwork anyway. But you're not a bad catch and you're only in your thirties . . .'

'Just coming up for the final year.'

'Oh, yes. I nearly forgot. Still, you needn't worry. People leave it much longer now before they get married. Most don't seem to bother. And if you get someone younger you've still time to have children.'

'If you've quite finished planning my life for me . . .'

She looked up at him, winked and tugged at his arm. 'Sorry. I suppose I'm just an interfering old granny.' She smiled.

'You're incorrigible.' He smiled back.

'Oh, I do hope I am . . . So what now?' she asked.

'I don't know. I'm painting like a lunatic. Trying to get on. You know.'

'You need me to sort you out.'

'I thought *I* was sorting *you* out.'

'Bit of a joint venture, then.' She let go of his arm and rummaged in her cavernous crocodile handbag for the key. 'It's in here somewhere.'

'Let me.' He reached out for the bag, but she shot him a withering look.

'It's the light, not my sight.' She fished out a pair of glasses, put them on and continued to delve into the depths of the bag until, triumphantly, she located the key and slipped it into the lock.

It was certainly different from the house where Nick's grandparents had lived when he was a child. Until widowhood, Rosie's home had been a modest Victorian terraced house in Cheltenham, but inside it was neither the rebellious teak-filled home of Second World War veterans nor an antiquated Edwardian emporium furnished with chintz and a reproduction of Constable's

The Haywain on the wall. Instead the walls were barley white and peppered with bright prints and some of Nick's early paintings. The floors were polished boards, part covered with Indian rugs.

His grandfather had been easy-going about Rosie's taste: she had been the arty one, and he had deferred to that. He had been content to spend his retirement from the insurance company with the *Daily Telegraph* and the television. Then a stroke had robbed him of movement and speech, and confined him to hospital. Rosie had visited him twice a day for four years, until he had slipped away one evening while she was at home having supper.

She had wanted to stay in the family house, but Nick's mother had insisted it was too large and Cheltenham too far away. Rosie, normally strong-willed enough to stand up for herself, had allowed herself, in the wake of her bereavement, to be moved into a flat in a small, purpose-built block, where her daughter-in-law could keep an eye on her.

Nick watched her hang up her coat and adjust her hair in the mirror, then turn on the lamps in the sitting room and walk through to the kitchen.

'Coffee?' she asked, filling the kettle.

'Just a quick one.'

The events of the day caused him to look at her more critically than usual, as she made the coffee, then deftly collected cups and saucers from the dresser. Nobody would take her for eighty-seven. Sixty-seven, maybe, or seventy—but not three years short of ninety. She had always been Rosie to him, at her own insistence, never Granny. But was she finally losing her grip?

He pulled out a pine chair from the small breakfast table, sat down and looked around. A handful of dried lavender poked out of a painted jug and scarlet tulips swallow-dived from a square glass vase on the fitted worktop.

'Will you stay here?' he asked, curiosity getting the better of him.

'No.'

The answer came so quickly and decisively that it surprised him. 'Why?'

'Because I hate it.' She brought the cups and saucers to the table.

'But where will you go?'

'I don't know yet.' She dropped two spoons into the saucers. 'If I stay here I'll just sulk and fade away. Let's be honest. I probably haven't long to go.'

'Don't say that.'

She leaned on the back of a chair and the piercing eyes fixed him. 'Now who's not being realistic?'

'It's just that—'

'You don't want to admit it.'

'No.'

'All right, then, we won't talk about it again, so long as you don't try to wrap me in cotton wool.'

'I don't think I could.'

HE LEFT HER at six, and, as he kissed her on both cheeks at the door of her flat, he noticed the photograph on a side table. It was a sepia-toned portrait of a girl with dark hair, fine features and a clear complexion. She stood in falling snow, which powdered the front of her high-buttoned coat. A pale scarf was wrapped round her neck, and her mouth was open a little, as if she was catching her breath in the ice-cold winter air. She stood to the left of a small boy in a thick, Barathea sailor suit, and a bearded man in a military uniform.

'She's still here, then.'

Rosie turned and picked up the photograph. 'Mama? Oh, yes. She always is. Doesn't she look lovely?'

'She does.'

Rosie replaced the photograph. 'We'll talk about it soon.'

'I'll call you. I can get back next week, if that's OK?'

'Fine.' As he walked out she called after him, 'You're not too cross with me, are you?'

'You're not very easy to be cross with,' he said and left with a wave.

Chapter 2

The northern coast of the Isle of Wight is divided into two by the Medina River. The eastern half looks towards Portsmouth and Hayling Island, and the western towards Lymington and Dorset. West of Cowes, between Gurnard and Thorness Bay, there is a craggy, crumbling stretch of coastline opposite the Beaulieu River. Cattle graze the pale green undulating meadows above the cliff, where a snaking pathway cuts its way between banks of blackthorn and quickthorn, brambles and gorse. In winter the salt-laden winds rip through the undergrowth, and heavy rains wash swathes of the greasy grey clay into the waters of the Solent. In summer, the

hedgerows are wreathed in dog roses and bryony, and clouded yellow butter-
flies flit over clover and vetches while the song thrush sings in the twisted trees.

For five years, Nick Robertson had lived in a clapboard cottage perched on
the top of this bare patch of coastline, just about making a living from painting watercolours and selling them through a local gallery.

His grandmother had impinged rarely on his life. He called her on the
phone every week or so, and she would ask how things were going with the
painting and his love life—she always spoke her mind.

His mother, Anna, having raised her three children—Alice, now married
and living in South Africa, Sophie, single and travelling in South America,
and Nick, the arty one, who studied at St Martin's and then decided to 'do his
own thing'—was doing an Open University degree in medieval history and
worked at her local library. 'It's my time now,' she had told her family, and
proceeded to live an almost independent life. After the children had gone, she
had told her husband she wanted out. He surprised her by saying that so did
he, then upped and left. Rosie had not been pleased.

Derek Robertson was known to most people outside the family as 'a bit of
a lad'. His ex-wife used less endearing terms to describe him. After a moder-
ately successful spell in the City he had cashed in his chips and devoted himself to the turf—often with surprising success. The *Racing Post* was his daily
paper, and when he wasn't placing bets on horses, he took a chance on anything vaguely entrepreneurial that came his way. His flat in Chelsea Harbour
suited him nicely. He loved his daughters, did his best to understand his son,
and enjoyed the wheeler-dealer life.

Which explained why, when Rosie was in trouble, she called on Nick, the
one member of her family who she knew she could always contact and would
get her out of a spot. Her relations with her son were good-natured but spo-
radic, and with her daughter-in-law, frosty and matter-of-fact.

Nick sat in his studio gazing at the sea, today the colour of pewter and
merging with the sky. The north island—the locals' disparaging name for the
mainland—had disappeared from view, as if it didn't exist. He liked the feeling of being cut off. As he was now—in more ways than one.

The phone rang, and he was surprised to hear his mother. 'Nick?'

'Hi.'

'The front page of the *Richmond and Twickenham Times* is plastered with
pictures of your grandmother chained to some railings. Do you know anything about this?'

'Well . . . yes.'

'And you didn't tell me? Why not, for God's sake?'

'Because I knew you'd be furious.'

'I am! The Russian embassy! She's not started all that again, has she?'

'All what?'

'About her mother being wronged by the Bolsheviks. She's not fit to be on her own any more!'

'Oh, come on, Mum. That's a bit much.'

'Well, clearly she can't look after herself. And your father's no help. I'm going round to her flat today to find out what it's all about.'

'Don't do that—you'll only upset her.'

'Too right. She has to know that she just can't do this sort of thing.'

He could visualise Anna at the other end of the phone: the grey mane held back with a black velvet alice band, the finely plucked eyebrows, the pearls, the black pashmina draped round her shoulders, the Jaeger tweed skirt and the black tights.

'Just leave it to me, Mum.'

'But what can you do, over there?'

'I can come over. I've already been once, as it is.'

'It's May. Aren't you up to your ears in painting?'

'Well, yes, but . . .'

'I must sort this out before she embarrasses us even more. Thank God I use my maiden name on the Open University course. At least nobody will guess I'm related to her.'

'That's not a very nice thing to say.'

'What she did was not a very nice thing to do. I'm going to get some brochures about nursing homes.'

'But she's not ill! Look, don't do anything yet. I'll talk to her.'

'It won't make any difference.'

'At least let me try.'

After a few more placatory remarks he put the phone down. It rang again, almost immediately, and the pompous voice at the other end made him smile.

'By my elegant little Cartier watch it's forty-eight minutes past the hour of eleven, which means that you are now exactly eighteen minutes late. As it takes a good half-hour to get to my little gallery in Seaview from your shack in the back-of-beyond, that means I shall not see you until lunchtime. Do I take it that you'll be requiring refreshments?'

HENRY KINROSS Fine Art was to be found at the top of a short flight of worn stone steps by a slipway that sloped down to the sea. The gallery had once been a boathouse, but the bitumen-painted feather-edged boards were now a delicate shade of eau de nil, and scallop shells had been fixed in a double row on either side of the door. As Nick opened the door, the bell pinged loudly. The gallery owner was holding a dreary seascape and frowning at it through half-moon spectacles. 'Look at this! Drive a man to drink.'

Henry Kinross was not a small man. He had a sizable belly, short legs, and the sort of face that looked as if someone had sat on it. His hair was grey, his cheeks were the colour of a Victoria plum, and his voice was refined by years of claret.

Nick glanced at the picture. 'Mmm. Do you want me to bring mine in?'

Henry laid the painting on the white-painted table in the centre of the room and took off his glasses. Then he waved at the blank wall at one end of the gallery. 'It'll look pretty bare if you don't. How many have you got?'

'About a dozen.' Nick propped open the door and began to carry in the framed watercolours.

'Wonderful. That should keep me going for a couple of weeks.'

'God! Longer than that, I hope. I'm not a machine.'

Henry began to line up the paintings against the wall. 'No gratitude, that's your trouble. Not everyone sells like you do, you know. Look at old what's-his-face.' He nodded in the direction of the grey seascape. 'That'll never shift. Too depressing.'

'Accurate, though,' Nick told him.

'If people want accuracy they can take a photograph.'

'Maybe mine will start to get a bit more dreary now.'

'Ah.' Henry put down the painting he was carrying. 'She's gone, then?'

Nick nodded.

'And you're feeling sorry for yourself. Well, can't say I blame you. She was a nice girl.'

'I don't need reminding.'

'I suppose not. But you probably need cheering up. Come on. Let's get out of here and into some food. Starving artist and all that.'

'I'm not hungry.'

'Well, I am, so you'll just have to watch me. Come and have a glass at least.'

Henry prodded Nick across the road and into the bar of the Red Duster. He ordered a bottle of the house red and two glasses. They planted themselves, on Henry's instructions, at a table just opposite the door. 'Cheers, old bean! First of the day.' Henry took a gulp of wine and sighed with satisfaction. 'Oh, little grape, how great thou art! Now, then . . . we'll wait to order food. Someone else is joining us.'

'Oh?'

'Artist. Wants me to take her stuff. I'm interested to know what you think. Thought you'd like to meet her first and then we'll look at her paintings.'

'No fear. I'm happy to meet her, Henry, but I'm not going to sit in judgment on her stuff. One artist criticising another?'

'That's all you lot ever do, isn't it?'

'In private, maybe, but not to each other's faces.'

The uneasy silence that might have followed was pre-empted by an almighty clatter outside the pub. All conversation stopped, and there was a general movement towards the door. Nick and Henry were first onto the pavement, followed by the barman and a couple of local builders.

'Bloody 'ell.' One of the builders had summed up the scene neatly, if not with clinical accuracy. In front of them, where earlier Nick's Morris Minor van had sat by the pavement, was a hybrid vehicle, half Morris, half Fiat, with no visible distinction between the two.

A dark-haired young woman was sitting at the wheel of the Fiat, her head in her hands. Nick tried to open the car door but it refused to budge. He ran round to the other side and tugged at the passenger door, which yielded. 'Are you all right?'

The woman lowered her hands.

'It's OK. Don't worry. Come on, let me help you out.'

She gazed at him apologetically. 'It was my brakes.' She began to shake.

'Best get her out,' offered Henry.

'Yes, come on. Can you slide across?'

She swivelled her denim-covered legs across the passenger seat and got out onto the pavement. She was slight, about thirty. Her long dark hair had been pinned back, but was now falling over her face—fine-boned and olive-skinned, but pale with shock. Nick put his arm round her to steady her. The baggy pink and white sailing shirt she wore made her appear waif-like.

'I tried to stop, but nothing happened,' she said.

Nick glanced at the fused vehicles. 'No.'

'God, what a mess!' said Henry, and the woman burst into tears.

'Thank you, Henry. We can see that.'

Nick eyed his van and realised that their long association was at an end. Then he looked at the Fiat. Not much hope there, either. In the back of the car, he spotted a tangled mixture of blankets and canvas, and grasped that the woman must be the artist Henry had been so keen for him to meet.

'Come inside,' he said to her. 'Let's get you a drink.'

By the time they had walked through the door of the pub and sat down at the table, a large Scotch had appeared courtesy of the barman. But the girl shook her head. 'Just water, please. Tap.' She reached into her pocket for a tissue and tried to smile. 'What a way to start.'

'Do you feel OK?' asked Henry. 'No bones broken?'

'I don't think so. Just a bit stiff.' She wiped her eyes with the tissue and thanked the barman for the water.

Henry took a gulp of his wine. 'I think I'm going to need this.'

'What about the cars?' asked the barman. 'Shall I call the Old Bill?'

'Not unless you want to?' Nick directed his question at the woman.

'But whose is the van?' she asked.

'Mine.'

'You'll want to claim on your insurance.'

Nick shook his head. 'Not worth losing my "no claims". But what about yours?'

'Same.'

'Shall we just call the breakdown truck to clear them away, then?'

'Are we allowed to?'

'Don't see why not. If we're quick.'

Within an hour the only trace of the collision was a scattering of dried mud and a bucketful of broken glass on the road. Passers-by had been hurried along, and the police—who were probably busy on the congested Newport Road—had failed to put in an appearance.

Henry never did get his lunch. Instead, he helped to salvage the paintings from the Fiat and carried them into the gallery.

It was a good half-hour before Nick discovered the identity of the woman who had written off his dear old van. Her name was Alexandra—Alex—Pollen and she turned out to be nothing like as frail as he had thought. But, then, you can't make judgments about anyone's character on the basis of having pulled them out of a crumpled car.

Over tea in the back room she explained that she'd discovered Henry's gallery the previous year on a day-trip to the island. She had thought he might like some stuff that wasn't run-of-the-mill, and had told him on the phone that her oils might be just that.

Nick admired her nerve, if not her paintings. They were vivid and simplistic, not at all his style, but they did have a raw energy.

'Can you sell them, do you think?' Alex asked Henry.

'Well, there's only one way to find out.' He looked across at Nick. 'What do you think?'

Nick did his best not to glare at Henry for putting him in such a position. 'I think they're . . . exhilarating.'

Alex wasn't fooled. 'Well, I can't expect everyone to like them. But I'll be happy enough if you'll give them a go, Henry.'

The remaining conversation was polite. Then it was time for Alex to leave.

'Well, I'd run you to the ferry, dear, except that I don't drive,' said Henry. 'What about you?' he asked Nick.

'I'd better hire a car.'

'I'm so sorry,' Alex said.

'No, well, you probably just moved things on a bit.'

A call to a friendly local garage resulted in a car being delivered to the gallery within the hour, and Nick took Alex to the Wight-Link ferry terminal at Fishbourne. 'Where's home?' he asked.

'Portsmouth.'

'Handy.'

'Very. That's why I wasn't too worried about getting home. I can walk from the ferry at the other side.'

She got out of the car, walked round to the driver's window and leaned in. 'Thank you for being so good about the car. I really don't know what to say.'

'Don't worry.'

'Just in case you change your mind.' She handed him a piece of paper on which she had written her name, address and telephone number. 'I expect we'll meet again soon. I like coming over to the island.'

He motored home, deep in thought, considering an Austin A30—and Alexandra Pollen. He was not considering Rosie. Until he saw her standing in the doorway of his house.

'What the . . .' He leapt out of the car and strode up to her. 'What are you doing here?'

'Getting away from your mother.'

'What do you mean?'

'She came round this morning. Did you tell her?'

'I didn't tell her anything. It was in the local paper.'

'Wants to put me in a home. Even had some brochures with her.'

Nick looked at her, laden with a small suitcase and two carrier bags. 'How have you managed?'

'I got a taxi—both ends.'

Nick unloaded her. 'Come on. Let's get you inside.'

Rosie glanced down the path to the road. 'Where's the van?'

'In a scrapyard somewhere near Bembridge.'

'Oh dear. Has it finally given up? Never mind—perhaps you can get a sports car now instead.'

'Will you stop changing the subject?' He fumbled in his pocket for the key, and ushered her in.

Over tea and biscuits the story tumbled out. 'She didn't even ask if I was all right.'

'I don't suppose she needed to.'

'Didn't care, more like.'

'Oh, now, stop feeling sorry for yourself.'

Rosie looked at him pleadingly. 'But to put me away!'

'She doesn't want to put you away, she wants to make sure you're taken care of. That's all.'

'Dreadful expression! Taken care of! Makes me sound senile. Just so that I don't get in her way.'

Nick realised this particular conversation was going nowhere. 'Why have you come here?'

'Because you're the only person I can trust.'

He smiled. 'You sound like a secret agent.'

'Mmm.' She paused. 'That would be fun.'

He shot her a look.

'I thought it might be a bit of a break,' she went on. 'Do me good.'

'Have you booked somewhere?'

'No.'

'Where will you stay, then?'

Rosie looked about her.

'Oh, Rosie! There's no space.'

'There's the little bedroom.'

'But it's full of painting stuff, and it's tiny.'

'You'll hardly know I'm here—and it won't be for long, just till I get myself organised. I won't get in the way.'

He sighed. 'It's not that I don't want you here, it's just that, well . . .' But when he looked into her eyes he knew he had lost: she wasn't going anywhere. And he was, as she had known he would be, a soft touch.

He bent down and kissed her cheek. 'I'd better clear out the little bedroom.'

'Thank you, sweetheart. You're a life-saver.' She squeezed his hand and walked over to the window. 'What a wonderful view.' She turned back to face him. 'What a lark, eh?'

MANY THINGS might have happened over the next few days: she might have irritated the pants off him; she might have been demanding; she might have fussed over him and driven him mad. In the event, she did none of these.

Over the first day she observed him at work and noted his *modus operandi*. By day three he worried that he was not looking after her enough. She had breakfast just after he did, then pulled on a pair of soft boots and a windcheater and went out. He didn't see her again until early evening when she joined him for supper and then went to bed early.

He was concerned about her walking along the cliff unaided, so he bought her a stick. She was indignant, until he explained that all proper walkers carried one like this, a modified ski pole.

By day four he pushed her a bit. 'Are you managing?'

'Yes, thanks. Are you?'

'Yes. Surprisingly.'

'You see, I told you I wouldn't be much trouble. And I'm not, am I?'

'Not so far, no.'

'Hmph!'

'Have you got enough clothes and things?'

'Oh, yes. I think so. I thought I might have a bit of an expedition, though. There's some nice sailing stuff in Cowes.'

He grinned at her. 'Don't tell me you're thinking of going sailing.'

'Oh, yes. I've booked the course.'

He nearly choked on his coffee. 'What?'

'At the sailing academy.' She saw the look on his face. 'It's for five days.'

'But you—'

'They've had older people than me doing it. The man said so.' She noted his look of wide-eyed astonishment but carried on, savouring the moment.

'I've always fancied getting out on the water, but your granddad never liked it, so we never did.'

'No.'

'Only little dinghies. Toppers, they're called. Quite fast, though.'

'Yes.'

'Should be all right as long as I can remember to keep my head down. Catching flies again?' she asked.

Nick closed his mouth hastily. 'You crack me up. You really do.'

'What a lovely thing to say. I must remember that.' As she went towards her room he heard her chuckle to herself, then murmur, 'You crack me up, you really do!'

NICK TURNED into the gravel path at the front of his cottage. 'The Anchorage' said the small slate sign. He couldn't help thinking that, as far as Rosie was concerned, the name was appropriate.

He walked along the verandah at the front of the house, between the forest of bright green montbretia leaves, and glanced into the tiny box-room next to the front door. It was the one place where he could tuck a computer. The desk lamp was turned on and Rosie was hunched over the keyboard.

Nick let himself in through the front door and poked his head into the little room. 'What are you doing?'

Rosie almost leapt out of the chair. 'You made me jump!'

He glanced at the screen, and then at his grandmother. 'When did you learn how to use a computer?'

'At night school when your granddad was ill. It took my mind off things.' Then she said brightly, 'I've found you a car. On the Internet. It's an MG.'

Nick sighed. 'But I don't want an MG. You can't get paintings into an MG.'

'Yes, you can. You can have a rack on the boot lid over the spare tyre. I've checked. And, anyway, the small ones would fit in the footwell at the front.'

'What about when it rains?'

She looked at him through narrowed eyes. 'It does have a hood, you know.'

There was nothing for it but to look over her shoulder at the screen.

'You see?' she said. 'Perfect. Very sporty. Bit of fun. Take you out of your-self. I'll print it off.' And then, evidently fearful that she had overstepped the mark, 'You don't mind, do you, about me using the computer?'

Nick shook his head. 'No. Not at all. I'm just surprised.'

The printer whirred and Rosie picked up the piece of paper and handed it to him. She stood up and indicated the finer points of the car. 'It's British racing green with a red radiator grille—you can't tell that from the print-out. And the hood is black. It says it's in its original condition and has had the same owner for the last thirty years.'

Nick read out: '"MG TC, 1949. Mechanically this car is superb. The engine, when being driven, has an excellent oil pressure and is entirely sound."'

'And it has the original logbook, showing owners back to 1963, and all the bills and receipts for the last thirty years. It was bought in 1969 for a hundred and fifteen pounds,' said Rosie. Her enthusiasm was infectious.

'How much is it now?' asked Nick, his eye drifting down to the foot of the page. 'Bloody hell! Eleven thousand two hundred and fifty quid! Not a chance! I haven't got that sort of money.'

Rosie's eyes lit up. 'I have!'

'What?'

'*I* could buy it.'

'Don't be silly.'

'I'm not being silly. I could buy it as an investment. I've got plenty saved up and nothing else to do with it. The banks aren't paying much interest. Much more fun to have a sports car. That way, you can drive it and I can come out for a spin occasionally. Can't I?'

'Well, yes. But no! I mean, this isn't right.'

'If you're worrying about your sisters and their inheritance, don't. I've sorted all that out.'

'But I want a van!'

'Don't be ridiculous. Can you hear yourself? "I want a van"! What a feeble thing to say when you could be spinning around in that.'

Nick looked at the print-out. It was indeed a lovely car. 'I don't know . . .'

'Do it for me?'

He folded his arms. 'And if I don't?'

'I shall be unhappy.'

'Where is this flash car?'

Rosie pointed out of the window. 'In Portsmouth. We'd be there in an hour.'

IT WAS LOVE at first sight. The rolling wave of the mudguard. The neatly spoked wheels. The crimson-reeded radiator grille. Nick ran his hand over one of the bulbous, glistening headlights and Rosie knew he was enslaved.

They hardly needed to take her out for a test drive. Nick knew how she would feel. Strong, but nimble. Spirited, but of a certain age. Obliging, as long as she was handled sensitively. The car had a lot in common with his grandmother.

He felt embarrassed when she wrote out the cheque, and tried not to look like a little boy who had just been indulged by his granny.

The salesman waved as they drove away like an excitable couple of newly-weds. From her position deep in the bucket-like passenger seat, Rosie glanced at Nick as they sped towards the ferry. He was beaming from ear to ear. She had not seen him so happy for a long while. It made her smile, too.

And then she remembered how it had felt to be taken for a spin in a fast car by a good-looking young man. She had been twenty-two. Her hair streaming out behind her, she was laughing and looking sideways at the handsome doctor, who brushed her knee lightly with his hand. For a month they were barely apart. Then he was called up, and she never saw him again. Six years later they engraved his name on the war memorial.

'Can we stop for a minute?' she asked.

Nick had been lost in his thoughts. 'Sorry?'

'I just wondered if we could pull up for a minute. My eyes are watering.'

He drew in to the side of the road. 'Yes, of course. Are you all right?' He watched her reach into her pocket for a tissue.

'Oh, yes. Just remembering.'

He leaned towards her, and kissed her cheek. 'Thank you.' He tapped the steering wheel. 'She's lovely.'

'Oh, she's a she, is she?'

'Of course.'

She pushed the tissue back into her pocket, pulled out a brightly patterned headscarf and tied it under her chin. 'Come on, then, or we'll miss the boat.'

AT SIX THIRTY the following morning he found himself leaning out of his bed-room window gazing dreamily at the car parked below.

He looked up at the sky, which was flushed with the amber glow of a clear morning. The sea was glassy calm, and there was no sound, except the distant kleep-kleep of half a dozen oystercatchers on the shore. He'd go to Sleepyhead Bay, find himself a quiet corner by some rocks, then paint the cottages and the little café. He hadn't felt like taking out his brushes for the better part of a week. Today he was anxious to get started.

'Will you be all right?' he asked later, as he loaded his bag into the passen-ger side of the car.

She was standing by the front door. 'Of course I'll be all right. Perfectly capable, you know . . . now that I've got my stick.' She grinned. 'I shall go for a little walk. Catch a bus somewhere. Not sure.'

'Well, take care. I'll be back late afternoon. We can have supper together if you want.'

'That'd be nice.' She waved, then went indoors as he steered the car down the track towards the village and out across the island.

WITH HIS BOARD on his lap, he was sketching the scene before him—the towering cliff, the neat row of cottages tucked in beneath it, the apron of rocks, girdled by shallow pools, and the children dipping for shrimps and crabs with their bamboo-poled nets. A couple of small yachts played nip-and-tuck half a mile out, and the lobster fisherman was carrying his catch up the steps to the little café. Nick had picked a good day.

He did not like being watched while he painted, but out here, especially during the school holidays, it was an occupational hazard. He had just finished the sky when he became aware of a child at his side. 'That's nice,' she said. Her dark hair was tied into plaits and she was leaning on her shrimping net to examine his work.

'I'm glad you like it.'

'It's better than my mum can do.'

'Does she paint?' he asked politely.

'Yes. She tries to sell them.' The child shrugged, dismissive.

'So do I.'

'I bet you sell more than she does.'

'Oh, I don't know.'

'I do. She hasn't sold one yet.'

'Oh. I see.' He laughed.

'Would you like to come and see her painting?'

'Well, I'm a bit busy at the moment.' He frowned, hoping she'd leave him in peace.

'She's only over there. And she'd probably appreciate some advice.'

He was amused by the child's conversation, which was older than her years. She was nine or ten, and was wearing a white T-shirt and a pair of baggy yellow shorts. Her feet were bare, her skin honey-coloured from the early summer sun, and her turned-up nose was dusted with freckles. She had the darkest eyes he had ever seen.

'What's your name?' she asked.

'Nick.'

'Nick what?'

'Nick Robertson. What's yours?'

'Victoria.'

'Victoria what?'

'I'm not going to tell you. My mum says I shouldn't—in case you're not very nice.'

Nick grinned. 'Quite right, too.'

The child pointed her shrimping net to the other end of the cove. 'She's over there. Will you come and look? Please?'

He could see that he would not get any peace until he did as she asked, so he put down his board, anchored it with a rock, and followed her as she picked her way nimbly through the sharp stones.

Around a particularly large and craggy outcrop they came upon a woman seated on a smooth, round boulder, with a stubby easel jammed among the smaller rocks in front of her. She was dressed like the child—in T-shirt and shorts—with her dark hair pinned up at the back of her head.

'I've brought someone to look at it, Mum.'

'Oh, poppet, why do you think . . .?'

The woman looked up. It was Alexandra Pollen.

Nick laughed.

Alex scrambled to her feet. 'Hello! Fancy meeting you here.'

The child looked from one to the other. 'Do you two know each other?'

'Well, yes,' Alex said, and coloured. 'This is the man whose car I crashed into.'

'Oh!' Victoria turned to Nick. 'I expect you're pretty cross with us, then.'

'No. Well, a bit. But not much.'

'We've got another one.' She prodded the net into the pool at her feet. 'It's not very good, but it was all we could afford.'

Alex brushed down her shorts. 'Sorry about this. She's a bit annoyed with me for pranging the car.'

'Not your fault when your brakes fail,' said Nick.

'It hadn't got an MOT,' Victoria chipped in.

'Oh. I see.'

Alex lowered her eyes. 'Sorry. I should have said . . . only I was due to take it in to the garage the following day. I hadn't noticed . . .'

'Daddy came round and she got in a bit of a state. She always does.'

Nick felt uncomfortable. 'I'd better get back to my painting.'

'Fancy a coffee?' Alex pointed towards the café.

'I really should get back. The light . . .'

'Ah, yes. The light,' she teased.

He saw the look in her eyes and gave in. 'Just a quick one.'

Alex turned to her daughter: 'Shall I bring you back an ice cream?'

'No, thanks.' She bent down to pick something out of her net. 'I'd rather have a Diet Coke, please.'

'OK.'

'She's quite a character,' Nick remarked as they walked towards the café. 'How old is she?'

'Ten, going on twenty-nine,' she said.

'I had no idea you had children.'

'It's just Victoria and me. I'm a single mum.'

'Oh?'

'Most of the time anyway. He keeps coming back—or trying to. We're over here for a few days to get a break.'

Nick said nothing, unsure how to respond.

Alex covered the awkward moment. 'Oh dear! This is all getting rather intense, isn't it? Too much information.'

'No—please, go on. I wasn't . . . I mean . . . Would you like that coffee?'

She laughed and broke the tension. 'Yes. And I'd kill for a biscuit.'

He ordered two coffees and some tartan-wrapped shortbread biscuits, then sat down opposite her at a little table on a sun-bleached deck among some old fishing nets. 'Shall we start again?' he asked.

'Third time lucky? Sorry. You must think I'm a complete wacko.'

'Only a bit of a wacko.' He tilted his head. 'Have you had a difficult time at home?'

'Yes. It's better than it was, but it's still a bit iffy. We married too young and stayed together for eleven years because of Victoria. He's not a bad guy, but we're just not suited and the rows seem to get worse.'

'What now, then?'

Alex shrugged. 'Who knows? He's starting a new job next week and he's going abroad on business for a few months. I wanted to be out of the way and I like it over here.'

He looked out towards the sea. 'Nobody knows about it, really.'

'About the island?'

'England's best-kept secret.'

'It's supposed to be for white-haired ladies and men with fawn anoraks, isn't it?'

'Well, I love it here. But, then, I'm not your typical thirty-something.'

'That's a relief.' Alex grinned.

'Thank you!' He sipped his coffee.

'So, what are you?' she asked.

'Almost thirty-nine.'

'And never been kissed?' she asked with a wry smile.

Nick frowned. 'Another disaster area, I suppose. Not much to tell. Just come out of a long relationship—well, not as long as yours, but three years. Debs went off to the States last week to see a bit of action.'

'Oh, I'm sorry.' Alex stirred her coffee. 'Are you in mourning?'

'Not really. A bit fed up. And hurt, I suppose.'

'Are you committed to staying here?' she asked.

'For now, yes. I love painting on the island—and I love it in winter when there's nobody about.'

'I think you're just a loner, really,' she told him.

'Maybe. Not always though.' He pushed a shortbread biscuit across the table. 'Another?'

'No. I'll wait until lunchtime. Are you staying?'

'Well, I've got a painting to finish . . .' He hesitated.

'Why don't you have some lunch with us? You can give me some advice on my painting.'

'I wouldn't dream—'

'Well, I'll settle for a bit of company, then . . . if you don't mind?'

HE WATCHED THEM as they pored over the menu, Victoria leaning over Alex's shoulder. They were like sisters, each advising the other on the best choice.

'You should have that,' said Victoria, pointing to 'freshly fried fish and salad'.

'What about you?' asked her mother.

'That.' Victoria darted a finger at 'Pint of prawns with brown bread and butter', then slipped the straw of her Diet Coke into her mouth and sucked.

'Can you peel them?' asked Nick.

Victoria nodded, without looking up.

'She's been able to peel prawns since she was little,' said Alex. 'We had a holiday in Spain, and she learned when she was three. She loves seafood.'

'Expensive tastes,' said Nick.

'Yes. She gets it from her father. I'm very low maintenance.'

Victoria sat back. 'How long are we going to stay on the island?'

'Just for the week,' Alex told her. 'Then we'll go home.'

'We can't see home from here, can we?'

'Not from this side of the island, but we can from the north side.'

'I prefer this side,' said Victoria. 'There's more sea.'

'Do you like the sea?' asked Nick.

'It's not that. It's just that it takes longer to get home from here.'

'Well, we can come back lots if you like,' her mother told her.

'Yes, please.'

VICTORIA FINISHED her prawns, leaving a neat pile of shells on her plate, while Nick and Alex were still eating. She excused herself from the table and went back to her rock pool. They watched her concentrate on fishing.

'Does she get on with her dad?' asked Nick.

'So-so. He spoils her rotten and he's not badmouthed me.'

'Will he still be able to see her?'

'Oh, yes. But if this new job takes off he'll be away quite a lot.'

'You get on really well with her.'

'Most of the time, yes. There is the occasional tantrum.'

'Well that's growing up, isn't it?' He smiled ruefully.

'That's what I tell myself. And I'm the only one she can let off steam with.'

'Grandparents?'

'No.'

'That's a shame.'

'Yes. I think she must get pretty pissed off with me sometimes.'

'You're a bit hard on yourself.'

'I deserve to be. I've made a real mess of things so far.'

Nick pointed to Victoria. 'Not with her.'

'No,' she said softly. 'Bless her. I'm just determined that things will get better. That's what keeps me going.'

'Is that why you're painting?'

'Partly. It's a bit selfish, too. I can escape when I'm painting. Go somewhere else. Be someone else.'

Nick watched as Alex traced patterns on the table with a finger. 'So you're not a career painter?' he asked.

'Oh, come on! You knew I wasn't a professional painter when you saw my canvases.' She looked worried for a moment. 'Do you think Henry knew?'

'Probably, but he doesn't care as long as things sell. He thinks you're worth a punt.'

Her face lightened again. 'Well, that's something, I suppose. A start.'

'What did you do before?'

'I was an English teacher. Then Victoria came along and I didn't want to be a part-time mum so I gave it up. But I can read a cracking bedtime story.'

'Lucky girl.'

'Oh, I hope so. I really want her to have a good life and I don't feel I've done very well for her so far.' Alex gazed at her daughter wistfully, then asked, 'What about you?'

'Well, no kids. Two sisters, both abroad. And a granny.'

'No Mum and Dad?'

'Yes. But the granny's the one who takes up most of my time.'

Alex laughed. 'Why?'

'She's a bit of a liability. Eighty-seven. Sharp as a razor but she has her moments.'

'How?'

'Oh, she's just taken it into her head that she hasn't lived enough so she's starting now, which is very nice in one way but a real pain in another. She's staying with me at the moment.'

'Here? On the island?'

'Yes. You ought to meet her. Why don't you come for supper one evening?' Then he worried that he had pushed himself too much. 'But perhaps . . .'

'It would be lovely,' she said.

They sat quietly for a few minutes, then Nick got up. 'I'd better get on. Painting to finish.'

'Yes.'

'Look . . .' He pulled a stubby pencil and a scrap of paper out of his pocket and quickly scribbled something down. 'This is where I am. I've promised my grandmother supper tonight, so if you two want to come you'll be very welcome. It would be good for her, too. And Victoria. They might be a match for each other.'

She took the note, glanced at the address and the map he had sketched.

'Are you sure?' she asked. 'We're a bit of a handful.'

'I'm positive.' He leaned forward and kissed her cheek. 'And thank you.' He turned and walked away across the rocks.

'My pleasure,' she whispered, as she slipped the note into her pocket.

'WHAT SORT of company?' asked Rosie.

'Female company,' said Nick, looking up from chopping the salad

'Ooh!'

'There's no need to say it like that.'

'I didn't say it like anything.'

'Well, that's all right, then.'

'Do I get a clue?' Rosie asked.

Nick sighed, then said, 'An artist and her daughter.'

'That's nice.'

Rosie put knives, forks and spoons, napkins and place mats on the pine table that stood in the bay window. She liked his little place. The outside walls were black-painted clapboard with yellow window frames and, inside, the wooden panelling was white. Nick's taste was minimalist without being cold: there were pieces of gnarled driftwood and shells on the doorstep, cream linen curtains at the windows and white-painted furniture.

The two bedrooms were warmer: brightly coloured quilts covered the mattresses and dried flower wreaths hung over the brass bedsteads. The bathroom sported a bath on ball and claw feet. It was the perfect seaside bachelor pad.

Rosie finished the table by placing a small bowl of wild flowers in the centre—dog roses, campion, grasses and buttercups.

'Where did you find those?' Nick asked.

'On the clifftop. I nearly got blown away picking them.'

'They're lovely. Thank you.'

Rosie smiled at him fondly. 'Now tell me about this artist.'

He told her about the crash outside the pub, about Alex's paintings, and about meeting her at Sleepyhead Bay. He told her about Victoria and about the child's father. About how Alex had turned from being an English teacher to being a painter and about how she was hoping to change her life.

By the end Rosie couldn't suppress a grin.

'Why are you smiling?'

'Because you're so happy to talk about her. And she has the most wonderful name.'

'Alexandra?'

'Yes. Very Russian.'

Nick frowned. 'How come you were called Rosie?' he asked.

'To put people off the scent when I was smuggled out of Russia. My real name is Alice Marie Xenia. All family names.'

He flopped into a chair. 'If you're so pleased that Alex has a Russian name, why on earth did you christen Dad Derek?'

'I wanted to call him Alexander, but your granddad put his foot down. Derek was the name of a good friend of mine who was killed in the war. A doctor.'

'And me? Was Nicholas your idea?'

'As luck would have it, that was your mother. All I had to do was sit quietly and smile to myself. But your father had the last laugh.'

'With my middle name?'

'Yes. I thought your mother must have been a bit dim not to understand, but your dad managed to pull the wool over her eyes—until after the christening at least. I did think he was taking his love of the horses a bit too far. Naming you after a Grand National winner.'

'It could've been worse.'

'Worse than Nicholas Silver?'

'Yes. If I'd been born a few years later I could have been called Red Rum.'

Rosie laughed. 'Sometimes you really crack me up,' she said.

Chapter 3

I don't know whether to feel guilty or relieved.' Alex was looking at the MG parked outside the house.

'Oh, think of yourself as a catalyst,' said Nick, a twinkle in his eyes.

'You do say the nicest things to a girl.'

'It's a way I have.'

'Are they all right in there, do you think?' Alex looked towards the house, where Rosie was showing Victoria Nick's treasures.

'Oh, yes. She's had lots of practice.'

Rosie had slipped into great-grandmother mode while Nick and Alex drank coffee on the verandah.

'She'll be reading her a bedtime story next.'

'Talking of which . . .' Alex looked at her watch.

'There's no rush,' said Nick. 'It's a lovely evening.'

He gazed at her sitting in the cane chair, feet curled under her. Her dark hair was still pinned up, but she had changed into a pale pink shirt and jeans. He could see the candlelight reflected in her dark eyes.

'It's the most perfect spot,' she said. 'You're very lucky.'

'I suppose I am.'

'So did . . . Debs live here with you?'

'Some of the time—when she wasn't abroad.'

'She travelled a lot?'

'A fair bit. Absence made her heart grow fonder . . . of somebody else.'

'How was it? The ending, I mean.'

'Strangely civilised. Scary, really.'

'Oh, don't be scared of civility. It's better than the other option.'

'I guess. But it's not very passionate, is it?'

Alex grinned at him mischievously. 'And are you a passionate man?'

He was about to reply when he became aware of another voice: it was Rosie's and she was getting into her stride. 'And then the princess met the most wonderful man.'

'How was he wonderful? Was he good-looking?' Victoria asked.

'Oh, yes. Definitely.'

'And did she fancy him?'

'Well, yes, I suppose she did . . . the princess lived in a country that was very large, and a lot of the working people didn't have much money. This meant that they didn't like the princess's family because they had too many lovely things, like Fabergé eggs and suchlike.'

'What's a Fabergé egg?'

Suddenly Nick grasped the drift of their conversation, and sprang up. 'Rosie!'

'Yes, darling?'

'What are you talking about?'

Before she could reply, Victoria said, 'A princess and a . . . What was he?'

'A pauper.'

Nick endeavoured to steer her away from what to him were uncharted waters and a possible source of embarrassment. 'Don't you think it's a bit late for stories?'

'Yes,' Alex put in. 'We really must be going.'

'No—I didn't mean—' He looked pleadingly at his grandmother.

She beamed at him innocently. 'It's only a quarter to ten—and they are on holiday.'

Alex stood up and slipped on her shoes. 'No. You're quite right. It's way past Victoria's bedtime.'

Nick tried to retrieve the situation. 'Don't go. It was just that—'

'We've had a lovely time. Perhaps we'll see you again before the end of our holiday. Say good night, Victoria, and thank Rosie for a nice evening.'

'Oh, do we have to? I want to hear the end of the story.'

Alex shot her a look.

'OK.' Victoria sounded resigned. 'Good night, Rosie, and thanks for having me.' She stretched up to give Rosie a peck on the cheek. 'Good night, Nick.'

'Good night, Victoria. Thank you for coming.' He was embarrassed now. He turned to Alex, but she was collecting Victoria's jacket from the back of a chair and did not meet his eye.

As they walked down the verandah steps together he tried to make amends. 'I'm sorry. I mean about . . . just then . . .'

'It's fine, really. Thank you for a lovely meal.' She squeezed his arm, then walked round their battered old Ford, let Victoria into the back seat and belted her in. 'Have a good rest of the week,' she said.

Nick watched the scarlet taillights disappearing down the stony track. How could a perfectly pleasant evening have soured so quickly? It was only minutes since he and Alex had been sitting on the verandah . . .

He stormed inside. 'You promised!'

'Promised what?'

'Not to go on about your past.'

'But I was only telling her about the princess and the pauper.'

'Oh, yes? A princess who had Fabergé eggs and lived in a large country where the poor people didn't like the princess's family.'

'Well, I was only embellishing it a bit with things I knew. I don't understand why you're so cross with me.'

'Because I worry about you.'

'But if you worried about me you'd care, and if you cared you'd listen, instead of treating me as though I'm stupid.' Rosie shook her head, blinking back tears. 'I might as well give up. Nobody really cares.'

'That's not true. Look.' He squeezed her hand. 'Let me get you a drink. What do you want? Tea? Coffee?'

'Scotch.'

'Scotch it is. And then you can tell me, if you want to.'

She looked up at him. 'Depends if you want to hear.'

'Of course I do.' He poured her a large Scotch, and one for himself, then went over to where she sat and handed her the glass. 'I'm all ears.' He sat at her feet and tried to look sympathetic.

'I didn't know anything about it until I was twenty. Until then I just thought my parents had given me away when I was a baby. They were poor and they had five children already—one more mouth to feed would have finished them off. I was brought up by a couple in Cheltenham. They told me I was properly adopted when I was about seven. My father died when I was fifteen. It was so sad. He had a stroke and Mum and I nursed him for months.'

'Like Granddad?'

'Yes, but it was worse in a way. I was so young. At least your granddad had had a good life. Then, when I was twenty, Mum was taken ill. I was desperate for her to get better, but she lay in bed getting paler and thinner. Just before the end came—a couple of days before, it must have been—she said she had something important to tell me about my real family, but that it might be better if I kept it to myself. All sorts of things went through my mind—that they might be criminals or something.' She paused.

Nick squeezed her hand. 'Go on.'

'She told me I hadn't been born in Cheltenham, as I had been told, but that I was born in St Petersburg and smuggled out of Russia as a baby to avoid a scandal. I thought she must be rambling but she kept on. She said that back in 1917 some sort of delegation was sent to Russia from Britain—to do with King George the Fifth and the Tsar. They were cousins, you know. Used to be mistaken for each other.' Rosie's eyes were misty.

'And?'

'The Tsar had five children. Olga and Tatiana were in their early twenties, Anastasia and Marie were in their teens, and their son, the Tsarevich Alexis, was about twelve. There was a young diplomat in the delegation. My mother didn't know his name. Apparently he'd got on a bit too well with one of the Tsar's elder daughters, as a result of which . . . well . . . I was the result.'

'*What?*'

'That's what she said.'

'But if it's true, why were you shipped out?'

'For one of the Tsar's daughters to have an illegitimate child would have been unthinkable.'

'But why didn't they just . . . get rid of you?'

'Abortion? Too risky. Imagine if anything had gone wrong.'

'But you're not . . .'

'No. No, I'm not. The Empress, the Tsarina, was the carrier. The Tsarevich was the only one of the Tsar's children who was a haemophiliac.'

'But how did they keep the pregnancy secret?'

'I suppose my mother was simply kept out of the public eye. I was born in 1917, just before the revolution, and spirited away.'

'How?'

'I've no idea. By diplomatic means, I suppose.'

'What does it say on your birth certificate?'

'Not much. Two fictitious names were given as my parents. I'd always thought the names must be made up, so about six months ago I went to check at the Public Records Office—the National Archive, they call it now—in Kew. They have no record of any married couple called George Michaels and Matilda Kitching.'

'So they were just made up?'

'Yes. By the people who smuggled me out, I suppose.'

'But you said your real name was Alice Marie Xenia.'

'That's what it says on my birth certificate, but my adoptive mum always called me Rosie.' She took a deep breath. 'As for the Tsar's family, I can remember the dates off by heart. The Tsar abdicated on the 15th of March, 1917, and on the 16th of July, 1918, the whole family was assassinated.'

Nick saw Rosie's fist tighten and her knuckles turned white.

'Wasn't there something about one of them escaping. Anastasia?'

'She was an impostor. Her name was Anna Anderson. The Tsar's cousin— another Grand Duchess Olga—escaped to Britain with her sister Xenia on a British warship, and she met all the impostors. She knew Anna Anderson was a fraud. No. They all died. They were herded into a basement room and shot. Even little Alexis. And my mother's dog.'

'So you know which one was your mother?'

'Yes.' Rosie got up and walked into her bedroom. She returned holding the framed photograph of the man in the army uniform, the boy in the sailor suit, the girl with the wonderful eyes and the clear complexion.

'That's my grandfather, the Tsar, my uncle the Tsarevich, and my mother, the Grand Duchess Tatiana.'

Nick took a deep breath. 'And you believe all this?'

'Oh, yes. I know it's true. I can *feel* it's true.'

Nick stared at her.

'But why should anybody want to believe me? I mean, I don't look like a grand duchess, do I? It's the most ridiculous story they've ever heard. It's the most ridiculous story *I*'ve ever heard.'

'But who told your mother—the one who adopted you?'

'I don't know.'

'So if it's true, it means . . .' He was trying to make sense of it all.

'Yes, love. You're in the line of succession to the Russian Imperial Throne. After your dad, that is. But somehow I don't think Tsar Derek has the right ring to it. Do you?'

NICK DIDN'T SLEEP much that night. There were a hundred unanswered questions in his head. Had Rosie really told no one else the full story? Was she telling the truth, or was she simply unbalanced?

Early the next morning, he got up, showered, and went out onto the verandah. A skein of mist hung over the sea and a watery sun was doing its best to break through. He shivered in the morning chill. It was six thirty. He loaded his painting bag, board and paper into the MG and folded down the hood. Then he released the handbrake and let her roll down the track before starting up out of Rosie's earshot.

The mist was clearing as he drove on past green fields and light woodland, then turned right on the narrow lane that led to Newtown Creek. He drew up on a rough gravel car park, took out his bag and board and made his way along the boardwalk that crossed the narrow inlets. He found a spot for his folding chair and easel and set to work. Three small boats bobbed gently in the river, their owners still asleep below decks.

For three hours he worked on the painting, until the light had changed too much. Then he packed away his paints and walked back to the car. He drove through sleepy Calbourne and sprawling Carisbrooke to Newport, and went into a bookshop. Under the section headed 'European History' he found what he was looking for: a book on the Russian royal family.

By the time he had returned to The Anchorage, Rosie had gone out. He made some coffee, and opened the book. Three hours later, he closed it and sat back in his chair. He was now acquainted with the Tsar's family, but he still couldn't begin to think of it as *his* family. Did it matter? Whether he was related to them or not, the story was compelling, and the way in which the Imperial family had met their end was shocking and inhumane.

He looked at his watch. Half past one. Alex would probably be out painting. He had her mobile phone number but was reluctant to call. Then his own phone rang.

'Hello?'

'Is Rosie with you?' It was his mother. She was not calm.

'Yes.'

'Bloody typical! I arrange for her to see two lots of sheltered accommodation and she buggers off.'

'Well, did you ask her if she wanted to see them?'

'I told her I'd—'

'Yes. You *told* her.'

Most daughters-in-law would have been only too willing to relinquish a relationship with their mother-in-law on the breakdown of their marriage. Not so Anna Robertson. Rosie was a loose end, and loose ends had to be tidied up.

'She'll have to come back. I've made appointments.'

'Well, unmake them. She's here for a while now. Till she feels better.'

'Now, listen, Nick—'

'No, Mum. *You* listen. She's getting on in years and she's a bit unreliable, but that doesn't mean you can shut her away.'

'I'm not shutting her away. These are nice places and they'll look after her.'

'Well, I'm looking after her at the moment so that's all right, isn't it? And she's having fun here. She's even booked to go on a sailing course.'

'*What?*'

'It's OK. She says they've taught people older than her.'

'Maybe, but I bet they had all their marbles.'

He changed the subject, careful to ask the question offhandedly: 'What do you know about her family?'

'Oh, it's quite ridiculous. She's got it into her head that her mother was somehow caught up in the Russian Revolution. She thinks she was smuggled out when she was a baby.'

'Does Dad know who her parents were?'

'Well, if he does he's never bored me with the story. Look, I haven't time

358 | ALAN TITCHMARSH

to talk. I've got a lecture in five minutes. I'm relying on you, Nick, to look
after her and see that she doesn't get into any more trouble.'

'Mmm.'

'Speak soon. Must dash. Oh, and don't let her spend any money.
Apparently her bank account is overdrawn.'

TROUBLES ARE like buses: they come in convoys. Nick had quite a collection
now. His grandmother's presence, his grandmother's state of mind, his
grandmother's apparent lack of funds, Alex's opinion of him.

Then two more buses turned up at The Anchorage. The pair were clad in
charcoal-grey suits and wore dark glasses. They were both sturdy men with
close-shaven heads and no necks.

'Mr Nick Robertson?' asked the shorter of the two.

'Yes.'

'Are you expecting us?'

'No. Should I be?'

The taller one looked down at the smaller one, then at Nick. 'Your father
hasn't been in contact, then?'

'Not for a week or two.'

'So you haven't got the package?'

'What package?'

The shorter hulk looked up at the taller hulk and frowned, then looked back
at Nick. 'Look, son, this is serious. We've come all the way across here because
we were told that this was where it would be.'

'I'm sorry, but I really don't know what you're talking about. Is this some
sort of joke?'

'No,' said the big hulk.

Nick felt uneasy. 'Well, I can call my father, if you like, but he keeps
changing his mobile so I'm not sure he'll still be on the same number.'

'No,' said the shorter man. 'That's the trouble.'

At this, the larger man took a step forward, almost crushing Nick against
the door frame. 'We don't mess about, you know.'

'Hello, I'm back,' said a voice. 'Had a lovely walk along the cliff path. Oh,
hello—I'm Nick's granny.' The two men wheeled round in time to see Rosie
hold out her hand. They didn't take it. They just stared, while Rosie twittered
on: 'Shame it's not brighter, isn't it? I expect you needed your sunglasses
when you set off, but it's a bit threatening now.' She looked up at the sky.

The two men froze as though they had been anaesthetised.

'Are you staying for lunch? I think we've some salad left from last night.'

Nick made to stop her, but the shorter of the two men spoke first: 'No, thanks, lady,' he said. 'We've got to be going.' He turned to Nick. 'We'll come back. You'll have it by then.' He gestured his companion towards the path, then nodded at Rosie. 'Take care, lady.'

Nick and Rosie watched as the pair lumbered down the path and out of the gate. They heard a car start up and drive away. Then Rosie asked, 'Did I do all right? I'm quite good at playing the harmless old lady. Did it help?'

'I'll say.'

'Who were they? Are you in some sort of trouble?'

'I have absolutely no idea.' And then, trying to sound casual, he said, 'When did you last hear from Dad?'

'A fortnight ago. You don't think they're anything to do with him, do you?'

'No, no. I just wondered if his mobile phone number had changed again.'

'Only one way to find out,' she said.

'Yes.' So he tried. The number was unobtainable.

THE LIGHTHOUSE at St Catherine's Point winked out over the sea as Alex and Victoria ate their picnic lunch on the clifftop.

Victoria was nibbling an apple. 'Are you cross with me?'

'Why should I be?'

'Because of last night. You know. With Nick.'

'What do you mean?'

'Do you fancy him?'

Alex looked at her admonishingly. 'What's it got to do with you?'

The child shrugged. 'Just wondered.'

They sat in silence for a while longer.

'What if I do?' asked Alex evenly.

Victoria examined her apple core. 'Don't you think he's a bit quiet?'

'Not at all. He's just . . . thoughtful.' Alex took a bite of her sandwich.

'I think he's quite nice.' Victoria put her apple core into an empty crisp packet. 'Will you see him again?'

'Who knows?'

Victoria stood up. 'You can go without me, you know. I don't want to cramp your style.'

'*What?*' Her mother looked at her hard.

'I don't mind if you want to be on your own.'

Alex patted the ground next to her. 'Come and sit down.'

Victoria flopped on to the plaid car rug beside her mother, leaned against her and gazed out over the sea. Alex stroked her hair. 'You've never cramped my style—understand? And I don't want you thinking you have to keep out of the way. It's you and me in this, OK?'

Victoria raised her face to her mother's and nodded. A few moments later she said, 'I liked Rosie.'

'Yes. Me too.'

'She's fun. And not old. Well, I mean she *is* old, but she doesn't *seem* old.'

'Some people are like that. They don't fit other people's preconceptions.'

'What are they?'

'Preconceptions? Oh, like prejudices. People don't always fit into boxes. Sometimes they surprise you.'

'Do you think Nick might be surprising?'

'Too early to say. Maybe.'

'So you will see him again?'

Alex stood up and brushed the crumbs off her jeans. 'We'll see. Anyway, we've only a few days left here so there may not be time.'

'Do we really have to go back? Couldn't we just stay here?' Concern was etched on Victoria's face as she got to her feet.

Alex folded up the rug. 'You've got school next week.'

The child pushed her hands into her pockets. 'They have schools here, too.'

Alex put her arm round her. 'Don't you think we're being a bit premature?'

Victoria shrugged.

'And you do know what that means, don't you?'

'Too soon.'

'Yes. Let's just take our time, shall we?' She handed Victoria the carrier bag that contained the remains of the picnic and set off for the car.

HENRY KINROSS had had a good day. He had sold seven paintings: four of Nick's, one of the gloomy canvases and two of Alex's brightest creations, which had been snapped up by a young couple from Fulham. He had a new *protégé*, and an attractive one at that. Perhaps he should ask Alexandra Pollen out to lunch. But Nick seemed to have taken a shine to her. It wouldn't do to fall out over a woman.

What he needed was a mature woman, someone with a bit of conversation.

Companionship was just as important as sex. The sad thing was that both were in short supply.

The sound of the bell broke in on his musings. He looked up to see Nick standing in the doorway with a bright-eyed lady on his arm. 'Henry, can I introduce you to Rosie?'

'Dear boy! Of course!'

OVER A BOTTLE of claret in the Red Duster, Rosie and Henry became better acquainted. After a few minutes, Henry realised that, had she been a few years younger, she would have been the woman of his dreams. He could not work out how old she was, but that made her all the more interesting. She was startlingly knowledgeable about art, easy to talk to and surprisingly coquettish for someone of her advanced years.

Nick was listening to the two of them talking, and marvelled at his grandmother. She could find common ground with anybody, whoever they were, raise her game, or lower it, to suit the occasion. He watched as she put away a couple of glasses of claret and a plate of steak and Guinness pie. She glanced at him occasionally, but Henry had her full attention, and she his.

By eight o'clock Rosie was living up to her name: her cheeks were brightly flushed. She was noticeably giggly, too. Nick saw the warning signs and decided to take her home.

'Oh! Do we have to go? I'm having such a lovely time.' She didn't slur her words, but there was a slight over-enunciation.

'Stay for another bottle, Rosie,' Henry said. 'Don't let this dauber take you home yet.'

Nick looked at Henry, whose countenance almost matched the liquid in his glass, and raised an eyebrow at his grandmother. For once she took the hint.

'No. Nick's right. We'd better be going. Things to see, people to do, you know. Ha-ha.' She pushed herself up and steadied herself on the table.

Henry stood up. 'Well, it's been a pleasure. Perhaps we can do it again some time.'

Rosie beamed. 'Oh, I do hope so. Thank you for your company.'

Henry ambled over to her as Nick helped her on with her coat, bent down and kissed her cheek. 'Take great care, precious lady.'

She beamed. 'To hell with that! Life's for living, and I'm going sailing tomorrow.' She took Nick's arm and walked out of the Red Duster, swaying gently from side to side in a decidedly regal sashay.

THE SILVER MERCEDES with the brand-new number plate completely blocked the track to The Anchorage.

'Bloody hell! Blooming holidaymakers! Think they can park anywhere.' He manoeuvred the MG onto the verge. 'Can you walk from here?'

'Of course. 'Snot far, is it?'

Her speech was sibilant now. He suppressed a grin. 'Take my arm.'

He walked her up the final curve of the track, and his heart missed a beat as the verandah came into view. Someone he had not seen in months was sitting on the step.

'Hello, Nick! How ya doin'?'

'Dad! What are you doing here?'

'Come to see you and Mum. Hello, old girl.'

Rosie screwed up her eyes. 'Derek! Who told you I was here?' And then, with a note of anger in her voice, 'You've not come to take me away, have you?'

Derek Robertson got up. 'What would I want to do that for?'

'Because of Anna. She wants me in a home.'

Nick's father shrugged. 'Nothing to do with me, old love. I'm happy as long as you are.'

They stared at each other for a few minutes, until Derek asked, 'Can we go inside, then? It's a bit nippy out here.'

Nick handed his grandmother over to her son, unlocked the front door and let them in. He put on lights, motioned Rosie and Derek to take a seat and asked his father what he would like to drink.

'Scotch, please, old lad.'

'Some things never change,' said Nick, wryly. He left his father and grandmother while he went into the kitchen to fix the drinks.

Derek Robertson could not have looked more different from his son. For a start he lacked height, and his manner of dress, while not exactly shouting 'spiv', had a showy look, from the slip-on buckled loafers to the black shirt. He even had crinkly dark hair and a thin moustache. He could have been taken for an Italian with Mafia connections.

Nick watched as his father sipped his Scotch. After a few minutes Rosie excused herself. 'I'd love to sit up and talk to you, Derek, but I'm afraid I must go to bed.' Rosie was doing her best to concentrate, but the alcohol had taken its toll. 'I'm completely done in. Knacked, I think, is the word. Yes, I'm completely knacked.' She giggled, pushed herself out of the chair and tottered elegantly towards her son, who rose to meet her. 'Good night, dear.' She pecked him on the cheek and wobbled unsteadily. 'Oops. Steady the buffs.'

'Good night, old girl. Look after yourself.'

'Oh, I don't need to. I've found somebody else to do that. I met a very nice gentleman today. In the pub. Henry. Art dealer. Very good company. Mmm. Lovely big hands.' Without a backward glance she walked carefully in the direction of her bedroom.

Derek looked at his son. 'Is she behaving herself?'

'Depends what you mean.'

'Always done her own thing, Rosie. Never been one to conform.' He winked.

'No.' Nick paused. 'Dad?'

His father was knocking back the remains of his Scotch. He put the glass down. 'Any more in that bottle?'

'A drop. Are you driving?'

'Only a small one, then.'

Nick poured the amber fluid into his father's glass and continued. 'Dad . . . I had two guys here today asking for you. Something to do with a package.'

'Oh, shit. I told them it wouldn't be here till tomorrow.'

'What won't be here till tomorrow?'

Derek Robertson knocked back the contents of his glass and reached into a pocket. He lifted out a small padded envelope.

'What's that?' asked Nick.

'You don't need to know,' replied his father. 'When those guys come back just hand it over to them, will you?'

'But why can't *you* give it to them?'

'Because I won't be here. I've got a plane to catch.'

'Dad!'

'I know what you're thinking, but it's all above-board. It's just better if I'm not here, that's all. It's just safer for all concerned if you do the handover. You don't need to know what it is.'

Nick folded his arms. 'I'm not doing it. You can't just swan in here like some shady character, pull out a package and expect me to hand it over to a couple of thugs without asking a few questions.'

Derek sighed. 'I'd like you to trust me.'

'I'd like to as well, but I haven't got much to go on.'

His father laid a hand on his shoulder. 'Will you or won't you? Just say yes or no and I'll be out of your hair.'

Nick struggled with his conscience. 'You promise it's nothing illegal?'

'Good God, no. It's just . . . well . . . private. That's all. Look, son, I just need you to do this one small thing for me. OK?' Then he played his trump card. 'It's to help Rosie.'

There was a silence. Nick was annoyed with himself for having been cornered. He had little choice. And his father knew it.

'OK—but I must be mad.'

'And I must be going. Those ferries are a bugger—never turn up when you want them to.' He slapped Nick on the back and made for the door.

'Dad!'

His father turned.

'When will I see you again?'

Derek Robertson shrugged. 'Not sure. Probably later rather than sooner.' He swung out of sight.

Nick ran after him, calling in his wake, 'What do you know about Russia?'

His father stopped dead in his tracks halfway down the lane, then turned to face him. 'What do you mean?'

'Rosie's past. What do you know about Russia?'

'Oh, that.' He looked thoughtful. 'Bloody big country, Russia. Lot of people.' He got into his car, slammed the door and drove off into the night.

Chapter 4

How she had managed to be up and out of the house before him was a mystery. Nick knew she hadn't had that much to drink, but it had affected her. He was rattled by her apparent self-sufficiency, and that he had not asked more about her sailing course. Then the absurdity of the role-reversal struck him and he felt slightly ashamed.

He ruffled his hair, yawned and gazed out at the sea. She had chosen a good day to start: enough wind to fill her sails but nothing strong enough to give trouble.

The ship's clock on the kitchen wall told him it was eight thirty. He went to fill the kettle, and saw an envelope propped up against it. He opened it and found his birthday card. He had quite forgotten. He was thirty-nine.

But the card lifted his spirits. It was not of the 'Happy Birthday to My

Favourite Grandson' type, instead it bore a black-and-white thirties photograph of a man in a suit holding the hand of a delicate-featured girl who was staring, rather distractedly, off-camera. The caption above it, in purple, read: *Emily is told that 'Philip's 12 inch' is, in fact, his television.*

He opened it and read the inscription: *Sorry! Thought this might make you smile! Thanks for putting up with me. All my love, Rosie xxx.*

He looked at the front of the card again and laughed out loud.

THE UNITED KINGDOM Sailing Academy nestles alongside the River Medina in West Cowes. It is a modern building with a slipway that leads down to the water; boats carrying sailors of little or no skill can be safely launched there. In the small classroom Rosie looked about her. She was the oldest by a good twenty years, but in her new baggy sailing shirt, pink cotton trousers and deck shoes she felt very much the part. Within a few hours she would be out on the water, and a lifetime's ambition would have been fulfilled. She thought, fleetingly, of her grandson, and hoped he would have a good birthday. But today the painter that held her attention would be made of rope.

NICK MADE himself a cup of coffee and walked over to the window again. The sun was glinting on the water. It was the perfect May day. The perfect day for a birthday.

What a joke. Here he was, with a mad granny who thought she was a cross between the Empress of Russia and Ellen MacArthur, and a package of heaven-knows-what waiting to be collected by a couple of heavies who would probably break his legs. Even the most optimistic soul would have to admit this was not a promising way to celebrate the end of your fourth decade.

And then he saw her walking up the lane. Alex, with a package in her hand. She saw him at the window and waved. She was alone.

'Hi! Come in.' He was at the open door to welcome her.

'You look happy.'

'Don't be deceived by appearances.'

She balanced on her toes and kissed his cheek. 'Happy birthday.'

'How did you know?'

'Grannies talking to ten-year-olds.'

'Ah!' He smiled apologetically.

'You're not having a good day, then?'

'Oh, just things.' And then he felt guilty for not welcoming her properly.

'Look, I'm sorry about the other night. I was a bit impatient with Rosie. I shouldn't have been, but . . . well . . . Anyway, coffee?'

'Please.'

Once inside, she turned to him and held out the packet. 'We made this for you, we girls. Victoria's with her friends, or she'd have come as well.'

He looked at the homemade envelope, which bulged at the seams, and at the scraps of coloured paper and feathers stuck to it. 'What is it?'

'You may well ask. Open it.'

Carefully, he pulled at the seams of the envelope and tipped the contents onto the kitchen table.

'Oh! Treasure trove!' He gazed at the objects that had tumbled from their paper wrapping: a tiny starfish, the black purse of a dogfish egg, green and blue glass shards washed smooth by the sea, two shiny razor shells, a piece of bleached white coral and a dozen or more shells no bigger than his thumbnail in creamy white, soft purple and dusky pink. 'They're beautiful. What a wonderful present.' His eyes darted over the treasures. 'Thank you so much.'

Then he looked at her in her loose white shirt and calf-length jeans, the shiny dark hair held back today with a tortoiseshell clip. He stepped forward, put his arms round her and gave her a hug. 'That's the nicest thirty-ninth birthday present I've ever had.'

She grinned. 'I'm glad.'

He bent down and kissed her forehead. 'I don't suppose you fancy a birthday supper, do you? I mean . . .'

'Just the two of us?'

'Well . . . if that's all right.'

'I'll have to ask permission,' she teased.

'Of course.'

She laughed. 'I'd love to.'

Over coffee they talked of Rosie's foray into the world of spinnakers and mainsails, and of Victoria's day on the beach with the friends she'd made in Sleepyhead Bay. Then Alex said she'd better be getting back before Victoria outstayed her welcome with her holiday chums, and he arranged to pick her up that evening. They parted with a double-cheeked kiss on the verandah.

He came back inside and went into the kitchen again. He picked up the padded envelope his father had given him the night before. It was fastened with staples. It would be a simple job to bend them back, open the end and examine the contents. Carefully he slipped the blade of a kitchen knife under each staple, prised back the teeth, then popped back the flap and eased out the contents. The self-sealing polythene bag seemed to be full of cotton wool. He pulled it open, and tipped the wadding onto the kitchen worktop. As he moved it apart, out fell four stones that glittered and dazzled in the light.

He had never seen such astonishingly beautiful diamonds.

He felt sick. Quickly he put them back into the wadding, careful to avoid marking them with fingerprints, then slipped the bundle back into the polythene bag, the bag into the padded envelope, and nipped the jaws of the staples into place. He put the envelope under a cushion in the sitting room and sat down to think. His heart was hammering and his mind raced. Were the stones stolen? Surely not. His father had always lived on his wits but had never been on the wrong side of the law. And yet he said he was leaving the country by plane. Why, if he had nothing to hide? And why couldn't he hand over the diamonds himself? What were they worth?

A knock at the door brought him to his senses. He looked up and saw the silhouettes of the two burly men.

IT WAS SIX o'clock when Rosie returned, her cheeks flushed with fresh air and excitement, but her eyes betrayed her tiredness. She flopped into a chair and said, 'Oh, yes, please!' when Nick offered her a gin and tonic. 'What a day. I don't remember when I last enjoyed myself so much. And the instructor says I'm a natural.' She took a sip from her glass, then looked up at him. 'How are we celebrating your birthday?'

'Ah.' A pang of guilt caught him. 'Well, er, I've arranged to go out.'

'Oh. Oh, I see.'

He heard the disappointment in her voice.

'With Alex. You could come if you like.'

Her face was like that of a spaniel who has just been chastised. Then she smiled. 'And Granny came too? I don't think so. You go and enjoy yourself. I'll have an early night. We sailors have to be up in good time. We're sailing at Gurnard tomorrow.'

He crouched in front of her and rested his hand on her knee. 'I'm very proud of you, you know. But you're not overdoing it, are you?'

'I'm pacing myself. I told you. And that reminds me. Could you nip into my bedroom and fetch the little parcel that's on my bedside table? I'd go and get it myself only my grandson tells me I have to be careful.'

He went to her room and returned with a small package that was, perhaps, three inches square. He gave it to her and she handed it straight back to him.

'Happy birthday, my love.' She took another sip of her gin.

He pulled off the wrapping to reveal a small box. For the second time that day, his heart thumped. He lifted the lid of the box. A diamond winked at him. It was the same size as those he had seen earlier in the day.

'But, Rosie, you've bought me a car, and now this and . . . I mean your bank account—'

Rosie raised an eyebrow. 'Your mother's been talking to you.'

'Yes.'

'I wondered how long it would be before she found out.'

'But how could you afford—'

'By being careful for the best part of eighty-seven years.'

Nick flopped down in a chair. 'I don't understand.'

'I got the idea from the Queen Mother.' Rosie took a restorative sip of her gin. 'She gave all her assets to her grandchildren. That way you can avoid death duties, provided you live for seven years after you've handed the stuff over.'

Nick looked at her with a plaintive expression. He was sure he'd read something about 'gift tax' or 'capital gains'. His thoughts were cut short.

'Oh, I know what you're thinking,' Rosie said. 'I'm eighty-seven, am I likely to last until I'm ninety-four.'

'No!'

'Don't interrupt. I looked at my bank account, and at how much interest had built up and it was pathetic. So I looked at the financial pages in the papers and worked out what the best investment was. And the financial experts seemed to think it was the right time to invest in diamonds. So I emptied my bank account and bought a few. This one's yours. At the moment it's worth about twenty-five thousand. Hopefully a bit more in a few years' time. And I've taken care of your sisters. Sophie and Alice have one each as well.'

'I see.' Nick gazed at the stone. 'It's beautiful,' he said.

'Yes. I'd take it to the bank and leave it there for a while, if I were you. Until you need to cash it in.'

Nick shut the lid of the box and looked at his grandmother. 'We've just got to make sure you live for another seven years, then.' His lips curled into a grin.

'Oh, I wouldn't worry about that. As far as the government's concerned I've just spent my money. No need for them to know where. It's yours now.'

'Rosie! Is that legal?'

'Probably not—but it's no more wicked than taxing old ladies so that they can't afford to live on their savings, is it? Anyway, hadn't you better be getting ready to go out for dinner? Don't want to keep Alex waiting.'

She winked at him. As he smiled back at her he thought that, royal or not, she was the most amazing person he knew.

THEY WERE GIVEN a candlelit corner table in the dusky, cream-painted restaurant. Nick ordered a bottle of Rioja, and a girl in her teens brought it to their table and opened the bottle rather hesitantly.

When she had left them, Nick lifted his glass of wine and clinked it against Alex's. 'Cheers!'

'Happy birthday! And lovely to spend it with you.'

Alex was wearing a loose-fitting white shirt and a pair of black trousers that hugged her slim figure. Her hair shone like ebony. Nick was entranced. As the evening wore on, he could not recall anyone, apart from his grandmother, to whom he found it so easy to talk. He watched her animated face over the glow of the candle. Her flashing eyes seemed almost jet black.

She told him of her childhood on a farm in Devon, of losing her parents when she was in her teens, of her marriage to Paul and their broken relationship, her hopes for Victoria.

'And what about you? What do you want?' he asked, over coffee.

'Oh, that's a big one. Don't really have time to think about me.' She looked away. 'I'm a bit scared, I suppose. Don't want to rush into something that might not work out. I can't mess it up any more for Victoria.'

'There she is again.'

'You see? It's impossible for any man to understand my responsibilities.'

'I think you might be underestimating any man.'

'You think so?'

'I think so.' He laid his hand on hers. 'Don't sell yourself short,' he said.

She wrapped her fingers round his and he squeezed her hand.

Their eyes met. Then the silence was broken by a plaintive voice: 'Was everything all right?' asked the waitress.

Nick began to speak, but Alex beat him to it. 'Oh, yes. It was lovely.'

HE OPENED the car door for her, then walked round to the driver's side and slid in. The engine roared into life and he steered the MG out of the car park. They said nothing, but he could feel her sitting closer than before. He caught an occasional whiff of her perfume. Suddenly it started to rain heavily.

'Oh, God!' He swerved into the side of the lane, beneath the shelter of the overhanging sycamores. 'It won't take a minute! Hang on!'

He leapt out of the car and fought with the hood. It took several minutes to fasten it in place, during which time Alex shrieked, at first from the shock of the freezing deluge, but then with hilarity as he battled with the canopy and its collection of poppers and zips that seemed to bear no relation to the fittings on the car. Eventually, she jumped out to help, and soon the car was shielded from the worst of the elements by the ancient black shroud.

'Get in! GET IN!' Nick roared, as he ran round to his side and stumbled into the damp interior. He was joined in the passenger seat by a drenched Alex, laughing until tears and raindrops were running down her cheeks in tandem.

'Look at you!' he exclaimed, and wiped the water off her cheeks. Then he leaned forward and kissed her gently, and with unexpected longing. Her scent filled his nostrils as he felt the softness of her lips on his. She made no move to resist, and he slid closer to her, in spite of the gear lever, finally resting his head on her shoulder as their breathing returned to normal.

Then he raised his head and looked into her eyes. 'Sorry.'

She shook her head. 'No, no. Don't be sorry.'

He stroked the back of her head, then kissed her forehead tenderly, before starting up the engine and driving her home.

THE FOLLOWING MORNING Nick was lying in bed, listening to the rain pounding on the roof. He replayed the events of the previous evening over and over again in his mind. He had not expected to be so affected by Alex, and wondered if she felt the same.

He slid out from under the duvet and padded across to the window. A stiff breeze was blowing the rain in diagonal sheets across the steel-grey sea and into the cliff face. Battalions of droplets rattled against the window of the cottage and trickled down the panes. Not a good day for sailing. He pulled on a bathrobe and went into the sitting room, expecting to find Rosie in her dressing-gown.

Rosie was fully clothed and pulling on a waterproof.

'What are you doing?' he asked. 'You can't go out in this.'

'Are you suggesting I'm a fair-weather sailor?'

'I'm suggesting you should be.' He looked at her with his head on one side. 'Have you seen the weather out there?'

'Yes.'

'And you're still going?'

'I'll take my stick.' She made the concession grudgingly.

'Well, that won't stop you being blown off the cliff. Look, give me a minute to get dressed and I'll drive you there. At least I can make sure you arrive in one piece.'

He showered quickly, threw on jeans, sweatshirt and trainers, and met her at the front door with his hair in a damp tangle. He put his arm through hers as they walked into the windy morning.

'Car smells nice,' she said, as he opened the door of the MG for her.

'It got a bit damp last night. Caught out by the rain.'

'First rain I've known that smells of Chanel No. 5.'

Nick said nothing as he eased into the driver's seat and started the engine.

'Same as I wear.'

'I know.'

'Did you have a nice time?'

He pulled out into the road. 'Yes, thanks.'

'Nice girl. Lovely dark eyes.'

They motored on in silence.

As he turned into the road that led to the sailing academy she tapped his arm. 'Here will do. I can walk the rest. Need a breath of air.'

The rain had eased slightly so he let her have her way. He watched her struggle, but resisted the temptation to get out and open her door.

Eventually she got out and straightened in the stiff breeze. 'Goodbye.'

'What about tonight?' Nick asked. 'What time shall I pick you up?'

'Oh, don't worry. I'll get one of my friends to drop me off.'

He leaned back in his seat and heaved a sigh. He hoped to God they wouldn't take her out on the water.

THE MAN at the bank took the package with little ceremony and assured Nick that he could have it back whenever he wanted. It was a weight off his mind to know that the diamond was somewhere safe, even though he was not sure that converting money into diamonds was a particularly sensible course of action. From what he had read, the diamond and gold markets were more volatile than bank interest rates, not less so, as Rosie had suggested.

But what worried him even more was the possibility that his father was involving his own mother in some kind of scam. If only he would answer his bloody phone.

VICTORIA WAS UNSURE of her mother's mood, and when you're trying to persuade a parent to buy you something, you need to be certain that your strategy is going to work. She had decided that she, too, was an artist, but rather than accepting the box of poster paints her mother was prepared to buy her, she had set her heart on a watercolour outfit in a varnished wooden box. She knew that now was not the moment to admit this, and settled instead for a guidebook to the Isle of Wight so that she could get to know it better. And, hopefully, find somewhere to live.

Alex, knowing that her daughter's intransigence could be epic when she put her mind to it, bought the modestly priced guidebook without demur and resigned herself to the fact that something was clearly brewing.

'Where are we?' Victoria asked, as she pored over the map in the guidebook.

Alex peered over her shoulder. 'Here.' She pointed to the bottom right-hand corner.

'And where is Nick?'

'Here.' Alex indicated the northernmost tip.

'How far away is that?'

'Well, look at the scale. There you are—that line. Five miles is about as long as . . . your finger.'

Victoria measured the map with her finger. 'Fifteen miles. Is that close?'

'Fairly.'

'What about you and Nick?' she asked casually, as she folded up the map. 'Are you close?'

'I think he's a very nice man, that's all. And I've only just met him.'

Victoria folded her arms. 'Honestly, you're like Elinor Dashwood in *Sense and Sensibility*.'

'Don't be ridiculous. That story was written nearly two hundred years ago and this is the twenty-first century.'

Victoria gave her a quizzical look. 'It's funny how some things don't change, isn't it?'

THE RED DUSTER was unusually busy, but Henry, having forewarned his friend the landlord of their arrival, had secured a table in the corner of the bar, albeit with only one chair. With a pint in one fist and a piece of bentwood furniture in the other, Nick elbowed his way through a group of yachties and eased himself opposite his patron.

They had barely begun to converse when a voice cut through the crowd.

'Sorry! Thank you so much. Excuse me!' And there she was, standing before them, with a gin and tonic.

Rosie smiled at Henry, who attempted unsuccessfully to stand up. He bowed over his bottle of claret and indicated the chair that Nick was putting down. 'Dear lady!' he exclaimed. 'What are you doing here? Afternoon off?'

'Oh, no. Just a lunch break. Too lumpy out on the water. They've brought us to see some special boats that they make here.' She raised her head and looked at Nick, who, having given away his seat, was standing beside the bar.

'Nick, dear, Henry will take care of me, won't you, Henry?'

'Of course. My pleasure.' Henry laid a large hand over hers. 'So, what's it to be? Lamb hotpot or red snapper?'

'Oh, the snapper, I think. Sounds so much more sparky, doesn't it?'

'A bit like you,' offered Henry, with a roguish tilt of his head.

Nick raised his eyes heavenward and drained his glass.

ROSIE PUT her head through the doorway of the tiny room where Nick was finishing off a couple of picture frames and asked, 'Coffee?'

He turned to answer her, and saw that, although she was smiling, her eyes were filled with tears. 'Hey!' He got up and enfolded her in his arms. 'What's the matter?'

'Oh, nothing. It's just that . . . Oh, I'm so silly . . .' She pulled a tissue from the pocket of the pink sailing trousers she was wearing.

Nick released her and stood back to look at her. 'What do you mean?'

'It's just that I don't remember being so happy in a long time.'

'That's not silly, that's lovely.'

'I suppose it is.'

'What do you mean you suppose? Of course it is.' He gave her a squeeze. 'Is it to do with Henry?'

'Oh, no, not really. Well, maybe a bit. He's very attentive. Only he believes I'm younger than I am.' Rosie looked away. 'I told him I was sixty-nine.'

'What?'

'Oh, I know it was silly of me but . . . he was so nice, and I didn't want him to think I was some senile old woman. Sixty-nine would make me only eleven years older than him, and it's not too much of an age gap, is it?'

Nick was surprised. 'Well, no, but—'

'He's asked me out on Friday night,' she interrupted. 'But I can't go. It's the final evening at the sailing academy. We're all going out for a drink.'

'I see.' Nick was trying to keep a straight face. 'Couldn't you go out for a meal afterwards?'

'Well, yes, I am. But not with Henry.'

Just for a moment, Nick felt like the father of a teenage daughter who was enquiring after her movements. 'Who with, then?'

'There's a man at the sailing academy. He's single, too. In his sixties.'

'And have you told him how old you are?'

'I said I was sixty-six,' Rosie said sheepishly.

AT TEN O'CLOCK Nick tapped on her bedroom door. 'Can I come in?'

'Of course.'

He opened the door and peeped in. She was tucked up under her duvet, with just her head visible. She pushed herself up a little, and Nick spotted the lace on her nightie. She was elegant even in bed. 'I'm sorry for being a stupid old woman. Mutton done up as lamb.'

'Don't be silly.' He sat on the edge of her bed. 'But, you know, I still don't understand you. You're supposed to be out of touch and helpless, and here you are on a sailing course with people half your age—'

'Be careful!' she admonished him.

'—but you hold your own in conversation with anyone and line up dinner dates like there's no tomorrow.'

'Well, there might not be.' Rosie laughed. 'You are funny.'

'Me?'

'Yes. You. You're thirty-nine and far more staid than I am. If I were you I'd start to live a bit.'

Nick sighed. 'Am I in for an advice session, then?'

'No. Well . . . maybe just a bit of *friendly* advice.' She looked right at him. 'Get on with it. Don't hang about.'

'Get on with what?'

'Your relationship with Alex.'

'There *is* no relationship.'

'Exactly. But there could be. You should be having a bit of fun. She's a lovely girl and she should be having fun, too.'

'What about Victoria?'

'Oh, don't worry about her. She's got her head screwed on. She's older than all of us.'

'You think?'

'Oh, yes. Funny, isn't it? Victoria's ten, but more like forty. You're thirty-nine and more like seventy, and I'm eighty-seven going on thirty! Nobody's the age they seem, are they?'

'You know, there are days when I think you'll live for ever,' Nick said. 'Where do you get your energy?'

Rosie nodded at the empty glass beside her bed. 'Out of a bottle.' Then she became serious. 'Oh, sometimes I have to work hard to get up. But I tell myself it's only natural at my age. You have to fight it. I just grit my teeth and get on with it. Other days I have a good cry, and feel completely done in. Then the sun shines and I feel better.'

'You're a star.'

'Oh, no. I'm quite scared, if I'm honest. I feel a bit funny some days. A bit disconnected. It's me and yet it isn't me.' She picked up a small black book. 'I always keep this by my bed. The Book of Common Prayer. Lovely language.' She looked up at him and asked evenly, 'Do you say your prayers?'

Nick nodded. 'Sometimes.'

'I say mine every night: "Gentle Jesus, meek and mild, look upon a little child; pity my simplicity; give me grace to come to thee—but not yet." I always put that bit in. Hope it makes Him smile.'

He watched as she lay back on the pillow. Calm now. Peaceful.

'He knows, doesn't He?' she said. 'Where I came from.'

Nick nodded again.

Rosie squeezed his hand. 'Try to find out for me.'

He sighed. 'If you want me to.'

Rosie smiled contentedly. Her eyes were closing and soon her conversation was replaced by gentle breathing. Nick turned out the light, kissed her cheek and quietly shut the door behind him.

THE NEXT MORNING, as Nick switched on the computer he wondered if Rosie had been searching there before him. He called up assorted sites with the word 'Romanov' in the title and, after some sifting, found one that looked promising. He felt a frisson of excitement as he started to read:

> The Romanov Dynasty began with the ascension of Tsar Mikhail
> Fedorovich to the Russian throne in 1613. Though still a young
> dynasty, by the 18th century the succession was seriously tested
> but with the accession of Peter III the crisis ended. In 1797, at his

crowning, Peter's son, the Emperor Paul, issued Succession Laws.

Under the 'Pauline Laws' the succession followed a certain sequence, based on seniority. The Emperor as head of the family and after him his eldest son was heir, then son of the eldest son and so on.

He scrolled up: 'If the male line died out completely, then the throne would pass to a female closest in relation to the last reigning Emperor. Also, no member could now be denied their succession rights, except those who had voluntarily relinquished them.'

He slumped back in his chair and took a deep breath. If Rosie could prove she was of the female line, and should the monarchy be reinstated, Rosie could legitimately claim her position as heir to the Russian throne. For one brief moment, Nick understood what it was like to be a male Cinderella. He could be only a hair's breadth away from becoming Tsar Nicholas III, after Tsar Derek had taken over from Empress Rosie. No: Empress Alice Marie Xenia. There was no denying it had a certain ring to it.

And then he read the paragraph that followed. It ended his reverie and brought him down to earth with a welcome bump:

The laws were further altered in 1820, and to be considered a member of the Imperial House, members of the family had to marry a person of equal rank; meaning persons from another sovereign house.

Accordingly, the offspring of these marriages were considered dynastic, while children of morganatic (unequal) marriages were not considered members of the Imperial House.

So if Rosie had indeed been next in line to the Imperial throne, she had relinquished her claim when she had married his grandfather.

He read the rest of the article, and discovered that the current heir to the Russian throne was Grand Duchess Maria Vladimorovna, who was now forty-one and living in Madrid. She had had the foresight to marry Prince Franz of Prussia, keeping the marriage dynastic, and they had a son and heir: Grand Duke George Mihailovich 'the present successor to the Russian Throne'.

So that was that. If Rosie had once been heir to the House of Romanov, she was heir no longer. And neither was he. But if Rosie had surfed the Net, how was it that she had not found this particular site, or another offering similar information? He would ask her when she came home.

But that night Rosie didn't come home: she went instead to Queen Mary's Hospital in Newport, with a broken hip.

Chapter 5

'She's been sedated,' said the doctor. 'It was a clean break and we've put her back together again. It wasn't the artificial hip, fortunately.'

'And will she be all right?' Nick sat by the hospital bed in which Rosie was sleeping.

'Well, at her age it's difficult to say. It's likely that she'll be less mobile than she was before. That said, she's fit for her age.'

Nick stroked Rosie's hand and listened to her breathing.

'We'll need to keep her in for a while, get her on her feet as soon as we can, and then I would suggest a period of convalescence in a home. There are one or two good ones on the island—unless you want her to go back to the mainland so that she can be nearer her friends?'

'I'd rather she was here, but I'll have to check with the rest of the family. My mother's on her way.'

'Yes, of course. We can talk about it later. She's in good hands for now.'

Nick looked back at Rosie. Her hands lay on top of the bedcovers, a plastic identity bracelet on her right wrist. It was all he could do to hold back the tears.

The sound of shoes on a hard floor broke in on his thoughts. He looked up. His mother was standing over him.

'WELL, HOW did it happen?'

'She slipped. On a boat.'

'Oh, Nick! What was she doing on a boat?'

'I told you, she was on a sailing course.'

'Stupid idea.' Anna Robertson's face was a picture of righteous indignation.

'Well, you were right, weren't you? And I was wrong. I just wanted her to have a bit of fun. And so did she.'

'And this is where it's led. So, what happens now?'

Nick was leaning forward with his elbows resting on his knees. They had left Rosie to sleep and were in the hospital waiting room, where Nick delivered the information to the floor, rather than to his mother. 'They'll have to keep her in for a while, and then they recommend a convalescent home.'

'Of course. Whereabouts?'

'I suggested here, but I thought you'd probably have an opinion on that.'

'It's out of the question. She'll have to come back to Richmond where I can keep an eye on her.'

'Lucky her.'

'Nick!'

He sat up. 'Well, we want her to get better, don't we? And she'll need encouragement for that, not you barking at her all the time.'

'That's not very kind.' She looked hurt.

'No, but it's accurate,' Nick continued stubbornly. 'You know you don't get on, and it would probably be better for both of you if she stayed on the island.'

Anna shrugged. 'Does your father know?'

'Not yet. I've tried ringing him but there was no reply. I think he was going abroad.' He avoided meeting her eye. There was no way he would mention the package, or explain that contacting his father had proved impossible. 'He's probably changed phones yet again.'

'More than likely.' She drummed her fingers on her handbag. 'Is she likely to be asleep for long?'

'A few hours. She's only just come out of theatre.'

'I see.' Anna glanced at her watch. 'I've a meeting tonight and I really can't miss it. If you think I should . . .'

'No. You get back. I can keep an eye.'

'Well, if you're sure . . .' His mother got up and laid a hand on his shoulder. 'We'll talk tomorrow, yes? Work out what to do.'

He nodded and turned to look out of the window as the purple haze of dusk settled on the hospital car park.

A PHONE CALL to the hospital at nine o'clock the next morning confirmed that Rosie had had a comfortable night and was now sleeping peacefully.

'Peacefully' sounded as if she'd given in, and that wasn't Rosie. He admonished himself for the thought and confirmed that he would visit her at lunchtime when she would be sitting up, they said.

He went into Rosie's bedroom. It was tidy and ordered, the photo of the Tsar, and a smaller one of Granddad, on the bedside table. He could see her nightie peeping out from under her pillow. Her travelling alarm clock ticked loudly, but the house was strangely quiet without her. Life was quiet.

And then he remembered: it was Alex and Victoria's last day on the island. He wanted to tell Alex what had happened, but more than that he wanted to see her. He punched in her mobile phone number and waited for it to ring. Her phone was switched off so he left a message: 'Hi. It's Nick. Just to say hello and . . . hope you're OK. Sorry I've not been in touch. Rosie's taken a bit of a tumble. She's OK but she's in hospital. I'll tell you all about it when we can speak. Er . . . that's all, really. Hope I'll speak to you soon. 'Bye.'

He looked out of the window at the pale grey day. At least it was fine. He grabbed his windcheater. He would buy some flowers to take to the hospital. Better still, he would pick some from the clifftop. She'd like that.

THE YOUNG WOMAN on the Isle of Wight ferry looked nothing like Nick. She was short and well rounded, with close-cropped hair and a tanned complexion. The rucksack on her back gave away nothing about her travels, but her brown legs and well-worn boots showed that she had been out of doors for some time. Sophie Robertson was back from South America and had headed straight from Heathrow to the ferry at Portsmouth.

Since arriving on the island, she had walked the couple of miles to The Anchorage, only to find that her brother was out. Not to worry, she would wait. She had food and water in her rucksack, and would make herself comfortable in a chair on the verandah until he returned.

She had been sitting there for an hour, reading, when a woman with a young girl walked up the drive. They seemed surprised to see her. Sophie got up and leaned over the rail. 'Hi!'

'Hello. Is Nick in?'

Sophie glanced at the house. 'If he was I wouldn't be sitting on the verandah.'

'Of course. I just wanted to tell him we're leaving the island today.'

'Oh. Righto. I'll pass on a message, if you like.'

'I tried to ring him on my mobile, but it's bust. If you could just say that Alex and Victoria called.'

'Fine. I'll do that.' Sophie sat down again and picked up her book.

'Yes. Right. Well, we'll be going, then.'

'OK. Goodbye, Alex and Victoria. I'll tell him you came.'

ROSIE WAS INDEED sitting up in bed when Nick arrived. His relief was unbounded as he bent to kiss her. 'Hello!'

She smiled, with what seemed like an effort, and whispered, 'Hello.'

He sat down on the chair by her bed and lifted the flowers for her to see: red campion and buttercups, stitchwort and cow parsley. He saw her eyes glint and her mouth force itself into a smile. 'Lovely,' she mouthed.

'I'll find some water for them in a minute. How are you feeling?'

'Sore,' she said.

'I'm not surprised. You had a bit of a tumble.'

Rosie nodded and closed her eyes.

'What am I going to do with you?' he asked gently.

'Don't know.' The voice was resigned, lacked energy, but that was hardly surprising. She opened her eyes and beckoned him closer. He leaned towards her. 'They want to get me on my feet, but . . . there's no . . . life in me.'

He held her hand and rubbed his thumb on the back. 'Oh, don't you worry, there will be. You're just a bit woozy from the anaesthetic.'

A nurse walked purposefully towards the bed and spoke in a loud voice: 'Hello, Mrs Robertson. We're a bit out of it at the moment, aren't we?'

'Mmm.' Rosie sounded distant.

The nurse tucked in a wayward length of sheet. 'We'll soon have you back on your feet, though. Would you like a drink? Cup of tea?'

Rosie shook her head and murmured 'No, thank you.'

Nick was alarmed. He had prepared himself for her to be frustrated and difficult, but not compliant or world-weary.

The nurse read the concern on his face: 'Still a bit under the weather, but she should pull round over the next day or so, get her bearings. We're just a bit confused, aren't we, Mrs Robertson?'

Nick wanted to explain that, although his grandmother was of a certain age, she was neither ga-ga nor deaf, and that she was a 'you' not a 'we'. But he thought better of it.

'Shall I put those in water for you?'

'Please.'

The nurse took the flowers. 'You could probably leave it until this evening if you want, Mr Robertson. She should be with us a bit more by then.'

'I'll just sit with her for a while, if that's all right.'

'Sure. No problem.'

He stayed by the bed for half an hour, while Rosie slept, then reluctantly headed for home.

THE SAILING to Portsmouth was uncharacteristically quiet. Victoria had her nose buried in the guidebook, occasionally writing something down in a small exercise book.

Eventually the Wight-Link ferry lowered its ramp onto the Portsmouth soil, and they got back into their car and drove off.

It was then that Victoria broke the silence. 'Who do you think it was?'

'I told you, I don't know,' Alex said curtly.

Victoria paused for a moment and then said, 'Maybe she was his old girl-friend come back.'

Alex had been doing her best to put that thought out of her mind. She had seen the rucksack with the airline luggage label beside the tanned stranger on Nick's verandah, and had concluded that Debs had returned. 'Look, can we just stop speculating and wait and see? We don't know who it was, and no amount of guessing is going to help us.'

'Are you cross?'

'No, I'm just a bit tired of being asked questions.'

'All right, all right. I'm sorry.' Victoria folded her arms, pursed her lips and stared out of the window at nothing in particular.

Alex felt mean. 'I'm sorry, too. It's just that . . . well, it's all very confusing, that's all.' She tried to placate her daughter: 'What have you been writing in your book?'

'Now who's asking questions?'

Alex sighed. 'I'm only interested.'

'No, you're not. You're just trying to make conversation.'

Alex laughed. 'Listen to us. We sound like an old married couple.'

'Yeugh!'

'Exactly. So, you tell me what you were writing and I won't snap your head off if you mention Nick.'

'We-ell,' she hesitated. 'I was writing down good places to live.'

'Ah, I see. And what conclusions did you come to?'

'Shanklin and Sandown are too busy, Newport is too far from the sea, and Cowes is too full of boaty people.'

'So you didn't find anywhere nice?'

'I like Sleepyhead Bay.'

'But there are only about ten houses, and I don't think you'd want to live there in winter.'

'I thought of that. Godshill is pretty, and it's not too far away.'

'Mmm. A bit chocolate-boxy for me.' Alex wondered why she had insti-gated this conversation. If their suspicions about Nick's visitor were accurate, the Isle of Wight was the last place she wanted to be.

'YOU DIDN'T TELL me you were coming home!' Nick flung his arms round his little sister.

'Didn't know I was until a couple of days ago.'

Nick took a pace back and eyed her up and down. 'You look so well!'

'All that walking.'

'So where did you get to, and why have you come back?'

'Well, if you let me in I'll tell you.'

Nick sat and listened as Sophie talked of her six months in Costa Rica, of tropical rainforests and coffee plantations, and of transiting the Panama Canal on a banana boat.

'You haven't said why you came home.'

'Dunno. Just felt I needed to for a bit.'

Nick grinned. 'I'm glad you did. Will you go back?'

'Not there. Chile, though, and Peru. Give myself a couple of weeks to get my breath back and then I'm off.'

'What will you do for money?'

'I've got some saved. I worked quite a lot of the time. Didn't earn much, but I don't need much.'

'Well, you might have a bit more than you think.'

'What do you mean?'

Nick filled in his sister on the events of the past weeks—of Rosie's relocation to the Isle of Wight, her sailing course and the accident, and the diamond legacy that was also Sophie's. He did not mention the Russian royal family. It seemed unnecessary, especially now that he had discovered there was no immediate danger of the Robertsons being called upon to take the throne.

'But why's she doing all this?' asked Sophie.

'For the same reason that you came home, I suppose. It's her time.'

'What does Mum think about it all?'

'She's furious that I let it all happen. Well, she was at first. I haven't told her about the diamonds. She knows Rosie's bank account is empty but she doesn't know why. She's probably just putting her head in the sand.'

'Just wants to get on with her own life, I suppose,' Sophie mused. 'But this diamond you say I'm getting. I suppose it will make things a bit easier. Where do you think it is?'

'In a bank somewhere, I imagine. Are you going to blow the lot on first-class travel, then?'

'Don't be stupid. Do I look like the sort who travels first class?' she scoffed.

'Er, no. A steerage girl if ever I saw one,' Nick told her.

'I tell you what I could do with, though. A bath.'

'I thought you'd never ask. I was just going to open all the windows.'

'Cheeky bugger!' She lunged forward to swipe him with her hand, but he caught it, spun her round and kissed her cheek.

'Nice to have you home,' he said. 'Get yourself cleaned up and then I'll cook you some dinner before we go and see your granny.'

'Now, there's an offer a girl can't refuse.'

TO HIS RELIEF Rosie was sitting up in bed, and something of her old self had come back. 'Where've you been?' she asked.

'Waiting for you to come round. You were a bit out of it before.'

'Huh. I'm bored stiff, stuck in here,' she grumbled.

'I've brought someone to see you.'

'Oh, not your mother. Tell me you've not brought *her*!'

'Ssssh! Keep your voice down. No, I haven't brought Mum. She came while you were asleep.'

'That was good timing.'

Nick beckoned to the figure hidden behind the door.

'Sophie! Oh, my love, what are you doing here? I thought you were in . . . wherever you were . . . South Africa.'

'South America. Hello, Rosie.' Sophie bent to kiss her grandmother.

Rosie, in a surge of affection, put her arm round Sophie's neck and hugged her. Then she spoke rapidly, through mounting emotion: 'I thought I'd never see you again. This is so lovely. So lovely.' She stroked the back of her grand-daughter's head, ruffling the golden stubble. Then she let Sophie stand up but took her hands. 'Look at you! You're brown as a berry! But your hair! There's not much left, is there?'

Sophie grinned. 'It's easier if it's short out there. Insects and stuff.'

Rosie frowned slightly. 'I think you're fairer than you were. Aren't you?'

'Sun probably.'

Rosie smiled again. 'Now there's only Alice, but I don't expect she'll be home for a while.'

'Not if you behave,' offered Nick. 'And her home *is* in South Africa.'

'Hey!' said Rosie. 'I haven't forgotten—it's just that it's easy to muddle South Africa and South America.'

Nick patted her hand. 'I know.'

'Now, we should be able to get some tea,' said Rosie, 'And you, Sophie, can tell me everything you've been doing.'

Nick could not remember when he had last felt so relieved.

SOPHIE EASED herself into the sleeping-bag on the sofa in Nick's sitting room. 'I'm knackered.'

'I'm not surprised,' Nick called from his room next door. Then he laughed. 'What does this remind you of?'

'When we were little,' his sister said.

He laughed again. 'You always wanted to talk and I always wanted to sleep.'

'Well, I shan't keep you awake tonight.'

'That's a relief.'

'Oh, that reminds me,' murmured Sophie, as she fought to stay awake. 'I almost forgot. A woman and a little girl were asking for you this afternoon when you were out. Alex and Victoria. Said she'd been trying to get hold of you but that her phone was bust or something. Does that make sense?'

HE HAD WANTED to ring her the night before, but it had been too late. He called her on her home number as soon as it seemed decent to do so—at around eight thirty. Victoria answered. 'Hello?'

'Victoria? It's Nick Robertson. Is your mum there?'

'No. She's out.' She sounded distracted.

'Oh.' Nick was flustered. 'Could you just say I rang and that I'm trying to get in touch with her? Maybe she could ring me later.'

'Will you be there all the time?'

'I have to go out to do a few things.'

'What about lunchtime? Will you be in then?' she asked.

'No. I have to go and see Rosie.'

'Isn't she with you any more?'

'No. She's had an accident.' Nick sighed.

There was silence at the other end of the line.

'Don't worry,' he said. 'She's OK, but she's in hospital.'

Silence again.

'Look, if you could pass on the message, and I'm sure we'll manage to speak some time today. OK?'

'OK.' And she hung up.

'Damn,' muttered Nick. He had wanted to tell Alex everything that had happened since they had last seen each other—and he'd wanted to tell her about Rosie himself.

He left The Anchorage and walked towards the cliffs, where he set up his easel. He worked all morning until half past twelve, when he packed up his brushes and drove to the hospital to meet Sophie at Rosie's bedside.

When he arrived the two were deep in conversation.

'How are you today, Duchess? Have they started you walking?'

'Have they? I'll say. Up and down the ward like a sentry. Ooh, yes!' Her eyes lit up. 'That reminds me.' She looked up at Nick. 'Did you tell Sophie'—she glanced from side to side, like a spy—'about the legacy thing?'

'Well, I did mention it.'

'But, Rosie, it's really not necessary,' Sophie told her.

'No buts. It's all sorted out. I've given Nick his and he's put it in the bank.' She turned to him. 'You have put it in the bank, haven't you?'

'Yes.'

'Well, I'll give you yours, Sophie, and you can do the same. As soon as your father comes back.'

Nick was horrified. 'Dad?' he managed weakly.

'Yes. I gave them to him for safekeeping. I couldn't get to the bank so he said he'd take them for me.'

SOPHIE KNEW something was wrong. All day Nick was preoccupied, and she assumed it was to do with the woman and little girl who had come to the house. She kicked herself for having forgotten to give him the message earlier.

During the afternoon Nick called Alex several times but there was no reply. Then, at around five, the phone was picked up by Alex.

'Hi!' He felt as though someone had opened a valve in his head, so great was his relief at hearing her voice. 'I'm sorry I missed you. I didn't get the message that you'd dropped by until late.'

'Oh. I see.' She sounded cooler than he had hoped. 'What's this about Rosie? Victoria said she'd had an accident but there was no need to worry.'

'She's broken her hip, messing about in boats, but she's on the mend. She was a bit dopey at first but she's almost back to her old self.'

'Oh, good. We did worry.'

'Yes. Sorry. Look, I couldn't see you again, could I? Soon.'

'Oh, well . . . it's a bit tricky . . . Victoria's back at school and . . .'

She seemed distant. Nick tried again. 'Perhaps I can ring you tomorrow?'

'If you like.'

'Is everything OK? It's just that . . . well, OK. I'll call tomorrow.'

He put down the phone. Why had she gone so cool on him? He ambled out to the verandah and flopped into a chair. Bloody hell! He'd cocked it up again. But this time he had no idea why.

'MAVIS?'

'Yes?'

'It's Nick. Any news on Pa? Has he done a bunk?'

Mavis was a sixty-something, amply proportioned spinster who lived with five cats on the edge of Epping Forest. She had devoted the last twenty years of her life to Nick's father—as his secretary-cum-personal assistant—but six months ago Derek had decided that he wanted to be more independent.

'Oh, I shouldn't think so. He'll just have gone to ground until the deal's done.'

'What sort of deal?'

'Now, you know better than to ask me that. There was a time when I would have known all, but your father prefers to work as a free agent nowadays.'

'Agent? What sort of agent?'

'Don't be dramatic, dear. He's never done anything on the wrong side of the law and I'm sure he's too old to start now. I'll give you a new phone number and you can keep trying it, but other than that I've nothing to offer.'

Nick tried the number. The line was dead as a doornail. Just like his love life.

'COME ON, then, what is it?' Sophie popped a piece of melon into her mouth. 'You've not said more than half a dozen sentences all day.'

'Oh, just girl trouble.' Nick nodded in the direction of the mainland.

Sophie looked guilty. 'Maybe I've frightened her off—by being here.'

'Don't be silly. She's not that feeble.'

'Certainly didn't look feeble. She seemed very . . . capable.'

'She is.' He laid his fork on the table and leaned back in his chair. 'Was she OK when you saw her?'

Sophie shrugged. 'Suppose so. If anything, she looked a bit disapproving. I saw her eyeing up my rucksack. Probably thought I was some sort of traveller.'

Nick sat up. 'Did you tell her you were my sister?'

Sophie hesitated. 'I . . . don't think so.'

Nick stood up and pointed at the rucksack in the corner. 'That was on the verandah, with airline labels all over it and you didn't tell her who you were?'

'No.' Sophie looked bewildered. 'What have my stickers got to do with it?'

'Alex comes here to tell me she's leaving and she sees you sitting on the verandah. And she knows I had a girlfriend who ran off to America.'

'Oh.' Sophie sat quite still, and then said, 'Oh, God!'

'Yes. Oh, God. She only thinks that Debs has come back.'

'YOUR SISTER?'

'Yes.'

'Oh.' There was a pause, then Alex chuckled and said, 'How silly.'

'Silly of her not to say.'

'And silly of me to jump to conclusions.'

'Typical Sophie. She's a great sister—love her to bits—but she can be a bit short with people she doesn't know.'

Alex brightened and made to brush it aside. 'Yes. Well, never mind.'

'No, but I do mind.' There was a pause. 'More than I realised.'

'Oh. That's very nice.'

'Look, can I see you tomorrow night?'

'Well, I . . . yes . . . I suppose so.'

'Shall I come over to you? I mean, you've been over here a lot lately.'

'No. No. I'll come to you. I'll just have to find a sitter, that's all. Oh, and I have a new mobile phone. Same number.'

'Right. See you tomorrow, then.'

Moments later Nick's mother rang. She had been giving some thought to Rosie's convalescence, and had decided, she said, that perhaps it would be best if Rosie stayed on the island. Her resigned manner spoke volumes.

He hung up. It was a defining moment. To all intents and purposes, his grandmother's future care was in his hands.

'I DON'T REALLY want to go out,' grumbled Sophie, the following evening.

'I know, but you owe it to me, don't you?'

'Mmm. I suppose so.' She was changing in the bathroom and talked to him through the half-open door. 'I'll be back about ten.'

'What?'

Sophie grinned to herself. 'Only teasing. I've booked a room at the Royal London—I'm meeting up with a few old drinking mates.'

Nick back-pedalled: 'Look, you can come back here. Nothing's going to happen. I just want to have a bit of time on my own with Alex.'

'Of course. And who'd want their sister hanging around, even if she has only been home a couple of days.'

'Soph!'

She came out of the bathroom wearing a T-shirt and jeans. 'You're *so* easy to wind up.' She reached up and ruffled his hair. 'Better clean yourself up a bit, though. Don't want to put her off.'

'I will—now I can get into the bathroom.'

HE MET ALEX at the ferry terminal, in the MG with the hood down.

'Is this wise?' she asked. 'Having the hood down?'

He leaned across and kissed her cheek. 'No rain forecast.'

'Where are we going?'

'I thought we'd eat in. Try to do a bit better than last time.'

Alex grinned. 'That's nice. No need to worry about anyone else.'

He looked at her meaningfully. 'No.'

They didn't speak much on the journey, just sat back, happy to be in each other's company.

She smiled at him as he opened the door for her to get out of the car once they had reached The Anchorage. 'Here we are,' he said. 'Dry as a bone.'

'In more ways than one.'

'Oh, don't worry. The Cloudy Bay is on ice.'

'Cloudy Bay? Are we celebrating or something?'

'Yes,' he said. 'The end of a misunderstanding.'

He ushered her up the steps and onto the verandah, where a small table was laid for two. Alex sat down and Nick disappeared into the cottage. He returned with a bottle of the New Zealand wine and two glasses. He poured, they drank, and looked out over the sea as the sun sank below the horizon.

'Do you ever take this view for granted?' she asked.

'No. It's never the same twice.'

'A bit different from my view in Portsmouth,' she said. 'You're so lucky.'

He smiled at her. 'I know.'

Over supper—lobster, bought from the fisherman at Sleepyhead Bay—he told her about Rosie's accident. Then, feeling the need to unburden himself, he explained about Rosie's preoccupation with her Russian ancestry and his researches into the royal family. It no longer sounded ridiculous. He found himself talking easily and she was attentive, absorbed.

Finally he said, 'Unbelievable, isn't it?'

Alex shook her head. 'No. Unusual, but not unbelievable.' And then, 'Oh my God!'

'What?' He stared at her.

'Our names.'

He sighed with relief. 'I know. Silly, isn't it?'

She grinned. 'I think it's rather sweet. Did Rosie notice?'

'Immediately.'

'I'm not surprised.' Alex looked more serious. 'And you still don't know for certain who her parents were?'

'No, and I don't really know where to start.'

'Maybe I could do a bit of reading. Research.' She hesitated, not sure if she'd overstepped the mark.

'That would be great!' Nick said enthusiastically.

'You jot down the facts and the names you know, and I'll have a dig around, if you're sure you don't mind.'

'I'm pleased you want to bother—that you think it's worth it.'

'Of course! It's fascinating. It'll be a bit of an adventure.'

'As long as you want one.'

She looked across the table at him. 'Oh, I think so.'

Then he asked, 'Do you have to go?'

Alex stroked the hair back from his forehead. 'I should really say yes.'

'But?'

'Victoria's with friends—I couldn't get a sitter.'

'Stay, then?'

'Yes, please.'

Chapter 6

He watched her as she woke. The early-morning light caught her dark hair and made it shine like polished jet. Nick could not remember ever feeling so calm as he did at that moment. Lying next to her in his bed. Feeling her warm and naked body next to his.

She stirred, then opened her eyes, squinting at the rays of dawn. For a moment he thought she might not remember where she was. Might suddenly regret the impulse of the night before, jump out of his bed and throw on her clothes, but she didn't. Instead, she smiled at him and snuggled closer. 'Hello, you,' she murmured.

'Hello, you,' he echoed.

They lay still for a few moments, silent except for their soft breathing. Then they made love again, and afterwards lay in each other's arms.

Soon, Alex rose from the bed and went to the bathroom. He watched her go, captivated by the sight of her. When she came back, she slid in beside him and laid her arm across his chest. 'What are you thinking?' she asked.

'About you.'

She raised herself up on one elbow and looked him in the eye. 'You don't think I was . . . well . . . a bit fast.'

He nodded. 'Like lightning.'

'Oh God! I didn't mean to be. I'm not usually . . .'

'Hey!' He squeezed her shoulders. 'Just kidding.'

'Oh. Well, that's all right.' She relaxed. 'I wish I could stay.'

'Can't you?' He looked at her, his eyes hopeful.

'No. The neighbours will take Victoria to school—with their little girl—but I've got to get back. There's shopping to do.'

'What?' Nick sat up and looked at her incredulously. 'You're lying in bed with me and all you can think of is doing the shopping?'

'It's all right for you! You have no responsibilities, but I have another mouth to feed.' She kissed him lightly on the forehead, slid out of bed and asked, 'May I have a shower?'

'Only if I can join you.'

HENRY SAT by Rosie's bed while the nurse arranged a bunch of red roses in a vase on the bedside cabinet. 'They're beautiful,' said Rosie, her eyes shining.

'Cut them myself this morning,' said Henry, with a wink.

'Dreadful man. They must have cost a fortune.'

'Worth it to see your face, dear lady. I've been a bit worried about you. Glad to see you're on the mend.'

'Slowly. Very slowly.'

'So, what happens now?' he asked.

'Another week or so in here, and then I've got to go into a nursing home.' She grimaced.

'What?' He looked horrified.

'Oh, not permanently, just to convalesce. Nick's going to arrange it.'

'Here or on the north island?' Henry still looked worried.

'Here. I don't want to go back there just yet.'

'Oh, good.' He reached out his hand and held hers. 'I wouldn't want to think you were going away.'

Rosie smiled. 'You're very kind, Henry.'

'Not kind at all. Just, well . . .'

'Whatever it is, I'm grateful.'

Henry gazed at her, sitting there. Somehow Rosie didn't fit here. She was a doer, and doers are always up and about, not lying in bed. She caught his eye. 'Not much fun is it?' she asked. 'Getting old, I mean.'

'No,' Henry agreed ruefully.

'But we're no different from the way we've always been, really.'

'Except that some bits don't work as well,' Henry said wistfully.

'I just wish younger people would understand.'

'Understand what?'

'That you never stop being you. That you still have feelings just as much as you did when you were younger.' Rosie sighed. 'I mean, I'm every bit as passionate and interested, it's just that somehow it all gets . . . blunted.'

'Is that how you feel now?' he asked gently.

'When I'm a bit down, yes. I just wish I could feel the joy in life that I felt when I was younger.' She looked distant, distracted.

'I think you should try to get some sleep.' Henry patted her hand, worried that her fighting spirit had been dented. It must be the medication. 'It's only natural,' he said. 'Probably something to do with the anaesthetic. It's still wearing off. We've got to get you back on your feet as soon as we can and out of this place. Then, perhaps, you'll let me take you out to dinner.'

Rosie looked anxious. 'Henry, there's something you should know. You remember when we were talking in the pub?'

'Mmm?'

'I was less than honest with you. I didn't want you to think that I was a feeble old lady so . . .'

Henry cleared his throat. 'If you're about to say something about your age, then I should mention something before you do. I lied to you about my age. I'm not really fifty-eight. I'm actually sixty-three.'

For a moment Rosie's face bore a look of surprise.

'Will you forgive me?'

She looked at him with mock admonishment, then melted. 'Of course I will.'
'You're very kind. Very generous.'
Rosie squeezed his hand. 'You know what that means, don't you?'
Henry raised an eyebrow.
'It means that you're only six years younger than me.'

IT WAS eight thirty that evening before Nick had a moment to phone Alex. After the mundanities of life—doing his own shopping, taking the car for an oil change, repairing a window at The Anchorage—and visiting Rosie in hospital, he dialled the number.
'Hello?'
'You got back, then? Shopping successful?' he asked sarcastically.
'Yes, thank you!' She was stifling a laugh. 'And thank you for last night. It was very . . . special.'
'Yes.' He paused. 'Yes, it was. I'm glad you stayed.'
'Me too.'
'And how's Victoria? You weren't in trouble?' he enquired.
'Not exactly. I got a few what you might call "old-fashioned" looks. You know—about staying out all night.'
'It's going to be tricky, isn't it?'
'I suppose so,' she said forlornly. 'But don't worry—I'll handle it. It's my problem. Just give me a couple of days to sort myself out.'
They said goodbye fondly, but he felt uneasy. He told himself to give her time. To give them both time. This was something not to be rushed.
He got up and walked outside onto the verandah. Dusk was falling. In the far distance, through the rising mist, the green light of a container ship floated across the water. Another day, another night. He was alone with his thoughts—of Rosie, his father, wherever he was, and Alex.

WHATEVER ELSE Nick expected to happen the following morning it was not Henry's arrival on his doorstep. 'Are you feeling all right?' he asked. 'Normally you never venture this far without your passport and immunisation.'
'There's no need for that. I'm on an errand of mercy.'
'That sounds ominous. Do you want some coffee? Even you can't drink claret at this time of day.' Henry glared at him. 'Sorry.' Nick felt he might have overstepped the mark. 'What's the errand?'
'I went to see Rosie yesterday.'

'That was kind of you.' Nick was busy with the coffee and didn't look up.
'She was talking about what will happen when she comes out of hospital.'
'It won't be for a couple of weeks yet.'
'Three days, actually.'
'What?'
'I asked the nurse. The consultant had just done his rounds. They can get her a physio in her rest home and they reckon she'll be fit to go there by the end of the week.'

Nick put down the kettle. 'They didn't tell me that. I haven't sorted anything out yet.'

'I thought that might be the case. Anyway, she'll probably be happy to get out of the place.'

'But she's hardly mobile yet.' Nick was worried. 'And it will be difficult to find somewhere at such short notice.' He could hear the panic in his voice.

'I'd thought of that. I might be able to help.' Henry fished into his inside pocket. 'My card.'

Nick took the small rectangular business card. It was a little crumpled at the edges. *Henry J. Kinross, MCSP, SRP*, it said, in minute copperplate.

'Henry, why do I need this? I know where you live.'

Henry pointed to the letters after his name. 'MCSP stands for Member of the Chartered Society of Physiotherapists. And SRP means State Registered Physiotherapist.'

Nick stared at him. 'You're a physiotherapist?'
'Correct.'
'But you're an art dealer.'
'The two are not mutually exclusive. And I wasn't always an art dealer.'
'But . . . how long is it since you practised?'
'Ooh, about half an hour.'
'What?'

'Why do you think I open the gallery late every morning? It's not because I have a hangover. I have a few private patients. It keeps the old skill going and it takes my mind off temperamental artists. I spoke to the consultant at the hospital and he agreed that Rosie could stay with me. I have a niece on the mainland who can come over and keep an eye on the gallery, and Rosie will recover more quickly than she would in some impersonal nursing home.'

Nick was stunned. The kettle whistled and he took it off the hob. 'You never said anything.'

'Dear boy, if there is one thing in life that I've learned it's that it doesn't do for people to know everything about you until they need to.'

Nick handed him a mug of coffee. 'You know,' he said, with a twinkle in his eye, 'I'm not sure I should trust you with my grandmother.'

'Dear boy. I never mix business with pleasure.'

'Good.' Nick laughed.

'But in the case of your grandmother I'm prepared to make an exception.'

ALEX HAD JUST got home from a trip to the library, where she'd done some research into Rosie's past, when there was a knock at her door. Whoever else she had expected to find when she opened it, it was not her husband.

She looked at him, standing there with his hands in the pockets of his well-cut suit. He was six feet three, darkly good looking and immaculately dressed. His self-assurance had once attracted her but now she found it repellent. They had grown to realise that they were, fundamentally, different in outlook, always had been, but they had put it to one side and allowed the physical attraction to carry them along.

'What are you doing here? I thought you'd gone.'

'Not till tomorrow. I was delayed. I came to say goodbye to Vicks.'

'She's at school. She'll be home any minute.'

'Can I come in and wait?'

'No. No, you can't. Look, we've been through all this. You know it will only upset her. Last time you saw her it was supposed to be for the last time. She had nightmares for days afterwards, Paul.'

'Don't exaggerate.'

'I'm not. It's not that she doesn't love you, it's just that . . . she's frightened of you.'

'But that's ridiculous. I've never touched her.'

Alex tried to sound sympathetic. 'I know that, but she needs stability. She can't cope with this whirlwind who descends on the house, rows with her mother, then takes off again.' She shook her head. 'No, I'm sorry, you'll have to go. Right now she just needs to get her mind round the fact that her mother and father don't live together any more.'

Paul leaned against the wall. 'So that's that, then?'

'Yes. That was that three months ago—three years ago.'

'Oh, don't bring all that up again. She's not coming with me.'

'Only because someone else is.'

Paul looked away.

'Go on. Go to America. You can see Victoria when you come back.'

He walked towards the door, then turned to face her. 'It didn't have to be like this, you know.'

Alex sighed. 'Oh, it did.'

ROSIE WAS SITTING up in bed, her lipstick freshly applied, holding out her hand as a manicurist varnished her nails.

'I thought this was a hospital, not a beauty clinic,' Nick said, as he arrived beside her.

Rosie looked up at him and beamed. 'Hello, love! I'm just having my nails done. They come once a week. Useful, isn't it?' She nodded towards the young woman in the pink nylon overall who was bent over her right hand. 'This is Clare. She's come to get me ready for my trip.'

'Trip?'

'To Henry's.'

'Ah, yes.' He smiled at Clare, who, evidently aware that a family heart-to-heart was about to ensue, packed away her varnishes and bustled off.

Nick sat down by the bed. 'Are you sure about moving in with Henry?'

'Oh, I'm not moving in with him like *that*! We're not—what do they call it? Co-something.'

'Cohabiting.'

'Yes. I'm not doing that.'

'Well, you'll be under the same roof.'

'Not in the same bed, though.'

Nick spluttered. 'I should hope not.'

Rosie looked at him with a serious expression on her face. 'Would it be so terrible if we were?'

'Rosie!'

She shook her head. 'People your age are all the same. Always imagining that sex is something for the under-fifties.'

Nick glanced around apprehensively. 'Will you keep your voice down?'

Rosie grinned. 'You don't stop suddenly, you know, when you've had your children.'

Nick leaned back in his chair. 'Are you trying to shock me?'

She looked him in the eye. 'Maybe.'

'Well, thanks for being honest, at least.'

Rosie leaned back on the pillow and closed her eyes. 'I'm tired.'

'I'm not surprised.'

She opened them again. 'But I'm happier. I've got something to look forward to now.'

Nick paused, more serious now. 'Look, don't you think you'd be better off where they can look after you properly?'

'Henry can look after me properly,' Rosie insisted.

'But he has a gallery to run.' Nick took her hand. 'All I'm saying is that I don't think Henry knows what he's letting himself in for.'

Rosie squeezed his hand. 'Shall I tell you something? I know he doesn't.'

'You're a wicked old lady!'

'I know. But it's more fun that way!' She grinned.

Nick laughed, relieved that her old spirit was back.

'I'm going to stay with Henry,' Rosie continued. 'He likes the prospect of looking after me, but I expect it will wear off. I'm ready for it, though, so I'll take the chance.'

'Do you take more chances now?'

'Heavens, yes. She saw his face and smiled. 'I know I'm odd, and your granddad found it wearing—he was happy to do the same things every day, bless him. But I can't. Too many things I've not done, and not much time left to do them.' Then she said, pointedly, 'It's in my blood.' Then came the expected question: 'Have you found anything out?' she asked. 'About my parents?'

'A tiny bit,' he said, 'but nothing very helpful.'

Rosie pushed herself up in the bed a little. 'Well?'

Nick explained the difference between marriages with members of sovereign houses, and morganatic marriages, and told Rosie about the true heir to the Russian throne.

'So we're not in line, then?' she asked evenly.

'No.' He paused. 'But you knew that, didn't you?'

Rosie was silent for a moment. 'Yes. But I wanted you to find out for yourself. I wanted you to be curious about your family history.'

Nick said nothing, just looked at her lying back on her pillow, eyes a clear forget-me-not blue, skin soft and smooth, lips perfectly made up. She was, he had to admit, the eighth wonder of the world.

'And what about you?' she asked. 'Alex. Is it going well?'

'I think so.'

'Don't want to rush it? Is that why you're not seeing more of each other?'

He nodded, looking preoccupied. 'She's still married—separated, but not divorced—and there's Victoria to think about.'

'Oh, those things will sort themselves out.' Rosie was dismissive.

'You seem very sure.'

'Stands to reason. If she wants you as much as you want her then the first one needn't be a problem, and Victoria—well, I think she knows a good man when she sees one. Take things a day at a time. Just chill out.'

'What?'

'Chill out.' Nick laughed. Rosie looked concerned. 'What's so funny?'

'You are.'

'Why?' She was indignant now.

'Nothing. It's nothing.'

'Some days I worry about you,' Rosie told him.

'Yes,' he replied. 'And some days I worry about you. Though for the life of me I can't imagine why.'

He sat with her for another hour, and when he left he felt strangely confident. He knew it wouldn't last, but for the moment he would enjoy it. Outside, the rain that had been threatening all day was now falling, that fine rain that soaks you to the skin. He had already put up the hood on the MG, and drove home with the inefficient wipers doing their best to clear the windscreen.

He made a dash for the verandah and, as he slipped his key into the lock, he heard the telephone. It took him a moment to recognise the voice at the other end of the line, who was gasping out seemingly disconnected phrases between the sobs: 'Paul . . . goodbye . . . Victoria . . . school . . . missing.'

WHEN HE COULD finally make sense of what Alex had said, the seriousness of it sank in. Paul had been to see her. He had asked if he could say goodbye to Victoria. She had refused. Victoria had not come home from school. Alex thought it likely that he had taken the child with him. She'd rung him but there had been no answer.

'Have you told the police?'

'No. Not yet.'

'Well, I think you should.'

'Oh God!'

Nick could hear the rising panic in her voice.

'Has she taken anything with her?' he asked, not knowing why that should be important but clutching at straws. 'Clothes, washbag, that sort of thing.'

'No. Only the clothes she was wearing. And her school bag.'

'And she didn't say anything this morning?'

'No.' Her desperation was audible.

'Was she OK?'

'She's been a bit distant lately. Her mind's been elsewhere. She always has her head buried in that Isle of Wight guidebook she made me buy her . . . Oh, Nick . . . you don't think she's gone to the island, do you?'

'It's possible. She didn't *say* anything about coming here?'

'Nothing.'

'I think she's most likely to be with Paul, if you want my honest opinion, but I'll go and look in all the places she knew. Sleepyhead Bay and the place where you stayed. I'll ask Sophie to wait here in case she shows up.'

'But how will I get in touch with you?' Alex asked.

'Ring The Anchorage and let Sophie know if anything happens. I'll give her both your numbers so that she can call you.'

After a few more placatory phrases he put down the phone and went to the yacht club to find Sophie.

'SHE'S WHAT?'

'Gone missing.'

'Oh, hell! Any clues?'

'Well, her father, Paul, came round just before Victoria was expected home from school and Alex wouldn't let him stay to see her.'

'Was that wise?'

'Victoria's always in a state when her father's been. I think Alex was just trying to keep her on an even keel. Anyway, she thinks Paul might have taken her, and it does seem likely. The only other thing is that she was welded to an Isle of Wight guidebook. I think she's fallen for the place.'

'Oh, poor Alex.' Then the organiser in Sophie came to the fore. 'I'll get back to the house. Have you rung the ferry company to see if she was spotted coming over? No? Then I'll do that. You go and look wherever you think she might be. Now, take this.' She handed him a mobile phone. 'It's new. I've stuck the number on it so I don't forget. I'll ring Alex and give her the number, then she can ring you—or ring me at The Anchorage—if she hears anything. Now get off and look.' Sophie strode off up the lane in the direction of The Anchorage.

'Thanks!' he yelled after her.

THE SUN was sinking below the horizon as he walked down the steps to Sleepyhead Bay. The rain had stopped, but the rough wooden planks were wet and slippery, as were the rocks in the cove. He hopped from one to another, looking for a small girl he hoped might be fishing for shrimps.

He knocked on the doors of the small cottages, but with no luck. Nobody had seen a small girl on her own. He tried the hotel where Alex and Victoria had stayed. They remembered mother and daughter, but had seen neither of them since. On he drove, to places where he knew Alex had taken Victoria, but his enquiries yielded nothing and it was getting dark.

At half past eight he rang Sophie. 'Have you heard anything?' he asked.

'No. But they had a school party on board the last ferry. They said it's just possible she could have slipped on without them seeing.'

'Damn.' He tried to think straight. 'Oh, Soph, what do I do now?'

'Ring Alex and tell her you've no news—bad or good.'

He did as Sophie suggested, and told Alex where he had searched.

'Is there still no sign of Paul?'

'No. The police have alerted the airports and the ferry terminals and they're talking to the Newport station.'

'Look, I'm not giving up. We'll find her. You mustn't think the worst.'

'I'm so glad you're there,' whispered Alex. 'I don't know what I'd do without you.'

As he set off again on his search, patchy cloud gave way to small expanses of sky, studded with stars, and the moon ducked in and out. Victoria was out there somewhere. But where? Where would a child go if she was disturbed by her parents splitting up and was looking for some kind of escape? She'd look for somewhere comforting. Somewhere she felt at home . . .

His reverie was broken by the shrill ring of the mobile phone in his pocket. He pulled over and answered the call.

'Nick?'

'Soph?'

'I think I've seen her. I was making some tea about five minutes ago and I glanced up at the window and I'm sure I saw a face. I ran out as fast as I could but I couldn't see anyone. I'm sure I didn't imagine it, though.'

'And you think it was Victoria?'

'Well, I only met her once and I wasn't taking that much notice, but I'm as sure as I can be that it was her. Do you want to phone Alex?'

'Not until we're certain.'

He slipped the phone back into his pocket and gazed up at the moon in the hope that it would offer inspiration. But the moon wasn't playing. It slid tantalisingly behind a cloud.

The phone in his pocket rang again. This time it was Alex.

'The police say they can't do anything until morning now. Have you found anything?'

He was unable to keep from her the glimmer of hope. 'Sophie thinks she saw a face at the window of the cottage and that it was Victoria's.'

'Oh God!'

'Now, stay calm. When Sophie ran outside there was no sign of anyone. But I reckon if she's here on the island she's probably sheltering from the rain and there's no way we're going to find her till morning.'

'No,' she said flatly, trying to hold on to her emotions.

'Why don't you try to get some sleep?' Nick said gently.

'I can't.' She let out a sob and the phone clicked off.

He wished he could be with her. He could only imagine what she was going through. He replaced the phone in his pocket, drove round for a while longer, and then returned to The Anchorage. He found Sophie dozing in an armchair. She started up when he walked in. 'Any news?'

Nick flopped onto the sofa. 'Nothing. Nothing at all. I'm beginning to wonder if it was your imagination. Maybe it was just rain on the window.'

Sophie shook her head. 'No, it wasn't. Unless rain wears a woolly hat.' She held up a lavender-blue knitted hat. 'Found it in the rosebush by the window.'

'Why didn't you ring me?' he asked angrily.

'I did. You had no signal.'

'Bloody mobile phones! I'm going to phone Alex. I don't think she'll be asleep.' He walked over to the phone and dialled the number.

Alex answered almost immediately. 'Hello.'

'Alex, it's me. Does Victoria have a blue woolly hat?'

'Yes. She always wears it to school, even when it's sunny. In case it rains.'

'Thank heavens! We've found it outside the house. On a rosebush. She must be over here.'

WITHIN THE HOUR the police had turned up at The Anchorage, and searched the house and garden. They sat down with Nick and Sophie and questioned them in detail about their knowledge of and relationship with Victoria. When they finally departed, dawn was breaking.

Sophie pushed herself out of the chair. 'Better have a shower. No. Come to think of it, you look terrible. You have one.'

'No. I can't. I need to start looking again.'

With the bossiness reserved for sisters, she ushered him to the bathroom, then cooked him breakfast.

'How do you feel now?' she asked, as he slumped down at the table.

'Better than I should,' he replied, rubbing his face.

'Nervous energy.' Sophie put her hand on his. 'Victoria will be fine. You'll see. She'll be cold, fed up and hungry by now. When you're cold and hungry two things become irresistible.'

Nick looked at her questioningly. 'Warmth and food?'

'Exactly.' Sophie came to the table and sat down opposite him. 'What's Victoria like? Do you get on?'

'I think so, but it must be a bit hard, seeing your dad and mum break up, then having your mum find a new friend so soon.'

'I guess so.'

'But it just sort of happened. I don't think either of us was looking to start a relationship. It just . . . crept up on us.'

'Love on the rebound?'

'No. I don't think so. She's fun, good company. No. It's more than that.'

'Hey! There's no need to defend yourself. You know what I think?'

Nick shook his head.

'I think you're in love. You're a changed man—you're cheerful, fun to be with. Not like you were with Debs.'

Nick raised an eyebrow.

'Sorry, but it's true. She did put a bit of a damper on you.'

He nodded. Seeing it clearly for the first time.

'Are you sure you can take on a ready-made family, though?'

'I think that depends on whether or not she's prepared to take on me . . . but it was Victoria who introduced me to her mum.'

'She was quite bold, then?'

'Yes. It's since then that she's got more thoughtful. She came round one evening with Alex. She was talking to Rosie. They seemed to be getting on really well, then Rosie started talking about the Russian royal family thing.'

'What?'

Nick realised he'd put his foot in it. 'I forgot to tell you—well, I didn't, actually. I was waiting for the right moment.'

'For what?'

'This isn't the right moment either, but, in a nutshell, you know Rosie was born in Russia?'

'Ye-es?'

'And she never knew who her real parents were?'

'Ye-es.'

'Well, she's got this bee in her bonnet that she's related to the Tsar.'

'*What?*'

'Exactly.' Nick got up from the table. 'I haven't really got the time to tell you now—I need to get out and start looking again—but the long and the short of it is that Rosie thinks her mother was Grand Duchess Tatiana who was assassinated with the rest of the Russian royal family in 1918, but she doesn't know who her father was.'

Sophie cleared her throat. 'This is all a dream. I'm hallucinating.'

'No, you're not.' Nick was pulling on his coat and making for the door. 'You're just part of a family with some colourful history.' He opened the door. 'Wish me luck.'

Chapter 7

He drove to Carisbrooke. Maybe the castle ruins had captured her imagination. Victoria loved Jane Austen, Alex had said, and Jane Austen had loved the Isle of Wight. Maybe there was a connection.

Leaving the car outside the towering walls, he circumnavigated the castle. It was so large, so impregnable; the vast hill on which it stood must have been capable of withstanding the most determined army. And yet he felt that there was no threat in the air. The castle was protective, benign. Its bloody history was behind it now, and it sat, like some battle-scarred leviathan, on its hill, ready to offer shelter to all who needed it. Perhaps he had become an incurable romantic, but he wanted to believe that the islanders were good people who, on seeing a lost ten-year-old, would take her in, find out where she was from, and get her safely home to her mother.

Then he remembered what Rosie had said during their tea at the Ritz. 'People think what the newspapers and the television tell them to think.'

Of course there were more good people in the world than bad. It was just that you never heard about them.

Rosie. He had put her out of his mind—there had barely been room for her during the events of the night. She had got on so well with Victoria and would be desperate when she heard the news. Unless . . . He slipped back into the car and drove to the hospital.

He walked down the long corridor, then turned the corner that led into Rosie's ward. She lay in her bed, sipping her morning tea. 'Hello, love!' she said. 'Guess who's come to visit me?'

At first he could see nobody. But then, as he approached the bed, he saw, at Rosie's shoulder, a small figure sitting on a chair. She was bedraggled and tired, and her face bore a worried frown. 'Have you been looking for me?' she asked.

THE PHONE CALLS were the first thing. Alex burst into tears at the news, said, 'Thank you, thank you . . . oh, thank you,' then hung up to rush for the ferry. He called the police, and then Sophie, who agreed to meet Alex at the ferry terminal. Then he sat down in the hospital waiting room and talked to Victoria, trying to understand.

'I just wanted to see if Rosie was all right,' she said.

'I thought you knew she was?'

'I wanted to see for myself.' She looked up at him now, suddenly shy. 'And I wanted to see you.'

Nick felt stunned. 'Why?'

'To try to understand what was going on.'

Nick put his arm round her. 'Is it very confusing?'

Victoria looked at the floor and nodded.

'It's just that . . . well . . . things happen sometimes and you don't have much control over them,' he said.

She looked up. 'Like you and Mum?'

'Yes.'

'I just wanted to know if you love her as much as she loves you?'

Her candour took his breath away. 'Do you think she loves me?'

Victoria nodded. 'Oh, yes. I just think she's a bit scared.'

Nick cleared his throat. 'I think we're all a bit scared. What do you think?'

She managed a weak smile. 'That you're very nice.'

Nick gave her a hug. 'I think you're nice, too. But why did you run away?'

'Because of Dad. When I was going home from school I saw him going to the house. I didn't want to see him, so I walked into town and got onto the ferry. I didn't want to make Mum worry. I was going to go back when I'd seen Rosie and you. But it took longer to get to your house than I thought. Then I looked through your window and that lady was there, the one we saw when you were out.'

'My sister?'

'I think so. She saw me, so I hid under the verandah, in case she stopped me finding Rosie. When she'd gone, and I knew you weren't there, I walked into Newport. Was Mum cross?'

'She was very worried.'

'What about Dad?' She looked frightened now. 'Is he coming?'

'No. He's gone. We thought you might have gone with him.'

She shook her head violently.

Nick wondered whether he should ask the question, but found it impossible not to. 'You don't seem to get on with your dad.'

Victoria shook her head again.

Nick sat and waited. He didn't like to probe.

Eventually she said, 'He's all right with me, but he's not nice to Mum.' She looked up at him. 'You make her happy.' She had a quizzical look on her face. 'Are you a good man?'

Nick was taken aback. 'Well . . . I try to be.'

'Because I think she deserves a good man.'

The power of speech temporarily deserted him—such old-fashioned, adult conversation from a ten-year-old! 'So do I,' he stammered eventually.

'I hope you're not wasting her time.'

There was no possible answer to this, so Nick said, 'We'd better get you cleaned up. Do you want to come back to the cottage and wait for your mum?'

'If it's not too much trouble.'

'Oh, it's no trouble. No trouble at all.'

'THIS PLACE is beginning to seem like a seaside hotel.'

They were sitting round the small table at The Anchorage—Alex and Victoria, Nick and Sophie.

'Not for long. I'm off next week,' said Sophie.

'It wasn't a hint,' said Nick, 'just an observation.'

Alex had been waiting for Nick and Victoria on their return from the hospital. Nick had left them to talk while he and Sophie had gone food shopping.

When they returned, they found mother and daughter curled up together on the sofa, Victoria lying against Alex, who was stroking her hair. They got up when Nick and Sophie came in, and then they had all set about preparing lunch. Nothing more had been said about Victoria's adventure. Until now.

'I'm sorry for all this,' said Alex, 'but I think we've cleared it up now.' She stood up, clearly wanting to change the subject. 'How's Rosie?' she asked.

'She comes out of hospital in a couple of days.' Nick told them about the plan for Rosie to stay with Henry.

'Henry? A physiotherapist?' asked Alex.

'I've tried to tell him that he'll have bitten off more than he can chew,' Nick said, 'but he's insistent. As soon as the consultant gives the nod, Rosie's going back to *chez* Henry for rest and recuperation.'

'He's mad!' opined Sophie. 'She'll drive him bonkers.'

'No, she won't,' Victoria chipped in. 'She has lots of good stories.'

'Well, I just hope he's appreciative,' said Sophie.

Alex asked softly, 'Is this wise?'

'Probably not,' said Nick. 'But if you can stand in the way of those two when they've set their minds on something, you're a lot braver than I am.'

'You talk about them as if they were a couple.'

'Well, they seem to be, in a funny sort of way. Rosie's old enough to be his mother but they've taken a shine to each other.'

Victoria, who was eating ice cream, said, 'I don't think age matters. It's whether or not people are suited that matters, not how old they are.'

Without thinking, Sophie said, 'And you're an expert on this, are you?'

Victoria nodded. 'A bit. Mummy and Daddy were the same age and they didn't get on. But Nick is much older than Mummy and they do.'

'Excuse me!' protested Nick. 'I'm only—'

'Ahem.' Alex coughed.

'—slightly older,' he murmured.

'So, what happens now?' asked Sophie, and began to clear away the plates.

'I think we'll head home,' said Alex, looking at her watch.

'Can't we stay here?' asked Victoria, turning her attention fully to her mother and putting down her spoon.

'No, sweetheart. We ought to get back to normal.'

'But you can come back soon,' offered Nick.

'How soon?'

'We'll see,' said Alex. 'We'll see.'

THROUGH THE OPEN door Nick and Sophie held their nightly conversation.

'Are you as knackered as I am?' she asked.

'No. I'm more knackered. Stop talking and go to sleep.'

'Victoria's wonderfully old-fashioned, isn't she?' she said thoughtfully.

'Comes of reading too much Jane Austen.'

Sophie heard a rustle of bedclothes and then he was standing in the open doorway. 'Do you think she's just old-fashioned or a bit scary?'

She sat up in bed. 'She's not scary, just scared.'

'Scared of her mum getting it wrong again?'

'Yes.'

Nick sat on the edge of Sophie's bed. 'With me?'

'Oh, no. Quite the reverse. I think she's worried her mum will let you go.'

Nick looked stunned. 'Are you sure?'

'Yes. And Victoria's pretty astute, too. She's got a great mum in Alex but it's not enough. She needs a dad, too. Look at me, I should know.'

Nick looked bewildered. 'You didn't say anything . . .'

'Of course I didn't. I wasn't going to admit it. But it was grim. For me Mum was always just beautifully turned out, and Dad was just never there.'

'But you . . .'

'Oh, I always jollied myself along. No point in getting depressed about it. But I got out as soon as I could. That's what makes me keep on travelling. Stupid, really. One day I'll have to stop and face up to it. Life. Relationships. Someone like you, that's what I want. Someone pleasant and malleable.'

Nick pushed her shoulder so she fell back against the pillow. 'Pleasant and malleable? Is that how you see me?'

'It was meant as a compliment,' she said seriously.

'I'll take it as one.' He laughed. Then he became serious. 'It's a big step, isn't it?'

She sat up again and looked him in the eye.

'Oh, yes. Just make up your mind whether you're ready to become a dad as well as a lover. That kid is not the sort to watch her mum having loads of boyfriends. She wants to believe that all relationships turn out well in the end, like in her Jane Austen novels—that's why she's hooked on them. They're her escape into a world she'd like to live in. I know it's all happened so suddenly, but if you're not serious about Alex—and about Victoria—then get out of this thing right now. Or I'll never forgive you. And I'm your sister.'

SISTERS! DONCHA love 'em? thought Nick. Just when you think you've got enough on your plate, they can't resist slinging in their own two-pennyworth and giving the whole lot a stir.

The next morning, he took his keys from the table and closed the door quietly behind him. Sophie was still asleep. For a moment he stood on the verandah, leaned on the rail, and breathed in the fresh morning air. The sea was unusually calm, like a polished pewter plate.

His thoughts were interrupted by the postman. 'You look as if you've lost a shilling and found sixpence.'

Nick came to with a start. 'Mmm? Sorry?'

'It can't be that bad.'

'No, it's not. Morning!'

'I'm glad I caught you. I've got a special for you.'

Nick looked down at the package. It was addressed in his father's writing.

HE PULLED up on a small, rough track that looked out over the bay. He had not wanted to open the package in the house, where Sophie might have appeared and been curious.

He ripped off the tape, prised apart the staples and slid out the contents. A small white linen bag landed in his hand. He loosened the knot and tipped out the contents. In his palm lay four large diamonds. From memory they were not the ones he had handed over to the heavies at his father's request, but they were of a similar size and clarity.

He tipped them back into the bag and drew the string tight. Then he fished inside the envelope and pulled out a folded sheet of hotel writing paper. There was no date.

Dear Nick,

Sorry I had to ask you to do that bit of business for me, but it all seems to have turned out OK. I'd have done the job myself but I had rather pressing business here in Moscow.

The enclosed were given to me by Rosie to take care of. Well, their friends were. I'm sending them back now in the safest way I know. I think it would be a good idea if you put them in the bank.

Don't worry, old lad. It's all quite above-board.

Yours ever,

Dad

The note was, in his father's usual style, short and sweet. And what did he mean by 'well, their friends were'? If these were not Rosie's diamonds, had his father substituted fakes? He must get them valued as soon as possible, but for now he had to put them somewhere safe.

Nick folded the note and slipped it back into the padded envelope with the linen bag. Then he drove straight to the bank and deposited the contents.

By the time he arrived at the hospital his head was swimming, but Rosie was on cracking form.

'I think I've sorted them out.'

'Sorted who out?'

'The nurses here. One of them has boyfriend trouble, and the other one's husband has just run off.'

'Oh.'

'In a bit of a state, both of them.'

'So you sorted them out.' There was irony in his tone.

'Are you going to be unpleasant?' Rosie asked, her brow furrowed.

Nick felt suitably chastened. 'Sorry. It's been a bit of a morning, that's all.'

She was sitting up in bed, fresh as a daisy, her hair coiffed, her lipstick freshly applied and her cheeks rouged. She looked like a duchess about to receive visitors at a morning audience. How appropriate, he thought, and smiled.

'Victoria's all right now?' she asked.

'Yes, thank God.'

'And Alex?'

'As far as I know.' He looked distracted.

'Oh. That sounds ominous.' He didn't reply, so she took his hand. 'Sorry. I expect Sophie gave you the female point of view?'

'Yes,' he admitted.

'She's good at that.' Rosie chuckled. 'Headstrong we used to call it. It sounds old-fashioned now, what with all this feminism stuff.'

'Are you not a feminist, then?'

'Oh, yes. A different kind, though. Wily.'

'In what way?'

'Well, I look at all these women moaning on about men. Using a sledge-hammer to crack a nut. You don't have to do that. You can get where you want to go much more quickly if you gentle them along—flatter them, flutter your eyelashes, instead of all this bra-burning business.'

'But wasn't that liberating?'

'Only for breasts. Damned uncomfortable for everything else.' She was warming to her subject now, eyes glowing. It was good to see her back on form, bright as a button, trying to shock.

'And another thing. Breast enlargements Why do they make them so big?'

'Keep your voice down!'

'What sort of man is going to want to go out with a woman with a pair of footballs fastened to her chest?'

'Stop it!'

'I mean, she only has to turn round sharpish and she'll knock you over.'

She paused. Nick was squeezing in the sides of his mouth to stifle the laughter. 'Stop, stop!' he said.

Rosie lay back on her pillow. 'Better now?'

He nodded. 'Much better.' And then, with feeling, 'Thank you.'

'Don't mention it, love. And you just keep your end up.'

'Rosie!'

'Oh, I know. It's a difficult time, and lots of people's emotions are involved, but don't underestimate your own. Just remember that your feelings are as important as anybody else's. You're a good man, and Alex'll see that.'

'Victoria asked me if I was a good man.'

Rosie shook her head. 'Funny child. Astute.'

'And scared? Sophie thinks she's scared.'

'Oh, yes. But all children of that age are. They just have different ways of dealing with it. Some lash out. Those like Victoria go into their imagination.'

'So how do you solve the problem, apart from just giving it time?'

'If I knew that, love, I'd be sitting in the House of Lords.' She smiled.

'Now, there's a thought. You'd look good in ermine.'

'And I might have been, mightn't I, if things had turned out differently?' He watched her expression change. 'We will find out, won't we?' she asked.

'About my mother?'

'Of course.' He stroked her hand.

'Only I would like to know before . . . Well, soon.'

HE PHONED ALEX from the hospital. They had not spoken for thirty-six hours. He did not know how she was feeling or what she was doing. He wanted to ask if she and Victoria would like to come over and stay for the weekend, though he was fearful of putting the question; afraid of being turned down.

'I'm not sure,' she said. She sounded preoccupied, hesitant. It was as if the passion and conviction they had shared only a few days ago had evaporated.

'Do you want to meet first? To talk?' he asked.

'Yes. Yes, that might be best.'

'Shall I come to you?' He knew at once what the answer would be. She seemed anxious to keep him out of her world.

'No. I'll come to you. I'll get the seven o'clock ferry.'

'Fine. I'll pick you up.'

And she was gone, with no talk of love, just a brief goodbye.

WHEN HE GOT back to The Anchorage Sophie was packing her bag.

'I thought you weren't going until the weekend?'

'Given you enough grief. Thought I'd better move out.'

'Don't be stupid!'

'No, it's all right. You need your space. Especially now.'

'But you can stay. I don't mind.'

Sophie stopped folding a shirt. 'What I said last night. Sorry if I got carried away. Too much wine.'

'Don't worry—you were quite right. I was talking to Rosie today and she was telling me her side of the story.'

'Poor Nick. You're getting it from all sides, aren't you?'

'Oh, I can cope. I'm made of tough stuff.'

Sophie zipped up her bag and picked up her jacket. She put her head on one side. 'Do you know? I think you are!'

HE WAS WAITING for her in the MG at half past six, in case the ferry was early. They never were, but tonight he wanted to be sure.

Eventually the ferry shimmied up to the slipway and the ramp descended. Cars flooded off, and to either side of them came foot passengers: teenagers with rucksacks, parents with children, old men and women, some with sticks. There were a couple of dogs and half a dozen cyclists, but no sign of Alex.

Perhaps she was waiting until all the traffic had disembarked. Yes, that must be it. But after ten minutes, when the last car and pedestrian had walked up the slipway, and the cars for the return crossing were being driven down to the water's edge and up the ramp of the ferry, he realised she had not come.

He got out of the car, ran across to the booking office, bought a ticket, then drove onto the ferry. He had her address. If she wouldn't come to him, he'd go to her.

The ferry seemed to take an age, waltzing around the Solent as though it were on a dance floor. He looked at his watch. A quarter to eight. With any luck he'd be there within fifteen minutes. Thirty at the outside.

HE FOUND IT difficult to talk in front of Victoria, and so did Alex. 'Why don't you pop up to your room, sweetheart?' she said.

Victoria looked from one to the other. 'Do I have to?'

'Yes,' Alex told her.

'OK.' She paused in the kitchen doorway and said, 'Goodbye, Nick.'

He raised a hand, then turned back to Alex, who was filling the kettle. 'Why did you say you would come?'

'Because I didn't want to disappoint you.' She looked agonised. 'I'm sorry, I really am.' She motioned him to sit at the kitchen table.

'What is it?' he asked. 'It seemed to be going so well. Even when Victoria went missing we found her together.'

'I know. It's just that . . .' She seemed reluctant to meet his eye. She looked embarrassed, ashamed. 'I just think we'd better stop seeing each other.'

'But why?'

'Because I don't want to upset Victoria any more. She's been through a lot lately, what with her dad leaving, and then going missing . . .'

'But she only went missing because she wanted to see Rosie.'

'No. She went missing because she was upset, unsettled and frightened.'

'Is that what she said? She told me it was because she wanted to see Rosie.' He hesitated. 'And me.'

Alex studied him carefully, then came and sat down. 'I can't risk anything going wrong between her and me. I just can't. She's all I've got.'

Nick sat back. 'She's not. You've got me, you know you have.'

Alex shook her head. 'No, I don't. I know we've had a good time, but I don't really know you. And you don't really know me. It might be fun for a few more weeks, months even, but what if it all ended then? Where would that leave Victoria?'

Nick bridled. 'How can you say that? How can you say that we simply "had a good time"? You know it was more than that.'

She spoke quickly now. 'You just can't see why I have to do this, can you?'

'No, I can't.'

'But then you've never had a child.'

He was stung, and hesitated a moment before he spoke. 'It doesn't mean I can't see how important Victoria is, and why it's important that she's happy. But you can't simply live your life for her.'

'Why not? I brought her into the world. She's my responsibility. I can't mess up.'

He was exasperated now. 'Why this obsession with "messing up"? It can't be right to shut yourself away and not have any relationships of your own.'

'The point is that Victoria's life—'

'Victoria, Victoria, always Victoria! What about Alex?' Nick stood up. 'You have a bright child up there,' he pointed in the direction of Victoria's room, 'and she'll know it makes no sense for her mother to be alone.'

'She's only ten—'

'Yes, and she's sharper than many fifteen-year-olds. But she's not emotionally equipped yet, and treating her like some china doll isn't going to help her.'

'And neither is a string of boyfriends.'

'Oh, I see.' He was angry now. 'You reckon I'm first in a long line, do you?'

'No. But that's what might happen.'

'It might. But that's not my intention. I came here because I love you and I want to be with you. And *I've* thought about Victoria, too. I know how important she is to you, and she'll become important to me, if you give me a chance. But if you just shut yourself away because of what *might* happen, then you'll never know joy. The sort of joy that we knew the other night. Or am I the one who's fooling myself?'

'No,' she said quietly. 'You're not. But you can't promise that it will turn out all right.'

'No, I can't. But I can promise you I'll try—with every fibre in my body. If it doesn't work out in the end I'll have done everything I possibly can to make it work, and that must count for something.'

The kettle's shrill whistle brought a halt to the conversation. Alex got up and turned off the gas. 'I'm sorry. It's just that with Paul coming back and Victoria going off the rails . . .'

'She didn't go off the rails.' He spoke softly now, his tone conciliatory. 'She just got a bit . . . lost inside herself.'

'And I wasn't there.'

'You were. It's just that Paul was there, too, and that threw her.'

Alex turned to face him. 'I'm sorry.' She lowered her head, and he could see tears flowing down her cheeks. He walked across to comfort her, but she turned away from him and stared out of the window. Then she wiped her face with the back of her hand. 'You'd better go now. It'll be for the best. Sorry.'

He stood for a moment, one hand outstretched as if it was frozen. He lowered it. 'What a lot of sorries,' he said. And then, quietly, 'Goodbye.'

As he left he did not turn back. If he had done, he would have seen the face of a small girl framed in the upstairs window.

Chapter 8

Henry was beside Rosie's bed as soon as the hospital doors opened. 'You're amazing!' he said.

'Why's that?' she asked.

'Look at you! It's barely eight thirty and you're all done up and ready to go!'

'Well, they wake us up so early, and I've never been one to hang around. Not that I've got much choice on that front.'

'How's the walking coming along?'

'Slowly. And it's a bit painful.'

'More than a bit, I should think.'

'We won't go there. Anyway, I've been thinking.'

'That sounds dangerous.'

'Be serious, Henry. If I do come and stay with you . . . well, there are one or two things I want to sort out.'

'Yes?'

She was clearly trying to measure her words. 'Well . . . I will have my own bedroom, won't I?'

Henry roared with laughter. 'Of course you will! Good heavens! The very idea! I'd be struck off.'

Rosie brightened. 'Well, I knew I would, really. It's just that we've never talked about . . . arrangements, and I thought we should.'

'Quite so.' Henry tried to suppress a smile, not altogether successfully.

'And then there's the problem of getting dressed. I'm very self-sufficient— but at the moment it's a bit difficult to . . .'

Henry patted her hand. 'I've thought of all that. The niece who's coming over to help me in the gallery is a sweet girl, and she can do all the bits you wouldn't want me doing.'

'I see.' She looked thoughtful. 'Why are you going to all this trouble? I'm no catch, you know.'

Henry laughed again. 'On that subject, madam, I beg to differ.' He smiled at her, his eyes twinkling. 'Do you really want to know? Honestly?'

Rosie nodded. 'Yes. Honestly.'

'There are two reasons.' Henry pushed his hands into his pockets. 'One is because when my mother grew older I saw what an amazing lady she was. I was too late to help her at the end and I never managed to tell her that.'

'I see. So you're salving your conscience by looking after me?'

He looked up. 'A bit,' he admitted. Then he looked directly at her. 'The second reason is that I don't think I've ever met anyone like you in my life.'

'Oh, Henry!' She smiled, then looked down coyly.

'It's true! You make me laugh and you make me glad to be alive.'

'Well . . .' Rosie glanced away. 'I don't know what to say.'

Through the dampness in his own eyes, he saw the tears in Rosie's. 'Don't say anything, then.' He cleared his throat. 'Don't they serve coffee here?'

'Not until nine o'clock, but if you turn on the charm with that nurse over there I'm sure she'll oblige. In a manner of speaking.'

ALEX THREW back the covers, got out of bed, stretched, then caught sight of herself in the mirror, standing there with her dark hair tumbling over her shoulders, her body encased in a baggy white T-shirt. God, she looked old. Wearily she crossed the landing.

She tapped on Victoria's door, then opened it. The child was sitting up in bed with a book. 'Don't you ever stop reading?' asked Alex, teasingly.

Victoria shook her head, still concentrating.

'What is it today?' She pushed back her hair.

Victoria held up *Sense and Sensibility*.

'Again?'

Victoria shrugged. 'I like the stories.'

'Do you know how many other ten-year-olds read those books?'

'No.'

'Very few.'

'It's not wrong, is it?' Victoria asked anxiously.

'Of course not.' Her mother ruffled her hair.

'Read a bit to me?'

'Oh, love, I don't think I can focus at this hour.'

'Please!' There was insistence in her voice, but not of the sort that foretold a tantrum. Not the sort of insistence that says 'if you don't I'll make your life hell for the rest of the day.' Just a positive note that made Alex sit on the edge of the bed and take up the book.

'From there,' instructed Victoria, pointing to a passage in the book.

'Budge up, then.' Alex slipped into bed beside her daughter, who rested her head on her shoulder as she read.

' "Marianne Dashwood was born to an extraordinary fate. She was born to discover the falsehood of her own opinions, and to counteract, by her conduct, her most favourite maxims. She was born to overcome an affection formed so late in life as at seventeen, and with no sentiment superior to strong esteem and lively friendship, voluntarily to give her hand to another!"' Alex stopped.

'Go on! Go on!'

Alex spoke more softly now. '". . . and *that* other, a man who had suffered no less than herself under the event of a former attachment . . ."'

She closed the book. 'Oh,' she murmured.

IT WAS MIDWAY through the afternoon when the hospital called. Nick was cleaning a wooden garden bench with wire wool. It was a mindless task, but the only thing he could settle to. When the phone rang he dropped what he was doing and ran inside, hoping it might be Alex. When he discovered it was a nurse, his heart sank.

'Mr Robertson? It's Sister Bettany from the hospital. It's Mrs Robertson. She's a little under the weather and we wondered if you could come in.'

'Of course. I'll be there as soon as I can. Is she . . .?'

'She's comfortable at the moment, but she'd like to see you.'

'Yes, of course.'

His mind raced as he made the short drive to the hospital. As he walked down the corridor to the ward, Sister Bettany put her head out of her office and beckoned him in.

'Is it serious?' he asked.

'It's difficult to say,' she said. 'She has a urinary infection. She was fine earlier, but she's declined over the day.'

'But will she recover?'

'Oh, we hope so. She's strong for an old lady, but we must take account of her age.'

Nick was more worried than ever now. Nobody took account of Rosie's age, because she took no account of it herself. He walked along to her bed. Her eyes were closed. He sat down and took her hand. He squeezed it gently and she opened her eyes. When she saw him she smiled. 'Hello, my love. How are you?' she whispered.

He was appalled to see her so weak.

'I'm fine, but what about you?'

She tried to say something, failed, and drifted off again.

He sat with her for an hour as she slept fitfully. Then he walked down to the office and waited for Sister Bettany to return from her rounds.

'We'll keep a close eye on her for the next day or so,' she said. 'Pop in whenever you want.'

'Thank you.' It was all so sudden. Things seemed to have been going so well. He asked the obvious question. 'Does this mean she won't be coming out quite so quickly?'

'Yes, I'm afraid so. We'll just have to play it by ear now.'

'Yes, of course.' He hesitated. Then he asked, 'How serious is it?'

'Serious but not critical,' she said. She smiled kindly.

HENRY WAS INCREDULOUS. 'But I was with her first thing this morning and she was in fine fettle.'

'I know. Apparently it happened quite suddenly.'

Henry plonked himself down on a wooden captain's chair, which creaked under his weight. 'Well, I'll be . . . you wouldn't have . . . she was so . . .'

Nick nodded. 'I know.'

'So I suppose I can stand my niece down.'

'Yes. I'm afraid they don't know when she'll be coming out now.'

Henry looked at him. 'And are you all right?'

'Yes. Yes, I'm fine,' he said distractedly.

'Well, you don't look it. You look exhausted. Let me make you some coffee with something stronger in it.' Henry pushed himself out of the chair.

'Thanks.' Nick wandered through to the back room in the wake of his burly patron.

Henry switched on the kettle. 'And that's not all, is it?'

'Mmm?' Nick was distant. Preoccupied.

'There's something else, isn't there?' And then, seeing he was not getting through, 'Woman trouble, is it?'

'What?' Nick came to. 'What do you mean?'

'Look, dear boy, I've not asked any questions—I've been very circum-spect, and after all, it's none of my business, but if two of my *protégés* are at a tricky stage in their relationship I'd just like to know.'

Nick hesitated, then tried to speak but settled instead for a sigh.

Henry busied himself with cups, sugar and coffee, and spoke over his shoulder. His tone was gentle, his language considered. 'Look. It was never going to be easy, was it? There's a lot of history there.'

Nick was staring at the floor. 'It's all so confusing,' he murmured.

'Oh. Right. Well, if we're going there you'll need quite a large tot.' He tipped a generous measure of Famous Grouse into the coffee, and handed the cup to Nick. 'She did talk to me, you know,' Henry went on. 'Alex.'

Nick took a sip of the brew and gasped at its strength.

'Nothing intimate. Not about you,' Henry assured him, 'but about . . . what was his name? Paul'

Nick said nothing.

Henry continued. 'He wasn't the most faithful of husbands, you see. He was a serial adulterer, by the sound of it. Travelled a lot, woman in every port—that sort of thing. She never found out until about three years ago, when he started living a double life, half in the States and half over here.'

Nick was shocked. 'She didn't tell me about the women.'

'No? Well, it's not something to boast about. Eventually she told him she'd had enough. He agreed to go—there was yet another woman. Now she just wants to give her daughter a fresh start.'

'I know. That's the trouble.' Nick paused. 'She doesn't seem to set much store by her own happiness. She'd rather stay on her own so that Victoria has a stable upbringing.'

'Shame,' said Henry.

'That's what I think.' Nick drained his cup. 'I'd better be off.'

'What are you going to do now?'

'Who knows? I'll go back and see Rosie this evening. Nothing else to do except,' he pointed to the walls of the gallery, 'fill these, I suppose. But I can't get into the mood.'

'Look,' said Henry, 'there's no pressure. I have enough to keep me going for a week or so. You'll need time to sort Rosie out, and yourself. Concentrate on the important things for now.' As Nick closed the door, he shouted after him, 'Both of them.'

BY EVENING Rosie seemed to have rallied a little. Nick sat with her, holding her hand, for the better part of two hours. Sometimes she drifted off to sleep, sometimes she woke and lay with her eyes open but said nothing. Then her eyes would close again.

He worried about her long-term prospects. She couldn't die! She was never ill! Watching her now made him anxious, and irritable. He needed her to get better and listen to him. Then he was ashamed of his selfishness.

Someone touched his shoulder and he looked up.

Alex was standing over him. 'Hello,' she said.

He slipped his hand out of Rosie's and got up. 'Hello,' he said uncertainly.

They looked at each other, then Alex put her arms round him and laid her head on his chest. 'I'm sorry.'

At first he thought she was talking about Rosie. 'They think she'll be all right, but they can't be certain yet,' he said stiffly.

Alex nodded. 'I do hope so.' She stepped away from him.

'Thank you for coming,' he said, hoping that she'd leave soon and not prolong the agony.

'I had to come. Too many things to say.'

Nick looked at her quizzically.

'I was a bit hasty,' she went on. 'Like you said, if I shut myself away in case of what might happen, I'll never know joy . . .' There was a catch in her voice. 'And I'd quite like to know joy. So, if it's all right with you . . .'

Nick held out his arms and said, 'Come here.'

Alex saw the tears welling up and wrapped her arms round him again.

'I'm so glad you're back,' he whispered. 'So glad.'

Later that evening, he took her to the ferry, kissed her tenderly, then watched the lights of the vessel recede into the distance. She had gone again, but this time he knew she would return.

Tomorrow was Sunday, and she had said she would bring Victoria over for the day. His pleasure at the prospect was tempered by concern for Rosie. He looked up at the star-filled sky and hoped with all his heart that both of the women he loved would make tomorrow a day to remember.

'I HAVE a surprise for you,' said Alex.

They were sitting in a café at Seaview, breakfasting outdoors in the early-morning sun, before they drove to Newport to see Rosie.

'I've had enough of those,' said Nick.

'This is a nice one,' Victoria told him. 'Mummy's been researching.'

'That sounds very official.'

'Well, I promised you I'd do some digging around to see if I could discover anything about Rosie's parents,' Alex said. 'And I've been at the library in Portsmouth.' Alex dug into her rucksack. 'You know you said that Rosie's mother's name—I mean her real mother—was given as Matilda Kitching?'

Nick dipped a piece of croissant into his coffee and popped it into his mouth. 'Well?'

'And her father's name'—Alex flipped through her shorthand pad until she found the page she wanted—'was George Michaels?'

'Yes.' Nick nodded as he chewed.

'Well, as Rosie said, there was no mention of either in the National Archive at Kew. Not with the right dates, anyway.'

'No joy, then?'

'Not until I started to look at the names of other people involved, who might have been around at the time.'

'And?' Nick took a sip of coffee.

'George Michaels was supposed to be part of a British delegation, wasn't he? I tracked down that particular visit. It struck me that I'd often seen pictures of the two of them—George the Fifth and the Tsar—in naval uniform. I found a naval archive in Portsmouth library that dealt with diplomatic relations between the British and Russian navies during the late nineteenth and early twentieth centuries. In 1917, the British sent a secret delegation to Russia. It was during the First World War, remember, so it must have been difficult.'

'They didn't give the names of all the people involved, did they?' asked Nick excitedly.

Alex paused, the better to build the tension. 'Oh, yes, they did. The junior naval attaché at the Admiralty was called . . . George Carmichael.'

'You clever thing!' Nick made to take the pad from Alex's hand.

'Not so fast. I've not finished yet.'

Victoria beamed. 'She's very clever, isn't she?'

'Brilliant!' he agreed.

'That was too much of a coincidence to pass over. But what it didn't do, of course, was give me any information about the mother. It also failed to show any meeting between the grand duchesses and the delegation. In fact, they had been in two different places—the delegation was sent to Murmansk, right up north on the Barents Sea. Murmansk had only been linked to St Petersburg by rail in 1916 and was just about to become an important port because it remained ice-free all the year round. Anyway, when the delegation was in Murmansk, most of the royal family were in St Petersburg, more than five hundred miles away, and there is no record of the delegation going there. They sailed from Portsmouth, up round the Norwegian coast and the North Cape, direct to Murmansk, where they met the Tsar. They did not go via the Baltic to St Petersburg and take the train north.'

'Which knocks Rosie's theory on the head,' said Nick, despondent.

'Well, it does seem to rule out the grand duchesses.'

'I feel a but coming on,' said Nick.

'And there is one. Before he was married the Tsar had a mistress. Now, I can only guess at this, and I may be wrong, and there are a lot of ifs.'

'Go on.'

'If the Tsar had not relinquished his mistress, and they still had liaisons, and one happened to be in Murmansk during the occasion of the naval delegation . . . and if the mistress did not confine her attentions to the Tsar . . .'

'You're right—there are a lot of ifs.'

'It would hardly stand up in court. Pure conjecture, that's all.'

'But what was the mistress's name?'

Alex spun the book round and showed him. 'Mathilde Kschessinska.'

He was stunned. 'Matilda Kitching?' he wondered aloud.

'It's possible.' She smiled tentatively.

'What happened to her?'

'She eventually married one of the Tsar's cousins, Grand Duke Andrei, in Cannes in 1921.'

'They escaped the revolution, then?'

'Yes, although Mathilde's mansion was ransacked. She eventually ran a ballet studio in Paris—even taught Margot Fonteyn.'

'But she's dead now?'

'Oh, yes.'

'So I don't suppose we'll ever know for certain?'

Alex shook her head. 'It seems unlikely.'

Nick squeezed her hand. 'Thank you for going to all the trouble.'

THE THREE of them walked down the long corridor towards Rosie's bed, Victoria in the middle, holding Nick and Alex's hands.

As they rounded the corner, they saw Rosie propped up on a mountain of pillows. She raised both hands in greeting and Victoria rushed across to plant a kiss on her cheek.

'Hello, sweetheart!' Rosie murmured. 'How lovely to see you.'

Nick and Alex bent down and kissed her too, and Nick asked, 'How are you?'

'Oh, you know. A bit feak and weeble,' she said to Victoria, who grinned at the little joke.

'Mummy's been finding things out,' volunteered Victoria. 'About your mummy and daddy.'

Rosie's face brightened. 'Has she?'

Nick cut in: 'She's been working very hard, but I think we should tell you later when you can take it all in.'

Rosie did not demur. She half closed her eyes. 'Weary. Sorry.'

Nick glanced at Alex, who read his mind. 'Come on, Victoria. We'll let Rosie rest for a while,' she said. 'We'll come back later.' And then, softly, to Nick, 'We'll wait for you by the car.'

He nodded in agreement, and they left with a wave. Then he sat on a chair and leaned close to Rosie's head.

'Sorry,' she whispered. 'It was lovely to see them both.'

'Yes.'

'Lucky boy.' She opened her eyes and nodded in the direction Alex and Victoria had gone. 'Special. Very special.'

'I know.' He stroked her cheek lightly. 'You sleep now,' he said. 'We all need you better.'

She smiled weakly and closed her eyes again.

'WOULD YOU COME with me to the jeweller's to have them valued?' he asked Alex quietly.

'But isn't it a bit personal? I mean, do you really want me to know?'

They were sitting on the verandah at The Anchorage, sipping coffee after an early dinner.

Victoria was sitting in Nick's dinghy, pulled out from beneath the verandah and beached on the rough grass in front of the house. Her head was buried in a book, and she absent-mindedly curled a strand of hair around her index finger as she read.

'I don't want to have any secrets from you. Not even financial ones.' Nick was adamant. 'Could you bear to come over again tomorrow?'

Alex smiled resignedly. 'I'm turning into a commuter. But I'll have to be back for Victoria coming out of school. If I catch the nine o'clock ferry over, I could take the two o'clock back. Would that be OK?'

'Fine. I shall miss you, though, when you go. I always miss you.' Nick stood up, lifted her off her chair and sat down with her on his lap.

'Hey!' she said. 'I'm far too heavy for this. You'll regret it.'

'Never.' He put his arms round her waist, and they watched Victoria in the boat until the sun sank behind the Dorset hills and it was time for the main-landers to go home.

Chapter 9

Nick was nervous. He had the entire contents of the bank safety-deposit box in the inside pocket of his jacket. Before they made their way to the jeweller's he opened the bag in the car to show Alex.

'Oh my God, they're huge!' she said. 'Are you sure they're real?'

'Well, no, I'm not—apart from the one Rosie gave me.'

Alex pushed at them with her finger. 'I've never seen anything like them. And you don't know where they came from?'

'Not exactly. Rosie said she converted her savings into diamonds—bought in London presumably—then handed them to Dad for safekeeping, but she kept mine back to give me on my birthday. That's this one.' He indicated the smallest of the five stones.

'And you think the other four came from Russia?'

'That's what the hotel writing-paper said.' Nick had already explained about the visits from his father and the two heavies.

'And the note said nothing about where they were from?'

'Here it is.' Nick handed the note to Alex.

Alex read it. Then she repeated: '"The enclosed were given to me by Rosie to take care of. Well, their friends were."' Then these aren't the diamonds Rosie gave him.'

'No. But are they better ones or fakes?'

Alex looked thoughtful. 'Well, he wouldn't have sent fake diamonds by recorded delivery, would he?'

'Unless he wanted me to believe they were real.'

'Would your dad really do that?'

Nick shook his head. 'I don't want to believe he would.' He tipped the stones back into the bag. 'But there's only one way to find out, isn't there?'

ELLIOTT WILLIAMS, the jeweller, reached under the counter and took out a roll of dark blue velvet, which he smoothed out across the glass surface.

Nick handed him the small linen bag and watched as he undid the top and tipped the stones out onto the fabric.

At first the jeweller said nothing. He put the magnifying loupe into his eye and held up each stone to it for what seemed an age. As he lowered the last of the five stones, he removed the glass from his eye and cleared his throat. 'Yes, well . . . We have here three different grades of diamond.' He gently pushed the one Rosie had given Nick towards the front of the cloth with his little finger. 'This one is pretty good. Not flawless, but very fine nevertheless. Value? Around the twenty to twenty-five thousand mark.'

'That's what I thought,' said Nick, involuntarily. Elliott Williams shot him a look. 'Oh, that's the only one I was given a value for.' Nick added.

'Right. These three here'—the jeweller pushed a matching trio forward—'are internally flawless and worth probably around seventy-five thousand apiece.'

'Gosh!' Nick tried to hide his surprise.

'And this one,' Elliott Williams pushed forward a diamond the size of his fingernail, 'is flawless. Quite beautiful and very well cut. It will be worth between seven hundred and seven hundred and fifty thousand pounds.'

Alex gasped. Nick said, 'Good God!' and Elliott Williams said, 'You're a very lucky man.'

'Yes. I suppose I am.' And then, 'Are you sure I don't owe you anything for the valuation?'

'Absolutely not. It was my pleasure to see them. And if you need them set—in a ring or a pendant—I'll be happy to do the job for you.'

'Thank you. Yes. Thank you very much.'

The jeweller scooped up the diamonds, tipped them back into the bag, pulled the drawstring tight and handed it back over the counter. 'I'd get to the bank as soon as you can, sir,' he said.

'Yes. Thank you. We will. And thank you again.'

When the diamonds were safely back in the custody of the bank, they treated themselves to lunch in a wine bar, with a particularly fine bottle of sauvignon blanc.

ONCE ALEX was safely on the ferry to Portsmouth, Nick drove to the hospital, and was delighted to find Rosie sitting up in bed, hair and make-up in apple-pie order.

'Look at you!' he said.

'I did. In the mirror. Much better,' she retorted.

'Are you back to your old self?' he asked.

'Getting there. Oh, I did feel ropy, but I'm on the mend, I think.'

He bent to kiss her, and was relieved to smell Chanel No. 5 once more. 'You really had us worried,' he said, patting the back of her hand.

'Oh, I'm a tough old bird,' Rosie replied, but he noticed that her voice did not hold its usual conviction. 'What have you been up to?' she asked.

'I found a girl, and she found me.' He sat down, and tried not to sound too pleased.

'Anyone I know?' she asked.

'Oh, yes.' He beamed.

'Two girls, then? That's nice.'

'Are you sure you're OK?' he asked. Something about her seemed not quite right.

'Yes, of course,' she said. 'Anyway, I'm glad about you.' She smoothed the blanket. 'You said yesterday that you had some news for me, didn't you, about my mother? Or was I dreaming?'

Nick hesitated. 'Yes. But only when you're ready.'

'I'm ready. Go on. Tell me.'

The prospect of disappointing her filled him with dread, but he told her of Alex's researches, the delegation and George Carmichael. Then he mentioned Mathilde Kschessinska. 'MK, the same initials.'

'Well I never. So instead of using my real mother's name, Tatiana, they used one belonging to the Tsar's previous mistress to avoid suspicion?'

Nick found it impossible to contradict her: she thought the naval attaché had had an affair with Grand Duchess Tatiana and that the Tsar's former mistress had been brought in as a smokescreen.

He shrugged. 'That's as much as we've been able to find out,' he said.

Rosie's eyes were shining now. 'So they did exist. This man, George Carmichael, did go there. And it's true.'

Nick could only smile, he hoped not deceitfully.

'Oh, what a relief.' Rosie flopped back on the pillow and closed her eyes.

After a few moments she opened them. She put out her hand and took his.

'I knew you'd come through for me.'

'Not me. Alex.'

Rosie nodded. 'Good girl. I knew she would, too.' She looked at him pleadingly. 'Do something for me?'

'Of course.'

'When you next hear from your dad . . .' She beckoned him closer. 'Thank him for sorting out the diamonds.'

'What?' He was astonished.

Rosie pointed to her bedside cabinet. 'There's a letter from him in there.'

Nick opened the door, and among the cotton wool and tissues, he found a letter on identical stationery to the one he had received from his father.

'How did he know where you were?' he asked.

'Oh, your father seems to know everything. Open it.'

Nick did so, and unfolded the letter.

Dear Rosie,

I hope this finds you well. I took care of the stones as you asked, but I had an opportunity to make them grow a bit. Don't ask how.

There was nothing underhand about the deal (I know you worry about that!), but I've been doing a bit of business over here—Russian capitalists are grateful for all the help they can get from wide-boy westerners like me, and have interesting ways of showing their gratitude.

I've sent the stones back to Nick—the slightly better versions of them—and told him to put them in a bank for safekeeping. I'll leave you to tell him what they're all for.

See you soon. And don't worry.

Your boy Derek xxx

'So, does Dad keep in touch with you then, when nobody else knows where he is?'

'Sometimes. When he feels like it.'

'But the diamonds . . .'

'Mmm?'

'I had them valued today.'

'Did you? Well, don't tell me,' said Rosie. 'I don't want to know.'

'As well as the one you gave to me, there are four, one large one and three smaller ones.'

'That's right. Now, can you make sure that, of the three smaller ones, one each goes to Sophie and Alice—wherever they happen to be. I know Sophie's gone off on the toot again because she came and told me. And Alice is in South . . . well, you know.'

'I'll make sure they get them,' he assured her.

'And you've got yours, haven't you?'

Nick nodded.

'But it was a bit smaller than the ones your dad sent back, or so he said.'

'Oh, that doesn't matter,' he said, dismissively.

'Well, hopefully it doesn't. You see, the third one is for Alex.'

At first he thought he had misheard her.

'What do you mean?'

'Well, I could see that you two were made for each other. And it wasn't just that you were called Nicholas and Alexandra. I'm not that stupid.'

'You can't—'

'Oh, I can. Old lady's prerogative. You can't stop me.'

'I suppose not.'

'And the last one . . . the last one is to be sold and the proceeds are to be put into a trust fund. I don't know what it will amount to, but it should make sure that the brightest little girl I've ever encountered gets a decent education.' She looked hard at Nick. 'I take it you're managing to keep up?'

'Victoria?' he asked.

Rosie nodded. 'Yes. Something tells me she's going to be very special.'

'But this is so sudden! How do you know—'

'How do I know that you'll stick together?'

Nick nodded.

'I don't. I just have a feeling. And it's such a strong feeling that I see no reason to question it. Sometimes you have to rely on your instincts. You're a good man and she's a good woman. You're also crazy about each other, and the child. Anyone can see that. You've got your heads screwed on. You'll manage.'

Nick's face bore the expression of someone with concussion.

Rosie leaned back on her pillow mountain and smiled. 'Go on,' she said. 'Say it for me.'

'Say what?'

'Oh, I think you know.'

For a moment he looked bewildered, and then he smiled. And as he smiled, so the tears welled up in his eyes. 'You know,' he said, 'you really crack me up.'

Chapter 10

Just three days later Rosie Robertson died peacefully in her sleep. Nick was with her, holding her hand. There were no last words, just a sigh, and a great calm. He eased his hand out of hers and kissed her forehead. Unable to stop the tears cascading down his face, he sat with his head in his hands for a while and wept, remembering nothing but the good times.

Victoria, too, took it hard. It was her first experience of death.

Alex was a rock to them both, and a comforting shoulder to cry on. There were lots of tears, but Rosie had left many happy memories—and quite a lot of money. It was some time before Alex could come to terms with her bequest, and her daughter's legacy. 'For now,' she said, 'do you mind if I just leave it in the bank?'

The day of the funeral was warm and sunny. There were few people at the Newport crematorium. Henry spent most of his time blowing his nose into a large red and white spotted handkerchief, and blaming the pollen from the flowers. Rosie would have liked that.

There were no hymns, just prayers of thanksgiving, and Rosie had asked that Nick read something for her. It took all his willpower to get through it, but get through it he did. With clarity and with great feeling he spoke the words of a poem that Rosie had loved:

> 'Do not stand at my grave and weep;
> I am not there. I do not sleep.
> I am a thousand winds that blow.
> I am the diamond glints on snow.
> I am the sunlight on ripened grain.
> I am the gentle autumn rain.
> When you awaken in the morning's hush
> I am the swift uplifting rush
> Of quiet birds in circled flight.
> I am the soft stars that shine at night.
> Do not stand at my grave and cry:
> I am not there. I did not die.'

And then came the only piece of music in the short ceremony, which gen-erated both smiles and tears as it rang out from the speakers at the front of the chapel. Rosie's coffin disappeared to the strains of 'Lara's Theme' from *Dr Zhivago*. Whether or not she had come into the world as a Russian princess, she certainly went out as one.

It was only as they emerged into the sunlight, that Nick noticed the soli-tary figure laying a wreath of lilies under the card that bore Rosie's name, where the family flowers had been placed.

Nick walked over and introduced himself. 'Hello. I'm Nick Robertson. Thank you for coming.'

'My pleasure,' said the old man, with a neat bow. He wore a dark coat and was tall, with iron-grey hair. He had a thick accent.

'I'm afraid I don't know who you are,' Nick confessed.

The man bowed once more. 'I am sorry. I should have introduced myself. I am Oleg Vassilievsky.'

'Ah.' Nick hesitated. 'You must have known my grandmother.'

'Not exactly. But I was aware of her. Your grandmother was from Russia. She was a Romanov.'

'Ah, yes. Well, she thought she might have been, but we've discovered that it was very unlikely.'

The old man shook his head. 'She was a Romanov. Not a legitimate one, but a Romanov nevertheless.'

Nick was incredulous. 'How do you know?'

The man smiled kindly. 'We know all the members of the family. We try to keep track of them.'

'That sounds a bit sinister.'

Oleg Vassilievsky shrugged. 'It is not intended to be. We like to think of it as loyal support.'

'I don't understand . . .' Nick looked over his shoulder at Alex and Victoria, who were deep in conversation with Sophie.

'We had rather lost track of Mrs Robertson until our attention was drawn to her.' He nodded at Alex.

Nick began to feel as though he were having a bad dream. 'So who were her parents?'

'Her father was an English naval officer.'

'We'd worked that out. But what about her mother? It wasn't really Grand Duchess Tatiana, was it?'

'No, it was not.'

'Thank God for that.'

'It was her sister, Grand Duchess Olga.'

Nick looked for something on which to steady himself. He found nothing. After several seconds he managed to speak. 'How can you be sure?'

'We are sure,' he said firmly.

'But . . . what does this mean?'

Oleg shook his head. 'Very little now. Your grandmother is dead. We came to say goodbye. That is all.' He offered his hand. Nick shook it and asked, 'Who is "we"?'

'You will not have heard of us. We are a small group of people loyal to the Russian royal family. Please accept our condolences. Good day to you.' He turned and walked towards a black car, whose engine was already running, and got into the rear seat. The car moved off and disappeared from view.

'YOU'RE NOT saying much.'

'Sorry?' He jumped, startled.

'You're very quiet,' said Alex, as they sat at the table in the Red Duster.

'No. Just thinking.' He smiled, giving her his full attention.

'Well, it's been quite a day. I think she'd have been happy with her send-off.'

'I hope so.'

Casually she asked, 'Who was that man you were talking to?'

'Just an old acquaintance of Rosie's,' Nick said.

'He looked a bit scary.'

'No. Not really. Just wanted to pay his last respects.'

One day he would tell her about the man. And about Rosie. But not now. For now he just wanted to take the two of them home, and try to start a new life. A normal life. A life as a husband, and as a father. When he felt the moment was right to ask them.

He watched as the two of them smiled and chatted together. There was nobody with whom he would rather spend the rest of his life.

His thoughts drifted off once more. To Rosie. 'Goodbye, my love,' he murmured. 'And thanks for everything.' And as he did so, all he could hear was the music from *Dr Zhivago*.

ALAN TITCHMARSH

Born: Ilkley, North Yorkshire, May 2, 1949
Autobiography: *Trowel and Error* (2002)
Website: www.alantitchmarsh.com

Throughout a varied and successful career, gardening has been the bedrock of Alan Titchmarsh's life. Hardly surprising, perhaps, since both his great-grandfather and grandfather were gardeners and, as a child, Alan loved nothing better than to potter about on 'Grandad Hardisty's' allotment. By the age of ten he had developed a burning desire to be like Percy Thrower, then the 'king' of gardening, whose television programmes he watched avidly. 'Like all children I was entranced by the glamour of telly, but stronger than that was the love I had for gardening and a need to share that passion. That's what Percy did. I wanted to do it too.'

At school, however, Titchmarsh's talents lay undiscovered. 'I was your classic late developer. My brain seemed fuddled, filled with fog. There was plenty of enthusiasm there . . . but it's hard to build self-esteem after being told you have nothing to offer. My old French teacher stopped me in Ilkley car park a couple of years ago and said, "We never thought you'd amount to much."'

'My old French teacher stopped me in Ilkley car park a couple of years ago and said, "We never thought you'd amount to much."'

The past two decades have seen Alan confound his French teacher's estimation of his abilities in every way. He went on to train and work at Kew Gardens, before taking an editorial job in the Gardening Department at the Hamlyn Publishing Group, who at that time were the publishers of Percy Thrower . . . And the rest, as they say, is history. Fate took Titchmarsh into broadcasting—*Trowel and Error,* his 'touch of the memoirs', tells the details—-and he has gone on to become one of the best-loved faces in Britain, presenting *Gardeners' World* for six years and *Ground Force* for five.

Recently, Alan Titchmarsh appeared in another new role, presenting *The Natural History of the British Isles*. 'It's not just about the pretty things that flower or feed, it's about how the land was formed,' he says. 'I was a bit daunted at first. I mean, this is David Attenborough territory and he's a childhood hero. But to get such an opportunity to explore the British Isles has been wonderful.' Not content with just one new venture, next year he will also be fronting *The 20th Century Roadshow* for the BBC, a contemporary version of the much-loved *Antiques Roadshow*. Experts will assess and value all sorts of things from the last century—everything from pop posters to Art Deco jewellery—and Titchmarsh says he's looking forward to it tremendously since he's a keen collector himself.

He has also thoroughly enjoyed his role as presenter of *The Last Night of the Proms*. 'I have loved classical music since I was ten or twelve. Handel's *Zadok the Priest* blasting out extremely loud in my barn [where he writes]; that's the kind of thing I listen to, and Vaughan Williams's *The Lark Ascending* has to be the best piece ever written.' This comes as no surprise, for there's something quintessentially British about Alan Titchmarsh, whose favourite author is P.G. Wodehouse, and whose favourite meal is steak and kidney pie.

ON WRITING

'Just cut out to be a gardener' . . . and a writer.

'I have to garden and I have to write. They are the two most fulfilling addictions I know. By the mid 1990s I had written more than thirty gardening books but there was a niggle at the back of my mind. Why couldn't I write stories? I wanted to exercise that part of the imagination which most grown-ups have to keep locked away. It is the supreme luxury—discovering characters, dreaming up a story. All authors are asked, "Where do you get your ideas from?" My reply is always the same. I have no idea.

'Once I started to write fiction I discovered that I write romantic fiction. This may sound odd. Aren't you supposed to plan the sort of book you write? Maybe you are . . . I have a basic idea for the plot, which I try to arrive at when I'm mowing the grass or weeding in borders. It's a rough structure. Rosamunde Pilcher describes it as a washing line, on which ideas and events can be hung.

'When I finish one novel I have not the faintest idea what the next one will be. And success genuinely surprises me. Where fiction is concerned, I still have the feeling that I've been allowed to play with the grown-ups.'

GLENN MEADE
WEB OF DECEIT

Paul March has been missing for
two years when a corpse, thought
to be his, is discovered frozen into
the icy wall of a Swiss glacier.

Jennifer, his daughter, sets off for
Swizerland to identify the body—only
to find herself caught up in a deadly
conspiracy to hide an explosive secret.

PART ONE

At 3 a.m., in New York, Jennifer March came awake in the dark, sensing a presence in her bedroom. A storm raged outside, lightning flickering beyond the window, rain lashing down. When she opened her eyes she was aware of the terrifying feeling that there was someone near her.

As she pulled back the covers and started to get up off the bed she saw the figure of a man standing over her. 'Don't move,' he ordered.

Despite the warning, Jennifer struggled in panic, but the man slapped her, a stinging blow across the face. *'Stay still!'* A flash of lightning flooded the bedroom and she glimpsed the intruder's face.

He had no face.

He wore a black ski mask, dark eyes visible through the slits, and he held a butcher's knife in his leather-gloved hand. When Jennifer went to scream the man's other hand went over her mouth. She curled up with fear, and her nightgown rode up her legs. Carefully the man placed the knife on the night stand. She felt a hand crawl over her flesh as he forced her legs apart.

'Stay still or I'll cut your throat!'

The man unbuckled his trousers and moved on top of her. Jennifer March was more frightened than she had ever been in her life.

SHE WOKE with a scream, clutching a pillow to her chest. This time the wakening was not a nightmare, but for real. Panting with terror, she gulped air.

Jennifer March let go of the pillow and threw back the covers. She switched on the bedside light, fumbled out of bed and moved to the window. Forcing herself to breathe slowly, she became aware of a harsh murmur. Rain. Heavy, incessant torrents that hissed out there beyond the open window.

New York was asleep, but she was wide awake. As always, the dream came during a storm. And as always, it swamped her soul with fear and anguish.

She found her way to the kitchen, switched on the light, took a bottle of water from the icebox and poured a large measure into a glass. She took a long drink, then padded back to her room and sat on the bed. Placing the glass against her forehead, she stared at the green numbers on her digital clock: *3.05.*

On a clear day she could see across the inlet from the condo in Long Beach, Long Island, to Cove End, her parents' deserted house. She had moved to the apartment hoping to make a fresh start, unable to live in the house any more, but she hadn't made any kind of start at all. She was trapped in her past. The nightmare still came. The memories still haunted.

There was only one person she could talk to about her despair in the middle of the night, or at any other time. She picked up the phone, punched the back-lit numbers on the keypad. Seven miles away in Elmont, Long Island, the line rang for a couple of seconds before a man's sleepy voice answered, 'Hello?'

'It's me.'

'Jennifer? Are you OK? Is . . . is everything all right?'

'I'm sorry, Mark. I know it's been a while, but I didn't know who else to call.'

'It's OK, Jennifer. I'm here for you.'

'I woke you.'

'It's all right. I guess you were dreaming, Jennifer. Is that why you rang?'

'It was the same dream. He was so real, like always.' Her voice broke. 'I used to think it would get easier with time. But it doesn't. It's been two years, but sometimes it's like it all happened yesterday. I still miss them so terribly.'

'I know it's not easy, Jennifer. But you have to realise that the man isn't going to come back. Not ever. Please understand that. Now I want you to lie down and close your eyes, try to sleep.'

She heard the words, and let them comfort her as she looked over numbly at the rain sheeting down.

'Are you still there Jennifer?'

'I'm still here. I feel sleepy now.'

'Good night, Jennifer. Try and rest.' There was a tiny hint of laughter in his voice, deliberate, as if to try to ease her out of her anguish. 'If I was there, you know, and we had that kind of relationship, I'd offer to rock you to sleep.'

'I know. Good night. And . . . and thanks for listening, Mark.'

'What's a friend for? Rest now. I'll talk to you soon.'

The last words he said were 'Take care', then the line clicked.

Silence now, but for the silken lash of water drenching the window and a distant growl of thunder. When she put down the phone, Jennifer March lay on her side, staring out with misted eyes at the dark rivers of rain washing the glass, until the sleep she had longed for finally came.

JFK International Airport, New York

NADIA PRAYED for it to be over. If she survived these next few minutes, she would live. If not, she was dead. She clutched the baby to her breast, and held on to the hand of her two-year-old daughter. The airport was noisy and crowded, and she was frightened, even though the men had told her what to expect.

She was twenty-three, with soft blue eyes and an innocent face, which was why the men had picked her.

It was a difficult life in Moscow. Hard to survive in a small room on the fourth floor of a rat-infested tenement block. Nadia Fedov wanted a better life for her daughter. Tamara wasn't going to end up like her mother, working in a nightclub that was no more than a brothel. She was going to have clean sheets and hot water, a nice apartment in a good neighbourhood.

Nadia rocked the baby, wrapped in a blue blanket, and suddenly it was her turn. The Immigration officer beckoned her forward. He examined her passport and airline tickets. Her passport was an excellent forgery, undetectable, and the man was nice. Try not to be afraid, she told herself.

The man smiled at Tamara, glanced briefly at the baby, then stamped one of the pages of her passport and handed it back along with her tickets.

'Thank you, ma'am. Have a nice stay in New York.'

It wasn't over yet. Nadia retrieved her suitcase from the carousel. She paid for a luggage trolley, and approached US Customs, pushing the trolley with one hand, the baby still cradled in her free arm, Tamara holding on to the trolley.

Most of the passengers were passing through freely, the Customs officers hardly stopping anyone. One of the officers looked at her, and Nadia pretended to attend to her baby, rocking the child and whispering, 'Sleep, Alexei.'

'Is this your luggage, ma'am?' the Customs officer put a hand on her trolley.

Nadia's heart was pounding. '*Da*, my . . . my luggage.'

'Step over here, please.'

She pushed the trolley over to the desk, her legs like jelly. The man lifted her case onto the metal desk and said, 'Would you open the suitcase, please.'

Nadia fumbled to get her bag open, getting flustered. She finally found the key. Still holding the baby, she made to unlock the luggage, her hand shaking a little, but the Customs man said politely, 'Here, let me do that for you.'

He opened the suitcase and searched her belongings. A small gift-wrapped box was nestled among the cheap clothes, and it caught the officer's attention. He put it aside. When he had finished searching the case, he picked up the box and shook it. It didn't rattle. 'What's inside here, ma'am?'

'A gift. For my cousin. A scarf.'

The man studied Nadia intently. 'Which flight did you arrive on, ma'am?'

'The flight from Moscow. I arrive just now.' She rocked the baby, trying to soothe her own nervousness.

The man frowned a little and said, 'Is your baby OK?'

'It was a long flight. I don't think he is well.'

The man looked at the box in his hand, then he said, 'Would you mind stepping into the office, please.' He pushed her trolley to a door. Another Customs officer opened it for them—a woman, pretty, dark haired.

The man laid the box on the table, while his colleague stood to one side. 'I'm afraid I need to open this, ma'am. Do you have any objection?'

Nadia nodded, trying not to tremble. 'No, you can open it.'

While his colleague watched, the Customs officer carefully peeled off the wrapping paper, opened the box and found a cheap nylon scarf. He looked a little upset at not finding anything. 'May I see your passport, please.'

Nadia fumbled in her handbag again and found her passport. The officer studied the pages. 'These are your children?'

'Yes.'

'How old is the baby?'

'Three weeks.'

The officer looked at the bundle in her arms. Nadia said quietly, 'He hasn't been well. The long flight . . .'

'So you said. We won't detain you any longer, ma'am.'

The officer came round from behind the desk to hand back her passport. He looked down at the baby, wrapped up snugly in the blue cotton blanket, its face serene, its eyes closed. He hesitated, then some instinct made him reach over and touch the baby's cheek. He paled, his face shocked as he stared back at Nadia, his eyes telling her what she already knew.

'Ma'am, this baby's dead.'

THE 113TH PRECINCT in New York's Queens district is located in a pale brick building on Baisley Boulevard. The precinct covers the sprawling borough of Queens, and also one of the world's busiest airports: JFK International.

Jennifer March parked her blue Ford sedan on the street outside and went in through the main entrance. The desk sergeant looked up when he saw the pretty brunette with the leather briefcase come towards him. She wore a neat, navy two-piece that hugged her figure.

'Is Mark Ryan around, Sergeant?'

'He was heading towards his office last time I saw him, Counsellor March.'

'Thanks.' Jennifer walked down the hall and knocked on a door.

A voice said, 'Come in if you're good looking.'

She stepped into a tiny office. A plain-clothes officer sat behind a computer typing up some notes, sipping coffee from a plastic cup. He smiled boyishly. 'Hello, Jenny.'

Detective Mark Ryan was in his middle thirties, dark haired, with an easy, likable manner and cheerful green eyes. He came round from behind the desk and kissed Jennifer's cheek. 'What are you doing here?'

'They asked me to cover the Nadia Fedov case.'

'You going to be her attorney?'

'That's what the Federal Defender Division pays me for, Mark. I've got some free time before the presentment in court this afternoon so I thought I'd talk with her. And I was hoping you could fill me in on all the details.'

'Sure, Jenny, no problem, and it's good to see you, anyway.' Ryan's smile became a look of concern. 'How've you been since the other night?'

Jennifer touched his arm. 'Fine, Mark. I really appreciate you listening.'

Ryan nodded. 'Like I said, what are friends for?' He gestured to a chair. 'Take a seat. You want some coffee before we start?'

Jennifer sat. 'Thanks, but I'd like to get on with it.'

Mark sat on the edge of his desk and put down his coffee. 'I was working with a DEA task force at JFK this morning when the girl was arrested by Customs. She came in off an Aeroflot flight from Moscow with a three-week-old baby boy dead in her arms. The infant's body had been cut down the chest cavity and sewn up. Pathology found five pounds of pure-grade heroin inside.'

Jennifer turned pale. Mark Ryan looked at her. 'Are you OK?'

'Yes, I'm OK. How long had the child been dead?'

'About sixteen hours. Which means he died about four hours before the woman left Moscow. You sure you don't want a glass of water or something?'

'No, I'll be fine. Was he murdered?'

'The medical examiner suspects the child died of natural cases, but I haven't got the full report yet.'

Jennifer felt ill. 'What about the young woman?'

'She's twenty-three, a Russian citizen. It turns out the passport she had was a fake. It was stolen and professionally altered, with a forged US visa.'

Jennifer jotted down some notes. 'Was the dead baby hers?'

'She claims it was given to her at Moscow airport by a couple she never met before. She had another child with her she says is hers. A little girl, two years old, named Tamara. She's being looked after by the welfare office.'

'How is she?'

'The daughter?'

'The mother, the daughter, both.'

'The kid's confused and wants her mom. The mother's scared and lost. She knows she's going to be put away for a long time.'

'How much were they paying her?'

'She says ten thousand dollars.'

'What else did she tell you?'

Ryan shrugged. 'Nothing much. She won't really talk and she asked for a lawyer. She seems pretty frightened about something. My instinct tells me someone threatened her and made her do it, but right now she's not saying.'

'What's going to happen to her, Mark?'

'You ought to know. She's not a US citizen, so she won't get bail. We're talking about a federal crime. She carried a forged passport and visa, and used a corpse to smuggle heroin. That could figure up to ten years, if she's lucky. But she's definitely going down. Unless she talks, which I'm guessing she won't.'

'And her daughter?'

'She'll be sent back to Moscow. To relatives, if the kid has any. At worst, she ends up in some crummy State home.'

'Does the mother speak English?'

'Pretty well, so you shouldn't need a translator. But I'll get one if you want.'

Jennifer shook her head and gathered up her things.

THE DOOR of the interview room banged shut and Jennifer looked at the young woman who stood up behind the wooden table. She looked younger than twenty-three, more like eighteen. Her blue woollen dress was cheap and worn, and she had a look of despair on her face, her eyes red from crying.

Jennifer offered her hand. 'My name's Jennifer March. I work for the Federal Defender Division and I've been appointed to act as your lawyer.'

The girl trembled as she shook Jennifer's hand. 'They told me lawyer would talk to me.'

'Are you OK, Nadia?'

Tears welled in the woman's eyes. 'I want to see my daughter.'

'I may be able to arrange that later, but for now we have to talk. Sit down, Nadia.' Jennifer pulled out a chair from the table and the girl sat opposite.

'I have no money to pay for you.'

'The Federal Defender Division will take care of that. They represent, free of charge, individuals, even illegal aliens, who are charged with federal crimes and are unable to afford an attorney. Do you understand, Nadia?'

The girl nodded silently.

'You were caught with a large quantity of heroin in your possession. And a dead baby that may have been murdered for the purpose of smuggling heroin. Those are very serious charges. Tell me what happened from the beginning.'

Nadia Fedov wiped her eyes. 'I work in nightclub in Moscow. I have degree in economics, but in Russia life is difficult, and this is only work I can get. Two men who visit nightclub always have lots of money. And always watch me. One day one of them say to me, "Would you like to earn ten thousand dollars?" I ask how. They tell me I have to take something to New York. They will give me Russian passport for me and my daughter, with American visa. I ask what they want me to take and they tell me it is something important. Ten thousand dollars is lot of money, and with American visa I can stay in your country. So I say, maybe. Some days later, one of the men comes to see me again. He says I must take dead infant with me.' Nadia Fedov's voice broke, and tears streamed down her face. 'There would be drugs inside body. I say no, I will not do it. Then the men beat me. They say they will kill my daughter if I do not do what they want.'

'What were you to do with the dead child when you reached New York?'

'Someone would be waiting for me after I come out of arrivals. They would take baby from me and pay me. After that, I am free.'

'Why didn't you tell Customs at JFK you'd been forced to smuggle drugs?'

'Because the men said they would find us and kill us if I told police.'

'What were the men's names?'

'I don't know. And even if I did, I couldn't tell you. The men said it didn't matter if I was in prison, they would find me and kill me if I talked. Kill me and my little girl . . . But now I will never see her again.'

Nadia Fedov put her face in her hands and sobbed. Jennifer walked round the table and put her arms round her shoulders, trying to offer comfort.

MARK RYAN was waiting for her in the corridor. 'How'd it go?'

'She was a dupe, Mark. She was used.'

'The little people always are.' Ryan looked at Jennifer March's face and saw tears in the corners of her eyes. 'Are you OK?'

'I'll be fine. I just keep thinking about that dead baby and . . . What about the woman's daughter? Can she see her?'

Ryan put a hand on her arm. 'I'll see what I can do.'

'Thanks, Mark.'

'So how've you been keeping? And how's Bobby?'

'Bobby's fine.'

'I've been out to the Cauldwell to see him a couple of times. But it's been a few months. I guess I'm due a visit.'

'He'd like that.'

Ryan hesitated. 'Maybe this is a bad time to ask, but are you free for dinner this week?'

'I'm really sorry, Mark. But just at the moment I'm pretty much up to my eyes with work. How about another time?'

Ryan gave a valiant smile. 'Sure, whenever. You want some advice? Go home and try not to think about all this. That woman back there in the blue dress will be doing enough of that for both of us.'

JENNIFER WENT into the women's rest room and tried to compose herself. She loved her work, even if sometimes she got to hear horror stories like the one she'd just heard. And she could identify with the young woman: she knew what it was like to have your life destroyed by evil, brutal people.

She looked at herself in the mirror. She had a vivacious, interesting face, with a generous, sensitive mouth and intelligent blue eyes. But there was an air of aloofness about her. She knew it was part of the protective armour she had worn since her mother's death.

She had lots of acquaintances, a social life that revolved round going to the gym and having dinner with former college classmates, but she had few real friends. At almost thirty-one, she was unattached and in love with no one.

She'd known Mark Ryan since childhood, when he'd lived across her street and they'd been just acquainted enough to say hello. He was four years older than her and she'd always liked him. Since her late teens their paths had not crossed again until one day three years ago, when she was still a law student and Mark was one of a group of NYPD detectives who came to Columbia School of Law to lecture on police procedures. Afterwards, they'd had coffee and she'd learned he was going through a messy divorce. Though neither had shown the slightest romantic interest in the other, they'd struck up a friendship. They went for dinner together at least once a month and hardly a week went by when they didn't speak on the phone, but that was it. Mark was a true friend, maybe the closest she had, and though she liked him, even felt attracted to him, she knew she was afraid of getting too close to any man.

They had gone on a dinner date two months ago, and afterwards Mark had kissed her, and she had enjoyed the pleasure of feeling close to him, but as soon as the kiss started to get heavy, she had panicked and asked him to stop.

It had been over two years since she had gone out on a serious date. She knew her problem had to do with the trauma of the night of her mother's death. Today was the anniversary of her death, and she didn't want her to be alone.

CALVERTON CEMETERY on Long Island was deserted that sunny afternoon. Jennifer parked her Ford and walked to her mother's grave, carrying a bunch of roses. The inscription on the white marble stone always sent a shiver through her heart:

> *In loving memory of Anna March,*
> *beloved wife of Paul March,*
> *RIP*

It had been exactly two years ago, and not a day had gone by when she didn't remember the nightmare of her mother's death and her father's disappearance. The simple white stone hid so much and said so little, for there was so much more to her parents' past than any gravestone could ever tell.

Jennifer placed the roses on the grave, then stood back, letting the past wash over her, remembering it all . . .

DURING THE FIRST FEW YEARS of her life, Jennifer saw very little of her father. Paul March was an investment banker, a tall, handsome man with dark, gentle eyes. He was always travelling abroad on business—to Paris, London, Zürich, Rome—and Jennifer missed him terribly. But he remembered to send his only daughter a postcard from every new place he visited.

And then the day would come when she'd see her father come up the path. He'd be smiling, his arms open, waiting for her to run to them. Jennifer loved the feel of his strong arms sweeping her up. He always brought her gifts— chocolate from Switzerland, a rag doll from France, a colourful wooden marionette from Italy—but the warm feeling of security Jennifer felt in her father's arms meant more to her than any of them.

When she was twelve, Jennifer's father joined a small private investment bank in New York called Prime International Securities. He was ambitious, keen to make a success of his career. Paul March prospered, and her parents moved to a wonderful old renovated house on Long Beach, a grey-and-white-painted colonial property with its own private dock. Her mother had worked as a legal secretary, but had given up her job to take care of her daughter. She was warm, caring and spontaneous, but although Jennifer cherished her deeply, she felt closer to her father. Perhaps because of his absences he was more of an enigma, and that mystery made her love him more.

When Jennifer was thirteen her brother Robert was born, and she was no longer the centre of attention. Jennifer didn't mind much, because Bobby was a good-humoured little boy who smiled a lot and loved to be picked up and played with by his older sister. But when her father held Bobby in his arms, just as he had held her, Jennifer felt intensely jealous. Her mother explained that her new brother had been an unexpected miracle after years of trying for another child, and that it didn't mean her father loved Jennifer any less. She felt, though, that a part of her father's love was gone for ever from her life.

As she grew older, however, she realised that something more vital was missing from all their lives. She started to notice that there were no family photographs from her father's past. Her mother had parents, aunts and uncles and cousins who sometimes came to visit, but Jennifer's father had none.

And her father never mentioned anything about his relatives, no more than he spoke much about his work. It was as if he didn't have a past.

But she learned that he *did* have a past, and it came with a terrible secret.

One day, when she was fourteen, while her father was on one of his business trips, her mother had an errand to run and left her alone in the house. Bored, Jennifer had climbed into the attic, a part of the house she never visited. In a corner was a big wooden trunk. It had a sturdy lock but Jennifer remembered seeing a bunch of keys hanging in her father's study. Curious to know what was in the trunk, she went downstairs and found the keys. One of them fitted the lock. She opened the trunk, and found a file of papers inside.

She thought at first they were old business documents, but when she began leafing through the sheets she realised they were something entirely different. Years later she was to understand that they were copies of legal depositions, the statements made to the police by the victims of one man.

'*Joseph Delgado stole from my company . . . he's a thief . . .*'

'*Joseph Delgado is a killer who deserves to die for his crimes . . .*'

'*Joseph Delgado is a dangerous young man who ought to be put behind bars for the rest of his life . . .*'

Who was Joseph Delgado?

Among the papers in the trunk was a black-and-white crime-scene photograph. A picture of a man lying in an alleyway, a knife stuck in his chest. It was too much horror to take in and Jennifer couldn't bear to look any more.

As she started to close the trunk she noticed another photograph among the papers. When she picked it up and stared at the image, her mouth fell open in shock. It was of a dark-haired young man in a prison uniform. Someone had written a name underneath in black ballpoint ink: *Joseph Delgado*.

The face looked disturbingly familiar.

It was her father's face.

The discovery horrified Jennifer. Delgado was obviously an evil man. But her father wasn't evil. She was confused. When her father came back from his business trip, she said to him, 'Who's Joseph Delgado?'

Paul March became white faced. 'How . . . how do you know that name?'

Jennifer confessed to opening the attic trunk. 'The . . . the man in the photograph, he looked like you, Daddy.'

It was the first time she had seen her father angry, and there was a strange, frightening look in his eyes. He slapped Jennifer's face and stormed out of the room. She wept, sobs racking her body, and her mother had to console her. 'Why . . . why did Daddy get so angry, Mom? Why did he hit me?'

'You were *wrong* to go through your father's things, Jennifer,' her mother said quietly. 'You must *never* pry into your father's private business in future.'

IT WAS TO BE many years before Jennifer went up into the attic or pried into her father's private business again. And the next time it happened, it was by accident. By then, she was in her twenties. Her father had remained with Prime, which had been bought by a private offshore investor a year earlier. Soon her father was promoted to vice-president. He was earning more than ever and had gained more responsibility, but had grown distant and moody.

One day, Jennifer passed by his study. A pair of French windows led out to the garden, and the patio beyond had a view of the sea and the tiny private jetty where her father and Bobby would sit for hours in summer, fishing and talking until the sun went down. But this day the French doors were open and her father was sitting alone on the patio in his favourite deck chair, his face buried in his hands. When he looked up, it was to stare blankly out to sea.

As Jennifer walked through the study to join him, she saw a metal security box open on his desk. The box was empty, but there was a yellow legal notepad and floppy disk beside it. She glimpsed the word '*Spiderweb*' written on the notepad and several illegible paragraphs in her father's handwriting.

He suddenly noticed her, rose from his chair and stormed in through the French doors. 'Were you reading my papers, Jennifer?'

'No, I . . . I just came by to see if you were OK, Dad.'

Her father picked up the notepad and disk and placed them in the security box. 'Those are private papers and none of your business.'

'But I was only—'

'Don't ever do it again.' He took a silver key from his wallet and locked the box. His face was flushed with anger, the same anger Jennifer had witnessed when she was fourteen and had confronted him about the attic photograph.

'Is everything OK, Dad?' she asked.

He put the silver key back in his wallet and led her to the door. 'If you don't mind I'd like to be alone. I've a lot of work to do.'

'Dad, I didn't mean to—'

'We'll talk about it another time. Now please leave, Jennifer.' He ushered her out of his study and locked the door behind her.

A month later her mother was brutally murdered and her father vanished.

SHE WOULD ALWAYS RECALL the night it happened. Her mother had asked her to stay the weekend, an offer Jennifer gratefully accepted, and that same evening her father had flown to Switzerland on business. The tiny Manhattan apartment that Jennifer shared with another female law student was cramped and claustrophobic, and she was always glad of the luxury of sleeping in her own room and enjoying her mother's cooking.

But that night, a savage storm raged in the darkness outside her bedroom. The noise must have disturbed her, and when she opened her eyes she was suddenly aware of the odd feeling that there was a *presence* in the house.

Jennifer flicked on the bedside light. Nothing happened. She climbed out of bed, pulled on her bathrobe and opened her door. As she stepped out, she felt a freezing blast of air. A window was open at the end of the landing, curtains lifting and falling in the wind. It must have been blown open, she thought, and went to shut it. As she closed the window, the lights on the landing flickered on, then were extinguished. Frightened, she called out, '*Mom?*'

There was no reply. She opened the door to her parents' bedroom and stepped inside. A blaze of lightning exploded beyond the rain-lashed window. In the wash of electric blue light she saw that the room was in disarray. Drawers had been ransacked, clothes scattered on the floor. Blood was spattered on the white carpet and on the walls. She froze in horror.

Another crack of lightning illuminated the room, and she saw the bodies. Her mother lay across the bed, savage wounds in her chest. Bobby lay crumpled on the floor, blood seeping from a wound to his neck.

As Jennifer made to scream, a hand clamped over her mouth.

It was a man and he was powerful. As Jennifer struggled in terror, he dragged her across the landing to her bedroom. When she tried to fight back the man smashed a fist into her face, and when she fell he tied a gag over her mouth. The bedside light flickered on and she glimpsed his face.

He had no face. He wore a black ski mask, his dark, evil eyes and mouth visible through the slits. He held a bloodstained butcher's knife in one hand.

The man placed the knife on the night stand. Jennifer saw a pistol tucked into his waistband. She cried behind the gag, curled up with fear, and her bathrobe rode up her legs. Suddenly she felt a hand crawl over her flesh.

'Stay still or I'll cut your throat.'

Jennifer sobbed as the man forced her legs apart. She didn't dare move. But as the storm raged outside, the lamp flickered on again and Jennifer glimpsed the bloodied knife on the table and the sight of her mother's blood made her livid. She fumbled for the knife and stabbed the blade into the man's neck.

He screamed, then his hand went up to pull out the blade. Jennifer saw her chance to push him away and ran to the bedroom door. She raced down the stairs and out of the front door.

The nearest house was sixty yards across the street. Jennifer could just make out the white door in the downpour, the verandah in darkness. Her heart pounded as she looked back and saw the masked man running after her, the bloodied knife in one hand, his other clutching at his wound.

Forty yards to the door. Twenty yards. Ten.

Jennifer raced up the verandah steps.

She hammered on the door and screamed, '*Someone please help me!* . . . *He's going to kill me . . . Please!*'

And then all her senses seemed to go, and she fainted.

WHEN SHE CAME TO she was lying in a hospital bed in a private room. A man came into the room. He was in his late fifties, distinguished looking, with a handsome face and silver hair. Jennifer glimpsed a uniformed police officer standing guard outside, before the man closed the door.

He said quietly, 'How are you feeling, Jennifer?'

She was still in shock, trembling. 'I . . . I don't know.'

'Jennifer, I'm not sure what to say.' It was obvious the man was deeply upset; he seemed at a loss for words and she could see tears in his eyes. 'My name's Jack Kelso. I'm a friend of your father's. Perhaps he mentioned me?'

'No, he . . . he didn't. Are you a colleague?'

'No, but we're good friends, and I felt I had to come here as soon as I heard what happened. Your mom . . . she was . . . a wonderful person.'

Jennifer said hoarsely, 'My mom's dead, isn't she?'

Kelso nodded. 'Yes, Jennifer, she's dead.'

'And Bobby?'

Kelso sighed. 'Bobby's in intensive care at the Schneider hospital.'

'Is he OK? Is Bobby OK?'

Kelso hesitated. 'He's going to live. But a bullet shattered part of his spinal cord, and there's been some brain damage. I've been told he's going to have difficulty walking, and maybe talking, but . . . he's alive, Jennifer.'

'*Oh God.*'

'He's *alive*, Jennifer, and that's what matters right now.'

'Why would anyone want to kill my mom and shoot Bobby?'

Kelso shook his head. 'I don't know. That's where you might be able to help the police. They think that maybe your mom woke and disturbed a thief, and Bobby tried to intervene, and that's why they were attacked.'

'The . . . the man. He tried to kill me too.'

Kelso nodded, held her hand. 'Don't worry. The police will have an armed officer outside your room, twenty-four hours.'

Jennifer felt deeply confused. 'I . . . I want my dad. When's he coming back?'

'The police are still trying to locate him, Jennifer.'

'He's in Zürich, Switzerland.'

'Yes, they know.' Kelso made to leave. 'Try and rest. We'll talk again.'

Jennifer said, 'Something's wrong, isn't it? What's wrong with my father?'

Kelso sighed. 'I don't know, Jennifer. It seems the Swiss police checked every hotel in Zürich, without success. Right now, they're not even sure he arrived in Switzerland, and they don't know where he might be. But I'm told that Interpol is doing everything they can to find him.'

'What are you saying?'

'He's vanished, Jennifer. Your father's simply vanished.'

A POLICE DETECTIVE had come with her to close up the house on Long Beach. It was six weeks after the murder, and she still felt vulnerable. The police had informed her that Interpol had been unable to trace Paul March, in Zürich or anywhere else. As Kelso had told her, her father had simply vanished.

She told the detective she wanted to be left alone to sort through her things. He reluctantly agreed. 'I'll be out front.'

When he left, she walked through the rooms in a daze. Several drawers in her father's study had been left open, and upstairs a number of the closets were in disarray, as if the house had been recently searched, and she guessed it must have been the police. She opened the French windows and looked out to the jetty and the boathouse and heard the soft sound of the sea.

She walked down to the jetty and sat on the edge, near the boathouse, where her father kept the motorboat he used for fishing. The tide was out and her feet dangled over the wet sand, a metal ladder leading down. The afternoon air was cool, a chilly Atlantic breeze whipping up white-topped waves far out to sea. The boardwalk was where her father liked to come when he needed to be alone. Some summer nights, lying in her bedroom, she'd hear the echo of his footsteps on the boardwalk as he paced up and down, mulling over some problem or other.

She closed her eyes and cried: she'd never hear those footsteps again. Why had her father disappeared and where had he gone? Why had her mother been slaughtered and Bobby left for dead? She couldn't understand any of it. Kelso had said the police thought the motive was robbery, but days after the murder Jennifer had been visited again in her hospital room by two detectives from Homicide. They wanted to go over her story once more, wanted to know whether her father had been depressed, or had ever beaten her mother.

She answered no to each of their questions. Afterwards, she heard the detectives talking outside her room. They talked about her father as if *he* might have committed the crimes, or paid someone to carry them out. Jennifer couldn't believe that for a moment. It was too repulsive even to think about.

Returning to the study, she idly opened the drawers of her father's desk: there were lots of bills and sheaves of paper, but the security box that had contained the yellow legal pad was nowhere to be found. As she remembered how angry her father had been, she recalled the other incident when she had discovered the trunk in the attic and mentioned the name Joseph Delgado.

She saw the old bunch of keys lying on one of the shelves. She picked them up and climbed the stairs to the attic. When she opened the trunk it was empty.

BOBBY HAD been too ill to attend the funeral service, and the first time Jennifer was allowed to visit him he looked helpless, confined in a wheelchair, tubes in his nostrils and his fifteen-year-old face lost and confused. He couldn't walk and couldn't speak. The bullet that had shattered his spine had crippled and muted him. He still had some power in his hands, and a police psychologist had tried to get him to write down what had happened the night of the murder, using pictures and words, but Bobby was too traumatised. Every time the psychologist brought up the subject, he withdrew deeper into himself.

After months of trying to get over her anguish, Jennifer resumed her legal studies. Bobby's injuries meant he had to be taken into permanent care at the Cauldwell home, where she visited him every day. Jennifer couldn't bear to live alone in her parents' house but she couldn't bring herself to sell it either. She rented the condo on Long Beach, for she still had an inexplicable need to remain close to the place of her childhood, perhaps because she dreamt of the day when her father would return home and together with Bobby they could try to rebuild their shattered lives.

For a long time she wanted to talk to no one, and her friends and classmates found it impossible to get through to her. She learned to keep everyone at arm's length, never allowed anyone to get close.

Jack Kelso had sometimes come to visit her, and he often visited Bobby. But she had learned little about Kelso and he had never explained how he and her father had met. Gradually his visits dwindled.

For months after her mother's death, the police had occasionally come by, but only to tell her that their investigation was going nowhere. Did she remember anything else, any detail, no matter how small? She told them about the day she had found the papers in the attic trunk, told them of the grisly photograph she had seen, and the name of the man in prison uniform who had looked like her father: Joseph Delgado.

'We'll look into it,' one of the detectives promised.

But the next time they visited they confessed they'd still got nowhere. 'The name's drawn a blank. We'll get back to you if anything turns up.'

Months passed but the detectives never returned.

Jennifer finally graduated from Columbia School of Law. After four years of struggle, the dream of becoming a lawyer had come true. Now, as she stood in the cemetery, looking down at her mother's grave, she thought of the other dreams that had never worked out. The police never caught the man who had killed her mother and shot Bobby, and her father never came back.

The Swiss Alps

THE CHILL bit into Chuck McCaul's bones despite his protective clothing. He had finally reached the Wasenhorn glacier. As he paused for breath, he looked down at the solid mass of blue-coloured ice, covered in snow.

He was twenty-one, fit and muscular, with cropped hair. Metal crampons were attached to his boots to ensure a good grip, and the ice seemed firm underfoot. After thirty minutes, he was fifty yards from the far side of the glacier.

He paused for breath. The view from where he stood was incredible. In the distance lay Italy, rugged, picturesque Alpine villages with red pantiled roofs, clinging to the mountainsides, as if defying the laws of gravity.

Ahead, he could see a series of crevasses, narrow slits in the glacier that had been cracked open by altitude pressure and cold. Some went down only a couple of yards; others dropped to the bottom of the glacier, perhaps more than a hundred yards. McCaul counted three crevasses, one after another, each about a yard wide, with maybe five-yard gaps between them.

He could jump all three, one after the other, *no big deal*.

Carefully, McCaul prodded ahead of him with the tip of his walking stick. The snow appeared pretty solid and the crampons would give him a good grip. The first crevasse was just a couple of steps away. He moved back to take a run. He had run three long strides when it happened.

One moment his feet were on the ice and the next they were stabbing at the air as the ground beneath him seemed to disappear.

McCaul screamed, lost his balance, and plunged into the crevasse.

WHEN HE OPENED his eyes he was lying on his back. McCaul's body felt as if it had been beaten with a sledgehammer and his skull throbbed, but he was still wearing his safety helmet and he guessed it had saved his life. High above him he could see the mouth of the crevasse: a jagged, blinding slash of blue sky, which was reflected in the ice walls of the chamber.

Slowly, he moved his arms and legs. He ached all over but nothing felt broken. He lay on a mound of snow, created by a small avalanche when the mouth of the crevasse had given way. Presumably the snow had softened his fall. He figured it was at least eight yards to the top, but he could probably climb up, by bracing his back and legs against the walls.

He was just getting ready to climb when a dark object inside the crevasse wall opposite him caught his eye. It appeared to be embedded in the ice.

McCaul frowned and edged closer. All he could make out was a dark, rectangular form. Curious, he removed his backpack and fumbled for his ice axe. The object didn't appear to be far in. He began to chip away, breaking off chunks of ice. He hit something soft. When he prised away the last shards with his numbed fingers he saw it was a canvas rucksack. It was frozen solid and the back of it stuck like glue to the ice. McCaul got a grip on the canvas, gave a couple of sharp tugs, and the rucksack came free.

Jeez, it felt heavy.

Forget the rucksack, Chuck. Leave it and just get out of here.

He forced himself against the wall, locked one leg hard against the ice, then his other leg, and braced himself. Slowly, achingly, he began to climb. When he had gone only a couple of yards, he froze, his breath catching in his throat, and had to brace himself hard against the walls to prevent himself falling.

He looked straight ahead in horror. Locked inside the ice, staring out at him like a ghostly apparition, was the face of a man.

Italian–Swiss border

THE AGUSTA HELICOPTER circled once before it came in to land.

As the whirr of the rotor blades died, Victor Caruso climbed wearily out of the passenger seat. He was a small man in his early fifties, overweight, with a bushy handlebar moustache and penetrating grey eyes. As he tossed away his half-finished cigarette, a squall of wind threw rain in his face.

'A great start to the day,' he called back to the pilot.

'It could be worse, Captain.'

'I doubt it somehow,' Caruso said moodily.

He saw two blue-and-white Fiats parked a short distance away. Half a dozen uniformed men from the local Carabinieri station in Varzo stood chatting in the rain. A tall man in a sergeant's uniform came from the group, and saluted.

Caruso nodded. 'Sergeant Barti, I presume?'

Barti offered his hand. 'Good morning, Captain. Thanks for coming.'

Caruso glanced up at the grey clouds. 'Tell me what's good about it? Yesterday I was in Turin, looking forward to my first day off in a month, when some idiot from headquarters phones and tells me I'm being flown up north.'

Barti smiled. 'Sorry to mess up your rest day, but we needed expert help.'

Caruso lit another cigarette. 'So where's the stiff?'

Barti nodded up towards the mountains. 'Up there, about an hour and a half away, most of it on foot. The weather's too cloudy to use the helicopter.'

Caruso raised his eyes in despair. 'Can't we take a car?'

'Only as far as the Alpe Veglia. Then we've got to walk to the glacier.' The Alpe Veglia was a huge nature reserve in the Italian Alps, closed to traffic, except the reserve's four-wheel-drive patrol vehicles. But even they couldn't make it all the way up the steep rock-shale tracks that bordered Switzerland.

Caruso sighed. 'Terrific. So who's up there now?'

'Two of my men. One's a local who knows the glacier pretty well. And there's a forensic pathologist from Turin named Vito Rima.'

'You can always count on Vito hovering around wherever there's a body.' Caruso tossed his cigarette away. 'OK, let's get going. Fill me in on the way.'

They got into one of the Fiats. It was warmer inside, but not much.

'We had a call yesterday afternoon from the Swiss police in Brig,' Barti began. 'A young American climber staying at the Berghof Hotel in Simplon reported that he'd found a body in the mountains. The American kid fell into a crevasse on the Wasenhorn glacier and discovered the frozen corpse inside.'

'You said kid. What age?'

'Twenty-one. His name is Chuck McCaul. He's a tourist, who likes climbing. It turns out he also found a rucksack lodged in the ice near the body.'

Caruso raised his eyes. 'Did you find anything in the rucksack?'

'The American left it in the crevasse. I thought it best not to touch it until you and Rima arrived.'

'Wise. Go on.'

'The Swiss police sent a team up to the Wasenhorn. It turns out the body's on our side of the border. The Swiss can count themselves lucky it's our case.'

'Why?'

Barti halted the Fiat. It was impossible for the car to go any further. The cloud had cleared a little, and the drizzle had almost died. Soaring peaks of white-topped, jagged mountains stretched ahead, part of the range that forms the natural border between Switzerland and Italy.

Barti jerked on the handbrake. 'I checked our records of missing persons, people we know who got lost in this part of the Alps, going back twenty years. All were found and accounted for, dead or alive. The Swiss say the same. So it's pretty odd that we've found a body that no one knew was lost.'

NEAR ONE of the crevasses stood two young corporals. Both wore heavy parkas and boots, and they were making coffee on a small Primus stove. Cloud wisps swirled around the Wasenhorn peak in the cold sunshine.

Caruso was still struggling to catch his breath as the sergeant went over to the two men. A small blue bivouac tent had been erected nearby, and a square had been marked out in the snow, with short aluminium poles planted round the mouth of the crevasse, yellow plastic tape strung between them.

Barti came back with one of the corporals in tow. 'This is Corporal Fausto.'

The young man saluted. 'Captain.'

'Tell me what's been happening.'

The corporal indicated the crevasse. 'We've marked off the site, as you can see. The pathologist is still down there.'

Caruso turned to Barti. 'I'd like to see the body.'

The corporal led them to the edge of the crevasse. Caruso peered into a pale blue chamber, which got darker the further down it went.

Barti said, 'It's an easy enough descent.'

'I'll have to take your word for it. Lead the way.'

Barti slipped a harness round his waist, took hold of a rope and lowered himself down. Caruso followed. It was bone-chillingly cold. As Caruso abseiled down he saw a blaze of light below, and moments later Barti gripped his waist.

'OK, you're at the bottom.'

Caruso let go of the rope and his feet hit packed ice. Round a bend, several yards away, a couple of powerful torches illuminated the chamber floor. A thin man stood with a black doctor's bag open at his feet, his breath clouding in the chilled air. He had a grey goatee beard, thick metal-rimmed glasses, and wore a quilted arctic parka and heavy woollen gloves.

'About time somebody decided to join me,' he said sourly.

'How are you, Rima?'

'Cold as an undertaker's kiss.'

Caruso scanned the chamber's icy floor. 'Did you check the ground?'

Rima nodded. 'Nothing, apart from the rucksack the American found.' He pointed to a large clear plastic bag propped against the far wall.

Caruso picked it up. The plastic was ice cold and partly clouded. Inside was a canvas rucksack. It felt heavy, and had a metal snap lock. 'You didn't open it?'

'I tried, but it's frozen solid, so I thought it best to wait until the officer in charge arrived.' Rima smiled. 'I guess that's you.'

Caruso put the rucksack down. 'OK, let's have a look at the stiff. An accident, you think?'

'Impossible to tell until we thaw him out.' Rima jerked a thumb behind him. 'See for yourself. He's over there.'

Rima picked up a torch and they moved along the crevasse bottom for five yards. Facing the left-hand wall, Caruso saw a folding aluminium chair. To his left, he noticed a small square cut into the ice near the chamber floor.

'That's where the American found the rucksack,' Rima explained. 'The body's about half a metre above your head, lying horizontally. You'll need to stand on the chair to see it.'

Caruso stood on the rickety chair and shone the cone of torchlight onto the frozen wall. A man's face stared out at him grotesquely from the ice.

'Kind of gives you the creeps, doesn't it?' said Rima. 'The ice has kept the body perfectly preserved.'

Caruso shivered as he peered in closer. The skin was alabaster white and the eyes were wide open. 'How long do you think it's been here?'

'I really can't say until we cut it out and I have it on the slab. But at this depth, the body could have been here a long time. Years maybe.'

'I'll take your word for it. Are you through?'

Rima rubbed his freezing hands. 'Almost. The next step is to cut our friend here out of the ice. We'll use a chain saw.'

'I'll need to talk to the American. Where is he?'

'One of my men is picking him up from his Swiss hotel,' Barti explained. 'I've arranged for you to have the use of one of the offices in our station.'

'Good.' Caruso took another look at the entombed face, shivered and stepped down off the chair. 'OK, I've seen enough. Let's get back up.'

THE OFFICE in the small Carabinieri station in Varzo overlooked a tiny square. Caruso sat at the desk near the window, and picked up the plastic evidence bag. He slipped on a pair of disposable rubber gloves and removed the heavy rucksack. The ice had thawed, and the canvas was wet and soggy. He pulled out his Swiss army penknife, jammed the rucksack between his legs and levered the lock with the knife. After a lot of effort it snapped open.

He peered inside and saw a jumble of clothes: a suit, a shirt and tie and patent-leather shoes among them. At the bottom of the pile he saw an automatic pistol and what looked like a slim, black leather wallet. He slipped the blade of his penknife into the pistol's trigger guard, and laid the weapon down on the desk. Then he picked up the wallet. Carefully, he slid the penknife blade between the covers and prised it open. To his surprise, it wasn't a wallet but a passport cover. As he began to separate the pages there was a knock on the door and a corporal put his head into the room.

'Signore McCaul is here, Captain.'

'Give me five minutes, then send him in.'

CARUSO SAT on the edge of the desk and looked at the young American seated opposite. 'Tell me, please, how you found the body,' he asked in English.

McCaul told him. Caruso listened, then said, 'Did you find anything else besides the rucksack?'

'No, sir.'

'You're certain?'

'My father's a private detective. I wouldn't lie about police evidence, sir.'

Caruso nodded. 'When do you leave Switzerland?'

'I don't fly home for another four days. Is that it, Captain?'

'*Sì*. That's it.'

McCaul stood. 'You mind if I ask a question?'

'Of course not.'

'What's the story? Who's the guy in the ice?'

'According to the passport I found in the rucksack, it seems he was an American named Paul March.'

New York

LEROY MURPHY leaned his burly, six-foot-six black frame over the wheelchair and gently removed the Sony CD headset from Bobby's ears. They were in the conservatory of the Cauldwell home, the doors open, a cool breeze blowing into the hot room—Jennifer, Bobby and Leroy, the nurse.

Bobby sat in the wheelchair, head to one side, saliva running down his chin. Jennifer wiped it away with a paper tissue. Then she took a comb from her bag and combed Bobby's hair.

Leroy said, 'OK, man's had enough attention. Looks like he's ready to rock. Quiz time. Bobby here knows more about music than anyone I know. That right, Bobby? And we're gonna show Jenny, ain't we?'

Bobby gave a lopsided grin and nodded.

Leroy placed a notepad on Bobby's lap and handed him a pen. 'That's my man. Song called "Closer Than Close". Gimme the singer, gimme the year.'

Bobby gripped the pen hard, then scrawled across the page. '*Rosie Gaines.*'

'Tell me *when*, man. Don't let me down, now.'

Bobby wrote: '*1997.*'

'You're my man. Tough one coming. Coolio had a number one that stayed in the charts four weeks the same year. Gimme the song. Impress Jenny.'

Bobby hesitated for a moment, his face twisted in concentration, then he wrote on the pad and gave a tiny grin of triumph.

Leroy checked the answer, slapped a big, meaty leg. 'Man, you're a walking archive, you know that? Got a memory better than a damned elephant.'

He ruffled Bobby's hair and looked across at Jennifer, his broad face grinning from ear to ear. 'Man never lets me down. Could win himself a *big* quiz show. Cars. Holidays. Lots of dollars. Me, I'm gonna be his manager.'

Jennifer touched the nurse's hand as he stood to leave. 'Thanks, Leroy.'

'Any time.'

'So, how are you doing?' Jennifer asked.

Bobby gave a nod and rocked back and forth in his wheelchair. He was seventeen but looked fourteen, with thick dark hair and pale, milky skin.

'Leroy tells me you haven't been eating too well. Is everything OK?'

Bobby looked uncomfortable. He turned his face away.

'What's wrong, Bobby?'

Bobby picked up his notepad, laid it on his knee. In the last year he had learned to use sign language, and so had Jennifer, because mostly now Bobby signed his responses, but when he was upset or angry he preferred to use his notepad and write his reply. The game he played with Leroy was just to keep his mind busy, because Bobby had a terrific memory. But his memory didn't extend to the night of their mother's murder. Jennifer often wondered whether all the circuits inside his head that had to do with the incident had simply shut down, or whether the bullet that had skewered into his skull had destroyed that part of his brain. The medical experts hadn't been able to say.

Now Bobby scrawled on the page with the pen, then sat staring into space. He looked distracted. Jennifer picked up the pad. It read: '*I want to get out of here. People are nice but they're not family.*'

She looked back at Bobby. 'I think I know where this is leading.'

Bobby let out a deep breath and this time he signed his reply; she understood the meaning of his gestures as he pointed at himself, then at her, and crossed his fingers. When he finished signing she knew exactly what he meant. '*I want us to be together. I want to go live with you. Permanently.*'

'Bobby, we've been through all this. You know I love you, you know I want you to be with me. You stay with me most weekends, but for the rest of the week my work takes up most of my day. Sometimes I don't get home until late. Right now the Cauldwell is the best place, OK?' She leaned over, tried to hug him, knowing he was frustrated in a hundred different ways, but Bobby pulled away. Then she heard footsteps and looked round.

Leroy stood there. 'Sorry to disturb you, Jenny, but you've got a visitor.'

SHE WAS STARTLED to see Mark Ryan waiting outside in the hallway. 'Hello, Jennifer.'

'This is a surprise.'

'I thought I'd take a drive up and see Bobby. Leroy told me you were here.'

'He'll be glad to see you. Is anything the matter?'

'With me? No, nothing.'

Jennifer noticed tension around Mark's eyes and mouth. 'Are you sure?'

He shrugged. 'Well, maybe two things. It looks like the federal prosecutor will be pressing for a maximum sentence in the Nadia Fedov case.'

'She's just a kid, Mark. You really can't change their minds?'

'I tried. I'm sorry, Jennifer.'

Jennifer felt angry. 'A young woman loses her two-year-old daughter and gets locked away for the best years of her life. The people who made her commit the crime lose five pounds of heroin, and walk away to do it again.'

Mark looked away, as if there was something bothering him.

'You mentioned there were two things,' Jennifer reminded him.

Mark was pale. A door led out to the sunny gardens and the pond, and he gestured towards it. 'How about we talk outside?'

They walked down to the pond in silence. When they sat on one of the benches, Mark said, 'Jennifer, I didn't just drive up here to see Bobby.' He took out an envelope, removed a sheet of paper and handed it across.

She saw that the page was a police report from Interpol. The body of an American male had been found in the Alps, frozen in glacial ice. And then Jennifer saw the name.

She sat in stunned silence, still holding the page, hardly believing what she had read. Dazed, she finally looked over at Mark. 'This . . . this is really true?'

Mark nodded. 'I've been trying to get hold of you all day but your cellphone was down. The office said you'd taken the afternoon off and didn't know where you'd gone. I figured maybe you'd driven over here.'

Jennifer had turned pale. 'If my father's body has really been found . . .'

'He's been found, Jennifer. A climber discovered his passport nearby.'

Jennifer shivered. 'Who sent you to tell me?'

'A friend of mine with the Long Beach Police Department called me. He saw a copy of the report that Interpol sent to the detective unit. I offered to break the news. I thought it might be better coming from someone you knew.'

Jennifer felt confused, and anguished. 'Can I see the body?'

Mark nodded. 'You'll have to identify it formally. I checked with Interpol and they told me that the region where the body was discovered is on the Italian–Swiss border. The Carabinieri station that's running the investigation is in a town named Varzo, and a captain named Caruso is handling the case. It seems the best route is to fly to Switzerland and drive over the border to Italy. You could have the whole thing over and done with in a couple of days.'

'How did my father's body end up in a glacier? What . . . happened to him?'

Mark shook his head. 'All I know is what I've told you. Maybe this Caruso can tell you more.' He looked at his watch. 'I've got to get back, but if it's OK with you, I'd like to see Bobby before I leave.'

'He's always glad to see you, Mark. But please, don't tell him about this. Not just yet. It might upset him.'

Mark nodded. 'Are you sure you'll be all right?'

'I'll be fine.'

He stood up. 'If you need a shoulder to lean on, don't be afraid to call.'

IT WAS ALMOST MIDNIGHT when Mark Ryan finished his shift and drove home. It was pitch-dark as he pulled into the driveway of his two-bedroom town house in Elmont. Some of the street lighting was out, but as he climbed the steps to the porch he glimpsed a dark-coloured Buick sedan parked fifty yards back on the far side of the street. He'd noticed the car as he drove past. There appeared to be two men inside, but Mark couldn't be certain, and he was really too tired to care as he let himself in the front door.

The house had the look of a bachelor pad. He'd bought Ellen out after their divorce, and since she'd left he'd found it difficult to keep the place tidy. But he lived for his job, it was what had kept him sane after the divorce, and he spent so many extra hours at the precinct he didn't have time for housework.

He went into the kitchen, put the kettle on to boil for coffee and opened the refrigerator. Some hard cheese, a couple of cans of beer and Coke, a tomato, half a carton of milk, that was it. He found a couple of slices of rye in the bread bin, so he made a cheese sandwich and went into the living room while he waited for the water to boil. He didn't feel like watching TV, so he just sat there, hunched over the coffee table, eating the sandwich.

Some home life. He was thirty-five next birthday and there was no one special in his life. Miss Right still hadn't come along. He had once believed it was Ellen. A petite, fiery brunette with a terrific personality, she worked as a legal secretary for a firm of Manhattan lawyers, and they had married within three months of their first date. Seven months into the marriage he came home early from night shift, feeling lousy with a flu bug, and found Ellen on the couch with the slick, expensive lawyer they'd hired from Ellen's office to conveyance their house. It turned out he was an old boyfriend.

The marriage limped on for a few weeks, but it was pointless. Mark filed for divorce after Ellen left one fall weekend and didn't come back.

Some nights when he came home he longed to have someone to talk to, someone to rub his back the way Ellen used to. Tonight was one of them. It had been a lousy couple of days. The dead baby at Kennedy had upset him as much as it had Jennifer, only he didn't always wear his heart on his sleeve.

He liked Jennifer; she was the kind of woman he could go for. But he knew she'd been devastated by her mother's death and her father's disappearance, and the frenzied assault she'd suffered. The night of the murder she'd run to his parents' house and his father had heard the banging on the front door, and when he came down he'd found her unconscious on the verandah. Mark's old man was dying of cancer even then but, leaving Jennifer in the care of Mark's mother, he'd grabbed his pistol and headed out across the lawns towards the March property. He'd found Jennifer's mother stabbed to death and young Bobby with gunshot wounds, but whoever had committed the crime had fled.

It was five days before Mark was allowed to see Jennifer, but she didn't want to talk to anyone. Afterwards, she withdrew into herself, and it had stayed that way until she started to work at the Federal Defender Division.

They resumed having dinner occasionally, and he had tried to get close physically, but it hadn't worked out, though they'd remained good friends.

Even allowing for the fact that it was bound to take Jennifer a long time to get over the trauma of the attempted rape, Mark guessed he just had to face it: either the timing was completely wrong or he obviously wasn't her type.

Mark heard the kettle boiling and stood. Maybe it was his cop's mind, but he found himself wondering about the Buick. He flicked off the lights in the living room, went to the window and peered out. The Buick was still there.

He was about to let the curtain fall back when he saw a big black Pontiac pull up in front of his house. The driver's door opened and a man stepped out. In the wash of a streetlight Mark saw that he was maybe close to sixty, tall and distinguished looking, with silver-grey hair.

Two well-dressed young men got out of the Buick, and walked over to join the guy from the Pontiac. All three came up the pathway. The doorbell rang.

Mark had left the porch light on and he crossed to the door and peered through the fish-eye security viewer. The three men were outside the door, the silver-haired guy in the middle. They looked respectable enough, but he didn't intend taking any chances. He slid his Glock automatic from his hip holster.

'Who is it?' Mark called out, peering through the viewer again.

'Mr Ryan? My name's Jack Kelso. I wonder if we might talk.'

'Mr Kelso, it's past midnight, a little late for you and your friends to want to share a Bible reading. So who are you, and what do you want to talk about?'

He peered through the lens, saw Silver-hair bring out an ID, which he held up in front of the viewer. Mark lowered his gun.

'Mr Ryan. I'm with the CIA.'

Mark opened the door. The two younger guys wore neat two-piece suits and button-down shirts with ties, and he guessed they were CIA too.

'I apologise for the lateness of the hour,' Kelso said. 'But there's something we need to talk about. And it's rather urgent.'

Kelso offered his ID badge again and Mark examined it. The blue Central Intelligence Agency logo was on one side, inset with the American eagle. On the other side was a photograph of Kelso, taken when his hair was a little darker.

Kelso nodded to his companions. 'Agents Grimes and Fellows.'

The two men offered their CIA badges. Mark examined them and stepped back. 'I guess you had better come in.' He closed the front door and led the way into the living room. 'Take a seat. You want some coffee?'

Kelso shrugged, and said, 'Coffee would be good. Thank you.'

Mark made four mugs of Nescafé and brought them into the living room on a tray. Kelso sat in one of the easy chairs, the other two agents on the couch. Agent Grimes was about thirty, with slicked black hair and deep-set eyes. Fellows looked as if he wasn't long out of college, baby faced, with soft hands and a boyish haircut. But Mark guessed he was able to handle himself.

He handed out the coffee and sat in the last free chair. 'What's this about?'

'I'd like to talk to you about Jennifer March,' Kelso replied.

'Jennifer? Is it about the drugs bust at Kennedy?'

Kelso shook his head. 'No, it's not about any drugs bust. Would Jennifer March consider you a close friend?'

'I think you could say that.'

'Does she trust you?'

'Sure.' Mark hesitated. 'Look, why all these questions?'

'I think you already know that her father's body has been found. If I'm not mistaken, you informed her of that fact. Am I correct?'

Mark put down his mug. 'Sure, I told Jennifer. But what's that—?'

Kelso put up a hand. 'Before we proceed any further, Mr Ryan, I'd like to explain something. What we're going to talk about is *strictly* confidential. It's a sensitive matter that pertains to national security. I want your word that you won't mention the conversation we are about to have, not to anyone.'

Mark looked at Kelso, then at the other two agents. All three stared back at him. He shrugged. 'OK. You've got my word. So what's all this about?'

'The CIA, and your country, needs your help.'

Mark almost laughed. 'Why *my* help?'

Kelso sat forward. 'You know that Jennifer's father vanished two years ago. And I take it you're aware of the other tragic circumstances of that time?'

Mark nodded. 'So?'

'At the time of his wife's murder and his own disappearance, Paul March was working on a secret assignment for the CIA.'

Mark frowned. 'Jennifer never said that. He was an investment banker.'

'He was also working under cover for the CIA. Jennifer never knew.'

'Let me get this straight. You're saying her father was a spy?'

Kelso shook his head. 'All I can say is that he was involved in a highly dangerous covert international operation. I can't divulge what that was.'

'Are you implying that Jennifer's father didn't kill his wife?'

'To be perfectly honest, Ryan, I can't be one hundred per cent certain of that.'

Mark was confused. 'I don't follow.'

This time, Agent Grimes spoke up. 'You don't have to, Ryan. Just accept that lives may be in danger on account of Paul March's body turning up.'

'Whose lives? In danger from who?'

Kelso sighed. 'We can't give you those answers, Ryan.'

'You're saying very little and asking me to trust you an awful lot.'

'You're right, I am. But Jennifer needs your help. And so do we.'

'What kind of help?'

'I believe Jennifer intends to travel to Europe to identify her father's body. I want you to take some time off work—a week or so—and follow Jennifer.'

'You mean tail her?'

'It would be better if you could go with her as a companion, but if that isn't possible then we'd like you to tail her as inconspicuously as possible.'

'*Why?*'

'I'd like you to protect her. To be her guardian angel. You know Jennifer, and she trusts you. You're a familiar face. And when people get into trouble, that's exactly what they like to see. A familiar face.'

'Get in trouble? Jennifer? What the hell for?'

'Because, Ryan, someone is probably going to try to kill her.'

Mark sat there, shocked. 'Why? Who?'

Kelso shook his head. 'I can't tell you that.'

Mark thought for a moment, then said, 'Who *exactly* are you, Kelso? What do you do for the CIA?'

'I'm an assistant director of special operations.'

'What kind of special operations?'

Kelso shook his head again. 'That's need-to-know, Ryan. And right now, you don't need to know. Will you help us? Will you help Jennifer?'

'Just give me some clue, something that will make me feel like I'm not walking down a dark road. The way I see it, the CIA doesn't usually go out of its way to protect one of its citizens. Unless they're important people.'

Kelso glanced at Grimes and Fellows before he said, 'I'm compromising myself by even telling you this. But if it helps change your mind, then I will. Jennifer may be the key to helping us find a computer disk that vanished with her father. The disk contained information that's vital to a CIA investigation.'

'Does Jennifer know about this disk?'

'I don't believe she does.'

'So how can she be the key to finding it?'

'That's speculation on my part,' Kelso answered. 'The disk vanished with her father. If she finds out how he ended up dead in a glacier in the Alps, it may offer a clue to the disk's whereabouts. But other people will also want it, and they're the ones who will almost certainly want to kill her.'

'Which still tells me nothing. What's on the disk?'

Kelso sighed and shrugged. 'I'm sorry, Ryan. My hands are tied.'

'Why can't you use your own men to tail her? Why me?'

'The people who may try to harm Jennifer will smell CIA involvement a mile off. You are a legitimate friend, and a highly trained police officer, who can stay close enough to observe and protect her. I can have my men in the background, far enough away not to arouse suspicion but close enough to call on quickly. I'll ask the question one last time. Can you help me, Ryan?'

'I don't know. I've got cases I'm working on. I'm not sure if my captain—'

'Tell him you need leave. Tell him you're ill. Tell him anything you have to. If you really have trouble getting time off, tell me, and I'll see what strings I can pull. But don't tell your captain *anything* about what you'll be doing, or about the CIA's involvement. If you talk to anyone about this, I'll see to it you're writing parking tickets for the rest of your life.'

'You already made your point.'

Kelso looked directly at Mark. 'So you'll do it?'

'I'll do it because of Jennifer.'

'Thank you, Ryan. I deeply appreciate your help.'

'Would I carry a firearm?'

'Of course.'

'Do you want me to just ask Jennifer to let me accompany her?'

Kelso nodded. 'But don't push the issue. Bring up the subject casually. Tell her you think she might need moral support when she goes to identify the body, and offer to travel with her as a friend. If she says no, tail her anyway.'

'It might be a lot simpler all round if you just explained to Jennifer that she may be in danger.'

Kelso shook his head. 'Not possible, Ryan. Neither Jennifer nor anybody else must get an inkling that the CIA is involved. If they did, we'd probably put Jennifer in worse jeopardy and ruin any hope we have of finding the disk.'

'So what exactly do you want me to do?'

Kelso reached inside his pocket, removed an envelope, handed it to Mark. 'What's this?'

'Airline tickets, in your name. They're open, business class.'

'You must have been pretty damned sure I'd agree.'

'Just prepared,' Kelso said. 'My cellphone number's inside the envelope. Call me after you've talked to Jennifer. There's also five thousand dollars in cash, for expenses. And a Visa credit card in your name. Just sign the back and don't worry about any amounts you charge. But naturally, I'd appreciate receipts for any costs you incur, so we can keep Uncle Sam happy.'

Mark looked at the envelope. 'It seems you've got everything planned.'

'Have you ever been to Switzerland, Ryan?'

'In my dreams.'

'You'll love it.'

Switzerland

CHUCK MCCAUL stood on the viewing promontory at the Furka pass and thought: *Awesome!* Ahead of him, beyond the granite promontory wall, jagged lines of snowcapped crags filled the horizon, tinted by the sun's dying light. Down below, he saw the Audi strain up the steep, winding road from the pass.

His own hired Renault was parked nearby, and near the promontory there was a souvenir store for the tourists who came up here in season, but its shutters were down and locked, the place deserted, and McCaul was alone. The Furka glacier was behind the store, a vast oasis of blue ice.

The Audi made it up the last bend and came to a halt beside the Renault. A man wearing a green padded windcheater stepped out, a Nikon camera slung over his shoulder, and smiled as he came over. 'Mr McCaul? I'm Emil Hartz, from the *Zürich Express*. I'm sorry now we didn't meet somevhere varmer.' Hartz spoke excellent English, but he pronounced his W's like V's.

McCaul shrugged. 'Well, you said you wanted some shots near a crevasse.'

'So I did, and I thought this place might be perfect.'

The man was tall, wore glasses and had thick black hair, which looked like a pretty lousy-fitting wig. McCaul said, 'So what exactly do you want to do?'

Hartz smiled. 'As the glacier is out of bounds, I thought some shots of you there vould be just as good.' He pointed over to where the glacier ended. A white fountain of ice toppled over the edge of a precipice. There was a sheer drop down to the Furka valley, almost a thousand feet below.

'It's pretty dangerous out there, sir. And I didn't bring any safety gear.'

'Don't vorry, I'll make sure you're not in any danger. But I'd like a dramatic shot for the readers. It will be perfect vith the ice in the background.'

McCaul thought for a moment and shrugged. 'OK. When you phoned me at the hotel you mentioned you'd pay a fee. How much had you got in mind?'

Hartz took out a notebook. 'That can be discussed later. So, tell me, did you notice anything unusual about this corpse?'

'No, I couldn't see it clearly through the ice.'

'Did the police find anything on the body? Papers? Documents?'

'I think they had to wait until the guy thawed out to check his pockets and clothes. But I found a rucksack in the crevasse, right next to him, and I believe there was a passport inside in the guy's name. Paul March.'

'Really?' Hartz scribbled away. 'Anything else in the rucksack?'

'Clothes, I think, but the cop in charge, Captain Caruso, can tell you more.'

'Just for the record, Mr McCaul, vhat's your age?'

'Twenty-one.'

'And your address in America, so I can send you a copy of the article.'

McCaul told him. Hartz smiled and said, 'I've been to New York many times. Great city. You live there vith your family?'

'Just my old man.'

'Is he a climber, too?'

'No, he's a private investigator.'

'Really? How interesting.' Hartz finished jotting, then put away his notebook. 'Right, now let's get some pictures.'

As McCaul followed him towards the precipice, Hartz checked his Nikon for the light. The sun was fading fast. McCaul's accident had left him just a little frightened of mountaineering. Fifteen feet away from the sheer drop, he thought he'd gone far enough. 'Is this OK?'

'Excellent.' Hartz shot a couple of frames. 'Now step back a little, Mr McCaul. And smile, please. Not a vide grin, but try to look slightly amused.'

Slightly amused? How could you look slightly amused with a thousand-foot drop only a few steps away? McCaul glanced down towards the Furka pass and said nervously, 'I think I'm close enough, sir.'

'Fine. Now, look at the camera. Don't move.'

McCaul remained still. It was the first time he'd have his photograph in a newspaper. He'd told his old man about it on the phone that morning.

Hartz clicked a couple more shots, then came over and said, 'That's it. I think I have everything I need.'

'What about the fee you talked about?'

Hartz directed a long, thoughtful look towards the deserted valley, then looked back up and smiled. 'Oh, I'm afraid there won't be one.'

McCaul was puzzled. 'I . . . I don't understand.'

'I'm sure you don't; it's rather complex. And you're a pretty dumb young man to agree to meet a stranger in a desolate place like this, wouldn't you say?'

McCaul noticed that Hartz no longer pronounced his W's like V's. And he noticed something else, a sudden, chilling stare in Hartz's eyes. Something was clicking in McCaul's brain. 'You're . . . you're not a reporter, are you?'

'Most definitely not.'

McCaul turned ashen. 'Hey, what's going down here, man?'

Hartz's hand came up quickly. It took the slightest push for McCaul to lose his balance. He fell back, slid over the ice towards the precipice, his cry echoing round the mountains as he went over the edge and dropped like a stone.

Hartz smiled. 'I'm afraid you are.'

New York

IT WAS ALMOST NOON when Jennifer pulled up outside Mark's house. Mark opened the door with wet hair and only a towel round his waist, as if he had just stepped out of the shower. He looked embarrassed, but glad to see her.

'You're a little early. Come on in.' He led her into the living room and Jennifer saw that the place was in disarray. Mark smiled when he noticed her looking at the mess. 'I promise you it isn't always like this.'

'No?'

'Sometimes it's worse.'

Jennifer laughed and Mark said, 'Why don't you make coffee while I get dressed, and then we can talk?'

'Done.' She watched Mark as he left the room. He had a good body, well proportioned with muscular legs and broad shoulders. His looks stirred something in her that she refused to acknowledge.

He had phoned that morning and asked her to call by to discuss something. She was still wondering what it might be as she made the coffee. She had just finished when Mark came in wearing jeans, a white T-shirt and sneakers.

'Why don't we go into the living room, Jenny?'

She sat on the couch, and Mark in the easy chair opposite. She sipped her coffee and put down her cup. 'I'm glad I got the chance to see you before I left because I've got a favour to ask.'

He seemed surprised. 'Really?'

'While I'm gone I'd like to leave your number with the Cauldwell in case there's any problem with Bobby. I'll have my cellphone with me so you can call me in Europe at any time, if you need.'

She saw Mark go noticeably red. He hesitated. 'Sure . . .'

'You're certain it's not a problem?'

'No . . . I could handle it.'

'You still haven't told me why you called.'

'Did you make your travel arrangements?'

'I fly to Zürich tomorrow, from Newark. I've rented a car and I'm going to drive down to Varzo. Why?'

'That's what I wanted to see you about, Jenny. I've been thinking, how would you like some company?'

'You mean you'd want to come to Europe with me?'

'Sure.'

'But why on earth would you do that?'

Mark shrugged. 'Identifying your father's body is going to be traumatic, so I thought maybe you might need some emotional support. I figured I could arrange some time off and book a ticket this afternoon. What do you say?'

Jennifer sat back, surprised. 'That's very kind of you. I appreciate the offer, but I'd appreciate it even more if you were here for Bobby while I'm away.'

'I could have someone fill in for me if Bobby needs help.'

'But Bobby's not happy around people he doesn't know.'

'Think about it, Jennifer.'

Jennifer declined. 'It's too much to ask. And thanks for offering, but I think it's something I need to do alone.' She stood. 'And now I'd better be going. I've still got to pick up my tickets and pack.'

Mark looked disappointed as he led her to the door. 'How long are you going to be away?'

'I'm not sure. Three or four days, but I left my ticket open.'

'What time does your flight leave tomorrow?'

'Nine fifteen p.m. I get into Zürich before noon the next day. You could come with me to the airport if you like.'

Mark blushed. 'I just remembered, I've got something on.' He kissed her on the cheek. 'Good luck.'

'Thanks. The Cauldwell will be in touch if there's any problem.'

Jennifer went down the path and climbed into her car. Mark was standing in the porch. He waved to her but had a troubled look on his face. Jennifer drove away with the uneasy feeling that he was keeping something from her.

LOU GARUDA was pretty tanked up after five Jamesons and three Buds, and looked as if maybe he needed an ambulance to take him home, not a cab.

Garuda was a cop with a reputation as a ladies' man, part Hispanic, darkly handsome, with sleek brown hair. The beachside tavern had a happy hour between five and seven, all drinks half-price, but what put the cherry on the cake for Garuda were the three strippers dancing on the bar.

At thirty-eight, Garuda had been hitting the liquor hard for the last couple of years, which partly explained why he was no longer a detective but back behind a desk as a community officer with the Long Beach Police Department, pushing papers, which bored him out of his tree. He didn't see Ryan come up behind him, but he felt the gentle pat on the back.

'Hello, Lou. It's been a while.'

He turned, saw Ryan standing there, a pleasant smile on his face. They knew each other from way back, when Garuda had served with the NYPD and they'd been patrol partners for a year. Garuda grinned. 'So, you found the joint.'

'Sure, I found it.' Ryan leaned over, picked up Garuda's glass and sniffed. 'I'll take a guess and say Jameson?'

'There's a guy knows his liquor.'

'Only because it killed my old man, and cancer of the liver ain't a nice way to go.' Ryan put the glass down. 'You want to take it easy, Lou. You worry me.'

'Don't hit me with the stern lectures crap. You want a booth or a table?'

'The music's too loud. Let's take a booth.' He led the way to an empty booth at the back.

Garuda said, 'How about a beer?'

'Not for me, I'm driving.'

'So am I.'

'Lou, I catch you climbing into a car like that I'll arrest you.'

'Only kidding. I've had my bellyful. After this I'm taking a cab.'

'Good man.'

The waitress came and Lou told her he'd have a double Jameson for the road. Ryan ordered a Coke and said firmly, 'Make his a single.' Before Garuda could object he went on, 'The March case. Two years ago. You remember it?'

'I remember all my cases. But I thought you already sniffed that case inside out. You never stopped asking questions about it at the time.'

'Sure, because I knew Jennifer, and the murder happened right across the street from my folks' place. But it wasn't my case, Lou, it was yours. And I'd like to hear it again from the horse's mouth.'

The waitress came back with their drinks. Garuda took a mouthful of whiskey. 'OK, from the top. Detectives arrived at the scene about 1 a.m., fifteen minutes after the local cops got there, right after the call from your old man. We found the wife's body and the teenage son in the main bedroom. She'd been stabbed twice in the chest and once in the throat. The boy had been shot through the back, only the angle the bullet travelled, it came out the back of his skull as well as shattering part of his spine. By some miracle he was still breathing. The daughter was over in your pop's place, traumatised as hell.'

'That I already know. Go on.'

'There was no sign of a break-in. Whoever did it maybe had a key, or else they were real professional. The girl said she'd noticed an upstairs window open, but we found no evidence of a forced entry. She was certain it was a guy who attacked her. And you know we never found her old man.'

'Your partners figured it might be the father who set it up?'

'Maybe. The guy travelled to Zürich on business, flying American Airlines. We checked with the airline, and Paul March was aboard the flight, sure, but after the plane landed, he disappeared. The Swiss gendarmes checked every damn hotel in Zürich and couldn't find him. We were left with a likely "what if". What if March arranged to have his family murdered and then did a runner?'

'What about motive?'

Garuda shrugged and swallowed some more whiskey. 'Now there you got me. There wasn't any money involved, or a skirt he'd kept hidden on the side, as far as we could tell. The insurance policy on March's wife wasn't a bundle. And whatever there was, it went to the kids.'

'So you're saying no one came up with a motive?'

'The only thing we figured was, maybe his wife or kids knew some dark secret about him. Maybe he meant to change his identity and start a new life someplace else, without his family, but had to cover something up before he left. Either way, he could have wanted to have his wife and kids bumped off.'

'There were no other suspects apart from March?'

'Not that we could find. No strangers seen in the vicinity before or right after the murder. No prints around the house, except those of the family. And there's another factor. There was a bad storm the night of the murder. The airport closed down for four hours; all flights into and out of New York were delayed. March would have had time to check in, drive back to his house and do the business, then drive back to the airport.'

'You think March would have attempted to rape his own daughter?'

'You're a cop, Mark. You know as well as I do, there's a lot of weirdos out there. It's a sick world. But my gut feeling was that he paid someone to kill his family. Maybe he meant to go to Zürich before the event, then come back and play the innocent. But the airport delay fucked up his schedule, he got scared, and he vanished in Europe and stayed hidden, with a new identity.'

'That's a lot of speculation.'

'And that's all we had, speculation. Mainly because there was something pretty weird about March. What I said about a dark secret in his past that maybe he wanted to cover up—we didn't just pluck that out of thin air.'

Ryan frowned. 'What do you mean?'

'March had no past—none that we could find. No family background, no relatives we could locate. We tried the Feds, missing persons bureaus, Interpol, you name it. No one had anything on him. March was a mystery man who appeared out of nowhere, then disappeared. The trail started a year before he met his wife. An address in some hick town in Arizona that turned out to have been a room in a cheap motel. Jennifer claimed that when she was a kid she'd found a photograph of a man wearing a prison uniform who resembled her father. The name on the photograph said Joseph Delgado. But we checked into the name and searched the prisoner data base of every US prison. None of the names we turned up had any connection to Paul March.'

Ryan frowned, shook his head. 'What about his employer?'

'Prime International Securities is a small Manhattan investment bank, very discreet and respectable. March had been employed by them for sixteen years, and was made a vice-president a year before he disappeared. But his employee history told us nothing we didn't know already. We did some snooping around his office, questioned his colleagues. But there wasn't a shred of evidence that he'd been anything other than an upstanding employee. Most of the people who worked with him knew nothing about the guy, except he was ambitious, a workaholic who kept to himself. He had no close friends, or even enemies, as far as we could discover. He had money in a couple of bank accounts, but nothing significant, and none of it had been withdrawn.'

Garuda sat back. 'And that's all I can tell you.' He took a sip of his drink.

Mark stared down at his own glass. Finally he said, 'Is that pal of your old man's still with the CIA?'

Garuda nodded. 'Yeah, I think he's still at Langley. Why?'

'You still keep in touch?'

'Now and then, but it's been a few years.'

'I need to get the run-down on someone. His name's Jack Kelso. But I need it to be discreet. Very discreet. Can you see what you can do for me?'

'Who is he?'

'Some kind of assistant director of special operations, whatever that is. I don't know what section or department.'

'I'll make a call when I get home, see what I can come up with.'

Ryan smiled. 'You sure you'll be sober enough?'

'Listen, I've been a lot worse and still found my way to the can.'

'Thanks, Lou. You want a ride home?'

Garuda shook his head. 'Why did you want to talk about the March case?'

'One of your old buddies in the detective unit told me they got word that Paul March's body had been found.'

Garuda put down his glass, stunned. '*Where?*'

'The Alps. He's been dead a long time. Frozen into a glacier.'

Garuda gave a low whistle. '*Jeez*, I guess now I heard it all.'

IT WAS JUST after eleven that evening when Mark arrived home. Ten minutes later he was packing his suitcase for the trip when he heard the doorbell ring. He went downstairs, looked through the peephole and opened the door. Kelso was standing alone in the porch, carrying a briefcase.

Mark let him in and closed the door. 'Like I told you on the phone, I tried convincing Jennifer but it didn't work.'

'A pity. However, I've confirmed your seat on the American Airlines flight to Zürich tomorrow evening. You'll be picked up from here at fifteen hundred hours by Agents Grimes and Fellows and taken to JFK. The three of you will leave on the same flight, over three hours before Jennifer's departure out of Newark on Swiss Airlines, so you'll get into Zürich airport well ahead of her.'

'What happens after I get to Zürich?'

'Jennifer's travel agent booked her a car hire at the airport. There'll also be a hired vehicle reserved in your own name, at the Avis desk.' Kelso patted his briefcase. 'Now, there are some items I need to go over with you.'

Mark led the way to the coffee table and Kelso flicked open the briefcase. Nestled in soft grey foam inside was a mobile phone, a charging unit and spare batteries. There was a Sony transceiver, and a handheld device the size of a TV remote control, with a tiny retractable aerial. Mark also noticed a pair of miniature Zeiss binoculars, and several road maps in a plastic pouch.

'You'll be familiar with most of this surveillance equipment,' Kelso said.

'And by the way, here's a photograph of Jennifer's actual hire vehicle. Take note of the licence plate.' He handed Mark a snapshot of a white Toyota four-wheel-drive, its Swiss registration plate clearly visible.

'How come you know that this is the actual vehicle she'll be driving?'

Kelso picked up the handheld device with the tiny aerial. 'It's better not to ask. But there'll be a bug planted in the jeep, a simple electronic transmitter, and this is the receiver. It gives a magnetic heading that will help you keep track of the Toyota. And if you're following Jennifer in darkness, remember that the binoculars have a night-vision attachment.'

'It seems that once again you've thought of everything.'

'I try to.' Kelso picked up the map pouch. 'Road maps of Switzerland and northern Italy. The most likely routes Jennifer will take to Varzo have been marked. There's also a map of Zürich's Kloten airport.' Kelso unfolded the airport map. 'You'll notice that a slip road next to a gas station has been high-lighted, about a quarter of a mile from the Avis pick-up area. Jennifer has to pass that point on her way out. It's the only exit, so I suggest you wait there.' Kelso placed the Sony transceiver in Mark's palm. 'One of my men will call you up on this when Jennifer's about to drive out of the airport. You'll wait until she's driven past, then follow her Toyota at a safe distance. Questions?'

'What happens if I lose her?'

'Call me or my men immediately. My number's programmed into the first memory location in the cellphone. Grimes and Fellows will be in your vicinity every minute of the day or night. If you need them, call them up on the radio. I'll be a phone call away.' Kelso replaced everything in the briefcase.

'You said I'd have a weapon.'

'An envelope in the name of Charles Vincent Jones will be left for you at the information desk at Zürich airport,' Kelso explained. 'Inside, you'll find a luggage chit and a key. Take the chit to the left-luggage desk where you'll be given a locked holdall in return. Inside, you'll find a Glock automatic and three clips of ammunition.' Kelso closed the briefcase. 'And don't worry about carrying this case through Customs. No one's going to bother you.'

MARK WAS drifting off to sleep when the phone rang. He picked up the receiver and heard Lou Garuda's voice. 'Mark? You awake?'

'I am now. What is it, Lou?'

'I made a call to that pal of my old man's down in Virginia. He's retired from the CIA, it turns out, but we chewed the cud for a time, then I mentioned this guy from the Agency I'd heard about in passing, name of Kelso.'

'Tell me.'

'My man's been out to pasture a couple of years but he'd heard of Kelso. It seems he's one of their senior honchos, and a highly respected guy.'

'Did you try to find out which section Kelso belongs to?'

'That's when the shutters came down, and I didn't press it. All my friend could tell me was that Kelso was transferred to something called special projects some years back. He didn't tell me what special projects meant.'

'Thanks, Lou. Listen, I need to ask another favour. Jennifer March's kid brother, Bobby, he's in the Cauldwell home. I need someone to call by in the next couple of days, make sure he's OK. Could you do that?'

'Sure. You mind me asking why?'

'I promised Jennifer I'd keep an eye on him while she's out of town, but it turns out I'm going away tomorrow.'

'Where?'

'I can't say.'

'How do I get in touch?'

'You can't. But I'll call you.'

There was a silence, then Garuda said quietly, 'I don't know what you're up to, Mark, but if it concerns the CIA you keep one eye firmly on your ass, old buddy, OK? Those guys are dangerous. So watch yourself, you hear?'

'I'll try and remember that.'

'Sweet dreams, amigo.'

PART TWO

Zürich, Switzerland

Jennifer approached a clerk behind the car-hire desk at Zürich airport. The man looked up and smiled. '*Guten Tag. Kann ich ihnen helfen?*'

'*Guten Tag.* My name is Jennifer March. I have a reservation.'

The clerk checked through some papers. 'How long will you be needing the vehicle, Frau March? You didn't specify.'

'I'm not sure yet. Three or four days, perhaps longer.'

'Of course, as you wish. I'm afraid we're rather short of cars today, but I've arranged a four-wheel-drive at the same rate. It's not one of our usual vehicles, but I think you'll find that it's excellent transport. Will that be suitable?'

'I guess so. I need to get to Varzo, just over the Italian border, and also the Wasenhorn mountain. How long will it take to get there?' Jennifer had made up her mind that she wanted to see where her father's body had been found.

The clerk produced a map and showed her the route. 'It shouldn't take more than four hours. You may keep the map.' He filled in the documents, accepted her credit card, and had her sign for the Toyota. Then he handed her a set of keys. 'Enjoy your stay in Switzerland, Frau March. *Guten Tag.*'

As Jennifer walked away she didn't see the clerk observe her leave, then pick up the telephone.

MARK HAD LANDED in Zürich just before 8 a.m. He'd slept only a couple of hours and felt exhausted after the eight-hour flight. He'd seen Fellows and Grimes on the plane but neither man had approached him, and once the flight had landed both of them had quickly disappeared.

Once he'd reclaimed his luggage he went swiftly through Customs, and eventually found the information desk on the arrivals floor. The envelope in the name of Charles Vincent Jones was waiting for him. The ticket and the key were inside. When he handed in the ticket at the left-luggage desk he was given a small canvas holdall with a sturdy metal lock.

He found the men's rest room and locked himself in one of the cubicles. Inside the holdall he found a Glock 9mm and three ammo clips, as Kelso had promised. When he came out of the rest room, he walked into one of the airport tourist stores and bought an olive-green loden hat with a slouched rim that partly covered his face. Then he walked into the terminal wearing the hat and a knee-length reversible raincoat he had bought in New York. He caught a glimpse of himself in a shop window. He felt kind of ridiculous but he looked like a different man. He checked the arrivals board. Jennifer's flight wasn't due to arrive until 10.55, and by the time she finished at the car-hire desk it was going to be nearly noon. He glanced at his watch: 9.15 a.m. He had plenty of time to buy himself breakfast before he found the Avis desk.

A BLACK Opel Omega was booked in his name and he handed over the credit card and filled in the forms, then found the pick-up point. The Opel was a rugged sedan with dark-tinted windows, and he stashed his luggage in the back. It was raining as he drove out of the terminal, taking the avenue that led towards the Zürich ring road. He had the map on the seat and minutes later he saw the slip road just beyond the gas station and pulled in.

He took the Sony transceiver and the tracking monitor from the briefcase, switched both on, and placed them on the seat beside him. The tracking monitor gave him a heading back towards the airport and the indicator read-out told him that the transmitter bug on the vehicle wasn't moving. Mark reckoned that Jennifer's Toyota was still in the car-hire lot, waiting to be picked up, and he switched off the monitor. Almost two hours later he was going over the route when the transceiver squawked. 'Ryan, are you there?'

Mark almost jumped. 'I'm here. Receiving you loud and clear.'

'Good. This is Grimes. Get ready, the target's on the way. Good luck.'

'Thanks.' Mark switched on the tracking monitor and saw the heading indicator change. Jennifer's vehicle was moving. Five minutes later he saw a white Toyota drive past, Jennifer in the driver's seat, looking straight ahead.

Mark started the Opel and pulled out after the Toyota.

JENNIFER DROVE onto the airport highway and headed south. An hour later she had reached the pretty lakeside city of Lucerne, then she took the E2 east along the lake, before heading south again. She began the steep climb into the Alps, through deep pine valleys and past sleepy hamlets. And then suddenly she was climbing up through the winding roads of the mountainous Furka pass. Some of the roads had no side barriers, the edges dropping away thousands of feet below. The views took her breath away, but the drive was mentally exhausting. When she descended out of the Furka, she reached Brig, the ancient Swiss gateway into Italy. She skirted the town centre and drove further south, stopping at an Alpine café for lunch.

By the time Jennifer drove into the tiny Italian border village of Iselle, the sun had come out. She passed through the border post without any fuss, the green-uniformed Italian Customs police barely scrutinising her passport, and reached the small, sleepy town of Varzo ten minutes later.

She found the local Carabinieri station with no difficulty. An old three-storey villa with mustard-coloured walls, it faced onto a tiny cobbled square. She noticed an intercom box on the wall outside. She parked the Toyota across the square, walked over and pushed the button.

Up on the verandah a couple of sleepy-looking men appeared, rubbing their eyes. Jennifer guessed she had woken them from their siesta.

A young corporal came down the steps, hastily sticking his shirt inside his uniform trousers. *'Signorina. Cos'è accaduto?'*

Jennifer didn't speak Italian. She tried to explain why she was there, but with no success. Finally, the corporal called out, and a tall man in his late forties appeared on the verandah. He came down the steps. '*Signorina*.'

'Do you speak English?'

'*Sì*, a little. My name is Sergeant Barti. How can I help you?'

Jennifer explained. The sergeant led her up the steps and into a cluttered office. He offered her a seat and went to sit behind a desk.

'You will need to speak with Captain Caruso, who is in charge of the case.'

Jennifer said, 'May I see him?'

'His office is at Turin headquarters, but unfortunately he is in Switzerland on police business.'

'I'd like to see my father's body.'

Barti shrugged. 'I'm afraid that's not possible. It is in Turin, and Captain Caruso will need to be present for the identification.'

'Then I'd like to see where my father was found.'

'It would be better to speak with the captain about that. The place is far from here, and dangerous, and it would be dark before we could get there and back.'

'Very well, I'll speak to the captain tomorrow. What time would be best?'

'In the afternoon, I think. Say two. I will telephone his office and explain that you will be arriving in Turin.' Barti rose from behind his desk.

'Is there a hotel around here where I can stay the night?'

'There are two small hotels in the town, and several just over the Swiss border. The Berghof Hotel in Simplon is very popular with visitors.'

'Thanks.' All she had got out of the man was a hotel recommendation. As she was about to go, she said, 'I believe an American found the corpse?'

'*Sì*. A young man named Chuck McCaul.'

'Could I meet him?'

'*Scusi*, that's impossible.'

'Why?'

'I'm afraid he's dead.'

FIFTEEN MINUTES later, Jennifer drove back over the border into Switzerland. The sergeant had seemed reluctant to offer an explanation about the climber's death, except to tell her that the young man had had an accident at the Furka pass, and that the Swiss police were investigating the matter.

Ahead of her the road forked left into the village of Simplon. As she checked her rearview mirror, she noticed a dark-coloured Opel fifty yards behind her. She was certain it had been behind her all the way along the winding road from Varzo. She couldn't see who was inside because the vehicle had dark-tinted windows, but she had a feeling it was following her.

Simplon was a tiny village, just a couple of long, narrow cobbled streets, with a whitewashed church at one end. There were several hotels and inns, and she pulled up in a parking lot outside one with a sign saying: BERGHOF HOTEL. As she stepped out of the jeep, the Opel drove past down the cobbled street to the far end of the village, before it turned onto the main road and disappeared.

When Jennifer went up to the reception desk of the Berghof Hotel, a young, cheerful woman was chatting on the telephone.

She finished her call and looked up. '*Ja?*'

'Do you have a single room for tonight, please?'

'I have as many as you want.' The woman smiled, her English perfect. 'It's the end of the season and the hotel is almost deserted.'

She had Jennifer fill in a registration card and then led her up to a large, oak-beamed room overlooking the Simplon valley. The view was exquisite.

'I could ask the chef to cook you something if you're hungry, Frau March?'

'Thank you, I'd appreciate it.'

'*Sehr gut.* You may eat in the dining room or the bar downstairs, but the bar's probably better, there's a bit more life.'

Jennifer showered, changed into jeans and a sweater, went down to the bar and sat in a pine booth. A log fire blazed and half a dozen men stood chatting at the far end of the bar. The woman brought her a steaming bowl of *Jägersuppe*, a plate of cheeses and cold meats, a salad and a glass of beer. When she finished her meal she noticed the men at the bar staring at her. Finally, one came over and placed a glass of white liquid on her table.

'With my compliments,' he said in fluent English. 'The local schnapps. It's not that bad so long as you drink it quickly. You're an American, I believe?'

He was in his late twenties and pleasant looking. Jennifer pushed the glass away and said as politely as she could, 'Yes, I'm an American. And thank you for the offer of a drink, but I'd really prefer to be alone, if you don't mind . . .'

The man smiled and offered his hand. 'Of course, but seeing as you're my guest, I thought I'd say hello. Anton Weber. I run the hotel.'

Jennifer flushed. 'I . . . I'm sorry.'

'No need to apologise. Will you be staying long in Simplon, Frau March?'

'No, just one night. I'm passing through.'

'A shame, really. The area is quite beautiful.'

'So I've seen. But I understand a body was discovered nearby recently.'

Weber sat down, frowning. 'You're not a journalist by any chance?'

'No. Just curious. The story seemed intriguing.'

'A young American climber named Chuck McCaul found the body in the Wasenhorn glacier. In fact, he was a guest here at the hotel, but I'm afraid he died three days ago. Fell into the Furka pass. I understand from the local sergeant that it's uncertain whether his death was an accident.'

Jennifer stiffened. 'You mean he might have been murdered?'

'I really can't say. They're still investigating the matter. A couple of detectives came by yesterday to search his room and take away his things.'

Jennifer felt a shiver go through her. 'Could I see the glacier where the body was found?'

'Of course, but you'll need a guide to get to the Wasenhorn. It isn't safe this time of year with the snow melting. May I ask why you wish to see it?'

'Just curious, as I said. And I'm sure the glacier's quite a beautiful sight. Where could I find a guide?'

Weber laughed. 'Actually, you're looking at one. Before I managed this hotel that's how I made a living.'

'Could you take me? I'll gladly pay for your time.'

Weber smiled. 'Nonsense, there's no need. For you, I'd consider it a pleasure. There's no climbing involved really, just a rather tough hike. Do you have any mountain gear with you—boots and so on?'

'I'm afraid not.'

Weber shrugged. 'No matter. I'm sure my sister Greta will loan you anything you need. She's the young woman who checked you in, and I'd say she's about your size. I'll meet you down here at six thirty in the morning.'

Jennifer lifted her glass. 'Thank you.' She sipped the schnapps. It felt like liquid fire in her throat and she winced. 'Oh my God!'

Weber laughed. 'Don't say I didn't warn you.' He stood and again offered his hand. 'It's been a pleasure meeting you, Frau March.'

MARK DROVE back into the village. He passed Jennifer's hotel and noted that her Toyota was still there. Directly across the street was another hotel. There was a car park at the back that would be perfect for keeping the Opel out of sight. He drove into it, parked and went into the reception.

'I'd like a single room.'

The receptionist looked up. 'Of course, sir. For how many nights?'

'Probably just one. And I'd like a room facing the street.'

The man frowned. 'The best views are at the back, looking out onto the Alps. Wouldn't you prefer one of those?'

Mark handed over his credit card. 'I'm sure the views are terrific, but I'd like a room at the front.'

HE SAT in his darkened bedroom, the curtains open, the Zeiss binoculars in his hands. Everything looked green through the night-viewer attachment, but he could clearly see Jennifer's car and hotel. The town was quiet, apart from the storm that had kicked up, which thundered around the mountains. He saw Jennifer closing the curtains. Now the lights had gone out in her room.

Mark put down the binoculars and closed the curtains. He flicked on a bedside light and set the travel clock alarm for seven o'clock.

There was a mini-bar in the corner of his room. He was hungry and thirsty, and groggy from the altitude. He poured a beer and a Jack Daniel's, then ate a couple of packs of peanuts, a Toblerone bar, and some hand-made liqueurs.

He opened the window, undressed and climbed into bed, feeling exhausted. The stormy mountain air that blew in through the window was like a sleeping draught, and he was asleep almost as soon as his head hit the pillow.

THE MAN drove into the village at 3 a.m. and halted outside the Berghof. It was pouring with rain as he switched off the engine. He rolled down the window and stared at the darkened hotel for several minutes.

When he was certain the street was deserted he stepped out into the downpour. He walked over to the white Toyota four-wheel-drive, took the tools from under his wet raincoat and set to work. When he finished five minutes later, he climbed back into his car and drove out of the village the way he had come.

New York

LOU GARUDA spent Monday going through his notes on the March case, but when he finished he was none the wiser. He wondered what Mark was up to that he couldn't leave him a number in case he needed to talk. He also wondered about Ryan and Jennifer March both leaving town around the same time. And then he had a weird idea. He called a number at JFK.

A woman's voice answered, 'Debbie Kootzmeyer, Customer Relations.'

'Debbie, it's Lou Garuda. I need a favour.'

'Lou, I told you before, next time my husband's gonna divorce me.'

'Not that kind of favour, babe. You still got access to passenger manifests?'

'Why?'

'I need to know if someone travelled on a flight yesterday. Maybe out of JFK, maybe out of La Guardia. A guy named Mark Ryan.'

'Lou, you know I can't give you that kind of information—'

'It's really important, Debbie. Just one name. Mark Ryan. Next time I see you, I'll make it up to you, any way you want.'

Debbie protested. 'Jesus, Lou, have you got *any* idea how many people travel through JFK and La Guardia every day? Ain't you got a flight number?'

'It's just a hunch, but try flights to Switzerland first. The guy's got an address in Elmont, Long Island. Maybe that might help.'

Debbie sighed. 'I'll have to call you back.'

Fifteen minutes later, she rang back. 'A passenger named Mark Ryan with an Elmont address travelled on an American Airlines flight to Zürich last night.'

Garuda smiled. 'Debbie, you're a sweetheart. Just check one more booking. Was there a woman named Jennifer March on the same flight?'

Garuda heard keys tapping, and then Debbie said, 'No one by that name travelled on the same flight.'

'Can you tell me *when* she travelled?'

'Lou, you're really pushing it.' Debbie sighed, tapped away at her keyboard. 'What you doing next Tuesday?'

'Why?'

'There's a possibility my husband's out of town.'

Garuda grinned. 'You're a slut, Debbie.'

'Yeah, but you love it.'

GARUDA PUT DOWN the phone, walked to the window and stared out at the towering skyline of New York in the distance. He was puzzled. Why had Ryan and the girl travelled separately? It didn't make sense. Something weird was going on.

Switzerland

JENNIFER WOKE just before six. When she drew back the curtains the sun was almost up and it was a beautiful spring morning. The cobbled village streets were covered in rain puddles after the storm. After she had showered and dressed, she went down to the dining room. A couple of places were set at one of the tables and Greta appeared a few moments later, carrying a vacuum flask of hot coffee. 'I hope you slept well?'

She always found it difficult to sleep during a storm, and that night had been no different. 'Apart from the thunder waking me a couple of times,' Jennifer confessed. 'It got pretty noisy.'

Greta smiled. 'Storms in the Alps always sound like the world's coming to an end. Anton should be with you shortly. He stayed up late, drinking with some of the locals. He tells me he's taking you up on the glacier. I'll leave some of my gear and a pair of boots outside your room. I hope they fit.'

'Thank you, you're very kind, Greta.'

'My pleasure. Enjoy your breakfast.'

Anton appeared ten minutes later, as Jennifer finished breakfast. He wore a thick woollen sweater and high socks, knee breeches and heavy boots, and he carried a backpack and a pair of binoculars. '*Frau March, guten Morgen.*'

'*Guten Morgen*, Anton. And please, call me Jennifer.'

'Jennifer it is, then. When you're ready we'll get under way. You have transport, I presume?'

'A four-wheel-drive.'

'Perfect. We'll take that, if you don't mind; it's better able to handle the mountain tracks. They can be rather muddy after a storm, you know.'

THE VIEWS were incredibly clear. The clouds had vanished and the air was perfectly still. As Jennifer drove up towards the Wasenhorn, Anton pointed out the Matterhorn and the Eiger in the distance.

'Have you any idea what the man might have been doing in the area where they found his body?' Jennifer asked him.

Anton shrugged. 'There's a long history of people using some of the more remote mountain tracks in this area as a route over the frontier, if they want to avoid the border and passport checks. Fugitives and criminals mostly. And smugglers have used the tracks for centuries.'

The steep mountain track was wide enough for only one vehicle, and was cut into the side of the mountain along a sheer precipice. The wheels skidded a little in the soft mud as Jennifer drove.

'Easy does it,' Anton said. 'But it's coming down when we really have to watch. You go too fast or skid and we might be in trouble.'

As they came round a bend a magnificent sight met them. The Wasenhorn rose majestically like some enormous ancient fossil, and then suddenly they were at the end of the track. Anton climbed out, slinging the haversack onto his back and grabbing his binoculars.

'The rest of the way's on foot, I'm afraid. But I think you're going to enjoy it.'

MARK HEARD a sound like car wheels rattling on cobble and came groggily awake. The sound of traffic came from outside his window, and voices talking in singsong Swiss-German. His head felt lousy. And then he realised why: alcohol and altitude didn't mix. The drinks he'd had last night had knocked him out. He lay there, one eye open and focused on the alarm clock: *8.05*.

He climbed out of bed frantically. He remembered the alarm going, but he must have reached over and turned it off. He stumbled to the window and looked towards the Berghof's parking lot. Jennifer's Toyota was gone.

WHEN THEY reached the glacier, Jennifer marvelled at the breathtaking sight. A sea of ice stretched before them, duck-egg blue and cracked by crevasses.

'Careful now. The ice is solid enough, but stick behind me and follow in my footsteps.' Anton led the way and pointed to a crack in the glacier about a hundred yards from the far side. 'That's the crevasse where they found the body. It's just over the Italian side of the border.'

When they came near to the spot he had pointed out, Anton said, 'Don't step too close, Jennifer. It's really quite dangerous.'

She peered down and saw that the crevasse got darker the deeper it went. 'Do you have a rope and a torch?'

'Yes, in my backpack. Why?'

'I'd like to see where the body was found. Could you let me down?'

'*What?* Jennifer . . . don't be foolish.'

She was determined. 'It's got me curious. And if the police went down there, it can't be all that difficult.'

Anton sighed. 'And I thought you were just a quiet, unassuming American tourist.' He unslung his backpack, uncoiled a nylon rope and began to hammer some stays into the snow to secure the rope. 'I'd better go down with you. I'm sure the last thing the police want is another corpse on their hands.'

THE FIRST THING Mark did was switch on the tracking monitor. The signal sounded weak and the pointer showed a heading due north. The read-out indicated that the Toyota was stationary. He consulted the map and estimated that Jennifer was somewhere near the Wasenhorn. He dressed quickly, grabbed his bag and went down to reception.

'How do I get to the Wasenhorn?' he asked the receptionist urgently.

The girl shrugged. 'You will see the signposts when you take the road north out of the village.'

Mark didn't even thank her. He ran out to the parking lot, stashed his bag in the Opel and started the engine.

THE CREVASSE was incredibly cold, like being in a deepfreeze. As Anton played the torchlight around the chamber walls, Jennifer saw the hole in the glacier where her father's body had been cut out, and she shuddered.

Anton said, 'You look quite pale. Are you OK?'

'I'm . . . I'm fine.' Suddenly she noticed a smaller hole cut into the bottom of the crevasse. 'What's that?'

Anton shrugged. 'I heard from our local police that McCaul discovered a rucksack near the body. Perhaps that is where they found it.'

'What was in the rucksack?'

'God knows.' Anton frowned. 'You know, you're really a very curious girl, Jennifer. You're sure you're not a journalist of some sort?'

'Certain.' She looked up at the mouth of the crevasse high above them, light pouring through the narrow gash from the clear blue sky, then took a long, lingering look around the frozen chamber.

'Have you seen enough?' Anton asked finally.

Jennifer shuddered. 'I think so.'

THEY SAT resting in the snow and Anton took a flask from his backpack and poured them each a cup of hot coffee. 'That ought to keep out the chill.'

'Thanks, Anton.' Jennifer looked out at the view. It was stunning: Italy lay far below them, and it seemed as if they were sitting on top of the world. 'Which direction do you think the man might have been headed?'

'God knows.'

'Where's the nearest town or village?'

Anton pointed down into the valley to the Italian side. 'Over there. A village called San Domenico, about eight kilometres away. It's part of the Alpe Veglia nature reserve. That's where McCaul was headed when he found the body. It's the normal route for crossing the glacier from the Swiss side.'

'And there's nothing in between?'

'Nothing except a mountain hut. It's called a *Berghut*, a resting lodge for climbers and hikers. The Alps are dotted with them. If the weather suddenly turns bad, having proper shelter can mean the difference between life and death. There's a *Berghut* just over the Italian side of the border.'

'Could I see it?'

Anton checked his watch. 'OK, why not? It's only a short walk.'

It didn't take long to reach the hut. It was built of stone and wood with a slate roof, was large and solid looking, and stood on a ridge overlooking the valley. Anton opened the creaking door and they stepped inside.

Thick oak beams ran overhead and there were a couple of bedrooms with bunk beds, and a basic kitchen. Winter wood fuel was stored against the stone walls, and visitors had carved graffiti on some of the beams.

'That's it, I'm afraid. It's nothing much,' Anton commented, and he closed the door after them as they stepped outside.

Jennifer noticed what looked like a small village some distance away, far down in the valley. 'Could I borrow your binoculars?'

'Of course.'

Jennifer focused on a walled collection of buildings overhanging a sharp precipice. She pointed it out to Anton. 'What's that?'

'The old monastery of the Crown of Thorns.'

'It's still in use?'

Anton nodded. 'It belongs to an order of Catholic monks, but there aren't many of them left and the place is neglected. A pity—I hear the cloister's quite beautiful, and it used to be famous as a sanctuary. Climbers have been known to use it as a refuge when the weather turns really bad.'

'How do I get to see the monastery?'

'Once you cross the border, it's well signposted from the main road.' He checked his watch. 'And now I really think it's time we were getting back. Greta will be expecting me at the hotel.'

AS THEY DROVE BACK down the track, Anton said, 'Remember to take it easy. This part of the track is pretty treacherous.'

Jennifer drove slowly, but suddenly the track dipped down sharply and she pressed on the brake. Nothing happened.

She pumped the brakes again but the pedal was soft. The Toyota picked up speed on the downward slope.

Anton said, 'You're going too fast, Jennifer. *Use the brakes.*'

'I am. They're not working.' She shifted down a gear and the jeep slowed for a few seconds but then coasted faster and faster. It was becoming difficult to control the vehicle. Her heart pounded, and she was afraid to take her eyes off the road. 'Pull the handbrake!' she shouted at Anton.

Anton reached over and tugged the handbrake, but it had no effect. Jennifer shifted down to first gear and the vehicle jerked violently and slowed, but suddenly she saw a sharp bend ahead, curving round the edge of a rocky cliff. Her heart hammered. 'Oh God!'

Anton covered his eyes with his arms and screamed, '*Mein Gott!*'

Jennifer yanked the steering wheel to the right and the jeep skidded towards the edge of the cliff, which dropped away hundreds of feet below.

She knew she was doomed. Anton overcame his shock, frantically yanked the wheel from her hands and tried to steer them out of the skid, but it was useless, and the jeep kept careening across the track towards the edge.

Suddenly a blue Nissan four-wheel-drive came out of nowhere, moving slowly round the blind uphill curve of the road. There was a deafening crash of metal as the two vehicles collided and the Toyota came to a grinding halt. Jennifer was wearing her seat belt but the force of the crash lifted her bodily and her head struck the roof.

As the Toyota settled, Anton let out a sigh of relief. '*Gott im Himmel!*'

He looked white with shock but seemed uninjured. Jennifer sat there for several moments, too traumatised to speak or move, before she unbuckled her belt and climbed shakily out of the Toyota. When she looked towards the cliff she saw a frightening drop to a rocky valley below. The accident had saved them. She suddenly felt dizzy, and when she turned back she saw the driver step out of the Nissan, steam rising from its mangled hood.

'Are you OK?' The man's accent sounded American. He was good looking, ruggedly built, and appeared to be in his fifties. He wore a parka, jeans and suede desert boots. He came over to her. 'I asked are you OK?'

Jennifer blinked. When she tried to answer the words wouldn't come. She realised she was still in shock. Then suddenly the man's face went out of focus, everything became foggy and she fainted.

WHEN SHE CAME TO, Anton was gone and the man was kneeling over her, dabbing her forehead with a damp handkerchief. 'How do you feel?'

Jennifer felt a throbbing ache in the top of her skull. 'I . . . I don't know.'

'Let me have a look.' The man held her face, lifted her eyelids and looked into her eyes. He held up his fingers. 'How many fingers do you see?'

'Three.'

'Good. Just lie still.' He walked over and examined the Toyota, then his own vehicle. The Nissan's fender had buckled and a front wheel arch was crushed in against the tyre. 'Mine's bad enough, but yours is a damned mess.'

'Where's . . . where's Anton?'

'Your friend? Gone down the track on foot to phone for a doctor. He seemed pretty concerned, but I think you're going to be OK. You've just got some mild concussion and a bump on your head the size of a camel's hump.'

'What . . . what happened?'

The man nodded towards the cliff edge. 'I crashed into you. And lucky I did, by the looks of it. You came down that track like you had the Fifth Cavalry after you. What were the two of you trying to do—kill yourselves?'

'My brakes failed.'

'Your friend didn't mention that.' The man frowned, went over to the Toyota and pumped the brake pedal a couple of times before sliding under the chassis. He reappeared a few minutes later, wiping his hands. 'If you ask me, those brakes have been tampered with.'

Jennifer sat up. Her head throbbed. 'What do you mean?'

'The hydraulic hoses have been loosened. The brake fluid slowly leaked away every time you put your foot on the pedal. If the vehicle was old, then maybe those hoses could have worked loose. But that Toyota's pretty new. It looks to me as if it was done deliberately.'

'But . . . but why?'

'We can worry about that later. Where do you think your friend has gone for help?'

'I don't know. Maybe back to Simplon. I'm staying at the Berghof Hotel.'

The man looked surprised. 'I was headed there later myself. I think maybe we'd better try and get you to the hotel and not waste time waiting for your friend to return. With a little luck, maybe I can get this baby going.'

He went round to the back of his Nissan and came back with a sturdy metal wheel brace. He jammed the brace under the wheel arch, put his foot against the tyre and pulled hard on the brace. The muscles in his arms bulged with the effort. Finally he managed to free the tyre from the twisted metal.

'OK, let's try it.' He climbed in and the Nissan started first time. He carefully reversed away from the cliff, then jerked on the handbrake and climbed out. 'Looks like we're in business. Can you stand?'

'I think so.'

He helped her to her feet and made her take a couple of steps.

Jennifer's head still throbbed but the dizziness had gone. 'I . . . I . . . never thanked you. If you hadn't driven up the track when you did Anton and I could have been killed.' She offered her hand. 'I'm Jennifer March.'

The man's eyes narrowed the instant he heard her name, and he didn't shake her hand. He looked angry as he picked up the wheel brace and tossed it into the cab. 'I know who you are. You're Paul March's daughter. Now let's get you out of here, and then I think we need to talk.'

Jennifer was totally confused. 'Who . . . who are you?'

'My name's Frank McCaul. Chuck McCaul was my son.'

It took a moment for the name to register with Jennifer. 'The . . . the climber who died at the Furka pass?'

'My son didn't just *die*. He was murdered.'

'*STILL, BITTE.*'

Jennifer winced. Her skull felt painfully sore. She sat on the bed in her hotel room as the local doctor put a dressing and sticking plaster on her head while Greta looked on. The doctor said something in rapid German.

Greta translated. 'He says if you start to see double or the headache gets worse, you're to call him.' Greta shook her head. 'Poor Anton still hasn't got over it. But you're both alive and that's all that matters. I think you should rest here for a little while. It would be better, *ja*?'

Jennifer agreed, but ten minutes later, when Greta and the doctor had gone, she was bored lying on the bed. She got up and put on her sweater. She still felt a little shaken as she went down to the bar. The place appeared empty, Anton and Greta were nowhere to be seen, but then she saw McCaul sitting alone at the end of the bar, a bottle of Scotch in front of him.

He looked over. 'Feeling any better?'

'A little.' Beyond the panoramic windows Jennifer saw that a shroud of heavy fog had rolled in over the mountains. 'Where's Anton?'

'He seemed concerned when I told him about your brakes, so he went to see the local police sergeant. I guess he'll want to question you later.' McCaul picked up his Scotch. 'Want a drink? You look like you could do with one.'

'Thanks.'

McCaul fetched another glass from behind the bar and poured her drink.

Jennifer said, 'I'm really sorry about your son.'

It was all she could think of saying. She saw McCaul's face tighten with grief. 'It hasn't been easy. Chuck was my only child.'

'I'm . . . I'm sorry,' Jennifer repeated. 'Can I ask how you knew about me?'

McCaul sounded suddenly harsh. 'Because I made it my business to know.'

When he didn't elaborate, Jennifer asked, 'Why are you so certain your son was murdered?'

McCaul put his glass down. 'The evening before he died, Chuck phoned me in New York. He said a reporter named Emil Hartz from the *Zürich Express* wanted to interview him up at the Furka pass about finding the body. When I got the call from the Swiss police to tell me my son had died up at the Furka, I phoned the newspaper in Zürich and asked to speak with the reporter. Guess what? No one named Emil Hartz works for them, or with any of the other Zürich newspapers I contacted.'

'Maybe your son made a mistake about the reporter's name?'

McCaul shook his head. 'I asked if any of their other reporters might have made the call. None of them did. Besides, this Hartz had promised Chuck a fee for the interview. The newspaper said they would never have done that.'

Jennifer paled. 'Did you tell the Swiss police all this?'

'Sure. Not that it helped much. In fact, when we crashed I was on my way up to the glacier to see where Chuck had found the body. I intend to investigate his death for myself.'

'Why would you want to do that?'

'Because I'm a private detective. And my intuition tells me there's something weird about all this. Maybe you could tell me more.'

Jennifer blushed. 'Are you suggesting *I* might be involved?'

'Not until I know any better. But finding that corpse up on the mountain is about the only reason I can think of why Chuck was murdered.'

Jennifer put her glass down. 'You're beginning to make me feel like I'm a suspect. If you don't mind, I have to see about my jeep.'

As she turned to go, McCaul gripped her arm. 'I've been a private investigator for ten years, and before that I was a cop. You get to know when things smell bad. And this whole business smells worse than a cow shed. First your father's body is found, then Chuck dies. And now maybe someone's trying to kill you. Is there anything you're not telling me?'

Jennifer flushed. 'Let go of my arm, please. I'm sorry about what happened to your son. But I don't know any more about this than you.'

McCaul let go. 'Then how about I ask you a favour?'

'What?'

'I checked with the Carabinieri. They say you've made arrangements to see your father's body. I'd like to go along.'

'I'm sorry, but this is a personal matter.'

McCaul continued to stare at her. 'It's personal for me too.'

'Then you'd better ask the Italian police yourself. Good day, Mr McCaul.'

MARK WAS hopelessly lost. He had driven up three different mountain tracks and found himself in dead ends. He tried calling Grimes on the radio but all he got was heavy static. The cellphone didn't work either: when he tried to contact Kelso the service was completely dead. To make matters worse, a fog had begun to descend, and it had started to drizzle. Halfway up another rocky track, as he came round a bend, he suddenly saw Jennifer's white Toyota.

He pulled over, switched off the engine and climbed out. The Toyota was perilously close to the edge of a cliff but there was no sign of Jennifer. It looked as if there had been an accident; the jeep's chassis had been badly damaged, and there were gashes of blue paint on the white bodywork.

As he examined the damage, he noticed a pool of brown liquid under the right front wheel. He slid under the vehicle and saw that a hydraulic hose was loose, and brake fluid had seeped round the screw thread.

He stood as he heard a car coming up the track, then a police Volkswagen came round the bend and halted. A burly Swiss officer stepped out. He looked over at Mark's Opel and raised his eyes. '*Wer sind Sie?*'

'Sorry, but I don't speak German.'

'Are you English?'

'American.'

'I'm Sergeant Klausen. What are you doing here?'

'I saw the jeep and thought there'd been an accident and stopped to see if I could help. Do you know what happened?'

The sergeant scratched his head. 'There's been an accident, all right. An American lady had a narrow escape. A vehicle crashed into her, and lucky for her it did or she would have gone over the edge. Her jeep looks *kaput*.'

Mark tried not to appear overly concerned. 'Is she OK?'

The sergeant shrugged. 'The other driver took her back to Simplon. She had a few bruises, but I believe she's fine.'

As Mark walked back to the Opel, he saw the sergeant kneel down and examine under the Toyota. Mark was curious and went back. 'You need a hand? I happen to know something about cars.'

The sergeant grimaced. 'Are you a mechanic?'

'No, but I know about engines.' Mark pointed to the pool of brake fluid. 'Some hydraulic fluid's leaked out because the brake line has worked loose.'

'The man who crashed into the American lady thought the brake line had been loosened deliberately.'

Mark looked at the flakes of dark blue paint embedded in Jennifer's white Toyota. 'What kind of car was the guy driving?'

The sergeant looked at him suspiciously. 'A Nissan four-wheel-drive. Why?'

Mark shrugged. 'No reason.' Before the policeman could say another word, he walked back to the Opel, climbed in and drove back down the track.

JENNIFER STOOD at her bedroom window, watching a curtain of fog and rain descend over the Alps. What McCaul had said about her brakes being tampered with disturbed her. *Who would have done such a thing?* She remembered the dark-windowed Opel that had followed her into the village. Maybe McCaul was right. Maybe someone *had* tried to kill her. But *why*?

She thought about McCaul. She knew he must be going through terrible grief, having lost his son. She remembered what it had been like when her mother died. First disbelief, then anger, and then a livid need for revenge. She felt irritated by the way McCaul had treated her like a suspect, but she understood his emotions. Suddenly remorse got the better of her.

She went back downstairs to the bar and found him standing at a window, staring out at the mountains, smoking a cigarette. His eyes looked wet.

She said softly, 'Are you OK, Mr McCaul?'

McCaul nodded. 'I'm sorry I was harsh. I'm just impatient to find answers. And call me Frank. It's bad enough the Swiss being so formal.'

Jennifer went over to join him. 'Will you tell me how you knew about me?'

'Easy. When I had no luck with the Swiss, I called a detective friend at Carabinieri headquarters in Rome. He filled me in on the investigation, as much as he could, and mentioned you'd be identifying your father's body.'

'Were you serious about someone tampering with the brakes?'

'I'd say it's a possibility, but it might be difficult to prove. With all that rough terrain, it might appear that the brake hose worked itself loose.'

'Maybe I'm paranoid, but I was sure a car followed me here yesterday.' She explained about the Opel.

'Did you see the licence number?'

'It didn't occur to me to notice.'

McCaul shrugged. 'Maybe it's nothing. But if you see it again, it might do no harm to get the licence number and tell the cops.'

Jennifer hesitated. 'If you still want, and for what it's worth, you can come with me when I identify my father's body.'

'Why the change of heart?'

'I think I owe it to you after what happened this morning. Do you think your jeep could make it to Turin?'

'Let me worry about that.'

'I'll call the detective in charge of the case and try to explain.'

As Jennifer turned to go, McCaul said, 'You mind me asking what your father was doing up on the Wasenhorn when he died?'

'I honestly don't know. My father disappeared two years ago. I've never seen or heard from him since.'

'I guess that must have been tough on you.'

'Getting over the grief wasn't easy, though at least now I'll have some kind of closure. But I'm really not looking forward to the identification.'

MARK PULLED UP outside the Berghof Hotel. There was no sign of a blue Nissan in the parking lot and he tried to figure out what to do next. He was tired of the deception of tailing Jennifer, and after seeing the accident scene he wondered whether it was time to put an end to the whole charade.

But where the hell were Kelso and his men? He'd tried the radio again and got nothing but static, and the cellphone service was still down. He decided to tell Jennifer the truth and worry about the consequences afterwards. He stormed into the hotel and saw a woman behind the reception desk.

'I'm looking for Jennifer March. She's a guest here.'

'Frau March left for Turin half an hour ago. Are you a friend of hers?'

'Yes. But the police told me she had an accident . . .'

'You heard?' The woman shook her head. 'She's lucky to be alive. She left with Herr McCaul. He saved her life when he crashed into her jeep.'

Mark wondered where he'd heard the name before. 'Who's McCaul?'

'An American, like yourself. His son died up on the Furka pass. A terrible tragedy. He was a guest here at the hotel. It was quite a strange twist of fate.'

'What do you mean?'

'The young man discovered a body up on the Wasenhorn a few days ago.'

Chuck McCaul. The climber who had found Paul March's body. But now the woman was telling him that Chuck was dead. Mark wanted to ask her more, but there wasn't time. 'You say they left half an hour ago?'

'At least that.'

Turin

THE CARABINIERI headquarters was a modern grey-brick building, four storeys high, with an underground car park. McCaul parked the Nissan across the street and they went up the steps to reception. Jennifer asked for Caruso.

A minute later a small, overweight man appeared. He had a bushy moustache and grey eyes. He shook Jennifer's hand and said, 'I'm Captain Caruso, signorina. We spoke earlier on the telephone.'

Jennifer introduced McCaul and Caruso shook his hand. 'I was sorry to hear about your son's death,' he said. He was puzzled as he turned to Jennifer. 'But forgive me, do you *know* each other?'

'We met this morning. Captain, is there somewhere we can talk?'

'Of course, upstairs in my office.'

It was on the second floor. A red file was open on the desk and there was a photograph in a silver frame of Caruso and a handsome, dark-haired woman.

'You said you spoke with the Swiss police about Chuck's death,' McCaul said.

Caruso looked at McCaul. '*Sì*, yesterday.'

'What did they tell you?'

'That they believe his fall was an accident.'

McCaul said angrily, 'That's horse shit. It was murder.'

Caruso raised his eyebrows. 'And what makes you say that?'

McCaul tossed his business card on the desk. 'I'm a private detective, and there are a couple of things about Chuck's death that just don't add up.'

Caruso studied the card, then said, 'The Swiss examined the scene of his death, and they are usually very thorough. They found no evidence to suggest murder. There were no footprints, apart from your son's.'

'Footprints in the snow are easy to get rid of.'

'The Furka pass is quite dangerous, Signore McCaul. There have been many accidents over the years when tourists have fallen to their deaths. Is it not possible your son had an unfortunate accident?'

'I told you, Chuck didn't have an accident. If anything, he would have been more careful after his fall. And there's something else you should know. Someone may have tried to kill Jennifer.'

'Is this true, signorina?'

'The brakes on my jeep may have been tampered with.' Jennifer told him what had happened that morning.

Caruso scribbled in a notebook. 'Most strange. Can you think of anyone who might want to harm you, Signorina March?'

'No, I can't.'

Caruso shook his head. 'What happens on Swiss soil is outside my authority. However, I will ask that these matters are investigated thoroughly.'

McCaul was about to speak again but Caruso raised his hand. 'We are forgetting the reason for this meeting. Signorina March, you are here to identify your father's body.' Caruso picked up the red file on his desk. 'Just one more thing, signorina.' He opened the file and Jennifer saw a passport, which Caruso opened on the photograph page. 'Is this your father's passport?'

Jennifer swallowed. Her father looked just as she remembered him: dark hair, blue eyes, a smiling, handsome face. 'Yes.'

Caruso stood. 'Thank you. And now, if you would come this way, we are expected at the morgue.'

A WHITE SHEET was draped over a human form on a stainless-steel table in the centre of the autopsy room. A small, cheerful man with a grey goatee beard and metal-rimmed glasses was scrubbing his hands at a washbasin when they entered. He dried himself, came over, and Caruso introduced them.

'This is Vito Rima, our forensic pathologist.'

'A pleasure to meet you.' Rima shook their hands.

'How . . . how did my father die?'

'In my opinion, he probably froze to death,' Rima answered. 'There were bruises on his chest, arms and legs, which may have been caused when he fell into the crevasse. The autopsy will tell us more. However, many of the tests that determine time of death depend on body and organ temperatures, and obviously they are impossible when the corpse has been frozen. But the belongings we found should help prove that your father died almost exactly two years ago.'

'I will explain later,' Caruso told Jennifer, 'after our business here is done.'

Rima slipped on a pair of surgical gloves and led them to the steel table. He gripped the edge of the white sheet, his eyes asking Jennifer whether she was prepared. She nodded.

As Rima started to pull back the sheet, Jennifer closed her eyes, suddenly unable to watch. In her mind she saw her father as she remembered him, saw him come up the garden path with open arms and smiling face.

She felt McCaul's hand gently grip her waist. 'Take your time, Jennifer.'

She forced herself to open her eyes, and looked at his face. His features were distorted, his skin the palest white, and his blue eyes were open and stared up at the ceiling. Overcome, Jennifer looked away.

Caruso said quietly, 'Jennifer March, I must ask you formally to identify the body you see before you. Is this your father, Paul March?'

This time Jennifer took a long hard look at his face.

'Signorina, is this man your father?' Caruso repeated.

Jennifer trembled, stared down at the corpse, the words spilling out in a torrent. 'I've never seen that man before in my life.'

'HOW ARE you feeling?'

Jennifer looked at Caruso as they sat in his office. 'Shaken, but I'll be OK.'

Caruso handed cups of coffee to her and McCaul, but Jennifer ignored hers. She said to Caruso, 'What was the man doing with my father's passport?'

'For now, that is a mystery, signorina.'

'Where exactly did you find it?'

'In the rucksack. There was also an automatic pistol.'

'Could I see what else you found?'

'Of course. I have to tell you, signorina, some of it has me puzzled.'

THE WHITE FIAT telecommunications van pulled up 100 yards from the Carabinieri headquarters. Two men in blue overalls sat in the front seats. The passenger's cellphone rang, and he took the call. The conversation lasted less than ten seconds, then he switched off the phone, and the driver started the van and drove across the square to the mouth of the HQ's underground car park, where a corporal was on duty.

The driver handed over a company ID and a work sheet, as he said in Italian, 'We've got some phone lines to check. It shouldn't take long.'

The corporal examined the ID and work sheet. 'Who requested this work?'

The technician shrugged. 'Some bastard of a captain, no doubt.'

The corporal smiled, handed back the ID and lifted the barrier.

CARUSO SLIPPED ON a pair of rubber surgical gloves and removed the contents of the evidence box. Each item was individually wrapped in a clear plastic bag: a heavy blue parka, a white woollen scarf, a green sweater, thick woollen trousers, climbing boots, and a vest and underpants. There was also a canvas rucksack, and in two other plastic bags were more clothes and an automatic pistol. Caruso opened the one containing the clothes: a white silk shirt and striped tie, a pair of black, patent-leather shoes, a pale blue suit.

'We found these in the rucksack. They are the kind of clothes a business-man might wear, and it seems this man had expensive tastes. The suit is American, and the shoes are Italian and handmade. The shirt is English, and made of silk. What's wrong, Signorina March?'

Jennifer stared at the clothes, resisting the urge to touch them. 'I . . . I think some of these belonged to my father. I'm almost certain.'

'What about the other belongings? Do you recognise any of those?'

'No, only the clothes from the rucksack.'

Caruso frowned. 'I would like you to look again at your father's passport. Do you have any doubts it's him in the photograph?'

He opened the red file, placed the passport on the desk, and Jennifer studied the photograph again. 'No, it's definitely him.'

'Your father and the dead man have the same hair colour and face shape, and would appear to be about the same age, but I could not be sure they were not the same man until you identified the body. I will have our lab in Rome examine the passport to see if it is a forgery, but it looks in order.'

Caruso opened some small plastic bags and laid their contents on the desk: a slip of torn paper and two ticket stubs. He handed Jennifer and McCaul each a pair of surgical gloves. 'Put these on before you touch the evidence.'

Jennifer picked up the slip of torn paper. It was faded, and some of the numbers at the bottom of the ragged page appeared to have been dissolved, perhaps by melting ice, but the rest of the note was clearly distinguishable.

H. Vogel
Berg Edelweiss
705

'What does it mean?' Jennifer asked.

Caruso shrugged. 'H. Vogel may be a name. And Berg means mountain in German. However, there is no Edelweiss mountain in Switzerland. As for the numbers, some of them appear to be missing, but they could be anything. Part of an account number, or a phone number perhaps. Who's to say?'

Jennifer handed the paper to McCaul as Caruso showed them the ticket stubs. 'These were in the man's trouser pocket along with the slip of paper.

Two one-way railway tickets from Zürich to Brig, second class, dated 15th of April two years ago, and clipped, which could mean that the victim travelled to Brig with a companion before he made his way up to the glacier.'

Jennifer examined the ticket stubs. 'What else did you find?'

'This.' Caruso opened another evidence bag and held out a small silver key. 'It was found in a pocket of your father's clothes. Did you ever see it before?'

Jennifer's heart skipped as a memory jolted her. 'I think so.'

'Explain.'

'A month before my father vanished, I remember he was anxious about something. One day I went to see him in his study and noticed a yellow legal pad on his desk. Across the top of the pad he'd written the word "Spiderweb". It was all I had time to notice, because he realised I'd seen the pad and got angry. He said I shouldn't have been reading his private papers. Then he locked away the pad in a security box, along with a computer floppy disk.'

Caruso frowned. 'What do you think "spiderweb" meant?'

'I've no idea. But the box was one of those metal fireproof ones that they sell in business supply stores, and I remembered it had a silver key.'

'Where's the box now?'

'I searched my father's study after he vanished and couldn't find it.'

Caruso pursed his lips. 'Strange.' He hesitated. 'I learned through Interpol of the terrible crime that happened before your father vanished. It occurred to me that he may have been running from the law. That he may have killed the man on the glacier and left behind his own passport and clothes, hoping that if the body were ever found it would appear to be that of Paul March.'

Jennifer flushed and her eyes met Caruso's stare. 'Captain, I knew my father. He would never have committed murder.'

There was a knock on the door and Rima entered. 'The autopsy is almost complete. Perhaps you'd like to know what I've found so far?'

Caruso nodded. 'You'd better tell us.'

'There were no internal injuries, and the bruises look like they were caused by the fall into the crevasse. It seems the victim simply froze to death.'

'Thanks, Vito. That will be all for now.'

'You see, there's no evidence of murder,' Jennifer said as Rima left.

'It seems not,' Caruso admitted. 'But the mystery remains. Where are you both staying?'

'At the Berghof Hotel in Simplon.'

Caruso closed the red file, swiftly gathered the evidence bags and replaced them in the box, not noticing that Jennifer still held the silver key. He took a card from his breast pocket and wrote something on the back. 'My home number, in case you can't reach me here. If you have any more accidents, I would appreciate it if you called me at once.'

'Thank you,' Jennifer said, slipping the key into her bag.

'And now, I must say good afternoon.' Caruso took his jacket from the back of his chair, gestured to the photograph on his desk and smiled faintly. 'When an Italian wife cooks dinner, it is wise not to be late.' He turned to McCaul. 'I again offer my sympathy, and I assure you I will speak once more with the Swiss and ask them to look into your son's case more closely. But may I suggest that you leave the investigation to the proper authorities?'

'As a private citizen I can investigate all I want so long as I don't break the law.' McCaul's voice flared angrily. 'I mean to find whoever killed my son. No one's going to tell me to keep my nose out of this, including you, Captain.'

Caruso took the outburst calmly. 'I can imagine how you must feel. You have suffered a terrible loss. But if you insist on a personal investigation, try not to get in the way of the police.' He stuffed the red file in his briefcase. 'I will study my case notes on the evidence tonight. Perhaps there may be some small clue I've missed. If there is, I promise I will contact you at once.'

IN THE UNDERGROUND car park the two men worked quickly. They reversed the van towards a thick metal fuel pipe that ran from a massive storage tank that supplied the building's heating fuel. Next to a stairwell, they noticed the black-lettered sign with the outline of a finger, pointing up: MORTUARIA.

One of the men took a remote control device out of his overalls and used it to arm the detonator in the hundred pounds of Semtex high explosive packed under the floor of the van. The other watched the car park, clutching a silenced Beretta pistol in his pocket. Five minutes later, both men removed their overalls. They wore business suits underneath. They locked the van and crossed the car park to the stairs that led up to the ground floor. No one challenged their exit, and two minutes later they stepped out of the front entrance.

CARUSO WENT down to the basement car park and squeezed into his white Lancia. He started the engine and drove up to the exit. As he checked for traffic, he saw two men climbing into a black BMW parked across the square.

Both wore dark business suits; one was thin and blond, and the other short and stocky, his head shaved close to the skull. Caruso frowned. For a moment he thought he had passed the same two men in the car park stairwell. Perhaps he was mistaken. He thought no more about it as he swung left, out onto the square. Fifteen minutes later he was already halfway home.

MARK PULLED UP outside the HQ building and saw a blue Nissan across the square. He felt a surge of relief. He figured Jennifer was still inside the building, identifying her father's body. He noticed a trattoria that had a good view of the HQ building. He decided to have a coffee and wait there.

As he locked the Opel, he saw Jennifer come down the HQ's steps in the company of a tall, rugged man. They were no more than thirty yards away when, to Mark's horror, Jennifer suddenly glanced in his direction.

He averted his face and walked away. Sixty yards up the street, he mustered the courage to glance back. To his relief he saw that Jennifer and the man had crossed the square and entered the trattoria.

THE TRATTORIA was almost deserted. Jennifer and McCaul each ordered paninis and a glass of red wine. 'You look shaken,' he said.

Jennifer stared out of the window. 'I just saw a man as we came out of the building and he looked the absolute double of someone I know.'

'Who?'

'Mark, a friend of mine. I'd almost convinced myself it was *really* him, but that's crazy. He's back in New York.'

'What happened in the morgue probably upset you more than you realise. A shock can set your mind running wild.' McCaul excused himself to make a phone call. 'I've got to make arrangements to have Chuck's body flown home.'

'Is there anything I can do to help?'

McCaul was grim. 'Thanks, but I guess not.'

Jennifer watched him walk towards the telephone at the back of the restaurant. He looked as if the burden of his grief was wearing him down. She looked out onto the street and noticed a black Opel with dark-tinted windows parked across the square, near the front of the headquarters building. Could it be the same car that had followed her in Simplon?

McCaul came back. 'It's done. They're going to fly Chuck's body home just as soon as the Swiss authorities sign the release.'

He looked brokenhearted and Jennifer touched his hand. 'Are you OK?'

'I guess I'm just about holding up. What about you?'

'I don't know. I came here believing I was finally going to see my father, and instead I saw a stranger. But why did he have my father's passport and clothes? A moment ago I was even convinced I saw the black Opel again.'

'What are you talking about—*Jesus!*'

A tremendous explosion erupted across the street and the windows in the trattoria shattered. A violent draught of air swept through the room.

McCaul pushed Jennifer to the floor. 'Get down!'

He flung himself down beside her as a thick cloud of dust rolled in from across the square, and then they heard a sound like a heavy clap of thunder.

MARK WAS in the Opel, observing the restaurant and wondering whether Jennifer had really spotted him, when suddenly there was a burst of brilliant white light and a sound like thunder exploded in his ears.

The Opel rose several feet off the ground, then Mark felt the full force of a powerful blast and his car was turned violently on its side. As it rolled over, his skull cracked against the roof. Seconds later there was another explosion and his gas tank ignited.

WHEN THE NOISE died, Jennifer struggled to her feet. The entire HQ building was demolished. Fires raged in the debris, a vast cloud of dust rose above the building, and several cars parked across the square were in flames.

Jennifer put a hand to her mouth. 'Oh my God! What . . . what happened?'

'It sounded like a bomb went off.' McCaul was ashen.

People streamed out of nearby buildings, some screaming, others trying to help the injured. Soon the sound of sirens filled the air.

McCaul grabbed her hand. 'There's nothing we can do. Let's get out of here.'

THEY TOOK the autostrada that led north out of the city. Ten minutes later they drove off the highway and into a village, no more than a cobbled street, a church and a bar. McCaul halted at the kerb. 'Are you OK?'

'I . . . I think so.' Jennifer was shaking.

McCaul nodded towards the bar. 'I reckon we both need a stiff drink.'

Inside, a young man stood behind the counter, polishing some glasses. McCaul ordered two whiskies, and led Jennifer to a window seat.

Her hands shook as she swallowed the whisky. 'How can you be so sure that the blast was caused by a bomb?'

McCaul ignored his drink. 'Whatever ripped that building apart, it sounded like a pretty powerful explosive, and from the look of the damage whoever was inside didn't stand a chance. If it was deliberate, that would make sense.'

'What do you mean?'

'Think about it. First Chuck is killed, then your jeep is tampered with. A little while ago you thought you were being followed, and now this. All the paperwork on the case was probably stored in the building, as well as the body, the most importance evidence of all. Getting rid of both would make it almost impossible for Caruso to carry on with the investigation. If you ask me, someone doesn't want this case to go any further.'

'But why? Who'd do such a thing?'

But McCaul wasn't listening. 'Give me Caruso's card.' She handed it to him. 'Maybe now he'll believe there's something weird about this whole business.' He stood and walked towards a wall phone by the bar.

McCaul dialled several times without getting through, then put the phone down in frustration. He asked the bartender for a phone directory, searched through the pages and jotted something down, then spoke with the bartender again and came back. 'There's no reply from Caruso's number.'

'He's probably still on his way home.'

'We need to talk to him.' McCaul waved the slip of paper he'd written on. 'He's listed, and I got an address from the phone number. He lives in a village called Osoria. According to the bartender, it's half an hour from here.'

THE VILLAGE of Osoria was a jumble of stucco and cut-stone houses set below thickly forested hills. Darkness was falling, but McCaul found the street they were looking for: a winding, hilly road lined with modern detached villas. They counted off the house numbers until they found Caruso's. A gravel drive led up to a two-storey villa with a steep garden of pear and olive trees. A garage was off to the right, and a white Lancia was parked in the driveway.

McCaul climbed out of the Nissan and Jennifer followed him to the front door. He rang the bell half a dozen times, but when no one appeared he tried the handle. The door was unlocked and he pushed it open. 'Anybody there?'

When there was no reply, they stepped into a narrow hallway. McCaul opened a door to the left. They found themselves in a large, deserted living room. They moved back out into the hallway and opened another door.

As they stepped into a kitchen, Jennifer froze. The room was in disarray, chairs overturned, broken crockery scattered on the floor. A body lay face up in a pool of blood. It was the dark-haired, middle-aged woman she had seen in the photograph on Caruso's desk. She had been shot through the head.

McCaul knelt and felt the woman's wrist.

Jennifer watched in horror. 'Is she dead?'

McCaul nodded. 'But not long. The body's still warm.'

'What . . . what about Caruso?' Jennifer asked.

McCaul stepped towards the door. 'Stay here, and don't touch anything.'

'No, please, I'd rather go with you.'

They searched upstairs but there was no sign of Caruso. The bedrooms were undisturbed. McCaul found a pair of household rubber gloves in the bathroom, slipped them on, and warned Jennifer again not to touch anything. 'The police will dust the house for fingerprints.'

One of the bedrooms at the back of the villa was used as a study. Lying on top of a writing bureau was Caruso's briefcase. McCaul flipped it open. 'Remember the case file that Caruso took home? It's gone.'

Jennifer saw some papers inside, but there was no sign of Caruso's red file.

McCaul searched through the bureau's drawers. There was nothing but writing pads, domestic bills and receipts. The last drawer was locked. He found a metal letter opener in one of the other drawers and forced the lock. A pistol lay inside. It was a Beretta automatic. McCaul checked that the pistol's seven-round magazine was fully loaded and stuffed it in his pocket.

'What are you doing?'

'What do you think? I like to be prepared, Jennifer. What happened here wasn't some kind of domestic argument gone wrong.'

They went back down to the kitchen and McCaul opened the back door. When they stepped out onto the patio they saw another door leading to the garage. McCaul opened it carefully. It was pitch-dark inside and he fumbled until he found a light switch and flicked it on. A light came on overhead.

In the centre of the garage was a small red Fiat, which Jennifer guessed had belonged to Caruso's wife. She noticed a figure in the driver's seat, and recognised the face at once, though blood had congealed on his mouth and spread down his throat. It was Caruso.

McCaul opened the passenger door and felt Caruso's wrist. 'He hasn't been dead for longer than half an hour.'

Jennifer turned away, unable to look at the grisly scene.

She felt McCaul's hand on her shoulder. 'Take it easy, Jennifer.'

'I'm OK. I'll be fine.' She steeled herself to look at Caruso again. Clutched in his right hand was an automatic pistol. His thumb was still caught in the trigger guard, the gun lying on his lap, as if he had put the weapon into his own mouth and the force of the gun discharging had propelled it away.

'If you ask me, someone did a pretty neat job,' McCaul said.

'What . . . what do you mean?'

'Think about it. What I said about the scene in the kitchen not being a domestic argument gone wrong. But maybe somebody meant it to look that way. Fixed it so it appeared that Caruso killed his wife then shot himself.'

A terrifying thought occurred to Jennifer: whoever had executed Caruso and his wife might be the same people who had killed her mother. Old sorrows came rushing in, and she felt like breaking down, but McCaul took a firm hold of her arm and led her back to the house.

As they stepped into the living room again, McCaul suddenly pointed towards the window. 'We're about to have company.'

Jennifer saw a police car approaching fast from the village. The flashing blue light disappeared behind some trees, then reappeared.

'Either someone alerted the cops or they're on their way to tell Caruso about the blast. Let's go.'

'Shouldn't we wait for the police?'

'That's the last thing we want to do. They might suspect *us*. And after seeing what happened to Caruso I'd say nobody's safe around here, not even the cops. We'd better paddle this boat on our own until we figure out what's going on.'

Before Jennifer could protest, McCaul led her out to his jeep. He started the engine and shifted into gear, but left the headlights off until they had sped down the driveway and were heading in the opposite direction to the village.

'Where are we going?'

'I wish the hell I knew.'

PART THREE

Italy

Half an hour after leaving Osoria, McCaul drove into a lay-by. Dusk was falling and rain clouds gathered overhead. He took a tourist map and a Maglite pencil torch from the glove compartment.

'Shouldn't we keep going?' asked Jennifer.

'We can't just drive aimlessly. We need to find out where we are.'

Jennifer was still shaking, but she forced herself to climb out of the jeep and join McCaul as he sat and opened the map out on one of the benches.

'I've worked some weird cases in my time, but this thing takes the prize.'

'Why . . . why would anyone have wanted to kill Caruso?'

McCaul looked at her. 'It seems to me like someone's desperate to stop this investigation going any further. First the corpse is destroyed. Now the paperwork has disappeared and the detective in charge of the case is murdered.'

'What would be the point?'

'You got me there. But I reckon there's got to be something in your father's past, or even your mother's, that points us in the right direction.'

'What do you want to know?'

'Everything, Jennifer. Everything you can remember.'

'Seeing Caruso and his wife brought everything back to me,' she said. She told McCaul about the night the masked intruder broke into her home, and about her life before and afterwards.

'It sounds like you had a pretty rough time.' He put a hand on hers, then said, 'What about the security box you saw in your father's study? Is there somewhere special he might have kept it hidden?'

Jennifer shook her head. 'If there was, he would never have told me.'

McCaul was frustrated. 'We're getting nowhere with this. OK, let's think about what we *do* know. Someone using your father's passport makes his way up to the glacier, probably to cross the border illegally. But there's probably a snowstorm and the guy winds up falling into the glacier or, as Caruso suggested, he's pushed by an accomplice, who plants the passport near the body. But what were the two people doing up there? And where were they headed?'

'I stopped to look at a *Berghut* when I was on the Wasenhorn with Anton.'

McCaul looked up, confused. 'A *what*?'

'A mountain hut. It's a rest stop for climbers.' Jennifer pointed to the area on the map. 'Close by, I saw an old Catholic monastery, the Crown of Thorns. Anton said it's used by mountaineers when the weather turns bad. Whoever tried to cross the Wasenhorn that night had to be heading in the general direction of Varzo, and the monastery's the first place they would have reached.'

'What are you suggesting?'

'Someone there might remember if anyone came looking for shelter that night. We could be at the monastery in less than an hour and then find somewhere to stay in Varzo.'

McCaul got to his feet, just as rain started to drizzle down. 'OK, we'll give it a try. I guess the monastery's all we've got, apart from a bunch of questions.'

Turin

MARK CAME awake to the sound of a female voice and opened his eyes. He was in a hospital bed, apparently in a private room. A nurse leaned over him as she adjusted his pillow. '*Come sta?*'

He looked up, groggy and confused. Beside her an elderly, white-coated man with a cheerful face said something in rapid Italian.

Mark suddenly noticed Kelso standing by the door and said, 'What . . . what happened?'

Kelso came over. 'I'll explain later. Right now, the doctor wants to examine you. By the way, the nurse asked how you felt.'

'Apart from a pounding headache and ringing in my ears, pretty confused.'

Kelso translated for the doctor, who shone a small torch into Mark's eyes, then went to work with his stethoscope, before checking his pulse.

'I need an explanation, Kelso.'

'Don't you remember?'

'There was an explosion. My car caught fire . . .'

'You were pulled free. The doctor tells me you suffered some cuts, bruises and mild concussion, but your X-rays show no obvious damage.'

Mark put a hand to his throbbing forehead and felt a sticking plaster where he'd cracked his skull against the car's roof. 'How long have I been here?'

'Several hours.'

The doctor finished his examination and spoke again in Italian.

'He says you're to rest,' Kelso explained. '*Grazie, dottore.*'

'*Prego.*'

The nurse and doctor left, and Kelso pulled up a chair. 'You look like shit.'

'Spare me the concern, Kelso, and just give me the lowdown.'

'The Carabinieri headquarters is rubble. I heard they counted six dead, five of them cops, and dozens more are seriously injured.'

'What caused the explosion?'

'A local radio report suggested that a fuel storage tank near the basement may have ignited. But there's no telling with any certainty until the forensics teams have sifted through the pieces. Personally, I suspect it was a bomb.'

'A *bomb*?'

'The blast seems too much of a coincidence. If it was deliberate and someone didn't want this case to go any further, then they sure went about it the right way. I went to see the damage for myself. The basement morgue was completely destroyed and probably the corpse and any evidence along with it. Which pretty much puts paid to any swift progress being made on the case.'

'But why? Who'd want to obstruct the investigation?'

Kelso's face showed his concern. 'Let's just worry about Jennifer for now.'

'The last time I saw her she was in a restaurant across the square, seconds before the explosion.' Mark told him exactly what he had seen.

Kelso jotted in a notepad. 'Did you get the Nissan's number?'

'It's in a notebook in my jacket, wherever the hell my clothes are.'

Kelso found Mark's jacket in a locker beside the bed. He rummaged through the pockets and handed the notebook to Mark, who read off the licence number. Kelso wrote it down. 'You say this guy McCaul was at the hotel?'

'The innkeeper said he was the father of the kid who found the body on the glacier. The kid's dead.'

'So I heard. The Swiss police claim he had an accident at the Furka pass, but it seemed suspicious to me, so I'm having it looked into.'

'And there's something else.' Mark explained about Jennifer's accident. 'Someone may have tampered with the brake hose on her jeep.'

Kelso was sombre as he put away his notebook. 'We tried calling Jennifer's cellphone. If she answered, we could at least have figured out where she was by having the signal triangulated. Her phone was switched off. Until she turns it on again we haven't a hope of locating her, but we'll keep trying.'

Mark was exasperated. 'I thought your two buddies, Fellows and Grimes, were supposed to stay on my tail this morning.'

Kelso looked embarrassed. 'Their vehicle broke down.'

'You've got to be kidding me.'

'They tried to contact you on the radio, but got no response. Mountain terrain can play havoc with radio reception. By the time they got their vehicle going again they'd lost you. They found out at the inn where you'd gone and arrived at the headquarters building moments after the explosion. And in case you're wondering who pulled you from your car before it went up in flames, it was Fellows and Grimes. So maybe fate played a hand.'

'Look, Kelso, how about you telling me what's going on here?'

'I told you, it's not within my authority. So cut the questions, Ryan.' Kelso walked towards the door. 'Meanwhile, I'd better try to find out if this guy McCaul is who he says he is.'

'Kelso, wait!'

But the door closed and Kelso was gone.

DARKNESS HAD FALLEN and the rain was still pouring down. Jennifer tried to relax as McCaul drove. The truth was, she felt secure in his company, even though he was a total stranger. There was a strength about him that was reassuring, and it felt comforting to have the protection of a fatherly figure.

'Tell me about your son.' The words were out before she realised the hurt her question might cause. She saw the pain in McCaul's face, but for the next few miles he opened up to her. Chuck was his only child, whose mother had left them when the boy was five, moved to LA and never came back.

After that, he talked mainly about himself, and how he had quit the NYPD to work for a private investigation firm. 'A couple of years back I started out on my own, handling matrimonial cases mostly.'

They reached Varzo. The narrow streets of pantiled houses looked deserted in the heavy rain. McCaul drove past a broad plaza. 'You said the monastery was outside the village?'

'That's what Anton told me.'

A few minutes later, beyond the edge of the village, they saw a narrow road that rose up steeply, and a sign that said: MONASTERO. McCaul turned onto the road and drove up a hill to a tiny cobbled square. In the wash of the headlights they saw a stone cloister surrounded by mustard-coloured walls, with a pair of wrought-iron gates in the middle and an ancient bell pull beside them.

McCaul said, 'You speak any Italian?'

'No. Do you?'

'The kindergarten variety, a couple of words here and there. Better pray there's someone here who speaks English.'

They stepped out into the pouring rain, McCaul illuminating their way with the pencil torch. He yanked the bell pull and a tinkle echoed deep inside.

They heard footsteps. A figure scurried out of the monastery to the gates. It was a young monk in a brown habit, holding a torch and an umbrella. '*Sì?*'

'You speak English? *Parla inglese?*'

'*No. Non parlo inglese. Momento.*' The man darted back into the monastery. He returned a moment later in the company of an older, bearded monk.

'Do you speak English?' McCaul asked.

'Yes. I'm Father Angelo Konrad. What do you want here?'

'We need to speak with whoever's in charge.'

'The abbot is away on Church business.' The monk glanced at the Nissan parked outside the gate. 'Are you lost, or have you a problem with your car?'

'No, but maybe we could explain inside?' McCaul suggested.

'I'm very sorry, but it's late.' The monk sounded impatient. 'We have just finished vespers, and we retire early. Come back tomorrow.'

The monk made to go, but Jennifer persisted. 'Father, believe us, this is important. It may even be a matter of life or death.'

Standing there in the downpour, the monk seemed to take pity on his visitors, or perhaps curiosity got the better of him. He sighed, took a bunch of keys from under his habit, slid one into the lock and opened the gate.

He led Jennifer and McCaul across the rain-soaked courtyard. They ducked under the shelter of a darkened archway until they came to a solid wooden door at the end. Flashes of lightning exploded in the darkness and they were all drenched as they stepped inside. Father Konrad shook rain from his habit, then held up the storm lamp to illuminate the room.

'A terrible night, not helped by the fact that our electricity and telephone were knocked out by lightning. Sit down, please.' The room was a tiny office, with a floor of worn terracotta slabs. The monk placed the lamp on a desk as he addressed Jennifer. 'You said this was a matter of life and death.'

'Five days ago a body was discovered on the Wasenhorn glacier. The Carabinieri believe it had been in the ice for two years.'

The monk shrugged. 'It's not unusual to hear of such stories in these parts. But may I ask who you both are?'

McCaul made the introductions and offered his card.

Konrad studied it. 'I don't understand. Why should an American investigator be involved in this matter?'

'We can talk about that later. The fact is, the man who died may have had an accomplice when he tried to cross the glacier.'

'Perhaps there was a blizzard that night,' Jennifer explained. 'We think the accomplice could have headed for the monastery. I'm told it's not uncommon for climbers to look for shelter here in bad weather.'

Father Konrad nodded. 'True, but I'm not sure I follow.'

'Do you keep a record of visitors?'

'*Sì*, the abbot keeps a record in his journal. The journal for two years ago is probably stored in the cellar archives. But it is unlikely that every visitor has been recorded.' Father Konrad looked impatient. 'Where is all this leading?'

'Would it be possible for you to check your records, Father?'

Father Konrad firmly shook his head. 'Signorina, it's late, and on a night like this I'm in no mood to go searching in the cellars.'

'Father, I wasn't misleading you when I said it was a matter of life and death. People have already died because of this.'

Father Konrad was baffled. 'Because of what?'

'I can't explain why exactly, but I can tell you this. If I told the police you may have information that's important to their investigation, they'd be swarming all over the monastery, keeping you up all night.'

'This is preposterous,' the monk spluttered. 'We are simple men of the cloth here. We have done no wrong. For what reason would they do that?'

Jennifer grabbed the storm lamp from the table. 'It's complicated, Father. But if you help us I'll forget about contacting the police for tonight.'

JENNIFER, MCCAUL and Father Konrad descended a winding granite stairway to the monastery cellars. The young monk who had met them at the gate was leading the way, carrying a couple of lanterns on a pole. Konrad was sullen.

Jennifer tried to soften his mood. 'Tell me about the monastery, Father.'

Konrad shrugged. 'What is there to tell? There are only four of us left at the Crown of Thorns, including the abbot. But many years ago our little church was quite famous, mostly because of these very cellars.'

'What's so special about them?' Jennifer asked.

'You'll see.'

At the bottom of the stairs was an ancient oak door with a sturdy, rusted lock. Konrad took down a big key from a nail on the wall, inserted it in the lock, pushed hard, and the heavy door creaked open. Steps led down to a chamber with stone archways on either side, in almost total darkness.

'The Crown of Thorns has an interesting history,' Konrad said. 'This part of the building is especially fascinating, but I warn you, you may be shocked by what you are about to see. Show them, Brother Paulo.'

The young monk raised the lanterns and Jennifer saw that the cellars were part of a crypt, with the bones of the dead everywhere, cemented into the walls, piled high in corners. Most horrifying were the skeletons, some lying down, some seated, others hanging from metal hooks in the cement. Some retained skin and hair, and the tattered remnants of clothing.

'What's all this?' McCaul asked, horrified.

'These people are monks,' Father Konrad told him. 'And wealthy landowners and aristocrats who down the ages chose to be entombed here.'

They passed an ancient throne in faded white marble. It protruded from the wall of the crypt at an odd angle, as if mounted on hinges. A decayed figure dressed in an ancient Cistercian robe was ensconced on the throne, hollow eye sockets peering out from beneath the hood.

Father Konrad said, 'Padre Boniface, our prior at the beginning of the eighteenth century. A saintly man, and the keeper of a long-forgotten secret.'

'What do you mean?' Jennifer asked.

'Look behind the throne,' Konrad said, and the young monk brought the lanterns closer. McCaul and Jennifer saw that the angled marble was attached to the wall by a pair of massive, ancient hinges, so heavily rusted they had long ago seized up. A two-foot-wide gap between the wall and the back of the throne revealed a dark passageway with tunnels leading off.

'The tunnels date from Napoleon's time, when the French invaded the region,' Konrad explained. 'An escape route if the monastery was ever attacked.'

They went on and paused outside a heavy oak door. Konrad unlocked it and they stepped into a large room, with high stone walls and vaulted ceilings. A lectern stood in the centre, and around the walls wooden shelves sagged under the weight of old ledgers, journals and bundles of documents.

Father Konrad searched the shelves until he found a handful of journals, and took them over to the lectern. 'Two years ago, you say. Which month?'

'April. The week of the 15th.'

MARK WOKE with a start and sat up. His headache had gone, but he still felt groggy. Thunder cracked beyond the window, and he guessed it had woken him.

The nurse had given him a sedative, and he'd drifted in and out of an uneasy sleep. He wiped the perspiration from his face and fumbled for his watch in the bedside locker: 7.30 p.m. He'd slept for over two hours.

He climbed shakily out of bed and removed his clothes from the locker. He had to do something to find Jennifer. He dragged on his trousers, slipped on his shoes, and was about to put on his shirt when Kelso opened the door.

'Thinking of going somewhere, Ryan?'

'I've had it, Kelso.' Mark pulled on his shirt. 'I'm getting out of here.'

'And going where?'

'I'll think about that later. Have you found Jennifer yet?'

Kelso sighed and closed the door. 'No, but I've got some news about our friend McCaul. He arrived in Switzerland on Tuesday to identify his son's body, and it seems he was once a detective with the NYPD.'

Mark stopped buttoning his shirt. 'I've never heard of him.'

'I had a photo emailed from New York.' Kelso sat down, took an envelope from his pocket and opened it. 'Was this the guy you saw with Jennifer?'

Mark looked at the grainy computer print-out. McCaul's face stared out at him: handsome, rugged, with high cheekbones. 'It looks like him.'

Kelso slipped the photograph back in the envelope. 'At least Jennifer's not in any immediate danger. From what I've been told, this guy McCaul can look after himself. He's a private investigator. And if the NYPD are to be believed, a very capable one at that. I thought at first he might be a complication we could do without, but on second thoughts I feel a little more secure that Jennifer's with a guy who might at least be able to help protect her.'

'Whatever you say,' Mark said flatly. 'It's been nice knowing you, Kelso.'

'Where do you think you're going?'

'I told you before, if you can't at least give me an idea of what this thing is about, I'm out of here. I'll find Jennifer myself.'

'If *I* can't find her, then what hope have *you* got?'

Mark grabbed his jacket. 'Maybe if I told the newspapers her story and got her face splashed on the front pages it might get some results.'

Kelso's face darkened. 'I told you before. This is a sensitive, covert operation. You can't do that. I won't allow it.'

Mark moved towards the door. 'Try and stop me.'

Kelso sighed in defeat. 'OK, Ryan, you win.'

'You're finally going to tell me what this is about?'

'I spoke with my superiors and they agreed I could give you a limited amount of information, *in extremis*, enough for you to know what we're dealing with here. I guess this is *extremis* enough.'

IT DIDN'T TAKE LONG for Father Konrad to find the correct journal. The entries on the lined pages were written neatly in black ink, but in a language neither Jennifer nor McCaul could understand. They watched the monk thumb the pages until he came to one that began *Aprile 15*. 'See. I told you. Nothing.'

Jennifer's heart sank. 'Are no visitors mentioned in the following pages?'

Konrad flicked over the page. 'Just one, five days after, on the 20th.'

'Who?' McCaul asked.

Konrad scanned the lines again, then frowned and fell silent.

'What's wrong?' Jennifer asked.

'I recall it now. A man arrived here. A stranger. The entry was written by Padre Leopold and reads: "*A visitor arrived last evening. He claimed he had got lost while hiking; he needed medical attention.*"' Konrad looked up. 'I remember now. He had suffered frostbite to his face and feet.'

Jennifer felt a shiver go through her. 'What else do you remember?'

'That he was hungry and in distress. We wanted to call a local doctor for him, but he refused. The abbot tended to his injuries with temporary dressings and suggested he visit a hospital.'

'What age was the man?'

'Middle aged.'

'Did he give a name?'

'If he did, none is mentioned, and I don't recall it.'

'Was he Swiss? Italian?'

'No. Foreign. He spoke English, I believe.'

Jennifer opened her bag. Her hands were shaking as she showed Konrad her father's photograph. 'Was . . . was this him?'

Konrad studied the snapshot, then shrugged as he handed it back. 'Perhaps it was the same man, but I can't be certain. We are talking about two years ago.'

'Does it say anything else about him?'

Konrad indicated some lines on the page. 'There is only one other mention. The man left us two days later, on April the 22nd. The abbot mentions that he took him to the local railway station.'

'Where did he travel to?'

'I really have no idea.' The priest snapped the journal shut. 'Now that we're finished here, let me take you back upstairs.'

They left the crypts and moved back up the granite stairway, the young monk leading the way, carrying the lamps on the pole. They came to the entrance hall and Konrad opened one of the doors. The storm was still raging.

'Where are you staying tonight?' Konrad asked them.

'We thought we'd find somewhere in Varzo,' McCaul replied.

'There are not many hotels in the village.' Konrad looked out at the rain, as lightning lit up the hallway. 'Perhaps it would be wiser if you remained here. Our guest rooms are basic, but comfortable. You are welcome to stay.'

'That's very kind of you, Father.'

Konrad shut the door. 'Brother Paulo will show you to your rooms.'

'One more thing, Father. Do you know of a mountain in the area called the Edelweiss?' Jennifer unfolded a slip of paper on which she'd written: *H. Vogel. Berg Edelweiss 705.*

Konrad studied the paper. 'What is this?'

'A similar note was found on the body. We don't know what the words and figures mean, apart from the fact that *Berg* means mountain in German. The paper had partly dissolved and some of the numbers may be missing.'

Konrad scratched his chin. 'Vogel is a common name on the Swiss side of the Wasenhorn, especially round Brig. But I've never heard of a mountain of that name in these parts.' He handed back the paper. 'And now, good night.'

He left them, taking one of the lamps from the pole. With the other, the young monk guided Jennifer and McCaul along a stone-flagged corridor, lined with oak doors. He showed them two rooms, side by side, with white-washed stone walls. Each room had a tiny window set high up, a wooden chair, a night stand, a fold-up metal bed, and a simple bathroom.

'*Momento. Prego.*' The monk crossed to another of the rooms nearby and came back with an armful of coarse grey blankets, fresh white sheets, soap bars, and a couple of thick candles, which he lit from the lamp. He handed one candle each to Jennifer and McCaul. '*Buona notte, signorina, signore.*'

'Good night. *Grazie.*'

'*Prego.*' The monk left them, his footsteps fading down the corridor.

McCaul gestured to the rooms. 'Pick one, then I'll help you with the bed.'

Jennifer stepped into the room on the left, and put the candle on the night stand. McCaul came in a moment later, opened out the fold-up and helped her fix the sheets and blankets.

'So, what do you think about the stuff Konrad told us?'

'I . . . I don't know. It's confusing.' Jennifer recalled Father Konrad's words: *Perhaps it was the man, but I cannot be certain.* What if the man who arrived at the monastery was her father?

'I know what you're thinking, Jennifer, but the guy who showed up arrived five days after the date on the train tickets. The person we're looking for couldn't have survived on the mountain in freezing cold for five days.'

'He could have found shelter in the *Berghut*, then made his way up here.'

'Why wait five days?'

'Maybe the mountain was impassable. Or he couldn't move because of his injuries until the weather improved.'

McCaul nodded. 'Fair enough. What Konrad said about the name Vogel may be a help. We can drive to Brig tomorrow and check it out.' A gust of wind rattled the window. 'You could do with some rest. You sure you'll be OK?'

'I think so. And thanks for helping me, Frank.'

'What's there to thank? We're in this together.' He put a hand on her shoulder. 'You'd better get some sleep. You need me, just call, OK?' Then he went out, closing the door behind him.

Jennifer sat on the bed. She had felt something like a small electric shock down her spine when McCaul had touched her. It was the first time in a long while a man had had that effect on her, but for some reason it didn't worry her.

Though she could acknowledge the spark of attraction between herself and Mark, she found it difficult to deal with that situation. But she could deal with her attraction to McCaul. It didn't feel awkward; it felt like something she could act on. Maybe because he was older, and she trusted him. And he made her feel safe in a way that reminded her of her father.

For now, she put such thoughts from her mind. Her luggage was back at the hotel in Simplon, and all she had was her tote bag with some underwear, a T-shirt and a pair of jeans. She undressed and scrubbed herself at the enamel basin, then slipped on a fresh T-shirt and panties and climbed into bed. The mattress was hard, but tonight she was just grateful for somewhere to rest.

Her tote bag was on the floor beside her and she plucked out her cellphone and powered it on. She was tempted to phone Mark and check on Bobby but her battery was almost down and she had no way of recharging it. She switched it off again; she would call Mark tomorrow. Finally, she blew out the candle, lay back in the darkness and tried to sleep.

Turin

'WHAT'S THE BIGGEST long-term threat to US national security, Ryan?'

The hospital room was quiet. Mark sat on a chair facing Kelso and said, 'You tell me.'

'Terrorism? Some rogue state with nuclear weapons and a grudge against America?' Kelso shook his head. 'It's organised crime. To be more specific, Russian organised crime. The Red Mafia. In the last five years the CIA estimates that the Red Mafia has had a worldwide turnover in the region of fifty *billion* dollars. They make the Italian Mafia look like a bunch of Boy Scouts.'

'I appreciate the lecture, Kelso. But what's it got to do with Paul March?'

'I'm coming to it. The Red Mafia purchase real estate, stocks and shares, and legitimate businesses. They gain control of these businesses to launder their illegal profits, because a legitimate business is the perfect laundromat. And guess where they invest most of their money? In the United States.'

'I get the picture. So what about March?'

'The company he worked for, Prime International Securities, was wound down a year ago. Before that, it was to all appearances a legitimate investment

WEB OF DECEIT | 515

bank. Except that it was owned by the Red Mafia, through a shell company in the Cayman Islands, and it laundered vast sums of dirty cash for them. It was part of an ongoing international operation run by a bunch of criminals you probably never heard of, the Moscaya clan.'

'I haven't. Who are they?'

'The Moscaya clan operates from behind offshore banks and companies and has always kept itself well insulated with an intricate bureaucracy. They have made it a policy never to get their hands dirty: that only happens to the little guys who work for them, people way down the chain. Four days ago you investigated an incident at JFK. An infant's dead body was used to smuggle drugs from Moscow. The Moscaya clan was almost certainly responsible. They don't care what heinous crime they have to commit to make a profit.'

'Why did they close down Prime?'

'Because we were getting too close to them. My team spent four years trying to get a strong case together on the Moscayas. We called it Operation Spiderweb. We tracked their illegal accounts, tapped their phones, tailed their top mobsters, all the usual stuff, but we got nowhere. So we decided we needed someone on the inside of one of the Moscaya companies. Paul March was one of Prime's top executives, the ideal guy, and we reckoned that with his help we could get access to some of the company's secret files.'

'You're saying he knew what Prime was up to?'

'He claimed he didn't, but he sure knew once we put him wise and made him the kind of offer he couldn't refuse.'

'What do you mean?'

'We did background checks on Prime's top employees. When we turned up nothing on March's early life, we dug deeper, and bingo. His real name was Joseph Delgado. He was orphaned at ten, spent most of his early life in foster care, with a couple of spells in juvenile prison for theft. When he was nineteen he got a year in jail for embezzlement, but as soon as he was released he killed a guy in a knife fight outside a bar in Phoenix. March claimed the fight was provoked and got off on a manslaughter charge. But he put his four years in prison to good use, and after his release he legally changed his name, got a college diploma and moved to New York. He turned his life around, and soon he was climbing the career ladder. Some years later he joined Prime. Then four years ago, it was bought by a shell company owned by the Moscayas, right after March was appointed as the company's financial controller.'

'What did you do? Promise you'd keep his past a secret if he played ball?'

'March was promised half a million dollars and witness protection for his family if he helped us nail the Moscaya clan's US and Caribbean operation. He readily accepted and made only one demand. He wanted all public evidence of his past life as Joseph Delgado permanently destroyed. Prison records, records of his court case, every shred of evidence that pointed to his previous existence. My people agreed to his demand.'

Mark thought: So that's why Garuda couldn't find any trace of the man's past. 'What precisely did the CIA want March to do?'

Kelso took a deep breath. 'Once or twice a year, March would take a business trip to Switzerland where Prime had several accounts. His job was a simple one: to make sure the books were in order and report back.'

'Go on.'

'A week before March flew to Zürich, we got a tip-off that the Moscayas were arranging a big deal with an Italian trafficker, which required them to pay fifty million dollars for a number of major drug consignments, forty million in gilt-edged bonds, the rest in diamonds and cash. One of the Moscaya's top henchmen, a gangster named Karl Lazar, was going to make the payment in Zürich. We learned from March that he'd been instructed to withdraw the cash, bonds and diamonds from safe deposit boxes in a Zürich bank used by Prime, and hand them over to Lazar. I had my team set up in Zürich. We'd tail Lazar every step of the way until it came time to catch him red-handed.'

Mark nodded. 'I'm listening.'

'March lands in Zürich, meets Lazar, visits the bank and makes the withdrawals. With the fifty mill in bonds, cash and diamonds stuffed into four large briefcases, he and Lazar walk to their hotel, three minutes away, to check in.' Kelso sighed. 'Then it all took a weird turn.'

'What do you mean?'

'March never checked in to his hotel, nor did Lazar. One minute they were being tailed as they walked to the hotel, next minute they'd vanished into a maze of side streets. We scoured every street for five blocks. We had the airports watched, but that turned up nothing. Paul March and Karl Lazar had disappeared, and one or both of them had stolen the fifty million.'

Mark frowned. 'You think March would have risked stealing fifty million from dangerous international gangsters?'

'Put it this way. Karl Lazar was a criminal to begin with, so I wouldn't have put it past him to steal from his own organisation. But I can't ignore March's criminal record. Fifty million dollars is a big temptation. March would have been hiding for the rest of his life under our witness protection, but with fifty million he could have afforded to hide in a lot more comfort.'

'I still haven't figured out how the body ended up in a glacier.'

'One of the ways the Red Mafia moved dirty money into Switzerland is using "mules". The Moscayas would hire someone trustworthy, kit them out as a hiker and give them a rucksack stuffed with cash. They'd make their way illegally over the Alps, hand over the cash to the bagmen the other side, and the money would be laundered and moved on to the US or the Caymans. Whoever took the fifty million knew that their chances of getting out of the country legally with that kind of stash would have been nil. So I reckon they'd decided to use an illegal route over the mountains, maybe one of the routes used by the Moscaya's mules. I'd say that was the plan, but then a storm blew up, and one of them fell into a crevasse and froze to death.'

'You mean March.'

Kelso sighed. 'The body on the mountain wasn't Jennifer's father.'

'*What?* But the missing person's report—'

'Said the victim had a passport in the name of Paul March. But I had Interpol send me a photograph of the victim in the glacier. It was compared electronically to the one in March's passport and it didn't match.'

'Then who *did* the body belong to?'

'There's a chance it was Karl Lazar's. But we can't be certain unless the Italians manage to scrape DNA evidence out of the ruins of the morgue.'

The door opened suddenly and Grimes came in, carrying a map. Kelso stepped over to the door and the two men held a whispered conversation over the map, until Kelso said urgently, 'Go get the car. I'll be right with you.'

Grimes left and Mark said, 'What's up?'

'Maybe we've got a lead, maybe not. Jennifer switched on her cellphone briefly five minutes ago. The triangulation was pretty rough, but it suggested somewhere near Varzo. Fellows has just called the Berghof Hotel, and spoke with the manager, some guy named Anton. He didn't know where Jennifer had gone but he mentioned that when he took her up to the Wasenhorn she seemed interested in a monastery called the Crown of Thorns, outside Varzo.'

'Why?'

'Who the hell knows? Grimes showed me the place on the map. It's about forty minutes away. Fellows is on his way. Grimes and I will meet him there.'

'I'm going with you, Kelso.'

'I thought you were told to rest . . .'

Mark reached for his jacket. 'Forget it. I'm not staying here. And there's a lot more you need to tell me. Such as why Jennifer's life is in danger. And if it wasn't Paul March's body, then where the hell did he disappear to?'

THE TWO MEN in the black BMW halted outside the Crown of Thorns. They spotted McCaul's Nissan parked near the monastery gates, and the driver doused his headlights and reversed under a clump of trees. Both men wore leather gloves, dark raincoats and black ski masks. They climbed out of their car in the drenching rain, and moved towards the gates.

One of the men produced a torch and directed it on the lock while his accomplice took a leather tool pouch from under his coat. He had the lock open in a minute and both men moved inside. They crossed the courtyard and slipped under cover of the archway until they came to the oak entrance door.

The man with the tool pouch went to work again, and the big wooden door sprang open. He nodded to his accomplice, and both intruders unbuttoned their coats to reveal Skorpion machine pistols slung round their necks. They readied their weapons and moved into the monastery.

FATHER ANGELO KONRAD came awake in the darkness. He thought he was having a nightmare and he couldn't breathe. Two black-masked intruders had invaded his cell. One of them had a hand over Konrad's mouth while the other flashed a torch into his face. As the startled monk struggled for breath, he felt the steel tip of a knife press into his throat.

'Don't move or talk unless I tell you to,' the intruder whispered. 'Otherwise you die, understand?'

Konrad nodded, terrified, and the hand came away from his mouth.

'You will answer my questions. Lie to me and I'll cut your heart out.' The threat in the hoarse voice was truly frightening, and Konrad nodded again.

'Where are your two visitors?'

Konrad was silent. Anguish welled up inside him, and he feared the worst.

The intruder pressed the knife tip into his throat. '*Answer*. Or I kill you.'

Grimacing in pain, Konrad told him everything.

'How many others are in the monastery? And where, precisely?'

'Two . . . two others. Bro . . . Brother Paulo is three doors away. Brother Franco is in the first cell past the next corridor.'

The intruder's hand came up to cover Konrad's mouth and he slid the knife across the priest's throat.

JENNIFER WOKE with a start. Her breath came in ragged bursts and her heart beat wildly. It could have been hours or minutes after she'd fallen asleep, she wasn't sure. The storm was still raging, splashing ghostly electric shadows on the walls, and she was bathed in perspiration. Her nightmares had come back again and she shuddered at the memory as she sat up in bed.

A second later, she heard a sound. From somewhere outside in the corridor.

Then she heard it again. Footsteps, the soft slap of leather on stone. The noise faded. She listened again, but heard nothing.

Jennifer forced herself off the bed, moved towards the door in the pitch darkness, and put her ear to the wood. Silence. The footsteps had stopped.

A moment later she heard another noise, this time a faint rattle.

The door handle was turning.

Jennifer staggered back, terrified. '*Who . . . who's there?*'

And then suddenly the door burst open. As she tried to scream, a hand went over her mouth, and Jennifer was forced back into the room.

A man's voice whispered, 'Don't make a sound.' Panic seized her and she struggled. The voice hissed, 'For Christ sakes, Jennifer, do as I say!'

McCaul's hand came away from her mouth and his Maglite torch flashed on. Jennifer saw that he had dressed hastily and was in his stocking feet, his shoes hanging round his neck by the laces. He put a finger to his lips for her to be silent, then closed the door. She saw Caruso's pistol in his hand.

'What . . . what are you doing?'

'Keep your voice down,' McCaul whispered. 'Just get your clothes on and come with me, quick as you can. We're leaving.'

'Why?'

'Because we've got company, that's why.' McCaul gripped her arm. 'Just do as I say, Jennifer, and right away. But do it quietly. And carry your shoes.'

Jennifer dressed as McCaul went to listen by the door. When she finished, she grabbed her bag and shoes and went to join him. 'What's happening?'

'I heard a noise in the corridor. As I went to see if you were all right, I saw two guys wearing black ski masks come out of one of the cells. I ducked back inside my room and grabbed the gun. When I looked again, they'd disappeared. I checked the cell. It was Father Konrad's. He's dead, Jennifer. His throat's been cut. A little down the hall I found another monk dead in his cell. Same thing. The third one's probably dead too, or soon will be. It's time we got out of here.'

McCaul raised the gun and flicked off the torch before he opened the door. He listened, then stepped out, Jennifer behind him. They had gone twenty yards when they came to the winding stairway that led down to the cellars.

Twin torch beams cut through the darkness as two men suddenly rounded the end of the corridor. Jennifer saw the men raise their machine pistols.

'*Run, Jennifer!*' McCaul pushed her down the staircase towards the vaults.

He flicked on the torch as they hurried barefoot down the stairs. They heard racing footsteps in the corridor above as the two men came after them.

Jennifer reached the bottom of the stairs and saw the oak door, the key hanging from the hook in the wall. She inserted it frantically in the rusted lock and turned the handle, The door opened with a creak of protest. McCaul shoved Jennifer into the darkness and moved in after her. As he locked the door from the inside the footsteps grew louder on the stairwell.

'Keep moving,' said McCaul, and pushed Jennifer into the crypt.

He flashed the torchlight on the walls, and pointed along the passageway. They could hear the intruders kicking savagely against the door behind them.

They pressed on. The light from the torch became weaker, but there was no mistaking the macabre sight of death everywhere. Jennifer shuddered as they reached the enthroned figure of Padre Boniface. McCaul shone the torch into the narrow gap behind the marble throne, and they saw the dark tunnel beyond.

Behind them came an almighty crash of splintering wood. McCaul pushed Jennifer into the narrow gap, and squeezed in after her. They had barely gone a dozen yards when the light from the torch weakened to a glimmer.

'The batteries are almost gone.' McCaul handed the torch to Jennifer and fumbled for his cigarette lighter. He flicked it on and the cavern lit up.

Jennifer saw rough-hewn walls, glistening with water. Stacked against the base of the walls were more human bones. McCaul pushed on until the tunnel was barely high enough to stand up in. They felt their way deeper into the passageway, and every few seconds McCaul flicked on his lighter.

Then they came to a dead end: a mound of rocks piled high against the passageway wall. It seemed hopeless, and McCaul grabbed at the larger rocks, tossing them aside, his despair turning to blind rage. When he had cleared away a good part of the mound, he waved the lighter flame over the remaining rocks and a weak draught of wind made the flame quiver.

'There's air coming from somewhere. Give me a hand here, quickly.'

Jennifer helped him clear away the debris until a hole appeared, followed by a rush of cold air and the sound of heavy rain.

'It looks like Konrad wasn't spinning us a yarn.'

McCaul crawled through the hole, pulling Jennifer after him. They were out in the open, on a ridge of high ground that ran along the monastery walls. The earth fell away steeply, covered in stones and wild brush, a dark ravine below. The thunder and lightning had stopped but the rain was constant.

'Get your shoes on, the ground looks pretty rough.'

Voices echoed behind them and they looked back through the opening in the rocks. A moment later a powerful torch beam shone from the darkness. McCaul aimed the Beretta into the passageway, fired off a volley of shots.

They scrambled down the incline, over loose stones, through thickets of coarse brush. When they reached the ravine they ran until they came to a narrow track. Soon they found themselves back at the monastery gates. They raced to the Nissan and McCaul slipped the key in the ignition. He started the engine, swung the jeep round and accelerated down the hill.

FIVE MINUTES later, McCaul sped into the village of Varzo. He skidded onto the rain-swept main plaza, hung a left into a narrow cobbled lane and halted.

'Why are we stopping?' Jennifer asked.

'We need to decide what we're going to do.'

Jennifer was on edge. 'Shouldn't we be trying to find the police?'

'Jennifer, even if the cops believe our story, which I doubt, they'd lock us up for our own protection. You think that's going to keep us alive? Whoever those guys are working for, they murdered Caruso and his wife. You think some two-roomed local cop shop is going to stop them from killing us?'

'How could they have known we were at the monastery?'

'My guess is, they used electronic surveillance. All they've got to do is plant a bug on the jeep and they know where we're headed. It could be anywhere. We could be looking for the damned thing for hours.'

'You mean they know where we are *this minute*?'

'Exactly. And if we stay in the jeep we're sitting ducks.'

CARLO PERINI was bored. He wished he were back in his flat with his girlfriend, but instead he was stuck behind the ticket booth at Varzo railway station.

He looked up as a couple approached the booth. They were both like drowned rats, but the woman was a looker, and had a good figure.

'*Sì?*'

'*Parla inglese?*' the guy said.

Carlo shrugged. '*Un po*' . . . a little.'

'We need two tickets on the next train out of here.'

'The train . . . that comes soon . . .' Carlo said, '. . . go to Brig, in Svizzera, via the *galleria* Simplon.'

'When?' The guy was agitated, pointing to his watch.

The train was late because of flooding on the line, but it was due in the next five minutes. Carlo held up five fingers. '*Cinque minuti.*'

The guy slapped a fistful of banknotes on the counter.

Five minutes later, the train for Brig pulled up. Carlo saw the couple climb into one of the carriages. The train pulled out. Carlo didn't see the powerful black BMW that drew up outside the station.

As the train disappeared down the tracks, two men in raincoats dashed up to the ticket booth and one of them said urgently in Italian, 'Excuse me, but I think we missed our train. The one that just left, where was it headed?'

Carlo looked at the guy. Blond, tough looking, with a scar above his right eye. His companion had a shaven head and dark, menacing eyes. 'Brig.'

'Does the train that left stop anywhere?'

'Sure. It stops at Iselle in about twelve minutes. But the way the storm's been, it will probably take longer. There are holdups all along the line.'

The blond smiled. 'Thank you so much.'

MARK AND KELSO were speeding towards Varzo in Kelso's Opel.

'You still haven't answered all my questions, Kelso. Who exactly is Jennifer in danger from and why would they want to kill her?'

Mark was in the passenger seat, Grimes in the back. The rain had stopped but Kelso kept his eyes firmly on the wet road.

'All I've got is a theory. Whoever stole the fifty million would have laid low for a time, maybe got themselves plastic surgery and started a new life. But the body turning up on the mountain presents a problem. Because now the cops will be sniffing around, and maybe the Moscaya clan will be doing the same, hoping to find out what happened to the fifty million. So the culprit is going to want to stop the bloodhounds picking up his trail.'

'You think that's why Jennifer's life is in danger?'

'I reckon that's part of it. There's something else you ought to know. The detective investigating the case was a man named Caruso. He and his wife were found shot dead this afternoon.'

Mark was stunned. 'Who killed them?'

'The information I got was that the crime scene looked as if Caruso shot his wife and committed suicide. But I figure they were murdered, by someone desperate enough to want this case closed, *permanently*, and on their terms. Either Paul March or the Moscaya's henchmen.'

'Why them?'

'I told you there was a computer disk. On our instructions, March was able to make a copy disk of a bunch of Prime's Swiss account numbers. Once we had the disk we'd be able to link them to the Moscayas. March refused to hand over the disk until after he'd been paid the half-million and he and his family were safely in witness protection. But the disk vanished with him.'

'Where does all this leave Jennifer?'

'A bunch of personal items were found in a rucksack near the body, and may just offer a clue about what happened to March and the disk. I've got a gut feeling the Moscayas will think the same. Once they get their hands on Jennifer, they'll find out all they can and kill her.'

Before Mark could reply, Kelso's cellphone rang and he flicked it on. 'Kelso. What is it?' Mark couldn't hear the caller but he saw Kelso stiffen. 'You're sure they're not there? . . . OK, we'll be there in half an hour. Don't touch a thing, Fellows, you hear me? Not a damned thing.'

MCCAUL HAD PICKED a carriage near the middle of the train and they had found an empty compartment. Jennifer was on edge. She slid open the compartment door and checked the corridor. She reassured herself that the two men were not lurking in the corridor, then slid the door shut and sat down.

McCaul came over and put an arm round her shoulder. 'There was nothing we could do, Jennifer. Nothing. If we hadn't escaped we'd be dead too.'

'Why would they slaughter Father Konrad and the others if they were only after us?' Jennifer got to her feet. 'There has to be a reason.'

'Like what?'

She paced the compartment. 'The only thing I can think of . . . You said yourself that someone's desperate to destroy every shred of evidence. What if that's why Konrad and the others were killed? They *saw* the man who survived the storm. They were witnesses—the journal entry was evidence of that.'

'Maybe you've got something there.'

'The man mentioned in the journal *has* to be the one we're looking for, so why don't we just go to the police right now?'

'I told you, Jennifer, we could be putting ourselves in danger.'

Jennifer felt a stab of fear as McCaul moved towards the door. 'Where are you going, Frank?'

'To find a washroom and clean up. Unless you want to go first?'

Jennifer declined. McCaul had fared the worst as he'd led their scramble down the embankment, and his clothes were muddied and ripped. But she still felt uneasy being left alone. He seemed to sense it, and touched her face.

'Don't worry, we're safe for now. I'll be back soon. Keep the door shut, OK?'

As Jennifer sat alone in the carriage, her imagination was unable to suppress the images of slaughter at the monastery, and her stomach churned. For some reason she had a desperate urge to phone Mark and make certain that Bobby was all right. She searched in her tote bag but couldn't find her cellphone. She must have dropped it during the scramble out of the monastery.

The train slowed, interrupting her thoughts, and she looked out of the window as the lights of a station came into view.

McCaul came back just as the train pulled out of the station. He shut the compartment door. 'The nearest washroom's three carriages down. Maybe there's a dining car where I can get us coffee. You want some?'

Jennifer flushed. Still preoccupied with the gruesome image her mind had conjured of Father Konrad with his throat cut, she felt bile rise in her throat.

'What's wrong?' McCaul asked. 'You don't look too good.'

She got to her feet. 'I need to use the washroom.'

As THE ICE-COLD water cooled her wrists, Jennifer's nausea subsided. She examined her face in the mirror above the basin. I look a mess, she thought. She tidied herself as best she could, then dabbed her wet clothes with water to clean away the traces of mud and grime.

As Jennifer made her way from the washroom back to her carriage, her nausea returned and she had a desperate need for air. She was at the end of the corridor and there was a glass vent near the top of the carriage window. She yanked it open and a cool draught washed her face. The engine changed pitch as it entered a tunnel. They had started their journey through the Simplon pass. Moments later, the door slid open at the end of the carriage.

A man stepped in. He was blond, with a thin scar over one eye, and wore a dark raincoat. Another raincoated man stepped in behind him; he was bald and stocky, with sinister eyes. Both men had cold, impassive faces, and there was something infinitely dangerous about them.

Jennifer knew instinctively that they were the men from the monastery.

The men lunged towards her. Jennifer screamed and ran back along the carriage. At the end of the corridor she glanced back. The men were gaining ground. She grabbed the door leading to the next carriage and yanked it open. Darting through, she stumbled into a crowd of students.

'*Scusi! Scusi!* Please let me through!' She pushed forward, her eyes locked on her compartment, twenty yards away. She knew her only hope of staying alive was to reach McCaul. *He has the gun.* She looked back. The men were ten yards behind, pushing their way through. Jennifer reached her compartment door and yanked it open. '*Frank! For God's sake help me!*'

But McCaul wasn't there.

She dashed out into the corridor again. The men were less than fifteen feet away. As they broke through the crowd and lunged towards her, she ran.

When she reached the next carriage she tore open the door. In her panic she'd barely noticed the compartments she'd passed, but now she realised she was in an empty section of the train, with not a single passenger in sight.

She noticed two exit doors, left and right. A window was open in one of them. She thought of jumping from the train. But it was speeding through a tunnel at sixty miles an hour. She kept moving.

As she started to yank open the next carriage door she heard a rush of feet behind her and the bald assailant appeared, carrying a machine pistol in one hand. He lunged forward. Jennifer tried to fend him off but he slapped her, a stinging blow across the face, and then his hand went round her throat. She struggled but the man pushed her head back through the open window.

As a razor-sharp blast of air slashed at Jennifer's face, she fumbled blindly in her bag. She found something long and hard, recognised the feel and shape of a ballpoint pen. She got a firm grip on the end and with all her remaining strength plunged the pen into the man's cheek.

He screamed and staggered back, dropping his weapon, clapping a hand to the pen embedded below his left eye.

Jennifer pulled herself in from the open window. The man lay writhing in agony on the floor, blocking her path. In her panic she yanked open the exit door. The man reached out blindly and grabbed her leg.

Jennifer saw the machine pistol on the floor. She reached for it and twisted her leg free, then brought up the weapon and squeezed the trigger. The Skorpion stuttered, a round hitting the man in the shoulder. He staggered back, falling through the open door with a scream.

As Jennifer turned away in horror, the carriage door behind her burst open and McCaul rushed in, clutching the Beretta. He took the Skorpion from her hand and guided her back into the carriage.

'You're OK, you're safe,' he reassured her, breathless. 'What happened?'

A body lay in the corridor and Jennifer saw it was her attacker's blond accomplice. 'Is . . . is he dead?'

McCaul held up the Beretta. 'No, but I had to hit him a couple of times with this before I knocked him out.' He knelt and took the machine pistol from underneath the man's raincoat, removed the magazine and emptied the round of ammunition from the breech, then did the same with the second Skorpion, before he tossed both weapons from the train's window.

Jennifer noticed that McCaul's face was badly scratched, and there was a nasty gash across his right eye. 'Where . . . where did you go?'

'To see if I could get some coffee. When I came back I saw a commotion. That's when I had the punch-up with our friend here. What went on back there?'

'I . . . I killed a man . . .' And then suddenly she was in McCaul's arms, fighting back tears as she told him what had happened.

'Calm down, Jennifer. You had to protect yourself.'

'I'm sure they were the two men from the monastery. How could they have found us again?'

'We'll talk about that later. It's time we got off the train.'

McCaul found the emergency stop lever in the next carriage. The train had left the Simplon tunnel and was speeding along a flat run of track towards Brig.

McCaul pulled the lever. For a couple of seconds nothing happened, and then Jennifer heard a ferocious squeal of metal as the brakes bit the tracks. The train shuddered violently, throwing them off-balance, and the carriages ground to a halt. McCaul yanked open the exit door and jumped.

He held out his hand. 'Jennifer, jump!'

She grabbed his hand and leapt off the train.

PART FOUR

Switzerland

The farm was remote, more than three miles from the nearest village. The man lived there alone, except for his two Dobermans, which gambolled about his feet that foggy evening as he finished milking the cows in one of the barns. As he carried the metal pails to the farmhouse, the dogs started to bark and leap with excitement. '*Sitz, Hans! Sitz, Ferdie!*'

The Dobermans came to heel instantly. The man set down the pails in the kitchen. He was sturdily built and wore green rubber boots and a frayed work jacket. His dark hair was patched with grey and his weather-beaten face bore the ravages of frostbite. Despite the efforts of his plastic surgeon, a chunk of flesh was missing from the tip of the man's nose, and to make matters worse he'd lost the tips of three fingers on his left hand.

He peered through the curtains, then turned back towards the table. A clutch of newspapers lay there, and a pair of binoculars. He picked up the binoculars and pointed them towards the main road. There was no sign of the car or the men, but they were out there, he was certain. He had lived in fear since he'd heard of the discovery of the glacier corpse. For three days he'd seen the car with two men watching his property. He put down the binoculars and took a pistol out of his jacket pocket. He checked that it was loaded.

'Hans! Ferdie! Kommt, meine Liebchen!'

The dogs bounded over and he patted their heads. The Dobermans would kill instantly on his instruction: their savage jaws could rip a human throat to bloody shreds in seconds. *'Ferdie! Hans! Draussen! Wartet draussen!'*

The dogs rushed towards the door and went to sit in the front porch. The man diverted his attention to a corner of the kitchen. A TV/video security screen was linked to two cameras that monitored the front and back of the farmhouse. He flicked a switch on the monitor and the image altered to a view of the barn and the garage. Satisfied, he tucked the pistol back in his pocket. He was fearful that his secret had been compromised by the corpse's discovery. But he was prepared to deal with any unwelcome visitors.

New York

LOU GARUDA sat at his desk at the Long Beach Police Department offices on Westchester Street. He had trawled the Internet for information on Prime International Securities and found little. Prime was no longer in business, but one of its former vice-presidents, a Frederick Kammer, now worked for another Manhattan investment bank, Cavendish-Deloy Securities. Garuda found the number and picked up the phone. He got through to Kammer's secretary.

'Who shall I say is calling?'

'Officer Lou Garuda. I'm with the Long Beach Police Department.'

There was a pause, then the woman said, 'I'll put him on.'

A man's impatient voice came on the line. 'Yes? This is Frederick Kammer.'

'Hello, Mr Kammer. My name's Lou Garuda. I have some information that might interest you, sir. It's about a former colleague of yours when you worked for Prime Securities, Paul March.'

'Is this an official call, Mr Garuda?'

'Not exactly. Two years ago Paul March vanished on the same night his wife was murdered. I covered the case at the time.'

'Yes, it was very tragic. March was a fine employee and much respected. However, I had been with the company only a year and hardly knew the man, so what has this got to do with me?'

'Why did Prime fold?'

'I've got no idea. Business seemed to be good, so you'll have to ask the registered owners. But I'm sure they had their reasons.'

'Who are they?'

'A shell company in the Caymans.'

'I'm not with you.'

'The company was owned by another company, which in turn may even have been owned by another. That kind of convoluted corporate ownership structure can be for tax-efficiency reasons or for reasons of anonymity, frequently both. Now, about this important information you claim to have.'

'OK, here's my news. March was found dead five days ago, frozen into a glacier near the Swiss–Italian border.'

'I . . . I'd no idea.' Kammer sounded surprised.

'I'm thinking of getting back on the case. Maybe you could help by answering some questions?'

'I'm sorry, but I've helped you all I can. Good day, Mr Garuda.' The line went dead.

Next, Garuda dialled the number for the Cauldwell home. He had promised Ryan that he'd keep and eye on Bobby so that was what he'd do.

Italy

'I COUNTED three bodies, two with their throats cut, and the third looks like he hanged himself.'

'Who were they?'

'Monks.' Fellows shone the electric torch ahead of them as he addressed Kelso and led them hurriedly in through the monastery gates. 'When I got here I found the gate unlocked and let myself in. The place is deserted.'

'You're positive there was no sign of Jennifer or McCaul?'

'Two of the cells look like they were occupied, but now they're empty.'

'Show me the stiffs, and let's be quick about it,' Kelso said grimly.

Mark followed Kelso and his men across the courtyard. Fellows led them in through a pair of oak doors and along a corridor into one of the monk's cells. Mark saw the lifeless body of a young man, dressed in nightclothes. He hung by his neck from a rope tied to the bars on the window. The chair beneath his feet was toppled and a bloodied stiletto knife lay on the bed.

Fellows escorted them into two other rooms down the hall. When Mark saw the bodies with their throats cut, he wanted to throw up. 'What went on?'

'The way it looks,' Fellows suggested, 'is that maybe the young one went crazy, killed the other two, then decided to top himself.'

'That's the way it's *meant* to look.' Kelso studied one of the victims, closely examining the slash across his neck. 'The stiletto we saw in the other cell isn't the kind of weapon a man of the cloth is likely to carry, now, is it? I suggest we get out of here before the local cops discover they've got three dead monks on their hands. Fellows, you go with Grimes. Ryan, stick with me. We'll scour the town and see if we can get a bead on Jennifer.'

HALF AN HOUR later they found the blue Nissan parked on Varzo's deserted main piazza. Mark recognised the licence number. It was Grimes who had spotted the vehicle first, and when they pulled up he was probing the chassis with a torch. Kelso went over to talk to him, then beckoned Mark. 'Grimes thinks it's been abandoned. The keys are still in the ignition.'

'Where did Jennifer and McCaul disappear to?'

'I checked the railway station,' Grimes said. 'The guy on the ticket desk remembered a couple resembling McCaul and Jennifer who bought tickets about an hour ago for Brig.'

Kelso reached for a map and torch in the Opel's glove compartment. 'I don't believe in coincidences. Get moving, Grimes, we'll follow you to Brig. Ryan, come with me.' He climbed into the Opel.

Mark slid into the passenger seat and Kelso tossed the map over to him. 'Why would they abandon the jeep and take a train?'

'Grimes found a bug planted under the Nissan's chassis.'

'You mean someone's been tailing them besides us?'

'Exactly. And judging by the blood bath we just saw, they followed them to the monastery. What happened after that only Jennifer or McCaul can tell us.'

'What's happening, Kelso?'

Kelso started the engine and swung out of the piazza with a squeal of tyres. 'There's a pattern here, Ryan. Those monks deaths were made to appear like a tragic act of violence—like Caruso's. But why did they have to die? Because they knew something, or were part of the evidence, and someone wanted to cover up that fact.'

'Who's the someone?'

'That's the fifty-million-dollar question.'

Switzerland

'WE'D LIKE two rooms for tonight. Adjoining singles.'

'Have you reservations, sir?' The receptionist at the Ambassador Hotel spoke in immaculate English and studied them with mild suspicion. Jennifer wasn't surprised: it was well after midnight, they were dishevelled and had no luggage except for her tote bag. They had trekked from the railway line towards Brig's outskirts, then hailed a cab to the centre of the town.

McCaul produced his credit card. 'Our car broke down outside town and we got caught in the rain. We don't have a reservation.'

'We have no adjoining single rooms available but we have two single rooms three rooms apart: 306 and 309.'

'They'll have to do.'

When they had filled in the registration cards, the receptionist checked their passports. He took an imprint of McCaul's credit card before returning it with two plastic door cards. 'The elevator is across the lobby.'

Room 306 was the closer as they stepped out of the elevator, and McCaul opened the door with the key card. 'I'd better let you get some rest,' he said to Jennifer. 'I'll call you at seven, OK? After breakfast we'll see about buying ourselves some fresh clothes and hiring another car.'

He made to leave, but Jennifer said, 'Please don't go.' There was a frantic need in her for company, and it had nothing to do with sex. It was a need for someone to hold her, to reassure her that she was safe.

McCaul stopped and turned. 'What's wrong, Jennifer?'

'I don't understand why this is happening. I don't understand how I've become a person who could kill a man. I don't want to be alone right now.'

McCaul came over and gently touched her face. 'I understand. But I don't know the answers, Jennifer. We've got to work out what it is you know or have that someone wants. If we can do that, we'll be ahead of the game.'

Jennifer held on to McCaul's hand. 'You really think so?'

'For sure.' McCaul nodded, slowly letting his hand fall away. 'Try and get some sleep. We'll see what we can turn up on the name Vogel in the morning, even if it means scouring every street in Brig.'

'WHAT'S THE PLAN, Kelso? Do we have one?'

Kelso had halted on Brig's market square and jerked on the handbrake. The town was in darkness, the streets deserted.

'It's one thirty a.m. Too late to start prowling round town questioning hotel clerks. We'll find somewhere to bed down for a few hours. My guess is that McCaul and Jennifer can't be doing much else at this hour.'

Kelso flashed his headlights as a Volkswagen pulled up in front. Grimes stepped out and walked back. 'Sir?'

'I want you to find us a hotel. Then I'll tell you what we're going to do.'

JENNIFER STOOD by her window, staring out at the lights of the town. Her body was drained of energy, but her mind was so troubled she found it impossible to sleep. As she stood there an idea came to her.

McCaul had warned her not to leave her room, but she wouldn't take long. She took her key card from the night stand and quietly let herself out.

THE HOTEL was in an alleyway near Brig's railway station. The sight of four Americans with only overnight bags didn't seem to unsettle the night porter. He had them fill in the guest registration cards before marching them upstairs to four single rooms. 'Breakfast is from six, *meinen Herren. Ich wunsche ihnen guten Nacht.*'

'Wait a minute, I'd like a word.' Kelso spoke to the man for a few moments on the landing, then handed him a generous tip and came back. 'Leave your bags in your rooms and meet me in mine in two minutes.'

Mark unlocked his door. He knew he ought to call Lou Garuda and check up on Bobby, and he estimated that it was a little after 7.30 p.m. in New York. Knowing Garuda, he'd stop off in a bar on the way home, so he decided to make the call straight after Kelso's meeting. He left his overnight bag on the bed, slipped out into the hallway and knocked on Kelso's door. Grimes and Fellows were already seated at either end of the single bed. Kelso beckoned him inside the cramped room.

'I figure they'll need transport,' Kelso began. 'So they'll probably hire a car or take a train or bus first thing in the morning. According to the night porter there's just one major car-hire office in town—it's a Hertz—so we'll stake it out before it opens. Ryan, that'll be your job. Fellows will watch the bus depot. I'll take the train station. Grimes will phone round the hotels and find out if Jennifer or McCaul have checked in anywhere. I'll call Langley and have them hack into the data bases of every hotel chain within fifty miles of here and check their booking records. Any questions? Good. I've told the porter to call us at six. That gives us just under four hours in the sack.'

MARK GOT UNDRESSED. He sat on the bed and dialled Garuda's home number. His answering machine kicked in and he left his hotel and room number, along with a message to call him back.

He peered out between the curtains at the lights of Brig. If Kelso was right, Jennifer was out there somewhere with McCaul. They'd looked pretty close as they strolled to the restaurant in Turin, and he wondered just how close they'd got. With that thought, he lay down on the bed and closed his eyes.

The telephone buzzed. He fumbled for the receiver. It was Garuda.

'I called the Cauldwell like you asked, old buddy. But what the hell's going on, Mark? What are you doing in Switzerland?'

'It's too long a story to go into right now, Lou, so just listen up. I wanted to ask after Bobby, and I've also got something I need you to do for me.'

Mark explained what he wanted Garuda to do.

'Is this anything to do with that CIA gorilla, Kelso, you had me check up on?'

'Lou, please, I can't go into it right now. I've got my reasons.'

'You know what I was thinking? It's time I got out from behind a desk and went back to being a detective. And maybe this is my big chance. Maybe we can work on this together, solve this case once and for all. What do you say?'

'I'll think about it.'

JENNIFER WOKE at six thirty. She had slept soundly, exhausted by the events of the previous evening, but pleased with her discovery.

She showered and dressed, then went along the corridor and knocked on McCaul's door. He was dressed, but his hair was still wet from the shower.

'Sleep OK?' he asked.

'As soon as my head hit the pillow.' Jennifer was excited. 'I think I may have turned up something. Let's go down to breakfast and I'll tell you.'

The hotel restaurant was crowded. A waiter led them to a corner table, and they helped themselves to fresh rolls, cheese, ham and coffee.

Jennifer explained that before she turned in she had gone down to the reception desk and asked to borrow a local phone directory. The clerk had handed her one for the Canton of Valais, of which Brig was a part, and back in her room she had searched the directory. At least a dozen people named Vogel were listed, but none had the initial H. 'So then I called the telephone operator and told her I was an American tourist looking for a Swiss relative living near Brig who I couldn't find in the phone directory. She found two unlisted people named Vogel with the initial H. One in a place called Murnau, about five miles from here, and another near the same town.'

'Did she give you their addresses and phone numbers?'

'No, she said it was against the law if they're unlisted. But she suggested we try the town hall in Murnau. They have the addresses and telephone numbers of everyone in the locality on their register.'

McCaul finished his coffee eagerly. 'Let's go hire a car and find Murnau.'

Most of the stores in Brig opened their doors at 7.30. By 8 a.m., Jennifer had purchased a sweater, jeans, underwear and a waxed jacket. McCaul bought jeans, T-shirts, a new bag and a jacket in green loden material. They changed into their new clothes back at the hotel, then checked out.

'We need to hire a car,' Jennifer told the desk clerk as they settled the bill.

'Of course,' the woman answered politely. 'There's a car-hire firm I can recommend. Let me give you directions to their office.'

MARK WAS WATCHING Hertz from across the street. He wore his raincoat and the hat he'd bought at the airport.

The Opel screeched to a halt at the kerb. Kelso was agitated. 'Get in.'

Mark jumped into the passenger seat. Kelso gunned the engine and did a U-turn on Brig's main street. Drivers honked their horns in fury.

Kelso ignored the protest. 'The data-base trawl turned up two guests in their names who checked into a hotel last night at one fifteen a.m.'

'*Where?*'

'Right here in Brig. A hotel called the Ambassador.'

As they pulled up in front of the Ambassador, Grimes ran to join them. 'The desk clerk said they checked out half an hour ago, and went to hire a car.'

'They couldn't have,' Kelso told him. 'Ryan had the Hertz office covered.'

'It wasn't Hertz. It was a small local operator the hotel likes to recommend.

Fellows called round and the guy there said they left in a dark blue Volkswagen Golf fifteen minutes ago. Fellows got the licence number. They asked for directions to the town hall in a place called Murnau.'

JENNIFER TOOK the main road out of Brig, and they followed a tortuous road through stunning Alpine scenery.

Ten minutes later they reached Murnau, a pretty village with dozens of small inns and ski lodges. The town hall was a centuries-old limestone building. They parked the car, entered the building and found a clerk.

'*Grüss Gott.* How may I help you?' the young woman said pleasantly.

Jennifer explained what they were looking for. 'Do you have the addresses on your register?'

The woman tapped on her computer. 'Herr Hubert Vogel lives in Bauer Strasse, near the old market square. He's a retired policeman. The second man, Herr Heinrich Vogel, lives at a farm five kilometres from Murnau. His occupation is given as mountain guide and climbing instructor.'

'Do you have their phone numbers?'

'*Ja.*' The woman wrote out the numbers.

Jennifer saw that the figures 705 were the last three digits of Heinrich Vogel's phone number. 'How do we get to Heinrich Vogel's address?'

'The property is about a ten-minute drive. It's quite remote, near the northern slopes of the Wasenhorn. But if I give you directions you should find it easily enough. The farm is called the Berg Edelweiss.'

TWO MILES from Murnau, a narrow track branched off from the main road. McCaul consulted the directions they'd been given. 'Hang a left.'

Jennifer turned onto the track. A mile further on they arrived at a pair of open wooden gates with a metal mailbox to one side. An inscription on the box said: BERG EDELWEISS. A big, traditional farmhouse with a collection of outbuildings loomed in the distance, shrouded in early-morning fog.

Jennifer halted the Volkswagen on the gravel driveway. She saw a barn and a double garage at the back of the farmhouse. The garage doors were open, revealing an old brown Mercedes. A pair of Doberman pinschers sat outside the farmhouse front door. They didn't move or make a sound.

McCaul stepped out of the car. 'Stay beside me and walk slowly.'

They took a couple of paces and the dogs growled, baring their fangs. Jennifer halted and McCaul gripped her arm. 'Just stand still a minute.' The

Dobermans stared menacingly, but they didn't budge. McCaul started to take another step, but the dogs snarled and rose off their haunches, as if to attack.

'*Sitz, Ferdie! Sitz, Hans!*'

A man appeared in the doorway and the dogs obeyed his command instantly. He looked to be in his fifties, with greying hair, and wore a frayed work jacket, his left hand tucked inside the front pocket. Jennifer saw that a chunk of flesh was missing from the tip of his nose.

'*Sprechen Sie Englisch?*' Jennifer asked.

'Yes, I speak English,' he said.

'We're looking for Heinrich Vogel.'

'I'm Heinrich Vogel. Who are you?'

'My name is Jennifer March and this is Frank McCaul.'

'If you wish to hire a mountain guide to take you up to the Wasenhorn, I suggest you look elsewhere. I'm busy right now.'

'We don't need to hire a guide. But we do need to talk.'

Vogel frowned. 'About what?'

'Herr Vogel, I'd really appreciate it if we could talk inside.'

Vogel pursed his lips and whistled. The Dobermans bounded into the house and their master jerked his head towards the open door. 'Come, follow me.'

They stepped inside. Vogel allowed them to enter first, then the Dobermans took up position in front of the door, as if blocking retreat.

The room was a typical Swiss kitchen, with a big pine dresser and an open wood stove blazing in a corner. A pine table dominated the centre, and scattered newspapers and a pair of binoculars lay on top. Mounted on a wall near the dresser was a video monitor that displayed a picture of the front yard.

Jennifer noticed several framed photographs on the dresser. One was of a group of four men, all wearing mountain gear, posing for the camera on a rocky ledge. One of the climbers was Heinrich Vogel. Beside him stood a dark-haired man with a thin face, a slash for a mouth and thick black eyebrows. He wore a blue parka. Jennifer thought his face looked familiar.

Vogel gestured for them to join him at the table. 'What's this about?'

Jennifer began by explaining about the Wasenhorn corpse. 'Perhaps you heard about it, Herr Vogel?'

Vogel glanced towards the video monitor before he shifted his gaze back to his visitors. '*Ja*, I heard talk about it in the village.'

'The police found something on the body that might interest you.' Jennifer removed the note from her bag.

Vogel's left hand remained in his jacket pocket. He took the offered paper with his right, carefully studied it and frowned.

'The name "H. Vogel" is clear,' Jennifer said, 'along with the words "Berg Edelweiss", and the last three digits of your phone number. Might you be able to explain why the dead man had this note in his possession, Herr Vogel?'

'I have no idea.' He studied them cautiously. 'Are you police?'

'No, I'm a private investigator,' McCaul replied.

Vogel glanced at the monitor again, then towards the window, and anxiously licked his lips. 'I am a mountain guide, and often take people up to the Wasenhorn. Perhaps this man once used me as a guide. What was his name?'

'The police didn't identify the body,' McCaul answered. 'They probably never will. The morgue in Turin where it was being kept was destroyed yesterday by an explosion.'

Vogel shifted slightly in his chair. '*Ja*, I read about the explosion this morning.' He pointed to the front page of a Swiss newspaper lying on the table. 'But I really don't understand why this man should have my name and address.'

Jennifer had the feeling that Vogel was playing them for fools. 'Is your guide business legal and registered, Herr Vogel?'

'Yes, of course. Swiss law is very strict about such things.'

'Then I imagine you have to keep a record of the people who hire you?'

'Well . . . yes . . .'

'Perhaps you could look at your engagements for around April the 15th, two years ago. The police think the victim died around that date.'

'Are you suggesting that *I* guided him up to the mountain?'

'No. But if there's a chance the victim once hired your services, then your records may help prove his identity.'

Vogel didn't reply, and McCaul said, 'Herr Vogel, the police no doubt will want to ask you the same questions. What harm can it do if you help us?'

Reluctantly Vogel got to his feet, and removed his hand from his pocket. Jennifer saw that the tips of three of his fingers were missing.

'Frostbite,' Vogel explained, noticing her stare.

'I'm sorry.'

'*Nein*, it is me who should apologise, for being so cautious. But I live alone, and one has to be careful these days. Now, if you will excuse me, I will see if I can find my records.' Vogel left the room, his footsteps fading down the hall.

Jennifer stood up and crossed the room to the dresser, the Dobermans watching her. She pointed at the photograph of the group of men. 'Look.'

McCaul joined her. 'What is it?'

'There's something familiar about the man in the blue parka. Look at his eyes, Frank. And his mouth. I know I've seen . . .'

'What's the matter?'

'*Oh my God*. The man in the ice. It's *him*.'

McCaul studied the photograph. They heard the dogs snarl. When they turned Vogel was standing in the doorway, a pistol clutched in his hand. McCaul made to reach for the Beretta but the dogs bristled, ready to attack.

'Take your hand out of your pocket,' Vogel ordered McCaul, and waved his pistol at Jennifer. 'Reach over very slowly and remove his weapon.'

Jennifer's hand shook as she prised the Beretta from McCaul's pocket.

'Place the gun on the table.'

She obeyed, and Vogel reached across and slipped it into his pocket.

He waved the pistol, indicating the chairs. 'Sit, and keep your hands on the table. Attempt to move and I will kill you both.'

'We didn't come here to harm you, Herr Vogel,' Jennifer said as she sat down. 'Only to look for information.'

Perspiration beaded Vogel's brow. 'Don't lie. You had a gun.'

'The gun was for our own protection.' She pointed at the photograph on the dresser. 'One of the men in the photo is the Wasenhorn victim, isn't he, Herr Vogel? And you know his identity. But he wasn't alone on the glacier when he died. My father may have been with him. Maybe you know that, too?'

'Your father? What are you talking about?'

'My father went missing two years ago. The police found his passport near the body—that's the reason we're here. I have his photograph in my bag. If I could show you . . .'

Vogel's eyes flickered with suspicion. 'No, hand the bag here. Do it slowly.'

Jennifer laid her tote bag on the table and Vogel rummaged with his free hand until he found the photograph.

'My father's name is Paul March. Have you ever seen him before?'

Vogel turned ashen as he studied the snapshot. He didn't lower the gun, but suddenly his expression changed from suspicion to curiosity as he looked back at Jennifer. 'Tell me *exactly* why you came here.'

WHEN JENNIFER FINISHED, the only sound in the kitchen was the ticking of the clock. Vogel's face was white and his hands trembled.

'You know the man who died on the Wasenhorn, don't you?' Jennifer said.

'*Ja*, I know.'

'Who was he?'

'My brother, Peter,' Vogel admitted hoarsely.

'What was he doing up on the mountain?'

'The night before he died, Peter drove here with two men he had picked up from Brig railway station. One of them was Karl Lazar, the other was this one . . .' Vogel tapped the photograph. 'The man you say is your father. I'd never met him before, but I knew Lazar. For many years he visited Murnau to ski, that's how he became acquainted with my brother and me.'

'Why did they come here?'

'Lazar asked me and my brother to guide them . . . no, *told* us to guide them across the glacier into Italy. They were very anxious. It was only later that I learned they were trying to flee from their Russian Mafia friends.'

Jennifer was stunned. 'I don't understand.'

'I thought you had come here to kill me. I thought you were one of them.'

'Herr Vogel, who was Karl Lazar and why was my father with him?'

Vogel was suddenly alarmed. He got to his feet and studied the security monitor. 'There isn't time to explain. They will be here soon. I understand now why they were watching the house. *You* were the reason. And when they come, they will kill us all.'

'What are you talking about? *Who* will come? *Who* will kill us?'

'You have to leave right now.' Clutching the pistol, Vogel moved to the window.

The Dobermans started snarling. 'Call them off!' McCaul shouted.

'*Sitz, Ferdie! Sitz, Hans!*' Vogel ordered.

The dogs growled defiantly, then sat still.

'Tell them to move outside.'

'*Draussen! Draussen sofort!*'

The dogs scampered into the hallway. McCaul slammed the door shut, wedging the table hard against the frame. He lunged and wrenched the weapon from Vogel's hand. but as he did so Vogel fumbled in his pocket for the Beretta.

'Frank!' Jennifer screamed as a shot exploded, slamming into McCaul's arm. Jennifer flung herself at Vogel and tried to prise the pistol from his grasp. Eventually McCaul staggered over and wrenched the gun away.

'Please . . . please . . . don't shoot me,' Vogel begged. 'I didn't mean to harm you. I meant only to protect myself. I swear . . .'

McCaul clapped a hand on his arm. 'Find something to stop the bleeding.'

Jennifer found a towel and tied it tightly round McCaul's arm until the bleeding subsided. 'Are you OK? Let me see.' She found two holes where the bullet had drilled through his jacket and passed through his upper arm.

They heard the sound of a car and Vogel became alarmed. 'They are here. I told you they would come.'

Jennifer moved to the window and saw a powerful black BMW speed in through the gates and roar up the driveway. The car halted on the gravel in front of the house. McCaul joined her at the window, dragging Vogel after him, just in time to see the car doors open and two men climb out.

One was the blond from the train. He had a sticking plaster across his forehead and spoke into a cellphone. This time his accomplice was a fit-looking man in his thirties carrying a machine pistol.

McCaul said to Vogel, 'Who are those guys?'

'I . . . I don't know. They could be the men who have been watching the house for days now, ever since reports of the body were in the newspapers. They follow me when I travel to the village.'

'Who do you *think* they are?'

'Russian Mafia. The same people Lazar worked for.'

The blond finished talking on his cellphone. He took out a pistol, nodded to his companion, and they moved forward.

McCaul stepped away from the window. 'You'd better have a back way out.'

'That way.' Vogel pointed to a door at the rear of the kitchen. 'It leads to the basement and out the back, to the barn and garage.'

McCaul opened the door and flicked a light switch, revealing steps leading down. 'You're coming with us. Where are the keys to the Mercedes?'

'In the ignition. But my . . . my dogs. I need to call them—'

'There's no time. Get moving.'

McCaul locked the door behind them, and they hurried down the stairs to a basement room used as a fuel store. Logs were piled high against the walls. At the far end was a door. They heard the Dobermans barking upstairs, followed by a scream, then shots rang out.

Vogel gave a distraught cry. 'They're shooting my dogs!'

'We'll be next if we don't get out of here.' McCaul handed Jennifer the Beretta. 'If anyone comes down the stairs just point it and squeeze the trigger.' McCaul lifted the door latch. 'I'll be back as quick as I can.'

'Where are you going?'

'To take a look outside.'

THE SOUND OF GUNFIRE died and suddenly the silence in the house was overpowering. Vogel was still distraught. 'Those bastards killed my dogs . . .'

'Please, Herr Vogel, keep your voice down.'

'You're mad if you think we can escape alive . . .'

'What happened the night you took my father up to the mountain?' Jennifer spoke in a fierce whisper.

'Lazar had a gun and said he'd shoot me and Peter if we didn't guide them over the border. I warned him that they were risking death, crossing the glacier at night, but he wouldn't listen. He wanted climbing gear for him and your father, and three rucksacks. Once they'd dressed for the journey I saw him stuff some briefcases into two of the rucksacks, and put some clothes into the third. We set off before midnight, and reached the glacier two hours later, just as the weather turned ugly. It became a terrible blizzard, impossible to see more than a couple of metres in front of your face. Then I heard a scream and Peter was gone. I knew he'd fallen into a crevasse.'

'What happened to my father?'

'I lost him and Lazar in the blizzard, but I really didn't care. I just wanted to get off that mountain and back here. It took me four hours and cost me my fingers and half my nose, but I was lucky to be alive.'

Jennifer heard a floorboard creak upstairs. How long could it be before the men found the basement? Her heart pounded.

'Why didn't you tell the police what happened to your brother?'

'How could I? It was easier to tell the locals that Peter had gone to live in Zürich. Otherwise, I'd be cutting my own throat.'

'What do you mean?'

'Years ago Lazar hired me as a courier for his Mafia friends. Every few months, I'd cross the Wasenhorn into Italy to pick up a package—a big rucksack full of money—and then I'd hike back across the glacier. Lazar's friends would take the money to a bank in Zürich where it was laundered. I knew what I did was illegal, but I didn't care; the Russians paid me too well.'

'Was my father part of this conspiracy?'

'How should I know? All I knew was there were two desperate men trying to escape with a fortune.'

'What do you mean by that?'

'As we made our way up to the glacier Lazar told us that he and your father had stolen a fortune from the Russian Mafia. He said that Peter and I would be paid generously for our help but that we'd have to keep our mouths shut.

But we had the feeling that once we helped them over the border they would murder us. That's why I fled when I had the chance.'

'Did you speak with my father?'

'No. Lazar did all the talking.'

'I need to know if my father could have survived the blizzard.'

'Impossible. The snowdrifts were several metres high. He and Lazar couldn't have found their way out of treacherous weather like that.'

'But *you* did.'

'Only by a miracle.'

'Didn't you go back to look for their bodies?'

'*Ja*, six weeks later, when I was well enough. But there was no sign of the bodies. They probably fell into a crevasse.'

'You're wrong. One of them survived and reached the Crown of Thorns monastery five days later.'

'No one could have stayed alive in those snowdrifts for five days.'

'There's a mountain hut nearby where they could have found shelter.'

Vogel didn't look convinced. 'Believe me, you are clinging to a vain hope.'

Suddenly the doorknob rattled at the top of the stairs. Jennifer's pulse raced, then she heard another noise and spun round. The door leading to the outside began to open slowly. She raised the Beretta and prepared to fire.

'It's me,' a familiar voice whispered, as McCaul appeared.

'They're upstairs, Frank. They're trying to open the door.'

Sweat beaded McCaul's face as the doorknob rattled again. 'There's a guy with a machine gun covering the back of the house and he's coming our way. Both of you get back against the wall.' McCaul took the Maglite torch from his pocket, flicked it on, and stepped over to the light bulb in the centre of the room. He raised himself on his toes, and used his coat sleeve to grip and loosen the bulb. The room was plunged into darkness, except for the weak glimmer from the torch.

Jennifer and Vogel pressed their backs against the wall and McCaul put a finger to his lips for them to be silent. Then he picked up a heavy log from the wood pile, stepped back behind the door and flicked off the torch.

Seconds later, the basement door creaked open. Daylight trickled in and the barrel of a gun appeared. The door opened wider and one of the intruders entered, clutching his machine pistol. Just then the door rattled on the landing above and he looked up in alarm. 'Dimitri?' the man called out softly.

McCaul lunged out of the shadows wielding the log, and struck the man's arms. He yelped and dropped the gun and McCaul struck him across the back of the neck. The man gave a muffled cry and slumped to the floor.

As McCaul grabbed the machine pistol, the door above crashed open and the blond appeared. Vogel panicked and bolted towards the far door. The blond fired his pistol from the top of the stairs, hitting him in the back. McCaul raised the machine pistol and fired in reply, a rapid burst that gouged plaster and chipped the landing walls. The blond tried to back out of the door but McCaul fired again, stitching the wall above the man's head.

'Put your gun on the floor!' McCaul screamed. 'Put it down or you're dead.'

The blond dropped his gun. McCaul was up the stairs in an instant, and grabbed the man by the coat. The blond staggered halfway down the stairs before he lost his footing and landed in a heap on the floor.

'Get up,' McCaul ordered, as he reached him.

The blond got to his feet, and McCaul searched him for weapons. Jennifer looked around. The other assailant was lying near the door, still unconscious.

She went to feel for Vogel's pulse, but there was none.

BACK UPSTAIRS McCaul pulled up a kitchen chair and pushed the blond onto the seat. 'Who exactly are you, Dimitri?'

'Go fuck yourself,' the man answered.

'Why are you trying to kill me?' Jennifer asked.

'If I had wanted to, I could have killed you long before now.'

Jennifer persisted. 'Who are you working for? What do you want from me?'

The blond remained defiantly silent. McCaul grabbed him by his lapels and hauled him to his feet. 'She asked you a question.'

The man sneered. 'Go ahead and shoot, but that's all you'll get out of me.'

McCaul struck him a blow to the jaw, then another, punching him hard. As he made to strike him again, Jennifer grabbed his arm. 'No, Frank!'

McCaul let the man go. He collapsed into the chair, barely conscious, and his head lolled to one side, blood trickling from his mouth.

'This guy's not going to talk. We're wasting our time.' He searched the man's clothes and found a wallet and a set of car keys, then took Jennifer by the arm and led her back down to the basement, where he searched through the second assailant's pockets. The man was still unconscious. McCaul found his wallet and stuffed it into Jennifer's tote bag, then removed the man's trouser belt and tied his hands behind his back. 'Now let's get out to the car.'

A GAS STATION lay ahead and McCaul slowed the Volkswagen and pulled in. His shoulder had started to throb. He removed his jacket and Jennifer examined the wound. The bleeding had stopped but the flesh was raw and angry.

'We ought to find a doctor, Frank.'

'Forget it. I visit a surgery with a gunshot wound, first thing you know the cops will turn up. The wound's pretty clean. We'll find a drugstore later and dress it properly. Now how about we see what's in that bag of yours?'

They searched through the assailants' wallets and found an assortment of Swiss and European currency, but no ID.

'We've reached a dead end here. Have you still got your passport?'

'In my bag. Why?'

'The trail's gone cold and all we've got is the stuff Vogel told us. I think we ought to hop on the first plane home and try to find out what happened to your father's security box. Whatever's inside may be the key we're looking for. And maybe we'll learn who's been pulling those guys' strings.'

THEIR FIRST SHOCK had been the bullet-ridden Dobermans and the entrance hall drenched with blood. They stepped past the dogs and Grimes led them down to a basement. They saw the body sprawled by the door.

Kelso finished examining the corpse and stood to address Fellows. 'Did you take a look upstairs?'

'It's empty. Grimes found this in one of the bedroom closets.' Fellows showed them a driving licence bearing the dead man's photograph and the name Heinrich Vogel. 'And there was some correspondence lying around. Seems our friend Vogel here was a ski instructor and mountain guide.'

Kelso examined the licence. 'We may have found our mule. Go examine the BMW outside. Find out if it belonged to Vogel.'

As Fellows and Grimes left, Kelso studied the blood-spattered floor.

Mark was tortured with worry. 'Where is she, Kelso?'

'I'm not a psychic, Ryan, but it looks like we've got another blood bath, and I'm not exactly hopeful.'

Mark charged across the room and pushed him back against the wall. 'Why couldn't you have told Jennifer the truth from the beginning? You had to play your stupid games and put her in jeopardy. This is all your fault, Kelso. And I promise you, I'm going to nail your ass for what you've done.'

Kelso turned ashen. 'Get your goddamned hands off me.'

Mark released his grip, and crossed the room to examine the blood trails.

He followed them out into the yard, looked up towards the roof and frowned. Then he stepped back into the basement and headed towards the stairs.

Kelso was close behind him. 'What are you doing, Ryan?'

'Saying my prayers.' Mark raced up the stairs.

Kelso followed him into the kitchen. '*What?*'

'There's a camera out front,' Mark explained, 'and another on the roof. If the cameras are working, they either have a live video feed with no playback, or else the feed's recorded. I'm praying it's the type that's recorded, because that means there's a chance we might learn something about what happened here.'

Mark followed the wires from the back of the TV security monitor down to a cupboard near the sink, and yanked open the cupboard door. '*Bingo*.'

Inside, on a shelf, was a video recorder with a tape running in the slot.

GENEVA WAS DAZZLING in the spring sunshine. Water cascaded down from the giant Jet d'Eau fountain out in the lake like a million cut diamonds. Trams trundled past luxury shops, and in the cobbled streets elegant cafés and jewellery stores gave a feeling of solid Swiss respectability. It seemed so normal that Jennifer found it hard to take in what had just happened.

McCaul drove along the lake shore and the Rue Versonnex until he pulled up outside the magnificent Hôtel du Lac, the most luxurious in Geneva.

'Why stop here?'

McCaul pointed to a plush-looking travel office next door. 'It's better to buy plane tickets here than hang around in a queue at the airport ticket desk. This way, if anyone's watching the terminal they'll have less chance of spotting us.' He emptied the assailants' wallets and counted their cash, which came to over five thousand in US dollars. 'This ought to cover our tickets.'

He disappeared inside the travel office and came out fifteen minutes later.

'Well?' Jennifer asked as he climbed in beside her.

'There's no direct flight to New York until tomorrow. But there's one to New York via Paris, leaving Geneva in just under an hour.' He waved a wad of airline tickets. 'If we hurry, we might make it.'

THEY WATCHED the tape and saw Jennifer and McCaul arrive at the front, and later depart by the track at the rear of the house. They saw the two armed assailants step out of the BMW and advance towards the house, then later the blond drag his comrade out to the garaged Mercedes and speed away. From the time display on the tape, Mark calculated that Jennifer and McCaul had left in the Volkswagen only fifteen minutes before he and Kelso had arrived.

The next hour was a frantic blur to Mark. They sped towards Murnau, scoured the streets for half an hour, then headed north towards Zürich, trying to get a bead on the Volkswagen, until Kelso gave up in frustration. He took out his cellphone and ordered Fellows to pull into a gas station while he made an urgent call to CIA headquarters in Langley.

MCCAUL ABANDONED the car in the Geneva airport lot. They stopped off at a line of shops in the terminal. At a pharmacy, Jennifer bought antiseptic cream, sticking plaster and gauze, and a pair of non-prescription reading glasses. In a gift store next door they purchased two overnight bags, a Tyrolean hat, a baseball cap, a woollen scarf and sunglasses. As McCaul donned the hat and reading glasses, Jennifer said, 'Shouldn't we dress your arm?'

'There isn't time. I'll take care of it after we board. They'll be looking for a couple. Stay near me, but not so close that it might look like we're together.'

McCaul handed over her tickets. Jennifer slipped on the sunglasses and the baseball cap and wrapped the scarf round the bottom half of her face.

They checked in without a hitch and headed towards the boarding gates. Fifteen minutes later, Jennifer and McCaul started to board the Air France flight to Paris, with an onward connection to JFK, New York.

FORTY MILES away, Kelso was talking to Langley on his cellphone as the Opel hurtled along the autobahn to Geneva. According to the CIA's computer wizards, at six minutes past noon an international airline booking computer in Paris had recorded that a Frank McCaul and a Jennifer March had purchased two tickets from a Geneva travel agent for an Air France shuttle to Paris, departing Geneva at 12.45, with an onward connection to New York.

Kelso switched off his phone. 'It's done. Undercover agents will tag them the moment they land at JFK. Langley's hacking into the airline computer. We'll know the moment they board. I've arranged for three undercover agents from our Paris station to board their flight at Charles de Gaulle and baby-sit them until they reach New York.'

'So what do *we* do? Sit on our asses until the next flight?'

'Langley's booked us on a private jet to New York.'

'And then what?'

'Maybe you were right, Ryan,' Kelso confessed. 'It's time we dropped this charade and told Jennifer what's going on.'

PART FIVE

New York

Lou Garuda arrived at a suite of offices in downtown Manhattan. He took the elevator to the sixth floor and found the room he was looking for. The sign in scratched gold lettering said: FRANK MCCAUL, PRIVATE INVESTIGATOR.

Garuda knocked, and when he got no reply he wandered down the hall to another office. The door was open. A sign on it said: CAROLE LIPPMAN SECRETARIAL SERVICES. A middle-aged woman sat typing at a computer.

The woman looked up and smiled. 'Can I help you?'

'Frank McCaul, the PI down the hall. He ain't around?'

'He left for Switzerland a couple of days ago. I'm afraid his son had a tragic accident in the Alps.'

'Gee, I'm real sorry to hear that. You know Frank well?'

'Sure, he's had his office here for quite a few years. I do most of his secretarial work. Were you thinking of hiring him?'

Garuda smiled, flashed his badge. 'No, I'm with the Long Beach Police Department. You mind if I ask you a couple of questions about Mr McCaul?'

THE AIR FRANCE 747 climbed above the rain clouds over Paris and when it reached cruising altitude levelled out to begin its flight across the Atlantic.

McCaul touched Jennifer's shoulder. 'You can relax now. We're at thirty-five thousand feet. We're completely safe.'

The next five hours were a blank to Jennifer as she settled into a deep sleep. When she woke they were only two hours from New York.

McCaul was beside her and wide awake. 'How'd you sleep?'

'Like a two-year-old. How's your arm?'

'It could be worse, but I think I spoke too soon about us being safe.'

'What are you talking about?'

McCaul was uneasy. 'We're being watched by three passengers and I'll bet you a hundred bucks they're tails.'

'Which three?'

'Don't look now, but two of them are guys, seated together eight rows ahead. One's red-haired, wearing a grey business suit, and the other's in a navy-blue windcheater and glasses. The third's a blonde woman in a charcoal two-piece, a dozen seats behind us in row thirty-six.'

'How can you be sure they're tails?'

'Two of them passed our aisle while you were asleep. They tried to make it appear innocent, but I know an appraising look when I see one. Don't worry, they won't try anything while we're aboard. Walk to the washroom and take a look at the two guys, but don't make eye contact. On the way back, go to the galley and ask the stewardess for a drink. You'll see the woman on your way.'

Jennifer stepped out into the aisle and walked to the washroom. As she passed row sixteen she caught a side-on glimpse of the man in the grey suit. He was about forty, muscular, with thinning red hair.

When she came out of the washroom she passed the two men face on. The guy in the suit didn't look up, but the man next to him did. He wore a navy-blue windcheater, a checked cotton shirt and glasses, his hair cropped close to his skull. He gave her a casual glance as she walked towards the galley.

As she approached row thirty-six, Jennifer noticed a woman in a charcoal two-piece with short blonde hair, flicking through a magazine. Jennifer saw her glance up in her direction for just an instant, but it was enough. McCaul was right. She got a glass of water from the galley and rejoined him.

'How are we going to lose them?'

'Maybe I've got an idea.' McCaul pressed the call button.

A few moments later a stewardess came down the aisle. '*Monsieur?*'

'Does the aircraft have a satellite telephone system on board?'

'*Oui.* But only in first-class.'

'You'd better lead me to it. This is a personal emergency.'

WITH NO LUGGAGE to retrieve, Jennifer and McCaul were the first in the queue for Immigration. Once their passports had been scrutinised, they headed towards Customs, but halfway there McCaul suddenly diverted Jennifer towards the rest rooms. 'Wait here and pretend you're searching in your bag.'

'What are you up to?'

'Just trust me and do as I say.'

Jennifer pretended to rummage in her bag. To her left was a solid steel door with a sign saying NO UNAUTHORISED PERSONNEL BEYOND THIS POINT, and a security keypad to one side. She glanced right and saw a couple of armed police. Then she spotted the three passengers near a pillar: the blonde woman nearest, the two men behind her, all trying to appear inconspicuous. Jennifer heard the panic in her own voice. 'They're behind us, Frank.'

'I see them. My guess is that with the cops around they won't try anything until we're in arrivals. Except this is where we're going to lose them.' McCaul indicated the steel security door.

Jennifer was puzzled. They would need the code to open the door. 'How?'

'With inside help.' McCaul punched a number into his cellphone and spoke. 'Where the hell are you, Marty? We're waiting where you told me, by the staff entrance. You'd better move it, buddy. Trouble's right on our tail.'

As McCaul flicked off his phone, Jennifer looked at the two men and the woman still waiting by the pillar. They seemed to suspect that something was amiss but looked unsure about what they should do next.

Jennifer's heart jumped when she heard a sudden noise. She looked round as the security door burst open. An overweight man with a bushy black moustache stood inside. He wore an airport official's uniform with a peaked cap and carried a clipboard in his hand, a staff photo-ID dangling from a chain round his neck. The name on the ID identified him as Marty Summers.

'The hell kept you, Marty?'

'Got here as quick as I could.' The man spoke in a Bronx accent. 'We've got to do this thing real damned *fast*, so move it, pal.' He ushered them inside.

Jennifer was propelled through the door by McCaul. She looked back and glimpsed the two men and the blonde woman running towards the door, but they were too late and it slammed in their faces. As Marty led them along a corridor, Jennifer heard banging on the door but she didn't look back.

'Marty works for airport security,' McCaul explained. 'Lucky for us he owed me a favour. I once caught his wife in bed with a guy who worked at the Hertz desk and got the photographs to prove it. Didn't I, Marty?'

'Sure did. The slut was sleeping with half the frigging airport. Best thing I ever did, saying adios to that bitch. Who were the assholes following you?'

'A long story. What about the car?'

Marty handed McCaul a set of car keys. 'It's in lot three, as you come out of the elevator on level four. A blue Chevy Impala. And I'd like it back in one piece, man. I still owe two years' repayments, so drive gently, you hear?'

'That's a promise.'

THE CHARTERED GULFSTREAM touched down thirty minutes behind the Air France 747 and Kelso was the first off. As they raced down the steps to the tarmac his cellphone sounded. When he answered, Kelso's voice became hoarse with anger. 'You've got to be kidding me. *How did that happen?* ... I want the airport scoured, every exit watched. Just find them, you hear?'

'What's wrong?' Mark asked.

Kelso was livid. 'Jennifer and McCaul have given my people the slip.'

THE MAN NAMED Marty watched from the doorway as McCaul and Jennifer headed towards the parking lot. He removed his uniform cap and tossed it into a garbage bin by the door. Then he punched his cellphone keypad.

A voice answered. 'What's the story?'

'They're heading for the Chevy.' The Bronx accent was gone.

'How'd it go?'

'She fell for the double act. Nick and me played it along, stuck to the script, and everything went real smooth. No hitches.'

'Perfect. Now let's finish the job.'

GARUDA'S NEXT visit was to a peaceful-looking neighbourhood in Hempstead, Long Island. He found the address at the end of a cul-de-sac. Frank McCaul's home was painted grey and butter-cream. Garuda noticed a teenager skateboarding at the far end of the cul-de-sac, and a guy tending his lawn in a garden across the street, but neither paid him much attention. He locked his car, strolled up to McCaul's verandah and rang the bell. No answer.

The house was protected by a thick hedge and no one could see him from the street. He rapped on the door and called out, 'Anybody home?'

No answer. Garuda opened his wallet and took out a penknife he'd confiscated years ago from a burglar. He slipped one of the filed blades into the lock, fiddled it around until he felt the tumblers click, and the lock sprang open.

Garuda wandered along a hallway and into the lounge. He spotted a bunch of photographs on the walls, mostly of a guy he assumed was McCaul, some of them taken with a kid wearing climbing gear and a helmet, with mountains in the background. Garuda wandered upstairs to a narrow landing. He was about to search the bedrooms when he heard footsteps in the hallway below.

The stairs creaked. He wrenched out his Glock and stepped onto the landing.

A guy was coming up the stairs. Middle aged, balding.

'Hold it right there, pal.'

Garuda recognised the neighbour he'd seen tending his lawn across the street. The guy carried a pair of leather gardening gloves in one hand. When he saw the Glock he took a couple of steps backwards down the stairs.

Garuda flashed his badge. 'Police. What are you doing in here?'

The man's fear vaporised when he saw the badge. 'I could ask you the same question, Officer. Saw you come in here and didn't know what the hell was going on. Name's Norrie Sinclair. I live across the street. We've got a damned good neighbourhood watch programme around here, I'll have you know.'

'Glad to hear it.' Garuda put his gun away. 'Frank McCaul lives here, right?'

'Sure. I usually keep an eye on the place when Frank's away.'

'Yeah? When did you see him last, Mr Sinclair?'

'A few days back. He had to travel abroad. His son, Chuck, died, you know.'

'So I heard. When exactly did Frank leave?'

'On Sunday afternoon he flew to Zürich. He was pretty cut up, could barely hold himself together. Some people came to take him to the airport.'

Garuda frowned. 'You said Sunday. You're sure about that?'

'Of course I'm sure. Why, what's the problem here, Officer?'

Garuda frowned again. 'Who came to pick him up?'

'Two guys I'd never seen before, in a dark Buick sedan.' The neighbour looked suspiciously at Garuda. 'You mind me asking how you got in here?'

'The front door was open.'

The neighbour looked back at the porch. 'That's weird. When I checked yesterday it was locked. What did you say your name was, Officer?'

Garuda headed down the stairs and out of the door. 'Detective Smith.'

MARK STOOD outside the JFK arrivals terminal, watching Kelso have an argument with a blonde woman and two men. Mark reckoned they were CIA; it was obvious Kelso was lambasting them. Then he barked a bunch of orders, the group dispersed into the terminal and he strode over and said bitterly to Mark, 'Some guy opened a security door in the Customs hall and they got away.'

Grimes and Fellows appeared and Kelso beckoned them. 'Take the parking lots. The others will search the terminal and the public transport queues. I'll take the car-hire and limo desks. Give it fifteen minutes, and meet back here.'

As the two men raced away, Kelso said to Mark, 'Take the bars, restaurants and the men's rest rooms. If you haven't spotted them within fifteen minutes, shift your ass back here.'

MARK TOOK the escalator to the mezzanine and passed between the busy restaurant tables. There was no sign of anyone who looked remotely like Jennifer or McCaul. Next, he tried the bar, then the men's rest rooms near by and the coffee dock, but without any luck.

A hundred yards across the mezzanine he spotted the blonde woman and her two companions, frantically searching a sea of passengers. As he turned back, Mark noticed a payphone. He realised this was the first chance he'd had in the last twenty-four hours to call Garuda. He stepped over to the payphone and rummaged in his pocket for change.

Garuda answered his cellphone on the second ring. 'Where the frig are you, Mark? You were supposed to call me back.'

'I'm in JFK arrivals. Just got in twenty minutes ago. I'm listening.'

'Well, I did some digging into McCaul's background like you asked, and called out to his address on Long Island. It all looks pretty legit, but there's something fishy that I don't understand.'

'*What's* fishy?'

'According to a neighbour, McCaul left for the airport last Sunday after he was picked up at home by a couple of guys in a dark Buick. Which meant he should have arrived in Switzerland on Monday morning at the latest, but you said he didn't get there until Tuesday, so there's a whole day missing from his schedule. The woman at McCaul's secretarial service said he'd definitely booked to fly direct to Zürich on Sunday evening. So I had a friend of mine at JFK check the bookings. McCaul's ticket for the Sunday evening was cancelled an hour before he was due to travel, and rebooked for the following night. Does that make any kind of sense?'

'No.' Mark's mind was working overtime. 'Is that everything?'

'That's it. So how about telling me now what's going on?'

Mark suddenly saw Grimes come up the escalator. 'I've got to go, Lou.'

'Hey, wait a sec, that ain't good enough,' Garuda protested.

Mark said, 'Lou, I really can't talk about this.'

'And here's me thinking we were working together.' Garuda hung up.

MCCAUL SWITCHED on the headlights. It was five o'clock in the afternoon, but the sun was buried behind a mass of dark clouds. They had been driving for half an hour. Every few minutes Jennifer had checked over her shoulder, but in the heavy traffic it was impossible to know whether they were being followed.

'Stop worrying, Jennifer. This time we've given them the slip.'

She hoped he was right. 'Why are we going this way?'

'I thought it was the quickest route to Long Beach.'

'Frank, I need to see Bobby first. I need to know if he's OK. The

Cauldwell's only a ten-minute detour. Please.'

'OK, but do you think you could do the driving? I've got a call to make.' He pulled in, got out of the car, and Jennifer slid into the driver's seat. McCaul climbed into the passenger side and opened the glove compartment. She saw an automatic pistol and a cellphone stashed inside. McCaul took out the pistol, laid it on his lap, and punched in a number on the cellphone.

Jennifer stared at the pistol. 'Why is there a gun in there?'

'Shut up a minute.' McCaul cradled the phone to his ear. Jennifer heard the faint click at the other end of the line, but she couldn't hear who McCaul spoke to. 'It's me. I'm heading for Cove End. Meet me there in half an hour.'

He flicked off the phone and Jennifer stared at him, perplexed. There was a cold edge to his tone as he said, 'Start the car.'

'Frank? Frank, what's going on?'

He picked up the gun. 'And you can stop calling me Frank. Now do as I say. Start the car and drive towards Long Beach.'

MARK FOUND Kelso waiting outside arrivals. He was talking on his cellphone as a black limo driven by Fellows drew up at the kerb.

Kelso flicked off his phone, strode over to Mark and said, 'Get in the limo. The others are going to stay here and continue the search, just in case.'

'I thought you told me you had Frank McCaul checked out?'

'So I did. What about it?'

'I did my own investigating and there's something not right about McCaul. Either you lied to me, Kelso, or else you made a grievous mistake.'

At that moment Grimes rushed out of the arrivals building. Fellows got out of the limo. Kelso said to Mark, 'This isn't the place to have this conversation. If you want to talk, get in the car.'

Mark was livid. 'I'm going nowhere until I get the truth,' he yelled. 'And I want it now. What are you and the CIA really up to, Kelso?'

Passers-by began to stare. Fellows cupped a hand over Mark's mouth and opened the rear door as Grimes grabbed him in an arm lock and forced him into the limo. Kelso held an ID up to the pavement audience. 'Police. This man is in our custody. There's nothing more to see here.'

Kelso climbed into the back, balled his fist and struck Mark a blow to the face. 'You *idiot*. That's for shooting your mouth off in public.'

Fellows climbed in the front to start the engine and the limo screeched away from the kerb.

Mark's jaw was on fire. 'Where are you taking me?'

Kelso said, 'Grimes spotted you on a payphone in the terminal, Ryan. So you'd better tell me who you called, and *fast*.'

'You're breaking the law by holding me against my will. It's kidnapping.'

'Right now I *am* the law. Now answer the damned question.'

'I had a friend of mine run a background check on McCaul. He called at McCaul's address on Long Island and discovered something odd.'

Kelso raised an eyebrow. 'What?'

'You told me McCaul flew to Switzerland on Tuesday. According to his neighbour, he left Sunday and was picked up by two men in a dark Buick.'

Kelso stiffened. He removed the envelope containing the photograph of McCaul from his pocket and flicked on the interior light. 'Take a look again at McCaul's mugshot. Are you still sure this is the guy you saw?'

Mark studied the photograph. 'It's a lousy photo and I only got a brief look at him, but he had the same general appearance, same hairstyle, hair colour . . .'

Kelso shook his head. 'That means nothing, Ryan. A haircut and a cheap bottle of hair dye would take care of that. Now I think about it, McCaul's presence at the scene of Jennifer's accident seems just too convenient. It could have been a set-up, and McCaul may not be who he says he is.'

Mark's face drained. 'You said his background checked out.'

'His *background*, Ryan. But unless we can identify him in the flesh we can't be a hundred per cent certain.'

'Then if he isn't McCaul, who the hell is he?'

'WHO ARE YOU?'

They were on the highway, driving east on Long Island. The sky had opened up and an icy sleet beat against the windscreen. Jennifer had the wipers on.

'You can call me Nick Staves. I work for the CIA.'

Jennifer stared at him. 'What happened to the real Frank McCaul?'

'McCaul's being looked after at a safe house outside New York.'

'Why did you impersonate him?'

Staves tucked the gun inside his jacket. 'So I could get close to you. Protect you from the people who intend to kill you.'

'Who intends to kill me?'

'A man named Jack Kelso. He once told you he was a friend of your father's, but that was a lie.'

Jennifer was stunned. 'Go on.'

'Kelso works for the CIA, and a couple of years back he ran a covert operation code-named Spiderweb. Its target was Prime International Securities.'

'*Why?*'

'It was owned by an offshore company run by the Moscayas, a Russian Mafia clan. Their fortune was invested in the US from illegal offshore accounts. Spiderweb was meant to shut down their business, permanently.'

'The Russian Mafia *owned* Prime?'

Staves nodded. 'They used it to launder their dirty money. Your father had no idea that the company he worked for was involved in criminal activity, until Kelso appears, tells him the truth, and convinces him to help get the paper evidence the CIA needed to nail Prime's owners.'

For the next mile, Staves explained about her father's criminal past. 'Kelso had his court and prison records destroyed as part of the deal. Fixed it so Joseph Delgado never existed. That's why the cops hit a brick wall with the name.'

Jennifer's mind was reeling, and she struggled to hold back tears. 'What was my father doing in Switzerland?'

'He was given instructions to withdraw fifty million from a Zürich bank used by Prime, and hand it over to a Moscaya gangster named Karl Lazar. Except it was all a set-up. Kelso had spun a web of deceit.'

'What do you mean?'

'He and a couple of his corrupt CIA buddies had struck a secret deal with Karl Lazar to steal the fifty million between them, and frame your father for the theft. They meant to kill him, get rid of his body, and make it look like he'd disappeared, so that the blame would fall solely on Paul March.'

'But why?'

'Greed, pure and simple. Had the plan worked it could have made them a fortune. Karl Lazar would force your father at gunpoint to cross over the Wasenhorn with him, where he planned to murder him along with the Vogels, dump their bodies into a crevasse, then later share the stash with Kelso and his people. But then the storm blew up and the whole thing went haywire.'

'Why didn't you tell me before now? Why did you put me through all this?'

'I was under CIA orders. The less you knew the better, at least until we found the disk and nailed Kelso. We couldn't even make Kelso's team aware that we knew he was crooked, in case he got to hear of it.'

'*We?*'

'The guy who helped us escape from the airport is one of my team. They'll be right behind us all the way.'

Jennifer's mind was in turmoil. 'Who killed my mother?'

'Kelso. He meant the attack on your family to appear as if it was all part of some game plan that your father had concocted before he vanished.'

'What . . . what happened to my father?'

'He probably died the night of the blizzard and his body's still somewhere up on the mountain. That's being realistic, Jennifer.'

'But *someone* survived . . .'

'We don't know that. The guy at the monastery could have been anyone.'

'It was my father. It *had* to be.' A surge of grief overwhelmed her, so intense that she couldn't focus on the road. She pulled in and laid her head on the steering wheel. Sobbing racked her body.

Staves put a hand gently on her shoulder. 'I'm sorry . . . You do believe me, Jennifer, don't you?'

She wiped her eyes. 'I don't know what to believe.'

Staves reached into his pocket and removed an ID wallet. He opened the flap and Jennifer saw the CIA logo on one side, and an embossed photograph of the man next to her on the other. The ID said his name was Nicolas Staves.

'How about you let me drive? You're in no fit state. And then I'll explain what Mark Ryan and Kelso have been up to.'

'*Mark?* Been up to? What are you talking about?'

THE LIMO was heading towards Manhattan. It had started to rain, a torrent of icy water hammering on the roof.

Mark said, 'You never explained how the Moscayas found out about the disk.'

'That's right, I never did.' Kelso turned round in his seat. 'Pull in, Fellows.'

Fellows did so. Kelso took out a pistol, screwed on a silencer and levelled the weapon at Mark.

Mark paled. 'What the hell are you doing?'

Even Grimes looked uneasy. 'I could ask the same thing, sir,' he said.

Kelso suddenly swivelled the Glock. It coughed once. The bullet hit Grimes in the chest, killing him instantly.

Fellows turned in his seat, confusion on his face. Kelso fired again, hitting him in the head, and his body jerked and collapsed against the steering wheel.

Mark attempted to lunge at Kelso, but the Glock was suddenly pointed at his chest again. 'Don't be a dumb asshole.'

'Are you insane, Kelso?'

Kelso rolled Grimes's body onto the floor and stepped out of the car. 'Get out. Put Fellows in the back and lie him on the floor.'

Mark dragged Fellows's corpse from the driver's seat and slid him into the back of the limo, rolling him onto the floor to join Grimes.

Kelso slammed the rear door. 'Now get in the front seat and drive.'

STAVES TURNED onto the highway for Long Beach. Jennifer peered beyond the rain-lashed windscreen. The storm was getting worse.

Staves said, 'You were right about seeing Mark in Turin. He and Kelso have been following you since you landed in Switzerland.'

Jennifer was shocked. '*Why?*'

'Kelso needed someone close to you in case you discovered evidence of his involvement. He probably intended to have Mark make his presence known to you, tell you he'd followed you out of concern. After that he'd have stuck with you, which would have kept Kelso on the inside track, but I entered the picture and messed up his plans. Mark thinks Kelso's out to protect you.'

'What does Kelso want?'

'At first, when the body was discovered, he just wanted to find out what happened to his share of the fifty million, but now he knows the disk exists he'll want it, to sell to the Moscayas and make up for the loss of the money. We also believe he or one of his people met Chuck McCaul to find out what evidence he'd found in the rucksack. They murdered him, probably to cover their tracks.'

Jennifer was fraught with worry. She wanted to believe everything Nick Staves had said, wanted to trust him and feel safe with him again.

'You said you didn't know where your father hid the box. But you've *got* to think again, Jennifer. If there's a chance it's still in the house, or if your father left some clue to where he hid it, we have to find it before Kelso does.' Staves reached across and gently touched her hand. 'Will you help me?'

'I . . . I guess so. Yes.'

The rain was pelting down as they turned in towards Cove End. The house was in darkness and the gate unlocked. They had arrived.

FIVE MILES from Long Beach, the limo sped along the highway. Rain lashed the windscreen and Mark tried to keep his eyes on the wet road.

Kelso said, 'Take the next turn for Long Beach and head for Cove End.'

'Is that where Jennifer is? This all has to do with the disk, hasn't it?'

Kelso gave a tiny smirk. 'Just take the next exit.'

'You made it look like March stole the fifty million but *you* took it.'

'Close. It was me *and* Lazar. We did a deal, except the fifty million vanished on the Wasenhorn. For all I know it's probably so far down a crevasse it'll never be found. Just like the bodies of March and Lazar.'

'That wasn't the way it was supposed to pan out, was it?'

'Lazar was meant to walk away with the fifty million, I'd get half, and March would wind up dead, along with the Vogels.'

'Didn't you search for the fifty million afterwards?'

'Lazar never told me where exactly he intended to cross the border. I left that decision entirely up to him, which was my big mistake. Until that body turned up, I had no idea where to look.'

Mark said, 'The explosion at the morgue, Caruso's murder, the killings at the monastery . . . That was all your doing. Why? Was it just to make sure that no evidence of your involvement in Paul March's death ever showed up?'

'Have you any idea what the disk is worth? The Moscaya clan will have no problem paying at least another fifty million to keep out of prison.'

'Don't tell me—and then you vanish, permanently?'

'After thirty years with the CIA I know how to cover my tracks.'

'Why are you doing this, Kelso?'

'You get tired of seeing assholes like the Moscayas pocket millions while you play good guy and put your life on the line but don't turn a nickel's profit, and all you've got to look forward to is a shitty pension plan. You get to think that it's time you put to good use all those dirty tricks the CIA taught you.'

'So where's the disk?'

Kelso grinned. 'I've got a feeling Jennifer may be able to help me answer that question, once I use a little leverage to jog her memory.'

LEROY MURPHY had never seen the two white guys before, but the ID badges they showed him said they were NYPD detectives. One of them was blond and had a bruised jaw. As Leroy led him and his buddy down a corridor in the Cauldwell he said, 'So how come you need to see Bobby?'

The blond had a look of concern on his face as he walked beside Leroy. 'His sister Jenny's been hurt in a car smash.'

'*What?* When did this happen?'

'Late this afternoon. She just got in off a flight and the cab she was travelling in was involved in an accident.'

'*Jeez*, that's lousy news. Jenny's the only family that Bobby's got. Hey, it's going to upset him to hear the news, don't you think?'

'The kid will have to come with us. Jenny's asking to see him.'

Leroy halted outside a windowed door.

The men looked in and saw Bobby sitting in a wheelchair by the window, doodling on some paper. 'That him?'

'Yeah, that's Bobby. But I ain't got the authority to let you take him . . .'

'I got all the authority you want right here.' The blond pulled out a pistol and struck Leroy a blow across the temple.

The big nurse was dazed. Then the other guy stepped in and slammed a cosh hard across the top of his skull, and he passed out.

The two men dragged his unconscious body across the floor. They dumped him inside a janitor's closet and locked the door. 'Let's go get the kid.'

JENNIFER STEPPED out of the Chevy into the rain. Staves shone the torch as he led the way. They were both drenched when they reached the verandah.

Jennifer unlocked the front door. A burst of lightning bathed the hallway in electric blue light, bringing back a flood of anguished memories.

'Where do you think we should search, Jennifer?'

'Maybe the study first, then the attic, basement and boathouse, if need be.'

The study was in darkness as Jennifer stepped inside. She fumbled to find the light switch and flicked it on. She forced herself to rifle the drawers while Staves went to work on the empty shelves, searching for a hidden recess, but after ten minutes they gave up.

They searched the attic and then the basement, but when they found nothing they moved into the kitchen. Staves unlocked the back door and a gale swept into the room, almost knocking them off their feet. A split second later the lights went out and the kitchen was plunged into darkness.

Staves flicked on the torch. 'The storm's knocked out the power lines.'

Jennifer saw that the gardens were deluged, trees waving angrily, the night sky crackling with lightning, ferocious waves pounding the boathouse dock.

'Don't let go of my hand. I don't want you being swept out to sea. Ready?'

'I think so.'

Staves pulled up his coat collar and ushered Jennifer out into the storm.

'PULL IN HERE,' said Kelso. He still had the pistol aimed at Mark.

Mark pulled into the kerb, 200 yards from Cove End. Across the street he saw his parents' house, the lights extinguished. His mom was away, staying in Phoenix with his sister.

'Leave the engine running but turn off the headlights. Then drive forward, very slowly.' Mark obeyed, and when he was within fifty yards of Cove End Kelso said, 'Stop here and kill the engine.'

Mark halted and turned off the ignition. Cove End was bathed in darkness.

A moment's silence followed, and then he heard the roar of the storm as a violent gust of wind shook the car. Kelso checked his watch. 'We're early.'

'What's that supposed to mean?'

'We wait.'

WAVES LASHED the boardwalk, and Jennifer was drenched as Staves forced open the boathouse door. He shone the torch over the motorboat and the shelves of engine parts and rusting tools.

'Get in the boat, Jennifer. Search every nook and cranny.'

She stepped into the boat and began to search the tiny cabin and wheel-house, while Staves played the torchlight into the engine compartments and felt around with his hands. When he found nothing, he went to search the shelves, tearing down tools and motor parts, a dangerous look in his eyes.

When he'd emptied the shelves he suddenly kicked out savagely at the boat. 'Where's the box? *Think, Jennifer!* Where could it be? *Where?*'

She moved out of the boat, and without warning Staves turned on her and grabbed her by the hair, twisting it viciously, before he struck her across the face, sending her staggering against the wall. 'I asked you a question.'

Jennifer was too stunned to reply. She trembled as she straightened up.

Staves was in a frenzy now, rage in his voice as he came to stand next to her. 'The box has got to be *somewhere* in the house. *Now where is it?*'

'I . . . I told you, I don't know.'

Some instinct made Jennifer rush for the door, but Staves came after her and grabbed her by the wrist. 'Where do you think you're going?'

There was a crazed look on his face, and at that moment Jennifer had no doubt he was capable of anything. 'You're . . . you're hurting me. Please . . .'

He dragged her from the boathouse and out across the flooded lawn towards the kitchen door, ignoring her protest. 'Keep your mouth shut.'

When they reached the door, Staves took out his cellphone and punched in a number. 'It's me. I want him in here *now*. Bring him round to the back.'

He finished the call and seconds later Jennifer saw headlights sweep into the driveway. A car braked to a halt and an overweight man with a black moustache struggled out. Jennifer recognised him as the man named Marty from the airport. His companion climbed out of the rear and she got another shock: it was the blond assailant from Vogel's farm. They bundled someone out of the back of the car then hauled him towards the house, head slumped, legs dragging on the gravel. Suddenly Jennifer saw who it was . . .

'*Bobby* . . .*!* ' She moved towards her brother but Staves grabbed her hair.

'Get him inside,' he ordered the men, and held on to Jennifer as he made another call, shouting into his cellphone, 'I gave it one last shot and it didn't work, Kelso. *Nothing's worked*. The bitch doesn't know where the box is. What do you want me to do now?'

'IT'S OK, BOBBY, I'm here. It's OK. Are you hurt?'

The two men had dragged Bobby into the kitchen and sat him next to Jennifer at the table. His eyes were swollen from crying and there was an angry bruise on his left cheek. As Jennifer clutched him, his body was racked by a fit of sobbing, and she felt a powerful urge to protect him.

'You bastard! He's been hurt . . .'

'Big deal,' Staves sneered. He jerked a thumb at his two accomplices. 'Kelso's on his way, and he's got company. One of you get out front and stay in the car and keep watch. The other had better stay in the back yard.'

Jennifer tried to comfort Bobby as the men went out. Moments later their car started up and reversed down the driveway. Staves searched the kitchen drawers, but when he found them empty he pulled up a chair and sat.

Jennifer heard footsteps outside the kitchen door, then it opened and Mark stepped in, followed by Kelso, who held a gun to his back.

Mark came towards her, but Kelso prodded him with the gun. 'Sit at the table.' He pushed Mark into a seat, slammed the door and said to Jennifer, 'I see you've met my partner in crime. Nick's quite an actor, I think you'll agree. He's always been one of the Agency's best when it comes to deception.'

Mark turned to Kelso. 'I assume he's not McCaul?'

'You're right. His name's Staves and he's CIA. And if you want his motive, let's just say he liked my pension plan better than Uncle Sam's.'

'What about the other men? Who are they?' Jennifer asked.

'Guns for hire, nothing more. One of the benefits of working for the CIA is that you get to know the best. Professionals who'll do whatever you ask so long as you pay them handsomely. The one you killed on the train was only meant to frighten you, but he probably played his role a little too earnestly.'

Mark looked at Kelso angrily. '*Why?* Why pretend to hunt Jennifer down and at the same time have Staves act like he's protecting her?'

'Put someone in danger, then make it look like you've helped them out of that danger, and they'll trust you with their life, maybe tell you all their secrets. The deception led us to Vogel. And we found out about the security box.'

'And where did I fit into your plan?' Mark asked.

Kelso grinned. 'You were our back-up in case Jennifer didn't take to Staves. Our original idea was that you'd travel with her and get close to her, but when she didn't want you to come with her we moved to plan B. She even thought she was being tailed by your Opel, so you frightened her as well.'

Jennifer stared at Kelso. 'What happened to Frank McCaul?'

'Oh, he's dead, I'm afraid. Like young Chuck.'

'You're an evil bastard, Kelso. You killed my mother. You shot Bobby.'

Kelso glanced at Nick Staves. 'You told her?'

Staves nodded. 'Even the part about us and Lazar setting up her old man.'

'Unfortunately, it's all true,' Kelso said calmly to Jennifer. 'There was nothing personal, it was just business.'

In a fit of anger Jennifer lunged at him, but he caught her wrist, twisting it behind her back. Mark jumped to his feet and made a grab at Kelso but Staves was quicker and in an instant he had his gun pointed at Mark's head.

Kelso shoved Jennifer into her chair. 'Give me the key to the box.'

Jennifer opened her bag and handed over the silver key.

Kelso tossed it in his palm, then slapped it on the table in front of him. 'Hard to believe that a little thing like this could cause so much trouble.'

Jennifer said defiantly, 'I don't know where the box is.'

Kelso removed his pistol from his pocket, produced a black metal silencer and screwed it onto the barrel. 'If that's the case, we've nothing more to say to each other.' He pointed the silenced pistol at Jennifer's head. 'I had thought you were holding out on me. But every trick we've used to try to loosen your tongue hasn't worked, so you must be telling me the truth.'

Kelso smiled thinly, then laid the pistol down on the counter and sat back. 'However, I still think the box may be somewhere on this property. You know why? Two years ago I surveyed every bank in New York State to see if your parents had a safe deposit box in any of them. They didn't. Now, what does that tell you? Either your father got rid of the box, or he hid it. If I had something that valuable, I know I'd hide it somewhere real safe, and close by. So you'd better start racking your brains, Jennifer. If you don't come up with some ideas, *fast*, I'll kill Bobby. Then I'll kill Ryan. Then I'll kill you. But you help me find the box, maybe you'll all live to see another day.'

'That's a lie. You'll kill us all anyway.'

Kelso gave a tight smile and picked up his pistol. 'Then the choice will be between a protracted, painful death and a very quick one. It's your call. I'm sure you don't want Bobby to suffer. Have I made myself clear?'

'Yes.'

Kelso pointed his pistol at Bobby's head. 'No one's ever asked your brother if he knows what happened to the box. You think he might know something?'

Bobby squirmed from Kelso's aim, retreating into Jennifer's arms.

'Please, don't harm him . . .' she begged.

Kelso pursed his lips in thought. 'Tell you what I'm going to do. I want you to put your heads together, and try and come up with some answers. Though I reckon Bobby here might respond more favourably if he didn't feel threatened, so Nick and I will leave you all alone to have your chinwag.' Kelso let the gun fall to his side and turned to Staves. 'Where's her cellphone?'

'Lost.'

'Is the house phone working?'

'No.'

'Any kitchen knives in the drawers?'

'No, I checked. The drawers are empty.'

'Good.' Kelso nodded to Staves, who opened the kitchen door and went out.

They saw him through the window, pacing up and down in the storm, dragging fiercely on a cigarette as he glanced at them through the glass.

Kelso walked over to the internal door, but as he opened it he looked back at them with a threatening stare. 'Nick's going to keep an eye on you from the garden. Me, I'll be out in the hall. So there's no way out of here. Stay at the table and don't move. Try to escape or call for help, and you're dead.' Kelso checked his watch. 'You've got ten minutes to come up with answers. After that, if I haven't got the box, I kill every one of you, starting with Bobby.'

THE ONLY SOUND was the wind raging beyond the kitchen door—the storm showed no sign of abating. Kelso had stepped out of the room, slamming the door, and Jennifer saw Nick Staves looking frozen as he paced about the garden. Every few seconds he glanced in at them through the window before he continued his guard duty, keeping the blond assailant company.

Mark said, 'I'm sorry, Jennifer, I thought I was helping.'

He started to speak again, but Jennifer put a finger to his lips. 'Let's not talk about it. Please. It's not important right now.'

Mark studied the kitchen. He noticed a small red domestic fire extinguisher hanging on the wall, then pointed to a door off to its right. 'Where does the door lead?'

'To a pantry. It's not an exit. Just a cupboard.'

Jennifer felt Bobby grip her hand. He looked so confused, so utterly helpless. She knew he was on the verge of tears again, and so was she. And as she looked into Bobby's face, she thought: What kind of man could turn a young boy into a cripple, shoot him in the back, without a shred of remorse? What kind of man could destroy an entire family because of greed?

Her eyes were wet as Mark touched her shoulder. 'Jenny.'

She was so caught up in her anguish that she barely heard what Mark said next. 'Jenny, Bobby's trying to tell you something.'

She came out of her reverie, and saw Bobby's hands signing to her.

'What's he saying?' Mark asked impatiently.

'That he's scared.'

'Join the club,' Mark said, and put a hand on Bobby's shoulder.

Bobby's eyes were red from crying. Jennifer said to him, 'I know now what happened to Dad and why Mom was killed. I want you to tell you everything, Bobby, but it would take too long to explain now and we don't have the time. But you know that the men you saw here are bad, don't you?'

Bobby nodded. He made a sign with his hands. *Did they kill Mom and Dad?*

Jennifer inwardly recoiled from the question, but she had to answer. 'Yes.'

Bobby's hands went limp.

Jennifer said, 'Did you understand what the men said? That they mean to kill us if we don't tell them where the box is?'

Bobby nodded again.

'Did your mom or dad keep a gun?' Mark asked.

'No,' Jennifer answered. 'Both of them hated guns.'

'If only we could get across the street there's a good chance there's a thirty-eight revolver in my folks' house. My old man always kept one in a bureau near his bed. Unless one of my family moved it, it ought still to be there . . .'

Mark hesitated just as Bobby made another rapid hand sign, and Jennifer paled. 'You're *sure*, Bobby?'

'What the hell's he saying?' Mark asked.

'He says he thinks he knows where the box is.'

Jennifer waited until Bobby had finished signing then she looked at him in amazement. 'You're sure about this, Bobby?'

He nodded, and Mark said impatiently, 'Where is the box?'

'A week before Dad disappeared, just after dawn, Bobby was woken by a noise. He looked out of his window and saw Dad pacing the boardwalk, carrying a grey metal box and looking as if he didn't know what to do with it.'

'What *did* your father do?'

'Bobby says he went into the boathouse and came out with a black plastic bag, tied up with blue nylon rope. There appeared to be something heavy inside, as if he'd put the box in the bag. Then he climbed down the boardwalk ladder to the water, until Bobby couldn't see him. But when Dad climbed up again a couple of minutes later, he didn't have the black bag.'

Mark frowned. 'If he threw it in the water, why did he go down the ladder?'

'Maybe he didn't want anyone to hear the splash. Or maybe he had the motorboat tied up at the bottom of the ladder, and meant to dump the bag out at sea. Bobby says the boat could have been tied up, because Dad often went fishing that early in the morning, but he's not certain because he went back to sleep.'

Mark shook his head. 'If the disk was in the box, your father wouldn't get rid of it. The disk was too important, so it's likely he hid it, but where?'

Jennifer looked towards the window, stuck for an answer. Staves was pacing like a restless animal. She shifted her gaze to the dark sea, then turned to Mark. 'About a hundred yards out in the bay there are some plastic marker buoys, warning fishermen of jagged rocks. If Dad dumped the bag overboard, he could have used one of the buoys as a marker to tell him where it was.'

'I guess it's a possibility.' But Mark didn't look convinced.

Jennifer watched Staves on the boardwalk with the blond. A thought struck her like a bolt of electricity. 'What if the box is still out on the boardwalk?'

'What do you mean?'

'What if Dad secured it underneath the walkway, or tied it below the water line? He could have attached the bag to one of the wooden support beams.'

'Assuming the box didn't get washed away in a storm, it sounds like a good hiding place. How much time have we left?'

Jennifer consulted her watch. 'About a minute.'

They heard footsteps behind the internal door. Mark shot a look at the red fire extinguisher before he whispered, 'I've got an idea that may buy us some time, but you'll both have to play it exactly as I tell you.'

'What's the idea?'

Mark explained, and Jennifer said, 'Kelso will kill us if we don't tell him.'
'He's going to kill us if we do.'

The door burst open and Kelso entered the room. He had the gun in his hand. Right on cue, Staves entered and slammed the door against the growling wind.

Kelso stepped over, and aimed the pistol at Bobby's temple. His finger tightened on the trigger as he stared at Jennifer. 'Well, your time's up.'

'I . . . I think I know where the box might be,' Jennifer stammered.

There was a moment's silence, and then Kelso's eyes sparked with triumph. 'OK, let's have it. Start talking.'

'YOU'RE TELLING me the box may be somewhere out in the bay, weighed down near one of the marker buoys? I don't believe it.' Kelso was enraged as he stared at the bay from the kitchen window. The storm was building to its climax, the wind so fierce that the swaying trees looked as if they would snap, and Jennifer doubted that he could see very far in the dark. Kelso turned back in frustration and went to stand over Bobby. 'You'd better be telling the truth.'

Bobby nodded.

Kelso said to Jennifer, 'If it isn't the truth, then I'm going to enjoy doing something I never got to finish.' There was a look of malice on his face as he tore open the top buttons on his shirt, pulled aside his tie and revealed the stitched flesh of a jagged knife wound below his neck. 'Remember this? Sure you do. I was lucky you didn't kill me that night.'

Jennifer regarded Kelso with unconcealed hatred, but he ignored her and crossed to the window again. 'Is your father's boat in working order?'

'It hasn't been used in years, so I can't say.'

Staves said to Kelso in disbelief, 'You're going out in a boat in that weather?'

Kelso gestured at Mark with his pistol. 'It won't be us, it'll be Ryan, but we'll have to wait until the storm dies down before he can check the buoys.'

'What are we supposed to do in the meantime?' Staves asked.

Kelso glanced out at the garden. 'Tell our friend out there to come inside before he freezes to death. Then take Ryan out to the boathouse and see if the motorboat is seaworthy. If he tries to get smart, kill him.'

IT WAS obvious to Mark that the boat wasn't seaworthy. A small amount of fuel slopped around in the tank but the engine appeared to be seized and the wood had splintered in places. 'It's a waste of time. I'd sink before I got ten yards.'

Staves kicked at the hull, his anger seething.

'I've got a proposition,' said Ryan. 'There's something Bobby neglected to mention, something that may form the basis of a deal between us.'

'What kind of a deal?'

'In return for letting us go, you get the box for yourself.'

'Spit out exactly what you've got to say.'

'The box may not be attached to one of the buoys. It may be elsewhere.'

'*Where?*'

'Under the boardwalk.'

When Mark explained, Staves was furious. 'You held back on us.'

'I figured I'd stand a better chance of helping Jennifer and Bobby walk away from this alive if I dealt only with you. I sure as hell wouldn't stand a chance with Kelso. I don't think you do, either. My instinct tells me you're not part of his final pension plan. My deal is, you get the box, if it's there, and you let us go, unharmed. That way, you don't have to share it with Kelso.'

Staves hesitated, considering before he replied. 'That's a big if. What if it isn't there? What if it's out there tied to one of the buoys, like you said?'

'We do the same deal.'

Staves pursed his lips. 'We'll see.' He grabbed an orange nylon rope from the motorboat and tossed it to Mark. 'Tie that securely round your waist.'

'What for?'

'You're going to take a look under the boardwalk, and I don't want you washed away.' Staves grinned. 'Not until we find what we're looking for.'

JENNIFER LOOKED at her watch—Mark had been gone exactly three minutes. It was time. She squeezed Bobby's hand, made a signal with her fingers so that he'd understand that things were about to begin. *Ready?*

His fingers moved in reply. *Ready.*

Kelso turned back from the window, saw Bobby's gesture and frowned. 'What's he doing?'

'He . . . doesn't feel well. He says he needs his medication, Dilantin, to stop him having an epileptic fit. It can happen if he's under stress.'

'Forget it. He'll do without.'

'My brother may die if he doesn't have his pills. Remember, Bobby's the last person who saw the box, and we haven't found it yet.'

Kelso considered. 'Where's the medication?'

'I keep a bottle of pills in my bag, in case of an emergency. It's in the car.'

Kelso tucked his pistol in his waistband and said to the blond, 'Shoot them if they try anything dumb.' He stepped out and banged the door after him.

The blond pulled up a chair and sat down, resting his pistol lazily across his lap. Jennifer prayed that the plan would work.

Bobby suddenly started to shake, his body racked by convulsions, and he collapsed in a heap on the floor. Jennifer moved to kneel beside him, but the blond pulled her away. 'What's wrong with him?'

'He's having a seizure. Please, I need a towel. Let me find one—'

The blond said warily, 'You stay there. I'll get it.'

He crossed to the sink and Jennifer took her chance. She grabbed the fire extinguisher from the pantry wall. As the blond turned back with a tea towel in his hand, she aimed the nozzle at his face and squeezed the firing handle.

Nothing happened.

Oh God . . . In her panic she'd forgotten to pull out the safety pin. As the blond dropped the towel and pulled out his gun, Jennifer swung the fire extinguisher and struck him across the jaw. There was a clang of metal and he grunted with pain, blood spurting from a cut in his jaw as he fell back onto the floor. He clapped a hand to his face, and with the other he reached out blindly to grab at Jennifer. This time she brought the extinguisher down hard on his head. There was a sickening thud. The man grunted and then lay still.

Jennifer went to pick up the man's gun. Bobby had stopped acting—he'd done exactly as Mark had suggested—but he was deathly pale and distressed.

'Please, Bobby, we don't have time to get upset, so you have to do exactly as Mark said.' She turned the knob on the pantry door and revealed a tight space surrounded by wooden shelves. 'Stay in there until you think it's safe to come out. You can't move, or make a sound.'

Jennifer helped Bobby into the tiny space and sat him on the floor. Fear was in his eyes as he stared up at her. She wanted to kneel down and hug him, but there was no time; Kelso would return any second—there was no medication in her bag. 'I'm closing the door now, Bobby. Try not to be afraid, please.'

She closed the pantry door and the catch clicked. Then she heard footsteps outside the kitchen and panicked. Kelso was returning.

'IT'S TOO DANGEROUS, Staves.' Mark finished tying the nylon rope round his waist, having secured it to a rung on the boardwalk ladder.

Staves pointed his gun at him and handed over the torch. 'Too bad. Lower yourself down and take a good look under the walkway.'

The torch had a grip string and Mark slipped it onto his wrist. He flicked on the light and waited until the next wave struck and began to recede. He began his descent down the ladder, and had reached the sixth rung when a wave crashed into the boardwalk. Ice-cold water hammered his body and he held tightly on to the rungs, but as the wave subsided he was swung like a pendulum by the sucking force of the receding water. He slipped, lost his footing, grabbed the rope and managed to pull himself back onto the ladder.

Another wave hit him four steps later. This time he maintained his footing. He was low enough now to see a crisscross of thick wooden beams under the boardwalk. But even in the torchlight it was almost impossible to see as the swells of water thrashed the beams. He waited until the swell had subsided, and just before an incoming wave was due shone the torch into a recess in the beams. Empty. He probed another recess. Nothing.

A wave smashed him against the ladder. He held on to the rope grimly, waited again as the wave buffeted him in the angry swell, and when it had washed away again shone the torch. Nothing. But a second later the torchlight reflected from something. His heart leapt when he saw a black bag tied to one of the crossbeams, the plastic slick with a sheen of salt water.

Mark struggled back up the ladder and onto the boardwalk. He was frozen. He coughed up a lungful of salt water, barely able to hear above the roar of the waves and wind as Staves shouted at him. 'Well?'

'It's . . . down there. I found a black bag tied to one of the beams.'

Staves's face lit up with excitement. 'Why didn't you bring it up?'

'It's tied to a crossbeam and I'll need something to cut the rope.'

Staves fumbled in his pocket and took out a Swiss Army knife. He opened a blade. As he handed over the knife there was animal caution in his eyes and he pointed his pistol at Mark's head. 'Try getting smart with the blade, Ryan, and I kill you. Got that? Now fetch the bag.'

JENNIFER HID behind the kitchen door as the knob began to turn. Her heart pounded as she gripped the gun in both hands. Her plan had been to race to Mark's parents' house and use the phone, but she didn't have time. She readied herself. She knew she had to shoot Kelso dead. It was the only way.

Her hands shook with fear. Could she shoot someone dead in cold blood? She wanted Kelso to pay the price for destroying her family, but what she was about to do would bring her down to Kelso's level, and that angered her.

Kelso stepped into the room. Jennifer found herself staring at the back of his head. She had a split second to act. She aimed just above the base of his skull, closed her eyes, squeezed the trigger, and the gun exploded in her hands.

Everything seemed to happen slowly. As the sound of the gunshot died, Jennifer snapped open her eyes and saw Kelso being punched forward by the force of the bullet.

Her heart pounded and her body shook from the trauma of what she had just done. Kelso was slammed into the kitchen worktop, then fell to the floor, shock on his face, but he was still alive and he clapped a hand to his neck, blood oozing between his fingers. Almost without thinking, Jennifer again aimed at his head and squeezed the trigger. The pistol exploded with a powerful recoil, and this time the shot hit Kelso's hand, slicing through a finger.

Kelso let out a scream, but he was already rolling towards the kitchen door, his shock replaced by rage. Jennifer had the feeling that she had managed only to graze his neck. Suddenly Kelso struggled to his feet and backed out through the kitchen door. His gun appeared in his hand.

'You bitch!' he screamed, then fired. 'You fucking bitch!'

A bullet grazed her arm. It felt as if a red-hot poker were searing her skin, and she yelled and dropped the pistol. There was no time to pick it up; she had to get out before a ricochet drilled through the pantry door and killed Bobby. She darted out into the hallway and reached the front door in seconds.

Now there was no going back. She had to stick to Mark's plan: *Get over to my parents' house and call 911. There's a chance the gun is in the bureau . . .*

She ran across the lawns in the pelting rain. Halfway across the street, her lungs on fire, she dared to look back and saw Kelso stagger out through the front door, clutching his neck. For a split second their eyes locked.

Then Kelso ran after her with a burst of speed.

MARK KNEW he was going to drown. As the waves slammed into his body, he sucked in mouthfuls of salty air and clung defiantly to the rope, Staves still up on the boardwalk covering him with the gun. Mark knew now he had little chance of escape. He'd hoped to get close enough to Staves to push him or trip him into the sea, but Staves had been careful and kept his distance. Cutting himself free from the rope and trying to swim away wasn't an option: the sea was too violent, and he'd drown before he got twenty yards.

He had cut the rope holding the black bag to the crossbeam, but he kept Staves's penknife clutched in his hand. The bag felt heavy, and he grasped it to his chest and struggled up the ladder, the icy sea water drenching him in endless salty waves.

Staves roared, 'Toss the knife up. Then get back up here. Don't lose the bag.'

Mark's hope that Staves's excitement might make him forget about the knife even briefly was dashed. He tossed the knife onto the boardwalk. Staves began to reel in the rope, pulling Mark up. When he reached the top of the ladder, Mark knelt on the boardwalk, exhausted.

Staves bent to pick up the bag. Mark braced himself to rush him, but suddenly a shot rang out. The noise was faint in the storm, but then came another shot, and another, a chorus of gunfire.

It came from the house. *Jennifer . . . Bobby.* Frantically Mark tried to get up but Staves grabbed the bag and kicked him back into the water.

'So long, sucker.' Staves fired once as Mark fell into the boiling sea, his body swallowed up by the waves.

RAIN LASHED against Jennifer's face as she ran to the white door as fast as her legs would carry her. The sky exploded with thunder and lightning, and her heart pounded as she raced up the verandah steps, too afraid to glance back.

She knocked over the flowerpot and found the spare key underneath, where Mark had said it would be, then fumbled the key into the lock and pushed open the front door. As she stepped into the hallway, she flicked on the light switch and the hall blazed with light. She saw the stairs ahead. Without a second's hesitation she bounded up them.

The landing didn't resemble that in her parents' house. Jennifer faced six doors, all closed, and she didn't know which was the master bedroom.

She opened the nearest door and found herself in a box-room. She moved on to the next room and pushed open the door. This room was bigger than the last, overlooking the rear garden, but it wasn't the master bedroom. She heard a noise in the hall downstairs—someone clattering onto the patio. *Kelso.*

In desperation, she flung open the next door and darted inside a large room, but didn't turn on the light. She heard footsteps on the stairs, and looked around the room in panic. The curtains were open, flashes of blue lightning drenching the walls. She saw a wooden writing bureau with a chair, framed family photographs and a phone on top. She was in the master bedroom. No time to use the phone. She had to find the gun.

Kelso's footsteps were coming closer, racing up the stairs.

She ran to the bureau and pulled away the chair. Six drawers. Which one held the revolver? Mark hadn't even been certain the gun was still there. She yanked open the top left drawer. Empty. She tried the top right. Empty.

Kelso was on the landing . . . she heard him trying one of the doors, then a few seconds later heard him push open another door.

She tried the next drawer. She fumbled madly, but there was no gun inside, only a jumble of erasers and paperclips . . .

She heard a noise and looked round. Was the door handle starting to turn? In a frenzy she tried the next drawer. Empty. And the next—

The door burst open. Bright light exploded into the bedroom from the landing, and Kelso was framed in the doorway, his face in shadow.

'Well, well. If it isn't the bitch who shot and knifed me.'

Jennifer stepped back against the bureau, petrified.

Kelso stepped forward, a self-satisfied look on his face as it materialised out of the shadow. He put a hand to his neck, then took it away to stare at crimson fingers, one almost severed at the knuckle. His eyes flashed with rage. 'It seems you have a bad habit of doing me harm. Where's Bobby?'

Jennifer didn't reply.

Kelso flicked on the light and stepped closer. 'Don't worry, I'll find him. But first, you and I have some unfinished business.'

Jennifer was paralysed with fear. Kelso was two feet away and she could smell his sour breath. A flash of lightning flooded the bedroom.

'Please . . . please don't . . .' she begged.

'What? Rape you?' Kelso grinned. 'Now that it's time to teach you a lesson, I confess I'm looking forward to it.' He brushed her cheek with the back of his hand. 'And afterwards you're going to tell me exactly where Bobby is. Do that, and maybe I'll make it a quick death for him. Otherwise, if I've got to find him myself, your kid brother's going to suffer. Have you got that?'

Jennifer pressed her back against the bureau, twisted her right hand behind her and fumbled in the open drawer. She felt some papers . . . but no gun.

Kelso inched closer, then his hand came up suddenly and grasped her throat. Jennifer struggled but he tightened his grip. 'Stay still, or I'll hurt you.'

Jennifer felt desperately in the next drawer. A notepad . . . and then her fingers felt something hard, metallic. Blunt at one end, stiletto sharp at the other.

Kelso's face was right up against hers, his sour breath on her skin, and he said hoarsely, 'Maybe you'll enjoy it too. What do you think, Jennifer?'

'I think you're going to hell, Kelso.'

His grin vanished as Jennifer brought up her free hand and plunged the brass letter opener into his chest. His body jolted and he lurched back, dropping his gun, his eyes wild as he clutched at his wound. Jennifer grabbed his pistol from the floor, aimed and squeezed the trigger.

The shot tore into Kelso's chest and he flopped sideways. Jennifer fired again, hammering Kelso's body against the wall, then he crumpled to the floor. She kept firing until the weapon gave an empty *click*, then she fell to her knees.

A second later, she heard footsteps on the stairs.

She looked round just as a figure stepped into the doorway. It was Staves, and he held a gun in one hand, a wet black plastic bag in the other. Jennifer panicked, raised her pistol and squeezed the trigger.

Click. She had forgotten the gun was empty.

A grin spread over Staves's face, and he glanced at Kelso's body. 'I guess I don't have to share, after all.' He raised his gun, preparing to shoot. 'It's nothing personal, honey, just something that's got to be done.'

The howl of a siren sounded in the distance and Staves hesitated. But Jennifer knew it was too late. She was about to shut her eyes and wait for the bullet that would kill her when a shadow appeared on the landing. There was a flash of lightning and she saw Mark, his figure outlined in the hallway, inching forward. His clothes were drenched and he had a pistol clutched in both hands.

She saw the anger on his face, heard it in his voice as he shouted, 'Staves!'

Staves spun round, caught off guard, and as he went to aim, Mark fired. The shot hit Staves in the head, killing him instantly.

IT WAS 8 P.M. and the storm had moved on, the black clouds driven away by icy Atlantic winds. Jennifer had comforted Bobby, had told the police everything she knew, and when she could take no more she told them she wanted to be alone, and she walked down to the boardwalk and sat on the edge.

A little later a uniformed officer came by and put a rain cape round her shoulders. It was a cold night, he said, and asked whether he could take her back up to the house, but she said no, she wanted to stay a little longer, and so he left her there and walked away.

She felt the breeze on her face, heard the water lapping beneath her feet, a swell still there, and she was suddenly more tired than she had ever been in her life. She heard the footsteps but didn't look round.

'You'll catch cold out here.' Mark came to sit beside her and slid his legs over the jetty's edge. He had told her everything: how Staves's shot had missed him as he had hit the water, how the rope round his waist, still tied to the ladder, had saved him from being swallowed by the waves. After he'd struggled out of the water he'd made it to the front of the house and seen another of Kelso's men, the one named Marty, heading towards the verandah at his folks' place. That was when Garuda's Porsche and two black-and-whites arrived, and Kelso's man was confronted. He had tossed down his pistol and given himself up; Mark had grabbed the weapon and pursued Staves into the house. 'But what about you? How are you coping?'

She wiped her eyes. 'I'll be fine.'

'Bobby's doing OK. He's confused, sure, but he'll come through. Right now he's wondering where you are and wanted me to come and find you.'

'I just needed a little time to myself. Can you understand, Mark?'

'Sure.' Mark put his arm round her shoulder and she leaned into his chest.

As he held her close, stroking her hair, something struck her: she realised that she hadn't been able to move on because she was waiting for her father to come back and hold her, the way Mark wanted to hold her.

'I can see that for now you just need to be on your own,' he said.

She didn't want him to go, didn't want to lose that secure feeling, but he seemed to sense that she needed to clear her head. His arm fell away but he held her hand as she said, 'For a little while longer. What about the Moscayas?'

'They're not going to be interested in you and Bobby. Now the Organised Crime Division has the disk, they'll have their own worries trying to run for cover from criminal charges that are going to tear their organisation apart.'

She bit her lip. 'I knew my father would never hurt us. I knew he'd never have deliberately put us in jeopardy. But you know what I keep thinking? I don't want him to lie cold and forgotten on a faraway mountain.'

Mark squeezed her hand. 'I'll do everything I can to make sure they try to find his body. That's a promise.'

Jennifer knew that he meant it. 'There's someone else I keep thinking about.'

'Who?'

'The young woman at the airport, Nadia Fedov. Seeing as the Moscayas are going to be busy in court, they mightn't care so much about her.'

'What are you saying, Jenny?'

'If I can convince her to turn federal witness, would you try to help her stay out of prison?'

A smile flickered across Mark's face. 'You don't give up, do you?'

'She's an innocent, Mark. She doesn't deserve to pay for a crime she was forced to commit.'

'I'll talk to the federal prosecutor's office, see if I can convince them to go for it. But if I ever get into trouble, I want you for my attorney. Deal?'

'It's a deal. Will you do one last thing for me, Mark?'

'What?'

'Will you bring Bobby down here? There's something I need to say to him.'

'I'll try and get a chair from the paramedics.' Mark slowly let go of her hand, stood and looked down at her face. 'I don't give up either, you know.'

'I know.'

'If you need a shoulder to lean on, don't be afraid to phone.'

She heard the words, wasn't immune to them. 'You're always the first person I call, Mark. I've a funny feeling you always will be.'

JENNIFER HEARD his footsteps as he walked away, the way her father used to walk away. She still missed him. Missed so many things about him.

In her heart she knew that it was impossible, but someday, somehow, she had to learn to live in peace with the demons that haunted her. She was for ever trapped in her past, and she knew why. Sometimes memories were all she had of the life she had shared and lost with her father and mother.

A little later she heard a noise behind her and turned. Mark stood there, behind Bobby's wheelchair. He nodded silently to her then turned and was gone, back towards the house, leaving them alone.

Jennifer crossed to her brother, knelt and looked into his face. He still seemed confused and lost as he rocked back and forth in the chair. A breeze blew in from across the bay and ruffled his hair, and she patted it down. She took his hand. 'There's going to come a time very soon when we have to talk, Bobby. Not just about tonight but about everything, about all the things we never discussed because they were too painful. You know that, don't you? You know it's the only way we can move on with our lives.'

Bobby nodded, and she squeezed his hand. 'You're sure?'

She wanted to say so much more, to reassure him that no matter what they would always have each other, that they were tied together, the same flesh and blood, but she knew that Bobby knew this already. She hugged him. He started to cry. She pulled him close, his cheek against her shoulder, and they clung to each other, swayed together in the cold Atlantic wind, as if the other was all either of them had in the world, and they would never let each other go.

GLENN MEADE

Born: Finglas, Dublin, 1957
Favourite hobbies: Travel and research
Former job: Training pilots

Are writers ever truly off-duty? Glenn Meade doesn't think so, and proves his case by saying that the idea for his new book came to him when he was on holiday in the Swiss Alps. 'I stayed in a small hotel in a beautiful mountain hamlet near the Italian border, and the owner told me that an unidentified body had recently been discovered in a nearby glacier. Apparently, climbers and hikers occasionally come to a bad end by falling into Alpine ice crevasses, and sometimes their bodies are never found, or they are locked into the ice for years, before melting ice in the shifting glaciers uncovers them. Like most writers, who always have their ears open for a good story, I got to thinking, what if? A few months later, the plot for *Web of Deceit* was born.'

Researching the book meant that Glenn Meade had the happy task of visiting the Swiss Alps several times to familiarise himself with the terrain. 'It seems as if I walked and climbed almost every inch of that area and I still have the callused feet as proof. And, yes, I walked across the glacier mentioned in *Web of Deceit*, and the views and experience were pretty breathtaking.'

Meade's imagination was fired by the idea of the Russian Mafia when he was in Washington researching his previous novel, *Resurrection Day,* and came across some reports on global organised crime. 'They turned out to be fascinating reading and made me realise that the Russian Mafia is a far bigger global threat than the old Italian Mafia clans ever were. I guess I couldn't resist using such disturbing, but interesting, ready-made bad guys in *Web of Deceit*.'

Despite the fact that the success of Meade's first four novels, *Brandenburg, Snow Wolf, The Sands of Sakkara* and *Resurrection Day*, made him an internationally best-selling author, he was nervous about giving up his 'day job': training pilots for Aer Lingus in Dublin, where he lives. Two years ago, however, he finally took the plunge. He enjoyed pilot training, but, in the end, writing proved the stronger passion. 'Although I can honestly say that it hasn't got any easier! I wish it had. Writing a book is still like climbing Everest, every time, but it's always worth it.'